667 S077

VOLUME II

the QUADRANT

Blessings on all
your journeys!

Kim Ridenour Raikes

at the
CROSS-
ROADS
of ANJIER

KIM RIDENOUR RAIKES

The Quadrant Volume II:
At the Crossroads of Anjier

Copyright © 2013 Kim Ridenour Raikes

ISBN: 978-1-938883-44-6

Designed and Produced by
Maine Authors Publishing
558 Main Street, Rockland, Maine 04841
www.maineauthorspublishing.com

The time for journeys would come and my soul
Called me eagerly out, sent me over
The horizon, seeking foreigner's homes...
But there isn't a man on earth so proud,
So born to greatness, so bold with his youth,
Grown so brave, or so graced by God,
That he feels no fear as the sails unfurl...
No harps ring in his heart, no rewards...
Nothing, only the ocean's heave;
But longing wraps itself around him.

—excerpt from *The Seafarer,*
anonymous origin, Old English

at the
CROSS-
ROADS
of ANJIER

XIII

JAMES ROBERTSON
North Atlantic—Maine, July-August, 1842

As we made our hard-fought way up the seaboard I gathered strength by degrees in the sickbay, skimming the magazines Melchett had lent me, or listening on the sly to the ceaseless banter in the saloon: talk which both fired my excitement about our approaching landfall, and fed my urge for more news about Melchett. Lying propped up against the pillows, old issues of Portland news sheets before me, I dreamed over the drawings of schooners and harbors, imagining from their shapes his native beaches, or the architecture of his inner shores.

We were now off the coast of New Jersey, gently rolling on a quartering sea; and as I read I absorbed the inconsequential chatter to which I'd become accustomed in the past few days: Haggai complaining about Melchett's cat, unperturbedly begging in the pantry; McCabe going on about his geraniums in the skylight, and plaintively asking Haggai—apparently not for the first time— for coffee grains to restore their vigor; Haggai protesting that he was overworked; and Melchett caustically retaliating with a snort, "Why'n't ye stay home an' cook chops for the mayor?"

The same fitful airs and somnolent breezes which had made it possible for me to catch this chaffing below had, along with our jury rig and crank cargo, retarded our progress up the seacoast; and as a result—far from setting a record—we were several days behind the schedule which Melchett had set for us in Havana. Kept below and fairly idle—McCabe firmly counseling against active labor, and Melchett fiercely scowling at me when I argued, with a glint in his eye

3

which bluntly informed me that he hadn't forgotten my defiance off Bermuda—I chafed at the weakness which prevented my working; and snatching chances when my superiors were on duty, I took to helping Shad and Haggai with lighter tasks about the saloon.

By the time I was finally permitted on deck for an afternoon of sun and fresh air, we were thirteen days out of Havana, and drawing near to the end of our voyage; and dazed by the sunlight and the preparations for homecoming, I stood in the waist dumbly gazing around me, marveling at the changes which met me. Besides the jury rig at the foretopmast and the massive slings which fished the main—alterations obvious at a glance—there were more subtle signs from stem to stern of recently repaired storm damage; whilst my shipmates were busily engaged in bestowing the last-minute touches for our grand hour in Portland. Because I railed against my inaction, particularly in view of the industry around me, McCabe set me to balling spun yarn by the old winch—the task of a boy or, at most, an ordinary seaman; but so overjoyed was I to be nearing the Maine coast that I cared nothing for ribbing, not even Howland's.

Zealously winding yarns by the bulwarks, I reveled at the sights and sounds around me: at the fine spray at the bowsprit, the roll and sway of the vessel, the hum and twang of the rising wind in the halyards. Periodically deadening our headway, Melchett called for deepwater soundings; and looking up each time at this land-nearing drama, I abandoned my work as the line was ranged along forward, bent to the heavy lead with its coating of tallow, then hove into the sea at McCabe's signal. With "Watch, ho! Watch!" ringing over the vessel—with length after length running out of the hands of each man, as the weight plunged down toward some unguessed flooring—McCabe counted out the knots of the fathoms, till enough line was out to show there was no bottom. Then ordering the line hauled in and snatched, he had the studdingsails set once again— only to repeat the whole performance in another couple of hours when, the line bringing up by the lead's touching on bottom, we had soundings at 60 fathoms.

The soundings of the Atlantic coast being regular—black mud, dark sand, white sand, silt or shells signifying specific banks or ledges to those who, like Melchett, could read their cipher—we soon knew where we were; for the lead having brought up a sample of clay, characteristic of the continental shelf off southern Maine, word swiftly went round we were off Jeffrey's Ledge. Adjusting our course for a more westerly direction, we tried to keep our eyes off the horizon, all hands being on deck now in the dog watch, and talking jubilantly of our homecoming; while McCabe came forward to jest with us kindly, relaxing the discipline which had so long ruled us: a clamor of shore plans competing for his ears, and expectations running high that we would fetch the Maine coast by nightfall.

Going down to supper with McCabe—Melchett and Spooner joining us soon after—I put away a hearty meal, my appetite sharpened by anticipation and fresh air, and by my growing conviction that the closer we drew to shore, the nearer I came to knowing Melchett as a comrade—to experiencing the familiarity of two men who are equals, as if the land would obliterate the distinctions between us. So close did I feel to new rights and freedoms that when Haggai brought in a bottle of port to celebrate our last evening at sea, I slyly put my glass forward, and received a liberal portion: McCabe giving me an indulgent nod, but Melchett cocking a severe eye at me—only the twitch at the corners of his mouth giving him away as he muttered, "Just *one,* you bastihd."

Whether or not he shared my excitement beneath the light words with which he addressed me, it was impossible to tell; for despite the festive mood which permeated the table—the only mess I'd ever heard of where all inmates aft broke bread with the captain—he was business as usual, immersing himself in his papers and charts as soon as our supper was cleared away. Hooking his spectacles over his ears—transforming his broad, weathered face with their frail gold, a contrast which never failed to inform me of his softness—he at once spread out a broad map of the Maine coast, all riddled with the depths of soundings, and mottled with the names of shelves and ledges. Then snatching the moment to instruct me— characteristically utilizing every occasion for learning, even the eve of our debarkation—he jabbed here and there with his blunt finger to trace the trajectory of the day's course, or outline the route still before us.

Looking down I could straightaway see that he had made this chart himself—that it represented the patient accumulation of data, probably over the course of years and in concert with coastmen like McCabe; and moved by the painstaking care he had taken despite his direct and impatient nature, I leaned my head close by as bidden, and followed his dartings across the parchment. Seeing my interest, he rose from his chair, and fetched the samples we'd so far hauled from the bottom: holding out bits of clay, shell and mud in the palm of his great hand, and detailing to me the undersea basins which each specimen represented. Almost lovingly prodding at each, separating out particles of sand, dirt and clay which made up the particular samples, he spoke of channels, ridges and floors, lobster beds and the grounds of cod, describing the bottom as if he'd swum there; while McCabe and Spooner, of old fishing stock, chimed in with opinions of their own, and Shad and Haggai debated the finer points with the vigor of connoisseurs.

That all this should have been inspired by a palmful of mud was touching enough; but so keen was the light on Melchett's face, so eager the gleam by which he informed me that he was sharing his heart's work, that I fell instantaneously silent, as I had when he'd shown me the shell in Havana—fell hushed as at some rare unearthing, some unique excavation or find. Perhaps it was the effect of the wine, taken on a stomach too long unaccustomed to food; perhaps the aura of confidence between us; but the saloon with its rosy lamps and yellow pine took on an immutable hum and glow, as if this were its true state to those not too hurried to notice. Deep in thought, it was all I could do to make replies to the others: Haggai at once seizing the chance to rib me for my low tolerance, but Melchett gazing at me out of the corner of his eye with quiet satisfaction, and an understanding as wordless as it was knowing.

Into this silent communion there suddenly shot the long, glad cry of "Land ho!," borne to us aft on the now quieting evening wind; and scarcely had its jubilant note died out than every one of us had scattered from our places, and tumbled up on deck to find all hands to larboard, looking out on the low, dusky sweep at the skyline. Having taken a moment to snatch up his spyglass, Melchett was the last one to appear; and bracing an arm in the mizzen ratlines, he took turns scanning the coast with McCabe, while Haggai, Shad and I, indeed every hand on board, ranged at intervals along the bulwarks, gazing entranced on the beckoning offing. Faint and hazy in the early evening light, commingling with the cloud shapes on the horizon, it was still but a glimmer of the salt marsh and granite to come; but afire at the thought of nearing its promise, I dreamed on it as I had on Melchett's magazines below—till feeling a hand at my shoulder, I looked up in surprise, to find Melchett himself offering me his glass.

Accepting it gladly, I trained it on the distance, while Melchett pointed out the sure, sweeping arc of Orchard Beach, the low, rocky bluff of Cape Elizabeth, the outermost islands of Casco Bay, and the long, broken coast stretching into oblivion northeast: shapes which resolved themselves over the next hour, as we adjusted sails and worked our way westward. With our anchors off the bows and our cables ranged on the foredeck, we crept along on into the evening until, having left Cape Elizabeth with its light astern, the wind went ahead and the tide turned against us; and in sight of Portland Head Light and numerous islands, we glided to a halt, dropped anchor, and waited for the tide to take us in at daybreak.

Having turned down the services of a pilot—in keeping with obstinate family tradition—Melchett took us in himself next morning, shortly after the tide turned at first light: dawn giving us a fair wind and bright seas for our homecoming, with clear skies and a tang of wet wharves to the breezes. In the midst of the commotion of weighing the anchor, I managed to slip to the deck unnoticed, and lend a hand here and there where needed: McCabe keeping a weather eye on me once he'd seen me, but allowing me to carry on light tasks without censure. As we made our way deeper into Casco Bay and gradually bore down on the city, we passed a cluster of shimmering islands, slipping by us off to starboard; and looking out on their summery green and silver, or the blue glinting swaths of the sea between them, I eagerly explored their hillsides, or wandered over their banks and beaches.

Gazing out ahead and to larboard, I drank in as well the details of the mainland: the low, green flatland with its sand stretches, the granite outcroppings with their rose tincture, and the city of Portland on its narrow peninsula in the foreground; and in the background a dusky line of hills, broken rises on the horizon. As we'd threaded our way between the isles and the mainland, we'd taken in the studdingsails and rigged in the booms, coiling away gear with a lively chorus; and now as we drew in toward the city, Melchett ordered in the royals and flying jib—two of the boys furling the royals since the wind gave us leeway—then called in the topgallants and bade us haul up the foresail, till *Charis* was under topsails, jib and spanker.

Gliding in toward the wharves—catching sight of the tangle of warehouses and sheds, sail lofts, masts, yardarms and rigging which fronted Commercial Street its whole length on the harbor—we clewed up the maintopsail and put the helm down, jubilantly letting go the anchor off Howland's wharf; and in an instant the decks were surging with people of every walk of life and description. Mothers and sisters hugging Howland and Reuben; dandified gents calling for friends; merchant types hailing Melchett and Spooner; newspaper agents inquiring for news; and waterdogs, idlers, longshoremen and drifters all competed for an ear in the uproar; and so beseiged were we that we were hard put to hear orders, or to carry out our final tasks. Running amongst the clutter ashore to haul her into the wharf, we made the last turns fast to the pilings: McCabe taking charge of the ship as soon as we were finished, and Melchett getting off at once with the mail.

We hadn't been a day in Portland—had scarcely begun to break out cargo, with me transferred back to my old berth in the forecastle— when I saw the folly of my conviction that touching shore would put Melchett and me on equal footing, or give me the chance for the meetings I sought. Far from being in his company more often, I scarcely ever saw him; for he was—as I should have foreseen— compelled to take up residence with his uncle Elkanah, Reuben's father and head of the Melchett clan in Portland, for diplomatic and business reasons. There, in some great house on Congress Street, he remained entrenched for our stay, so swamped with Portland relations and in-laws—so caught up in shipyard and counting house transactions—that he seldom came by the ship save to check on the progress of the cargo.

Even when I did see him he was surrounded by Melchetts and Howlands, and in an irascible humor; so that it wasn't long before I'd understood that his family hierarchy ashore would be as relentless a force to contend with as maritime procedures at sea. Lying in my bunk at night, missing his characteristic sounds and nearness—the ritual of waking and reading, record-keeping and Haggai-baiting which for days had spoken to me of his presence—I felt more separated from him than ever, of a different society entirely; and I wondered disconsolately how I'd fit in with his family—how I'd expected I'd even be invited to their tables.

Though he did little to change his style of dress, bowing to convention only enough to wear a sack suit, a highly informal trowsers and jacket which contrasted humorously with the frock coats of his kinsmen; though neither he nor the others knew anything for certain about my past in Boston, or my unpalatable months in Liverpool and New York; though he himself seemed to care nothing for the distinctions between us, we were kept apart by the responsibilities of his station in life ashore as surely as we had been at sea, and my lack of schooling in his shoreside traditions was plain.

To complicate matters even further, there rose up within me, these warm nights in the forecastle, the old ghosts of fear and pursuit and exposure; for now that I was on the same shore as Boston—now that I was within reach of the arm of Lomond—my old concerns for my name and safety, almost forgotten in my days at sea, were once again at large and active. Exactly how Melchett had handled my signing of the Articles, that day I'd penned my name at Hannah's— whether he'd registered me at the Boston Customs House, as he was legally bound to do, or somehow, against character, manipulated matters in the more lenient Rio to make it appear as if I'd signed on there—on this my safety ultimately depended. But which course of action he had then taken, I couldn't bring myself to inquire—knew both he and McCabe would suspect a guilty conscience; and so I could only dumbly conjecture as to whether my trail was covered or no.

Those of us—like Howland and Reuben—who actually resided in Portland, simply went home upon our arrival, reporting for work each day at seven and knocking off, like the rest of us, after six; but the bulk of us, who expected to go on to Cape Damaris, continued to live on board, with Sundays and evenings at our leisure; and it was during such free time that I pursued my attempts to acquaint myself with Melchett's shore life. At first I went out little, eating supper on board, then wandering the wharves in the relative calm of the evening, listening to accents and looking at faces, testing the bounds of my new terrain; but as the week wore on and I became stronger, I took to joining Paul and the others for drinks at some of their favorite haunts, and so gradually widened my explorations of the city which was Melchett's home away from home.

Counting houses, ship's chandlers, the great mercantile houses of Portland: these were the interstices of the city's system of commerce, and a part of Melchett's regular beat; but I longed for a glimpse of his more personal orbit—yearned for a look at the place he was staying, or the home where he'd courted Anne before marriage. Walking back to the ship one night after drinks and a jaunt through the center of town, I finally had the chance I sought; for our way took us past both the Melchett house on Congress Street and the Howland establishment not far away, and Paul spontaneously pointed them out.

Taken aback by the size and grandness of both places, despite the fact I'd long known of the wealth which distinguished the Melchetts and Howlands—fascinated by the profusion of windows, the configuration of porches, gables and ells which suggested the complexity of the rooms within—I took to wandering about on my own in the coming nights, discreetly crossing and re-crossing on the opposite side of the street, trying to memorize every detail. So familiar did I become with Elkanah's house in particular that I could almost read its windows and doors, as I'd learned to cipher the lines in Melchett's face—understanding, from the intricacies and obligations of its structure, the scope of its demands on his time, and the explanation of his set and harried expression.

One night, near the end of July—but a day or two before our departure for Cape Damaris, when we'd nearly completed ballasting the ship—I took off by myself the whole evening, and set out on foot to explore Elkanah's one last time. It was a sweet, fragrant summer's night, with the little lifts of the breeze in the vines, and the clatter of horse hooves on the cobbles; and as I unobtrusively approached on the far side of the street, I saw that the Melchett place was the setting for an elaborate evening party: the colored lights on the lawn, the canvas awning over the walkway, and the brightly illumined windows all proclaiming the occasion even from a distance.

Opening the doors of arriving carriages, helping the occupants down, numbering the vehicles and arranging their parking, the serving men could be seen bustling about in bright jackets; while richly dressed men in kid gloves and tail coats, with top hats of silk or satin or beaver, and elegant ladies in brocaded frocks, with finely-embroidered capes or mantillas, floated up the walk to the door. Knowing that Melchett must be within, I slipped to the lee of a broad tree nearby, and pretended to pass the time with a cigar: dutifully puffing—though I cared little for smoking—and peering discreetly at the house, or listening to the strains of the music like a child yearning over a banister rail.

Even though I knew that Melchett himself despised such gatherings, I longed for the privilege of being there too—of being able to go where he went; and I felt intolerably apart and alone. Out of nowhere I wanted, as I watched, a passport into that cryptic world, coveted it because it was his; wanted, as he had, the right to reject it. Fascinated—both repelled and attracted—by what I was discovering of his life, I looked on while the wind stole about me in whispers, bearing the distant aroma of jasmine, or rustling the leaves on a nearby clapboard wall.

As I stood gazing at the bright windows—as I picked out the motions of swaying figures, and wondered if Melchett had ever danced—there all at one rose up in my mind's eye the squalor of my life in New York, the immigrant cellars, their berths alive with vermin, or the bleak attic cells of Ann Street; and giving a sudden bitter laugh—tossing down my cigar, and crushing out its ash—I set my course for the neighboring gin house I'd visited once or twice with Paul, and ordered myself a mugful of grog. A mixture of rum, beer, sugar and water, it wasn't the drink for one lately ill; but I followed it up with another and another, till I'd so effectively lost track of my thoughts, and the passage of the hour, that I wound up missing curfew by several minutes. Cocking an eye, McCabe reprimanded me roundly; but Melchett gave me a long look when word got back to him next morning, and my shipmates commenced talking robustly about it, till by noon I'd supposedly spent the night drinking, and ended up in some bed house or brothel.

If I'd been anxious to glimpse the architecture of Melchett's shore life, the ten days or so we'd been docked in Portland, I was even more keen to walk his native ground in Cape Damaris; and as we squared away on the last day of July for the final stage of our voyage, I was as enthusiastic as any of my shipmates. Less than a working day's sail from Portland, our entire route lay within sight of the coast; and with the southwest wind behind us, we exalted in the changing shoreline. As we manned the halyards and braces one last time, we gloried in the spruce which spiked the headlands, the rocks and inlets which tortured the shores, and the historic islands which slipped by off either bow: Damariscove, long, low and timbered; Monhegan, rock-boned landfall of seamen; and the complex group of the Two Bush Channel, Metinic, Mosquito, and the Spruce Head cluster.

Bright and enthused as any of the hands, Melchett held forth on the quarterdeck; whilst I, fully employed on deck for the first time since my illness, reveled in the rhythms of my labors. Cutting in toward Penobscot Bay—passing Sheep Island and Monroe to larboard, and the isle of St. James, birthplace of the McCabes, to starboard—we at last rounded Damaris Point, and trimmed our yards for the last mile of our journey: fetching first the lighthouse, set on a low, wind-bare cliff—next the line of spruce-clad bluffs which stretched toward the harbor—then finally the harbor itself, and Cape

Damaris overlooking it on an arena of hills.

A resounding cheer went up from the men, dimly echoed by those waiting across the water; while I halted in my work to stare with eyes devoid of doubt or worry. These were the shores which had witnessed Melchett's boyhood, and the passage of his life into manhood; and as we drew in toward the town I beheld them with delight, with a dazed kind of hush that I was actually here. White squares—green masses—the hills' rolling profile—the steeple of a church—bare masts in the harbor: each unencumbered, spare line or angle, each resolute, practical structure spoke to me of the character of the town's shapers; and I felt as I traversed the clean, stalwart townscape that I'd come home to it many times already—that I was discovering forms long known but forgotten, like signposts recalled out of distant journeys, or landmarks beside roads long ago traveled.

As we eased into a berth out near the end of one of the great piers—as we made fast to the pilings amid competing chanteys, and the exclamations and shouts of the mob which poured over the bulwarks—I saw that half the town had turned out to meet us; and struggling not to lose my foothold midway out the mainyard, I cast about for a sight of Melchett's family. Spotting him still entrenched on the quarterdeck, I fumbled to make out those around him; but so engulfed was he by men of all ages, some rudely dressed, some finely attired, and all clapping him upon the back or shaking hands, that I couldn't hazard a guess who they might be, till they passed in a body below me on their way to inspect the jury mast, and I picked out one or two who might be his brothers.

As he came forward amongst them the gangplank went down, to the accompaniment of urgent children's voices; and picking out the shrill, piping sound, he hastened down toward a group at the edge of the wharf where a cluster of townspeople anxiously waited. Darting ahead with a quick, eager eye, I spotted a woman, fashionably dressed and hatted, with a number of straining children in hand; and I knew even before he caught up the young ones that these were indeed his wife and children. Scarcely even pretending to work, I watched as he fondled each of his offspring, all having turned up except the baby; quietly, reservedly greeted Anne; inclined his head toward a short, silver-haired lady who I knew must be his mother; and gave a brotherly embrace for a bright, fair-haired young woman who I guessed at once was Keziah.

Then catching the two oldest children, Tom and Jean, in either hand—briefly tipping his cap to the crowd around him, and patting the impatient twins, who remained with Anne—he plowed a path for the young ones back on board toward the bow, pointing out the jury rig to his mother and sister, who'd followed, and who seemed by their gestures to take as intelligent an interest in the structure as the assembly of brothers and townsmen around it. Whenever I seized a glance after that, he was standing in the midst of the throng, whilst the children were handed about over the heads of their elders, and travelers' tales of the race to Rio or the hurricane in the Florida Straits rose to my ears in competing snatches; then turning over the ship to McCabe, he headed back with Tom and Jean for the gangway, flinging the bag he'd set there over his shoulders.

Disembarking with his children, he gathered up Anne and the rest of his party, while I watched with a sudden desolate sting— tipped his cap once again to the thinning crowd on the wharf, and made his way through its ranks to a handsome brougham waiting nearby; then helping the others to a seat within, he disappeared inside himself, and drove off down the street with his family.

As cut off as if I'd been left behind, I finished out my duties in silence, squaring the yards, coiling up rigging, and bunting up the sails while choruses of "Round the Corner" rose from the hoarse throats of my shipmates, and echoed along the increasingly quiet wharf; then clearing out with my gear like everyone else, I left the ship which had been my home for four months. Though we had still a day's work before us, hauling out the last of the cargo and moving *Charis* for repairs to the shipyard, all such final tasks were slated for the morrow to allow the hands the rest of the day for homecoming; and every one of my shipmates had gone off with his family.

Feeling disoriented and alone after their departure, I stood on the quay with my trunk on a handcart, looking about for McCabe who, like all the others, had stopped by at the counting house to pick up his last month's wages—I myself having decided to forego my salary, as I scarcely felt I had earned it. When at last I spotted his lean, mild mug bobbing toward me in the midst of unfamiliar faces, and realized he was coming to meet me, my spirits immediately cheered a degree; and giving a wave as I pushed my cart toward him, I allowed him to escort me to the Seven Seas Inn across the way—the place where, having refused the hospitality of my shipmates' houses, I'd some time ago agreed to let him engage me a room for a month.

With the prospect of lodgings ready and waiting in an establishment owned and run by McCabe's uncle, I felt my heart rise afresh with excitement; and as we entered the Inn—a big, rectangular, white clapboard building with dormer windows along the roofline— and found the lower halls darting with a brisk flux of tradesmen, seamen, and well-dressed women bound to dinner, I was filled again with adventure. Meeting Jimmy McCabe, a kindly, gnarled, white-maned old man with a fatherly manner and a twist of the sea to his visage, bolstered me further; and by the time I'd climbed to the third floor with my trunk and fitted my key to the lock in my door, I felt again as I had when I'd first seen the town—as if I'd come home to familiar moorings.

As soon as I swung open the oak-paneled door, the room completely took me aback; and I stood for a moment on the threshold, uncertain whether even to enter. Expecting the ordinary bare, nondescript chamber of a typical seaman's lodging—and even that several cuts above anything I'd ever lived in—I felt a catching at my throat; for before me was as homelike a place as any I'd ever heard tell of or imagined.

In one corner rose a spacious four-poster, neat, plump, with a quilted coverlet of obvious value—in another a pine wardrobe with drawers beneath, a dresser with mirror, and a well-appointed washstand; whilst along one wall ran the fireplace and mantle, and upon the floor lay colorful round, braided carpets. The walls—far from bare—were papered, and boasted one or two fine paintings of vessels under a press of sail; while at the windows white muslin curtains were stirring—the dormers overlooking the waterfront and town, and a fan-shaped pane facing the harbor.

Though I'd known even at Hannah's that there might be such a room—though I'd thought that, if ever I were to settle on land, my desire would be for a place such as this—my joy at the prospect of realizing my vision was shattered as soon as I came to my senses; for within moments my daze had diminished enough to permit me to perceive that—despite McCabe's assurance that the room was within my means—there must be some arrangement with Jimmy, no doubt initiated in Portland, to lower the price or to allow someone— probably Melchett—to pay the balance. Torn between gratitude for the gesture and anger at having been accommodated—divided between a yearning for the lodging before me, and a recognition that I should not accept it—I felt a sudden sting to my eyes; and utterly uncertain how to proceed, I remained mute on the threshold.

"Will this do, d'ye think?" I heard McCabe ask me, his voice— always offhand and understated—now coming a trifle anxious; and struggling to collect my wits—resolving at last not to let on that I knew, until I had actually confirmed my suspicions—I got out a smiling "Aye," and assured him that I would be fine here. Without further ado we entered the room, opened the trunk and unpacked my kit; then putting a hand under my elbow, McCabe steered me round the Inn—helping me make arrangements for laundry, directing me to the boarders' parlor where I'd take my meals, and finally treating me to supper at the *Seven Seas* dining saloon, where we were engulfed by a tumult of land and sea stories.

Fortified by a spread of sumptuous seafood and eager to investigate the town before nightfall, I sallied forth with McCabe after dinner, accompanying him as he bought up supplies for his homecoming, and hired a trap to convey us to his cabin. As our way took us down Water Street, the main thoroughfare of the town—a broad, shop-lined artery cobbled with bricks, directly on the clear, curving dock-front—I managed to view a good deal of the seaport, and all of the wharves save those of the shipyards behind me. Stationers', apothecaries, general stores, saddleries, and small shops filled with wares from foreign ports passed me by on the right, while the ships which had supplied them filed by on my left; and as we worked our way through the early evening traffic, my heart kept pace with the rapid rhythms around me.

Anticipating a glimpse of the Melchett family house on the edge of town, and further on, Melchett's house out the peninsula road, I peered first one way and then another, as the shops began to give way to homesteads: my eagerness to set eyes on Melchett's homesites swallowing up even my trepidation that I would be out of place within them. Mindful of what I had seen in Portland, I scrutinized the houses now approaching, now slipping past us at either hand; but I quickly perceived that all were unpretentious, tall and narrow, a century old or more, with widows' walks at the rooflines and shutters at the windows: their character a unanimous proclamation of the simplicity of the hands which had wrought them.

Suddenly upon my right there appeared one great house, set back a distance from the street, and beyond it, behind a white fence, a broad, open yard dotted with majestic maples and oaks. Three stories high and with a wing at the rear as large—square and severe as a box, topped with a blunt cupola, yet graced with numerous green-shuttered windows—undeniably grand, the seat of a sprawling and successful family—it nonetheless was in every way as forthright and plain as the old captains' houses we had just passed, and it looked as welcoming and home-like. Understanding at once I looked at it, abashed, yet inexplicably relieved; and reading the wordless side glance I cast at him, McCabe smiled.

"Aye," he responded, drawing rein for a moment, "this here's the Melchett family house. Ben growed up here; his Pa owns the place, an' Joseph lives here with his children, along with the youngeh brothehs an' Keziah. Old Abigail, Ben's grandmotheh, she lives here too."

Still silent I continued to gaze at the dwelling, torn between my gratitude for its simplicity and my awe at its imposing size; between my impression that it was accessible, and my instinctive awareness that its hierarchy of inmates and code of life rendered it oppressive. Looking at the building I directly understood why Melchett had fled its confines with Charis, and taken to hanging about the bait sheds of Fishtown; appreciated the challenge of making one's mark in this superstructure of family and business, and hence the competition which had sparked the race to Rio; read it all as plainly as if the house were a map, and its legend the index to Melchett's nature.

"We'd best move on, we'll be seen for suhtain—old Abigail misses nothin'," McCabe murmured, recalling me with a touch to the shoulder; and giving the horse a flick of the reins, he headed down the street toward Fishtown. "Ye'll be comin' here soon t' dinneh, no doubt," he went on, with something like a mischievous glint in his eye. "But I had a mind t' let ye see it t'day, t' rid ye of this notion you won't fit in."

I saw he was grinning and stared at him in wonder, for I'd said nothing to him of the true state of my feelings—nothing of either my long-standing apprehension or of my present ambiguous reaction. "It's as simple inside as out, though I don't deny they've some fine old treasures brung back from here an' there," he added. "You c'n put youhr feet on the table though, b'lieve me!—except in the drawring room, an' hahdly anybody eveh goes there. As t' youhr clothes—" his grin grew wider. "Well, you've seen the rags Ben wears—I sweah he's had that jersey for ten yeahrs...an' that jacket! It drives Anne near t' distraction. But his fatheh's just the same. On the street ye'd take him for a gooney."

With a smile which conveyed both my gratitude for his words and my lingering doubts and misgivings, I turned my thoughts back to the road before us; and giving me a pat on the knee, McCabe headed over the narrow river which bounded the Melchett property on our right, and flowed along the sandy road to our left till it emptied into the nearby harbor. There I could see a collection of weathered docks and buildings gathered on either side of its mouth; and gazing the half-mile or so to the hamlet, I descried shingled cottages set up on low stilts, and mewing gulls wheeling over the bait sheds, or perching in crowded rows on the rooflines.

"That's fish town," McCabe pointed, "place where Paul lives, 'n Johnny Kalkman an' the Coombs brothehs. A fair amount of oystehs 'n cod they haul in with them schoonehs an' scows! We're in the McCabe paht of town now," he grinned, with a comradely glance at me; and taking at once to the clutter and disorder, the haphazardness of roof, wharf and building, I felt a flash of accord with the village, and an unexpected rush of kinship with McCabe.

Then a thick stand of spruce intervened on my left and obscured both my reverie and line of vision, at the place where Water Street veered into the Point Road; and I found myself driving along the peninsula, along the mile-long lane which led to McCabe's cabin, Melchett's home and the Cape Damaris lighthouse. From my left came the hollow drone of the surf, louder whenever the trees thinned or opened; while nearer at hand came the muffled clopping of hooves and the hush of the wagon wheels cushioned in sandy gravel—sounds so low that I could pick out the thump of my heart as I sensed the approach of Melchett's house

"We're comin' up on my cabin now," McCabe suddenly broke the silence; and following his hand as he gestured, I spotted a sandy drive on the left, and traced it to an opening in the tall pines—to the guess of a log dwelling between the branches, and the grey line of the sea beyond the grass bank. "It's tight as a newly-caulked ship an' twice as tough," he smiled, explaining as we drove by that Melchett and his brother Tom had helped him build it. "It'll stand foreveh."

In two minutes more we were at the foot of Melchett's drive, marked on either side by an old fieldstone fence, and surrounded by a wilderness of pines and hardwoods. "Take a quick look," McCabe said, "I expect they're all there to suppeh." Snatching a rapid glance as bidden I noted how the drive curved around to the left and disappeared from view en route to the stable; took in the carriage-filled parking area ahead, and the back of the house which faced us. Painted an old yellow, with dark green shutters—two stories high, with a kitchen ell at the rear, attic dormers and a widow's walk—roomy but modest, unassuming, spare, it seemed to have sprung right out of the sallow shore around it; seemed to have been shaped out, like the twisted pine boughs above it, by the forces and exigencies of nature.

At first sight I would have said that it wholly reflected both the man who'd built it, Trevellyan, a reclusive eighteenth century captain, and the man who'd later bought it—Melchett, on coming into his property at twenty-one; for it was perched on the edge of the bank as on a frontier, as close to the open sea as one could get on land, as if uneasy at the thought of being ashore, or full of disregard for the amenities of town. But on closer view I could discern discrepancies which clearly suggested Anne; for carved out of the underbrush which grew haphazardly everywhere was a kitchen garden which looked to be well tended, its ordered rows running beneath the ell windows; while on the right an area had been wrested for roses, and for the formal flower beds flanking the detached parlor entrance. Brick walks, potted plants, and wrought-iron lamp-posts too seemed to be out of place in the country, as if someone had been dissatisfied with rural life, and contrived to simulate the setting of a townhouse.

The final result was a subtle air of contradiction, an unspoken contention between the isolated establishment of a seaman who shunned the convention of town, and the domicile of a well-bred society matron who missed the environment in which she'd been raised. Transfixed by the antipathy I sensed in the house, by the cross-currents which seemed to vie for the grounds, I lingered to gaze on the area slowly; then suddenly spotting a rope swing in the beech tree which stood at the bend of the drive nearby us—spotting further signs testifying to the presence of children—I felt my thoughts turn to other channels.

"They must love it here," I heard myself murmur, the words out of my mouth almost before I knew it.

Seeing the direction of my gaze, McCabe took my meaning at once. "The young 'uns? Aye. I ought t' know: I growed up on this shore m'self. It's a grand raisin' for a child. It's on account of them, as much as hisself, that Ben won't heahr of movin' back t' town."

Alert at once to his implication—surprised, for he was not one to stoop to gossip—I turned to look at him thoughtfully, recalling all the scuttlebutt round the forecastle table about Anne's resistance to locating so far out on the peninsula; then turning back to the house I felt a flash of hunger for what she apparently disregarded. Almost as swift as the hunger came my incredulous reaction to the revelation that I wanted, indeed coveted such a place for myself; that I, of pure Romany stock and teaching, raised to disdain permanent dwellings, stood in the road desiring someone else's home and belongings.

Taken aback by my own feelings—forced to confront the fact they'd been growing, side by side with my yen to know Melchett, ever since I'd resided at Hannah's—I cast about for a way to forget them; and as if understanding McCabe shook the reins, and turned the horses in the rutted road. As we turned away the parlor door suddenly opened, and a party of callers headed down the walk to their carriage—visitors who'd come to welcome Melchett home, or to see the new child, or both; and hastening on—appreciating at once that a continuous flow of guests, on top of his obligations to shipyard and family, must be characteristic of Melchett's life ashore—I rode beside McCabe in silence, mulling over my impressions.

Driving back toward the town we returned to McCabe's cabin, where we put on a pot of coffee; soon I was engaged in helping him unpack, or set to rights his newly stocked shelves, and so I forgot my thoughts for a time. Forgot them completely later that night: for we both drove to the tavern at the Inn and, under Jimmy McCabe's direction, got half-seas over on some fine West Indies rum.

Yet my moment on Melchett's shore was not my last news of him that evening; for when I returned to my room sometime after midnight, there was a note stuck in the doorway—a small square of paper which caught the glow of my candle, and set my heart to erratic thumping. Fumbling with the key and the candle—in no condition to manage more than one task at a time, and struggling not to burn up my missive—I at last succeeded in entering my chamber; and shakily setting the light on my desk top—scanning the small card which leapt up at me, and instantly recognizing it as Melchett's—I threw myself into the chair to read it.

On one side was the standard businessman's legend, printed in unpretentious typeset: "Capt. Benjamin G. Melchett, Melchett Bros., Inc., 31 Water Street, Cape Damaris, Maine"; and in the lower right corner was the even smaller postscript, "Res., East Point Road." But on the back was a handwritten message, uncharacteristically slanted and hasty, though typically direct and pointed, bereft of either greeting or closing: "How about supper at my place tomorrow? McCabe'll be by around 6 to pick you up—B."

Not even bothering to undress, I fell into bed with the note in my hand, sinking into the feather ticking as into the depths of a warm ocean billow, so full of conflicting recollections that I dropped at last into a swirling slumber, and knew nothing till Jimmy called me at daybreak.

The next day saw us so busy with our final duties to *Charis* that I not only saw nothing of Melchett, but had no chance myself to prepare for dinner; and when at last I knocked off at five and hurried back to my room for a clean-up, it was a disheveled sight which looked out of my mirror. Washing up, shaving, donning my best white duck trowsers, and pulling on the only jacket I had, the square-cut blue coat common to sailors, helped a little; but in my plaid shirt and worn-out patent leather pumps, with no better hat than my sea-going tarpaulin, I was no match for a society matron, and knew it.

Promptly at six McCabe pulled up at the Inn door, wearing the same half-professional, half-laboring garb he wore when he was on deck, though I knew perfectly well he owned better; and hopping aboard I sat down beside him, too on edge to exchange more than a greeting. Giving me an understanding nod, he at once whipped up his mare; and we were off with a creak and a clatter through the bustling traffic of town, passing the shops and homesteads of Water Street, the Melchett family house and the wharves of fish town, till at last we reached the peninsula junction, and headed out the Point Road for Melchett's.

As we left behind the landmarks and pointers I'd become acquainted with just yesterday, I rejoiced in the wind's gusting and blowing, for its restless, unceasing sound and motion seemed to move in time with my own pent-up energy, as though my spirit were a conductor.

When we approached McCabe's drive he slowed the buggy, as if—having reflected on the likelihood of my social shortcomings and concluded, correctly, that they were many—he'd decided to start off at scratch, and take a moment to instruct me. "If ye want t' impress Anne," he began gently, making an effort to be tactful, "all ye have t' do is follow her lead. That's jest the way things're done here on such occasions. Don't shake her hand unless she offehs; take her int' the dinin' room when suppeh's announced, if she approaches an' gives ye her ahrm; set at her right hand, pass whateveh she passes, use the forks n' spoons in the ordeh ye find 'em, don't put youhr elbows on the table, don't say ain't, don't pay much heed t' the young 'uns, an' don't go on about sea life if ye c'n help it."

"Will it help Ben if I butter her up?" I asked bluntly.

"It always makes things easieh if she accepts his friends," came his typically laconic reply; and flapping the reins he bypassed his driveway, and headed down the road to Melchett's.

Parking the buggy in the bend of the drive, we approached the house on foot, McCabe leading the way down the path toward the ell, and me eagerly gazing about as I followed. Rising before us, the house—tall, square and airy, with its companion buildings grouped near the stable—reminded me suddenly of *Charis*; for like a ship it had obviously been shaped to accommodate nature, wrought with a geometry of light, wind and seasons; while at the same time it had been designed to replenish itself with its gardens, well-house and woodpiles and tool sheds.

Yet recalling my impressions of dissension yesterday, the very path we walked divided, one branch heading off for the parlor doorway, the other continuing on toward the ell; and giving his thumb a jerk toward the parlor—steering me meantime up the ell pathway, which I took to be the tradesmen's and family's entrance— McCabe grinned, "That's not for the likes of you an' me, mate," with his usual half-wry, half-philosophical humor.

As we came up the walk past a couple of pines which till now had screened a part of the yard, we heard the ringing of an ax, and the good-natured barking of a dog; and over-run at once by a zealous spaniel, we found ourselves confronted by Melchett, chopping kindling near the kitchen woodpile. Looking up from his work he gave us a wave, his face lighting up with glad recognition; and sinking the ax into a log by the woodpile, he abruptly crossed over to meet us, the eagerness of his eyes belying the awkward reserve of his manner.

As he gestured about in the flutter of greeting, he pointed out for me the path which led to McCabe's cabin, then drew my attention to the incoming schooners, and the low-lying outline of St. James Island, barely visible in the haze eight miles out: his shabby shirt and baggy trowsers, big, knotty hands and tow-bleached hair, all making him appear at one with the shore. Beckoning us at length to follow, he led the way up the back steps and through the enclosed porch—neatly stacked with a mountain of wood which at once informed me there'd been no need for him to chop kindling—and thence into a magnificent country kitchen, long and low and heavily raftered, as much like a ship's galley as any place on land, where Sadie the housekeeper contended with supper.

As energetic as a mate in a gale, she set to and hugged McCabe, embracing him like a long-lost brother—indeed, I later found out they were cousins—then warmly turned and welcomed me, her plain, earthy face and ample curves somehow in keeping with the prodigious hearth, and the long pine plank table laden with dishes. Informing us that Anne had gone upstairs to tend the baby, she sent us summarily away, shooing McCabe away from the kettles, and promising supper within the hour; and leading us on down a short hallway which housed the stairs, Melchett ushered us into the sitting room, a square, well-lit chamber which fronted the sea.

Collapsing gratefully into an armchair I gave my attention at once to the hearth, where two-year-old Seth and Courtney were playing and tugging with Melchett's cat Bo'sun. "These're the twins," introduced Melchett, characteristically unable to light in a chair, and kneeling down by the young ones to start up a fire. "This here's Seth," he said, grabbing the nearest, then propelling him firmly in my direction; and the boy trotted obediently up to me with the sublimest air of indifference I ever saw in a child. He was very fair, his hair straight and silken, his eyes brightly blue; and like all New England children of means, he was attired in a long gathered dress, embroidered and flounced at every twist and turn.

I wanted to hold him, wanted to stroke his smooth tresses—but he was wary of my aims, and entirely disinterested: stopping just short of me, giving a smart salute, then sidestepping my hands as I grasped him. "He's damned hahd t' get hold of," grinned Melchett, as the boy headed back to his game with Bo'sun, "don't I know it myself! Here's Courtney; she's ouhr charmeh," he added, giving his daughter an encouraging prod; and leaning down toward her as she approached, I saw at once she was that indeed, blue-eyed and fair-haired liker her brother, with long golden curls and a delicate air.

"May I hold you?" I asked, longing to touch her; and her face lighted up at the words.

"Yesh, matey," she lisped, holding up her arms, oblivious of her father's explosion of laughter.

""Christ, Melchett, ye'll have 'em splicin' ropes by Christmas!" choked McCabe, as soon as his own guffaw had subsided.

"Hope so," smiled Melchett, turning back to the fire; but there was something less than a smile in his voice, and I looked at him thoughtfully as I stroked Courtney's hair.

It had been years since I'd held a child, not since I'd left Wales, certainly not since New York; and my heart swelled with awe as I caressed Melchett's young one—swelled till it ached when she stole her hands round my neck, and tucked her head under my chin. With Courtney nestling familiarly on my knee and Melchett before me, building up the fire; with McCabe in the easy chair filling his pipe, and Seth teasing Bo'sun with a spool and string, I had a moment to catch my breath, and take a look at the room around me: the drone of the sea, the crackling blaze, Seth's cheerful babbling to the cat, and McCabe's intermittent, pacific puffing the happy accompaniments to my gazing.

It was a bright, airy room, illumined by three windows, and set about with a comfortable sofa and chairs: the net result so inviting and warm that even I, who'd never sat in a room such as this, felt gradually less and less out of place. Yet for all its simplicity of form and purpose, Melchett seemed ill at ease in its confines, even apart from his awkwardness as a host, and his offhanded clumsiness with his children; seemed far less at ease than on the deck of his ship, as if the room were too small to contain him; and I found myself frequently alternating my glances at cupboards and books, shadows boxes and carvings with glimpses of his demeanor and face.

As I gazed about, young Seth wandered by within reach of his father, who'd finally settled on an ottoman near the fire: I saw Melchett's big, abrupt hand dart out, grasp the child by the folds of the skirt, and swing him up to a berth on his lap. From his unexpected perch atop Melchett's knee, Seth crowed and clapped his hands with laughter, as if in glee that he'd been outwitted; and Melchett cast a triumphant glance at me. For all his ungainly show of affection, he looked surprisingly natural with a child on his knee, though the two of them made an amusing contrast: rugged Melchett with his rough brown clothes, his blunt, square hands and broad thighs and knees, and small blonde Seth in his absurd dress, patent leathers and white stockings, with his head cocked to one side and his eyes on father's face. A look flashed between them which showed they were kin, after all; a wave of wistfulness washed over me, and when it had passed, I was aware of Anne's step on the stairs.

Depositing Courtney hastily on the floor, I apprehensively got to my feet, just as Anne swept into the room—tall, stately, self-assured as a dancer, with the baby still held in the crook of her arm. Remembering not to offer my hand—nodding at Melchett's brief introduction, and struggling to keep an awkward note from my greeting—I stood before her with whatever poise I could muster, while she graciously welcomed me and acknowledged McCabe's presence; studied her with quick, oblique glances—finding in her cool genteel beauty, stylish fair hair and searching blue eyes, evidence of breeding and money. Not till I'd met her could I have imagined a more obvious complete contrast to Melchett; and overcome by the impact of her distinction and the ambiguity of my impressions, I found myself floundering to keep the talk going.

Casting about wildly for something appropriate to say and catching sight providentially of the baby, I held out my arms with an impulsive "May I?"; and smiling for the first time since she'd entered the room, she transferred her bundle to my arms. Overjoyed to have something to hold onto—pushing back the blanket to see young Nat's face, and murmuring a reassuring word or two—I sat down with him in my lap, propping him so Courtney could see him; while Melchett,

no less at ease around an infant than around a loaded cannon, went
back to his ottoman and lighted a pipe, making no move to claim his
new son, in fact eyeing him askance, as if he were about to explode.
Accustomed as I was to hordes of Romany young ones, I easily got
acquainted with small Nat, sandy-haired and grey-eyed like his
father; and finding him good-natured after his nursing, I played with
his hands or tickled his feet, while McCabe asked Melchett about his
habits, and Melchett responded with offhanded affection.

Gliding to the doorway to summon Tom and Jean in from
play—looking in on us with a quiet "See to it they really do come in,
Benjamin"—Anne excused herself for a moment and drifted down the
hallway, probably to help Sadie; and glad of her absence I toyed with
the baby, conscious of Melchett's eye on my face. At length getting to
his feet with a grunt, Melchett went to the door and commanded—in
his finest quarterdeck bawl—"Thomas! Jean Charis!"—a summons
which brought a distant "Aye!" from somewhere out on the wind-
rustled bank; and barking back "Get youhr tails in here! *Now!*"—an
order which elicited a vigorous "Aye, *aye!*"— Melchett returned with
his characteristic air of finality to his ottoman and his pipe, while
McCabe chuckled familiarly from the depths of his chair.

Melchett's pipe was scarcely re-lighted when a banging came
from the hallway entrance, and Tom burst in upon us with Jean.
Flinging himself at once down by the cat—shoving Seth aside
none too gently—Tom made himself at home on the hearth; while
Jean paused wordlessly in the doorway, studying me with a timid
sharpness. Melchett's other children were bright and playful, as
conventional as other young ones their age; but there was nothing
ordinary about the child now before me, and I gave her back stare
for stare without censure.

At five she was small and slim, with wild, pale fair hair, almost
flaxen, dangling in wisps about her shoulders, and a worn calico dress
hanging limply to her boot-tops. In her face was something of both
of her parents—Anne's delicately refined features, Melchett's grey eyes
and willful brow; while her fragile limbs, with their airy lightness,
brought to mind the gossamer threads of nature—the dew-spangled
webs, the fine veins of leaves, the beaded filaments of spindrift.

But it was chiefly her eyes which arrested my notice, for they gave lie to the frailty of her body: their rain-colored gaze at once young and old, innocent and knowing, stalwart and tender. They could have been set in any face of any age, but in hers they brought out the delicate cheekbones, the pointed chin, and the small determined brows, and gave her a look of unearthly perception. Not since I'd left Wales had I seen eyes like these—the eyes of a vibrant forcible spirit, too large for the body which housed it, as if it threatened the slender walls of its dwelling.

"Hullo, Jean," I murmured softly, longing to break through the reserve of this, Melchett's favorite child; but she refused to respond to my greeting, rooting herself instead at McCabe's elbow, and eyeing me from a cautious distance. It was all I was to see of her for the moment; for Anne—returning just then from the kitchen, and finding her and Tom still not dressed for supper—dispatched them at once upstairs, and they obeyed without a word. Excusing herself once again from our midst—by the tightness of her mouth, obviously vexed, though her manner showed nothing of it—Anne followed them out of the sitting room door; and a moment later I heard her step on the stairs, as she headed up to aid their efforts.

It was apparent to me, even in my inexperienced state, that things were not going as smoothly for her as desired—that for so large a house, and so young a family, she was decidedly short of help; but Melchett seemed to notice nothing of it as he drilled McCabe about the day's business, or reached in now and then to poke at the fire.

Anne was back amongst us in record time with Tom and Jean in their Sunday attire; and there followed a rather stiff and formal half-hour as we sat together waiting for supper—the children divided between sitting primly in their chairs, at Anne's bidding, and wandering freely about, at Melchett's. We were an odd lot as we sat together, so odd that we inspired amusement—the children in their velvet-trimmed breeches, watered-silk dresses and satin ribbons; Melchett looking like a lumberjack who'd just barreled in for a plate of beans; me in my seaman's poor best with my long hair, and a gypsy's neckerchief tied at my throat; Anne in her elegant silk and lace trappings; and

McCabe walking the line between working man and professional in his seedy frock coat and seagoing trousers; and it was all I could do to contain my rising laughter.

Nor was the conversation any less awkward, Melchett cross-examining me about my room at the Inn or McCabe about the details of moving *Charis*, Anne vainly endeavoring to bring the talk round to social topics, and the children now and then bursting out with questions, encouraged by Melchett, promptly hushed by Anne. When at last Sadie came in to announce supper, I was indescribably relieved; and remembering McCabe's words I let the others go first, entering the dining room with Anne on my arm and seating myself quietly at her right, while McCabe automatically anchored himself by Melchett, and the children ranged themselves in between. Following Anne's cues I unfolded my napkin, managing not to spill the roll wrapped within it; and I could see that Melchett was about to attack the oysters already set on his plate, when Anne checked him with a quiet "We must have grace first; it's youhr turn, Thomas."

Sitting bolt upright in his chair, Tom folded his hands on the table, while all the other children, even the twins, followed suit; and the rest of us bowed our heads as Tom recited rapidly, "Thank you God for this good food amen."

With an amused grin tugging at the corners of his mouth, Melchett again addressed his oysters, while a line of vexation divided Anne's brows. But nothing more being said about Tom's abbreviated effort, the children too dug in, beginning with their rolls and butter; and for the next several minutes I was so busy trying to sort out the tasks before me—passing dishes, helping Courtney, fumbling with the amazing array of silverware, and watching Anne and McCabe for cues—that I completely forgot the moment. So long accustomed to such meals that he gave scarcely a thought to the art of serving, eating and timing the finish of each course, Melchett seemed not to notice the triumph of my correct responses; but I sensed that Anne was aware of my efforts, no doubt pleased to discover I was not wholly ignorant of the amenities.

As I put away in rapid succession the simpler courses leading up to the veal—as I watched Melchett carve, then serve the meat with Sadie's help—I gazed at the dining room about me, and at the parlor visible through the French doors across the way. Chock full of mahogany, rosewood and china, brocaded sofas and Persian carpets, the parlor looked to be Anne's particular haven; but the dining room was warm and simple; and it brought a relative calm to my spirit as I sought to address my unfamiliar tasks.

Deprived of the topics which consumed his interest—shipbuilding, navigation, maritime law—Melchett was a poor conversationalist; and without recourse to the social doings particularly congenial to her, Anne did not fare very much better. With talk of both sea and town out of the question, there was a regular dearth of subjects; but I hit upon the idea of asking about the children and so succeeded in pleasing Anne, while tactful McCabe and the oblivious young ones carried the day with their simple banter. Yet the meal did not pass without incident for all that; for as the children prattled on with their youthful exchanges, I was aware of the dense undercurrents which riddled the air between their parents. Not that their contention was visible in the form of retorts, frank remarks or disagreement, for both were too self-contained for that; but it showed in their careful self-control, their strained and humorless words and glances, and in the brittle atmosphere which pervaded the table.

Amongst the potential causes for dissension was surely their conflict in attitude toward the children; for Anne ignored them save to instruct them, her affection evident only in her strict standards, while Melchett spoke to them like miniature seamen, with a kind of encouraging, indulgent gruffness. When Jean declared her desire to become a sailor—swiftly seconding Tom's intention—discernible lines appeared between Anne's brows, though she said nothing to dissuade her; while Melchett quickly applauded his daughter, countering Tom's mocking "Oh, ho! A girl a sailoh!" with a half-comic, half-caustic "An' I s'pose Charis Spooneh was a man, eh?"

But it was the innocuous question of grammar which seemed to spark the hottest contention, and allowed me an uneasy glimpse into their conflict. Having picked at her food throughout the meal, Jean had eaten little and said even less; and finally taking notice Melchett barked, with his usual mixture of affectionate brusqueness:

"What's the long face for, hm?"

"Is my face long?" Jean asked curiously, looking over at him with thoughtful grey eyes.

"You bet it is, 'bout a mile an' a half."

"Well, I've been thinkin'," the child informed him.

"Don't drop your g's, dear," Anne interposed, in a voice no doubt meant to be kind, but which nonetheless brought a wince to Jean's features. Perhaps it was the effect of a long day, or of the preparations for so formal a meal coming on top of the festive responsibilities of Melchett's return home; but there was an edge to Anne's tone that hadn't been present earlier, and the child could plainly detect it.

"Well, I've been think*ing*," she automatically corrected, with just a trace of her own resentment.

"Good Lohrd! At the table?" bawled Melchett, while the lines faintly deepened between Anne's brows.

"Aye, suh."

"Well, does your thinkin' have t' keep ye from eatin', hm?" persisted Melchett, dropping his g's with obstinate abandon.

"No...but I ain't especially hungry," Jean confided.

"You know better than to say 'ain't,' daughter," Anne stepped in again; and this time Jean's eyes dropped to her plate as she toyed with her fork and said nothing further.

I could see that the simple reprimand had brought the child to the brink of tears, for her fingers trembled as they handled her silver; but her sensitive reaction was as nothing compared to the silent explosion which occurred between her parents. Their eyes met for just an instant, but Melchett's glance was as fierce as an onslaught— worse than anything I'd ever received from him, even after the fiasco in Rio. If he'd ever looked at me like that, I'd have withered on the spot; but Anne was perfectly equal to it, giving him glare for glare in a wordless duel which brought a veritable chill to my spirit. Then all was conversation once more, as if the moment had never happened; and I found myself seeking refuge in my dinner, too shaken for the time to meet anyone's glances.

Accustomed as I was to displays of temper, vented at once and without regard to appearance, this suppression of anger was utterly foreign to me, much more frightening than even my uncle in a royal eruption at my aunt, grandmother, and the entire Welsh constable force together; and it was long before I could shake off my disquiet. Though the appearance of enjoyment and well-being was preserved throughout most of the rest of the meal, the air remained full of oppression; and I couldn't say I was sorry when at last Anne pushed back her chair, preparatory to clearing the table for the children's Scripture, and Melchett, McCabe and I adjourned to the library for a scotch and soda.

Like the sitting room, the library—or captain's room as they called it—commanded a view of the shore and the sea; and I could tell at a glance that of all the chambers in the house, this one revealed the most about Melchett. Generously stocked with a battery of gun cases, barometers, thermometers, and every conceivable periodical on maritime interests; set about with comfortable, indestructible armchairs upolstered in pigskin or polished leather; lined from ceiling to floor with bookshelves and cupboards packed with ship's lore, it was plainly a seaman's refuge, a captain's reference room and meeting place for cronies. Within its confines a sensible atmosphere prevailed, and the others clearly sensed the same ease in air as I did; for McCabe at once threw himself down in a chair, putting his feet up with a contented sigh, while Melchett—having handed round generous glasses and pipe fills—settled down to his drink with satisfaction.

As the talk went round with the ring of new places, Kittery, Kennebunkport, Bath, Wiscasset; as I learned for the first time of the Portland Melchetts' moves to press *Charis* into the opium service, owing to her fleeting lightness, and listened to Melchett vent resistance—I kept my eyes for the most part on his features; saw that, removed from the circle of his family, he seemed almost himself again, with his long legs stretched out and crossed at his boot-tops. I was just beginning to understand that the burden of his sprawling family, the shipyard ashore and *Charis* at sea, was but a part of his story; was just beginning to perceive the extent to which he was, in truth, a discontented and frustrated man. Because of his passion for work and the zest with which he attacked his duties, he'd never struck me till now as unhappy; and I wondered if he had seen, himself, his failure to find the same satisfaction as others in the conventions and mores of the town.

Scanning the room as I mused I suddenly stumbled upon a little glass cabinet near the window; and realizing with a hush that it contained shells—that this was the house of Melchett's collection—I was at once on my feet to see it: Melchett setting down his drink and coming to stand beside me with an eagerness which wiped the last strain from his features. Unlocking the glass door, lifting out his favorites, schooling me in their names and places of origin, or recalling the times and shores on which he'd found them, he placed them in my palm with unsteady fingers; and marveling at their array of shapes and patterns—seeing Melchett's animation as his burly hand held out each dainty for inspection—I felt my volatile spirits soar.

Drifting in through the open window, the breeze from the shore wafted about us, stirring our hair as we bent over the shell case; and at one point rattling the nearby papers—gusting in harder as if to steal our attention—it swept through the room like an invitation. Following Melchett's restless gaze out the windows—suddenly longing to be away from the house, as if instinctively knowing how to reach him—I impulsively appealed, "Take me t' find some?" At once jumping at the chance—shutting the glass case and heading immediately for the door, then remembering McCabe, still sitting in the chair from which he'd been indulgently watching—he called back over his shoulder, "Want t' come?"

Diplomatic as ever, McCabe drained his glass, saying "Thanks, but I b'lieve I'll head home 'n digest.... Stop by for a cup o' coffee lateh"; and collecting his pipe he got unhurriedly to his feet, while Melchett took off to fetch his jacket. Trying to look McCabe in the eye, I wondered if he had read my thoughts, or if his departure were a mere coincidence; but he seemed serenely oblivious of his acts as he warmly thanked Anne for supper, then ushered me out the front door to the dune. Heading off for the path to his house, he ambled easily into the trees, giving me one last jaunty wave; and gratefully returning the gesture, I settled myself on a bench, and waited thoughtfully for Melchett.

The slam of the porch door announced his approach; and getting immediately to my feet, I waited with my hands in my pockets, while he stumped down the path with his jacket over his shoulder. Shrugging into it as he walked, he produced from one pocket a ridiculous brown cap with a visor, which he clapped unceremoniously onto his head. He now looked as much like a hunter as a seaman; but wholly unconscious of his appearance, he headed without further ado for the beach steps. "Nice day for a sail!" he called over his shoulder, the only words he had spoken since he'd come out to meet me; then lapsing at once back into silence he led the way down the steps to the seashore, and we were engulfed by the tumult around us.

Setting a course for the lighthouse on the Point—striding now just ahead of me, now at my side, and picking his way familiarly amongst the rocks—he waved me over to bits of flotsam, shellfish in the rock crannies and pools, while I peered over his shoulder with wonder. The tide was low, revealing much of the shoreline, and leaving behind caches of snails and mussels; and impulsively shedding our shoes and stockings, we waded out in the sand and mudwrack, picking up shells he called razorbacks or scallops—the surf rising and rushing and ebbing about us, and the gulls veering and dipping just above. Though we said nothing, as if mere words might rob the power of the moment, or distract from the potency of the shoreline, we exchanged knowing glances often, as though we shared an unspoken language, an understanding conveyed direct from mind to mind. Once he helped me to clamber onto a ledge, taking my hand to aid me up the last step; and here we stood side by side for a moment, looking out on the last flush of the sunset, unthinking as two lads on the great lap of the earth.

Then drawing nearer to the lighthouse, we walked along the broad shelves of granite, squatting down over the tide-pools, gazing at minnows a-flash in their basins, or spotting starfish half-hidden by rockweed: our shoulders so close that his arm brushed my own as he poked into the briny waters. At last leading me to a flat rock just below the lighthouse, Melchett came to a halt and sat down; and as soon as he did so I understood that this was his spot, a place to which he'd come many times since boyhood; for it was so secluded that it invited one into its shelter, as into some secret center of nature. Far out on the seaway the running lights of a vessel shone out like twin stars in a dusk-colored heaven, while the beam of the lighthouse swept silently before us, touching the wave-tops with luminescence. Taking off his cap, Melchett rubbed his forehead, the wind blowing his unruly sandy hair free; then leaning against a rock, his eyes sought the ceaselessly on-running sea. For a long time we sat there in wordless contentment, while the light of the flare-path deepened to silver, and the lamps of the vessel slipped into the sea mist.

When at last he stirred and stood up to go, picked up his cap and slapped it against his knee, I felt as if we had grown to the shore, my entire being protesting our leave; and as if to signal his understanding, his hand came down fleetingly to tousle my hair. "McCabe'll drink that whole pot o' coffee if we don't go 'n help him— c'mon," he prodded, in his usual offhand manner; but his grip as he hauled me to my feet was kind, and his arm for a moment brushed comfortingly on my shoulder as we set off down the shore for the cabin.

In the coming days I saw him often, but more briefly than I would have liked to; for I was busy settling in at the sail loft, while he was caught up with a vengeance in his shore tasks—on 'Change every day by seven, seldom ready to leave the counting house before six. Missing his company during the noon hour and evenings—the only leisure I had myself besides Sundays; steering clear of the sailors' haunts on the harbor for fear of running into seamen I'd known in Boston, I filled in my extra time by exploring: going over every inch of the shipyard, and searching out all the landmarks Melchett had mentioned, including Cy Spooner's Curio Shop.

At noontime—having met Cy himself and seen his workbench, piled high with majestic figureheads and trailboards, and having invested a little money in apple wood, which I removed to a small work shed Cy had finagled—I took to carving my own creations, unbeknownst to any of the others. And at night I sometimes visited Paul in fish town, hiked out to McCabe's cabin or to the Point—always snatching the chance to walk past Melchett's shore front, and look up at the lighted windows. One warm eve, longing for his company—too drawn by the unknown behind those windows to break away from them so early—I simply slept on the beach, curling up in a hollow below the house with my jacket spread over me to keep out the fog, then getting up at sunrise and hiking back to town.

As I settled in at the Inn Melchett stopped by fairly often, usually unannounced, always for brief spells, putting his feet up with a drink before heading homeward, or quizzing me in the doorway about my work in the sail loft. I'd already given him a copy of my key—having had several made, since I knew I would lose some; and obviously pleased, he was not shy in using it, for frequently on coming home from a day in the shipyard I found signs that he'd been in my room in my absence—found things that he'd left to make life more comfortable or practical. This was chiefly the result of our tug-of-war over money; for Melchett, having early on discovered that I hadn't collected my last month's wages, and having no doubt deduced the reason, set about with characteristic obstinacy to pay them.

On the day after I'd been to supper at his house, I found $17 on my mantle, which I left conspicuously on his desk in the counting house when he was out to luncheon with his brothers; whereupon he burst into my room the same evening with a fat, dusty tome in hand, hauled out his spectacles, hooked them over his ears, irately opened to a marked page, and began to read from the chapter and section of the maritime act of 1835, which directed that seamen be paid their wages even when taken ill, even though foreign. Slamming the book shut, he put the money back on my mantle; and when I hotly commenced to argue—incensed as I was, since I'd already ascertained, through my own discreet channels, what the true price for a week at the Inn was—he immediately stomped out of the room.

His display of temper notwithstanding, I put the money back on his desk at noon the next day, right on top of the note he'd left me ordering me not to do it; but he eventually had the last word—winning the battle by investing the dollars in things for my room, or in personal gear. First it was a spirit lamp with a supply of whale oil and all the makings I needed for tea, which appeared one day when I came home from supper; next it was a penknife and friction matches, the sort of conveniences or practical inventions for which he had an eccentric passion; and soon thereafter I came home to a rope ladder, stowed away under the dormer window.

"Melchett, what's the hell is this?" I asked, holding it up when he stopped by later.

"What d'ye think it is, you ass? It's a ladduh!" he growled, pouring himself a drink from the decanter he'd already established on one of the shelves of my cupboard.

"But what the devil is it doin' *here*?" I persisted, undeterred by his end-of-the-workday temper.

"It's t' use in case of fiyeh, you farmeh! D'je neveh stop t' think of what on earth ye'd do if this place was t' go up in smoke, an' you stuck up hehre on the third flooh?"

But it was the canvas tent—neatly folded on top of my trunk, with a note giving me leave to camp anywhere on his shoreline, and listing other places I might try as well— which most clearly conveyed his protective attention; and the small, steady words blurred as I read them. Whether he'd spotted me curled up on his beach, or merely intuited my longing to taste again my old customs, I couldn't guess; but in this, as in many other ways, I knew he was looking out for me, and my heart swelled even as it railed with exasperation.

If he was looking out for me ashore, he had the sea in mind as well; for he wasn't long in marching me out to his beach, and personally instructing me in how to swim. Vowing he'd see to it I never set foot again on any Melchett ship till I learned—scrounging round in his deckhouse, built near the dune, and coming up with a bathing costume which fit me—he had me out in the surf that first Sunday, and every Sunday afternoon thereafter, till I was too waterlogged to paddle. As diligent, exacting and unrelenting a teacher as he was a taskmaster on deck, he had me kicking and splashing no matter what the weather; and whenever I showed signs of flagging, he bodily tossed me into the combers—standing by judiciously to watch me flounder.

What Anne must have thought of this abuse of the Sabbath, I could not begin to imagine; but she never appeared not even to bring refreshments, Melchett himself going up to fetch lemonade for the children. The twins never showed up to join us either, perhaps because Melchett felt he had his hands full teaching me; but Tom and Jean were there in white flannels, with sailor's collars and belts at their middles, and McCabe often ambled up to watch their antics. Taking comfort from the ease with which they'd mastered swimming—concluding that if even small Jean could do it, I too could eventually manage to triumph—I gradually made fair progress; but it was the sight of Melchett dressed for the sea, the gruff strength of his big hands and body which brought me back again and again to my lessons.

As my skills advanced I discovered many small things about his family, just as, with time, I was learning the rhythms of his shore life: the twelve-to-fourteen hour workday, with the hour on 'Change to begin with, then the incessant meetings with business partners, the luncheons at the Inn with his brothers, the meticulous inspections of vessels taking shape on the ways, and finally the drinks to unwind at the end. On weekends there were the Saturday dinners in rotation at different Melchett houses, the whole clan showing up for baked beans and brown bread; and the Sunday arrival en masse at church, eight or ten Melchett carriages meeting at the Ship Street Bridge, and driving on in a courtly body.

Of the church they attended—the Congregational—I knew nothing, less even than about the Church of England, whose hymns I'd sometimes heard on Welsh roads, or the Methodist, whose wandering ministers had plied us with tracts; nor did I actually know much about Melchett's religious life, save what I'd gleaned from instinct or conjecture. Sunday services at sea had always been left to McCabe, or sometimes handed over to Spooner, Melchett persistently foregoing the tradition. But I guessed—from the intensity of his Abolitionist sentiments and the integrity of his business dealings, as well as from the spirituality I sensed in him—that it was his awkwardness about the depth of his convictions, rather than any lack thereof, which had persuaded him to take a back seat.

Whether he attended church in port at Anne's bidding, of his own free will, or through some silent compromise between conviction and convention, I again could only conjecture, though I strongly suspected the last; but at any rate he never missed a Sunday, even dressing for the occasion, and escorting his whole family at the reins of his carriage. Watching that first Sunday from beneath a store awning—seeing the entire cavalcade roll by, led by Sarah, Abigail and the family house inmates, and followed in due order by Melchett's uncles and brothers—I picked out Ben on the box of his brougham, scarcely recognizable save for his broad shoulders and beard: so refined and imposing in top hat and starched collar, solemn cutaway coat and grey trowsers, that I was as abashed as if he were President, and turned away in flushed confusion.

As most of my shipmates on the voyage to Rio were making arrangements to ship out with Tom Melchett when he squared away for Havana at the end of August, and as it was expected to be a short journey, lasting little over six weeks, I felt compelled to sign on as well; and far into the warm summer nights at my Inn room, I lay and wrestled with my decision.

Though I longed to remain in Cape Damaris, the exploration of which I'd just begun; though I regretted even a short separation from Melchett, the source now of daily strength and power—I was concerned at how it might appear if I only sailed with him, the one lengthy voyage or so he took a year; and as he wasn't due to ship out till after Christmas, four or five months off at the soonest, I tilted in favor of the trek with his brother. Bewildered, too, by my diminishing freedom—by the consternation which overcame me whenever I considered my deepening bond with him, or even my attachment to the Inn, a place as far removed from a tent on the moor as I'd ever expected to live; confused whenever I looked at myself, my commitment to Melchett Bros. or my room at the Inn through the expectations of my father's eyes, I anguished over my direction.

In the end—preferring the trip to Havana, on the whole, to any other voyage, since at least it would be warm, and since I knew the city—I finally signed on as an able-bodied seaman, taking heart from the fact I surely needn't ship out again till Melchett did, and from the news that Reuben and Howland would be out of my hair: Reuben due to ship as supercargo. and Howland spending the autumn in Portland. Even Keziah, Melchett's sister, finished with her first year at Bowdoin, and reputed to be a crack mathematician, was getting ready to go as navigator; while of all Melchett's brothers, Tom was said to be most like Ben in command and humor. With Bill Worthing preparing to head out at the same time, his full-rigged ship bound for Kingston, Jamaica, and set to race Tom's to the Straits of Florida, the whole town was a-brew with bets and rumor; and the anticipation made it the easier of me to carry through my decision.

Yet, once signed, I carried my departure date as a constant nagging reminder, the days peeling off the calendar faster than I could have imagined; and it was the sting of my impending parting which spurred me to eke out every last bit of knowledge from the land voyage I'd devoted to Melchett.

I hadn't been a week in Cape Damaris when an invitation—finely written in gold, ornate letters—came from Sarah Melchett for luncheon on Friday, a meal to which Ben and his brothers as well had been welcomed; and even more apprehensive about this occasion than about my earlier visit to Ben's house, I sent back my acceptance at McCabe's direction, relieved that he too had been invited, and privately guessing that Ben had asked him to see me through.

By now I'd had my hair cut and had had a good shirt made, from a bolt of fine Indian nankeen; but apart from these improvements I looked as much the part of seaman as ever, the day I strode up to the Melchett family house with McCabe. Greeted at the door by an actual butler—invited into a spacious hallway, brightly clad with Persian carpets and dominated by a lofty stairway, then ushered into a well-appointed parlor, I was profoundly ill at ease; but my anxiety fell from me the instant I met Sarah Melchett.

Rising at the moment she saw me and warmly extending her small, gracious hand— addressing me by my given name, and coming straight to the point with a huskily whispered, "Thank you for the life of my son," she made me feel as if I were kin; and seeing in her straight, stalwart carriage, her determined brows and simple garments, many of Ben's most basic qualities, I felt doubly at home and welcomed. Nobody else having yet arrived, she set to work putting me at ease, indulging me as I looked round the room, or sitting beside me on one of the sofas: her rustling silk dress, bluish-grey with a matching lace cap, as understated as her low accent, and quietly concealing a firm, hardy frame which, despite its smallness, was plainly anything but fragile.

Not long after we'd sat down her second son Joseph, known far and wide as a daring, hot-headed master, swept in with an ebullient bow and flourish; and close on his heels came Jared and Matthew, the youngest of the Melchett brothers, the former having recently received his captain's papers, the latter already a journeyman shipwright. Intimidated by the showy Joseph—put off by his confident, flashy demeanor, in part because I instantly fathomed how it must have overshadowed Ben and the others—I might have found conversation awkward; but I was happily spared the endeavor, Joseph so charged up by the events of the morning, Jared so busy baiting the slow-fused Matthew, and Sarah so intent on putting each son in his place, that I had no chance to get a word in edgewise.

Hearing the noise no doubt from her chamber, Keziah came breezing in from the stairway, greeting me, then immediately throwing herself into the skirmish; and the aged Abigail, tapping in with her cane, her stiff, old-fashioned, brocaded gown bristling, ignored me and instantly fell to haggling. Erupting into the house in the meantime—slamming the door, and stomping into the sitting room in his absurd work clothes, barking out "Motheh" with a wave of his hand, "Robertson, McCabe" with a nod and salute, then throwing himself down into a chair with the announcement "When's dinneh? I'm stahved!", Ben brought a comical lull to the tumult; and conversation might have been diverted into other channels, had not Jared brought him into the fray with,

"Have ye heard the news? Cabot's suin' the yahd for that wharf space!"

"A' course I've heard it!" Ben bellowed back, shouting like all the others as if the whole clan were deaf; "what d'ye think I've been bustin' my ass oveh all mohrnin'?"

With a glance at the heavens Sarah asked "Where's John?", managing to make herself heard without raising her voice; and putting his boots up on a low, graceful table, Ben answered bluntly,

"Right on my tail. I b'lieve that's him at the dooh now."

"*He* shuts it quietly," muttered Sarah, with a wryness which spoke of both exasperation and humor; then John was amongst us, the eldest brother, the yard's lawyer, his easy, assured manner recalling something of his mother's as he bent to kiss her and offered his cheek to Keziah. "Sorry I'm late," he murmured kindly, shaking my hand as I rose to meet him, and nodding at his suddenly subdued brothers. "Tom's going to be even lateh—sent me on to tell you to staht eating without him. Is dinneh ready?"

"We were only waiting for you," smiled Sarah, getting to her feet and offering me her arm; and leading this eccentric company of kinfolk, we swept into the dining room together.

Sitting down at the long, broad table which dominated the bright, cheery room—abashed by the elegance of the service, and by the number of servants who stood by to assist us—I fell back again into an uneasy silence; but all of the others, including McCabe, were soon oblivious of their surroundings, for immediately after John pronounced grace, they straightaway got down to business. Shouting out shipyard news, arguing over plans, challenging prospects or one another's intentions, they scarcely seemed to heed one another: their eager, excited, insulting manner so vividly recalling my old suppers round the fire that I, too, at length forgot myself in the clamor.

Far from polite intercourse, there was no pretense here, no thought for a balanced conversation, indeed for any topic save the vital concern which had birthed the family; just commerce, the shipyard, maritime law, and the nautical did-does of every Melchett man, woman and child from the seventeenth century on down to the present. Filling the air were the tensions and conflicts which I'd known riddled the family since my first week aboard *Charis*, the jealous, competitive, internecine strains which manifested themselves in the curt words and blunt frankness bandied by all save John and Sarah; but so covered were they by genuine comradery, so undergirded by family loyalty, that I was at a loss to discern the fine line between repartee and hostile candor.

Chaffing Abigail with talk of cutting down her oak—the tree which Winslow had eighty years ago planted—to mast an upcoming Melchett vessel, provoked an acidic "I'll see you in couhrt first!" from the undaunted, sharp-tongued old lady; and she looked so capable of resorting to litigation that I couldn't decide if she spoke in jest or not. Yet on other subjects the whole clan was united, as in opposition to the Portland Melchetts' pressure to enlist *Charis* in the opium trade, or in support of John's efforts to crack down on the runners at Portland boarding houses, his specialty at law being seamen's rights; and then their intense family strength was apparent, even to a rank outsider.

Listening to the vigorous, unceasing debate around me—studying the respect which John and Joseph, the eldest, commanded from their rest of their kinfolk, John so educated and socially prominent, Joseph with such an obvious flair as a master—considering the niche which every one of the others had been obliged to find in the shipyard, in order to make his name in the family—I realized more forcefully than ever that Ben had had a good deal to live up to; appreciated the unspoken pressure which had driven him to achieve and perform.

Whether the competition which drove him was truly to his taste, or merely an unconscious engine, I couldn't say for certain, though I tended more and more toward the latter; but unwilling or no, he was caught up in its motion, as I could see from his passion for breaking sea records, or his preoccupation with building a bigger, even faster ship than *Charis*; and the lines of his face, as I looked over at him, took on a new meaning in the light of his kinsmen.

As I listened and studied the faces around me I was aware that several were missing from their number—Ben's father Galen, not expected till September; Tom, the third son, due any minute; and all of the wives and young ones of the four married brothers. In the midst of my tallying a door opened and shut in the distance, firmly but not loudly; Sarah's face at once lighted, and I realized that she must know the entrance habits of every member of the family.

"Whehre in blazes is everybody?" a booming shout echoed, followed by a steady, heavy footfall.

"It's Tom!" came a chorus of delighted voices, their tone informing me that he was the general favorite, and the brightening faces around me confirming the news; then John called out in answer, "We're in the dining room, of course!"

Looking more like Ben than any other the others, almost as large, nearly as fair, though not so handsome—his big, plain face alive and good-natured, but unlighted by the vision which illumined Ben's glances—Tom came ambling in to greet us, with a glint to his eyes and unrestrained smile which spoke not merely of a well-developed sense of humor, but of the mischievous streak of a prankster. This was Ben's closest brother, not only in age but in friendship, and I could readily understand why; for here was not just a kinsman but a comrade, a companion with whom one would gladly share burdens, and a master for whom one would willingly work a vessel. "Good Gawd, is thehre anything left for me?" he bellowed, casting a dolorous eye round the rather vacant table.

"Only this!" laughed Ben, about to pitch a buttered roll.

"Throw that an' I'll rub it in youhr hair, Benjamin!" Tom threatened, in a tone as teasing as it was taunting.

Ben would have thrown it, of course—his wrist already braced for the toss; but reaching over with parental mien, John neatly snatched it and set it aside; and what with brotherly insults and re-telling of news, it was some time before we could settle back down. When we did it was with a new tack in conversation, Tom's talk brightening and buoying the whole table. As he spoke—now jesting, now baiting Ben, or murmuring absurdities to Keziah—I studied him with quick, covert glances; for by this time I knew I'd be shipping with him, and I wanted to get a sense of him as a master. By the final dessert I'd but confirmed my first impression: that here was a fair-minded, steady man, not given to rash acts or taking chances, likely to be considerate of his men and ship, and less driven than Joseph or Ben to win honors—on the whole a likeable, practical seaman, built to get the job done with little fuss, and even less flourish and fanfare.

Though I'd been listening to Tom with particular attention—though I'd kept one eye on Ben, and eagerly absorbed his reactions—it was to Sarah my mind turned again and again with interest; for under Tom's benevolent influence her reminiscences had begun to flow freely, and by the end of the meal she'd taken over the table, keeping us all in thrall with her tales of the childhoods of the grown men and women who listened. Such stories as these I'd been longing to hear; and I harkened, entranced, as she spoke of the early years of her marriage, sailing from port to port as a sea bride—of the hardships of 1812 and after—of the plight of the shipyard, reduced to inactivity by the 1807 embargo—of the arrival of her oldest five children, and their rearing in the cabin and on deck. For the first time I heard of Ben's birth at sea—off the south coast of England, near the Isle of Wight— with a blood-stirring surge of kinship, his birthplace so much closer to mine than I'd imagined that I almost felt he was my countryman; heard stories of his antics on deck, as a young lad coming to know sea, sky and weather.

But more important even than Sarah's accounts was the wall we passed on the way to the library, as we finally adjourned from dinner; for here was a veritable gallery of portraits, all gathered together like a family history, so that I could actually see the faces of those who'd figured in the old tales I'd heard. Finding me paused, riveted before them as the others flowed on past me into the library, already lighting cigars and passing decanters, Sarah showed me my way amongst them, going over each frame and face like a guide who knows each tree of his terrain. Fascinating one and all—from the likeness of Sarah and Galen as a young couple, to the rendering of Abigail and Winslow in formal, elegant middle age, to the touching painting of Charis, not very long before her death—they moved me as deeply as if they revealed my own ancestry; but it was the portrait of Ben as a lad of nine or so to which I returned over and over, elated.

Looking almost flaxen, his hair was lighter, and neatly parted and combed to one side—its clean, trim line, and the stiff, severe sweep of his sober suit and collar, bringing out his fine, perceptive eyes, the sensitivity of his strong chin, and his boyish, vulnerable face. Pinned not on the viewer but on the distance beyond, the wide grey eyes revealed an innate honesty, a nobility, a capability born and bred with them—yet as well a discontent, and an eager, troubled searching which profoundly recalled the gaze I'd met that night at Toby's. Standing hushed as before a landmark on a journey, before a feature newly discovered yet somehow remembered, I paused for a moment before him—paused to wonder at my instinctive progress; marveled, hovering there in the hallway, that my passage was as much a mode of recognition as of finding, like that of a salmon heading up the river to spawn, somehow knowing it from all other rivers as its birth-bed.

XIV

BENJAMIN MELCHETT

Cape Damaris, Maine   August, 1842

When he heard we had horses—not merely carriage cobs, but thoroughbreds—he could hardly contain himself, his face blazing up with a sudden swift animation, and his eyes afire with the delight of a wayfarer who unexpectedly finds himself on familiar ground. Jumping to his feet he sprang for the window, craning his neck for a view of the stables, all the while attacking us with quick, eager questions. Till now he'd been self-restrained and respectful, disciplining his impulsive spirit with the same determined vigor he'd shown at sea, or since then in any untried situation: his native warmth bursting out in rare flashes as he responded to Mother's stories, or overcame his reserve to ask Tom about his ship. But now his constraint fell wholly away, and we saw the natural man beneath, ardent, instinctive, spontaneous as a brush fire, as he strained for a sight of the horses out the window, or drank in the details of their pedigree and rearing.

Catching us up as a wind snatches spindrift, his excitement carried us all away; and soon every one of us—even Mother and Keziah, who'd left us to our own devices in the library after dinner—were on our way out of the house, and down the winding path to the stables. As we walked I rejoiced at the turn of events, for I'd wanted my family to see him as I had; and my heart rose as he pressed ahead with Tom, his open, ringing laugh floating back to us on the breeze.

Old Ezra had the horses out exercising in the south pasture near the house, and we all climbed up on the fence—Robertson perching himself on the topmost board like a boy, and leaning forward eagerly with his elbows on his knees. Tom and I pointed to each horse in turn and gave its name and some of its history; there were six in all, including my bay and Joseph's sable yearling, and the colt which Keziah had brought down from Portland. But one animal in particular caught his attention: Tom's horse, a bright, spirited mare with a shining red coat; and he was plainly bursting to ride her. "Well, let's go!" said Tom, jumping down to whistle her over, and catching up one of the bridles on the fence near the stable. "If you c'n stay on her," he laughed over his shoulder, "you'hre welcome t' make youhrself to home here!"

Dancing up in response to his call, Damariscotta nuzzled his hand, then willingly accepted her bridle; and settling myself more comfortably on the fence, I glanced over at Robertson with anticipation. To my amazement he'd already stripped off one of his boots, and his fingers were working excitedly at the other; at the same moment Tom threw a blanket across the horse's back, and was about to lift the saddle when Robertson looked up.

"Marry, what're you doing?" he cried, as if Tom was about to commit some atrocity.

"I'm only saddlin' her up, man! Don't tell me y' want t' ride her bareback?" Tom answered, one of his hands still poised on the pommel.

"May I?" Robertson asked, standing before us barefoot and shirt-sleeved—stockings and jacket having followed boots in due order—and looking at Tom as appealingly as a boy begging for his first gallop.

"Hell, she'd love it—but I hope you don't bust youhr ass!" Tom told him, with obvious reservations.

Unable to keep silence any longer, Mother looked prayerfully up at the heavens. "Here we go again," she intoned, crossing over to where Robertson debated with Tom. "Jim, be careful; she's a spirited animal—well-trained, but willful and skittish. Lord, I've picked up more than one son out of this pasture, and I don't want to see you in splints before the aftehnoon's out."

Robertson threw her a look of easy familiarity and confidence—

he might almost have been her son already—with a radiant smile in which his white teeth shone, and a flash of dark blue, exuberant eyes. "Don't you worry!" was all he said, giving his head a toss as he turned; then approaching the horse with a calm, assured murmur, he spoke a few quiet words in greeting, stroking her nose and neck with his fine hands, and making overtures, not in English. Perhaps the muttered words were Welsh, perhaps Romany or a mixture of both; I still couldn't tell the difference. As he spoke Tom looked at me with one eyebrow raised, and Keziah rubbed her hands together; but we needn't have been apprehensive, for 'Scotta nuzzled him in a friendly way; and in one spring he was up on her back with his bare feet dangling at her sides, and the reins hanging trim and sure in his hands.

Then they were off, in a mad, joyous run as much like a dance as a dash on the meadow; they might have been one animal, so completely did he anticipate her moves, so effortlessly did she interpret his signals. She cantered, she turned, she trotted and pranced, in answer to his invisible signs; and finally she galloped freely across the pasture, running like a colt newly released from a paddock—her long mane rippling like wheat in the wind, and her red tail streaming out behind her. From where we sat we could plainly see them, dashing first one way and then another, navigating the shrubs at the edge of the pasture, then crossing the open plains of the hill: each change in tack, each switch in direction the product of an unseen give and take, or the gist of an unheard conversation. For the life of me I couldn't have said how he stayed aboard; she moved as if she hadn't a rider, rearing up on occasion almost high enough to spill him, as if in sheer exhilaration—as if her will and spirit exactly matched his own.

As he came to know her he became more daring, springing round on his seat till he faced her stern, or swinging his legs from one flank to the other: doing what I knew had to be the patterns of old circus tricks. Sometimes his ringing laugh was carried back to us by the wind, sometimes the neighing of 'Scotta; and as I listened I realized that he must have ridden many such a horse, in just this fashion, across the meadows of Wales as a boy—felt that time had rolled back to reveal this living, breathing memory.

Suddenly it seemed like a gift: the sunlight grew brighter, the new grass greener; I felt newly born into the world myself, with eyes too tender to bear the dazzle. With a catch to my breath I saw Scotta's red coat, and the blades of the pasture beneath her hooves; saw the dome of blue sky and Robertson's dark head against it, his tousled hair blowing freely in the breeze. It was as if the years had peeled back and stopped, and I stood gazing, awed, at some tableau poised in space, contemplating its beauty. Then man and horse moved on again, rousing from the frame of the moment like a portrait which is no longer frozen; and I saw that they were returning to us.

All this time we had hardly spoken a word, as though we had all held our breaths for that quarter hour or so. But now I heard Keziah exhale, as if she had just surfaced from a wave; Mother said "How beautiful!" in her lowest tone, and I knew from its pitch that she was deeply moved. Tom let out a whistle. "This is the kind o' picture you was tryin' t' paint of him on deck, I guess," he turned and said to me; "I undehstand now what you meant. By God, I neveh saw anybody ride a horse like that!"

Then they were before us, man and horse; 'Scotta's sides were heaving, and I looked up to see Robertson's transformed face: cheeks flushed, forehead damp, eyes ablaze like vivid blue fires. Tumbled about his face, his wet hair clung in ringlets; while his throat labored with the effort of breathing. Grinning his widest grin, he nodded; and we found ourselves running up to him, our voices full of exclamations. As he drew rein I put up both my hands; and slipping confidently down into them he came barefoot to the ground. Tom was beside us by then, with Mother and the others close behind him; at once there was a commotion of cries, and a tumult of competing shouts.

"Well, I'm damned!" Tom said ruefully, and Robertson turned his shining eyes toward him.

"May I ride your horse again sometime?" he asked.

"Hell, you c'n *have* my horse!" laughed Tom.

If he'd won over my family in record time with his arsenal of nautical skill, well-mannered charm and disarming spirit, he was just as fast in taking on Cape Damaris, adapting to the townsfolk—and they to him—much more readily than I would have expected. Aroused by the same curiosity about his past which had tantalized us, one and all, aboard *Charis*—seeing in the quality of his seamanship, and the discipline with which he carried out his tasks in the sail loft, not just another fly-by-night sailor—the town regarded him with immediate interest; and wherever I went I was aware of the same undercurrents of fascination which I'd so often detected at sea.

With his worldly ways and knowing air, yet his attitude of self-command—with his curious mixture of the nautical and the foreign, such talismans as his figured neckerchiefs giving a decidedly faraway aura to his common seaman's gear—he was an instantly recognizable figure, easily standing out even in the wharf traffic. Even if no one knew quite how to take him—even if he aroused controversy, as he did at once for not attending church—they were drawn to him anyway by his attraction. Captivated by his looks and undisclosed past, Keziah and her set, and even settled matrons like Mother, were straightaway caught up in romantic speculation; while his frank, congenial ways and ready wit won him many comrades amongst both the fishing and mercantile circles—cottage kitchens and town parlors alike vying for his company at dinner.

Getting to know the town and its inhabitants in turn with a speed which considerably amazed me, Robertson too was making adjustments; for frequently I spoke to tradesmen who'd previously made his acquaintance, or paused to introduce him to some shipwright or chandler only to find they'd already met, over a drink or on the street or down to the yard. Often when I stopped by to visit him at his room, I found he'd gone off, for a few hours or for the night; and though uneasiness always made me suspect the dance halls, I usually discovered him toasting dorymen at Eli's, or later heard of him at one of the cottages in fish town. Sometimes he was at Paul's place, sleeping off a Friday night on the sofa, or at one of the McCabe's fiddling and dancing—picking up the intricacies of the fisherman's stomp; but at others he was much farther afield, so that

I discovered, astonished, that he'd ridden abroad as far as Belfast, though I never found out how he got there.

But his impact on the town and its imagination was still as nothing compared to his continuing influence on me; and nothing brought home his profound effect more clearly than the changes he'd wrought in my attitude to my work, and the habits and duties of my shore life. While he grappled with coming to live in a new town, indeed in an entirely new society and order, I floundered in my old ways and customs, struggling to make sense of old patterns, once legible but now stale and muddied. Formerly I'd looked forward to my work in the yard, to launching one ship or getting another underway, my enthusiasm at seeing a new bow part the water offsetting the detestable office work; but now I was so completely preoccupied with him that I could scarcely keep my mind on my business. Forced to re-do calculations, re-copy ledgers or unscramble bills of sale, I frequently fell behind in my work; and even when I managed to catch up, I asked myself what it all meant, anyway.

Till now I'd desired the acclaim of my family, the recognition of colleagues from Castine to New York—had longed to make my name as well known in shipping circles as Brown and Bell or Smith and Dimon; knew I had it in me, as none of my brothers or cousins did, to lay out a design with innovation and experience, sail it at optimum speed and bring home a profit, all three. But now all I wanted was the admiration of a man whose existence I hadn't even imagined when *Charis* slid down the ways a few short months ago; and the result was total upheaval, the loss of all my old goals and directions, and the founding of new under less than ideal conditions.

Committed to the teeth at the shipyard—up to my ears in responsibility to family, not only the one I'd sprung from, but the one I'd started—I was in no position to change tack; yet I longed to chart a course with fresh visions, yearned to venture, dream, discover, do anything but the tasks at hand; and I found my thoughts drawn again and again to the room on the third floor of the Inn, where Robertson dwelt in eccentric disorder. What he did, what he thought, how he lived, these were the matters which held my attention; and I found myself waking up every day to the undeniable tug of adventure—

found myself gazing ahead like Magellan to the draw of unplotted horizons, prey to the irresistible tang and pull of discovery.

Finding excuses to look in on him at the Inn became a daily preoccupation; and I took to getting up from my desk on impulse, leaving my papers in limbo and heading to his room on the chance I might run into him at home. Since he was far from easy to find—at dinner time being mysteriously absent, during the evenings invited to supper, or off roaming the town with a shipmate—I wasn't often successful even during leisure hours; but as I had a key to his room and usually things to deliver, I always stepped inside for a moment, almost as glad for a chance to see what the place looked like, to sense his character from his belongings, as I would have been to meet him. Standing in the doorway at first, then—as I came to feel more at home—taking the chair by the harbor window and helping myself to a fill for my pipe, I looked around with eager interest, taking in the signs of his presence—the tangle of bedclothes, the jumble of towels, the characteristic clutter on his desk—with a cheerfulness which heightened my senses.

Though scrupulously clean, the room lacked the discipline of order and neatness to which I'd always been accustomed; reflected instead his mercurial existence, every object free to drape or fall or wrinkle; and the result was an irrepressible aura of movement, the air of a nomadic caravan or campsite, as if the whole place were on wheels or horseback, poised for a moment in the act of rolling. Despite my passion for shipshape order I felt the tensions of work and family fall away from me as soon as I clapped eyes on this jumble—felt a vitality in their potential for action which enlivened and refreshed me; and the longer I stayed and looked around me, the more invigorated my spirit.

Knowing that he loved to go off on his own, I seldom attempted to arrange times to see him, and tried not to regret missing him if chance failed me; but when he didn't come home at night, or returned to his room at an outlandish hour—when he took to hiding out day after day for dinner—I couldn't suppress an anxious disquiet. Lunching at the Inn with my brothers—sitting home on the beach steps after the children were in bed, wondering where he was and what he was doing—I tasted a distance I'd never known before; rebelled against the obligations which divided me from him, and hosted an unreasoning loss and suspicion. Resentful of his many new associations—not wanting to share him, or the bond we'd created, with anyone else who came into the picture—I begrudged the companions who took his time, even as I welcomed his swift adjustments, and even though I knew, at bottom, that no one else could usurp my place in his feelings.

I was particularly provoked by a few intimates of Keziah's who'd taken a romantic shine to him, my hackles instantly up whenever I came upon their whispered conversations and understood that he was the topic of interest. Driven to eavesdropping to learn what was going on—my pulse taking a jump every time I caught his name, or heard little anecdotes in which he figured—I listened with utter disregard for politeness, needing to hear their tales of his doings, yet hating their obvious, eager interest. Though Robertson did nothing to encourage their notice—though he spent little time in mixed company, and scrupulously observed all the social niceties which would prevent others from thinking him fast or forward—several of Keziah's friends, amongst them Damaris, had met him in the Winslow or Spooner parlors, and so had the privileges of women formally introduced; and they didn't hesitate to press their advantage.

Nor was I any less grudging of Robertson's shipload of male companions—old friends like the Talbots welcoming him like a cousin, Paul and Shad taking him trawling, and new acquaintances like Jimmy and Eli looking after his wants with fatherly affection. Leaving home after my family had retired—restlessly roaming the beachfront toward town, hoping to run into him on his way somewhere—hanging around the deserted wharves, from which I could watch the lights of the Inn, drawn as a galleon to the glint of gold—I passed many an evening shuttled between hope and resentment; yet all the tosses of mood were worth it when I spotted the yellow arc of his window, and knew that at last I had a chance for a visit.

Even when we did get together I oftentimes shared his company with others, his room increasingly overrun with the traffic of fishermen, sail makers, carpenters, and ostlers, any of whom might be expected to drop by at any hour; but on those infrequent occasions when I saw him alone, I savored the moments all the more for their rareness. Unwinding with a drink by his window after work, running into him at the sail loft and showing him round the yard, I slowly came to know him better; and as August wore on and we became more accustomed to one another, it became easier for me to find ways to approach him. Less and less fearful of disrupting his privacy, I took to grabbing odd moments when they happened, regardless of the place or the hour—anxious to snatch whatever occasions presented themselves, since I knew he would be shipping out by the end of August.

Wanting to be guided around, shown all my old haunts and the high points of the town, Robertson was an eager companion; and commandeering him before he could slip off at noon, I rode him out to the harbor with a basket from Eli's, fed him lunch on the rocks overlooking the dock front, or shared a meal from the saddle as we roamed the side streets. Nor did I confine my efforts to daytime; for once when I found him camped on my beach in his tent—which he was liable to pitch almost anywhere—I went down before dawn with a pot of tea, some loaves of bread and a round of cheese, waked him and shared this Romany breakfast while the sun rose red in the haze of the fog, and the sweet morning breeze rustled the grasses.

Loving to jump on a horse on short notice and ride with me for a spell after supper, he was an ideal journeyer's comrade, ready to climb back out of bed if I stopped by after hours, or rise before four if I dropped by that early. Each time I caught up with him the glad light in his eyes led me to be more impulsive the next; and snatching time when I should have been working or attending to matters of family and home—cutting corners which I never would have cut before, with an unconcern which amazed me when I paused to consider—I gave myself up to the delight of his presence, even Anne's disapproval of my impromptu sallies, and her cool silences when I returned, unable to draw the zest from my outings.

Wrangling one Saturday afternoon off for both of us, I took him by foot into the woods nearest my house, heading west toward the peninsula's center, and instinctively making for the small, log-sided lodge which Tom and I had built on the shores of a lake. Whether or not we'd have time to reach the place—it being some three or four miles inland, and Robertson's inclinations being unpredictable—I wasn't certain; but I wanted to give him a taste of the woods, longed to get him away from any chance of interruptions so I could have him all to myself. It was the first time we'd been alone together for any length of time since we'd met—the first time Robertson had really been in the woods at all, he confided, since he'd left Wales three years ago; and as the trees closed in behind us—as we were engulfed by the cushioned hush of the forest, the sea only a hollow drone in the distance—we exchanged jubilant glances.

Picking our way amongst the saplings, then letting the unplotted lanes carry us on, like chips of wood in a meandering current, we exchanged recollections and stories, or discussed how the Maine woods differed from the Welsh: stooping, kneeling, touching moss, or running our palms along the trunks of white birch, as if we'd never seen any of it before. Eager to share my fund of discoveries, I imparted my woodsman's knowledge, a combination of childhood finds, shipwright's technology and Indian folklore: pointing out everything from the different species of spruce—white spruce being fit for spars, ship knees and joists, black spruce for the making of beer—to the hemp which the Indians had used to string bows.

When I'd emptied myself of my bits of treasure—wrapping things up by pointing out local dangers, since I knew he'd sooner or later camp here—Robertson took over with his own brand of science, putting me to shame within a few minutes with a knowledge much more profound than mine, which he shared with his habitual eager shyness. Greeting old botanical friends with delight—giving me their names in three languages, then carefully stowing leaves, roots and stems in his pack—he collected dandelion greens, elderflowers, peppermint, yarrow, woodsage and ground ivy, wild rye, coltsfoot, cowslips and foxglove, not to mention about 20 kinds of bark, all to be used in various combinations to make hot or cold teas or infusions for everything from the common cold to bronchitis.

Old memories stirring under his teaching, I brushed aside a mulch of pine needles to reveal the heart-shaped, glossy leaves of gold-thread—dug into the sand to expose the gold root, its bright yellow mesh running in all directions. Drawing it forth to dry it for use in the winter, I reached up to pinch the pitch off white pine, good for use as a salve, when applied to a wound and bound with a cloth: Robertson clearly suspicious of any remedy he hadn't tried, yet anxious to learn just the same from my customs, and putting my things with his in his pack. In the golden light of the afternoon his vivid smiles, cast back at me as I followed, together with our deepening closeness, filled me with a buoyant elation; and as if the woods too rejoiced at our rapport, they signaled their gladness with a brilliance of leaves, and the springy resilience of the forest floor.

Coming out all at once, after a couple of hours, on the clear expanse of the lake—which I'd left as a surprise—I pointed out our cabin beside it; and taking it all in with unchecked excitement—the trim, log-sided dwelling, the placid waters, the ridges and hillsides of spruce in the distance—Robertson darted about like a sparrow; stood with me on the rude porch with quiet delight, and wandered about the lodge's small kitchen, past the built-in bunks, the cabinets and plank table with the hush of one stumbling on something long-desired.

Taking down a couple of cups from the shelf, we drank our fill at the stream, a stone's throw or so from the door; then looking ahead to our next meal, we debated ways to scare up some supper. Though there were rifles in the gun case, and I had my own with me—though there were birds and small game in the woods in plenty—I was somewhat relieved to discover that Robertson was completely ignorant of firearms and their use, certainly far less familiar than with the knife which I'd restored to him since our return from Rio, and which he now no doubt wore again in his boot; and thinking longingly instead of a trout dinner, we decided to try our hand at fishing.

Getting out poles and lines for the two of us, I led him from place to place in the little rocky stream which, moving down out of its source in the Camden Hills, threaded the pine vales and fed the lake: me showing Robertson how to cast, since he'd plainly never fished with such equipment before, and Robertson catching on with some skill and patience, though he obviously regarded the gear as cumbersome. Between his beginner's luck and my own experience, we caught our supper within an hour; and as we bent over our assortment of trout and bass, cleaned and fileted them with satisfaction, I asked: "Have you really neveh fished with a pole an' line b'fore?"

Shaking his head, he smiled, "I never have."

"But you poached in ev'ry riveh in Wales," I prodded slyly, thinking of all the times he'd confessed to Romany filching, sneaking and thieving.

"Oh, every chance we got," came his good-natured answer.

"And you neveh used any kind of pole?"

"No... too much equipment t' pack around, when you're obliged to travel light; an' no way t' hide it when the warden comes lookin'... Fishing with a pole is a gadje invention."

"Then how do *you* do it?" I challenged, with interest.

Giving me a smile, he led the way upstream till he came to a sort of pool in the shore, a sheltered recess under a grassy bank; and lying down quietly on his stomach—staring for a while till he spotted a trout, shading itself in the lee of a rock—he reached carefully in with his fingers. Barely even parting the surface, then slowly immersing his hand and forearm, so gradually I could scarcely detect his progress, he at last closed in under its belly; and lightly stroking it with his fingers, apparently mesmerizing it with the motion, he gently, patiently tickled it upward, until—with a swift and unexpected movement—he deftly snatched it out of the water.

"Well, I neveh!" I breathed, in frank admiration; and determined not to be out done, I immediately laid down and tried it myself. Spotting another fish was difficult enough, getting my hand into the water without scaring it off even harder, while coming near enough to touch it proved impossible; and I quickly discovered—to my chagrin—that I had nowhere near the grace of movement to imitate

Robertson's performance: a fact which he confirmed with a teasing laugh, and an affectionate, indulgent eye.

Longing to camp out of doors by the lakeside, instead of stoking up the stove in the kitchen, Robertson talked me into building a campfire; and using a pan or two from the cupboard, a few of his herbs, and potatoes and flour from the wood bins, he made a sort of chowder and some biscuits, while I fried the remaining fish in a skillet. If he'd ever appeared elated before—ranging about on deck in the wind, roaming the north pasture on Tom's horse, meeting my children or sitting by me at the lighthouse—his joy was as nothing compared to his gladness now; and as I poked and prodded at my skillet, my glance went repeatedly to his bright profile. Fixing his concoctions, adjusting the fire, collecting last-minute spices or tools, he revealed skills I'd never realized that he, as one of a nomadic people, had been forced to develop; and as I cooked and ate beside him, I was consumed by admiration.

Sitting and talking, listening and watching, picking out the splash of a fish, or the cry of a loon on the distant lakeshore, we ate as if we'd never eaten before, appreciating each distinct tang or flavor; and so fulfilling was the simple meal that washing up when it had ended, taking apart the campsite and dousing the fire, putting away the poles and preparing to head home, silenced us with desolation. Turning away as I locked the lodge, Robertson kept his face averted, and refused to meet my eyes when I'd finished; and instinctively putting an arm to his shoulders—groping for some way to ease my own loss—I huskily promised a camp trip come autumn, after his return from Havana, late October being the standing date of my annual outing with Tom and McCabe.

Characteristically quick to respond, Robertson's spirits soared at my gesture, as bright with anticipation as they'd a moment ago been clouded; and as we turned into the old logging road—a seldom-used lane which came out below the Point, and which Tom and I often took to shorten our journey—his eyes were once again clear and eager, and the tenseness left his face and shoulders. Grilling me with innumerable questions—how long we'd camped together, where we usually went, whether we used a tent or the lodge, hunted or fished or a combination of both—he dwelt with delight on the coming outing; then at last lapsing into silence, he attended to the lay of the land, and the hues of the gradually waning day.

As he walked I noticed that he was scanning the roadside, obviously looking or searching for something, with an air which told me it was important; and though I seldom forced him to confide, I couldn't help but query: "Jim, you surely ain't lookin' for any more plants? There can't possibly be any you ain't stowed in youhr pack."

Grinning at me, he shook his head, and confessed that he was searching for any sign of the gypsies I'd told him frequented the summer carnivals roundabout. Touched that he'd remembered the story I'd recounted of me and Charis running away—this being the first time he'd referred to it since I'd shared it that night at sea—I asked,

"How would you know any had passed?"

"By the roadside," he explained. "If they really are gypsies, not merely tinkers—if they're Rom that've been sent across, for example, for breakin' the law in Britain, or whatever—they'd leave patterins for those on the road behind them: messages made from grasses and twigs t' show their direction or destination if they know it, the time that they passed, the number in their party, an' so on."

"What do they look like?" I prodded, eager with interest.

Stooping, he made up a few in answer, showing me how to combine stones, leaves and branches to plot out an image of place, time and direction—the result so natural that one might easily pass it by, unless one happened to be deliberately looking. As always when he spoke to me of his past, or allowed me to read a page of his travels, a sense of awe crept over me, as if I were receiving something rare for safekeeping; and I stored in my mind each design and meaning the same way I'd memorized the signs for buoys, lights and reefs and channel markers in standard use on charts for seamen.

Too moved for speech I watched as he laid out one last patterin stating who we were, a Romany chal—a gypsy fellow—and a gadje, heading south toward the lighthouse, then east along the Point road on foot, a few days after the full moon in August; watched as he scattered his other examples, leaving his last to any who could read it; then in silence we went on our way, following the shore road to the lighthouse.

Walking now under the starlight, we tasted the nighttime moods of the forest—the stirrings, the hush, the occasional hoot of an owl, the snap of a branch beneath a deer's hoof: Jim displaying a keen sensitivity for sounds, especially now that we were in darkness. In the sweet, fragrant warmth of the August night—in the pale, diffuse glow of the moonlight—the criss-cross of pine needles shadowed his face, as if he were looking through a netting; and so fine was his fairness—so timeless, yet so youthful and fleeting—that I felt it as much like a pain as a pleasure. Walking beside him, I wanted to take his arm, to seal the afternoon with something as concrete as the brush of a shoulder; but abashed by his presence, I scarcely dared look, and walked on quietly beside him.

Reaching McCabe's still wrapped in silence, we burst in and helped ourselves to his kitchen—McCabe emerging sleepily from his chamber, and mixing us drinks with neither surprise nor comment; then Jim curled up like a cat on the sofa and fell asleep instantly, sailor fashion; and reluctantly leaving them there by the hearth, I barely had time to snatch a few hours' rest at home, before seeing the family off to church the next morning.

That he possessed a particularly fine sense of humor and roguish love of practical jokes was even clearer now that we were in port; and as August slipped by he caught me up and rolled me along with his playful zest, making me laugh for what seemed to me like the first time since I was a boy. But if we were growing daily closer together—if such outings as our trek in the woods, or such pranks as he played on me with affection, were strengthening the already fast bond between us—our relationship was by no means idyllic; for the amount of our affinity and fellow feeling was also the measure of our contest of wills.

Driven by the same instinct to protect him I'd felt the first night we'd met at Toby's, I took to providing whatever I could for him—to meeting his needs almost before he'd recognized them; and offended by a patronage which curtailed his independence, he never failed to hotly resist me, responding often with an explosion of temper. How far I could push him it was difficult to determine, especially as there were times when he seemed unconsciously to invite me, or to appeal with wordless glances, so that I was commonly at a loss how to walk the ill-defined line between his pride and his need. On some occasions I was so convinced I was in the right—as in the matter of paying his wages—that I felt justified in putting in my oar; but at other times I was forced to admit that he was entitled to resent my intrusion, as when I put him to the test in the water.

He'd been swimming at my place for three weeks or so, coming over on Sundays and sometimes after dinner, when I concluded he'd taken my instruction lightly, as something between a sport and a lark. Taking the chance to teach him a lesson on Tom's sloop one evening as we skimmed the calm harbor, I resorted to the same trick my father had used on me: reaching over and deliberately pushing him overboard, then tossing him the life-ring and watching him toil to it, my heart in my mouth and my body poised for a rescue. Grappling for the ring he cursed me, hurling out the finest assortment of oaths I'd ever heard—calling down calamity on me and my heirs for at least the next ten generations; and immediately on being hauled back on board, he straightaway pushed *me* over, then refused to speak to me for two days.

Since neither of us could ever bring ourselves to apologize, or at any rate, to gracefully back down—since he wouldn't own defeat on the question of his wages, and I never repented of pushing him into the drink—we might frequently have come to a stalemate; but so mercurial were his spirits, and so powerful my urge to know them—so ready was I to fall in with his moods, even as he learned to fall in with mine—that unexpectedly our ill will was forgotten, or evaporated in the enthusiasm of our next meeting.

Some of my maneuvers to protect him he never knew of or discovered, since to circumvent fireworks I simply worked behind his back, as when I took Tom and his first mate aside to ask them to look after him at sea; but others he managed to uncover, and of these none provoked him more than the arrangement I'd made with Jimmy to lower the price of his room at the Inn. Since I'd hammered out the agreement by letter from Portland before we'd even hauled into Cape Damaris—since Jimmy could be trusted to take a secret to his grave, and McCabe was the only other one in on the business— I'd thought the conspiracy was air tight; and I'd congratulated myself many a time since on providing both a homelike berth for Robertson and a steady boarder for Jimmy, paying over the extra dollars myself once a month.

So secure did I feel that as September drew nigh and with it Robertson's departure, I'd further arranged for Jimmy to hold his room—the six weeks or so he was to be gone—at a purely nominal rate, since he'd not be taking board in the interim; for I wanted above all for him to have an established place to come home to, and feared that if he were forced to give it up, as were most foremast hands when they put to sea, there might come a time when he didn't return. But when Jimmy approached him with the proposal, offering terms carefully calculated not to be so generous as to arouse suspicion, Robertson balked; and when I stopped by later that evening to see if I could talk him round, he straightaway turned on me and exploded.

"Ain't it enough you've already conned Jimmy int' lowering the price behind my back, then gone an' paid the difference yourself?" he cried, his features ablaze with indignation. "Now here you come back again with your propositions! You c'n take your money an' go to the devil! I'll live where I please an' pay what I can, on the same terms that everybody else does!"

Instantly losing my own temper—partly out of fear of losing the arrangement and chagrin that he'd somehow stumbled upon it, partly out of anger at his bullheaded refusal to bend his obstinate pride to my will—I found myself shouting unreservedly at him, hurling out insult for insult with pleasure: finding an unlooked-for delight in his fury, a relish in knowing that I could take him on, that I could fling oaths and match wits and vent ire in a way I'd never done in my tense conflicts with Anne. "I didn't do this just for *you,* y'know, you son of a bitch!" I shot out at last, while he gaped at me in stunned silence; then having revealed more of myself than I'd intended, I stormed out of his room like a cyclone, while he stood by with his features unexpectedly softened.

The upshot of it all was that next day I discovered he'd gone to Jimmy and accepted his offer; and that night at McCabe's it was as if nothing had happened: Robertson playing his pranks on me at supper, and me chasing him outdoors into the rain—chasing him up beach and down hill and round forest in the most violent thunderstorm of the summer, while the lightning rent the skies into ribbons, and the thunder out-boomed our uproarious laughter.

If we were plagued by frequent conflicts of will, we were divided as well by the differences of habit, the extraordinary distinctions in outlook brought about by our widely divergent backgrounds. Sometimes sitting by him in front of his fire on a chilly summer evening, on those rare occasions when no one else was present, I contemplated how dissimilar the two of us were, struck even more by our differences on land than I had been at sea; shook my head, disbelieving, that someone so unlike me had come to so profoundly pervade my thoughts.

Though he was obviously attracted to material wealth—though tales of our holdings, investments and earnings never failed to prick up his ear, and he was settled enough to own some things himself— he was completely independent of objects; not just in the sense that things had no real hold over him, but in the sense that he never acted as owner, never arranged or ordered or defined his belongings, or viewed them as distinct from anyone else's. I could not imagine him, for example, engaged in a lawsuit such as we were, to establish our claim to a few yards of wharf space; could not imagine him even lining up his tools in the sail loft, or docketing his few receipts, bills and papers. Of the little he had, everything was allowed to run free, so that I never knew from one day to the next where I might find his clothes, gear and notebooks—never knew if they'd be on his shelves, hooks and mantle, or even if they would be in his room.

Accustomed for years to living by method, to keeping each thing in its own proper place so that I could readily fetch or replace it, I had virtually everything I owned organized in shipshape fashion, where it could be depended upon to remain; but Robertson's belongings, like headstrong beings, were scattered about all over town. Jackets, hats, papers, combs, changes of clothing and sheath knives and boots, palms, needles and fids for his work, even his pocketbook and money, were likely to turn up almost anywhere; and hardly a day went by when somebody didn't return something he'd left behind, or when we didn't have to institute a search for some item unaccountably misplaced.

Having ordered my hours as thoroughly as my belongings, such wasted time drove me almost witless; but with the acceptance of a man forced for a lifetime to travel light and improvise, he took searches and losses in stride. Nor was his view any different toward money; for though as far as I knew he wasn't in debt, he certainly was not saving either, spending his wages with the same lack of design with which he handled time and belongings. Buying a few clothes— to which he was plainly attracted, and which he wore well—or footing the bill for drinks at Eli's, after he'd set aside funds for room and board, he spent his money until it was gone; and it was plain to see that he was perfectly capable of continuing thus indefinitely— spending what he had, enjoying what he bought, then borrowing or improvising the items he needed, or philosophically doing without.

Frequently during our hours alone we shared our views on a host of subjects—Robertson volunteering very little in a personal way about himself, but offering whatever I wanted to know about Romany life in general; and in this manner I learned more about our differences in background, and came to appreciate how difficult he must have found it to adjust to our customs. Thinking the gypsies to be utterly free of convention—under the influence of popular literature on the subject, which portrayed them as flamboyant, if not downright licentious—I was surprised to learn of the strict moral codes, harsher than any law in New England, which governed the internal life of the clans; laws severely overseen by the *kris,* a sort of judicial council of elders. In addition to injunctions relating to morals, there was another set of commandments regarding what was considered *mukado*—unclean—and why: the word referring not just to a condition of dirtiness, but to a kind of personal contamination, stipulations surrounding everything from the contacts with women to the processes of washing and eating.

Listening to Robertson talk I began to understand many of the oddities about him—his reluctance to share cups or to eat a meal when he didn't know how it had been prepared; his horror at chamber pots, water closets and outhouses, even the "seat-of-ease" in the head aboard *Charis;* his stringent personal cleanliness and peculiarities of toilet, about which there had been many jokes in the foc's'le and galley; and finally his respect and modesty around women—every one of these old customs and restraints still governing his ways, despite his contact with *gadje* life for several years.

Hearing him detail the punishments for infractions—everything from temporary untouchableness to expulsion—and considering the constraint with which he spoke of the *kris,* the brevity and suppressed indignation and anger, I began to entertain the suspicion that he'd at one time clashed with his elders, guessed that he may even have been expelled; yet I couldn't begin to fathom what he might have done at so young an age to merit so extreme a measure, unless it were some act of violence. Nor could I ask point-blank what had happened, any more than I could voice any number of other personal queries, such as whether or not he'd had a sweetheart—as rumor so persistently maintained—or even whether he'd had a brother or sister. It wasn't just my respect for his restraint which forced me to check my countless questions; for I saw early on that he tired easily from set queries, as he had that night he'd cried aboard *Charis*: his fatigue then due, as I understood now, not just to illness and emotion, but to the bewilderment with which he regarded logic, the relentless order of interrogation.

Whether or not his bepuzzlement at method—at the spoken give and take of information, as much as at the arrangement of objects— was a characteristic of his own nature, or an attribute of the Rom as a people, I was still too uninformed to decide, though I was beginning to suspect the latter; but in either case I was forced to develop ways to learn what I longed to know of his past, without tiring him with my passion for order, or offending his pride and reserve. Listening to him these nights by his fire, I learned to time my few careful questions, as I'd learned to time my maneuvers at sea—learned to ask one or two things, when his mood seemed receptive, then let him drift and meander in answer; let him wander the paths of old recollections, then culled what I wanted to know from his roaming.

If the laws which governed Rom internal life were strict, they were much more relaxed with regard to gadje—outsiders being fair game for duping and thieving, and their gullibility one of the principle means of making a living. Though Robertson described the respectable modes of employment in which the different clans specialized— though besides such unique trades as harping and carving, fiddling, smithying and horse dealing, there was always seasonal labor—the universal method of raising money was simply fleecing the credible gadje: ring dropping, pig poisoning, petty thieving, poaching, horse swindling and fortune telling. Through his eyes I saw not only the perceptiveness of the Rom—their ability to gauge degrees of wealth, past history and even gullibility from apparently innocuous detail— but also the blurring of ethical borders I'd long thought inviolate and rigid.

Besides seeing the absurdity of fences and purses—of staking out objects in personal parcels—I saw too a new slant on the alleged advances of Romany coquettes and dancers: saw not gypsy sirens enticing gadje or responding to suggestive offers, but shrewd businesswomen bilking unsuspecting gentry of gifts or money or at least, dignity, without actually compromising their virtue. Turning to Robertson I saw this same shrewdness in his propensity for lying, or to speak Romishly, for suiting answers to the moment—in his astuteness at wheeling and dealing, a skill which he'd revealed in Rio—and in his exasperating amorphousness, as demonstrated by his changes of name and age, or his vagueness about his personal past; saw too that many of his relations with gadje since his leaving of Wales had been a kind of deliberate thumbing of the nose.

His relations with Walker, for example, appeared now to be not just the contest of an unruly young seaman at odds with a belligerent master, but the clash of a hostile and resentful exile, probably either ostracized or shanghaied, working out his anger at a wholly different society and taking satisfaction at causing it trouble, in resisting its alien customs and standards. Looking back in my mind over Walker's papers—contemplating whoever had been opposite him in his fight in Boston, then mulling over his contention with Reuben and Howland—I realized that his conflicts with gadje had been many; and I was wordlessly thankful that whatever it was he'd found in me that night our eyes had met at Toby's, it somehow transcended our separate cultures.

Not that he still openly embraced the Rom life, or attempted to practice the majority of his old customs. After years of mingling with the impure gadje, he'd by now adapted—at least outwardly— to our lifestyle, maintaining, besides a number of unconscious old habits, simply an integrity of nature, the essence of Rom pride and independence. Whether, indeed, he privately regarded himself still a gypsy, or was beginning to view himself as a man in transition, a member of the very culture he'd been taught to revile, I wasn't sure; but remembering that he'd told McCabe in Rio that he didn't expect to go back to Wales, I tended to believe he was homeless, either no longer welcome by other Rom, or no longer willing himself to rejoin them.

Longing to know if he was aware of his change, to find out in what light he now saw himself, I finally got up the nerve to ask; but to my "D'ye see youhrself still as a Rom, even though you've lived for yeahrs with the gadje?", he responded with barely veiled anger.

"I don't know," he answered, his face at once clouding with doubt and confusion, while his eyes swiftly darkened with resentment; and it was plain that the subject was not open to discussion.

Covering up my mistake as best I could, I hastily steered the talk to new channels, while he in turn let the matter pass; but his unexpectedly taut reaction was another sign of the strains and conflicts I knew he harbored—tensions which had led to his breaking down that night aboard *Charis,* and which I guessed, despite his generally bright demeanor, hadn't yet been resolved. Whatever the answer to my question—whatever his own private conviction—he was to my eye a man between cultures, obviously torn in both directions; and to my efforts to make him feel at home—to familiarize him with the mysteries of digging for clams, or prying the last tender bit from a crab leg—I now added a deeper sensitivity to his past, making it easier for him to hold onto old customs, and protecting him from the misunderstandings of others.

That he rejected many of his native conventions—that he was detached enough to see their constraints, now that he'd been away for several years—it was at any rate plain from the outset; and he had no objection to discussing such matters, as long as I didn't force him to draw conclusions.

"I never thought much about it when I was growing up," he mused, one night when I asked if all the regulations regarding *mukado* hadn't been a burdensome prison. "It was just the way things were done. We were taught not to drink out of the same cup as a gadje, that cats were *mukado* and horses not, the same way were taught t' keep clear of the fire, or t' help strike the tents when it was time to move on." Glancing over at me with a candid look, he gave his shoulders a rueful shrug. "Now that I'm outside I c'n see the oddities of the system—what must look to you like constrictions.... But then, there's peculiarities here too, and penalties of another sort that're just as binding," he added slyly, giving me a sidelong look. "Calling cards, visiting days, chaperones an' introductions, the number of forks 'n spoons at the table: I still can't seen t' make much sense of it."

Hearing him confess his bewilderment at the very restrictions which had always suffocated me, I was unexpectedly touched; moved that here was another who, like me, stood outside the bars of convention. Yet even though it was clear that he'd turned aside from many of the strictures of his own culture; though he could plainly see the constraints of ours, and the social pressures which enforced them, he was not one to engage in a debate on the ideal society— on the system which might house the benefits and rejected the drawbacks of our separate cultures. For one thing he still knew too little of ours to realize its particular virtues; for another the subject was too abstract to arouse or hold his interest. He much preferred the solid, the concrete, the sensual immediacy of the moment, to any theoretical discussion.

Though he rejected slavery on principle, for example—holding freedom of personal movement almost above all else; though he listened to me expound on the propositions which had led to the founding of this nation, he was not a man to espouse causes or weigh issues, and he obviously found much of what I said incomprehensible. Yet this was to say nothing against his level of intelligence, which was clearly of the first order—as could be seen from his maneuvers to outwit me, the agility with which he anticipated my motives, the sharpness and clarity of his perception, and the depth with which he comprehended my moods, or intuited my thoughts and needs: all with a swiftness which seemed to bypass logic, and which frequently took me by surprise. His was simply a different way of perceiving, of rendering detail into knowledge; and as the weeks slipped by I struggled to time and harmonize my knowing with his.

If I found that we had much in common in wanting to shrug off the ties of oppressive social structures, I realized that we were leagues apart on life views I'd always regarded as prevailing before: outlooks on life, death, and religion especially. That we had no mutual ground at all on such matters came as a bolt out of the blue to me, though I couldn't have said why I should have expected different. Having never attended Sunday worship while at sea, though virtually all of his shipmates showed up at least on occasion—having foregone church now that he was ashore, though there were services which catered especially to seamen, and demanded little in formal attire—Robertson had already been judged heathen by the regular churched community, and I'd concluded he had little regard for established religion. That the town was already talking about his absence—especially since he'd set up tentative residence, and was fair game for the Congregationalists, Methodists and Baptists—I knew as well, not just from general gossip but from Anne, who took him to task behind his back almost daily.

Yet even with all this it came as a shock when one night I managed to set him talking about religion, and he revealed the odd mixture of mythical and spiritual beliefs of the Rom—beliefs in which many god-figures flourished, and death was a finality save for a restless and shadowy, half-human after-domain. That we did not share a belief in one supreme God—that Robertson knew nothing whatever of Christ, that he did not believe in life after death, at least not in any Christian sense—came as a profound jolt to me; and I spent the days afterward—when I should have been working—trying to sort out my reactions.

Forced by his beliefs to confront and evaluate my own convictions in a new light—to consciously consider them, for the first time, from the shifting perspectives of varying values, rather than as inflexible standards—I suddenly felt wholly unsettled; and it was no help whatever that from the point of view of the churched, he was doomed to hell eternal—that our disparate outlooks pointed at best to separate and widely divergent futures, a prospect already intolerable to me.

We differed too on political matters—not in a clash of views or opinions, but rather in degrees of interest, Roberston being sublimely indifferent to the whole structure of government from the village on up, while I'd been born and raised in a climate of issues. Utterly ignorant of American principles and history—equally oblivious of the British and Welsh—only vaguely aware that Tyler was President, that the Maine-Canadian border had just been settled—unacquainted with what Thomas Jefferson had done, with the purpose of the Revolution, even with the fact that there *had* been a Revolution, he sometimes seemed like one dropped from another planet, struggling to make sense of my references and language. Yet despite his lack of political tutoring, he was possessed of a profound worldliness, far greater than mine, for all of my travels; with an aura of sophistication and knowing, a sensuality of thought and gesture, which pervaded his very mood and manner.

There was no doubt whatever in my mind, for example, that though I was married and he was not—though I was nearly ten years his senior, and he only a short time removed from boyhood—he knew far more about amorous matters than I did. Just how and where he had come by his knowledge—in Liverpool bar-rooms or East River boarding houses, certainly outside Rom circles—I had no clearly defined idea; but my conviction persisted that the marital relation was far less a mystery to him than to me. I thought of my one visit—with my brother Tom—to a Boston brothel just before our weddings, and blushed again at the recollection. Nor could I say I'd fared better since; for turning to the present I considered my inadequate relations with Anne, obviously the worse for my want of schooling—then contrasted my uncertainty with Robertson's poise, his unconscious air of sureness and knowing, and felt my shortcomings even more vividly than before.

Having had, before marriage, one or two stabs at romance, my boyhood flings made equally terse reading; while romantic theories about Robertson's past continued to abound, fed by bits and pieces of rumor. It was true that I could still find nothing concrete in them; that, though he'd confessed on the Line—as a part of his baptismal ordeal—to interludes with a Liverpool barmaid, and had never denied scuttlebutt of a Welsh sweetheart, I'd discovered the easier information came from him, the less likely it was to be honest; so with regard to specifics, I was still none the wiser. Yet his reluctance to disclose what he withheld, his mix of regret, restraint and attachment were so strong that my opinion persisted that his had been a wide and varied experience; and even as I longed to unveil his secrets, I couldn't but contrast my own lack of practice, and rue my poverty of background.

Whatever his actual exploits had been, he was at any rate much freer with touch, much less inhibited in body than I was. Watching him as he moved through his duties, his hands bringing to life surfaces, textures, contours; looking on as he tended my children, seeming to know just how to hold them—feeling his way round their needs and defenses as handily as a mariner through the shoals of a harbor; seeing how my young ones took to him in return, clustering round his body like cubs about a bear, I marveled at his physical prowess—at the effortless way he related to others. Ashamed that he should prove a better parent than I was—stung by my detachment as a father, a negligence I felt sure was unknown in Rom families—I began to try to imitate his manner; commenced to care for the children in ways

I never had, particularly young Nat, whom I'd never even held, and who like all infants terrified me.

Finding him crying once when I came upstairs, I tried to settle the matter myself, instead of calling Anne, as I habitually did; lumbered up as gracefully as I could to the cradle, and peered down at this squalling five-month-old baby, red-faced as a shellback on a binge in a tavern.

"Well, what's the problem, eh?" I asked, trying not to sound like I was on the quarterdeck, and feeling awkward as a suitor on his first call. To my amazement Nat hushed at once, looking up at me in the midst of his wailing with the startled interest of one tapped on the shoulder—forgetting all about his discomfort, no doubt, in his astonishment that this man with a beard had addressed him. Circling him warily—wondering if I should hold him—wondering, indeed, just how to go about it—I finally got around to bending down, Nat all the while watching me like a rabbit; then at last managing to get my hands under him—finding his body somewhere in the blankets which, with his petticoats, wholly encased him, and lifting him out gingerly as a rocket, I sat down with him in a chair by the window, trying to remember how Robertson held him, and finally propping him up against one of my knees so I could look him in the eye.

"So you'hre my son, you little farmeh," I muttered, cautiously touching his fingers and face; and cocking his head in a comical fashion, Nat patted my hand as if to say, "So you'hre my old man, you big old beahr, you." Touched, I stroked his short, silky hair—saw that it would be sandy, like Tom's; traced the cleft of his chin, his beautifully defined lips—Nat meantime sucking my fingers or pulling at the hairs on the back of my hand. Investigating him for the first time, I looked at his fat legs under his dresses, then took off his booties and tickled his bare feet as I'd so often seen Robertson doing: Nat responding with a chortle, and reaching up to clutch at my beard.

At last getting up I carried him to the window, and held him up to look at the sea: his eyes adjusting to the bright light, and focusing on the distance in wonder. "Look here, this here's the single most impohtant thing I c'n show ye—that's what fathehs're s'posed t' do,

ain't it?" I expounded, still holding him up to the open window.
"Well, this here's the sea, the life an' blood of this planet, the source of
the food on youhr plate an' the clothes on youhr back, not t' mention
the grist for youhr spirit: that's all ye need t' know—don't forget it."

Whenever I passed by his cradle after that, whether he was
upstairs or down, his plump little arms reached up to greet me; and
so encouraged did I feel by the success of my venture that I took
to courting the other children, finally even getting up the nerve to
reach out once and rub Robertson's hair: the leap of my heart a-clang
in my ribcage as the crisp, cool dark waves slipped past my fingers,
and Robertson's eyes flashed into gladness.

By the last week or so before departure, I was spending time with
him almost every day—usually early in the morning when no one
else was around: tiptoeing into his room to find him still tumbled
in sleep, half-dressed and tousled in the tangled sheets, then setting
up breakfast while he wakened and stirred—sometimes laying out
Romany fare, the best tea, freshest loaves and cheese I could find,
sometimes my own favorite grub, crabcakes, brown bread, shipjack
and coffee. Hiking the shore before parting ways for work, we shared
our last hours together in silence, while the quiescent ripples lapped
at our feet: Jim pacing beside me subdued with restraint, and me
yearning to voice my clumsy regard, yet reluctant to presume upon
him. Aware as I was of the profound feeling between us—of his
intense, if unspoken, devotion for me, and of mine, equally wordless,
for him—I was as distressed by our coming parting as if it were
slated for years, not weeks—my discomfiture heightened by vague
premonitions whenever I thought of the trek to Havana.

Far from relenting to logic or reason, my uneasiness deepened
to superstition despite my lifelong disgust with such notions; and
nothing increased my anxiety more than the dream which struck me
a couple of nights before they were due to put out for Cuba: a dream
which began with the shock of understanding that Robertson had
just been lost off the jibboom, and the ship hauled to for the fruitless
rescue. Hovering in spirit over the quarterdeck, I saw Tom reading
out the brief service, all the others clustered round him hatless and

downcast—even Howland and Reuben looking sober as stones; then after a silence—according to custom—all Robertson's gear was brought up from the foc's'le, and Tom began to auction it off.

Trunk, ditty box, dungarees, duck trousers, tarpaulin hat, sou'wester and oilskicks, sheath knife, palm and fids, even razor, all were placed in a desolate heap on the poop, while I looked on the scene with mute anguish; but as Tom held up his father's waistcoat, the one Jim had worn doing stunts in Havana—as Paul stirred himself from the reserve of his grief, and made a move to bid for it—a searing pain wrenched me from my silence, and I found my voice for the first time. Shouting over Paul's words, I cried "No, you can't have it; it's mine!"—but no one there could hear or see me.

Waking up in a sweat I climbed straight out of bed, and spent the rest of the night pacing the beach till I could see Galt Wingate, Tom's mate: coming straight to the point—and ditching the whole of ship custom—by begging him to keep Robertson off the jibboom. Hearing out my entreaty with an incredulous patience, Wingate of course denied the petition, and even as he spoke—striving to recall me to my senses, in the manner of one reasoning with a deranged uncle —I realized I was powerless to forestall disaster, as powerless to protect Jim at sea as I was to prevent a recurrence of his fever in Havana.

The last day I took him out to sit for a spell near the lighthouse, before parting ways with him at McCabe's cabin. Though he'd left his trunk—his most treasured belonging—in his room when he'd overhauled his gear earlier in the day, and taken one of my old chests instead; though he'd left me his keys and bidden me to look after his room, all gestures which encouraged me to believe he'd return—I felt the sheer force of his absence as I'd never felt any loss since Charis' death; and it was next to impossible to stand around the next morning in the midst of the last-minute dockside preparations, and not give vent to my desolate feelings. I hadn't wanted to see the ship off, but with Tom and so many of my kinsmen aboard, I'd been obliged to put in an appearance; and now I stood on the crowded wharfway, flush with the gangplanks of the *Amanda Howland*, trying to look cheerful or, failing that, useful, while Tom's officers and crew shambled up with their handcarts.

When Robertson came up—in company with Paul—and caught sight of me despite my quick about-face, he strode straight over to say goodbye, his tense, stern-set features and disciplined manner at least as revealing as his halting words; and huskily muttering "Watch youhr step on the jibboom," I slipped a small box—housing my shell from Havana, the one he'd admired that night at dinner—into his pocket without his seeing. Ludicrously, we shook hands on the dock, neither of us looking at the other; then he was aboard, sharing jests with his shipmates, and rallying to obey Galt's orders. The windlass creaking to the mournful cries of "Shenandoah"—the anchor slowly breaking the surface—the ropes casting off—the sails shaking out—*Amanda* was swinging clear of the pier, while the last of the landsmen jumped for the planks; then leaning over to a favorable NW wind, trembling as she took to her course, she steadied and headed out of the harbor.

It was the last day of August, the ship was due back around mid-October, expected to be gone a mere six weeks or so—but not till her departure did I fully appreciate the power and invigoration Robertson had brought into my life; for as she skated the wind to the Point—as I hurried out to the headland at the lighthouse, to see her stand out for the Mussel Ridge Channel—the intensity of the sunlight relented, the blush faded from the buds of the roses, and the textures and grains vanished from the granite.

XV
EBEN MCCABE
Cape Damaris, Maine   Sept.-Oct. 1842

As soon as I seen the long look on his mug as he came ambling up to my door, I knew plain as rain what he'd come to say, whether he actually said it or not; knew it as plain as I'd known what was weighing on Robertson's mind, last night when he'd set down beside me at the table to say a few words before shipping out. Whether Jim'd finally decided he could trust me, after all them times I'd advised him, or was just too overcome to hold back any longer, he'd let his hair down and spilled his whole story—not that I was surprised by any of it, since I'd pretty much figured it all out by Rio; but Melchett, of course, said nothing at all, planting his stern on the sofa by the sea windows and calling out for a scotch and soda. Looking him over whilst I filled his glass, I soon'd tapped his thoughts anyway, since I could read his dour puss, his restless paws and shuffling boots as easy as the coastline from a trawler; and as I set down beside him I hid a grin.

After he'd talked of this and that for an hour, looking lost as a ship without a rudder—after he'd downed a cargo-load of spirits, far more than his usual moderate ration, and 'd given up on me for the evening—I thought I seen a spot to put my oar in; and as he got up to leave I blandly slipped in, "By the way, Robertson was by here last night for a spell, after he'd been out t' the Point with you."

His face lighting up before he could check it—the same way as a lamp will when you're trying not to wake others—he asked, picking up his jacket sort of casual, "Anything in p'ticulah on his mind?"

"Oh, a few last-minute requests he'd already mentioned," I

answered, knocking the last of the log into embers, "but b'fore he left he asked me t' keep an eye on *you*, for his sake, whilst he was gone; an' since he seemed t' mean it, I thought I'd let ye know I intend to."

Looking like a beach-head fought over by gulls, his face was a mix of joy, restraint and pleasure, all squabbling to get the upper hand; but all he said was—gruffly—"Well, whyn't ye tell me so in the first place, instead o' keepin' me waitin' an hour t' hear somethin', you sogeh!" Then downing the last drop in his glass he was off, in something between a huff and a halo; and I set for quite a while by the fire chuckling, watching the embers crackle and simmer.

It was the last time I seen Melchett with a bright look in his eye for the better part of a week or so—him being a regular bear to live with, whether he was at home, the shipyard or Eli's. Even at the big send-off next day for Worthing—the *Sabrina Fenwick* bound for Kingston, and every hand aboard her ready to race Tom both ways—he looked on with mild annoyance, like a man interrupted at reading the paper: this from a waterdog who'd lived for years for the thrill of commerce and competition. Catching sight of him now and again with his glower, I was damn relieved I was working for my cousins, making a new net and tanning old ones, instead of helping him out at the yard: the monotony of weaving meshes while Obed and Lem salted their catches, being a mile preferable to shuffling receipts while dealing with Melchett's cantankerous humor.

From what I could tell, as soon as the town'd settled down from the antics of seeing off two ships in two days, he pretty much throwed himself into his work, especially into his plans for a new vessel—old Seth and the other heavyweights at Melchett Bros. having been talked round to the dimensions of his lift model, and given the go-ahead to build come spring weather. Drumming up investors—including me, as usual—then lining up timbers, a master carpenter and joiners, teams of caulkers, sail makers and riggers to be ready for work when needed took the whole of his workdays and then some; and when he did drop by to see me, it was to talk over the developing vessel, not to discuss what really ate at him.

Though I was pleased he checked with me on her sail plan—

since I knew damn well I'd be fool enough to ship as mate aboard her, if and when she ever slid down the ways—I would of liked for him to open up; but being the most mule-headed barnacle-back on the coastline, he'd kept right on with his drawings and papers, driving every one of us to drink with his relentless outlines. Not till Robertson's been out a week and we had news of him one night at Eli's, did he give me so much as a breath of his real mind; and even then, it wasn't what I'd expected.

Eli's was packed stem to stern with a live crowd—it being Friday night, and all hands freshly paid off and celebrating—and Melchett and me was setting by the back windows, somewheres between our second and third, when Sage Haskett blowed in and breezed by us on his way to pick up his mug at the counter. "I s'pose ye've heard by now as t' how youhr blue-eyed Welshman has been at it again in Pohtland," he slowed down long enough to bawl over his shoulder at Melchett; and Melchett, who'd been looking tireder than I'd ever seen him, perked up his ears like a horse at the race track.

"What d'ye mean?" he barked, setting up in his chair and coming all at once into focus.

"You ain't had the story?" grinned Sage, swinging round and shambling up to us with a swagger—not at all reluctant to tell tales out of school about Robertson, since he'd never taken a shine to him in the first place, and hadn't bothered to revise his opinion even after Jim'd lassooed Ben off the Bermudas. "Ye'll have t' hear it from Haggai—say, Haggai! lay a course oveh here a minute!—he's just back from a month to his sisteh, an' seen *Amanda* while she was docked in Pohtland."

"Is she all right? What happened? She ain't listed as cleared in the papehs," pressed Melchett, getting brusquer by the minute.

"Oh, she's off—cleared afteh she'd been in poht three or four days," assured Sage, as Haggai broke away from his corner and began to navigate the commotion of shellbacks, tankards and chairs and tables between us.

"Three or four days! Tom'd expected a couple," Melchett exploded, running his hand through his hair like he always did when put out.

"There was some delay in shippin' the extra cargo—everybody

was in a stew about it, though by rights the race's from Pohtland t' Pohtland—but here's the man t' spin ye the story," Sage chuckled, making a bow as Haggai drew up within earshot.

"Evenin', Cap'n, Eben," beamed Haggai, watching Sage disappear in the throng at the counter; then "Don't mind as I do," as I cleared the old lobscouser a seat beside me. "I'm just off the *Maine,* ain't even had suppeh—ye know, that's my first run on a steameh—an' damned it is warn't as smooth a ride as they say—a bit noisy, a' course, an' the smoke, when the wind shifts, but—"

He would of launched into a stream of details—was busting with news of every last spigot and lever, down to the nuts and bolts in the engine; but Melchett, who thought all who rode steamers was no less than traitors—and who knew perfectly well Haggai knew it—straightaway froze him short with a look, and bringing matters to the point, barked: "What's all this about Robertson?"

"Ye ain't got word o' that here yet?" laughed Haggai, gloating over the fact he'd already got Melchett's goat, and fishing round in his pockets for his pipe and pouch. "Well, that there makes quite a yarn—I betteh do somethin' t' swab down my pipes—Eli! Eli! Pour me a refill! Make it a mug o' flip—an' bring me some chowdeh!—Nice t' be able t' make youhr own cousin wait on ye, heh heh... Well, y' see," he commenced, carefully filling his pipe whilst Melchett looked on with volcanic impatience, "t' begin with, though I was stoppin' to my sister's near the harboh, I was by *Amanda* pretty often, visitin' with Abby in the galley; so you might say I knowed more or less what as goin' on, even though I wasn't shipped aboard her.

"Well, they'd hardly got the hook down 'n stahrted takin' cargo—which there was a mix-up, so things got off t' a slow stahrt—when Howland, comin' by an' catching' sight o' Reuben dressed t' the teeth, an' hearin' about the race with Worthing, gets all fired up hisself, an' changes his mind about not sailin'. Decidin' t' sign the Articles afteh all, he goes b'low t' see Tom; 'n Tom, recognizin' as how Sal might be an advantage if the race with Worthing should come down t' the wire, agrees t' take him at the last minute: Galt puttin' him into his own watch t' keep him separated from Robertson, who'd gone into Tuppeh's watch already."

By now Melchett'd taken on the look of a man who knows for a certainty what's coming, and throwing a quick glance at me, he lit his pipe; but Haggai, saluting Eli as he came up with a mug and helping hisself to a generous swallow, went on with the story more or less gleeful. "Well, there was foul weatheh b'tween them two almost b'fore Sal'd got his trunk stowed down in the foc's'le, though I don't know the rights of it, except neitheh of 'em come t' blows—things bein' pretty much like they was afteh Rio. But b'fore Tom'd up anchor 'n stood out for Havana—roundabout three days ago now—they had a reg'lar squall oveh Howland's sisteh Sapphirer, who I'd seen down by the wharves fairly often: Sal watchin' out for her like he's always done eveh since their Ma passed on."

Breaking off for a moment to attend to his chowder, which'd come sailing up just then on Eli's tray, he left us dangling while he put away half a bowlful, one eye cocked on Melchett to gauge his impatience; till Melchett, having put up with his monkey business as long as he could stand it, snatched the dish and put his hand over it, snapping, "You don't need no more; what happened?"

"Now, skippeh, keep youhr shirt on; what's a good yarn if it ain't told propeh?" Seeing Melchett heave himself back in his chair, Haggai reclaimed his bowl and ate on in silence, grinning under Melchett's eye; then stoking up a fresh pipe, he at last went on.

"Anyways, as I was sayin', Sapphirer took t' comin' by the dock fairly often, her 'n Reuben's sistehs with her—s'posedly t' see her brotheh, but I noticed it was Robertson she had her eye on. Since I was by ev'ry day m'self, I seen her hangin' round watchin' the crew work, then sidlin' up t' say hello when they knocked off, an' headed for Widder Wingate's for suppeh. At first it was just a word or two t' the local boys; but it warn't long b'fore her 'n Felicier was chattin' up t' Robertson—'n since the gals was posted right at the dockhead, he had t' file past 'em t' get t' the road, an' couldn't get away without returnin' some talk. I s'pose Sal didn't like her takin' notice o' him— he *is* damn fetchin', an's turned otheh heads b'sides hers; but I hadn't no notion how hot Sal's feelin's was runnin' till long about the end o' the fourth day, when everybody's tempeh was gettin' short anyways, what with the delays 'n all."

Deadening headway again to polish off his flip—holding the empty mug aloft to catch Eli's attention, the same way as a ship hoists a distress signal—Haggai kept us waiting till Eli'd come by, and promised us a fresh round of spirits; then putting his feet up in perfect imitation of Melchett, he eased hisself back into the story.

"That's right...the end o' the fourth day," he warmed up, folding his arms and looking important. "Comin' up from the galley at knockin' off time, I seen Howland 'n Robertson face t' face on the dock, with both the watches crowded round, an' Saphhirer 'n Felicier 'n them in the background. Near's I could figure in the heat o' the moment, Howland'd accused Robertson of makin' time with his sisteh, 'n Jamie'd denied it, claimin' *she'd* made advances—which I leave it t' you which is the most likely. By the time I gets m'self a ringside seat, Jamie's whipped up t' where he's callin' Sal a liar; 'n Sal's warnin' him t' keep his distance from her, for the rest o' the stay an' in the future. I s'pose it might of ended then 'n there in a drawr, since everybody knowed Galt'd be up any minute, him havin' stayed b'hind in the hold t' give one last look around at the stowage; but Sal can't neveh resist tackin' on the last word—so stickin' out his chin, he belts out like a bullfrog: 'You ain't in no class with her, you Limey pimp!'

"At that Jamie up'n loses his tempeh—which he has a short fuse, I don't deny it; an' holdin' back Paul—who bolts out with his hands cocked—he dives at Sal like a fish hawk at a salmon. Expectin' he'd maybe throw a left or an uppeh, Sal's caught completely off balance; 'n down they both goes in a heap on the plankin', like a couple o' sloops knocked down by a wind shear. Rollin' 'n kickin' like a tub without ballast, gettin' t' their feet, then' blowin' each otheh down, they're in a flat-out, squallin' tempest—not as good as the one in Rio, which I kicks m'self for havin' missed, but a beaut: both of 'em bein' about the same size an' both of 'em determined as hellcats, though it's easy t' see Jamie has the advantage. Sal, he don't often get much practice, since folks mostly backs off when he growls; but Jamie's done his share o' scrappin', as I c'n see from his timin' 'n punches.

"Hollerin' out left 'n right all around, some of us is encouragin' Sal, but most is puttin' their dough on Jamie; an' sure enough if he don't finally pin Sal, haul both his hands behindst his back, drag him cussin' 'n twistin' t' his feet—'n give him the old heave-ho int' the harboh!"

By this time Melchett's face—which'd been looking grim— suddenly begun to twitch at the corners, pretty much like mine was doing in spite of my efforts to look sober; but managing to check ourselves for the moment, we gave ear more or less without comment, whilst Haggai plunged ahead with a relish.

"But that ain't the end of it—no, not near all; 'cause at that instant Reuben, just comin' up the dock from town—bein' dressed, as ye c'n picture, in hat 'n tails, actin' out the part o' supercargo t' the hilt—hoves int' view just in time t' see the heels o' Sal's boots hittin' the wateh. Not even botherin' t' take off his coat, he hurls hisself on Jamie's back like a wildcat, leapin' down from a branch on a hunteh; an' down they both goes like a birch gnawed by a beaveh, Reuben's hat flyin' off in one direction, an' his solid brass buttons bustin' like popcorn. Well, they tangles a bit, Paul 'n Abby holdin' down Sal who's climbed out o' the drink lookin' for more; but Reuben's no match for the likes o' Jamie—mostly clawin' 'n kickin' whilst Jamie is laughin', scramblin' for first one hand, then the otheh, 'n gettin' 'em both in his grip 'fore Rube knows it. Haulin' 'im t' his feet like a sack o' potatoes, Jamie gives 'im a swing or two in a circle, pickin' up speed 'n lettin' 'im go when he's flyin'—an' damned if Rube don't end up in the harboh, givin' a grand splash just as Galt clears the scuttle.

"Bearin' down on us all like a storm surge on a dinghy, Galt comes 'n busts things up in a hurry, tryin' t' look stern, the way he's s'posed to, but crackin' a smile in spite o' hisself—pretty much like you folks is doin'—when he sees Reuben clambeh up out o' the brine, salt wateh runnin' in streams down his nose, 'n squishin' out o' his patent leathehs. Well, he puts Jamie t' work at one end o' the ship, Sal at the otheh, 'n sends Reuben b'low t' post papehs, even if it is afteh hours—an' even if they is too sore t' lift feathehs; 'n that's the last I knowed of it all, since they managed t' clear harboh next mornin'— though I don't doubt Reuben 'n Sal're puttin' their heads t'getheh, 'n we ain't heard the last o' the story."

Till now we'd contrived to keep up a serious front, as befitting the former mate and skipper—not to mention the ongoing backers—of this fire-eating Welshman; but as soon as Haggai'd downed his flip and gone off to spin his yarn to others, Melchett gave a droll look over his glass, and both of us busted into uproarious laughter. Rolling out at last after having been pent up, our bit of a hoot somehow relieved not only Melchett's week of ill-humor, but the long-time constraint between us; and as he subsided—wiping his wet cheeks, and generally settling his feathers—his grey eyes looked out at me with new candor.

"Well," he sighed, shaking his head, and giving a honk or two into his handkerchief, "aside from seein' Sal 'n Reuben get their comeuppance, I can't say as I like it much."

"It ain't like Robertson t' take Sal's bait—leastways, not since Rio," I seconded, thinking that only the mightiest personal distress—commencing long before the run-in on the dock—could of led him to jettison his pledge not to fight. "I'm took aback...honestly thought he'd neveh cut loose again, after what we said t' him the last time."

"It ain't just that," Melchett muttered, giving me a thoughtful look, "—though I admit I'd hoped he'd carry my words in mind even when I wasn't with him." Pausing, he seemed to ponder something a moment, whilst the racket in Eli's ebbed off a little; then making up his mind, he went on with his musing. "It's the slow stahrt, when things'd been planned out so careful, an' when so much d'pends on keepin' t' schedule...the fight, when I could of sworn this'd be one time when both the watches 'd been set up without conflict..." Once more he halted, his face taking on a look both troubled and honest, as alert as a bird's when some danger threatens; and he seemed to be on the brink of confiding something important.

"What is it?" I prodded gently, deciding to risk a bit of a push.

"I don't know," he shrugged, whilst the noise around us sort of fell to a humming. "The slow staht, the fight... it's not a good omen for the voyage."

I'd never heard him speak of omens before, unless to jeer at others who talked that lingo; and my ears at once stood to attention. But instead of making an issue of it—as if knowing the best way to get him to talk was to play him along like a bass on a trawl line—I simply encouraged him lightly, "You think this run is jinxed, then?"

"I don't know," he struggled again, giving me a long look as if to judge how far he should go, or how fairly I'd listen; then apparently satisfied with what he seen, he plunged ahead with a quaver: "I had a dream the otheh night...just a couple o' days b'fore *Amanda* put out... an' damned if it didn't hit me again, roundabout night b'fore last. I dreamed that Robertson'd just been lost off the jib boom—that the ship was hove to whilst Tom read the service, an' auctioned off his clothes 'n gear." Breaking off he took a drink, trying to look crusty as ever; but I seen that his fingers quivered—and his voice, when he spoke again, was thick with feeling. "I tell you I sawr his stuff as plain as day—right down t' the buttons on his red shirt, an' the stitchin' on the collah...It was so real I woke up convinced it'd happen—even went oveh t' Galt, the first time I dreamed it, t' try t' convince him t' keep Jim off the jib."

Amazed he'd gone to such extremes—imagining at once what Galt must of thought of it—I managed to keep my mouth from popping open; and nodding instead, I tried to put things into perspective. "You think just b'cause you had a dream, then heard of the usual sorts o' delays 'n squabbles that plague any ship outward bound, that Robertson's numbeh is up?" I said kindly. "Remembeh with *Charis,* things commenced with us pickin' up Robertson in Boston after he'd been in a hell of a ruckus—which we still don't know the rights of; then went on in Rio with coffee too high, red tape 'n waitin' while prices fell, not t' mention a knife fight on liberty day; an' finally wound up off the Florida Straits with the biggest blow we ever been in—an' still we had a record run with no hands lost."

"I know that what you're sayin' makes sense," he allowed, his lips twitching at the points of my tally. "Hell, I'd of said it m'self anytime b'fore now! But I just can't shake the feelin' I had both times I woke up from that dream—not anything like worry oveh partin' from a shipmate, but like absolute certainty I'd seen the future."

"Ben, I can't recollect as I eveh heard you talk this way," I said, even the hum of noise in Eli's now fading to little more than a buzz in the background.

"I can't recollect as I eveh *felt* this way," he confessed, meeting my eyes head-on and honest. "Next thing y' know I'll be hearin' voices; an' from there it's only a step down t' the *Flyin' Dutchman*—or seein' phantoms in the crow's nest."

Chuckling at his stab at lightness, I clumsily tried to reassure him, though his words'd given me my own sneaking foreboding. But whatever the outcome of his dream, it'd opened up a new channel between us; and finishing up, we paid Eli and left, walking companionably back to my place. Long after he'd headed on up the shore for his house, I set thinking over his words at Eli's, and the changes which'd steadily crept over him ever since we'd hauled into the harbor with *Charis;* and the moon'd risen above the horizon before I finally put out the last lamp.

If I was aware of the changes in him others was too, though I doubted they could read his new attachments, and the anxiety his devotion gave him, from his gruff, edgy humor and preoccupation. What I seen was a slow revamping, an all-over altering in his nature and looks, like a brig taking on a new line in dry dock, or a lobster gradually splitting, then shrugging off its old shell. But what his kin seen— judging from their comments, or their looks of dumb amazement— was the unrelated bits and pieces of his uncharacteristic behavior; and they was as confounded as Tom had been when Ben'd cornered him just before *Amanda* put out, and asked him to watch over Robertson on board.

"What's got int' him anyhow: he neveh used t' give a damn about anybody else's hide b'fore," Tom'd appealed to me then; and he wasn't the only one over a barrel. Out of the blue hired by Ben to draw up a new will—supposedly to cover Nat and allow for his assets since *Charis,* though I suspected the real purpose was to provide for Robertson's financial future—unflappable John was struck all of a heap; and when he come by with a copy for me—since Ben'd saddled me as executor again—a week or two after *Amanda'd* cleared, he knit his brows as he went over the changes.

"Have you seen his one?" he asked me, dumbfounded, thumping the generous portion Ben'd set aside for Robertson. Following his

finger I managed to make out—from the usual tangle of legal chatter—
that Ben'd directed the sizeable figure to be put in a trust and doled
out monthly, probably to stump Robertson's flair for spending: John
dutifully passing on to me Ben's request that the entire provision
be kept secret, since he didn't want to offend Jim with premature
knowledge of the steps he'd taken to secure his future.

"What's going on with him, do you know?" poor John wound
up, as he neatly slipped the will back in its pocket. "What he's laid
aside for Robertson's in parity with the sums set for Anne and the
children. It's not like Ben to go off the deep end like this about his
own kin, much less somebody he hahdly knows. I like Robertson
myself—he seems like a good lad—but afteh all, Ben's only met him
a few months ago; and does anybody actually *know* anything about
him?"

Checking a grin I tried to reassure him that Robertson's head
was really worth the price; but he went off with his brow faintly
clouded—and I could see he thought Ben'd taken leave of his senses.

But nothing surprised anyone more than the new slant Ben'd taken
as a father—suddenly carrying on with his young ones as if he'd just
found out he had children. Now when I dropped by of an evening,
they was crawling all over him in his armchair, pulling his beard,
unbuttoning his boots, rumpling up his precious magazines and
papers—even Nat, who like all the babies had since birth been
cooped up in his cradle.

For years put out by his fatherly distance, stunned Anne seemed
to care for this opposite extreme even less—being one with most
of the rest of the town in believing that too much affection spoiled
children's natures. Rounding them up, disciplining them for being
rowdy, or banishing them to the parlor to memorize Scripture, she
seemed constantly on the brink of hot words with Melchett; but
Ben—in company at least—ignored her, fondling the young ones
or encouraging confidences pretty much like he'd seen Robertson
doing. Once I actually seen him reading them a story—some
nautical cliffhanger or other, of course: not as natural as Jim was at
it, a bit awkward and gruff around the edges, but to all appearances

satisfactory to the young ones.

Coming to his door—Spooner, Wingate and me, his brother Matthew and a couple of riggers, to meet one last time before lofting the new ship—we was taken aback, one and all, when he ushered us in with Nat on his shoulder, and both of the twins dangling from his hip pockets: Spooner and Wingate exchanging dumb glances at the sight of their crusty old shipmate with a babe in one arm and toddlers at his tail, like a loon with its chicks riding pig-a-back in the water. And when Nat come down with his first case of grippe—it being now late September, and the weather liable to abrupt changes—he was far more anxious than he'd ever been with any of his other offspirng, who'd all weathered their share of childhood illness. Even I, who'd grown accustomed to his changes and expected more than others of him, was brung up short when I heard from Sadie that's he'd taken it in turn with Anne to see him through the crisis, cleaning up diapers, soiled bedding and clothing he never would of touched before, while Nat quieted best when his pa was near him.

But there was other changes in Ben as well—less catching to the eye than his anxiety over the voyage, his concern for Robertson's welfare or his playfulness with his children—which I reckoned only I could see; and these small alterations delighted me as much as the big ones. Besides a fresh willingness to take chances and a shade of relaxation in his passion for order, I commenced to glimpse a new preoccupation with his personal looks and shore togs: his beard now neatly trimmed, his clothes changed more often, and his hair—though unruly as ever—thick and clean as a stand of dune grass. Though like everyone else he bathed Saturday nights—hauling down the tub in the kitchen, drawing and heating enough water to fill it, then waiting his turn while Anne and the baby, the girls, and finally the boys used it before him—he'd taken to coming by my place Wednesday eves as well, and using my copper for a mid-weekly refresher.

Happening on him once in Westcott's general store, I found him pawing over a new assortment of soaps and hair tonics brung down from Boston; and though he quickly moved on to the lamp oil, I later seen—out of the tail of my eye—that he quietly sneaked back and bought some. His working clothes, too: though he still wore the plainest garb, bowing to form only enough to sport a jacket—the short, square-cut coat all shellbacks wore—back and forth to the counting house and shipyard, what he did wear was uncommonly clean and mended.

At first sight he still looked like what he was, a hard-headed, hard-working downeast seaman, stubborn as the granite under his boots; but there was a kind of softness creeping over his features which caused me no end of satisfaction. Watching him as the days went by, his face worn by enforced patience and waiting, I seemed to see something like a light about his eyes and expression, like the glow of a lamp through the palm of your hand; and more than once I was struck by the new comeliness in him.

If there was changes percolating in Melchett, there was alterations brewing in the town's character as well—most of them reflecting back on Ben and his kinfolk, and stoking up upheaval in his personal and family life. Though there'd been—for example—a temperance union in town for decades, practically ever since Maine'd become a state, there was suddenly all at once four of them, the Washington movement having took over from Bath; and Anne—who'd for years abided by Ben's order to steer clear of all such tomfoolery—suddenly heeded the call from Brewster one fire-eating Sunday sermon, and joined the Washington Temperance Society. As if it wasn't enough she'd marched up to him and become a member—paying her year's dues out of her egg money, since Ben was too tight to let her have ready cash—then offered their house for the September meeting; and Ben all at once found hisself in the position of a man whose wife publicly chastises his drinking, then forces him to host a bash of like-minded townsfolk.

Though I knew he seldom exploded his feelings—his relations with Anne being pretty much a matter of mutual grin-and-bear-it affliction, kind of like the President and Congress—he must of let her have it when they got home that Sunday; for he erupted on me around dinnertime, having refused to take the family over to Sarah's, and put away a tidy nest of whiskey and waters before finally giving me an earful.

"Ain't it enough the state already tells me how t' spend half my money, run half the shipyard an' regulate my ship practically down t' the ringbolts?" he steamed, as we drank to personal freedom. "Now here's the town tellin' me what I c'n drink 'n can't—it bein' *my* stomach, for the love o' Pete! If I was a public nuisance it'd be a different matteh, but when've I eveh touched a drop at sea, or been out on the street when I was ashore? As for it bein' immoral—what gives them the right t' d'cide that for me? What d'they think Jesus was doin' at Cana—changin' wateh t' wine just t' put on a show? I d'clare, if Anne turns the house oveh t' that meetin', I'll set in the library an' drink t' their destruction!"

Of course he meant what he said, him being a Melchett; and of course Anne went through with the meeting, her being a Howland—so next Thursday there they was parading by my place, about thirty carriages and buggies filled to the brim with the town's foremost people: Rev. Brewster, shopkeepers, bankers and doctors, not to mention plenty of sea folk, the movement by now having spread right down to the wharves and onto the decks of the schooners. Sneaking through the woods I seen them park in Ben's driveway, or all up and down the road for furlongs, then swarm into the parlor entrance; and as the lamps come on with the fall of evening I could see them hobnobbing in the dining room and parlor, Anne having flung open the double doors between the two rooms to accommodate so many.

There was another light burning as well, this one round in front in the library, where I could almost picture bullheaded Melchett steaming over his sketches and decanter; and figuring that the place of a friend should at the moment be by his side, I pulled up my socks, brushed off my boots, marched up to the door—the parlor, not the kitchen—tipped my hat at the astounded Anne, and asked her leave to confer with Ben over the sail plan of the new vessel.

The sail plan, of course, had long since been decided, Ben having been shoving drawings at me since Havana; but not waiting long enough for her to answer, I gave a nod to the preacher, waved a hand at the others, tramped down the hall and bowed myself in to see Ben. Up to his eyebrows in papers—with a drink stubbornly set at his elbow—he was downright delighted to see me: motioning me to a chair and passing me the decanter with the strongest glint of affection I'd ever seen in his eyes. Nor was I the only one who stood by him; for there was soon a roomful of others, amongst them his brothers Jared and Matthew, and old cronies like Wingate, Spooner and Longworthy, who just happened to drop by needing to see him. Charts under their arms and polite words on their lips, they'd plowed their way through the throng in the parlor ; and time things got done we'd had a fine gamming and accomplished a deal more on the new ship in the bargain—though Anne didn't speak to Melchett for days, and no one could keep up a freeze better than she could.

Nor was that the end to the town's moral uprising; for not only did the temperance societies keep on in full swing—carrying the vote to deny licenses to sell spirits at the next town meeting, and leaning on merchants already holding them to turn in their papers— but the Baptists suddenly had something of a revival, filching Congregationalists and Methodists from their pews, and baptizing converts right and left in the river.

In the midst of it all Jackson DeMille—a classmate of Ben's a few years back at Bowdoin, and newly finished with the course at the seminary in Bangor—arrived on the scene at the Congregational church, accepting the call as junior pastor: him being a town son and hence something of a favorite, though opposite as day and night from Brewster. That they'd eventually clash everybody more or less expected, figuring to accept differences with Christian spirit; but nobody'd imagined that, whilst Brewster kept on more or less leading the temperance movement, Jackson—though a teetotaler hisself—would speak against it his first Sunday, calling on separation of church and state.

The town was in such an uproar after this kick-off that the next Sunday I thought I better go and hear the man myself; so brushing off my beaver hat—which I hadn't clapped on in quite a spell, having long ago given up on Brewster, since I couldn't make head nor tail of his preaching—I cast off for the Congregational church, and hove myself into the McCabe pew. Ahead of me five or six rows I could see

Ben and his team of children, Anne and the entire Melchett clan—easily some fifty in number—ranging up and down several pews; and before long every other seat was taken as well, the place being packed with members and townsfolk come to share in the excitement.

Still revved up from last Sunday's cyclone, Jackson throwed hisself into the service, his text being Matthew 6:19: "Lay not up for yourselves treasures upon earth...but in heaven; for where your treasure is, there your heart will be also." He hadn't gone five or six sentences into the sermon before I could see he wasn't going to tiptoe politely, or dull our wits with any of Brewster's flights of fancy: his baldheaded words taking the bull by the horns, direct enough to satisfy even the likes of Melchett.

"Hasn't the time come for us to own up to what is the incontrovertible truth: that all of us, from the wealthiest to the least, possess more than we need of earthly treasure, and possessing it, have the less to store up in heaven?" he commenced, while Farley Westcott ahead of me cast a doleful look at Deacon Allen, the banker. "Possess it, I say, though is not the reverse ratheh true: our goods rule us, our thoughts and time, our town's and business's direction and commitment; and the measure of their rule is in direct proportion to the diminishing sway of our heavenly store.

"And how stealthily their domination gains hold of our hearts and steers us! My grandfatheh, like yours, arrived on these shores with little more than the clothes upon him, hewed himself a crude home when he could spare time from the laboh which provided him with bread and meat, and gave thanks that the bare needs of his growing family were met by the roof, the hearth and the board. Nothing adorned the walls save the utensils of housework, nothing decorated the earthern floohs save the swishing arcs of the broom... As they prospered those walls were hung with weavings, while hardwood, then carpets covered the floohs; a second story was added, then an ell at the back; and finally the place was abandoned altogether, in favoh of anotheh more stylish, with room enough for the family treasures. Alert to the trend of the times, ships plied the watehs, bringing home, not just the necessities of life, but still more wares to fill the town's parlohs—going as fahr as Canton to satisfy our hungeh for dainties like porcelain and ivory.

"And where were our hearts all of this time: set upon the sights of heaven, or focused on the commerce at hand? Concentrated on the bread of life, or consumed by an appetite which demanded always more than the plenty before it? ... The more goods we required, the more vessels needed to transport them, the more trees hewn and stripped for the shipwrights, and the less time for storing up treasure in heaven—for something so elemental as the praise which springs from a heart awestruck by creation.

"Haven't we yet tasted the gall of maintaining the burden of our earthly possessions? What housekeepeh here hasn't known the exhaustion of keeping up with crowded rooms; what workeh hasn't felt the oppression of having to laboh to provide eveh more? How long will we continue to boast oveh our census, comparing it jealously with otheh towns'—lisiting our ships, our schoonehs, our wharves, shops and churches with the pride of schoolboys collecting marbles; and how long will we fail to contrast our inventory with Jesus', which contained nothing more than needed to sustain him, or with the twelve's, which contained neitheh spare cloaks nor sandals? How long will our shipping pandeh to the town's appetite for goods eveh furtheh removed from necessity, while but a day's ride away, a whole community—the Shakeh town at Sabbathday Lake—sets an example of ordered priorities in modern times?

"I ask you to pause and reflect: where will our present course lead us? Will we keep on building ships and fashioning wardrobes till the woods of Maine are stripped, and the mansions of heaven are bare? Already our forests are ravaged; even as I speak, the swampehs are combing the islands.

"Keeping in mind the example of Christ, I want to present you a challenge: Change course! Simplify youhr lives! Disinvest! Let our businesses concentrate themselves on what is needed; let our church rid herself of her excess baggage! Instead of looking for more, let us settle for what we have; or as Christ bade the rich man, give away surplus, and settle for less! In this way with one effort we will not only rid ouhrselves of the load of our so-called treasures on earth, but restore the balance of creation, and free our thoughts from objects—their use and upkeep—which tax our spirit, and draw our eyes down from the throne of heaven."

It was hard to say whose mugs looked the most dumbfounded—those of the tremendous shipping circles, three-fourths of the town being sea-related, or those of the shopkeepers who bought from them: the whole congregation pretty much gaping as if they didn't know which end was up. Unable to restrain hisself any longer, Cabot Lombard, who owned stock in half the enterprises in town, not to mention the only shipyard big enough to rival the Melchetts', actually got to his feet and cried out: "If folks like me staht to disinvest, what d'ye think'll happen to the economy of this town?"

Impulsively jumping to his feet in turn, Melchet—who'd been listening rapt as a bird dog, the few times I'd been able to glimpse him—countered hotly, "Jackson's right! How far no'th d'ye think we're goin' now for white pine; an' how many ships d'ye think are plyin' the China Seas for cargoes the likes of lacquer an' jade—when they ain't lyin' three or four miles off Woosung for a fortune in chests of opium?"

Looking like she wished she could sink through the floor, Anne turned several shades closer to scarlet; while Lombard—who everybody'd suspected for years of being engaged in the opium traffic, along with such stalwarts as the Howland Brothers of Portland—shot back with a withering look: "Well, let's see the Melchett yahd sell its ships then—or Jackson his shares in the bank 'n the papeh!"

Standing up calmly amidst the commotion, John Melchett—ever the peacemaker—put in sanely, "Gentlemen! Let's remembeh where we are! This is a house of worship, not the lyceum. As long as Rev. DeMille has the flooh, let's hear him out, and save debate for the propeh place and houhr!"

The pews settled down then—albeit with a grumbling—till Jackson pronounced the benediction; but such a buzz arose as folks filed out the doors that I could scarcely hear my own thoughts. Nor was that the end of the matter; for Jackson next day took up the gauntlet, divesting hisself of all the DeMille stock in the bank and his brother's news sheet—Eliphet for years having published a weekly;

packed up his bags, left his father's house—old Andrew probably wishing he'd never sent his son off to Bangor; and moved into a shingled cabin on the waterfront. There, with his books and papers, he no doubt begun to cook up his next sermon; while Melchett, looking troubled, went back to business, his mood even hotter than it had been.

As if all the hullabaloo over Jackson, the temperance crusade, and the departure of *Amanda* wasn't enough to unsettle Melchett, there was the upheaval at the shipyard: all hands trying to get as much work done as possible before cold weather shut down operations, and Melchett in particular struggling to set things in place so the new ship could take shape in the spring without him. Having hired Spooner again as master carpenter, and his brother Matthew as Spooner's assistant, Ben'd energetically set things in motion, like always watching over every step of production hisself, including lofting the ship at the end of September. Not wanting to miss the sight of him chalking out patterns on the dance hall-sized floor of the mold loft, I begged off a few days from net-making; and toting along a stool and a pipe, I plopped myself down to watch in out-of-the-way corners whilst Ben, Spooner and Matthew cleared the decks to commence working.

In the long, plank-floored room—big as a barn and almost as cold—they worked from daybreak to lantern-lighting, laboriously plotting points, then using battens to draw fair curves between them, as section after section—frame outline after frame outline—of the profile and ends of the ship was chalked out full-size on the floor, and patterns was made for the cutting of timbers. Measuring and drawing, Ben's big, sure hands seemed even steadier now that Jackson'd spoke his piece, as if guided by something more than practice; while his thoughtful face hovered without words over his chalk, as if he was gnawed by some doubt or dilemma, yet was bent till he solved it to do his best work. It was the same when he chose timbers to cut to pattern, the giant pieces for the keel, the great lengths for the frames, planking, knees, deck beams and deck planking: his hands running along the hard, seasoned pine, live oak and mahogany, hackmatack and teak as if they was living bones for a body.

Storing patterns in the rafters overhead, systematically numbering timbers, and putting heads together with Spooner and Matt over starting dates and procedures, he gradually lined things up for placement in spring; and since Melchett Bros. already had three other vessels under construction, all set to be launched and rigged in the next 30 days, the anticipation and pandemonium of building was pretty much non-stop and ear-splitting.

In the midst of it all Ben's Pa and brother blowed back into town from Valparaiso and Rio; and as always when Galen and Joseph was home, things picked up even more at the yard—their style on land as brusque and high power as Ben's was in the midst of a gale. To clear out his head—and maybe sort out his thoughts—Ben took to spending time in Robertson's room, as if he was calmed by Jim's lingering spirit; and once or twice I suspected he slept there, for I seen the lamp burn late of an evening, and stumbled on him at the Seven Seas breakfast uncommonly early next morning.

As September turned to October his mind suddenly swung to the other tack—the hectic pace of building, his confrontations with Anne, even the doubts that I knew lingered over Jackson's message, all firing him up with a kind of feverish excitement as the time for *Amanda's* arrival drawed nearer. To whip him up even further, we at last got word—by steamers out of New York and Boston—that *Amanda'd* made it to Havana by the 17th of September, after a respectable 12 day run; and with the official word for Melchett Bros. came the usual packet of letters, scrawled out by all hands them first days in port—including an actual note from Robertson for Ben, which he snatched up like money and raced out to read.

When I asked him later what Jim'd written, he said only: "He spent liberty day alone at Calzada de San Lazara, lookin' for shells"; but there was a contentment about him that I hadn't seen for weeks, and a flush to his face that made him look comely.

For three or four days he sailed through his duties, his mood for once actually good-natured; but all that come to an end with the second dispatch, which reached us around the fifth of October, with long letters from Tom for Elkanah Melchett, John Howland, Shad Talbot and Ben. As soon as he seen who they was for and who'd penned them, Ben's mouth sort of went down at the corners; and taking his up with a sigh he set down beside me, broke the seal and drawed out the pages. From where I set I could see Tom's writing, neat and small and even like Ben's, though with something of a character of hurry; and guessing too well the subject of the letter, I lit my pipe and impatiently waited.

Watching Ben's face from under my lashes, I seen his frown gradually deepen, his brows come together and his scowl develop, kind of like the stages of a no'theaster; but not a word would he say till he reached the end, when he shuffled the pages shut with an oath, stuck them in their envelop and tossed it to me. "Damn Thomas, anyway!" he cried—his use of Tom's proper name a sure sign of his turmoil; "they"ll all take feveh in that Havanner hell-hole!"

"Hell-hole?" I boggled, my face no doubt registering my lack of understanding.

"They're in jail," Ben said flatly, whipping out a cigar—since there was nothing bracing to drink in the office.

"In jail?" I echoed dumbly, such an end having been far from any of the spectacles I'd pictured.

"That's right, in the calaboose, all four of 'em—Robertson, Paul, Reuben 'n Sal: leastways they was when this was written, an' maybe they are still, for all I know!—Go ahead, read it!" he gestured briskly, beginning to gnaw his cigar as much as smoke it, exactly in the style of old Galen.

Shifting around in my seat I opened the letter, heaved a great sigh and scanned the pages. "Dear Ben," Tom'd written, beneath the date of 23 September, and the notation, "Havana Harbor":

"It's late, approaching midnight, and I'm still at my desk, hurrying to get these letters out by steamer tomorrow. I won't beat around the bush like I did with Shad or John or Elkanah, since I know with you I can come straight to the point. What I'm writing about is Robertson, Sal and the others; and I'm doing it now so you'll know how things stand when we finally haul back into Cape Damaris—assuming we ever make port at this pace.

"I can say in good conscience that the trek down went smoothly, not just with respect to the ship and day's runs, but with regard to both of the watches. I'd thought, after the tussel in Portland between Robertson and Sal, that I'd made a mistake in signing on Sal, even if I did take the precaution of putting him in the opposite watch from Robertson; but it looked instead on the way down as if I'd stumbled on a bonanza. With Sal leading Galt's watch, and Robertson Tupper's, the ship went great guns from Portland to Havanna: their rivalry better for progress than any other reward ever devised. I should have known that it wouldn't last, or that Sal and Reuben, at any rate, would be cooking up some mischief after that drubbing in Portland; but after the first day or two my mind was on other matters, and neither Galt nor Tupper had detected anything unusual afoot.

"Well, after we'd got the hook down in Havana, I sent Galt aloft to do a thorough check of the rigging, to get an idea of how much overhauling we'd have to do to get her shipshape for the run home. Back down he came again with a long face and bade me follow him up the mainmast; and laying out on the main topgallant yard, he pointed out seizing after seizing—sound on the outside but burnt in the center. There weren't enough to endanger the ship, even if all should happen to go—being calculated, you might say, to cause a nuisance in the first big blow on the way home, and land whoever'd been sent up to lay them on in hot water.

"Looking at each other, we both said 'vitriol'—though neither of us could believe that any of the hands would've resorted to such a low seaman's trick to get one of their number in trouble. To find out who'd done it, all we had to do was determine who'd laid on the seizings, then call aft his rivals, the odds being good that this beaut of a set-up was the long-awaited sequel to Portland. Since Galt knew the job hadn't been done by his watch, we straightaway fetched down for Tupper; and taking a look at the seizings, he said at once: 'They're Robertson's. I had him up here to work on the lanyards after that blow after Hole-in-the-Wall; but even without remembering that, I'd recognize the job as Jim's—the neatest, most sailorly seizings on the vessel.'

"Going straight down to Howland's and Reuben's berths—all

hands being at work on the docks—I myself went through their gear: something I've never done before, and hope I'll never have to again. In Reuben's chest and bunk we found nothing, but in Sal's we struck pay dirt: a bottle of vitriol, strapped under the berth plank. I told Galt to send them both aft, as soon as it was time to knock off for supper; and sitting down at my desk, I tried to sort out my approach. Bad enough if the two of them had thought out this set-up to get Robertson in trouble; but now I began to wonder if their purpose hadn't been more devious than that—to get Robertson in hot water, slow us down for repairs, and possibly cause us to lose the race to Worthing, thereby getting Robertson in even deeper. I even began to entertain the notion that Reuben and Sal had some secret money on Worthing, and had gone to these lengths not only to even the score with Robertson, but to handicap us and give Bill the edge, and rake in a bit of dough in the bargain.

"Well, all would have gone according to plan—meaning I would have had these two aft, and, since I had the evidence, would have got some story out of them—if the cabin boy, Orin's brother, hadn't been working t'ween decks, and eavesdropped on us on his way back to the pantry. Delighted to have stumbled on such a hot story, he went and spilled the beans to Robertson, who like the others was out on the wharves; and taking matters into his own hands—which is the chief fault I can find with him as a seaman—he at once confronted Sal.

"Being men of few words, they soon came to blows, Reuben halfheartedly helping out Sal, and Paul throwing himself in on Jim's side for good measure; and time Galt and I had called them to heel, the Havana police were on the scene—and you can imagine the god-awful chaos that followed. The men were brawling on public property, the police claimed, breaking this ordinance or the other—you know Havana—and were under arrest, to be jailed without trial—all this in a commotion of about fourteen different languages; and all but arrested ourselves for trying to halt the scuffle, Galt and I left Tupper in charge, and tailed the whole lot of them into the city.

"Unsuccessful in getting anything out of the authorities except a vague promise of release 'in a few days,' Galt and I headed for the

American consul, ready to pay whatever needed to be paid—but on the steps we turned and looked at each other, had the same thought, grinned, and headed back for the ship. In short we decided to teach them a lesson, and let them stew in their own beans for the night— all four of them in the same cell, mind you; and tomorrow we'll see what they've left of each other!"

Urging Ben not to be anxious about the outcome of the voyage— swearing to be off on time, and give Worthing a run for his money— Tom'd signed off with his characteristic scrawl; and feeling my mouth twitch at the corners, exactly like it'd done as I'd heard out Haggai's yarn—envisioning Sal, Reuben, Paul and Jim nose to nose in some steaming jail cell, Sal and Jim hissing like cats, and natty Reuben with a three-days' beard—then looking over at Ben's rueful face, I suddenly exploded into laughter.

"I'd like t' know what's so goddam funny," Melchett rumbled, hauling the cigar out of his mouth.

"Tom's right—you know Tom's right, an' c'n see yourself the sense 'n justice of it. Just think what an education it'll be for Sal 'n Reuben—three or four days without a shave or a wash, chewing the whole thing out with that wildcat Robertson... B'sides," I added, subsiding, and gentling my tone at the sight of his face, "I 'spect this ain't the first time Jim's sat it out in a jail cell: it won't work near the hardship on him as it will on dandies like Reuben 'n Sal. Cheer up: they must of got off days ago now, by the 28th at the latest— roundabout the same time Worthing was due t' quit Kingston. I expect they'll sight each otheh on the run home."

"If they ain't still in Havanner translatin' some court rule, or sittin' in quarantine with yellow feveh," Ben put in glumly, though I noticed the old dryness was creeping back into his tone, and his overcast brow was clearing a little. "Well, this'll make a pretty tale for the town, an' set Elkanah an' John back on their heels! About the best we c'n hope is, what with everything else that's goin' on around here, the whole thing'll eventually get lost in the shuffle, instead of gettin' blown out o' proportion."

Lost in the shuffle is where the tale indeed ended, after a brief explosive commotion; for close on the tail of this gem of a yarn came other news out of New York and Boston, of a tough hurricane season all up and down the Bahamas, Florida coast and Windward Passage: storm after storm taking its toll on the harbors and shipping in transit. Pouring over the papers or copies of Lloyd's Register—anxiously checking the lists of vessels posted overdue, or the insurance reports coming out of Portland—the whole town waited with teeth on edge for word of *Amanda* and *Sabrina,* or the half-dozen coastwise schooners which'd set out in recent days for ports like Appalach or Mobile. As October 10th neared and no word—good or ill—reached the papers of *Amanda,* Melchett grew first over-excited and over-expectant, as if any minute the signals might be run up, then anxious and finally—as *Amanda* and *Sabrina* was both posted overdue—sharply nerved up and worried: too restless to keep his mind on his work or attend to his chores at home.

Looking tense and preoccupied as well, the rest of the Melchetts—from cool heads like John and Sarah to firebrands like Joseph and Galen—kept reassuring each other with hopeful explanations: a delayed clearance from Havana, lost time in foul weather, or repair-work that could be done at sea; whilst the rest of the town—three-fourths of them with kin on *Amanda* or *Sabrina,* or one of the schooners that'd cleared for the Gulf—tried the same way to keep up their spirits. With virtually every vessel late it become plainer and plainer that the weather was in fact the culprit, though in the case of *Amanda* there was other possible causes; and Ben, setting down with me one night at Eli's—too wrought up to do more than sip at his tumbler—shook his head and gave a hollow chuckle.

"I don't know what picture's worse," he rumbled, running a hand through his unruly mop: "That Tom's hung up in Havana gettin' them four out o' the slammeh, or one or more of 'ems down with some feveh, or the whole lot of 'em are out in the eye of some hurricane tryin' t' keep the masts from goin' oveh. Whicheveh it is, I almost don't care anymore, so long as we get this waitin' oveh!"

To darken matters even further, other ill news meantime hit the town—the first in the shape of a case of smallpox which'd occurred, unbeknownst to any, aboard one of the brigs that'd moored here, before clearing to deliver a cargo in Portland. On receiving word from the Portland port physicians that the seaman in question had taken sick just after quitting Cape Damaris, and that the whole vessel was now in quarantine in Portland, the entire town was pitched into a panic, since these shellbacks had mingled ashore for five days. A batch of vaccine was at once brung from Castine, and all those unprotected straightaway vaccinated—a case of locking the barn doors after the horses was stolen; and Melchett, who'd worked night and day to convince Robertson to submit to vaccination before *Amanda*'d sailed, stuck his chin out at me and declared: "If I eveh *do* get that bastihd back here again in one piece, I'll see to it he's vaccinated if I have t' hold him down while you do it!"

The town'd hardly recovered from the anxiety of small pox—holding its breath for several days, at the end of which time, no new cases was reported—when the first of the overdue schooners hove in view, Malachi Pelham's, with a distress signal flying; and boarding her in droves, we found no one to man her but Pelham, and his second mate, Josey Coombs—the entire crew and the mate lost to intermittent fever. Stunned, we stood by while the bells tolled the six losses, one mass service commemorating the blow to the town; then descending on Pelham, we heard the tale in pieces—the fever having been picked up in Mobile, and the massive storms having drove the vessel—undersized and under-manned as she was—repeatedly off course thereafter.

"Same thing Jim had," was all Melchett said, comforting me in his gruff way for the loss of my cousin; and in common with most of the rest of the town's, it was plain that his thoughts was dark and uneasy.

On the fifteenth of October, in the midst of a hot spell, come another misfortune—not from abroad, but as close as the harbor mouth: the granddad of all thunderstorms shattering the peace around midnight, and a bolt of lightning striking my cousin Obed's cottage. Though all escaped —Obed tossing the young ones practically into the high tide, which always come up under the windows—the place was a total loss, the cheap pine and shingles consumed in minutes, and only the net-boxes saved by quick thinking.

At once the entire town pitched in—relieved, perhaps, to have a job to put its mind to: Melchett Bros. sending over wagonloads of prepared lumber, the lumberyard dispatching cedar shingles, and herds of Melchetts, McCabes and Talbots, Shields and Kalkmans, Coombs and Pelhams setting up flood lamps and working nights. In dungarees and work shirts—with hammers and wrenches poking out of their pockets, and with mugs of coffee passing from hand to hand—booklearners like John Melchett and Jackson, along with born builders like Ben and Spooner, put every spare minute into the project: Jackson curling up for catnaps on the shore grass, and Ben hardly sleeping at all, to my worry.

Working together in such a fashion, the town managed with an effort to control its anxiety over the missing, *Amanda* and *Sabrina* now ten days overdue; but hardly had the frame gone up on the cottage and partitions laid out inside, than a fresh mischance struck the community, and tried our endurance even further. Sailing alone one night in the harbor—having taken his sloop out for a quick run around sunset, probably to work off some agitation—Matthias Melchett, one of Ben's uncles, and the senior shipwright at Melchett Bros., was knocked overboard by a freak shift of the boom, and his body recovered down shore next morning. For years one of the chief powers on the board of directors, and a first rate skipper in his own right, his loss was a blow to the town, yard and family; but for Ben, who stood likeliest to all at once replace him, it was as abrupt and unlooked-for as a knockdown.

Not yet twenty-eight, he was suddenly in the position of one about to be called to take on a share of the real weight of the shipyard—a call for which he'd secretly yearned, I'd long guessed, though nowadays he'd maybe begun to have second thoughts; and the sudden prospect of responsibility, on top of all the concerns now pressing on him, must of made for some staggering burden. The funeral took place on the same day as *Amanda* and *Sabrina* was officially listed as missing; and by the time the service was over and folks'd filed off—stern and bareheaded—from the graveside, Ben was looking so played out that without asking his leave I myself drove him home with his family, handed the children over to Sadie, and put up the horses and carriage in the stables: it being a measure of his state of mind that he never raised an eyebrow in protest.

Taking him by the elbow I then herded him to my place, after a word or two to Anne; and throwing hisself down on the sofa by the front windows, he set staring absently out to sea, his waistcoat hanging open and his cravat tossed beside him. Obediently eating the small meal I put before him, he still couldn't bring hisself to talk; but when I'd set a pillow behind him and he'd stretched his legs out to rest, he suddenly looked up and met my eyes, and all at once broke into the silence.

"I'm scared," he faltered simply—the unspoken words "scared *for Jim*" hanging in the air between us, as if he feared further jinxing the voyage; and more painfully moved by his frankness—the first wholly honest thing he'd ever said to me—than by any of the misfortunes that'd wracked the town, I barely was able to make an answer.

"I know it," I said to him kindly, wishing I could find any words to encourage him, any sign in recent events to ease him—but simply accepting instead the stark fact of conditions.

Elementary as my response'd been, it seemed enough for him at the moment; and closing his eyes he drew an unsteady breath, as if trying to find the words to continue. Giving him time, I groped for my pipe, lit it and puffed a few times in silence—the toss of the trees and the wash of the combers only a droning outside the windows. So long was he quiet, and so even his breathing, that I figured he'd dropped off in his exhaustion; but raising his eyes at length with a frankness, he broke into a drowsy murmur. "Ironic, ain't it," he said then, his lips twitching with a kind of wry humor. "He blew int' my life without my so much as askin'...without my even knowin' I needed t' meet him...an' I actually let him go lightly...with nothin' more than a shell in his pocket."

As he spoke his voice fell off to a hush, his mouth turned up at one of the corners like he'd just drunk of something bitter; but before I could find a word to ease him, he closed his eyes again with a silence, as if speaking had used up the last push he had in him. Touching his hand, I seen he was asleep; and getting to my feet with a sigh, I carried the tray into the kitchen, then come back to set by him with my pipe.

Looking down on his face now, I seen that the bitterness was gone, the doubt and confusion and even the worry; and in their place was a simple quiet. Coming in through the windows the light shone full on him, and brung out every curve and line of his features, the way it does with the limb of a tree when it shows every twist and curl of the bark. Like a carving of someone who'd lived long ago or a figurehead ready to mount at a bow, his face was aflood with a kind of oaken beauty—not just a strength or a dignity but a sheen, as if the carver'd revealed his spirit. For a while I set looking, gratified and fascinated, seeing the valor of pain and devotion; then reluctantly getting again to my feet, I spread the afghan over his shoulders, and quietly drew shut the curtains.

XVI

BENJAMIN MELCHETT
Cape Damaris, Maine   Oct.-Nov. 1842

Not two days had passed since my uncle's funeral when I found the note on my desk I'd been dreading: a summons to meet with the board of directors. Wholly unprepared for the meeting—my mind at sea, my will undecided, and my limbs too weary to permit concentration—I found them all sitting round the counting house office: Seth, my father, my uncles Ephraim and Simon, even Abigail and my grandfather's cousin Jorab, so old now he could scarcely keep from dozing. Though he'd always been particularly close to Matthias—though his face still bore signs of carefully-checked grief—Seth was nonetheless crisp as a dollar, coming straight to the point with such matter-of-fact acceptance of the several tragedies which lay behind us, and of the uncertainties which still faced us, that I felt a chill descend on my spirit. Downright Rom in his stoic temper, he barked out as cooly as if no loss had convened us:

"No use pussyfootin' about, mate: Matty's gone an' you'hre the hand best qualified t' take his berth. So come Monday mohrnin' ye moves int' his office, an' your brotheh Jared moves t' your desk. The new ship is youhr first assignment; but there's the riggin' of the brig t' oversee, an' a ketch an' two schoonehs t' line up for next season. An' whilst we're gammin' I might as well tell ye that Galen's set up a cahgo for Mahch in Valparaiso; so youhr sailin' ordehs is January first. Just see to it ye doubles the Horn an' hauls back int' the harboh soon's possible afteh ice-out, so's ye c'n begin t' take oveh production."

Having plainly said all that was essential, Seth shoved back his chair and stood up; and the others—having just as plainly agreed to his words beforehand—followed suit, Pa giving his arm to Abigail and Simon helping Jorab to his feet. It never having occurred to any of them that any true-blooded son of theirs might want to contest his assignment, they all clapped me on the shoulder and filed back to work; and I was left standing in an empty office. Too stunned by the march of events to call them back to order, or to even know what terms I might want to press, I ushered myself back out to the street; and needing to go somewhere to sort out my thoughts, I instinctively sought Jim's room at the Inn.

Shutting his door behind me, I felt a measure of calm, as I always did when I entered his chamber; and sitting down by the harbor window, I wistfully looked around. Here in quieter days a month ago I'd unabashedly explored every nook and cranny, drawn by even the most innocuous of his belongings: fishing in drawers, poking into desk pockets, diving around in the wardrobe and cupboard— all of them too jumbled anyway to show my tampering, and all of them containing bits of things that I'd been hankering for months to fathom. By now there was only one crook I hadn't pried into, his trunk; and if he hadn't taken the key I'd probably have plumbed its depths as well. But now in my confusion of aim and purpose, I just wanted to absorb his presence—to warm myself in the strength given off by his belongings—as an animal in winter seeks out its mate's fur; and sitting in the easy chair by his window, I pondered the dilemmas before me.

Here I was with the berth I'd worked for ever since I'd studied at Bowdoin—with the recognition I'd coveted ever since I'd begun to wear long pants, and battle it out with my gifted brothers: the youngest man ever to sit on Melchett Bros.' board of directors, with enough responsibility and enough say in operations to keep me hopping till the turn of the century. At any other time in my life I would have gone out, and bought everybody a few rounds at Eli's; but now, drawn by the new vistas I'd glimpsed since I'd met Jim, and faced with the doubts which had assailed me ever since Jackson'd preached, the job seemed like an imprisoning burden.

Like a mariner who's gone for days without a sighting, or who's zigzagged so much to get a slant in a headwind that he's actually lost his bearing, I gazed out Jim's window for over an hour; then confessing myself beaten again for the evening, I hove to and tried to turn to new matters.

But as always when my hands were idle, my thoughts swung immediately round to Jim, and settled into a stifling worry: into the anxiety which had oppressed me in one degree or another ever since *Amanda*'d cleared for Havana. Here was the chief reason I lay becalmed, unable to shift from one tack to the other; for so numbed was I by my fear for his safety that decision-making was for the time hopeless. Aside from the witness of surviving ships to the season's twin perils of fever and weather, and my own all-too-vivid acquaintance with both, there was the awareness of my repeated dreams to warn me of the hazards which beset him; and whether the latter were accurate reflections of what was indeed happening to him, or simply indications of danger, I knew beyond a doubt that he was at risk.

My first dream—of Tom auctioning off his clothes, after he'd been lost off the jibboom—had been stark and unpalatable enough; but not even to Eben had I spoken of the one that'd come since, about the time *Amanda* was posted overdue: a brief, vivid flash of Jim's face deluged with water—too brief for me to see whether he was drowning, or simply overcome by a horrific downpour. The first time I'd dreamed it, I'd bolted awake with such a sickening dread that I'd at once jumped out of bed, run for the door to the upstairs porch— standing open in the uncommon hot spell—and lost my supper at the railing. Coming out still tying on her wrapper, Anne found me shivering on one of the deck chairs, set up to permit me a quick glance at the channel; and supposing at once I'd taken the ague, she'd gone back to mix up some powders. Since then the dream'd affected me a half dozen times; and so little did I now desire sleep that I was glad to work nights on Obed's cottage—or, if I did lie down, to have Anne beside me.

Sensing the state to which worry had worn me, and anxious herself on behalf of her own kin, she began to regard me with a cool kindness, the closest she ever came to affection; and thrown together by our mutual burden, we called a truce on our various warfronts. But welcome as our cease-fire was, I hungered for far more to sustain me; longed, as I hadn't longed for years, for the touch of a hand in the thick of my hair, or the bulk of a shoulder against my cheek. Casting my eyes around Jim's room, I suddenly fell on his white and blue jersey, draped where he'd tossed it on the arm of the sofa; and unthinkingly gathering it up in my hands, I buried my face in the scratchy wool. Drinking in the faint scents of the sea and his body—the vague tang of brine, hemp, soap and sweat—I felt inexplicably soothed and uplifted; and sustained even now by this bit of his presence, I summoned up the strength for the day's work, and leaving his room, locked the door behind me.

On the twenty-third of October—the day after my meeting with the board of directors, and the thirteenth day since *Amanda* and *Sabrina* had been due—I was called to Warren on business; and hating to go—longing to stay in town, in spite of the veritable pall which garbed it—I nearly bullied Jared into going in my stead. But somehow getting word of what was in the wind, McCabe talked me into riding with him, seeing the job through and coming home in the afternoon, after a bit of dinner at the Windward, a favorite stop of ours whenever we travelled inland. "Change o' scene'll do ye good; we'll take the stage if you're too tired t' drive," he wheedled; and against my better judgment I fell in with his plans, leaving word with Pa I'd be back by supper.

To my surprise the two-hour ride—past homesteads and hillsides familiar to me since childhood—did ease me, so much so I even dozed in spite of the stage jolts; and by the time we reached Warren and parted ways on the sidewalk, me for the counting house and McCabe for the town square, I actually was feeling somewhat rested. Squaring away at the meeting—me, Fales, Snow and Ingham—we made quick progress, setting up transactions for Jordan's Liverpool cargo; and I was just beginning to take a deep breath, now that I had a little distance between me and home, when Fales' brother burst excitedly into the office, picked me out in the midst of the group, and bawled: "Haven't ye heard the news? A rideh just galloped in from

South Thomaston—a ship's been sighted off Fisherman Island—an' word has it she's the *Amanda Howland*!"

Jumping up and leaving them—mouths agape—without a word, I barreled out onto the street, collared McCabe and tore across the way to the livery, where I threw down ten dollars—enough for a month—for two horses, tossed McCabe onto one and threw myself on the other, and dashed out of town in a cloud of street dust.

Knowing full well what'd happened, McCabe hung on for dear life, the two of us whooping like a couple of school boys; and back we galloped again to the harbor, fiften miles of relentless going. Topping the rise at Ship Street—wildly seeking out the signals—we found, not the Melchett house flag, but Worthing's; and there down at Brown's Wharf lay the *Sabrina Fenwick*. So completely cast down I couldn't go on, I instinctively drew rein and threw myself under a tree; and clambering down from his saddle, Eben sat down beside me, and put a kindly hand to my knee. For a long time we sat thus, gasping in silence, while our horses labored similarly beside us; then getting to his feet—looking out on the harbor, and listening to the jubilant ringing of church bells—Eben reached down and patted my shoulder.

"C'mon," he tugged, trying to cheer me; "you don't know but what they've news of *Amanda*—maybe sighted her or spoke some ship that has—they'd of sure been on the lookout for news all the way."

Not daring to hope after my supreme disappointment, I nonetheless got up and mounted again; and riding down Ship Street toward the pandemonium on the wharves—the entire town turned out to welcome its boys home, ringing bells, crying news, or simply dashing about wildly —we drew up at the Seven Seas Inn, and tossed our reigns over the posts there. On our way to Brown's Wharf, not far from the Inn, we were just turning down Water Street and passing the printer's—no one noticing us in the commotion of traffic— when McCabe at my side came to a halt; and clutching my arm, he broke into a murmur. "Well, look who's here," he half-drawled, half-marveled, like one torn between wonder and amusement; and giving a nod, he gestured across the cobbles.

My heart giving a jump at the strange note in his voice, I looked across the way to where he was pointing; and there, wearing a green monkey jacket that wasn't his, standing talking with Andrew DeMille as if he had all the time in the world, was none other than Robertson. Blowing in the breeze, his dark hair was disheveled, and he sported besides a rough three weeks' beard; but he gestured as jauntily to old man DeMille as though he'd been on the right ship and on time, and hadn't cost me half my natural life in worry. Too taken aback to move my feet—my heart stopped dead in my chest as well—I somehow managed to make use of my lungs; and letting out a roar they must've heard in Warren, I simply bawled out: "*Robehrtson!*"

Turning at once with a swift flash of joy—throwing us a dazzling smile—he hurriedly bade DeMille good day, giving a quick salute as he left; then dashing across the street toward us—narrowly missing a team and a cart—he sprang up the curb that edged the walk, and flung himself at me with a bound. Nearly crushing him in my clasp I simply held on to him like a bear; then breaking away he hurled himself at McCabe, who nearly smothered him as well.

"What has happened? Why're ye here? Where's Tom?" I cried, coming to my senses enough to perceive that something extraordinary had taken place.

"Tom's here—he's well," Jim answered at once, breaking loose from McCabe and recovering his breath, his cheeks above his beard flushed and his blue eyes dancing.

"What's happened? What're ye doin' on Wohthing's ship?" I kept at it, bellowing at him as if he was as deaf as Jorab.

"We foundered in a storm off Cuba—lost *Amanda* and all of the cargo. Worthing was right there on our stern—we'd rendezvoused not far from Matanzas, an' kept each other in view when the weather turned bad: he picked us up with a breeches buoy."

"Good Gawd! Poor Tom!" I gasped, too stunned to begin to take in the loss—neither cargo nor vessel insured—to Tom and the shipyard, or to contemplate the near miss in lives. "D'ye mean t' say nobody was hurt?" I exclaimed, scanning his limbs as my dream rushed back to me.

"Not a scratch. Tom got off her about five minutes b'fore she went down."

"Whehre's he now?" I kept on, overflooded with images of *Sabrina* with twice her capacity in men, beset with shortages of food and gear, and an almost inevitable confusion of discipline and order: all the hardships his terse words hid.

"Still down at the wharf with Worthing. As soon as we'd tied up he dismissed us, and sent us off to find our kin—whoever didn't show up at the dock. I'm supposed t' fetch Abigail an' whoever else is still at the house, an' drive them down to Brown's Wharf in the buggy."

It all at once dawning on me that he was actually here, talking to me with his collar blowing in the wind, I suddenly stopped and took in his face: saw that, beneath the brightness of homecoming, he looked worn, and more seasoned than he had, though perhaps it was the beard. Meeting my gaze with clear eyes and chin steady, he seemed to be taking stock of me in return; but McCabe recalled him with a tug at his arm, and his usual down-to-earth dry manner.

"We'd best get movin," he reminded, having collected his wits enough to take action.

"I know—I can't stop—I've been sidetracked half a dozen times already," Jim acknowledged, with a glance down Water Street where he was headed.

"Go right on—we've got t' see Tom. But meet us at Brown's Wharf afteh you drive up with the buggy," I urged him; and with a nod and a ringing "Aye!" he was off.

Approaching the wharves we ran into dense crowds; and elbowing our way in and out of the tumult we craned our necks for a sight of Tom: faces streaming past us with jubilant cries, exchanges of gladness or wonder or joy, the town too intent on the return of its loved ones to take thought of the loss of *Amanda,* or the burden many would have to reckon with tomorrow. As we drew near enough for a clear view of *Sabrina,* we both stopped short with an exclamation, her entire tophamper bearing signs of the battle—from the jury-rigged main topmast and the slung mizzen to the brine-soaked sails and double-rigged yards. The crew having been dismissed at once for homecoming, the loose ends of entering—the littered decks, the stray lines, the unshed parcels and battens still hung about her in disarray, intensifying her battered look. But she was home and more or less in one piece, the center now of a regular storm of townsfolk all jostling and sloshing and breaking against her, running up and down her gangplank or scrambling inboard over her bulwarks like so many seas in a gale on dry land.

In the midst of it all I spied Keziah, though it was hard to be sure that this waif was my sister: for there she was astride Joseph's shoulders, in a pair of breeches lashed in at the waist and a checkered shirt hitched up at the elbows, sunburnt as a shellback and just as undaunted. Clambering down from her perch she hurled herself in my arms, with a carefree laugh that would have done Charis proud; and like revelers at a party accosting latecomers, a host of McCabes, Coombs, Talbots and Melchetts surged in on us and crowded round as well, while jugs of ale passed hand to hand.

Coming at last on Worthing and Tom—both of them looking tense and exhausted, yet beneath the strain, grimly joyous—I hailed first one and then the other: Tom seeming as if he scarcely knew what was happening. Realizing of a sudden what a debt I owed Bill, I threw my arms about him as I had my brother; and surprised but pleased—clamping his old paw on my shoulder—he managed to say above the noise: "Ben, I only thanks Gawd I was there t' pick them up; no boat could of been lowehed in them seas."

In the chaos I contrived to get Tom aside on the fringes of the mob where I could hear him; and though he'd probably spun his story half a dozen times already, he ran it through for McCabe and me from the beginning, too overcome to have any emotion left save a kind of incredulous humor.

"Didje eveh hear of such a jinxed trek?" he shook his head at me with a lame grin. "When them four was in the calaboose in Havana, I thought sure thing's hit bottom, and we'd see the bright side on the run home. But no: first we had t' get them lubbehs out o' the slammeh, which took a deal more time and effort—not t' mention cash flow—than I'd expected. Then Tuppeh goes an' falls down the poop companionway, an' gets picked up at the bottom with a busted leg. How's that for a pickle? Three masts a hundred and more feet high, about a thousand hazards facin' him ev'ry day, an' he falls down a bloody laddeh! It bein' a compound fracture, too much for me, we had t' hustle about town t' find a doctoh; and when at last we finds one who both speaks English *and* appears t' know what he's doin'—there bein' plenty of one or the otheh, but damned few of both—we've lost anotheh day; an' then the watch still has t' pick us a fresh second mate."

"Who'd they choose?" I broke in, catching a look in his eye vaguely akin to a glint or a twinkle.

"Can't you guess?" Tom grinned at me, his eyes breaking now into a full sparkle. "Robehrston, of course!"

There being a sawed-off piling behind me, I groped for it and promptly sat down, for once in my life too taken aback to bark an order or question; but Eben, who'd been listening spellbound, lighted his pipe with a gratified chuckle.

"Since neitheh Sal nor Reuben was in his watch, I figured I'd go along with the vote—though it would've sat a little betteh with me if I hadn't just had t' spring 'im from prison... When they elected him he was the only one that was surprised, I reckon. Anyhow, we move Robehrtson int' Tuppeh's berth, brush off our hands, haul up the hook an' clear the harboh, thinkin' *now* we c'n head home an' lick Wohthing's ass; but we hadn't been underway a couple days when the weatheh settled in downright ugly, an' it was plain our troubles was just beginnin'.

"Wishin' t' sight a vessel bearin' south, so's we could find out what we was headin' into, what should we raise instead but a ship goin' our way, just comin' up out o' the old Bahama channel; an' damned if it doesn't prove t' be Wohrthing! We might've had us a grand race home; but drawin' near enough t' speak each otheh, we exchange a few thoughts on the weatheh, an' agree t' play it cautious an' stick t'getheh. B'fore the day's out we're glad we did, for by nightfall we're in the teeth of a monsteh storm, with a wind that splits the foremast like a toothpick. I b'lieve the old girl could've weathered that—*know* I could've seen her through any damage topsides; but around daybreak she gives a mighty lurch, toppin' some goliath with a roll t' leeward, an' settles hahd on her lahrboard beam. Knowin' the muscavado's shifted, I climb down int' the hold t' find not only the barrels out o' trim, but a series of leaks where the seams've stahted; an' seein' at once there's no hope t' retrim her, I dash up an' direct Galt t' marshal his watch for patchin', while I do what I can topsides t' relieve her.

"With her yahdarms in the sea an' her lines a shambles, there's clearly only one course t' follow; so callin' Robertson t' break out the axes, I range his watch along the foc's'le, with blades t' clear an' let go the riggin', while I take on the task of the foremast. I've always said if the cahrgo shifted I'd take out the masts m'self ratheh than lose her; so I chopped through first one an' then the otheh—leavin' only enough of each t' run up a signal, an' a bolt of canvas t' stay her—while the men followed through with the stays an' runnin' riggin'. As soon as she gets clear of that burden, she rights herself a few degrees, an' rolls with the seas a shade easieh; an' settin' Robehrtson's watch the job of juryriggin' staysails, I take Galt's b'low t' see t' the cahgo, an' t' locatin' an' patchin' the seams that've stahrted.

"Scared t' death with every roll them barrels'll shift again, an' crush one or more of the men workin' on 'em; equally scared we'll run up on the shoals, the Grand Bahamer Banks bein' not far t' windward, I hahdly breathe the whole time we're down there; but at the end of that time we still ain't righted the cahgo, an' we're still takin' on quantities of wateh, despite what seems like miles o' patchin', an' the men on deck pumpin' nonstop. Climbin' topsides around suppeh I see Jim's rigged two staysails—how he done it in all the blowin' an' lurchin', with half what he needed ovehboard or floatin', I still ain't managed t' get him t' tell me; but in spite of his capital work, an' in spite of the efforts we've made b'low, it's pretty much plain we're losin' the battle.

"Plain t' Robehrtson at any rate; Galt 'n me, concentratin' on the fight b'low, hadn't come round t' givin' up yet. Makin' his way oveh t' me when I show up around suppeh, an' cuppin' his hands t' yell in my ear, Jim insists on organizin' some plan for rescue—since it's clear what boats we've still got can't survive in them seas, even if they c'n be lowered without fillin' directly. With Wohthing still hahd on our larboard bow—stickin' close as he dares despite his own damage—

it's obvious the only thing that'll work is a ship t' ship operation; an' pressin' me for leave t' put togetheh a sort of breeches buoy, an' to signal Wohthing somehow our intention, he urges we get off Keziah an' the youngeh hands by nightfall. Convinced we cn'n weatheh the night I just the same have t' confess the sense of his plan; so giving him leave t' set up what he can, I go b'low t' inform Galt, an' help him set up an agenda for nightfall.

"Comin' back on deck an hour lateh, afteh linin' up the next stage of the cahgo, I find Jim's put t'gether a kind of canvas breeches, with a double cable an' set of tackle, while Wohthing's moved in t' a couple hundred yahds, an' hurled oveh a hawser with a weight 'n buoy; an' it driftin' toward our larboard bow with the seas, Jim at last hauls it in with a grapplin' hook. Attachin' his cable 'n tackle t' the stub of the mainmast, he makes both ends fast t' Wohthing's hawser, an' signals him t' haul it back; an' Bill, barely able t' make us out, but more or less feelin' by tuggin' that the hawser's ready, hauls it an' Jim's cable oveh the wateh. Attachin' his ends in turn t' his mainmast— leavin' plenty o' slack t' allow for our rollin'—Bill spins out the line t' let us know he's ready; an' settin' up the breeches buoy, Jim first helps Abby in it, thinkin' t' send Keziah an' little Martin next, when he's certain that it works.

"Since we c'n scarcely make each otheh out, can't send up a flare in the drenchin' downpour or make ourselves heard oveh the wind's roarin', we all have t' more or less feel our way, with the hope the otheh ship understands our manuevehs; an' ye c'n mahk my words that we're here now t' tell the story b'cause Jim an' Bill managed t' talk through that rope. Timin' every dispatch with the waves, Jim'd send a hand on his way, haulin' on one rope while Bill hauled on the otheh; then Bill'd send the empty breeches back, with a note wrapped in canvas t' say so-and-so'd made it, an' sometimes a word or two regardin' position an' timin'. Getting Abby oveh, we next try Keziah, dressed in dungarees an' foul weatheh gear; an' with her we send off some of the ship's papehs, wrapped in canvas inside her oilslicks.

"An' that's just the staht of a struggle that goes on till it's too dahk t' see. Afteh Keziah goes little Martin, then six or seven of the othehs—Jim sendin' off first the youngest, then whoeveh's married an' has children, while I switch the remainin' hands around t' make sure there's enough t' do the job both topsides an' b'low. I don't know how many times one of the cables pahted, snapped in half when one of the ships rolled away from the otheh; thank Gawd neveh when anyone was oveh the wateh.

"By daybreak the wind is shriekin' from the opposite quarteh, blowin' us both steadily toward the banks, while *Amanda* is ridin' loweh 'n loweh; an' now it's imperative that we get the rest of the men off—one hand afteh another makin' it safely t' Bill's. Well, it comes down at last t' us officers, me an' Galt an' Jim; an' there's Jim insistin' it's time for us t' go. He'd been gettin' more an' more impatient, as if there was some clock in him that spelled out t' him just how long we had; while me—I can't begin t' describe how I felt: like there was simply no force on earth that could get me off of that ship. I'd always thought it was somehow heroic, the way skippehs stuck t' the end with their crafts; but now I seen t'was nothin' heroic about it, just the plain muleheaded loyalty of a man doin' his job.

"So when Jim tries t' get Galt off, as the mate, an' Galt balks—when he stubbornly comes afteh *me*, I tell him I'm not leavin' on a bet. At that he gets simply furious with me—you'd of thought *he* was the skippeh! 'Damn this old tub!' he yells at me—'Let it go! It's nothin' but a chunk o' wood! But your life is somethin'—remembeh your family that loves you—Sarah an' Ben' an' Rachel!' That's what he did t' me—named all your names, an' made me see your faces. Till then I'd neveh given any o' you a thought; an' feelin' you all come alive in my mind, tuggin' me one way, *Amanda* the otheh—well, it was the longest five minutes I eveh spent, tryin' t' make up my mind what t' do. I felt if there was even a chance for *Amanda*—perhaps run up on the banks where I could still bring off the cahgo—I'd've failed in my duty not t've stuck by her. In the end Jim convinced me an' we got off in ordeh—him first, then Galt, then me with the log; but he wouldn't go himself till I'd sworn I'd come afteh; an' even as he was gettin' int' the breeches, he was hissin' at me that he hoped I'd burn in hell, if I didn't get off like I promised.

"Well, there we all are, safe an' sound on Bill's deck, woefully lookin' at what's left of *Amanda*, when Jim b'side me cries out 'Oh my

God, we've left Jack!' In a flash I remembeh all about poor Tuppeh, lyin' in the foc's'le with his leg in a splint—I hadn't given him a thought since the storm broke upon us. With all the urgent needs in the hold, an' Jim's incredible scheme above—with all hands at work day an' night on some task, ridin' the breeches an' shiftin' watches—I'd just plain clean forgot all about him! B'fore I c'n plan with Bill what t' do, *Sabrina* takes a long roll down a sea, whilst *Amanda,* settlin' by the stern, moves very little—the two ships convergin' so close t'getheh that Bill yells t' the helm, afraid of a collision; an' as the helm goes hahd up Jim leaps t' the bulwarks, makes a grab for a length of the cable, an'—b'fore I c'n get t' him t' stop him—swings himself back onto *Amanda.* Cryin' out b'hind me 'He can't move 'im alone!' somebody else jumps right on his tail; an' I'll be damned if it isn't Howland!

"Runnin' uphill t'ward the foc's'le, they're out o' view b'fore any of the rest've us knows what's happened; then comin' to with a jolt we shake a leg in a hurry, riggin' up a sling for Jack an' tightenin' up the cables 'n tackle, while Bill's men're workin' like blazes t' keep *Sabrina* clear of *Amanda.* Comin' up at last with Jack, Jim'n Sal carry him t' the rail, hangin' on t' what they can as they go, then hoist him t' the sling an' strap him in; an' haulin' on our line while they pull on theirs, we manage t' ship him to us. Getting our hands on him we lift him out, three or four of his watch at once seein' him b'low; while meantime on *Amanda* Howland an' Jim look like they're shoutin' it out at each otheh—if ye c'n b'lieve it, each of 'em insistin' the otheh go first! There's Howland pushin' Jim t'ward the sling, an' there's Jim shovin' it at Howland—both of 'em lookin so much alike in their oilslicks that we c'n scarcely tell 'em apaht. B'fore we c'n make out which one t' expect, another deluge is breakin' upon us, so hahd an' heavy it feels like hail, an' so thick we can't see our hands b'fore us; so we don't know till we feel a yank on the rope that someone's comin'—an' can't see till he's in our arms that it's Sal.

"We no sooneh than get the sling back t' Jim than a tremendous sea bears down on us both—*Sabrina* liftin' to it, but *Amanda* not; an' when it passes, we c'n see she's goin' fast, sinkin' stern first with her bow free of the wateh. But that's not the worst of it, for as we'd pitched an' rolled, the cables'd pahted again from the strain; an' she's just far enough away t' make sendin' anotheh impossible, even if there happens t' be time. Hollerin' t' the helm t' bear down on *Amanda*, Bill grabs anotheh cable while I snatch a weight; an' Jim, seein' his chance, scrambles out onto the jibboom—I've thought of that dream o' yours so often, an' Galt, it's got him converted t' voodoo—an' there he waits while the two ships swing t'getheh.

"Goin' down so fast now we c'n see her settle, *Amanda*'s takin' a washin' with every sea that rolls oveh, the jibboom bein' about the only point that clears 'em. Realizin' we've got not above a few minutes, Bill gives our line the best toss he c'n musteh, oveh the jib an' int' the wateh; an' makin' that end fast t' his waist, while we range ours around the mast, Jim waits for the best chance t' jump. Scared t' death *Amanda*'ll settle b'fore we c'n get him off, losin' him an' endangerin' *Sabrina* in the funnel, Bill keeps shoutin' the helm in closeh, while I wait in the waist with the life-ring an' a hook, an' every otheh man on deck works a sheet or a line; then seein' a great wave Jim takes a leap, misses *Sabrina* but rolls inboard with the sea, an' washes up at our feet like a fish...an' not five minutes afteh, *Amanda* goes undeh. I don't wondeh you look dazed," he finished, giving me a measured look; "it was a near thing."

As he'd spoken I'd felt such a tightening in my middle that I couldn't have said a word if I'd wanted; but now I managed to get out hoarsely, "Go on."

"Well, there was Wohthing with twice his capacity in hands— not enough stores or gear t' go round, an' not enough anything in the long run t' see us through the weatheh we still faced. Off Hatteras we hit anotheh gale, an' sprung the mizzen—we've slung it now; an' off Jersey there was anotheh storm waitin'. In the midst of it all there was Keziah, decked out in Abby's breeches 'n shirt, helpin' Bill by takin' oveh the navigation: gettin' sights wheneveh she could, an' dead reckonin' with a flair that would've put Pa t' shame. Poppin' up from her calculations she'd bawl, 'Boys, can't ye keep this tub on course? We'll be raisin' the Canaries at this rate!'"

Overcome already, I felt my eyes fill: it was so like what Charis would have said.

"Anyhow, that's it: ev'ry ship we spoke looked about as bad as us—we're home at last, an' I'm mighty glad, though I ain't a pahtic'ly happy man."

"Damn you, don't be an ass!"—this from Pa, who'd'd turned around: I don't doubt he'd listened to the whole story right through again. Putting his hand briefly on the back of Tom's neck—the only gesture of affection he had—he fished in his waistcoat for a fresh cigar, while Tom looked at him with a shaky smile. "By Jupiteh!" Pa went on as he struck a match, "I've got t' meet this son of a bitch Robehrtson! Where the hell is he anyhow? It seems I've got two sons t' thank 'im for!"

It wasn't long before he got his wish; for I was still sitting hunched on the piling, and Eben's hand had scarcely left my shoulder—where it had been resting since Tom's tale of the jibboom—when a buggy dashed up at the Water Street kerbing, and Jim jumped down to give a hand to its inmates. In the jubilant reunion that followed Tom endured another onslaught of questions, looking like he could sleep on his feet; and keeping my seat I watched Jim in the flurry, with a new and voiceless respect at his presence. Breaking in at last on the celebration, Mother and Rachel steered Tom to the buggy, Jared hopping up to drive them home; and even as they went, the crowds on the pier dwindled. But now there came another meeting, and one that I'd been looking forward to; for Pa ducked away from the crowd still clustered round Worthing and set a course for Jim.

"Damme, so you'hre Robehrtson!" he bellowed at Jim as he came up within hearing. "Jest step oveh here an' let me take a good look at ye!"

Throwing an unrestrained grin at me, Robertson did as he was told; and they stood facing one another in a patch of open sunlight: Pa short and burly, with his hands cocked on his hips—that ridiculous relic of a pea coat, and that cap!—and Robertson tall and graceful, his monkey jacket open and blowing, and the sun on his dark and wind-tossed hair.

"Aye, you'hre jest as Tom said," Pa concluded after a moment. "A hahd workeh, an' ye've got the devil in youhr eye. Oh, I knows a tempeh when I sees one!....Young bastihd, ain't ye!"

"I'm nineteen," Robertson spoke up defensively.

"Eighteen, Robehrtson, eighteen!" I called out to him, laughing; and I laughed all the harder when I saw that he flushed.

"Ah! A bit of a liah t' boot!" Pa barked, shaking his head. "Well, if I undehstands things aright, I've got two sons t' thank ye for—this farmeh hehre"—he threw a nod at me—"an' the one that's jest left. Neitheh of 'em's wohth their keep; but jest the same, they've a soft place in m' heahrt. Thank ye." Having had his say, Pa put his cigar back in his mouth and began to chew as much as smoke it, in that emphatic way of his; while looking somewhat overwhelmed—with amusement, solemnity, and a kind of awe—Robertson stood before him speechless.

Knowing that this was just the prelude to Pa's inevitable working over—knowing that after a moment, and with no transition whatever, he'd commence his interrogation, drilling Jim on every craft he'd ever sailed, or demanding to know his opinion on such innovations as double topsails, and all the other controversies dear to his heart—I interrupted long enough to call out,

"Robehrtson, meet us at Eli's when Pa's done with you—I'll treat ye t' a first rate dinneh!"

"Aye! I'll be there shortly!" he promised with a ring to his voice; and as Eben and I disappeared in the crowd I could see Pa open his volley, Robertson meeting it with obedient attention, and a play of laughter about his lips.

A babble of voices met us at Eli's—a regular tumult of excitement, as if every doryman, shellback and skipper, windjammer and pilot gathered within were fired by the same flame that raced in me; and picking a table by some smoky window, we sat facing the door and ordered a drink. Too overcome to exchange thoughts with Eben, I simply wanted to sit with an eye to the door; and divining my mood Eben said little, chuckling to himself now and then as if he recalled one of the high points of Tom's story—Reuben and Sal emerging dog-eared from prison, or Robertson stomping his foot at his skipper.

Unexpectedly breaking in on my thoughts, Eli whisked a tray

before us, with a clatter of decanters and glasses; and McCabe and I were clinking rims in silence and essaying a test of the strength of the brew when the oak door popped open, and Robertson stepped in. Shutting the door he gazed around, casting about for some sight of us; but he was stopped in his tracks by a crowd of seamen milling around the tavern entrance—the whole lot of them clapping him on the shoulder and assaulting him with a barrage of questions. A cheer went up from the table nearby us where many had heard all or part of Tom's story; and waving them quiet with an embarrassed greeting he broke away from the cluster around him, sighted us and headed at once for our corner.

"This has been the making of Jim," Eben said quietly as he approached our table, for we both saw a steadiness to his gait, an air of command about his expression that hadn't been there when we'd last seen him, before the demands of *Amanda*'s last voyage; and we couldn't fail to perceive the new maturity in him.

So overcome were we by our respect for his conduct—both as mate and as engineer of the rescue—that when he reached us we spontaneously got to our feet; and looking at us with an abashed silence he shook our hands while his flush deepened. "Have a seat, mate," Eben said with a grin, kicking out a chair for him; and he accepted it with a shaky laugh, hanging his jacket on a nearby peg. As he sat down I saw he was wearing a red jersey and a pair of duck trowsers that hadn't been his before; and reminded afresh of how close had been the margin by which he'd managed to get off with his life, I reached across the table and gripped his elbow—Jim responding at once by catching at mine. It was the only instant I was to have with him for the time being; for already the others were drawing up chairs or pushing and shoving their tables closer: not just old cronies like Spooner and Wingate, but acquaintances from as far away as Warren, and idlers from schooners out of Kennebunkport and Falmouth.

"Hungry?" I managed to ask him simply, thinking what three weeks on short rations had probably done to his appetite.

"I could eat the wharf," he confessed with a game smile, and an appreciative sniff of the aromas around him.

"I'll that care o' *that*—say, Eli! Get youhr tail out o' the galley a minute!"

Coming out still wiping his hands on his apron—catching sight of Robertson by us at the table—Eli made a beeline across the room, clapping his arms about Jim as he rose to meet him, and embracing him with all the hearty fervor of one grateful for the life of his brother. "Glad t' see ye was smaht enough t' know who t' send off first off *Amanda*," the old barnacle cried, giving Jim an affectionate cuff with his big paw.

"Knew if I didn't I'd never get any more free mugs out o' *you*, Eli," Robertson answered, shooting him a sly grin as he reclaimed his chair.

"Bring this man a tray o' steamehs—an' a steak or two t' go along," I cut in, getting down to business. "We won't pull up ouhr noses at anotheh round o' scotch neitheh. The whole thing's on me," I added quickly.

"It ain't neitheh—it's on the house," Eli insisted with a pat on Jim's shoulder; and even as he left others were calling out, "Next one's on *me* though, Eli"—enough rounds set up in the space of a minute to set the town on its ear for a week.

On half rations since Havana—on a dry ship, without a drink since he'd last seen Cape Damaris —Robertson wasted no time at the table, his first glass going straight off to his head; and though it was plain to me he was tired—though I dared to suspect that he, like me, longed for a few moments alone together—he fell in at once with the spirit of the party, doing his best to please the crowd about him, and doggedly answering all questions save those pertaining to his part in the rescue, which he waved quiet, or *Amanda*'s sinking, of which he'd say nothing.

Rising to the bait of the others—baiting them himself in return—he gave the place a whale of a time for an hour; then clearly beginning to list to starboard, he began to make free use of my shoulder, leaning against me with his knees drawn up at the table, as he listened to tales of shipwrecks told by others. But at last even his attentiveness gave way to stupor, and the fatigue of the past month's trials; and as the crowds at Eli's gradually thinned out, or lapsed into a sodden nimbus, he sprawled unabashedly against the arm I'd draped round him, with both of his boots up on Eli's table.

"Feelin' betteh?" I asked him dryly, in the comparative aloneness we now had in our corner.

"Aye," he managed to mumble, too far gone to muster much for an answer.

"Is that cavern in youhr belly filled up?"

"Aye."

"We didn't leave no chinks unfilled?"

"I can't feel them if you did."

From across the table, Eben was laughing.

"If Eben fetches round a horse an' buggy, d'ye think ye c'n make it back t' the Inn?"

"If y' c'n get me t' the door."

"I'll hoist ye with a grapplin' hook if I have to... I'll wageh you'd like t' have a sleep."

"Aye...a couple days'd be about right."

"Then that's what you'hre goin' t' do."

"You ain't plannin' t' ship out t'morrow?"

"I wouldn't think of shippin' out without one o' the mates."

Getting him into his jacket—no easy task in my own state—I saw him to the door still chuckling under my breath, my arm clamped tightly about his shoulders; and coming round with Eli's buggy Eben jumped down, and held open the well-worn door. Swaying into motion we cantered off down the street, the cobbles ringing beneath old Sabra's hooves; and stirring by me—all at once leaning toward me, like one no longer able to stave off his need—Jim stretched himself to rest on the seat, and nestled his head on the bench of my knees. Too tight for words, my throat swelled as I reached back, and fetched the lap robe to tuck about him; and giving a quiet sigh of contentment, he murmured, "Got somethin' for you in m' pocket," and was out.

Pierced with regret when the buggy turned, and told me with the sandy hush of its wheels that we were heading into the courtyard, I eased him up on the seat and, with Eben's help, saw him up to the stairs to his room at the Inn. Quickly lighting a lamp, Eben went straight to the hearth, and built up a fire to take off the chill; while I settled Jim on the opened bed, pulling off his jacket and stripping off his boots, and covering him up with a nest of quilts.

Seeing to our own ride, Eben went back downstairs, there to hustle the boots to re-saddle our horses; and loath to leave, I took my time with Jim's jacket, wondering whose it had been as I smoothed it—when all at once I remembered what he'd said in the buggy, about having something for me in his pocket. Eagerly reaching in one, I found a fid of twine, but in the other, two small boxes: one that I'd made in grammar school with a ship in full sail etched on its cover, and the Havana shell I'd given him inside it; and the other similar in shape, flatter and a little larger, obviously recently made by him.

Putting mine back in his pocket—keenly touched that he'd saved it, perhaps even daily carried it with him—I sat down with his in the chair by the bed, and looked at it closely in the lamplight: the lid carved with the central scene of his childhood, a tent pitched before a stand of pines, the moon and stars above and to one side, a campfire. Opening it, I found a shell—one he must have found liberty day in Havana, alone at Calzada de San Lazara: a sunrise tellin, as big as my palm, the most exquisite I'd ever seen. So aglow was it with the subtle gradations of saffron and pearl, oyster and salmon that it seemed like the sun cast its rays in my hand, or pulsed behind my flesh like a lantern. Battling to quell my reaction, I put shell and box deep in my own pocket, and slowly rose to my feet again—bent over Jim asleep on the bed, and looked down upon his face in the lamplight.

Suddenly I wanted nothing more than to see this man every year for the rest of his life, as time passed over him; age seemed like a friendly thing; I wanted to see the changes in his face, his shape, his mind, as simply and plainly as I longed to see the shifting shore, the aging trees, the ceaseless changing pattern on the surface of the sea. For a long time I stood looking down at him, imagining him in the ripening guises of time; then bending over, I blew out the lamp, and gently spoke in the unhearing dark. "You an' me, we got unfinished business," I murmured through the thickness in my throat; then buttoning my coat, I slipped out of the room, and noiselessly closed the door behind me.

It was late the next day before I could see him; for aside from the fact that he needed rest, I had my hands full at the yard: the whole of Melchett Bros. congregating and dividing up to tackle tasks. Moving *Sabrina* before Worthing could get wind of the shift, Joseph and Pa and a dozen others initiated a host of repairs; while the rest of us went to work in the counting house, coming up with ways to underwrite Tom.

Having already diverted the bulk of my savings to the building of the new ship, including every dollar I'd cleared on *Charis*, I was hard put to scare up cash; but with Jim home everything suddenly seemed possible, and I spent the morning cashing in everything that wasn't nailed down. Putting the whole thing together I drew up a check, and promptly transferred it to Tom's account; while everyone else did pretty much the same, us brothers meeting the loss of *Amanda*— at $40,000 one of the costliest vessels we'd built, more than half of her owned outright by Tom—and our uncles and cousins assuming responsibility for the cargo. That well underway I hightailed it to the Inn, thinking to catch an afternoon dinner, and look in on Robertson at the same time; and springing up the stairs I softly opened the door, and quietly slipped it shut behind me.

A glance at the bed told me Jim was still sleeping, though he stirred slightly as I came in: one jersey-clad shoulder free of the covers, and his dark hair—long again, after three months of growing—tousled about his forehead. Kneeling on the hearth, I set a fresh log on the fire, gently knocking a little life from the embers built earlier by McCabe; then looking up I found his eyes had opened, and he was smiling over at me. Gazing at me for a moment, he closed his eyes again, just as I sat down in the chair by the bed; and thinking he'd dozed, I took out my pipe, and was digging in my pouch for a fill, when he murmured drowsily at my side, "Still here?"

"You bet I am," I responded, taking a draw or two on my pipe. "How d'ye feel, mate?"

Slowly sitting up in the bed—propping both of the pillows behind him, and brushing the hair back from his face—he gave me a game, contented smile. "Better than when I first woke up," he confessed, a rueful glint or two to his eye. "Eben told me I had t' spend the day in bed...I didn't put up much of a fight."

"First sensible thing I eveh heard y' say... Jimmy's got some chowdeh settin' on the stove for you: feel well enough t' tuck it away?"

Willing to give food a try, he nodded; and going to the door I hollered the news down to Micah, Jimmy's errand boy at the Inn, then sat back down in the chair by the bed.

"You been at the yard?" he smiled again, his eyes on me.

"All mohrnin'. While you been up hehre sawin' logs, we've moved *Sabrina,* got some new sticks in her, an' cleared the countin' house books of *Amanda.*"

His lips twitching at my exaggeration, he asked, "Is all this enough t' convince your Pa t' finally take out some insurance?"

"An' give oweh good money t' line the pockets of them vulturous bastihds in Boston? Good Gawd, no! Thought you might've heard Pa's views on that subject yestehday."

His bit of a twitch broadened into a grin. "We covered quite a lot of ground, but I didn't dare ask him that one, and he didn't bring it up himself."

"Well, you'll get the chance t' hear more t'morrow; it's the first time in quite a spell that all six of us brotehs 've been t'getheh in pohrt with Pa, so Ma's puttin' on a whale of a dinneh—an' word has it you'hre invited."

He closed his eyes, though he was still grinning. "In that case I know I'm goin' t' take Eben's advice, an' rest up in bed till t'morrow."

Coming in with a tray Jimmy himself caught his words, and set the food before him with a chuckle; and gratefully digging into his chowder, Jim gradually began to look more chipper, asking me questions about the new ship, and begging for news about the children.

"Every one of 'em's ready t' eat you alive, they're so damned keen t' see you," I told him. " If ye want, you c'n come home with me afteh Sunday dinner, an' have a look at 'em youhrself."

Gratified, he gave me an eager nod, his eyes—as always when he heard about the young ones—shining; then pausing in the midst of his meal, he hesitated a moment, silent. Looking at me thoughtfully, he seemed to weigh his words, as if uncertain how to proceed; then "About your uncle Matthias," he ventured, suddenly making up his mind, "... I'm sorry."

Giving him a quick look, I searched his face, at once getting the idea that Eben had told him everything about what'd happened while he was at sea; and immediately I felt my heart lighten, for I couldn't have found the words to relate any of it, or trusted my voice to speak them if found. His eyes on mine, he seemed to know not only the afflictions of the past month, but my relief at not having to convey them—his gaze imparting his commiseration; and unable to meet it, I cast my eyes down, infused with the warmth of his understanding. "Will the new job be much of a burden?" he asked simply, as if we hadn't just, with a glance, transmitted more than a month's worth of tidings.

"I won't know till we get back in May," I told him, endeavoring to keep my answer steady. "I ain't neveh tried t' build more than one ship at a time, or t' keep tabs on half what Matthias kept track of. But at least it'll get me out o' the office."

His lips quivered wryly, but he said no more about it, asking instead after goings-on at the Inn, or apologizing for the loss of my trunk, which I'd given him so that he could keep his Rom chest ashore. "There was no time t' save anything but the ship's papers, or small things the hands could take off with 'em," he explained, letting me take his tray to the door.

"Good thing ye took it; it hadn't near the value of youhrs....You must be fresh out o' clothes, mate."

"Aye. I have these, an' my sou'wester an' oilslicks—the green jacket is Bill's, though he said I could have it."

"Keep it—ye'll need it. Winteh'll soon be upon us; ye can't go runnin' around hehre, or campin' with us, in a jersey shirt 'n linens."

His face blazened up at the mere mention of hunting. "You mean we're still going?" he eagerly asked me.

"Of course we'hre still goin'! Think we'd let a little thing like *Amanda* stop us? If I work like hell the next few days, I c'n see the brig through the riggers; an' we c'n staht Friday if you'hre ready. I already told Seth I was takin' Tom whetheh anybody liked it or not; an' he couldn't say much, since I've got as much clout now as he does."

"How far 're we goin'?"

"Not as far as I'd like, you c'n bank on that! There's no time now t' run you up the Penobscot; but we c'n use the cabin as a base, pack a tent 'n hike out from there, huntin' grouse an' maybe gettin' in some fishin'."

Sitting straight up in bed—rubbing his hands together in his excitement—he fired off questions about the tent, whose it was and how it'd been made, what we'd pack and how it'd be carried; and my spirits soaring at his anticipation, I felt a yen for the land I'd never known before, a yen no mariner in his right mind should harbor.

"I don't know," I said in answer to his look—for he'd read my expression with his usual skill. "I seem t' have a touch of land feveh... always do at this time o' yeahr. You ain't seen how beautiful it is hehre yet—you was dead drunk yestehday"—here he stifled a grin, without comment—"but the fact is it's an unusual late autumn, prettieh than it's been in a decade, an' I'm restless enough t' walk t' K'tahdin. So brush up youhr boots while ye've got the chance, mate: the Rom ain't the only ones that c'n make tracks in a wildwood!"

We set out at last near the end of October, on a mild, sunny morn of radiant oranges and yellows: me, Tom and Eben walking in step, carrying rifles and toting knapsacks; Jim cavorting and dashing between us, running ahead or falling behind; and the dogs leaping along through the bracken, their backs arching in and out of the grasses, like porpoises before the bow. Cutting across fields starred with fern and sumac, we jumped the crumbling walls of stone fences, their contours of rock round and full in the sun, and headed for the eaves of the woods: their boughs studded with the spare, brilliant golds of birch, or the lingering fullness of oaken auburns. Following no roads we kept to the woodlands, stopping now and then to adjust our heavy packs, or to pause spontaneously at some crimson treetop—at some sudden splendor of russet and blue sky, or of rainbow-hued hillsides in the distance.

Taking us through mixed fir and hardwoods—luring us through groves strangely quiet and insulated, the sea only a faraway droning sound, except for the distant toll of a buoy—our way suddenly led us more or less into the open, into a dell studded with young pine and sandy byways, and surrounded on all sides by the sloping eaves of the forest. Here there were evergreens, some a man's height, some taller, clustered in groups or scattered and lonely, our meandering course taking us between their full branches; and as we wandered across this secluded valley I was all at once swept by memories older than childhood—by recollections of roaming these paths long ago, long before I could have known them in boyhood—as if my formless, unbodied spirit had once wended its way along their courses, like a breath of wind at the skirts of the saplings, or nosed about the twigs and branches.

Hushed by the force of the recollection—strangely heightened by the rush of my recognition, as a child is when he stumbles upon an old haunt, or a cupboard he favored in his early days as a toddler—I gazed about me half in awe, half in fear; and sensing my mood Jim fell in beside me, looking to and fro as if he too remembered—as if he too meandered old trails in his memory, or traced again paths of ancient migrations.

Resting briefly about mid-morning, we perched ourselves on an old board fence, long abandoned, which had once marked the bounds of some forgotten homestead; and eating the apples Eben had scooped up at the last minute, we munched companionably in silence, while the dogs bounded back and forth at our feet. As I ate I looked down at the weathered grain of the old boards—at the whorls and patterns of dun, grey and umber, or the sharp, chipping bits of crack lines and splinters; then coming upon the strong lines of Jim's hand, I followed them to the red flannel of his sleeve, the grey nap of his waistcoat and the dark blue of his pantlegs. As I gazed the wind crept up around us, now whispering like a breath on our faces, now strengthening and stirring Jim's hair, or rustling briefly in the branches; then came a full gust, and our collars were rippling, and the shadows were flickering on Jim's hands and face.

How clear the shapes about me all looked! Had I really seen all this day after day, rambling about these woods as a boy, or climbing the Ship Street hill to the district school—the definition of the logs in the weeds, the riot of jonquil against the blue sky? I must have; must have seen it without words— with a different recognition; with nothing standing between my raw eyes and the rarity of what I perceived. How had I lost it, this force of perception; why did it only come to me now betimes? Had the others lost it as well, somewhere between manhood and youth—between crawling out into the garden unwatched, and shipping a handspike or hauling a line? Looking at Jim—at his bright, rapt face, alert as the ears of the dogs on the prowl—I suspected that the world was like this for him always; and I marveled again at the clarity and power that visited me in the zest of his presence.

Reaching the cabin, we set aside some of our stores, and picked up others needed for the evening—aiming to head inland a few more miles before nightfall, and stopping only long enough for a midday meal by the lakeside. Helping me with the fire, Jim brewed up some tea, while Tom cleaned the brace of grouse he'd flushed, and Eben cast a line into the water. As we worked the southwest breeze stirred the waters, rippling them all the way to the reed-filled marsh at the far end; while about us the riverside was alive with movements. Overhead the skies were in motion as well; for as we cooked we heard a distant honking, a discordant chorus of squawks that slowly grew louder, till the expanse over the lake was dotted with patterns: the haunting flight-forms of geese on their way south. Silent in this cathedral of sound and color, Jim and I filled our kids with hard tack and fried pork, exchanging glances as we set out shares for the others: a rush of thankful awe in my heart that in some mysterious way, my presence enriched the lakeshore for him just as his enhanced it for me.

In a moss-grown clearing amongst tall red pines—just above the banks of a stream, winding now toward its source in the uplands— we made our late afternoon camp and pitched our tent: the four of us working as harmoniously together as a crew of foremasthands on the deck of a ship. Eagerly taking charge of the tent, Jim whittled poles, bent at the top, twined them in pairs and staked them in the ground, arranging the canvas over their frame; while I cut boughs of arbor-vitae for our floor, and Tom and Eben took over the fire. Watching fascinated as I laid the boughs in the tent—row upon row, underside up, and with the stubs covered—Jim squatted beside me, asking questions; and asking him in return about the style of the frame, we exchanged habits, downeast and Rom. When at last it came time to lay out the bedrolls—when the matting was done, thick and aromatic, wide enough to sleep four men abreast, and long enough for two dogs at the foot—I spread my blankets by the tent wall on the left; and reaching through the door flap, he at once handed me his, then followed it with each of the others. Unrolling them one at a time—spreading his neatly out next to mine, then setting Eben's and, lastly, Tom's—I felt a jubilant flush in my midriff: without realizing it, I'd longed for this all day, to have him beside me at night.

Crawling out of the tent I went with him to help the others: Tom by now having readied a giant fire, a couple of yards long and half again as wide, and Eben busy setting out stores for supper. Anxious to supplement Eben's lake trout in the now failing light, Tom and I cut a couple of birch poles, climbed down the bank and tried our luck with pork bait, while Jim made a stew of the brace of grouse, and a few of the herbs and leeks he'd collected. By twilight we were supping stew from our kids, and eating fried trout on makeshift plates; and by dark we'd washed up our kettle of utensils, and were drinking coffee round the fire.

As moonrise came on and our pot gradually emptied, we amused ourselves with story-telling—the first conversation we'd shared all day, since we'd either been drinking in the splendors, or walking warily to flush out game. Now in the freedom of our leisure, we marvelled at the woods and the weather—none of us able to recall when we'd been favored by such mildness so late in the season—or answered Jim's questions about the Indians who'd dwelt here, and the animals which frequented the area still. Fascinated by our descriptions of moose— such a creature as he'd never seen—and Tom's fanciful tales of beaver and bobcat, the handiwork of the former in evidence down the river, but the tracks of the latter a rare sight in Knox County—Jim was particularly interested in bear; and it was plain that his curiosity was not unmixed with fear, though he did his best to listen offhand.

But it was the talk about ghosts—about the spirits of the woods, old Penobscot and Abenaki lore, or tales of the lumberjacks and swampers—that really riveted Jim's attention; and finding he'd struck the mother lode, Tom let loose with a barrage of legends, while Eben egged him on as a skeptic. Down below the lake—surrounded by fir-tops, blacker than the night-shades of the sky—was just visible in the bend of the stream; and about us the tree shadows, long and soft in the moonlight, criss-crossed the open ground and the water, silver with the sheen of reflection. His face flickering in and out of the darkness, first reddish with the bright warmth of the fire, then netted with the shift of the shadows, Jim laughed and played along, encouraging Tom to spin out yarns; but as time went on I could sense the chill that gradually settled over his spirit.

That he was superstitious—much more so than I'd guessed in the beginning, more even than his lingering use of Rom prescriptions might suggest—I already knew from the scuttlebutt, and from signs I'd observed on my own; and I watched with mingled sympathy and fascination as he struggled to control his expression. Nor was he entirely alone in his concealed reaction; for as night came on and the darkness deepened—as pauses occurred now and then in our talk, allowing us to hear the profound silence of the forest—I began to feel that the woods had come alive; that they were no longer only watchful, but suddenly awake with the night. It was as if a spirit of wildness pervaded all the passages of the woods—a spirit from which all the forms of the forest drew their life, and which we ourselves could perceive in an unguarded silence.

Just as I was about to speak up, or throw on a log or stretch my legs—whatever it took to dispel this portent—there came a wild cascade of yells, abrupt and throaty and swelling in volume, inciting a pandemonium of wails, like the yodeling howls of a host of coyotes; and at the sudden instant of silence, Jim instinctively clutched me by the elbow, the first sign of fear I'd ever known him to show.

Seeing his face—knowing the sound—and feeling, perhaps, a sense of relief themselves—the others burst into a roar of laughter, a chorus of yowls not unlike the one dying: trying to convince Jim, between whoops and hoots, that he had just heard a couple of loons, and making no headway with him whatsoever. Having heard—that eve he'd left the lodge with me—merely a series of trembling calls, and thinking that to be the full range of the loon, Jim was determined he'd just heard a spirit, the very voice of the wild which we'd been feeling; and he looked at them as if *they* were the lame ones. Deciding it was high time to put a stop to such talk, I broke in and settled the matter, with the sensible suggestion that we turn in; and throwing on an abundance of deadwood—Jim particularly fervent in his efforts—we called the dogs and crawled into the tent.

Each of us having brought two stout blankets, one to roll up in, and one to share, we actually had the benefit of three, both of our own and half of another's; and it was well for us that we did, for the night was clear, and promised cold. Settling in beside Jim— wrapping myself in my thick gray, and spreading my wool plaid and his extra across us—I pillowed my head on my half-empty knapsack, while the others set their boots near the flap, and the dogs bedded down to sleep at our feet. Dropping off in a matter of minutes, Tom and Eben were soon breathing deeply, after a final lingering chuckle; while Jim, rolled like a cocoon under the blankets beside me, seemed wakeful, curled on his side with his face toward me. Too contented myself to sleep—the smells of the canvas, the hush of the wind, the occasional brush of a leaf on the tent, and most of all the warmth of Jim's nearness, all swelling my heart with a happy tide—I gave myself up to my vivid sensations: to the scent of the crushed arbor vitae beneath me, and the sliver of moonlight from the door to Jim's shoulders.

Though he was wrapped in a blanket like me, I could feel the touch of his knee, and the press of his elbow under the covers; and I drank in his physical closeness—found a peace in sharing space I'd never known before: a sixth sense telling me that he partook of my feelings—that despite his soft breath and quiet lashes, he was alert, and strangely happy. In the bit of moonlight that slipped through the tent flap, I could see the curve of his shoulder, and the outlines of his face at rest on his knapsack; could make out the spill of dark hair on the canvas, and smell the cool, wool scent of his jacket.

Not wanting to sleep, I resisted to the last, murmuring exchanges with him across the covers, or enjoying the easy quiet between us: feeling secret as a youngster whispering confidences after hours. At length feeling my eyes close, I lingered still on impressions—on the scratch of wood against my throat, or the warmth radiating about me from Jim; dallied still on the vistas I recalled from the day's hike, or the views that yet opened up before me. For four more nights I could sleep like this—simple nights of body and shelter, of sparks and shadow and sheen on the river; simple nights on the down of fir branches, with the hush of Jim's breath a few inches from me.

On waking we rose to another fine day, clear and turning warm like the one before it; and so it went on the days that followed, the four of us crawling out of the tent to find the frost melting, and the early mist or fog dispelling in the sunlight. On some morns we lingered over breakfast, too content with filets of salmon, fried trout and a freshly-brewed pot of coffee to hurry into the day's activity; on other morns we were far upstream by daybreak, Tom, Eben and I with our lines in the water, while Jim rustled up a small cook fire and breakfast.

Sometimes it was Jim who provided the day's first meal, tickling up a trout or two from the bank, while Eben and Tom looked on, dumbfounded; other times one of the rest of us brought down a woodie, or scared up a couple more pat from the thickets, and so saw us through dinner or supper. Finding they liked to cook together, Eben and Jim experimented with the flour, coming up with camp biscuits much improved over hardtack, or new ways to prepare or spice up our catches; while Tom and I hiked out betimes and hunted, taking no more than what we needed, so as not to unnecessarily rob the woodlands.

Rising and cooking, eating and washing—Jim as meticulous as a gypsy gentleman, the Romany rye of his stories and rhymes, putting us to shame with his blade and small mirror—then straightening our tent, and heading out; returning to our camp before dark, which came early, fixing a big dinner and lingering over the fire, we quickly developed a harmony of habits, a pattern of living as elemental as hunger, or the worship which springs unbidden from wonder. Though in the beginning we'd planned to travel on each morn, and pitch out tent anew each night, we quickly became so attuned to our spot, to each other's ways and the needs of the day, that we had no desire to move on; and evening after evening found us still at our campsite, stirring pots or swapping yarns by the fire, or growing drowsy on our bedrolls on the pine boughs.

With the approach of the end of our week came an increase in my regret and sorrow, and an intensification of my already taut senses: each miniature sight or impression, each fleeting tang or scent or whistle, heightening with the threat of its ending. That Jim shared in my pain I knew; for kneeling by me at the banks of the river, filling the kettle or rinsing utensils—seeing the flotilla of bright leaves on the current, or the lichens on the contours of granite—he looked on with a poignant expression, a gaze which celebrated yet bid farewell to each moment.

Finding that he'd slipped away one morning, the day before the last of our stay— concerned about the state of his feelings, yet reluctant to break in on his aloneness—I at last made up my mind to follow; and heading out in his direction, I came upon him partway up a hillside, sitting thoughtfully on the edge of a hollow which stretched beneath a gigantic beech tree: the most prodigious I'd ever seen, surely a century old at the least. With a broad, silver trunk of magnificent girth, great roots protruding from the woodland floor, and massive grey limbs radiating in all directions, it was the grandest old tree of the forest: wide-spread as a maple, sound as an oak, towering as a white pine in the midst of a clearing. On Jim's rapt face was an expression of awe, as if he'd just stumbled on a bonanza; and he looked wordlessly up at me as I settled down beside him. For some time we sat together in silence, experiencing the benign might of the tree's presence—gazing up at the grey boughs in the azure sky, or picking up the beech nuts beside us; then suddenly we looked at each other, and a twinkle appeared in Jim's dark blue eyes.

Understanding one another, we immediately got to our feet, and promptly began to climb up the tree—me giving Jim a boost with my knee, and he helping me up with a hand; and sitting amongst the resplendent branches, forty feet or more above the ground, we looked out over the slope of the land, down toward the river and below it, the lake, with the free-moving wind astir in our hair. Winding between hillsides, the stream turned to rapids, the foam of white water plain from our perch; while upon either bank the forest marched upwards, bough upon painted bough toward the heavens. Clusters of gold, swaths of fir green or orange, bits of russet or moss or vermillion: all lay below us like a living mapland, left by a master hand for us alone to discover; and hungrily sating ourselves on its fairness we at last climbed down from our host, and walked back to the camp, still silent.

Though he rejoined the others with spirit, Jim remained unusually quiet, whether cleaning the fish or felling deadwood; and it wasn't till suppertime that evening, as we built the fire alone together, that he finally decided to break his silence. "You know," he began, with a lowness of tone that I'd long since learned meant he was about to confide, "I've seen that tree b'fore, or one like it."

Attentive to the uneasy awe in his voice, I looked at him carefully with an encouraging eye, while our cook fire crackled brighter and higher.

"It wasn't anywhere here or in Wales," he went on, his voice taking on an even lower timbre. "It was...in a dream I had a few months back, a couple o' nights after I met you in Boston, while we were all still staying at Hannah's. I was walking in a woods...rambling or roaming; yet drawn all the while toward something that pulled me. It wasn't as if I had some destination in mind...more like some destination had *me* in mind, and was sending out a call or signal."

He paused, giving a prod or two at the pine cones, and the other tinder in the midst of the fire; then giving me a thoughtful look, he went on. "Then all at once I saw what'd drawn me—a gigantic old beech, with limbs the size of average tree trunks, spiraling like a stair all the way to the crown. As soon as I saw it I wanted to touch it—to draw some of that power into me, or just to feel its solid sureness. A great wind came up, so I clung to its roots—to one of the big old knees that protruded from the forest floor. Then as it blew a hurricane, the tree bent to help me, its branches growing down into the ground; and I was in its center, protected." Poking at the tinder again—neither lifting his eyes, which had been averted, nor raising his voice, nor in any way altering the course of his statement, he finished simply: "Even in my dream I knew somehow... that it was bound up with my meeting you; and when I woke up I had a feeling of power—a feeling that I could accomplish anything that day."

Too moved to speak, I simply listened, stung by the many inexplicable ways we had of knowing one another—of exploring one another's grounds, or intuiting one another's homes. Here he had, in his dream, seen deeply into my midst, after only a couple of days—seen the knotty bulk of my facade, and the tenderness I could never voice; seen his unconscious need for my strength, and the protectiveness I'd instinctively felt for him. Shaken anew by our chance encounter I sat looking into the fire, while Tom and Eben came up from the river, and dinner somehow prepared itself; and far into the evening, as our talk unveiled the habits of moose, or recalled the orbits of wintering fowl, I sat pondering what he'd revealed—sat marveling that he had been, all along, wandering and traversing my trails, even as I'd been journeying his.

Perhaps it was the influence of Jim's dream, perhaps the intensification of leaving; but this last night before we broke camp and moved back down again to the cabin—this last night in our tent by the river, Jim lying tense and restless beside me, the others slumbering soundly and snoring—I fell at length into a deep sleep, and embarked upon a riverman's journey. With the gurgling of the stream in my ears—the ceaseless trickle and wash of the current, breaking in rills over the granite—I found myself plying the shores like a beaver, nosing out local lodges and hollows; exploring submarine outlets and channels, and tracing them to rooms under stream banks, or mud-walled dens above the water.

Then the dream changed, and I was in a dory, no longer on

the river but on the open sea, with a fisherman dressed in oilslicks and sou'wester; and as I watched he set his net and drew it, hauling in a seemingly inexhaustible harvest—every fish and crustacean imaginable, their bright scales and shells glistening and gleaming. Silver, green, opal, gold, copper, damask—lobster, scallop, mollusk and haddock—he shook them into the glow of the sunlight; and wet with brine they twisted and floundered, like a deck load of living jewels in the noontide. Though he looked familiar with his oilslicks and clay pipe, I didn't know him till he turned his face, and I saw that it was McCabe; but intent on his catch he didn't see me, peering unobtrusively over his shoulder.

In the midst of the haul—now in plain view before me, on top of a regular mountain of sea life—there suddenly appeared a blue lobster, that maritime rarity with the freak pigment: so uncommon that I'd never met anyone who'd caught one, though I'd heard yarns of their being trapped, and kept alive for a spell in a sea tank. With its great claws and fan-tail, its segmented armor, its black eyes on thin stalks and its long antennae, and above all its bizarre blue color, this amazing creature now filled all my sight; and seeing it by itself in this fashion, I marveled at its unique nature: at its sensitive feelers, its jointed shell, out of which it stepped as it grew, and the depth and breadth of its field of vision. As if it had somehow detected my presence, it suddenly began to speak to me—not in words, but mind to mind, its dark eyes stirring with thought and knowledge, and its feelers moving with expression; but though I woke immediately after—though I sat straight up in the tent in my blankets, with the whole of this vivid dream before me—I could recall nothing the creature'd conveyed; nothing save an unshakeable fellowship, and an unspeakable sense of wonder.

Not till our last day, hiking down to the cabin, did the heavens cloud over and the wind come up; but even so autumn's beauty lingered, the few remaining leaves brilliant in the grey sky, solitary notes all the grander for their sparseness. As we reached the cabin it commenced to rain; and as it was already past noon, with much unpacking and repacking to do, we decided to stay the night, and use our time to organize our stores for those of us who snowshoed out in the winter. With the rain on the roof and the wind at the eaves, we found contentment in our activities here too, despite our regret for the trip's ending: cooking at the fireplace, overhauling the cupboards, or sitting up late around the fire, telling tales of other treks in this cabin. When at last we locked up and set out the next day, I felt as bereft as if I'd left a loved one; and it was harder still when we reached the Point Road, for Eben and Jim quietly parted ways at my fence post, Tom borrowed a horse and rode into town, and I was left to walk up to my kitchen.

Longing to be alone—to sort things out, and get accustomed to the idea of being home—I was assaulted instead by my young ones, by Sadie and Anne and a parlor full of houseguests; and there was no chance to make a transition from the rhythms of camping to the routine of home life. As if the sudden change and noise weren't enough, there was the shock of the house itself, which I looked at with disbelief; for while I was gone it somehow had shrunk—kitchen, sitting room, parlor, none of them nearly as large as they'd seemed before. Like a man who returns to his childhood home, or the room in which he'd played as a babe, expecting to find the spacious floors he recalled, and discovering instead a small, ordinary chamber, so now I looked round as I unpacked my gear, confused as an alien in my own home, or displaced as a refugee after a windstorm. But most intolerable of all was turning in at night; for instead of the vast woodland at the tent flap, the stars overhead and Jim at my elbow—instead of the soughing of wind in the pine boughs, and the scent of arbor-vitae beneath me—there was the crowd of chests, carpets and mirrors, the chill between Anne and me in our silence, and the press of four walls which muffled the sea gusts, the wash of the waves and the whisper of branches.

Feeling that I would expire without air, I tried throwing open a couple of windows, much to Anne's sleep-startled protest; but finding rest impossible, I at last drew on some clothes, and went out to the woods between McCabe's place and mine. Wandering about for a moment—overcome by the free wind, and the unfettered sense of height, space and shadow—I at length sat down in a rift of dry leaves; and gazing out at the gleam on the seaway—remembering the sheen of the moon on the river, and the dance of the fire's reflections on Jim's face—I wondered where in this great night he lay sleeping.

Finding a slender beech at my shoulder, I instinctively lay my face against it, as if I expected it to console me; and at the touch of its bark I broke into sobs, low, wracking sobs which wrenched my chest, and plucked and pulled at the cords of my throat. I hadn't wept at all for years, certainly not since Charis had died, perhaps not even when I realized she was gone—not just because I'd been taught to contain pain, but because I could no longer will to express it. And now that it burst from me like a fire, blazing to life from a deep-buried ember, it burned all the harsher for its long smolder—searing me within like an iron, till I no longer cared how it branded or scorched me, or made me appear to the eyes of the forest: this big, cumbersome man with his arm round a beech tree, rubbing his cheek against the grey bark skin.

Returning to work was no easy task in my raw state: moving the ships out into the harbor, rigging up sound moorings for winter, and getting the smaller craft up into dry dock; completing arrangements for construction after ice-out; and above all getting ready for my own trek in two months—all seeming to demand more than I had to offer. On the home front too things were characterized by all the accelerated preparations for winter—closing off buildings, readying sleighs, chopping and piling up next year's firewood, transferring stores from the springhouse to cellar, and putting in enough stock to maintain ten until April: much of this without the lift of Jim's assistance, for he was quickly caught up in his own demanding routine. After the five uninterrupted days I'd just spent with him, I tried not to begrudge the Talbots and others who now swooped in to claim his evenings; but I found that, far from satisfying me, our week had simply whetted my yearning for more; and it was no consolation that half of the townsfolk shared my yen for his companionship.

Bad enough that all his old shipmates were available to pleasure him round; but worse still were the pressing attentions he was suddenly receiving from Keziah's circle—any number of her intimates following up their introductions with noticeable flirtations and favors. Besides Keziah—who'd arrived in port too late for fall term at Bowdoin, and so was home till after Christmas—our cousin Persis, Sabrina Winslow, Sally Wingate and Tabitha Pelham, Kate Haskett and Damaris Spooner—all of them with either enough financial security, or lack of class consciousness or both, to pursue any kind of match they wished—saw him regularly in their own parlors, as I always heard sooner or later from Sadie; for with the single exception of Kate, their fathers and brothers were his friends and shipmates.

That he never issued an invitation or made any obvious kind of advances seemed to dampen nobody's spirits; in fact seemed to make romantic hopes all the keener, since everyone presumed that, as an outsider, he was too modest to press his attentions. Nor did his lack of background work against him; for with his striking looks, his circumspect manner, and his sterling record as a seaman—on deck if not ashore—he had by now won a reputation; and what remained unknown about him only heightened everyone's interest. According to rumor, which I could tap in my own kitchen, Damaris in particular was smitten; while even Keziah, whom I'd supposed regarded him as a brother, carried on with him across the Thanksgiving table—her good-natured banter no different from Tom's, yet somehow stinging me into such an awareness that I dreamt uneasily that night of their marriage.

How he felt about all of this notice, it was impossible for me to guess; for the few times I saw him, at the Inn or at Eli's, he seemed to be either in his habitual high spirits, or stoically reserved and contained—giving little indication of his thoughts either way, though I could sense an unspoken strain. Each time I saw him and felt again the incontestable bond between us, I reassured myself of my place in his life; but all such confidences were thrown to the seas one Saturday night early in December, when I stopped by the Inn on the spur of the moment to see if I could finagle him for dinner, found his room empty and the hearth cold, and learned from Jimmy—with many a wink and chuckle—that Damaris had suddenly got up the gumption to invite him out herself to some doing.

"That's right—he borrowed m' buggy," the old barnacle gloated, warmly rubbing his hands with approval. "He's got a new set o' shore togs too—sawr him as he was leavin', an' damned if he wahrn't dressed up like a dandy. A bit too bright for the likes o' me, but then, folks from them foreign pahts dress fancy. I've got t' hand it t' Damaris, she's a spunky gal—a fittin' niece t' her Aunt Charis, an' a fine match for Jamie, if I do say so as shouldn't."

He would have volunteered a lot more if I'd shown signs of staying round to listen; but stung by a bitter sense of betrayal—no matter how groundless and unreasoning—my only thought was for a swift exit, and I was halfway to the front door before he could begin his next sentence. Once out in the cold night, I paced up and down, making false starts in half a dozen directions, while the red and green ship's lights at the Inn entrance flashed by me, and the horses at the hitching rail breathed curiously at me; then at last mounting my bay—literally heaving myself into the saddle, and giving a unnecessary yank at the bridle—I headed off toward the Point Road, thinking to throw open a bottle with Eben.

Crossing China street and seeing the commotion of buggies and horses partway up the hill, in front of what looked to be Amasa Spooner's place, I realized the shindig was at Damaris's grandfather's; and feeling doubly betrayed—Amasa having been my close friend for years, my master carpenter ashore and at sea—I cast a cool glance in his direction, a sudden suspicion stabbing my midriff that he had all along been playing matchmaker. Any number of small gatherings held in his parlor flashed back to my mind now that I was wary—gatherings to which both Jim and Damaris had been invited; and I wondered now if things hadn't been going on since August. Turning up the hill in spite of myself, I slowed my pace and passed by the buggies, hoping against hope not to find Jimmy's, but spotting it, and Sabra, close to Amasa's walk; while from the house, a tidy, clapboarded Federal, came the strains of violin and piano, punctuated at intervals by gay laugher and chatter.

Of all Keziah's comrades I'd always liked Damaris best, not just because she was Amasa's granddaughter, and close kin in more than blood to Charis Spooner, but because I found her sensible, strong and unspoiled, unlike many of her girlfriends. But now—picturing her in a watered-silk dress, with her hair done up in some fashion or other—imagining her playing games in the parlor, or favoring the guests with a bit of music—I found her insufferably offensive: her unemphatic, fine features, her greyish eyes and brown hair, and the quiet, knowing aura about her, grating on me like the grind of a steamboat. Robertson, too, in his bright garb and cravat, with a hat and probably kid gloves in tow, suddenly seemed no longer my friend, the man who'd dipped drinks with me from the river, but a stranger who'd unexpectedly appeared in town, bent on giving me a sleepless weekend; and try as I might, I could feel no good will for him.

Thinking to find solace from Eben—the one dependable mate I still had—I came about and rode to his cabin, thankfully found him astir by his fire, threw myself down into his vacant wing chair, and commanded a generous brandy; but though I left broad hints I was troubled, and considerably rumpled in spirit, he seemed oblivious to my openings, sipping companionably across from me, and blithely chatting of such inconsequential matters as trawling or shrimping or shipping. Now that I *wanted* him to pick my thoughts, his primary sport for almost a decade, he obliged me by saying nothing, like the perverse wretch he was; and giving up at last I departed, leaving him with a half-empty bottle, and the grumpy adieu I flung over my shoulder: my last glimpse of him catching his imperturbable expression, and the dry indulgence with which he regarded me, as if he was vastly amused by my visit.

Nor did things between Robertson and I always go smoothly the few times we were alone together; for even without his sashay with Damaris, we seemed to have entered upon another stretch of rocky waters, crossing one another as we sometimes had during August. When the Articles were finally ready for signing—when I'd formally been chosen as master, and in turn had roped in McCabe as first mate, Robertson came forward for the second mate's berth; and though this was exactly what I'd been hoping, I knew better than anyone the drawbacks of his strong nature: the disadvantages not so much of his temper, as of his obstinate willfulness. By regulating his watchmates we could checkmate his temper, since, without the likes of Howland and Reuben, he worked profoundly well and brightly; but containing his willfulness posed a first-rate challenge—especially on so lengthy a trek as planned, and on so demanding a passage as Cape Horn.

Before I handed him the pen and inkstand, I told him directly that he was to carry out orders, or pass them on to those working with him, with no additional interpretations, no second-guessing of my motives, and with none of the back-talk he'd shown me off the Bahamas; and though he agreed to the conditions—which were no different from those he would have encountered elsewhere—his chin came up, his eyes perceptively narrowed, and his brows came together in a dark slant. Taking the pen, he signed his name to the papers, with his customary vigor and flourish; but as he handed them back—before he could turn away—I detected a twitch, just a hint, as it were, of grim delight at the corners of his mouth, as if he'd already figured out how to get round me, and relished the challenge of the undertaking. Wondering just who was taking whom on, I was left sitting with a flood of misgivings, and the discomfiting feeling I'd just been had; and giving my head an aggrieved shake, I went back to work with exasperation.

When the disquiet over this interview had finally settled, there was the matter of his vaccination for smallpox to ruffle the surface of the waters between us; for having campaigned unsuccessfully for months to get him to submit to this crucial precaution, I'd finally tricked him into compliance, and he was not one to bear such wiles lightly. Having understood, while we were still camping, that the last day of October was my birthdate, he'd asked me what he could do to mark the occasion, when we got back into town in a few days. "There is somethin' I'd like ye t' do for me, if ye'd take the trouble," I'd wheedled gently, instantly conceiving of a way to catch him, and bend that obstinate will to mine for once. "I'll do it; what is it?" he'd unthinkingly offered, expecting, probably, some sentimental request; and trying to check my triumphant grin, I'd said simply, "Let Eben vaccinate ye for smallpox." Having made an open offer, he could hardly refuse, though his eyes sparked his opinion of my maneuvers; and now I saw to it he went through with the bargain, arranging with Eben to get the vaccine.

Appalled at the vaccination process—as appalled as any Rom ever was at any gadje medicinal flimflam—he submitted with considerable ill-grace and rancor; and when I stopped by McCabe's later that day to ask conciliatingly how it'd gone, Eben gave a nod at the stairwell, indicating he was still upstairs. "He's a bit undeh the weatheh—the usual feveh, along with a few otheh imaginary symptoms; an' I've given up tryin' t' convince him he ain't dyin' o' smallpox," Eben summarized for me dryly; and grinning widely, I sprinted upstairs, where I found him dozing on the spare bed, looking crumpled as if he'd just been clipped by a wagon.

Here was a man who'd stitched up his own knife wound, quietly endured all the indescribable hardships of the winter North Atlantic, and God only knew what besides, laid low by a simple vaccination; and restraining a wild inclination to laughter, I gently touched him on the shoulder. Turning a little, he opened one eye, scowled "Happy birthday, you son of a bitch," and promptly turned back to the wall, obviously signaling an end to my visit; and giving vent at last to my laughter, I indulged in a victorious guffaw, before exiting down the stairs, still chuckling.

But if my relations with Jim were fraught with upheaval—if Damaris had roused the first real suspicion between us, and his will and mine were frequently at odds—there was one thing that didn't fail me: our unquenchable partnership of spirit—the heightening of our week in the woods with me always, whether Jim was beside me or not, matching words or letting bygones be bygones. Like a steady hand on a deep inner rudder, it saw me through the rapids of rough words, or the whirlpools and eddies of doubt and distrust; and indeed it was the one thing that sustained me through all the rankling and scraping, this quiet awe at the life-forms about me—this storehouse within me of portraits by the river, radiantly pulsing for Jim's eyes and mine.

It was well for me that this wonder was with me; for besides my

sporadic contentions with Jim, there were conflicts at the yard—
all seeming to draw to a head with the advent of Christmas, and
the New Year's date of our embarkation. Along with the usual last-
minute wrangling over port-of-call arrangements, inventories and
schedules, there was the unexpected squabble over who was to
replace me, the short span between ice-out and my return to take
over construction; and it was little to my liking that the choice was
Joseph. Suddenly proud of my new place on the board—jealous as a
parent over the superintendence of my new ship—I was ill-pleased
that he, the least close of my brothers, and my rival in more sense
than one, was to stand on the ways in my stead for so brief a time as
even a day; and determined to counter his presence with someone
who could faithfully represent me, I actually talked Spooner, my
right arm at sea, into staying in port to lay the new keel.

Calling a meeting to work out the details of both the voyage
and spring construction—hauling in me, McCabe and Robertson,
Joseph and Spooner by the scruff of the neck, and sitting us down in
the main office—the board of directors at length ironed things out,
though not without a vigorous effort; and this being Robertson's first
counting house meeting, his face as he took in the mechanics was
a study. Bills of lading, manifests, consignees; Articles of Shipping,
proposed courses, sea stores; letters of introduction or checking or
credit: it was his inauguration into the real intricacies of sailing,
the responsibilities of the officers and owners; and though he said
nothing, he looked deluged.

But it was primarily the ill-disguised rancor between us
members which commandeered and held his attention: Seth riding
roughshod over my proposal; Pa reigning in my course even tighter;
Joseph arguing for changes in the keel's scarfing; and long-suffering
McCabe struggling to smooth things over. We'd drifted a little in past
days, Jim and I, chiefly because of my bitterness over Damaris—a
resentment I'd taken pains to conceal, though he must have felt it
in my brusque manner; but now as we sat together in Seth's study,
surrounded by safes and tables and ledgers, he seemed to sense the
weight of my office, and emanated an understanding—a sympathy
so genuine it melted my cool guard, and caused me to gratefully

answer his gaze. As the meeting broke up and we left the room, Seth actually apologized for his rough handling, lifting my spirits a degree more; but Joseph quickly stepped in and squashed things, tossing offhandedly to Seth: "No need for kid gloves; you know Ben—he ain't exactly a man o' feelin.'"

Though I said nothing, his thrust hit home, there being nothing more painful to me at present than my struggle to show emotion; and Jim instantaneously seemed to feel it. As soon as Joseph was out of earshot, he turned to me and said with a cool smile, "He doesn't know you very well, does he?"; and overcome by his perception—seized by the realization that, indeed, neither Joseph nor any of the rest of my kin knew me—I was moved to the quick again by Jim's sure sight.

That he saw me to the core was confirmed this same day in a wholly unexpected fashion; for after I'd retuned to my desk after lunch, I found a note from him, and a key—the note inviting me to supper at Eli's, and directing me meantime to the small shed at the yard where I'd frequently seen him entering and leaving. Taking the key I hastened off at once for the shed, unlocked the door and stepped within; and there, by the light of a solitary window, I beheld a regular carpenter's shop: a stock of wood, mostly apple and pine; a bench littered with a collection of toys, some carved and painted, some still being roughed out; augers, chisels, gouges and files of every particular and description; and jars of paint with sundry brushes. But most important, mounted on the wall across from the window, set so that the light would fall full upon it, was something tall and bulky with a linen cloth covering it, and a note attached: "For Ben—Merry early Christmas—from Jim."

Drawing off the cloth I found before me a figurehead—a ship's figurehead exquisitely painted—so meticulously conceived and carved that its eloquence took my breath away; but its majesty wasn't the only thing which gripped me, for I saw in an instant that its subject was me. The face, the pipe, the pilot's cap, the wind-whipped cravat and crumpled jacket, all were unmistakably mine; but the revelation was in the features and their expression; and I stared witlessly at them, amazed, for this was not the visage which peered at me each day out of the bedroom looking-glass. The face was broad, strong and weathered, with fine lines about the eyes and mouth, and bolder ones about the nose, cheeks and forehead; the hair was tangled; the beard square and brown; the mouth, despite its pipe, sensitive; the jacket, disheveled; the attittude of the head, determined—all recognizably me, it was true. But the sea-grey eyes were set on the distance with a mingled curiosity and purpose—a gaze directed by both a goal within, and an allurement without; and the whole was infused with a sense of nobility which put to flight the eccentric collar, the unruly hair and blunt, plain features.

Awed, I simply stood back and stared, as if I had never seen myself before—saw qualities of strength, refinement, direction; tempering them, a wonderful compassion, a quizzical, almost sheepish tenderness; and lurking beneath them, a fine suggestion of humor. But overriding them all was a veneration, whether my own or Jim's, I couldn't discern—a reverence which seemed to take up from where my present marveling left off. All the anger and dissension of the meeting that morning, the acrimony of recent encounters with Jim, even the self-reproach I'd felt when I'd understood that, while I'd been burning with suspicion toward him, he'd been working noon and night bodying out this image of his inner sight: all fell away, and I was left simply with the deepest upwelling of serenity and self-worth. When at last I became aware again of my surroundings, I found that I'd somehow sat down on a stool; and here I perched for an unknowable while, my mind so torn between my admiration for Jim's work, my awe at this manifestation of myself, and my understanding of why I'd been given it today, that I was at a loss what to do.

At length tearing myself away from the figurehead, I turned to the other things in the room—to the wood and tools, probably borrowed from Cy Spooner, and the toys he was making on the bench, probably the children's Christmas presents. Crossing over and inspecting the latter, I found there were several cars of what promised to be a train; and a wonderful large top, big as a saucepan, painted in multi-colored stripes. Having had no idea of Jim's gift as a carver, I was as dumbstruck by his command and deftness as I was by his evidence of knowledge of me; and I marveled at the form and luster of his models.

That he'd been quietly working—a common laborer amongst twenty—in the billows of canvas and duck in the sail loft, with this rare gift unexpressed inside him, when he could have had any artisan's berth in New York, fairly took my breath away; and not least amongst the convictions which swept me—as I finally stepped out and re-locked the door—was my determination to see at once to his transfer to fine carpentry in the joiner's shop, or to his establishment in independent practice: visions sweeping me in grand succession of the billetheads he could make to order, or the trailboards and figureheads he could create for the new ship.

It being by now late in the afternoon, and my mind fit for anything but work, I simply walked back and closed up the office, then went early to Eli's to wait for Jim: ordering a drink to pass the time, and sipping it at our favorite table near the wharf window. Joined by two or three of the others—Worthing, Longworthy and Wingate supping on chowder—I sat by quiet and uncommunicative, surrounded by a kind of cushioned hush, too moved for the light talk which dominated the table: my responses, when required, coming automatically, and my eye darting to the door every time it opened.

When at last Robertson stepped in—well-wrapped in a pea coat, his hat, gloves and muffler covered with snowflakes—spotted me, stomped his boots, and headed over, I rose impulsively and met him halfway, throwing my arms about him in a grateful embrace; and instantly yielding himself to my gesture, he instinctively clung to my shoulders. Walking side by side back to the table, we quietly nodded and sat down with the others—Jim shrugging off his snow-crusted peacoat, while Worthing fetched over an extra chair, and Longworthy drawled with an inquisitive eyebrow: "Well, what was *that* all about?"

"That was in thanks for an early Christmas present," I answered, casting a wordless look at Jim.

"Must of been some present," Longworthy grunted.

"It was," I averred simply.

After a supper of baked halibut—which we ate, as always, in company with many, our table getting progressively more animated and crowded, till it resembled the mess of a three-master's forecastle— the two of us managed an escape to the Inn, with a bottle of scotch and no one behind us; and while I built up a roaring fire on Jim's hearth, he kicked off his boots and lighted the lamps. It was our first opportunity to be alone together since we'd come back to town from our camp trip; and somehow knowing that no one would interrupt us, we settled ourselves with unspoken glee by the fire, the bottle and a couple of glasses between us: me stretched out on the carpet with my elbows to prop me, and Jim on his back with his arms behind his head, turning to his side now and again for a drink. So far not a word about the figurehead had been said; but now I asked him in quiet wonder, "Whehre on earth did'je learn t' carve like that?"

Immediately he smiled up at me. "My father," he answered simply. "He was a master at it—did all the fine woodwork for the *vardos*, our wagons—and in his spare time, around the fire in the evenings, he whittled playthings for my cousins and me."

"Like the top I sawr on youhr bench?" I asked gently, remembering all at once words he'd spoken in fever, lying ill in the sickbay after Havana: words recalling the swirling hues of a toy, whirling away on a bit of bare earth.

"Aye," he responded, while the fire snapped on the hearth before us. "I had one like it: it was large, and painted in a pattern of colored stripes. One of my earliest memories is of spinning it on the moor, wherever I could find a patch of hard clay."

This was the first time he'd confided such personal memories since our talk that night he'd cried in the sick bay—the night he'd told me he was a gypsy; the first time he'd referred to his father, or to the specifics of his own life. "What did youhr fatheh look like?" I asked, seizing this moment of closeness between us, and pressing him with a careful spirit..

He smiled frankly. "Like me," he answered, meeting my eager gaze. "At least, as I last remember him—I think that he looked then very much as I look now."

"His eyes were blue, like youhrs?"

"Aye. No one else we knew had eyes like ours—I think we must have got them from something British, through my grandfather. My cousins' eyes were dark, very black, even blacker than Romany eyes usually are. All in all, we were known far and wide for our eyes; my cousin Idris was even thought t' have special powers."

"You mean, the way we thought witches did hehre?"

He paused for a moment, reflecting. "Talk here always seems to connect witches with evil—with spite or fear or sudden misfortune. A *chovihani* has...a deeper sight, an ability to see backwards and forwards in time—not like fortunetelling, those are mostly cheap tricks for the gadje; and the Rom, anyway, are chiefly interested in the present." Pausing again, he turned a little, and took another sip from his glass; then settling back with his head on his arms—with his elbow brushing mine on the carpet—he went on with a confiding tone. "But a power like that, to see ahead or behind, or to make connections others don't notice—it's a gift, and it can be used in many ways: not just to startle or to win influence over others, but to heal or warn or to unite lovers. I s'pose its use d'pends mostly on the character of the *chovihani,* or the *chovihano* that has it... Idris began t' see visions when she was eight—she saw my grandfather's death and funeral, exactly as they later happened; and she often knew what was happening in the present, to other members of the family in Wales or England."

"Was she oldeh than you?" I asked, fascinated, and not without a backward look at my dreams of the summer, as I reached out to give a poke at the fire.

"A couple of years younger."

"An' you had otheh cousins?"

"About a hundred... but the closest were Idris and her brother."

"Did you neveh have a brotheh or sisteh?"

"No."

"But you travelled about with Idris' family?"

"Almost always."

"Were they Roberts?"

"Aye. My Uncle Culvato was my father's brother; then there was Fenella, my aunt, and Idris and Djemail, her brother. Taw, my grandmother, went about with us too: we usually slept seven or eight to a tent, with a couple of dogs tied by the door, an' three or four horses tethered t' tree limbs."

Moved to at last know who belonged to the names I'd heard him murmur in Boston or aboard *Charis*, I swiftly absorbed all his words, with a dozen new questions springing up inside me. "Was youhr fatheh much oldeh than you?" I asked next, sensing he was willing to let me proceed.

"I think only about twenty years or so. He married young, an' I was born soon after."

"What were his clothes like—how do Romany chals dress?" I pursued, eager to picture this man in my mind's eye.

"Would you like to see?" he offered warmly, with a radiant smile which burst forth like a fire, unfettered and flashing and full of promise.

Wordless, I nodded at him, too overcome by the dazzle before me, and by a sudden expectation, to give voice to even a simple answer; and getting to his feet, he went to his trunk, unlocked it, rummaged and withdrew from the bottom several folded garments, which he placed one by one on his knee. Catching these up, he sent me a glance, the kind of look a magician might signal; then crossing to the curtain he'd hung at one end of the room—a sort of alcove for washing and dressing, since he was Rom to the core when it came to his preference for privacy—he slipped within, and was absent for several minutes. Seeing to the fire, I stirred up the logs, and tossed on a couple more for good measure; and when I looked up, he was before me, in all the full garb of a Romany rye.

Taken wholly aback, I gaped dumbly at him, my eyes darting up and down him at random, as I struggled to take in the points of his costume: his coat, a dark blue broadcloth with short tails, well-cut; his waistcoat, the same pink satin with fine, embroidered flowers I'd seen him wear on Independence Day in Havana, juggling with Paul and the others; his shirt, a white holland, with a figured neckerchief at the collar; his pantaloons, plum-colored, of a velvet corduroy with unusually wide cords, the legs cut short just below the knees; his stockings or leggings, a lavender worsted; his shoes, a pair of highlows. In his ears he wore the loops of gold earrings, and on his head, a wide-brimmed, low-peaked hat of black beaver, while in his hand he held a whip, adorned with an elegant, roundish gold knob. The gold was genuine, as were the buttons which decorated his topcoat and waistcoat: half-guineas, doubloons, and seven-shilling gold pieces, all pierced and sewn on with reckless abandon.

Like a statue of some archaic squire, or the bow piece of some quaint, old barque—like a figurehead which has climbed down from the pinions of its mounting to address its audience with breath at its lips, so now he stood on the carpet before me, the flush of life at his cheeks and eyes; and moved to the depths I touched the smooth satin, the warm plush of the corduroy and the embossed gold of the buttons, like a child exploring a new-given gift, afraid to speak for fear of waking.

Satisfied at last that I'd missed nothing—hauling out my handkerchief, and giving a honk or two in it, not caring that he saw how he'd touched me—I turned away and sat down by the fire, pouring myself a stiff one while I was at it; while he set aside the whip, hat and topcoat, and sat down to remove the highlows.

"Did he always dress so fine?" I quavered, finally managing to come up with a voice. "Somehow I'd pictured him more in laboring clothes."

"Oh, this wasn't how he went about every day—though in public, an' even b'fore each other, the Rom look with high regard on those who c'n dress."

"Were most of these clothes actually his?" I inquired, carefully sidestepping the matter of how Jim had come into their possession.

"Aye."

"He had enough money t' make buttons o' gold pieces?" I asked dryly.

"I never remember us being very well off.... I s'pose because he made buttons of gold pieces," he confessed, equally dryly. Removing the rest of his outer clothing—handing me the waistcoat to look at more closely—he pulled on a woolen jersey; and thus comically attired, half sea dog, half Rom—still wearing earrings, neckerchief and stockings, with those incredible plum-colored pantaloons—he composed himself by me on the hearth, and proceeded to drink my health in Romany.

"Teach me some Rom words," I petitioned, after I'd finally managed to muster the *"Aukko tu pios adrey Romanes"* of the standard Romany toast.

His eyes bright and candid, he nodded. "Which ones would you like t' know?" he offered.

"Is there a word for sailing-ship?" I asked, smiling.

"Aye, *berro*; and a sailor is a *ber-engro*, a ship-man."

"Say it again."

He complied; and I tried with difficulty to imitate him—to match the strong points of his accent: the Latin resonance of the vowels, the Welsh fluidity of the consonants, and especially the strongly trilled r's, which always made his speech so distinctive. Since I barely pronounced my r's at all, or transformed them into something akin to an *ah* or an *uh;* since my consonants came out like gravel, and my softer sounds like slush in April, my efforts as a student were nothing short of hilarious; and he didn't trouble to suppress his laughter.

In this fashion I nonetheless learned a bit of the language—the words for I and me, *mande* and *miro;* for you, *tu;* for fire, *yag;* for wind and water, *baval* and *pani;* for mug, chest and chair, *coro, mufta, besh-engri;* for yes and no, *avali* and *ne;* and for brother, *prala,* or more affectionately, *pal,* a word I'd sometimes heard him call me. When I'd learned as many as I thought I could remember—when he began to show signs of fatigue, as he always did in logical discourse—I broke off for the time beings and replenished our glasses; and we sprawled drinking before the fire, with the easy silence that sometimes fell between us.

When he seemed refreshed, I looked down at him, his face unusually frank and open, and his eyes gazing up into mine with affection; and encouraged by their warmth and candor, I got up the daring to venture, "You've neveh spoken about youhr motheh."

"I know it," he responded without censure. "She died when I was very young, only four or five or so."

"D'ye remembeh her?"

"Aye—a little—small things, like her red cloak—her long, dark hair and bright-colored dresses."

"What was her name?"

He hesitated, and I suddenly realized that, as she was dead, it might not be proper for him to speak it. "Can ye write it down?" I appended; and looking relieved, he tore a paper from his desk top, dipped his pen in the ink, and hastily wrote "Narilla"—flinging the note into the fire as soon as he was certain I had read it.

"Was she a Roberts, like youhr fatheh?" I asked.

"No; she was a Wood, another of the Rom clans that travel in Wales."

"Do you know how she died?" I couldn't help pressing, my pulse gaining speed with each new discovery.

"No; but I remember her funeral—oddly, I remember that almost more plainly than anything else about her."

"What was it like?" I encouraged gently.

His eyes grew faraway and he became silent—not as if he was unwilling to speak, but as if he was casting his mind back to early scenes. "I remember the tents," he began slowly, "and the fires that were burning among them... it was night... there were two or three nights, and everyone came from miles around, all the Roberts and Woods... a number of others related by marriage. Spirits were pretty light, mostly—people eating and drinking, kettles going on the fires almost continuously, and everyone talking and telling stories—that's the way things're always done; no one's allowed to show signs of grief...

"There was one tent set aside where they had put her, and there were always two or three there beside her, with candles, keeping watch. I kept wandering in to look at her... at the coffin, which was filled with her things—dresses, jewelry, keepsakes—the pile kept getting deeper and deeper, as folks dropped off things of hers they'd found in their tents, or trinkets and such she'd given them. Once I tried to take some of them out; but my uncle, Tornapo, put everything back, explaining that she'd need it all—that we couldn't keep anything of hers anyway, it'd make her spirit restless. None of it was very clear—where she was going, or why my keeping her necklace would make her uneasy...

"Finally they buried her, and all of those things, near a churchyard somewhere, with a kind of service—we always used the Church of England; and afterward I understood what they meant, that we couldn't keep anything of hers—for when I came back to the tents, they were building a huge fire; and on it they flung everything she'd ever owned or used—our tent, our mattress and blankets, all of our utensils. They smashed the dishes and buried everything that wouldn't burn...they shot our horse, my dog... I kept crying and telling them my top was in the fire, but they hushed me—no one was allowed to show any feeling—that, too, would have made her restless.

"Finally the fire died down, and they sifted the ashes, burying everything that remained. There was nothing left to remember her by, or our early life as a family. My father made us another tent, and worked, and I worked too—tending sheep and filching gadje, and learning to make simple woodcrafts and carvings. We travelled with my uncle and aunt, and Taw; and gradually we accumulated other possessions. But it wasn't the same."

As he talked his simple words of loss and hardship filled me with an awe for the stark ways of his boyhood—with a deeper understanding of his restrained nature; and I looked down at him with fresh-seeing eyes. His face in the firelight was at once moved—transfigured with the power of recollection—and disciplined as by some inner hand, so that both feeling and dignified strength spoke out; and as I gazed at it I saw other memories, unvoiced remembrances of times fat and lean. In the warm glow of the fire his fine, candid brow, the clear, almost grecian cut of his features, took on a kind of inner gleam, an incandescence of flesh and spirit, as if they'd caught the flame in the grate; and in their sheen I saw new expressions, new details of tone and horizon.

I'd never noticed before how sensitive his lips were, how finely cut; how the short wisps at his temples softened his hairline, or shone with a reddish-brown in the lamplight. Like the purity of harbor waters, whose transparence discloses the sunlighted floor, his face as he spoke reflected his depths; and I looked at him with the awed joy of a carver, who's freshly set his tools at rest.

Plainly exhausted by his recollections, and spent as well by his narration—a lengthy speech for him—he fell silent; and thinking it best not to press him further—much as I longed to travel his memory—I let him drowse for a bit beside me, turned on his side with his head on his arm. Poking and prodding at the fire, I succeeded in coaxing a greater warmth, which helped to ease the chill in the room; then making a quiet foray in his cupboard, I came up with a loaf and a cheese, which I carried on their plate to the hearth. Using his ship's knife I sliced a few rounds, and poured a fresh glass; and partaking of these, I gazed at the fire, or let my glance drift round the points of the room. When at length he stirred and stretched, and looked up at me with a warm eye, I handed him a few shares of bread, a slab of cheese and his filled glass; and gratefully sitting up on the hearth, he silently ate and sipped beside me, while the fire snapped and hissed in the grate.

Realizing I soon had to be off—already hours later than I'd told Anne in my note—I nonetheless couldn't yet break away; and returning to the subject that had brought us together, I asked him the question I'd longed to all evening. "The figurehead," I ventured cautiously, thinking back with awe on its features, on the fineness—yes, the handsomeness—of its visage. "Is that really how I look t' you?"

Unhesitatingly, he said "*Avali.*"

"How did'je do it?" I asked simply.

He smiled. "I made friends with Cy Spooner, you know, not very long after we made port last summer. He caught me hanging around his Curio Shop, and took me back into his studio to see his figureheads, all in a row along one wall. As soon as I saw them I thought of something that'd happened to me just before I saw *Charis,* the day I met up with you at Toby's... Walking down the wharf, with the prows of the ships meeting from either side overhead, I suddenly realized I was in a kind of archway, made up of figureheads from every quarter of the world.

"I must've marched along avenues like that a thousand times in the past couple o' years... but this time a strange feeling came over me...as if I was walking down a gallery of ancestors... the sort of arcade you'd expect to find in a palace, or one of those crumbling estates we used t' pass by in England. Even though the figures were all so different—so obviously unrelated to each other, or to me—they were all somehow so familiar... as if I'd some way descended from them... or as if they'd somehow all sprung from my head."

He paused, while his eyes grew faraway and dreamy; then a smile touched his lips, like a gleam of memory. "I remember a soldier, a lascar... a kind of god-like figure like Neptune... a Spanish dancer, with a fan held up sort of flirting before her... and a Turk, whose face seemed to spark with allure and adventure. They put me in mind of those nights with my father, carving out figures by the light of the fire... or those rows of smithies beneath the archways in Tunis, hammering out metal in the firelit shadows.

"I wanted then to try my hand at one, to see what sort of face I'd find in the wood... and when I saw Cy's, I couldn't wait any longer. I showed him a thing or two I could do with his tools, and told him what I wanted to carve; and when he saw my work, he gave me some applewood, and taught me how to make a pattern. He's the one who set me up in the yard, in the little shed he'd used to store wood: he cleared it out, gave me the key, and promised not t' breathe what I was up to."

"Would you like t' try anotheh?" I offered gently, having listened to him with an awed silence.

Immediately his eyes lighted up. "What is it?" he asked, all at once in the present.

"Well, if this ship o' mine eveh slides down the ways, she's goin' t' need a figurehead; an' I can't think of anyone I'd ratheh see carve it."

"Do you have an idea who she's t' be named for?" he queried, his face alive with eagerness and pleasure.

"I ain't said a word t' anyone else yet—but right from the staht I've thought that, since she's gettin' on, an's mothered most o' the hands that run the yahd, it's about time somebody built a ship for my grandmotheh Abigail."

At once his eyes took on a luster, a light of silent thought and vision, as if he was already picturing her face, with its lean, direct, strong-willed expression, and imagining how to shape it out. "If I had Cy's backing...if he could help me choose the wood, an' advise me how t' prepare it for the weather...I think I could do it... I'd love t' try."

"Then you c'n make a staht as soon as we get back in May...I guess you know ye've got youhrself a job in the joineh's shop anytime you say the word—Bart Wingate'd take you on as apprentice in ship's cabins; or we c'n set you up on youhr own if you want...you could carve nautical pieces t'order, like Cy does."

"Could I do both?" he appealed. "I'd like t' know everything Bart's got in his head...I'd like t' help outfit the new ship...but I'd want t' keep on, after hours, at the shed, workin' on the figurehead with Cy t' teach me, till I felt ready t'strike out on my own."

"It's fine with me, so long's ye don't wear youhrself out...Anyhow, it's time t' get ye out o' the sail loft," I said dryly, getting to my feet with regret, and taking leave at last of his face. Looking up at me—sitting up a little, and leaning on one hand on the hearth—he was the picture of anticipation, of a kind of half-hopeful, half-fervent searching; but I could see in his eyes that, as when we'd been camping, another part of his past had found an outlet in his present, and ran true to the course for which he'd been seeking. Rubbing his hair warmly, I put on my boots, then went to fetch my hat and coat; and pulling them on, I tramped to the door, leaving him with what little was left in the bottle.

"G' night, mate," I said from the hall, lingering on the sight of him by the fire. "*Kushti rardi, pal*," he responded, with the hint of a wistful note in his voice; and the last thing I saw, as I shut the door, was the contemplative hush of his face, and the sheen of the firelight on his hair.

Next day getting dressed in the chill of our room—Anne already up helping the girls with their aprons, and Sadie and the boys down in the kitchen—I was standing at the mirror adjusting my collar, when suddenly I looked up and met my eyes: stared for a moment, then dropped my gaze back to my collar, feeling abashed and idiotic. It'd been years since I'd actually looked at my face, probably as long ago as those bleak days at Bowdoin, putting myself together for a rare social or outing; but now—remembering my figurehead —I again raised my eyes, and ventured a curious, half-sheepish survey.

Critical as ever, I saw the same broad, weathered face—somewhat improved by a neatly trimmed beard—that I'd come to expect, those few instants a day that I dressed; but undeterred—peering harder—I saw something else: a maturity I hadn't noticed, a ripeness which had somehow crept up on me; and awed, I realized I was beginning to resemble my uncles, Matthias and especially Ezra, who'd always looked so imposing on the decks of their ships.

Odd, too, how I'd never noted before the interesting, even intriguing hue of my eyes—not so dark as slate, not so pale as mist, but a kind of enigmatic sea-grey, soft or commanding with the change of mood, or the new, animated light in their depths. Looking closer—reaching up, and sweeping back my hair—I saw a strong, high, windbeaten forehead, enticingly marked with the scrivening of the sea; saw the thick, youthful shine of what I'd always taken to be an unruly thatch of sun-bleached tow hair. Remembering the soft wisps at Jim's temples, I looked at mine, and found hairs as fine as the down on Nat's head; scrutinized my brows, and saw they were smooth, strong and even, quizzically knit. My teeth—which I'd only looked at before when cleaning—were straight and white, almost as regular as the children's; while my lips—though not so ruddy as Jim's—were appealing, sensitive and neatly shaped: a readiness about them, indeed about the whole face, which suddenly made me break my gaze, and turn away from the glass, disconcerted.

In a flurry of activity the year's end was upon us: Anne's kin from Portland—her sister Charlotte, her stuffy brother-in-law William, and their even more insufferable children—arrived by stage for a lengthy stay; while my preparations for departure reached a hectic peak. Though there was, as usual, little celebration of Christmas—most of the shops remaining open, and several ships entering or clearing the harbor—Anne goaded us all into church after breakfast; and since Jim was so taken aback by our stark treatment of the day— the only date of the Christian calendar which interested him—I managed to talk Anne into inviting him to dinner. Arriving with an armload of gifts—which instantly made him a hero, even to my starched niece and nephew—he settled himself in the sitting room, relieved to find the young ones had at least hung stockings; and while we waited dinner, he delighted Nat on the hearthstones, winding and releasing the top-string, or entertained Charlotte and William with sketches of Christmas doings in England.

But the day was not wholly without surprise for him; for before mealtime Eben marched over on a pair of snowshoes, and the two of us led Jim out to the stable, where we'd been secreting the horse we'd bought him, a splendid, spirited, but well-trained pinto. Since no one knew horses like Jim did, we'd exerted our utmost in the purchase, calling in Tom's and Joseph's savvy, then sending all the way to a Portland breeder; and while we were at it I'd procured a saddle, and the best bit and harness that Longstreet could muster: my motives being not wholly unselfish, since I knew that every fresh bond Jim developed was an additional tie to home.

Though he needed a horse—though I felt certain that he'd value this one—his reaction surpassed my fondest expectations; for instantly he was wild with joy, flinging his arms around me, then pitching them about Eben, and exclaiming in three or four different languages, much to stodgy William's amazement—the latter having followed us to see what was up.

Up, down, and around the mare, rubbing her face, speaking Romany words in her ear, rigging up the bridle and throwing on the saddle, he was a whirlwind of excitement; while the mare for her part seemed as much taken as he, warming to his attentions and nuzzling inquiringly at him, or breathing and muttering as if in answer to his cries. Then they were off at a trot down the drive, navigating the new crests of snow—Jim without hat, muffler or gloves; and where they went none of us knew, for they disappeared somewhere up the Point Road, and were gone so long we went back to the house—Eben and I delightedly chuckling, and William looking tight-waisted as ever.

When at last man and horse came back up the drive, kicking up a froth of snow, dinner was already well underway; and I had to excuse myself, don hat and coat, and fetch Jim bodily in from the stable. Catching him by the collar, prying bucket and brush from his hand, I hauled him vigorously back to the table, where exasperated Anne was waiting: otherwise he would surely have spent the day in the barn.

At the table he was in excellent spirits, sparking conversation, amusing the children, even unbending Charlottle and William, scarlet-cheeked and brilliant-eyed; and after the meal, as we retired into the study, he persevered in the same vein: running on about the virtues of his horse, whom he'd already christened Dee—after a favorite river in Wales—and entertaining himself by trying to set William drunk. A teetotaler, William was drinking punch, which I myself saw Jim spike with the sherry; and checking a grin, I sat by, innocent, sipping my own hard-earned brandy and water, while Jim assiduously tended the bar. Becoming at first more conversational, then more given to jest, then to gestures and laughter, William gradually emerged from his shell, Jim slyly, stealthily encouraging his glass; and finally there was a wholly new man before us—not the retiring, stuffy banker, one of the first men on earth to bore me, but a shrill-voiced, animated reveler, prone to flights of aggrandizement and fancy, or to bursts of wheezing hilarity.

Not content with having created a spectacle in my study, Jim somehow inveigled us all out of doors, where he got William up on a pair of snowshoes; and while Eben and I lay helplessly back in a snow bank, gasping with uncontrollable laughter, he paraded poor Will back and forth, like a penguin navigating a hot stove-top. Since William had spent a lifetime at a desk, and had hardly so much as wet his boots in the slush; since Robertson himself was a novice, having only donned snowshoes the first time the past fortnight, it was hard to say which of the two of them was the more outlandish; and though it might have been the brandy, I could have sworn that, at the kitchen window, Charlotte and Anne were giggling behind the lace curtains.

Figuring he'd easily made my day, Jim at last took pity on William, and helped him jovially back to the house; then emerging once more, he took his leave with Eben, predictably by way of the stable.

Bidding me good day—lavishing affection on Dee—he underwent one of his characteristic about-faces in mood; and suddenly quiet, he reached into his coat pocket, and shyly slipped a small box in my hand. "Here's somethin' for you—it ain't much," he appended, with a lowness of tone which betokened deep feeling; then sparkling-eyed and bright-faced once again, he went tromping off with Eben, their laughter echoing in the still woods.

Not wanting to open the box before the others—desiring to clear my head anyhow of the brandy, and the reverberations of the children's noise—I went down to the deck at the edge of the dune, and brushed the snow from the planks of the bench. It was a fine afternoon, the sun shining full on the big, unmarked drifts, and the wind gentling in from the southern points of the compass: its cat's-paws, and the sun's rays, almost warm on my face. My hands fumbling, I quickly opened the box, and found on the top of a layer of cotton, a note; my heart giving a bound, I picked it up and read:

> "Dear Ben: I told you there was nothing left of my mothers's, but that wasn't exactly completely true. When Tornapo put back the things that I'd taken, the night before she was to be buried, he didn't find her golden locket, which I'd already slipped inside my sleeve. I've carried it about in my trunk all these years; but now I'd rather that you should have it. If you look inside it, you'll find a paper, and on it, my true name—the one I was given at birth by my father. Every Rom child has such a secret— it's whispered in his ear when he's born, to deceive any evil spirit about the child's real identity. When I last saw my father, he whispered mine again, so that I should always know it, no matter where my travels took me. It's the name of his favorite Welsh poet. As soon as you read it, be sure to burn it The two little drawings were made by my aunt. (Fenella). She was very apt with a pen.
>   Merry Christmas! —Jim."

My eyes were so blurred when I finished this that I could scarcely see to fold it, and lift the cotton on which it had rested. There lay the locket, shining on some yellowed paper. I could see at once it was old, far older than Jim: probably it had been used, for one purpose or another, amongst the Rom for generations. Its smooth oval shape was without ornamentation, save for the pattern, delicately etched, on the front; but it scarcely had need of decoration, as it was obviously exquisitely crafted, wrought—like its chain—of the finest gold. Laying it reverently in my palm, I picked up the papers on which it had been bedded, and unfolded them with trembling fingers: to my unspeakable joy, two small pictures sprang out, sketches I knew at once were of Jim as a boy.

The first portrayed him as a child of two, showing just his cherubic head and shoulders; and all that was fatherly and protective in me rose up at once to block my throat. He was already remarkably beautiful, not just with the irresistible purity of children, but with the poise and awareness which gave promise of the man. His dark hair was silken and waved about his face, and his features were rounded and babyish; but his forehead was already wide, his brows fine and straight, and his eyes large and full of a kind of urgent eagerness, precisely the look I saw so often on Jim. There was something else as well—something which lurked about his half-smile, or permeated his expression: a mischievious knowing, as if the child himself was subtly aware of his charms.

The other picture showed him at six or seven, and must have been rendered out of doors: it looked as if he had just been running, and stopped obediently for the sketch. His features were more boyish and defined, his dark hair longer, almost to his open collar; and everything about him from his tangled tresses, his wind-rippled shirt and rumpled trousers, to his scarcely-restrained bare feet, suggested an arrested motion.

Eyes wet, I looked up, the snow sparkling about me; I saw the bright sea, and the isles of the Mussel Ridges in the distance; but at the same time I saw the hillsides of Northern Wales, the flush of their heath and ling in the summer; I saw a dark-haired boy; saw him age; saw him run and look up at the sun; saw his life move forward and mingle with mine, as if there were now many tributaries between us, running in and out of time...as if, all along, I'd stood waiting like a river for them to reach me. Opening the locket, I lifted out the paper, and read the name, "Taliesin."

How long I sat there dreaming, gazing at the pictures streaming through my mind, or listening to the sound of this child's voice, I couldn't have said; but at last I realized I was very cold, almost frozen to the deck—suddenly saw my numb red hands, and felt the protest of my feet. Digging out a friction match, I struck it, and burned the evidence of Jim's name; took the locket and slipped it inside my collar, fastening the catch at my neck; carefully folded up the drawings, and hid them, with Jim's note, in my breast pocket; then standing up, I brushed off my pants, and squaring my cap, headed back for the house.

XVII

JAMES ROBERTSON
Cape Damaris-Valparaiso, Chile Jan. -March 1843

The following week found me caught up in Ben's world with a vengeance; for these were the last days before embarkation, and preparations were going forward at an accelerated pace. From Warren, Thomaston and Cape Damaris, an eccentric and varied cargo was being shipped in the hold under McCabe's supervision; mailbags were being taken down from their pegs and fetched from various exchanges; sea stores were being hauled in from the chandler's; spare rigging, timbers, spars and canvas were arriving from assorted lofts and sheds; cows, pigs, hens and ducks were coming in from surrounding farms, and being housed on deck in pens; and throughout town, in various sitting rooms and kitchens, seamen's trunks were being brought out, and neatly stocked with gear and sea togs.

In the midst of it all I began to see with vivid clarity my own distinct duties; and I dolefully perceived they'd be considerably more demanding than the brief obligations I'd met aboard *Amanda*, those few fleeting days before she foundered. For one thing, meticulous, exacting Ben wasn't the easy-going Tom; for another, starting the business from scratch here in port—an angle I'd missed, my short stint on *Amanda*—gave me the chance to appreciate the entire span of my duties. The bosun's locker with its pots of paint, ropes, blocks, tackles, marlin and sinnet; the pantry store with its casks of salt beef, salt pork and hard tack, its kegs of cider, molasses and ale, provisions to last a score of men several months; and above all the stowage for spare sails and canvas: all these were my particular province, their

broaching or doling out my concern; and as I went down their rows
with my pen and ledger, I was overwhelmed by what I was supposed
to keep track of.

If the lockers weren't enough, there'd be nine men under me;
and though Eben and I had already planned out our watches for the
minimum of friction, I felt a paternal responsibility such as I had never
experienced before; and with it came the reluctant comprehension
that I would have to step smartly to lead them. That our run would
take us around the Horn for most part in winter weather intimidated
me even more—every tale I'd ever heard of mountainous seas,
relentless head gales, ice floes, snow squalls, frozen hands and feet
coming back to me now with untimely clearness; and sitting down
on my bunk across the saloon from Ben's cabin—looking out my
lone porthole at the far horizon—I shook my head with wordless
disquiet, amazed at the lunacy of my undertaking.

Preparations were rendered even more hectic by private
considerations of my own; for now that we were so close to leaving,
lingering farewells were being spoken, in the form of dinners or the
exchange of keepsakes; and I suddenly found myself the focus of an
unexpected spurt of attention. The fussing of Sabrina and Sally—the
good-natured solicitousness of Keziah and Kate —I could manage;
but when I checked into my cabin one eve, prior to knocking
off for the day, and found on my mounted desk a small package,
containing a miniature of Damaris—an exquisite likeness etched in
enamel—I hadn't the least idea what to do. Returning it was out of
the question—an insult to her sensitive spirit; yet keeping it, the only
alternative, was bound to encourage expectations.

So far I'd managed to keep our acquaintance—the only genuine
friendship I'd ever had with a lady—on a fairly comradely level;
but her gift confirmed my growing suspicion—exacerbated by her
parents' attentions, and the suspect gestures of Cy and Amasa—that
her sentiments were something more than friendly. "Serious gals
like her fall hahd," Eben had already wryly warned me; and though
I hadn't paid him much mind, it suddenly looked like coming true.
Since I'd never had an experience with a woman like her—Rom *chis*
being coquettishly forward, but never frankly direct like Damaris—I

was utterly confounded by her manner; and I felt helpless to forestall her moves in a way which wouldn't result in stung feelings. Having not expected such developments at all—having never having imagined that I, a foreigner, a heathen, and more or less a pauper, as any number of townsfolk kept pointing out, would be a desirable match for anyone of any background—I was once again brought by the lee by her interest, and by the advances of her circle.

Being above all independent—finding it difficult enough to blend in with Melchett Bros., or to harmonize my will with Ben's— the revelation that others might have designs on my future, or that living here predisposed me toward certain ends, raised my hackles in no uncertain fashion; and along with my incredulity I began to feel a creeping, obstinate resistance. Yet—though Keziah aside, I cared little for the others—I had the sincerest regard for Damaris' feelings, over and above my own frustration; and I earnestly desired to spare her. All night I speculated how to respond to her gift, coming up with half a dozen notions; but whichever maneuver I considered, I made no perceivable headway.

Adept at starting my own rumors, I thought of adding fuel to the ones currently going—thought of hinting, perhaps, that I was already married; but I couldn't do so without offending the town's mores— without giving Ben in particular the wrong ideas, and tying my own hands at some point in the future. For the same reason I feared to say something vague, like "my heart is already given"; and at last, exasperated, I simply did nothing, finding a simple way to thank her, without committing myself or my feelings—and that done, I sped back post haste to *Charis*, and feverishly longed for embarkation.

My yearning to be off redoubled when, the Saturday noon before departure, I sat drinking at Eli's after knocking off for the weekend, and an eruption of sailors interrupted my tumbler. Looking up half-interested—hearing they'd just arrived by brig from Boston—I suddenly recognized one of them, a young seaman I'd encountered with Lomond in Ann Street; and the whole of my past straightaway assaulting me—every anxiety I'd put down since I'd come here re-assailing me in fresh doses—I precipitously rose from the table, got out in a hurry and rode Dee to Eben's, my heart a-hammer with my haste and panic.

Once in the sane surroundings of McCabe's kitchen, with reason reasserting itself and embarkation only two days off, I began to feel a little better, Eben as ever calm and reassuring; but even so I might have spent a restless weekend, hiding away with my nerves in tatters, if Ben hadn't come by just then with the cutter, on his way to the wharves to find me. "C'mon, let's go! We've got business in Warren—an' if ye set still an' manage not t' upset the sleigh, I'll treat ye t' a whale of a dinner!" So barking he climbed back into the cutter; and overjoyed to be on my way out of town—even gladder to be accompanied by him, and aboard a sleigh, a conveyance which till now I'd seldom ridden—I settled in beside him under the lap robe, giving Eben a wink and a wave as we drove off.

Our route taking us down the Point Road, which led straight back into town, then turning us up Ship Street at the busy square near the waterfront, I was assailed anew with consternation; but as we mounted the hill, leaving the town and harbor behind, and set out across country sparsely inhabited by farms, their snow-covered rooflines glistening in the afternoon sun, my veins coursed more and more swiftly with joy. Beside me Ben—wrapped in a pea coat, with perpetual pilot's cap and muffler, pipe clamped in mouth and reins poised in rough gloves—looked wordlessly smug and cheerful, as if he too were glad to snatch one last chance together before shipping out on Monday; and as the hillsides and firs slowly slipped by he glanced over at me and gave me a grin.

Riding together, uphill and down dell, the harness bells jingling, the runners sighing, and the northwest wind stinging our faces, we made it to Warren in a couple of hours, stopping first at Fiddler's Green, an eating tavern, where Ben treated me as promised to a magnificent dinner, the last we were to have in some time. Our appetites whetted by the winter air, we set to without undue talk or compunction, both of us shamelessly gorging on roast beef with half a dozen accompaniments; then staggering out, we wrapped up Ben's business, picking up the shipment he'd come for—one bag of mail and, to my amazement, $12,000 in specie, which he nonchalantly stuffed under the sleigh seat. Clucking at the horse again we were off, our shoulders and knees brushing under the lap robe; and silently peaceful we re-traced our route, while evening slowly deepened to night, and a host of stars took shape in the heavens.

In the pristine dark, with no sound but the sleigh bells, or the slipping of our blades in the snow—past the hushed, shrouded hills, their slopes blue in the moonlight, their valleys and groves folded in shadow—down the slow-winding road, driving now along pine-boughs, drifting now beside homesteads a-glimmer with candles—we glided homeward too awed for a murmur, too pained for even an exchange of glances; and not even when we drew up at Eben's and Ben helped me down, then saw me slowly to the door, did either of us break the silence.

Despite the ice in the harbor, which Melchett Bros. had to have broken, we got off as scheduled the fifth day of January, in a bitter wind and a cloud of flurries. Concerned about visibility Ben cursed the weather, stomping about as the crew came aboard; but I blessed its power of concealment, for bundled up in my pea coat and sea boots, with my hat pulled low and lashed on with sinnet, I felt inconspicuous on deck, even though a crowd—undeterred by the weather—had massed on the wharves to witness proceedings. Somewhere in the throng stood Damaris, whom I'd glimpsed in sober bonnet and mantle; and somewhere, perhaps, lounged the nameless sailor I'd spied two days ago at Eli's, come to study the innovative lines of *Charis*. In the front ranks I could plainly see Tom and Jean, swathed to the eyes in woolens and mufflers, and raised in the arms of a couple of uncles; and near them—their great coats flapping in wind gusts, their dark cloaks and mantles dusted with snowflakes—I spotted Galen and Sarah, old Abigail with her stout walnut cane, Keziah on John's arm, her brothers and their wives—indeed the whole Melchett clan, even Anne.

As Eben came forward to check on the rigging, the cat and fish tackles, all fair for business—as Ben bawled the kick-off, and we hove short on the anchor, me straining with the men at the windlass—as we hoisted and set topsails and braced the yards, then manned the

windlass again, tripping the anchor—as we raised the jib and felt her
pay off, the whole ship by now a-echo with chanteys—we heard the
roar of the crowd's approval, heart-making cheers behind the snow
curtain. The steeples and roof peaks gradually blurring, then fading
in the eddies and flurries, the town on its arena of hills fell behind
us; and with them went Damaris, the sailor, all trace and sound of
friends and kin, departing now from the bleak, wind-swept wharfway.

In their place we heard the toll of the bell buoys, their erratic clang
growing steadily louder, then dwindling as we left them astern; and
as we cleared the protective arms of the harbor—as we gave a wide
berth to the shoal round the Point, and felt *Charis* roll with the open
bay—the Mussel Ridge Channel hove into view, island beyond island
pale-hued in the snowfall. Making our way along the white-flurried
spruce, brine-stained granite ledges and slate-colored seaways, we at
last braced away for the roaring Atlantic, carrying as much sail as we
could in the quartering wind; and trying to get accustomed again to
the cold, to stiffened hands and stinging face, and to the pitching and
swaying of working aloft, I felt the indomitable rise of my spirits—
not just for the magnificence of our maneuvers, but for the prospect
of the untasted before us, and for the grace of unresolved cares left
behind.

The first leg of the voyage saw winter weather, unrelenting gales varied
only by compass—by the direction and intensity of the wind, and
the thickness and duration of the snow squalls. Miserable topsides,
our hands cracked and bleeding, and our spells of rest insufficient,
we were already asking ourselves why we'd shipped; but below in
my own little cabin near Ben's, in the routine peculiar to inmates
aft, I found satisfaction in the change of events. It was a novelty to
have my own private place, comparable to my room ashore, after the
strains and confines of the crowded foc's'le; and I liked the privilege
of the louvered door, the workspace of the desk mounted on the
bulkhead, the built-in bunk with its drawers down each side, and its
space for my sea chest in the center. Something in the simplicity of
the appointments reminded me of austere Ben; and though the two

of us were separated by the saloon, as well as by our distinction of duty, I already felt as if we were veritably housing together, sharing quarters and necessities as we had camping.

Like the prerogatives of my cabin, the routine aft was on the whole pleasant—permitting me to see Ben more often, and in a more casual setting, than I'd supposed when I'd first considered my berth; for though he and Eben, following maritime tradition, ate together while my watch was on deck, he was always still at table when I came below, taking coffee and going over his slates as I supped. At such moments when we were both free, we shared the sofa in the saloon, he studying charts or writing, his spectacles a-glint in the lamplight, and me making tentative sketches of Abigail, a comforter wrapped around me for warmth.

My position was made all the happier by the fact that here was none of the disdain for the second mate manifested on other ships— none of the pecking order which would have relegated me last; for not only was there no hint of superiority in Ben's and Eben's personal arrangements with me, but even Shad and Haggai were solicitous of my welfare, helping me with my cleaning and laundry, reserving plenty of choice food for me, and setting on the board, now and then, a bit of smoked fish or pumpkin pie, well-advertised favorites of mine. After the adequate but unimaginative fare of the foc's'le— salt beef, hard tack, pea soup and beans, dressed up every so often by molasses or plum duff—the menu aft was much to my liking: not so luxuriant as on the liners, where masters sat to meals in their coattails, and second mates were doled out the leavings—but hardy and tasty nonetheless, quintessential downeast cooking.

The general round of my work was to my liking too: short sleeps, short stints on deck—except when all hands were battling topsails, or wearing ship in heavy weather—and, since it was far too inclement for leisure on deck, short spells off-duty below for mending and washing, sketching or carving. Indeed if it were not for the cold, and the mischance of last-minute passengers—who'd been housed in the sick-bay next to Ben's cabin—I could have been wholly content, at least below; but the cold was a factor hard to forget, and the passengers, first cousins of Anne's bound for Chili on business, even more so. Man, wife and child, all three were a trial to the rest of us aft—particularly to Ben, who reckoned passengers the worst possible part of a master's duty, and who regarded them as considerably less than human.

Geared to doing his own work since boyhood, he couldn't begin to fathom Phillip, who sat reading his interminable financial journals with his feet up on the bolted ottoman, when he wasn't confined to his berth seasick; couldn't comprehend Priscilla, who paged the fashion plates of Godey's Lady's book with a vial of anti-bilious pills within reach, when she wasn't pestering Haggai in the pantry; couldn't understand even Sidney, a peaked, over-dressed lad of ten, who pushed his toy soldiers about underfoot all morning, and plagued him with incessant questions at mealtime. From Ben's point of view all three should have been working, paying their passage in labor, not cash—Phillip as a deck hand, his wife as cook, steward or seamstress, and the lad as a cabin boy; and he had no patience to boot with their poor seamanship. Seasickness he regarded as a constitutional weakness, as sure a sign of flawed character as sin; and it sat ill with him that he was expected to entertain them at meals and see to their needs, when he had but the scantest respect for their persons.

That they were passengers and had nothing in common with him were not the only strikes against them; for there were times when I suspected, from an impatient glance or a word let fall, that what Ben resented most of all was simply their presence at the table or sofa, when the two of us could have been alone together; and I couldn't but concur with his frustration, when so many of our duties already worked for our distance.

If matters were—passengers aside—essentially pleasant below, they were far otherwise on deck; for besides the bitterness of the temperature, there were the complexities of my duties, and the challenges of achieving tasks in foul weather. In the sub-freezing gales the wind at our bow seemed to cut through our multitudinous layers—stout-webbed drawers and socks, woolen trowsers and frocks, knit jerseys, thick pea coats, hats, mufflers and sea boots, all very awkward to work aloft in—like relentless blades through bits of tissue; and it wreaked havoc as well with our bare hands. What with the snow and the sleet and the surge-swept decks, we were seldom ever dry, there being no surcease from the chilling damp even in our longed-after berths; and the brine quickly galled our ankles and feet. As an officer I fared slightly better than the crew, since my cabin was small and located aft, neither so cold nor so wet as the wide, exposed forecastle; but even so I too was seldom warm, unless I lingered by Shad's stove in the pantry, the one source of heat on the ship abaft the galley; and I too waged a continuous battle to dry out clothes and gear before needed, or to thaw my frozen limbs between watches.

Besides the bitterness of the weather, there was the harshness of the work—my job obliging me to be the fastest and best workman, both on the running and standing rigging, no matter how numbed or fatigued I felt; to be the first to pass the weather earring, if we were called to reef topsails, reefing and shaking out being near-constant trials; to oversee the work aloft or out on the jib boom, whether that be shortening sail or repairing rigging, perilous tasks in the pitching and blowing; and to keep up with Ben's orders, passed along to me via McCabe each morning. There being no sail maker expressly shipped to cut canvas, the job fell to me and a couple of other seamen if a particular sail needed replacement; and it was my task as well to keep the key to the bosun's locker—to dole out such tools or seizing stuff as required by any given repair to the rigging.

And finally there was the loneliness of my station; for when work was not going forward due to the weather, it was my lot now to keep to the quarterdeck, alone and to windward if Ben was below, or across from him to leeward whenever he surfaced; and I missed the comraderie of the forecastle, the skylarking round the mess table and the long yarns spun at nightfall. I even missed my quarrels with Howland; for though he—as the ablest hand of Eben's watch—kept me relentlessly on my toes, striving to beat me to the yardarms when all hands reefed both topsails, or to outmatch my work on the rigging, we seldom ever came face to face, or found the chance to hiss an exchange.

In my own watch I counted myself lucky to have Paul and

Roan, Jack Tupper's cousin Garrett and Damaris' brother Mathias, along with a tried and true contingent of Coombses, Winslows and Wingates; but it frustrated me that I had so little contact with them, save to direct their work or shout a few words aloft. Coming into finer weather—leaving Hatteras astern, and raising a succession of beneficent blue skies—matters began to look up a little, all hands rejoicing in shedding cumbersome clothing, and manipulating ship with limbs thawed and limber; but still it was my first lengthy taste of the unremitting responsibility and loneliness aft; and I looked over at Ben pacing to windward with a new latitude of understanding.

By the time we caught the NE trades, a few degrees south of the Tropic of Cancer, we'd finally begun to hit our stride—barefoot, straw-hatted, shirt-sleeved and duck-trowsered, *Charis* carrying a full press in the fine, steady winds; and with far less adjusting of canvas required—with the cat roaming the deck, the livestock sunning, and a fleet of laundry a-flap in the halliards, a harmonious good will prevailed over all. Coming up on the poop at last to take the air, Priscilla in her billowing dresses, and Phillip and the lad in their linen suits, had a surprisingly civilizing effect on the vessel; while Eben and even Ben—always preoccupied on deck, bent on enforcing order and business—seemed given to unexpectedly light touches.

As the three of us had settled into our routine on the quarterdeck—far more formal and structured than our round below—we'd cautiously eased into our new relationships with one another: Ben and I at first tiptoeing around each other, uneasy and wary as two pugilists in a ring, and Eben tactfully refereeing between us. Accustomed to receiving orders from Ben through Eben as a foremast hand, I found it an adjustment to receive them directly—a challenge to interpret them not as personal dictates but as motions in the chain of command; and I struggled to overcome the feeling that I was his subordinate even harder than I had when I'd shipped as a seaman.

Determined to get out to Valparaiso and back by the early part of May at the latest, Ben tolerated no let-up in our pace fore or aft; and I labored under the stress of stretching myself to meet the onslaught of his demands, torn between wanting to facilitate progress, rebelling against his willful manner, and wondering if he ever noticed my efforts.

Despite the offhand informality of the whole ship—despite the respect and regard with which orders aft were dispensed—he was not only clearly in charge, but a man who clearly liked to take charge; and his sense of command frequently rubbed me the wrong way. Yet even at my most irate moments I had to frankly confess to myself, in the sweet privacy of my small cabin, that he was far better fitted than I to direct; that in spite of my habitual show of resistance, I was unarguably drawn to his hand—longed to surrender to it altogether as I had when I was ill with fever, or too fatigued or intoxicated to dissemble.

For his part, he seemed always on the brink of disquiet, as if trying to conjecture what freak of behavior I might take it into my head to perpetrate next, and bracing himself to meet or forestall it. My brief stints at the wheel he'd been willing to arrange, even though such employment for the second mate constituted a breach of long-standing tradition; but when—one Sunday eve on a warm, breezy dog watch, with the carmine sun going down in a peach-colored sea—I put in my free time with my men on the foc's'le, swapping jests and playing the fiddle, he summarily dispatched McCabe to fetch me aft, where he reminded me in no uncertain terms that my place was no longer on the foc's'le, even if I happened to be off-duty. Fighting the frustration of my ambiguous standing, I tried to campaign for wider latitude; but no sooner had I begun to launch my rebuttal than the line came down between his brows, and his eyes flashed steel-grey with annoyed impatience.

To his mind our three positions as officers were drawn out with indelible clarity, far more so on deck than below; and though as master he had virtual control of the vessel—though he could have re-written the rules in any fashion he wanted—he went by the book in the vast majority of cases, and expected the rest of us to follow suit. Yet—even though, perhaps, he scarcely knew it—he too chafed at the bonds of tradition, he too worried the leash of his office; and in no way did I see this more clearly than in the manner with which he handed me orders, his dictates more than once going beyond the maintenance of the ship to circumscribe my personal actions. That my protection and safety were his objective did nothing to abate my resentment, or excuse the abuse of his prerogatives; and as the voyage wore on—as we barreled along, every stitch and seam of the canvas drawing—our contest of wills over his mandates flared more and more frequently into the open.

Over no matter did we battle with greater insistence than the question of my work on the jib boom. Before Hatteras I'd felt him watch every move that I made whenever I assisted my men at this station—indisputably one of the most hazardous on any vessel; but he'd never attempted to restrain me, it being my plain duty to supervise my watch in furling the jib in heavy weather. But now that we skimmed lightly along, close-hauled, in a considerably improved clime, he directed me through McCabe to leave the three jibs to any of my ablest hands, Darcy or Paul or occasionally Coombs: the first real indication he'd given that his dreams of last summer still haunted him.

Conceiving it to be my job to superintend such work as commonly went forth on the jib boom—furling the sails or taking off the bonnets, or making repairs to the standing rigging—from the jib boom and not from any place else, no matter how clement the weather, I made up my mind to disobey; and I could feel the wrath of his gaze all the way from the quarterdeck some 160 feet away, the next time I hauled out over the bowsprit cap with Paul and a couple of the others.

What might have happened if matters had been allowed to run their course—whether he would have dispatched McCabe again, or even marched forward himself to collar me, and risked causing a certain sensation—or whether he would simply have swallowed his pride, knowing full well that I was right, and that he'd be unable to upbraid me before my watch for doing what was plainly my duty—I was never to discover; for suddenly, as I struggled to help Paul with the seizing, Roan at the helm failed to meet a sea, we lurched and directly I lost my footing. Such incidents had happened before so often that instantly I figured I could wrangle my way out of this one, even though the bottom had dropped out of my stomach; but to my dismay I couldn't recover the footrope, lost my grasp at the lashings before Paul could grab me, and felt myself falling an interminable time before I finally smashed into the water.

Stunned to feel myself plunging under—fighting to the surface, amazed to find myself off the vessel, disconnected from it or from anything solid—realizing I actually had to swim, to keep on top of the seas by some method or other—I felt a panic such as I had not experienced since the night of the fight with Lomond; and forcing myself to remember the lessons off Ben's beach—thanking God I was barefoot, with no heavy sea boots to drag me under—I treaded and splashed for all I was worth.

Immediately stopping headway, *Charis* drifted back, while every bench, board, buoy, plank and life-ring aboard her came flying out in my direction, and a tumult of cries, calls, commands and answers—amongst them Melchett's curt, brusque orders—came riding out to me on the wind. Striking out for one of the objects—alternately swimming, then giving way to fatigue, or momentary bouts of panic, and resting myself by floating spread-eagled—I made it at last to a bright-painted buoy, even as the quarterboat was lowered away; and overcome by relief, or by the long, even swells, on which I rolled and dipped like a mallard, I was all at once uncharacteristically seasick, straightaway losing my mid-day dinner. Thankful that Melchett was too far off to see me, I fastened myself like a barnacle to the buoy, giving a hail to the quarterboat to windward; and sighting me from the broad crest of a long sea, those aboard signaled me with an answering halloo, and a jubilant wave of an oar at the heavens.

From there it was simply a matter of awaiting their approach, clambering aboard into Paul's kindly hands, and sending up a signal to *Charis*, which, having sternway, was steadily drifting toward us, Melchett's clear, strident orders discernible over the waters. By the time we'd hove into plain view of the others, and positioned the quarterboat to board her, I'd recollected some of my wits, enough to disguise my unnerved condition; and when I dropped at last onto the planks of *Charis,* I was as cool as tradition demanded, managing not to kiss the deck in my gladness.

"Damn good thing somebody taught ye t' swim," was all Melchett had to say about it, on his way back to his post and his pacing; but there was a quiver to his gravelly voice as he said it—and a glint to his eye which clearly informed me that I hadn't heard the last of the matter.

That I hadn't misread him I wasn't long in discovering; for as soon as I emerged from my cabin—in dry clothes, and more or less in my right mind—there he was at the saloon table, his arms folded obstinately over his chest, the corners of his mouth turned downward, and his broad, sunburnt brow more obdurate than ever. Cocking a disgruntled eye at me, he indicated a chair for me with his foot; and suppressing a sigh I took it, wishing Priscilla or her irrepressible son would suddenly put in an appearance. One or the other could usually be depended upon for anything like an interruption; but now, just when a sudden spell of malaise or an onslaught toy soldiers would have been genuinely useful, neither of them erupted to spare me.

Finding me reluctant to meet his eye, Melchett took me by the chin, in a pinch neither pleasant nor respectful; and seeing that he now had my full attention, he proceeded to unburden his mind.

"I don't want y' out on the jib boom again unless it's absolutely necessary—thought I'd made that clear once b'fore; but since I didn't, I'll spell it out now: in foul weather, or in case of serious injury t' the boom or the stays, which won't admit of a lesseh hand or delay, you've got the job; otherwise, you'hre t' send Darcy or Paul, or anyone else y' think c'n handle the work."

Having plainly said all he considered essential, he prepared to get to his feet; but—stung by his high-handed pinch, and his manner—I stuck out my chin before he could rise, and declared with as much calm as I could muster:

"Then you'll have t' replace me, for I won't do it."

As if certain that he'd heard me incorrectly, or that I had taken leave of my senses, he stared at me for an instant dumbly; then obviously abandoning both suppositions, he broke into an open glower—a glare which conveyed unbridled impatience, confounded fury and exasperation more vividly than any gesture or statement.

"You know yourself I've got t' be out there the next time—if I'm not, the men'll think I'm afraid; an' anyway, you know it's my duty," I said shrewdly, before he could come up with a volley.

"Well, damned it I can't change what's youhr duty!" he exploded, with all the ire of a man who will not be thwarted. "What else have I got this infernal job for if I can't change a couple o' rules?…As f'r what the men say—small comfort *that'll* be next time, when ye've slipped youhr cable for Davy Jones! Y' hear it ev'ry day from incomin' linehs, or any otheh ship that tries t' make time like us: it's the second mate that's lost off the yahdarms or jib boom b'cause it's the second mate who's the most exposed, the second mate who takes the most risks. Well, I'm not makin' a note o' youhr loss in the logbook; so hang back a little when you ain't so needed, an' give the goddam odds a chance!"

"You're *afraid* t' let me go out," I challenged, out of a sudden longing to hear him say that he cared—out of a perverse determination to goad him into a confession.

"Afraid, hell!" he flared, cold to my tactics. "If you'hre d'termined t' shorten the odds, that's youhr business. But it's my job t' see to it we make good time, good money an' a completely safe passage, at least as fahr as men's lives are concerned; an' I'm goin' t' see to it I do it."

"An it's *my* job t' lead my watch on the lower yards, or out on the jibboom when work's goin' forward; an' I'm goin' t' see to it *I* do it," I countered, furious he'd managed to slip out of my hands.

"*Youhr* job's what I tell you it is!" he bawled.

"My job's what I *know* it t' be, what custom on both sides o' the Atlantic's always made it out t' be. I tell you, if you won't let me do what I know I'm supposed to, I'll resign an' you'll have t' replace me. Get Howland—he's dyin' t' ship in my berth."

He glared at me with the same withering glare I'd seen him send Anne when she crossed him—but I met it unperturbably head-on; and for a moment we contested our wills thus, speechless, as if words were no longer adequate to convey our contention. As he probed me in the eye and plumbed my whole mind and purpose—as I searched him in return, stripping off the covers of his thoughts and defenses—I saw in his face a succession of layers: wrath, resolve, exasperation, burden, honesty, regard, and finally, simply a naked anxiety and worry. It was at the sight of the last that I almost backed down; but I held fast until the end—and he, perceiving my unyielding intent, actually broke into a half-smile: one corner of his mouth going up in something between grim resignation and fondness.

"All right, mate—but damned if I won't leave ye in the drink the next time," he muttered, releasing my eye with a sudden softness; then as if afraid what gentleness he might reveal if he lingered, he heaved himself up out of his chair, and at once returned to the deck.

Yet our confrontations on deck made our casual contacts below all the sweeter and warmer by contrast; and as we fetched the Line 21 days out from Cape Damaris, and humbugged along in maddening light airs and calms, I began to count our days' successes not so much in miles run or sails hoisted, but in the latitudes raised on him as a person. Shipping aft gave me more private glimpses of him than I'd ever had at any time before, save camping; and in between our bouts of contention, I employed myself by looking out for new glances. That he'd actually begun to leave a few things of his lying about—under the influence, perhaps, of my perpetual clutter—I'd already noticed with appreciation; and now in my rare spells below in the heat, as I stumbled upon his pens and slate pencils, pipe rack and bits of dirty laundry, I welcomed these new familiarities of him, charmed.

Once, finding a couple of his shirts laid out for Shad to mend— the habitual serviceable, threadbare plaids he'd been wearing in warm climes ever since I had met him—I settled down beside them under the skylight, the early morning breeze in my hair, and McCabe's geraniums nodding beside me; and having some free time I proceeded to mend them, a curious joy thrilling me at their contact. Very handy by now with a needle, I made short work of the rents and loose seams; then, shirts aside, I even stitched up a prodigious pair of drawers, with a pleasure of service I'd never expected to know.

On other occasions I played practical jokes, when I knew they wouldn't disrupt shipboard routine; for I enjoyed watching him step out of character as sober master whenever he encountered Phillip's silk hose in his sock drawer, or his spectacles perched on the beak of the carved eagle. But above all I treasured the personal glimpses one attains of another when one lives close to hand—the snatches and bits by which I knew his body: the sights of him bent over his charts on a hot night, his collar open and his sleeves rolled up, and the sheen of sweat glazing his temple; the glances of him asleep in his cabin, easy to sneak now with the doors lashed open; rarer glimpses of him emerging from a bath in the copper tub, wearing little more than trowsers and slippers, his bare, oaken back carved with broad expanses. Proud of my own strength and capable build—determined to hold my own up on deck—I knew at such moments I was no match for him; and I yearned to cast myself on his rough bulk the way a lone seaman yearns for a sound mooring.

What he felt himself—when he wasn't furious with me for some fluke or confrontation on deck—I could only guess, for he was a man of few words, and even fewer affectionate gestures; and the hectic shipboard routine, his own demanding round, and the all-pervading presence of Phillip and family, added to censor his regard still further. That he savored our times alone together, by the taffrail looking out on some spectacle of the waters—the heaving and blowing of a lone whale, the slow, silent wheeling of the constellations on the velvety sheen of the night sea; that he relished our moments together over morning coffee—me recording distances and sail changes on the slates, he making a list of day's jobs for Eben—I knew, from the feel of the almost tangible bond between us, and the confessional warmth of his glances over his spectacles. In such moments of splendor or homely day's work, his unshakeable devotion pulsed on his features; but whether the course of his feeling ran in the same channels, and to the same ungovernable depths that mine did—even whether I'd be ready to meet them, should he ever give them expression—I was no surer now than I had been in Maine.

Once, waking suddenly in the middle watch below in my berth—feeling an eye on my face and my bare back, as I lay on my side in the heat of a Line night—I felt as if someone were looking at me; heard, as I stirred, a firm, barefoot tread departing from nigh my open doorway; but I didn't dare open my eyes, and never knew if it was he. Haggai and Shad, even Phillip and Priscilla, all got up and walked about in the night, sometimes to visit the water closet, sometimes to take the air under the skylight; and since all of our cabins, and the pantry and hallway which led to such quarters as the carpenter's and cook's and steward's, all opened out into the saloon, our paths as a simple matter of course criss-crossed before one another's doors. It mightn't have been anyone but Phillip, too restless to sleep—since he never worked—taking inventory instead of the cabins, to see whom he might find on deck for a smoke.

Yet if I couldn't be sure that Ben looked on me as I looked on *him*, these hot night on the Line, I couldn't doubt other clues to his feelings, let fall by chance or design by the wayside; and I'd learned to measure the fortune of day's runs by the meaning and fervor of their message. Displays of affection were not common between us, as if he feared to weaken them through overuse—as if he felt still too awkward to yield them, or too uncertain what to make of my mood; but he couldn't restrain the speech of his hands, even though they didn't touch me; and I could read much in their big, square shapes as they hovered beside mine over the day's slates, or handed me a cup for my coffee. Nor did they always fall short of their mission; for one early morn, as I sat exhausted at the saloon table, played out from a night-long battle on deck; as I sat with my head buried in my arms, and my bare feet luxuriating in the carpet, I heard a step in the entry behind me, and felt a warm palm on the back of my neck.

"Ye've got the toughest job on board, mate; don't think that I don't know it," came Ben's voice, his fingers kindly gentling my hair; then helping me to my feet, he saw me to my cabin, with hands which steadied and eased like no other—hands knowing as any master touch at a helm.

If the course of my friendship with Ben was jagged—its stretches of fair sea punctuated with storm swells—the run of my relationship with Eben was steady, as calm and sustaining as halcyon sailing; and I frequently rested myself in the latter. As the days passed I found

I was getting to know Eben better, in settings and ways I'd never encountered before; and I rejoiced in the moments which brought us together. It was true that I never saw him below—our two watches alternating so that he was always on deck, whenever I was free to descend; but since our changing of the guard obliged us to overlap on the quarterdeck while the helm was relieved, the course for steering given, and orders for the day's work repeated, I seldom parted him without a few minutes' chat, and an unfailing sense of support.

That he was as efficient in his role as mediator on deck as he was in his cabin ashore, I very early on discovered, he not only saving me from various pitfalls I mightn't have avoided without his tactful aid, but passing on to me—to my grateful pleasure—Ben's anxiety over my fall from the jib boom, or his gratification at my workmanship. That Eben was utterly free from the condescension with which first mates were commonly afflicted—that he looked to me as a partner, one whose contributions he could build and depend on—I'd also discovered within a few days; and I reveled in the alliance between us. But it was in his unexpected capacity as ship's preacher that I really saw new slants to his nature; and the first time I heard him tackle a service I listened from my surreptitious seat, transfixed—amazed by the scenes raised on his homely visage.

Since *Charis* was essentially a sober New England ship of the most old-fashioned variety—the product of local enterprise and mores, dry as a tea-shop, at least at sea—and reflective of various religious principles, Sundays were always staunchly observed: there being not only a surcease from labor, aside from the changes needed made in the sails, but a worship service between decks for those who wished to attend. All of the men having been strictly raised in any one of several denominations, the services were generally pretty well filled; and as always I marveled at the place religion had in their undemonstrative lives—at the importance it probably had in Ben's, though as with his affection for me, I never knew for certain how deep it went, or what shape it took, since he couldn't convey it.

Indeed for this very reason he'd always shuffled the responsibility for services— rightfully his—onto Eben, or anyone else who would take it; and Spooner, till now, had usually led worship. In Spooner's absence the job had fallen to Eben, who'd accepted somewhat dolefully, claiming he felt ill-equipped; and curious to find out what he was saying—word having it that his first two meetings went off well; eager to discover more about Ben's religion in a setting less intimidating than church, I accordingly took my place in the back row of a cluster of benches laid out between the fine freight and sail locker: Ben being on deck with a skeleton crew.

As soon as I sidled in and sat down—heads turning right and left at my unexpected appearance, all hands having by now given me up to the Old Harry—Eben saw me and sent me a warm glance, with a pleased, contemplative look on his face; and while I busied myself with trying to look unobtrusive, he sat on for a few minutes quiet, delaying a start even though we'd all gathered, as if rearranging his words for the day.

After a couple of hymns—which the others knew from memory, and to which I mutely listened—Eben hauled himself to his feet, fetched his testament from under his seat, placed it on the upended hogshead which served for the morning as a rude lectern, and—looping one hand through the strap above, *Charis* wallowing miserably in the dead air—calmly proceeded to address us. "The text t'day, boys," he embarked, his splendidly prosy, unadorned visage even more understated than usual, "is on the potteh an' the clay; an' since there's actually two or three separate passages I'd like t' submit t' ye this mornin', a couple from Isaiah, an' one from Jeremiah, I'll read 'em to'getheh stem t' stern."

Screwing up his brow he proceeded to intone: "Yet, O Lord, thou art ourh Fatheh; we are the clay, and thou ouhr potteh; we are all the work of thy hand..." Then turning a few pages: "Woe to him who strives with his Makeh, an earthen vessel with the potteh! Does the clay say to him who fashions it, 'What are you making?' or 'Youhr work has no handles'?..." And finally jumping ahead to a last mark: "The Word that came to Jeremiah, from the Lord: 'Arise, and go down to the potteh's house, and there I will let you heahr my words.' So I went down to the potteh's house, and there he was working at his wheel. And the vessel he was making of clay was spoiled in the potteh's hand, and he reworked it into anotheh vessel, as it seemed good to the potteh to do. Then the word of the Lord came to me: 'O house of Israel, can I not do with you as the potteh has done?' says the Lord. 'Behold, like the clay in the potteh's hand, so you are in my hand, O Israel.'"

Closing his Testament with a thoughtful expression—rubbing the bridge of his nose with his free hand, and shoving the brown locks back from his forehead—he commenced his bit of a sermon: "Now, boys, as most o' ye know, the usual thing t' do with these here texts is t' point out that the Lord is in chahge, an' that us folks is as clay t' his will. We was clay when he made us, an' breathed life int' us; an' now that we're walkin' about he's molding us still. He's the skippeh, so t' speak; we're the ship, an' he shapes oweh course. Or again, he's the shipwright, an' we're the timbers; he selects the right plank for each job, steams it or hews it an' sets it in place. If he don't like the looks o' what he's shapin' up—if we don't lay the course, that's t' say, if we ain't in good trim, or if we don't take the right curve afteh we're fetched from the steameh, due t' some flaw or stubborn streak or whateveh, why, he's free t' mash up the works, wad it back up an' staht oveh again, just like a tyke does with a ball o' clay.

"Now that's a threat, boys, t' sort of keep us in line—just like them furrows that plows Melchett's brow is a threat he'll set us back on our heels, if we don't toe the mark here on board." A gust of wry laughter swept over the rows, every man in the room knowing Melchett's brow well; and Eben's eye as he surveyed us twinkled on me. "And as I said, that's the usual way t' look at these here texts—the way we been lookin' at 'em since we was old enough t' set still in the pews, an' put our cent in the collection plate. But when I ponders 'em now, I sees something' more; an' it appears t' me, odd as it might sound at first, that what we're talkin' about hehre is marriage.

"In fact, at the risk o' soundin' downright addled, I think that's what most o' both Testaments is about—the joinin' t'getheh of two parties. It don't matteh if each o' the parties is single, the way we think of a conventional marriage—God on the one side an' each of us on the otheh; or if one party's single an' the other's many, like God an' *all* of us, or Christ an' the church. I know we ain't used t' thinkin' of splicin' in this fashion; but seems t' me we've got far too narrow a view o' marriage t' really appreciate what's goin' on in the Bible.

"Now, what we've got hehre, in the traditional view, is a picture of the Lord in command, an' each of us sittin' in his hand, bein' molded accordin' t' his purpose. I s'pose that'd match up t' ouweh idear of a skippeh directin' his crew. But I ask ye, is that the way it works out, eitheh in Scripture or at sea an' at home? T' begin with, the Lord ain't removed from what he's makin'; he's investin' somethin' of hisself every time he spins the wheel, just like the shipwright's puttin' his heart int' the vessel takin' shape on the ways. An' that vessel on the ways—that clay on the wheel: is it really a dumb thing, or does it have a say in the shapin'? It has a say, boys; a' course it does. I don't hold with some o' you othehs that the Lord is so completely in chahrge that none of us has a word in ouhr buidin': that's where ouhr own will an' nature comes in. We do have a word, even if it's flawed; an' he's got t' sort of take it int' account.

"Y'see, there's a kind o' give an' take t' the process—a kind of exchange o' cargo or whateveh—that not very many takes the time t' point out. A ship's carveh, now, when he bolts up his blocks o' wood, picks up his tools an' stahts workin'—when he stahts fetchin' out a face from that blank mass—he makes somethin' more than what's in his mind. If that figurehead's alive it'll talk back t' him, surprise him, sway his hand every minute. As all o' ye know, it's the same steerin' a ship: *Charis* ain't a dead thing t' yer palm, but's alive with initiatives an' answers. An' that's what I calls a marriage, boys: a conversation between us an' ouhr Makeh, an exchange of values or properties or whateveh that results in a genuine union—the kind o' union ouhr marriages here on earth is patterned afteh.

"*Results* in a genuine union, I say, though that don't by no means happen ovehnight, anymore than repeatin' weddin' vows results in a marriage, or signin' the ship's Articles results in a voyage. Practic'ly the first thing that happens, on embarkin' on a conversation with God, as on embarkin' on a commitment t' a mate, a ship or a crew or anything else, is somethin' like a clash o' wills. The Lord, he's got a picture in mind, a design he'd like t' throw off well; an' ye gets the impression, from the Old Testament especially, that he'd just as soon neveh back down. An' us pots—damned if we don't want handles when we ain't got 'em; an' damned if *we* don't resist backin' down. We don't like t' yield t' his hand, b'cause we figure it for a weakness—same's we figure it for a weakness when we surrendeh t' each otheh in some contest or otheh at home or at sea.

"But it seems t' me the secret of a successful marriage's that very yieldin' we're so resistin'. I ain't sayin' there ain't no place for backtalk—a healthy conversation's got t' have some o' that flow, an' I neveh reckoned it, m'self, f'r a sin. The Psalms is full o' that kind o' brass, the clay talkin' back t' the potteh; an' it strikes me that Jeremiah gripin', or Jonah grumblin', or Thomas doubtin', was conversin' just as true as Mary when she sweetly agreed t' be God's handmaiden. The clashin ' o' wills is part of the process that leads t' a stable understandin'—like the exchangin' o' cargoes t' steady two ships. But there comes a time when it's got t' end—when we faces up t' the self-loss of yieldin'. Didn't the Lord hisself learn t' yield—an' not just to the occasional pleadin' o' the prophets? The Lord ye sees in the New Testament's much more subtle an' givin'—he's invested much more o' hisself, in fact all of hisself, his Son, t' save his valuable marriage with us.

"What do I think it looks like, the perfect marriage—or mebbe I should say the seasoned marriage, the one where all pahties 've bowed t' each otheh? Well, I could show ye a ship in full sail, every man at his station, every yahd trimmed t' the wind—the hull tuned to the wateh, the helm t' the ruddeh; an' I s'pose it would look somethin' like that. Or I could throw open a door an' show ye a ship's carveh with his figurehead b'fore him—the figurehead guidin' the tools of the carveh even as it yields t' his hand.

"But it'd be pretty awkward t' place all that on this hogshead; so I brung along somethin' small an' simple t' demonstrate... This here's a spliced rope—I had Jamie make it up a whiles back, though he hadn't any notion what for: nobody makes a neateh splice than him. When it's done, the tapers're so clean ye can't tell where the one rope takes up, an' the otheh rope leaves off. They just kind o' bleed int' each otheh—rope into rope, God int' clay, mate int' mate.

"An' now, boys, it bein' a hot day, an' every motheh's son o' ye wantin' a breath of air, why, I'll just wrap things up with a prayeh, an' ye c'n take away from this service whateveh seems fittin.'" Putting down his pipe—which he'd lighted about halfway through, ruminating and smoking being exercises impossible for him to separate—he bowed his head into his free hand, and intoned over the lowered faces before him: "Lord...who's gave us not only these clay forms, ouhr bodies... but voices t' address ye, an' one anotheh...enable us t' remembeh that ultimate weddin' that each of us c'n pattern afteh... wisen us t' see ouhr paht in the splicin... an' help us t' yield when the occasion is fittin'—t' learn t' answeh each otheh's helm—whetheh dealin' with you or this here ship an' ouhr shipmates, or any of ouhr loved ones at home."

Then picking up his pipe once again—tucking his Testament under his arm, and casting a subtle glance at me, the only look he'd given me the whole service, he wordlessly headed aft for his cabin; and returning the benches to their bin for safe storage, the rest of us broke up with a shuffle, and the usual babble which attends dispersal.

It being Eben's watch on deck, he was soon on the poop to relieve Ben, while his men hastened off to various stations to while away the rest of the morning; and free myself for another hour—longing to spend my leisure thinking—I cast about for a suitable place to reflect, for a spot where I could be alone and quiet. There being a scanty number of such corners even in the most moderate of climes, not many niches suggested themselves; and I ran over them in my mind with irritation.

My entire watch already thronging the forecastle, and Eben's tucked away in various spots in the waist—save for the pair of hands posted at helm and lookout—only the quarterdeck held promise; but as Phillip and company were roaming the planks after rebuffs from Ben and Eben, I quickly foresaw they'd latch onto *me*, and dispatch any chance for quiet. There remained simply the masts; and longingly I thought of the maintop cross-trees—coveted its loftiness, its detachment, its access to broad views and airs—though of course, there might already be somebody there roosting. Even off-duty I had no business in this eyrie; but sneaking steadily closer to the ratlines, keeping a weather eye on the quarterdeck, I at last saw my chance and hastened aloft; and to my delight, I found my nest vacant.

Tucking myself neatly in its cup—propping my chin and arm on the ledge—I looked out past the network of rigging to the aquamarine haze in the offing, to the grandeur of unbroken seaway; and rocking and swaying with the ship's pitching, I timed my musings with the wide motions, while the white fields of canvas puffed, fell and slatted. With the indefinable reaches before me I dwelt upon the words I'd heard spoken, words which, till now, I'd only heard with my heart; saw that I'd been living their vision ever since I'd first looked on *Charis*, and followed the wind to her skipper at Toby's. As if my height gave me the gift of perspectives I'd been too close to discern, I saw that today another hitch had been taken in the bight that'd first been knotted in Boston, then again as we'd sailed from Havanna, when I'd bowed to the inevitability of my allegiance; saw that I'd been nudged another degree closer to a bond that was above and beyond my making.

What it all meant in the webwork around me, I left for those with the wit to answer; dwelt instead on my own patch in the weaving, on my own set of coordinates in the fabric. With the sting of shame I beheld the loose stitches, the immaturity of execution that betokened my part with Ben; then shame turning to wonder—to a kind of wry awe—I saw the needle that repaired the netting, saw Eben's shrewd hands poised in his twine—saw the knowing patience of his expression, and the nimble shuttling of his fingers. What art they possessed, these work-roughened members, I couldn't have said any more now than before; but as they knitted and wove I was pierced by a sweet will, by a disposition to blend, merge, ally; and the joy that flamed up in me knew no constraint. When at last eight bells rang from the binnacle aft and the calls went out to change the watch, I instinctively got to my feet, and prepared to assume my duty, no differently than my watchmates tumbling up from noon dinner; but the man who climbed down from the cross-trees that morning was not the same man who'd earlier climbed up.

That Eben was as capable of working with Ben to manipulate me as he was of conniving with me to maneuver Ben—that he'd quite probably cooked up that sermon some weeks ago, and kept it on the back burner till I showed up to hear it—even that he and Ben likely sat round the saloon table, calculating the success of their schemes, I'd by now pretty much concluded; but even the suspicion that I was being managed behind my back couldn't quell my newfound compliance. Now as we fetched the latitude of Rio and began to ready the old girl for the Horn—unbending her fine weather canvas, rigging in surplus booms and tackles, and bending anew her best Russian duck, the stoutest suit of sails on board—I began to feel less a subordination than a partnership with myself and Ben, an alliance which extended outward from me to include every hand who manned the vessel; and as I became more adept at giving myself up to the living union which carried us forward, I was astonished at how much easier my load was, at how much more smoothly things went on deck—at the harmony of signals and orders and responses which developed between myself, Ben and Eben.

From the way they replied to my earnest effort—with a kind of alacrity and welcome, and a perceptible recognition, as if I'd just all at once hove into view—I saw that they'd been waiting for this; while even my watch, as if sensing something newly seasoned in my till now rather mercurial performance, began to look to me with esteem. Feeling a newfound responsibility not just for the likes of Paul and Roan, whose part I'd always taken, but for Darcy and Coombs, several years my senior, and Matty and Garrett, whom I scarcely knew—feeling a broadened obligation not just for the success of my watch, but for its accord with Eben's—even feeling a new fraternity toward Howland, with whom I now tried to cultivate a kind of truce, I endeavored to pattern myself after Eben: the result being that we made better time than we had at any spell prior, and executed maneuvers so smartly that even Melchett was heard to whistle.

Looking at me the crew as a whole—even those which, on the last run, regarded me with a wary distance, or those who'd, on this trek, nursed a resentment that they'd been passed over for a veritable outsider—began to accept me as one of themselves; while Eben, channeling on orders for the day's work, began to confer with me more and more over the method of their dispatch, and to solicit my opinions. But it was for Ben that I struggled the hardest, biting my tongue when I felt a reprisal, checking my will when I felt challenged, subduing the impulse to goad him into taking me on when I felt recalcitrant—in short, risking myself as I seldom had since I'd met him, in order to match myself with his purpose.

For his part, he responded by promptly giving me new responsibility; for one day just before noon, as I finished up my midday meal, he emerged from his cabin after winding his chronometer and handed me his comparing watch and sextant, then wordlessly sat down to his dinner—obviously intimidating that it was my job today to observe the sun and calculate our position. My grasp of mathematics and hence, navigation, still being far from ideal, I simply gawked at him in answer, refusing to suppose that he could possibly mean for me to do what he seemed to; and seeing me hesitate he barked, "C'mon, shake a leg, it's almost noon!"

"But...this is *your* job," I gaped stupidly, mired somewhere between fear and wonder.

"Not t'day it ain't," he said calmly, addressing his tub of chicken and dumplings as stoically as if it was the usual order for him to hand over his precious equipment—worth as much as the saloon he ate in—to Eben, much less to me. "An' I don't intend t' check youhr work—so ye'd betteh get it right."

The sinking sensation in the pit of my stomach was not unlike the one I'd felt falling off the jib boom. "But...you never made Haskett navigate," I protested, still trying to grasp what was required of me

"Well now, youhr name ain't Haskett, is it?" he drawled, jabbing another forkful of dumpling and draining off half a cup of coffee. "Eben'll look afteh youhr watch long enough for ye t' finish; so hop to it—or he'll get a cold dinneh."

Accordingly I took his sextant, woefully mounted the companionway steps, and issued out onto the quarterdeck, where I shot the sun while Eben noted the time; then—having taken not just one or two, but three observations—I feverishly worked out my calculations below. Beads of sweat gathering at my temples, I figured the distance of the day's run, and recorded position, course and variation painstakingly on slate, log and chart, just as I'd seen Ben do it countless times: he meanwhile placidly eating, and making feeble efforts at conversation with Phillip.

Though I did my best to act unruffled—though compass, divider and parallel rulers, tidal and logarithmic tables yielded themselves one by one to my needs, and fell into place more or less as required—there was little of Ben's steadiness in my hands; and the thought that what I was plotting out now would determine where we'd be heading next did nothing to tranquilize my spirit. That we were nowhere near land at present, and hence in no danger of imminent grounding, offered me little consolation; for I was convinced that, building on my work, Ben would eventually make a blunder, and run us up onto the Antarctic shelf. Repeatedly I urged him to check my figures, too concerned for the lot of us all to be sheepish; but to all my petitions he turned a deaf ear—thinking, no doubt, to terrorize me into skilled work, into relying on myself and not him for precision—the navigational equivalent of tossing me out of Tom's sloop to learn swimming.

What he thought of my job, I'd no idea, since true to form he never said a word about it; but every third noon after that, weather permitting, he handed me his comparing watch and sextant, he and Eben taking it in turns with me to navigate; and through all of the latitudes down to the Horn—through autumnal skies and freshening breezes, and gusts of red dust out of Africa—I persevered, growing gradually less intimidated by my office. As if my stints at noon weren't enough, Ben had me eye to sextant at dusk as well, observing the moon with him and Eben, and at night measuring the altitudes of various celestial bodies; had me once again practicing obtaining back sights, in case the horizon below the sun was obscured by haze, and memorizing charts of the heavens—driving me almost wild by demanding rigorous identification of the stars. Acrus, brightest and most southerly orb in the southern cross; Atria, most vivid of three stars forming the southern triangle; Vela, the sails, or false southern cross; Canapus, second brightest star in the sky—all mapped themselves into perceptible patterns, till the heavens I'd known only as vague arrays from the campfire became comprehensible as traveler's landmarks, or patterins left by the roadside. Even in my sleep I could picture their bright pomp, their grand procession as *Charis* winged southward; could sense the linkage between their formation, and the architecture of our migration; could feel their invisible bond to our passage, as surely as a bird feels the link of the season, or a ship the defining hand of the wind-flow; and with the passing of days my faith increased in the inexplicable sway of their guidance—in the otherworldly aim of their steerage, and its correspondence to some instinctive homing within.

Now as we made our way steadily southward—unlike a bird, flying into, not out of autumn—the weather gradually deteriorated, the barometer falling and the temperature cooling; and we brought out once more our woolen trowsers, and hastened to repair our storm gear and pea coats. Looking out from the taffrail one morning, I beheld for the first time an escort of cape pigeons, swooping gracefully about the vessel—their black heads, white bodies and mottled wings speaking of bleak nesting grounds and lone islands; and before long they were joined by petrels and albatrosses, criss-crossing our paths with strange cries and lorn mewings.

It being but the threshold of autumn, we yet hoped to double the Horn in kind weather, battling the westerlies but spared storms and snow; but there was something inexpressibly foreboding in the starkness of the seabirds around us—something vaguely, obstinately discomfiting in the gradual thinning out of other vessels; and a series of minor mishaps on board did nothing to ease up our sense of disquiet. Old dogs like Haggai, knowing nothing of navigation, and little of the data which guided our choices, snuffed the air and muttered predictions, or looked on the irrational chain of mischances with the face of seers perceiving omens; while even Ben, who scoffed at superstition, and mercilessly ridiculed Haggai, seemed to me to be strangely alert, like one who hears, without knowing it, his instinct.

Blasting out of the Rio de la Plata—a hundred and twenty miles wide at its sea mouth—a sudden pampero gave us more grist for misgiving, blowing out, with a crack of thunder, the mighty 12,000 square-foot mainsail, and carrying away the upper maintopsail yard; then beating us to the foremast and jibboom, it immediately split, in resounding succession, the jib, the flying jib and foretopsail, the yards meantime bucking like reeds in a wind squall. In the roaring and booming—unable to hear orders—I had to rely on my history of Ben's will, on my understanding of his gestures and Eben's to carry out my part and my watch's; and racing to shorten sail and furl tatters—to secure started deck boats and stove-in bulwarks—I found I instinctively *knew* what Ben wanted, knew it without shouts or cries or instructions—knew it as plainly as I knew pain or hunger, as if I were an extension of his frame.

For his part—the job of directing the storm over—he was aloft at once with me, to see to the repairing of the maintopsail yard: a job which would have fallen to Spooner, but which he summarily now took on his shoulders, while Eben stepped into his harness below. Working beside him—watching his blunt, knowing hands, and glimpsing his stoical, comprehending face—I felt the calm I always felt in his presence, a calm which seemed to proceed from his worn garb and torn, roughened boots as much as his bearing. But there was no denying the unease which oppressed the rest of the ship in the storm's wake; for far from clearing the air its appearance, like a kind of gloomy forerunner or menace, had only intensified expectations of foul weather; and few were the men who prophesied a benign Horn.

Having worked the whole day on the main topsail yard—his back badly lamed from his labor—Ben came below that night to a late supper, looking more done in than I'd seen him since our battle off the Florida Straits; and—below myself for the first time that day, after the rigors of sending down tattered sails, then sending up and bending new ones—I was stricken by his condition. Though he made light of the storm's trials, and shrugged off my halting concern for his ailment, he dispatched his meal in silence, his movements slow and his mouth set with pain; and having never before seen him any way but hale, I felt a swift, unreasoning panic, an unsettling precariousness of footing, which affected me like a child's loss of direction, or of a brightly burning bed lamp.

In the swinging arc of the saloon lantern, his broad, comely face—beneath a thatch of thick hair, bleached almost tow by the tropic suns—showed a characteristic love of battle, as if he welcomed the fight to come, sensing that it would match his mettle; but there was something vulnerable in the bow of his shoulders which brought a sudden chill to my heart, and offset the calm I'd earlier felt in his presence. That this was but the beginning of the struggle—that we hadn't yet crossed the 40th parallel, and so faced a fortnight at least of the world's most demanding sailing—did nothing to enliven my courage; and though he tried to reassure me with the reminder, "Y' know the North Sea, an' the Winter North Atlantic," I personally felt far short of his grim joy.

As the following days bore out my suspicion; as the wind pulled ahead and we braced up sharp, sending down skysail yards and stun'sail booms—I felt a weight settle over my spirits; and it was not lightened by the yarns of my shipmates, trotted out in honor of our Horn rounding. There was nothing particularly cheering in the preparations going on either: storm lamps set out and hatches caulked tight, shutters drawn over the ports of the deckhouses, a bogey stove set up in the sail locker for the crew to dry their clothes between watches, Phillip and Co. ordered below for the duration, the cow dispatched—along with the last of the pigs—to spare them the rigors of the passage, and Haggai's beloved hens hustled between decks into a roost Melchett himself had knocked together.

As we fetched the 40th parallel, then the 45th, the barometer fell below 30 and stayed there, the days growing shorter and the skies massing leaden; and two or three days at a time passing now without observations, or with only a hasty shot at the moon, Ben again took over navigation, dead reckoning with the lead line and compass, though he insisted I work through the steps with him—the torturous calculations of miles, currents and driftage. Out of sight of land now for 46 days, almost always closed off from the heavens, we seemed to me to be on another planet, eerily sailing uncharted seaways; and I yearned for a stake in Ben's perpetual sureness, in his indefatigable sense of direction—longed for a share in his faith in the unseen, in his trust in the impalpable, the trackless.

"If I could just get a glimpse of land I'd feel better," I hollered to him one eve by the taffrail, as we clung to the mizzen shrouds and gazed shoreward; and his laughter blew into my ears with the wind's roar.

"Ye're jest like McCabe—so damned concrete!" he bawled at me over his shoulder. "I tell ye, the Falklands are there"—a jerk of his thumb off the starboard beam—"Cape San Diego's there"—a jerk of his thumb off the starboard fore channels—"an' Deceit Island an' Cape Horn's beyant"—a final jerk off the starboard bow. "Take it from me, you don't want 'em no closeh'!"

As we passed the fog-shrouded Falklands and commenced the actual doubling of the Horn—from 50th parallel to 50th, over one thousand miles of herculean sailing; as we braced the yards up for the westward traverse, *Charis* close-hauled and rolling heavily, high seas making breeches over her lee rails fore and aft, and filling the decks with a foaming welter—the battle for the Pacific was on, the prevailing gales blasting our faces, and *Charis* clawing for a slant in her favor. It was precisely the sort of contest Melchett loved—straining for another mile of westing, literally wrenching it from the hands of the wind; and looking at our painstaking progress—mapped out in zigzags on the saloon chart, WSW to SSW and back again, then WNW to SW for half a dozen switches—I could see why I'd long since lost all clear sense of direction; could see, in the constant beating back and forth—in the flurry of stars which indicated tacking, and the lengthy record which racked up the sail changes—the explanation for our exhaustion.

Determined to carry all prudent sail—to avoid lying-to at all costs, and obstinately tack to and fro till he triumphed—Melchett taxed us all to the limit, and none of us more unremittingly than *Charis*: the result being ceaseless wear on the vessel, all of which had to be renewed directly. Ripped from the ringbolts with a thunderous report, the main topsail went one night, blown to the darkness—the forestaysail whipped away not long after; while on deck the incessant pounding of head seas took out at whim whole sections of bulwarks, harness casks, poop ladders, belaying pins, hatches—the lot of which had to be replaced in the gale winds, in between sending up new sails, tacking and reefing.

Nor did our brief respites below bring much comfort; for in the miserable cold and wet, they followed the same inevitable pattern: off with our wet gear, hand up to dry—on with attire merely clammy and damp—down with a cheerless, unheated repast, Haggai, on deck, having long ceased to cook—up from the table without a word to our shipmates, including disheartened Phillip and Co.—into our cold, sodden bunks all-standing, even our sheath knives still at our belt loops—then up again before due to be summoned, averaging little more than an hour or two of rest at a stretch.

Far from being our only problem, fatigue and discomfort were but two of many; for injuries crowded thick and fast upon us: splits and cracks in exposed flesh from the cold, broken bones in our hands from deck falls, and lengthy gashes on skulls and kneecaps from high seas tumblings across the planking. Though by now I would have expected that all of us would have lung fever—especially the hands in the foc's'le, which took the deluging brunt of the head seas—there was scarcely a cold on board, our bodies somehow adapting to the chill and wet; but instead we were prey to sea boils, even with our boots strapped to our belts, scarves stuffed in our collars and sleeves lashed with sinnet; and fearsome bouts of earache and toothache, brought on by the inclement gales, took their toll of men from both watches, including Coombs and my right hand, Paul.

Despairing of his recovery forward, I at last brought Paul aft to my bunk for Shad's tending—Indian meal poultices, mustard plasters, and laudanum to enable him to sleep; while I took to sleeping in Ben's bunk, empty day and night of his presence. On deck constantly now for the battle, resting his back in a chair lashed to the poop, and risking himself to the erratic combers by sleeping brief spells in a cot in the coach house, he came below these days only to wind the chronometer, and synchronize his comparing watches. Downing hot coffee and a bite standing, he was riveted instead to *Charis,* listening to every throb of the rigging, every groan of the hull as he hurtled her forward; and I realized, as I watched his alert, almost husbandly bearing, that to him the ship was alive and speaking—her tightly-racked sheets pulsing and thrumming, her tautened duck booming and roaring, her shrouds and masts shrieking and droning: every sound sobbing a meaning to his ears, and eliciting an appropriate answer.

On our 53rd day out—the first of March—I got my wish for a glimpse of land; for the long, drawn-out wail of "Laaa-aand ho!" revealed the bleak, cold outline of Staten Island, eight miles off the starboard bow; and as Ben had said, I desired no closer view. With the dark closing in, we set a more westerly course, snugging *Charis* down for the fight; and as if in response came the full blast of the Horn, meeting us fist to teeth with its might. Heading into the mammoth rollers—a thousand feet from crest to crest, and mounting in unfettered height, as they swept unobstructed around the world—we accosted a gale raw with rain, and forebidding skies vaulting before us, prodigious and grim with the threat of wind; and bowing before it—our ship but a flyspeck—we ventured forward into the furor.

Beating back and forth for a slant, we battled on thus for two days, confronting the indomitable will of two seas; and as if aware of our obdurate contest, the Horn dispatched its whole arsenal at us, one storm after another with little transition between: some, fraught with rain, proclaiming the clime of fall—others, laced with sleet, stinging hail and pellets, and punctuated with thunder and lightning, seemingly betwixt the seasons—and others still, riddled with snow squalls, presaging the height of winter.

Constantly manning the pair of pumps now—*Charis* shipping 5" more water than she should have, what with the seas breaking over the bulwarks—we alternated one with another, and with the other posts of our duty: our tricks at the helm reduced to an hour, with two hands at the wheel for safety, and lookout stints shortened likewise. Not needlessly exposed to the tumult—to the whipping and flailing topmasts above, and the life-snatching welter of seas in the waist—we put in the majority of our time on the poop, all hands save the lookouts having been stationed aft, and the braces led to the topsides of the coach house; and in the dim chaos of sleet and snow, lowering skies and slate-colored seas, we seldom knew what was happening forward, till an added roar informed us of damage, or a sidewise lurch announced we'd been boarded.

Toppling in over the cathead, one roller submerged the entire length of the main rail, sweeping away all moveable gear on the main deck, before snatching the binnacle and smashing the skylight, then cascading through it into the saloon and aft quarters; and rigging a jury hatch over the skylight, I caught glimpses below of Priscilla—flounces turned up over her shoulders—rescuing Melchett's papers and journals, and Phillip and Sidney bailing out with buckets. Undeterred by the binnacle's departure, Melchett fetched a fresh compass to steer by—having secreted reserves in every niche of the vessel—while McCabe's watch tackled the denuded main deck, and mine lay below to rally with Phillip. But as if put out by our show of resource, the Horn retaliated again after darkness; for that same night, in the turmoil of steep decks, crest-slashing yardarms and threshing lee shrouds, we lost the main topgallant mast and maintopsail yard, the same spar on which Melchett had so obstinately labored: the wreckage dangling from the mainmast, imperiling all hands so long as the gale held, and dragging as well over the deck rails.

As soon as day broke and the winds moderated, most of us sprang aloft to clear damage—me going over the side with four others to recover spars and canvas in the water; and lashing the lifelines to us with his own hands, Melchett turned away to the mainmast, where he helped send down the snapped topgallant. The job over at last just as the winds rose—the spars and topgallant lashed to the pin rail, till such a time as we could hoist them—we discovered the mainmast was sprung, not very far above the maintop; and far into the night we were working with storm lights, me and Ben and picked men from both watches, to strengthen the mast and renew the damage.

On the 55th day came a freak change in the weather, the wind shifting south, then falling quiet, like an antagonist gathering strength between rounds; and in the midst of a dead calm—unnerving as June snow, or any other unnatural occurrence—the moon broke out of a rift of black cloud, enabling us to snatch an observation. Not that it was in any sense needed; for off to the north, distant about five miles, rising sheer from the floor of the sea like a dark fang, and piercing a thousand feet into the night sky, was the unearthly sight of Cape Horn, with its desolate accompanying land mass, broken and bleak as a planet's wreckage.

In the utter, vast loneliness—not a ship, not a whale, not a bird or a porpoise to break seas around us—we all paused in our work to gaze at it: Eben and Ben over the taffrail, me and my watch in the waist, the larboard watch over the spray rail— even Phillip and Co. topsides, having staggered out of bed and onto the poop at Ben's call, expecting to find the ship in her last extremity of need, and discovering instead this awesome silence.

If the night itself, suddenly tantalizingly silver, with silver black seas and sable cloud fields, delineated by the cold moonlight; if the ice-clad ship, with its poised sails, and its crew alone on the southern ocean; if the stark shore, with its abrupt shapes, its rock-hard, naked, chiseled outline, weren't enough to chill the flesh, there were the Tierra del Fuego place names, rolled off by Ben loud enough for all to hear: Famine Reach, Useless Bay, Deceit Rock, Desolation Island, Last Hope Inlet, No-Man's Channel—appellations to strike bleakness into the boldest of hearts.

And rising over it all like some evocative music were the no less chilling sounds of *Charis*: for frozen over in the night's calm, her disfigured tophamper encased in ice, and her decks like glass except our sand runway; encrusted head to foot in rime-frost, her canvas stiff and glacial with clear coats, and her running and standing rigging a-glisten, she was shrilling to the wind's fingers, shrilling and singing and soughing and sighing, like some gigantic crystalline harp-ship, set by her glassblower on a sheer sea. Shot with reflections from the moon's glow, stilled for a spell from the sea's roll, the water itself seemed like a clear pane, a window surface upon a deep bowl, from whose opaque depths uprose these bare land-forms, manifestations of a long-drowned scape; and stung to a man by the gravure before us, we paused as one to look on its stark shape, and listen to the lorn whine of its wind flow.

Then—the cloud-wrack shifting—the light went out, and the wind sprang up again from ahead; and taking leave of the rails and our thoughts, we scurried back to our stations post haste, bracing the ship for the sudden blast. Settling to a steady roar from the southwest, the gale attained its height and held, so that we, close-hauled, made several degrees of westing, wrenching them victoriously from the Horn; but the pain of handling the gaskets and sheets, inflexible as steel cables in their frozen state; the trial of reefing the ice-hardened sails, stiff and unwieldy as copper plate; and above all, the agony of sending back up the main topgallant mast and upper yards, and bending a new main topsail and main topgallant, in the teeth of biting head winds and sleet, constituted the most exhausting labor I'd ever undertaken.

My hands raw and white from the searing cold, from my having beaten them to start circulation—my face cut and slashed from the hail—I came down at last from the mast half-crippled, after a day and a night of almost respite-less work; for so many were laid up by now with bad hands, or, like Paul, with debilitating earache, that we could never rally more than seven or eight on the mammoth lower yards; and the heaviest work inevitably fell to me. Even the welcome rounds of Haggai's coffee could do little to lift my spirits; and when I finally drew a watch below, I crawled gratefully into Ben's cabin, passing up the breakfast which slid to and fro in the fiddles perpetually clamped to the table.

Passing Ben's mirror I caught a glimpse of my face, almost unrecognizable in the dim light: my full beard, the product of two weeks' license, all of us having ceased to shave after Rio de la Plata—my wild hair, as untouched by a brush as the rest of me by bath water—my soaking attire and sag of fatigue, all proclaiming our protracted struggle; but unmoved by either my appearance or discomfort, I elected to fall into Ben's bunk all-standing, my hands too numb to manipulate buttons.

Dumbfounded that men actually sailed thus of their own volition—that any vision of endeavor or commerce, much less the exchange of a few hundred barrels of flour for a like value of indigo and hides, was worth the travail which had so reduced us—I crawled under the blankets weakly, with a hollow laugh at our madness. When I woke it was so dark—darker, not lighter, than when I'd turned in—and I was so gnawingly, emptily hungry, that I knew at once something was amiss: that either it was eternal night, or I had somehow missed my watch.

Coming to in the midst of a panic, hearing the bells, then glancing hurriedly at Melchett's clock, I saw incredulously that it was five in the evening; and I suddenly realized with an astonished start that I had slept away nine hours, something I hadn't done since we'd left Cape Damaris. Hastening into the clattering pantry, I confronted a guilt-faced Haggai, from whom I discovered that Ben had stood the obligation of my afternoon watch, ordering him and Shad not to call me; and so furious was I for Ben's interference—for his taking my burden upon himself, when he already was overtaxed—that all my old recalcitrance flared up, and I refused to speak to him—save to answer vital commands—the whole next wretched couple of days.

That he could keep up a grudge as well as I could, he demonstrated once again; for furious in return at my temper, he turned his back whenever I approached, delivering his orders coldly, and ceasing to ask about my health, the state of my mind and the work of my watch: anxious concerns which I missed deeply, but which I would have died rather than confess.

At the height of our row the wind precipitously shifted due west, threatening to take out every last sail; and in the tumult of orders— "Up helm!"—"Keep her off!"—"In mainsail!"—"Furl foretopsail!"— "Loose forestaysail!"—"Reef main topsail!"—"Close reef!—Close reefs!"; in the chaos of flying lines and tackles, booming, resounding, thundering canvas, and running forms on deck and up shrouds, I found myself again up on the main topsail yardarm, battling the unmanageable canvas, beating my hands to keep them from freezing, and struggling to haul out the weather earring. With every sudden pitching of *Charis*, every unexpected shift in the wind force, the sail, getting aback, slatted wildly beneath, threatening to throw the lot of us off the footropes; but painstakingly beginning again, hauling taut the weather earring, then the lee, then one by one knotting the reef points, we slowly gained on the massive job.

In the midst of it all—in the sheets of rain, which passed at times leaving only the wind, powerful as an animate will, and riddled with flashes of what I took to be lightning—I saw the sail take on a strange hue, an almost incandescent azure; and looking up the yard, I saw corposants at the mastheads, throwing an eerie cast all about us, and turning our hands and faces bluish. Out on the yardarm next to me, Matty was stolidly knotting his reef point, his half-obscured form bathed in the strange light; and I was glad to have him near me, for something of the tranquil sweetness of Damaris transferred from him to me in the turmoil, and helped to ease my fear at its furor. In the rain-lashed dark I could at times barely see him, his face in and out of the periodic torrents; but I could descry him well enough to know the unutterable moment when he was gone—without a cry— into the reaches below.

My heart in my throat I screamed "Man overboard!", trying to make Coombs, the next man on the yard, hear me; but even at my loudest I could convey nothing, and had to rely on frenzied gestures—the alarm making its way up the yard torturously, slowly. In an indescribable panic I spotted McCabe, looking out for the sheets from below; and by a flash of grace the torrents abated, allowing me to send down an unmistakable signal. Toiling uphill aft—while we labored on the yard, making our arduous way to the mast, then one by one down the drumming shrouds—McCabe hailed the wheel and alerted Melchett, the two of them flinging overboard whatever they could lay hands on; but by the time *Charis* had deadened her meager headway—by the time we'd clambered pell-mell onto the poop, and helped Ben clear away the quarterboat, minutes, many minutes had passed.

Stricken, I thought how Matty had fallen 90 feet into frigid Antarctic waters, his sea boots strapped on, his clumsy foul weather gear lashed tightly—thought how the seas rolled in mountains and canyons—knew, from Ben's face, that it was over, that he was only going through the motions to satisfy the demands of conscience; yet even so—even as the quarterboat, with the greatest effort, was cleared away from its housing inboard, and lowered into the snatching waters—even as it filled directly, and disappeared from view in an instant—I couldn't confess that we had lost him. Begging for the other boat, I pressed my insistent way toward it, trying to rally another effort; but Ben's commanding grip closed on my arm, and putting his mouth to my ear, he hollered: "We can't spare it—we've got t' have boats—an' even if we could get her off, d'ye think I'd let ye go in it?"

Turning his back he ordered all hands to the coach house, in the lee of which he undertook a head count; but Eben put an arm about my shoulders and managed to convey to me kindly, "He's right, y'know—we've got t' go," as he walked me uphill to join the others.

Reassured we'd lost no others, Ben sent a few hands to finish close-reefing the main topsail, and a few to loose a couple more staysails, then coil up the lines that had been abandoned; and *Charis* reduced to little more than bare poles—lying-to for the first time since the start of the battle—the men returned as ordered to the lee of the coach house, where Ben had rigged up a canvas awning. The whole ship vibrating—even though off the wind—as in an after-shock of emotion, we gathered wordless beneath the shelter, in the circle of dim light from the hurricane lantern; and standing before us with his worn prayer book—adjusting his spectacles, which Priscilla, now standing in the circle with her downcast family, had considerately brought him—Ben began to read the service.

As he commenced I recognized the Anglican sentences—in common usage aboard merchant vessels—which I had heard a few times on past voyages, but which I knew Ben had uttered never; and as he pronounced the brief, simple phrases, his voice sometimes lost in the shriek of the wind's howl, but calm and steady when we heard it—as he clamped his rough hands on the sides of his volume, to keep the leaves from peeling off in the blowing—as he struggled to make out the print in the dim light, a pain assailed me from deep within, not for Matty now, but for Ben.

Though he arrived at the committal without breaking, intoning the old words—"Unto Almighty God...we commend the soul of our brother departed...and we commit his body to the deep...""; though those who stood in a circle around him, struggling to keep their footing with our roll, heard him out stoically, with restraint—there was such an unadorned power in his unemphatic expression that I could scarcely bear to behold it; and I had to dig the arcs of my nails into the raw wounds on my palms to check my answering outrush of passion.

When he next ordered Matty's small trunk up from the foc's'le, and prepared to auction it off—when he called all hands save the wheel and the lookouts into the sheltering walls of the coach house, and held up, one at a time, the wool jerseys, the warm flannel shirts and worsted trousers—when I saw on his face the freakish realization of his old nightmare of my own loss off the jibboom, it was all I could do to keep from crying out; and even as I bought up the things I knew Damaris would want, the mute ropework Matty'd last worked on—a sailor's cross, a fresh pair of beckets for his trunk—my hands trembled from the cramps of restraint.

Coming below at four in the morning—so beaten by the combined force of the weather, the relentless work and Mattys' loss that I could scarcely navigate the companionway ladder—I felt only the most compelling need for Ben's presence; and passing up my own bunk where Paul lay suffering—passing up Eben's, though it was empty—I dragged myself into Ben's cabin. With the ship lying-to, the gale stabilized, and the glass higher than it had been in days, he was in his bunk for the first time in two weeks; and stupidly I knew I had to be near him—knew it as plainly as a bird knows the urge which commandeers its flight with the seasons, as a bear knows its dying summons. Sitting down at his desk, I managed to get off my boots, and pull on damp trousers in place of soaked ones, fumbling to set things ready for a call with my last strength; then shutting the door, I crawled into Ben's bunk, seeking simply the fortitude of his body.

Coming to a little, he murmured, "Jamie?", his hoarse, muffled voice unsure with slumber; then "Come have a sleep, matey," he drowsily invited, in the most comforting tone I'd ever heard or hoped to hear. Burrowing my face on his wool-clad chest, and my feet between his great, stumpy calves—nestling my hands, broken and numb, in the radiant space between us—I abandoned myself at last to my need; and answering me even in his half-sleep—clasping me in a crushing embrace, his big, hardy arms rounding my shoulders and waist, and his blunt, warming hands closing me tight—he clamped me to him with compassionate sounds, burying his beard in my hair with a sigh.

As if freed for a moment by the extremities of the night, we lay thus together in half-conscious peace, in a contentedly dying awareness—as unmindful of our torn hands and wild hair, numb limbs and filthy, wet, brine-riddled garb, as we were of *Charis'* agonized tossing; then suddenly I knew that he was asleep. On the brink myself, I felt *Charis* lurch, heard the distant staccato of boots and harsh cries—but in the unparalleled haven of that embrace, I cared nothing for what it portended; had a fleeting thought, in those burly arms, that I didn't care if the whole ship went down with every living soul aboard her; then the next instant, I too was asleep.

The next thing I knew was a knock at the door, and the warmth of Ben stirring beside me, one great paw still clasped about me, exactly as we had dropped off. Vaguely aware of the knock repeated, I tried to grasp the rude elements of waking—the time, the place, the watch in progress, *Charis'* condition and my obligations; but strive as I might, I could clutch at nothing, save the comforting bulwark of Ben's body, till Shad spoke out from behind the panel: "It's 5:00—time t' wake, Cap'n."

"All right, I heahr you—thank'e, Shad," came Ben's voice, hoarse and faraway, yet near me; then slowly, with a sigh, drawing his arms from about me—carefully climbing over me, supposing me still asleep, and pulling the covers closer around me—he made his way across the room, took out his match safe and struck a match. As he lighted a lamp I heard his quick in-taking of breath, his startled, low hush of exclamation, then felt him gently turn me and look at my hands; and half-opening my eyes I saw that his woolen jersey was all mottled and dabbled with my blood. Going at once to the door he recalled Shad, asking for hot water and Eben; then drawing back the covers he stripped off my stockings, and quickly looked at both of my feet. I'd no idea how badly I'd split my hands, and wondered vaguely what I'd done to my feet; but as I could feel his touch at my toes, I didn't give another thought to it, sleep coming over me immediately again.

The next time I woke he'd taken the deck, and it was Eben bending beside me, dressing my hands with his deft touch, and offering me a pull of brandy; then I slept again till early in the afternoon, when I rose, determined to make myself useful. As I awkwardly pulled on boots, coat, sou'wester—my bandaged hands twice their normal size, and about as dexterous as a seal's flippers—a sense of bouyancy pervaded my spirit and lifted my being; and as vehemently as I'd felt last night that I could never hoist another clewline, I felt today I could hoist any burden. The pain of the night was not forgotten, neither my grief at Matty's loss, nor my bodily affliction; but a freshness coursed through my fatigued limbs, and invigorated my muscles and sinews, as if I had slept far longer than a few hours, or supped at a generously laden table.

Getting somehow up the companionway, I emerged from the hatch and took the deck, expecting to find *Charis* hopelessly beset, and my few resources in immediate demand; but what I found instead was a ship blithely flying, her cloud of sail drawing and her bow clipping water, like a petrel skimming and fishing the deep; for while I slept the wind had uncharacteristically veered east, as if the Horn had suddenly relented—and we sped before it now with the vigorous wing strokes. At work in the waist, without song, but with spirit, the larboard watch were renewing storm damage, the pale, wintry light on their tired faces; while on the poop, in a cluster as if they'd been conferring, were Eben and Ben, Priscilla, Phillip, and even Sidney, their hair blowing free in the beneficent breezes.

"If only it could've come twelve owehs sooneh," said Ben, with a bleak smile, as I hove up beside him; but the worn lines on his face looked less strained in the sunlight, and there was a gladness in his eyes as they met me.

We fetched the Diego Ramirez, dropped them astern, and headed north in rapid order, sometimes making 200, once even 300 miles a day, the very essence of Melchett's idea of glory: the east wind holding steady, then shifting south, as if all at once determined to favor. As I contemplated its abrupt switch from willful to fawning—

supervising my watch from the deck while my hands healed—I was chilled by the creeping suspicion that, as if appeased with Matty's body, the Horn sought nothing further from us; and though I did my best to shake off such notions, it lay back of my mind even at our work's height, as I knew it lay behind my shipmates'; for I caught their remarks and understood their faces.

As if determined to forestall such brooding, or at least keep our minds from our loss, Ben kept us relentlessly busy—there being no need for him to invent labor, as there was an abundant testimony before us. Never had *Charis* looked so bedraggled—as untouched by handspike, holystone and mallet as the rest of us by soap, brush and razor; and as vigorously as beards, grime and tangles fell from us, did the evidences of abuse disappear from our ship. Setting up the slack standing rigging, slacking off taut backstays, hoisting fresh-rove running rigging, and installing a new binnacle and skylight: such tasks kept us hopping all the way up the coast of Chile; and though there was no heart in any of us for a chantey, or even a song on the forecastle of an evening, there was a will to work and progress.

Joining us one by one from their sickbeds, those who had been laid up gradually emerged to tally on: Paul, out of pain at last, but likely permanently partially deaf; Pelham, recovering from a wrenched kneecap; and Darcy, whose ring finger McCabe had been obliged to amputate. On the 66th day we slanted in toward the coast, on the next overhauled our anchor chain and ground tackle, getting the anchors over the bows; and on the 68th—a full ten days longer than Ben had hoped, but still a remarkably fast passage, almost a fortnight faster than average—we at last made Angel's Point, and anchored down in 31 fathoms of water: Valparaiso Bay lying tranquil around us, and the city, enticing, beneath white-shouldered mountains.

The first thing Ben did, after going through the formalities of entering the harbor—handing over his manifest, Shipping Articles, and list of sea stores for inspection, all of them, as usual, in characteristically meticulous condition—was to clear away the jolly boat for a trip to the city, stowing Priscilla and Sidney in the bows, Phillip, their trunk, and the mail in the stern, and commandeering me to help row and translate, my French and Spanish being far superior to his. Delivering the mail, our first obligation, then seeing Phillip and Co. at last into their hotel—Priscilla almost kissing the marble floor, and even Phillip, who probably would not have shown any emotion in an avalanche, pumping hands with abandon—we next had the sad task of hunting up an outward-bound steamer, and putting aboard her, along with out satchel of letters for home, Ben's account of Matty's loss to his parents, over which he had painfully labored.

These tasks accomplished, we at last had the leisure to comprehend that we were actually on land—that we, for the first time in over two months, had the latitude to dash and explore, and the territory on which to venture; and as if in reaction to our weeks of strain, a kind of exhilaration swept us—a giddy gladness which commenced as a ripple and culminated in a wave of elation. Not alone together since that night on the Horn, when we'd so far forgotten ourselves in exhaustion—tentative at first in each other's presence, as if unsure what kind of face to put on our abandon—we exchanged hesitant glances, which gradually gave way before our celebration; till Ben, as much as I, was eagerly nosing about, up and down the long street which followed the harbor, and which bristled with pedestrians of all nations. Impulsively steering me into a grog shop, he treated me to a round, which turned out to be several; then festive as two boys bent on skylarking, we ranged in and out of the markets, ostensibly to buy goods for the vessel, but frankly to entertain ourselves grandly.

Laid out on the cobbles, on tables, in baskets, goods from a score of lands gaily beckoned: gaudy silks from the Orient, splashing folds on the grey stone; exotic fruits from the South Seas, gleaming round, grainy, mottled; baskets, weavings, slippers, straw hats, bristling with bold, regular Chilean patterns; and pottery, black, red, or earthen-colored, proclaiming the hands of Patagonian makers. The guardian now of 70 dollars—two months' wages, counting my advance money—I was dizzy at what I could buy; and even Ben—so tight he'd again shipped as supercargo to save wages, and signed a crew that would break and stow freight besides sail ship—was snapping up baskets of oranges and lemons.

When I came to a halt before the streamers of broadcloth, satin and nankeen and indigo-dyed weaving—when my fingers caressed in especial a fine silk, salmon-hued as a cloud after sunset, with the longing bright garb always stirred in me, it was Ben at my elbow who was shouting "Buy it!...Y' could have shirt made up like youhr fatheh's... y' should wear such things when ye' ain't workin'...y' c'n be proud of the stock ye come from...Hell, I'll buy it m'self!"

Before I could stop him he'd rolled off four or five yards, and bought them without stopping to bargain—handing me the bright folds with the glint of a grey eye, and the obstinate quirk of an eyebrow; and in like manner I came into possession of a wool hat, and a length of garish-striped cloth for a belt, while I bought him a pair of heelless jute slippers, not unlike Haggai's, which he'd always admired, and tobacco of a scent we'd never discovered at home. Added to these purchases were things needed on board, bananas, pineapples, squashes such as we hadn't tasted in weeks; a crateful of new laying hens for Haggai; an earring for Roan, to celebrate his first doubling of the Horn—Darcy having already pierced his ear; and an exotic plant to king it over Eben's geraniums.

But the most inspired purchase of all—made when we were already grotesquely overloaded, and feeling joyously idiotic—was a magnificent gold and green macaw, of limited— mostly profane— vocabulary and pungent humor, in a cage made of intricate jute-work: a find made by me but sealed by Melchett. "We'll give it t' Eben—God, it'll drive him crazy!" he crowed, a jubilant ring to his laughter; and plopping down all his packages, he hauled out his pocketbook.

By now we were so overloaded—and so incapable of navigation— that we needed a handcart to assist us: a vehicle which Ben, to my amazement, promptly confiscated when no one was looking—his grey eyes meeting mine with mischief. It was probably the first thing in his life he'd ever pilfered, and certainly the proper moment for the venture; but even with its timely aid—even with the macaw and hens perched upon it, and the heavier baskets of produce—we had our arms well-filled with bundles: so well-filled that Ben, unable to see the street before him, missed the curb at one of the corners, and went down into the gutter with all flags flying.

All might have been well, and the catastrophe righted, if I hadn't instinctively reached out to aid him, dropping two baskets and losing my balance, then going over, with the cart, into the same gutter: Ben, on his knees, preparatory to rising, promptly abandoning himself to his laughter, and wallowing in the hilarity of our mishap. The hen crate athwart me, a sea of oranges about me, and the macaw madly chanting "Sonuvabitch! Sonuvabitch!" at me, I was in no position to right things, and entreated Ben, between spasms of laughter, to get to his feet and make himself useful; but every time he made an effort, another rousing round from the macaw, or the sight of an orange mutely rolling into traffic, sent him back his length on the curbside.

Precisely at this unpropitious juncture there hove into view, dressed in immaculate gaiters, fawn-colored trowsers and tight dress jackets, a couple of gentlemen who seemed to know us, or at any rate to recognize Ben; for they checked their course and tacked in our direction before coming to a confused hover, as if uncertain whether they really desired to meet us. "Good Lord, d'y know who that is?" gasped Ben, grasping his aching sides between guffaws, and making a valiant effort to subside. "It's Joshua Snow an' Jeb Lombard from Pohtland, or I'm a dead man!" "Dead man! Dead man!" shrieked the macaw, as if recalling words heard on the high seas, maledictions hurled or prophecies uttered; then "Sonuvabitch! Sonuvabitch!" while I went into a fresh spasm, realizing these men to be the same Ben had courted, so far without a glimmer of success, and intended to court again this summer for business.

Seeming to feel they couldn't not claim acquaintance, now that they were practically upon us, yet clearly wishing they could instantly be conveyed elsewhere, Snow and Lombard gathered steam and drew nigh us, tipping their hats in wordless greeting, and looking down at us in more ways than one; and scarlet-cheeked from our suppressed laughter, not to mention several rounds of whiskey, we just as gravely tipped ours in return. Finding Ben Melchett in a Valparaiso gutter, with a disreputable-looking companion beside him, couldn't have improved their opinion of him, already dimmed by his refusal to join the temperance movement; and they made off as speedily as they had come, without having managed to find their tongues.

Words had utterly failed us as well, partly because we were holding our breath, struggling to contain our next explosion of mirth; but the macaw knew no such constraint, shrieking "Dead men! Dead men! Sonuvabitch!" at their hastily departing backs. As if released by this benediction, our laughter vented itself at last, probably before the two of them were out of earshot; and we lay there in the debris of marketplace and rainstorm for innumerable moments to come, helpless with renewed convulsions.

"Gawd, I hope nobody else we know is in pohrt," gasped Ben, when at last he could weakly get to his knees and begin stowing oranges back in their baskets; and inspired by his feeble efforts, I rallied to help him right the hen crate. Hen crate and bird cage back on the handcart, produce and dry goods in their respective parcels, and the exotic plant consigned to the gutter, we were finally prepared for a fresh start, heading off for our wharf with many a mirthful exchange, and an accompaniment of squawks and cackles. Our jolly boat miraculously where we had left it, and just as miraculously, loaded without mishap, we rowed ourselves back to the vessel, enjoying the hues of the sunset in the harbor—the shimmers and glimmers of aqua and rose, cream and jade and beryl green: the rhythmic work mollifying our spirits, and heightening the intimacy between us.

When at last we hove up and climbed aboard, unloaded our goods and headed for the saloon—me with Haggai's hens and Ben with Eben's macaw—it was utterly, sweetly dark, and the lights were coming out along the harbor. But if we thought the day had wound down to a tranquil end, we had another surprise in store for us; for as we tumbled down into the saloon, I heard Ben suddenly catch his breath, then quietly marvel, "Well, I'll be damned"; and there, sitting betwixt Eben and Haggai, accepting a light for his cigar from Shad, just as if he had always been there, was an old, hale, hearty ox of a seadog, whom I knew at once for Ben's Uncle Ezra.

XVIII

EBEN MCCABE

Valparaiso, Chile-Cape Damaris, Maine March-July 1843

"So ye finally got back! Figured ye'd have a load o' likkeh aboard ye," bellowed Ezra, who by now had quite a load aboard hisself; and unceremoniously dumping cages and crates, Ben tossed his arms about the old lobscouser, whilst Robertson looked on with a delighted sparkle, and Haggai made a dash for the hens. In betweenst the cackling and squawking, first-rate bird cussing and damn-ye's; in amongst the exchanging of gifts—Ben handing me over to this macaw with the glint of a Roman marching a gladiator into the ring—and the broaching of a fresh keg, things was pretty lively for a spell; especially since, what with the rousing effect of the whiskey, and the habit we'd got into of hollering off the Horn, we was all shouting at the tops of our voices.

But finally with the exception of Haggai, who'd gone off to put his hens to bed, we got ourselves settled down at the table, a box of cigars and a pile of mugs before us; and with the macaw swung from a makeshift perch just behind him, old Ezra cast a bemused look at our faces, the grizzled hairs round his ears poking out like a quill pig's.

"So ye'r Jasper," he bawled, eyeing Robertson through rather bleary orbs, as if trying to take in some of the details about him, but losing them as fast as he could collect them.

"James," corrected Robertson with a twitch at his lips, and a vastly amused glance at me.

"Close enough!" Ezra roared with a slap to his knee, and a handsome gulp of whiskey and water. "I'se been hearin' a few tales about ye, Jasper, whilst ye've been out t' town chasin' birds."

"They can't be any hotter than the yarns I've already heard about *you*," Robertson grinned, with his chin out and his eyes snapping in his old brazen fashion.

"Oh ho!" boomed Ezra with rowdy approval; and "Oh ho! Sonuvabitch! Sonuvabitch!" crowed the macaw, whilst all hands exploded into sodden laughter.

"Thanks, boys," I wryly addressed Jim and Ben, when at last they simmered down for a minute and the macaw'd quit screeching. "I really needed a demon at my sittin' room window."

"'Pears t' me he jest needs an old salt t' teach 'im some mannehs," blustered Ezra, wheeling round in his chair and peering at the offender, who hopped up on a bar to meet him beak to beak. "A little friendly chat'll tone y' down some... I neveh met a dumb critteh that didn't cozy up t' sweet talk. How about a drink there, Shorty?" he coaxed, saluting the cage with his tumbler.

"Jackass!" disdainfully hurled the macaw, with about as much coziness as a land shark; and another wave of guffaws engulfed the table.

"He don't say much; but his timin's perfect," gasped Ben, when at last he could catch a breath; and

"What I want t' know is, what am I goin' t' feed 'im?" wailed Shad, eyeing the bird like some beast in its den.

"Raw meat, t' judge from his tempeh," I averred, with a doleful look at Jim and Ben; and them two sinners laughed on, unrepentant.

"We would've brought you something nice," pacified Jim, "a flowery plant f'r your shelf —but we were obliged t' leave it in a gutter": this last with a straight face and a loaded glance at Ben, who read him off with a mirthful glimmer. Then them two went off into fresh convulsions, leaving us to ponder their antics; and we grinned vacantly at them over our glasses, speculating on plants and gutters.

"So how long have ye been here? How'd ye find us?" Ben drilled him, his face showing he was still dumbstruck by Ezra's presence.

"Oh, I seen ye tack int' the harboh—I had m' eye on ye from the beginnin', b'fore ye'd paid out y'r anchor cable. I says t' Shorty—that's m' cat—I says, 'Sharp ship like that, she's got t' be Yankee—in fact,

I'll lay ye two t' one she's out o' eitheh Searsport or Cape Damaris...'
When the stern swung around with the tide, I could see her house
flag; an' when I seen she was from the old burg, I claps ol' Shorty on
his fat head. 'With a rig like that,' I says, 'all laid out f'r speed, there's
got t' be a Melchett or two in her afteh quartehs; an' where there's
a Melchett, a' course there's a keg, an' a neighborly glass waitin' t'
be filled!' So I jest hops oveh, leavin' Shorty in charge, rows up an'
climbs y'r Jacob's laddeh, an' helps m'self t' what I could find—though
there weren't near what there should be, boys."

"He was settin' at the table with Shad an' Haggai, an' half a bottle
o' Scotch already empty, time I got out o' the hold an' found 'em," I
said dryly; whereupon Shad eagerly tacked on,

"But the dishes was scrubbed an' the pantry shut fohr the evenin',
jest like it's s'posed t' be, Cap'n," which touched off another explosion
of laughter.

"Figured ye wouldn't be able t' wait until nightfall, Shad," chaffed
Ben, his sunburnt cheeks all the redder for his share.

"Well, I guess we waited longer'n *you*," returned Shad, with a sly
look out of the tail of his eye at Melchett; and the table erupted again
into guffaws, punctuated by "Awk! Belay that! Take in the slack o' y'r
jaw, Jack!" and other censorious barbs from the macaw.

"So where've ye been? What're ye up to? Where're ye headed?"
persisted Ben, characteristically ordered even with his decks awash.

"Heh-heh, jest like the old Ben—always got t' be comin' from
somewheres an' headin' somewheres else," chuckled Ezra, digging
around in his waistcoat with a gnarled paw, and coming up with a
pocket knife, with which he cut a fresh cigar. "Well, let's see, when
did I see ye last? Not since I cleared the harboh with the *Hannah
Tuppeh*, eh? Well, boys, I didn't stay aboard her f'r long. Had a
change o' plans, or heart or whateveh. Long 'bout the time I hits Rio,
an' plunges int' all that buyin' an' sellin', loadin' an' unloadin', licensin'
an' translatin', which'd wear out Stormalong hisself, if he tried it—it
all at once dawns on me, I doesn't *have* to! I doesn't have t' do any o'
this f'r a livin'—in fact, I doesn't know why I'se eveh done it!

"So I sells the old girl, seein' as she's my ship, t' the mate an' a
couple interested Eastportehs; while I buys me up a tidy schooneh,

hires a cook an' a couple o' hands, puts in some ballast an' happily ups anchor! The harborh masteh, he wants t' know what port I'm clearin' for, an' me, I don't have the first idear; so I says t' the cook, a Malaysian lascar, who mebbe speaks a couple hundred words o' English, 'Where the devil dy'e feel like goin'?' 'Singapore!' he says; an' 'Singapore it is!' I echoes, an' shapes m' course f'r the Straits o' Malacca. In Singapore I meets his wife an' children, 'bout fifty or sixty of 'em, all of which adopts me; then off we heads f'r the Sandwich Islands, wherest one o' the hands has got a brotheh.

"Well, so it goes f'r a couple o' years, boys, or mebbe three—I can't remembeh: jest followin' our nose from port t' port, now an' then pickin' up a small cargo, or layin' oveh t' make repairs an' so forth. But somewheres along there it gets a bit wearin'—that big ol' schooneh, three hands an' quick cargoes; an' I sees I'll have t' trim things down a bit furtheh. It dawns on me I c'n do my own cookin', an' doesn't really need the old cook—no offense—" this to Haggai, who'd just looked in—"so I drops him off in Singapore one evenin'; nor does I really need them two hands, who was always fussin' an' scrappin' anyhow.

"So I sells the schooneh an' buys me a neat little sloop, which I c'n handle m'self, no matteh the weatheh; an' I sets out alone with a pantry an' stores, an' the rest o' my profit stashed in an airtight. 'Course, I takes with me m' cat; a man's got t' have *some* company, else he starts talkin' t' hisself like old Manasseh... I has a notion I'd like t' get t' know the Windwards, spend a couple o' years on the reefs an' beaches, sort o' rid m' system of fifty years o' Maine wintehs; so Shorty an' me drops by Grenada, an' moseys along Martinique an' St. Lucia. 'Long the way I finds the sloop seems a bit crowded, so I heaves ovehboard a couple o' chests, a chair an' most o' the pots n' dishes...keepin' a plate an' a cup, an' a couple extry f'r visitohs. With the cabin so trim, an' the small hold cleaned out, I'se room t' buy up green bananers, or oranges or whateveh I thinks southbound vessels is cravin'; an' I hauls out int' the trades now 'n again t' sell 'em, an' replenish the funds I'se got in m' airtight.

"An' that's the way it's been, boys, these past five or six years now: livin' the simple life, an' honin' things down when they gets cluttered. No house, no taxes, no dinin' room fixtures; no creditors, no payments, no business, no work hours; jest me an' the cat an' a fish now an' then... an' a crony in jest about every port when I gets lonely. Why, boys, ye'd be surpprised how much time there is f'r livin.... If folks back home knowed it, they'd stop the whole business—the whole hullabalu, 'buyin an' gettin' gain,' eh? An' the whole system'd come crashin' down ovehnight...

"But since most folks is busy headin' off in the opposite direction, the system's pretty safe f'r the moment... I put int' Valparaiso this past week, thinkin' t' carry out some repair work, then square off f'r Tahiti, which I ain't neveh seen yet...havin' a hankerin' like always t' explore new places; but now that y'r here, I'll tell Shorty there's a delay, whilst I sits around an' samples y'r likkeh...an' has ye oveh t' sample mine."

We'd all been giving ear pretty much spellbound, our chins in our palms and our glasses idle: Robertson with his blue eyes flashing, a-fire with restless understanding—his glance darting back and forth from Ben to Ezra, as if charting seas only he could fathom; Melchett with a look of envy, his grey gaze fond and discontented; Shad with his quiet, homely attention; and me with the simple delight of kinship I always felt in Ezra's presence. Three sheets in the wind and tired to boot from our day's work, we probably would of listened indefinitely on, the perfect audience for the old lobscouser, if Haggai hadn't broken the spell, buzzing back in with a tray load of grub, which he'd rigged up after bedding down his hens. In the hubbub of grabbing cheese and bread, sweetmeats, condiments and fruitcake, we all come energetically back to the present, and no one more industriously than Ezra, who set out tempting bits for the macaw; whilst Robertson, discovering much of his pet fare on the menu, dove into his plate with a relish, and a conspirator's grin of thanks at Haggai.

"Now, Jasper," attempted Ezra, when the table'd finally begun to look a little bare, and Jim'd happily dove into his second square of fruitcake. "I hear tell ye hails from Wales. I used t' ship there a heap o' times. I wants t' know what yer doin' amongst this pack o' lobstehbacks—that bein' what they all is, Benjamin included. Port

Talbot boy, now is ye?"

"No, sir," Jim answered respectfully, with the same mix of awe and indulgent humor he'd had on his face since he'd first laid eyes on Ezra. "I was born near Bala, but I ain't Welsh. My folks come from gypsy stock."

As soon as he said it—drunk as we both were—Ben and I looked at him, then at each other, with a kind of dazed but pleased delight, this being the first time he'd ever confessed his true origin to anybody else but us; while Shad and Haggai chimed in "Well, I'll be a monkey's uncle! I didn't have the first idear!", and old Ez lighted up like a bull's-eye.

"Ye don't say! So y'r a gypsy *chal* then, eh? Right sensible folk—one o' the few sensible folk I'se eveh knowed. Hone down y're belongin's, pitch 'em int' a tent, or int' the back of a little wagon, an' when it comes time, up anchor an' go! Neveh stay in one place too long, so's the mold doesn't grow on y'r roof or y'r soul! Why, I used t' visit the market in Port Talbot—got t' know a few o' the gypsy stalls there—damned if ye doesn't put in me in mind o' some o' the folks I knowed once—let me see—Lovell was one—Johnny Lovell, an' his partner was Manfri Lee."

A flash of elation passed over Jim's face, a brilliant, dazzling sunburst of gladness—and with it something else, a home-yearning and hunger, such as I'd never seen in his eyes before. Glancing at Ben, I seen that he'd glimpsed it too, for he was regarding Jim with compassion, and a sort of secret worry. "They're relations of my mother's," Jim shone, all unaware of our staring. "She was a Wood, and her mother a Lovell."

"Well, I'm damned!" roared Ezra, marveling. "Small world, ain't it—a reg'lar network o' family!"

"What were they selling? How were they dressed? Did they cheat you?" pressed Jim, his eagerness almost painful to see.

"Cheat me?" laughed Ezra with a slap to his knee. "The Lord only knows! I wasn't thinkin' o' money."

"They got your eyeteeth," Jim averred, nodding.

"If they did, they're welcome; I ain't neveh missed 'em," Ezra chuckled. "As f'r what they was wearin', why, I doesn't rightly remembeh, except they was colorful—a sight more colorful than the Welsh, an' a sight tidier than the Irish tinkers, with which they was busy hissin' an' fightin'. I likes t' see a bit o' coloh m'self, even if what I wears is work gear—an' *they* obviously thought they was becomin', for their chests was as puffed up as if they was courtin'."

"What did you buy from them? Did they invite you in?" Jim persisted, that awful hunger still writ on his features, till I actually ached to see him.

"Why, they was sellin' a couple o' horses, as good a' lookin' animals as I eveh laid eyes on—though I hadn't no need f'r 'em m'self; an' in the wagon they had things they'd made, baskets an' fish-nets an' such like; it was the baskets I needed."

"Johnny's," Jim nodded, his eyes dreaming.

"Well, I buys a few—this was some years back, an' I needed 'em f'r my own produce business; then we has some chat about roamin' an' tradin'. They hasn't neveh sailed themselves, so I'se a bit of an oddity to 'em; they hasn't no call t' go on the wateh. But we sees eye t' eye when it comes t' roamin', livin' out o' doors an' ejoyin' life's bounty; an' they certainly undehstands what I says about not wantin' t' ship with m' relations—for as soon as I say it out comes a heap o' abuse about their'n, which ends up with 'em almost fightin' each otheh."

Robertson clapped his hands with delight.

"But what struck me most—an' caused me t' remembeh 'em— was what a sharp eye they had f'r *me*; 'cause when I runs int' 'em again, a couple years lateh, at a different market, havin' put int' Aberystwth f'r a spell—when I hesitates a minute an' says t' myself, 'Is these the same chals or ain't they?', they at once hails me oveh, calls me b' name, an' ask how's m' sloop *Penobscot* doin'!"

Jim broke into a frank, merry laugh. "Business ploy," he nodded, grinning. "They must've made a fortune off ye."

"Well, fortune or not, they seems happy t' see me, an' shows me oveh all the stuff in their stall. I drinks tea with 'em this time—damn good tea, the best—an' meets a couple o' their children: black-haired chits a bit on the wild side, not as clean as what they could be, but good-lookin' as any young 'un's I'se eveh met. They tries t' do business too, an' fleece me o' whateveh their fathers hasn't; but I hasn't no need o' trinkets, an' as f'r fortunes, I ain't the least interested in the future. When they hears that, an' a bit more about m' boat, which they thinks of as a sort o' floatin' wagon, they seems t' take a bit o' a shine t' me; at any rate, they has me int' their tent, wherest a lady with long black horse-tails o' hair is chattin' with a few otheh ladies, an' a tanglin' heap o' children. We all winds up drinkin' more tea, the ladies sort o' off t' one side, me an' the men cross-legged on a blanket, an' the children an' lurchers in an' out an' about; then I has t' be off, refusin' more fortunes, but promisin' t' drop by the next time I sees 'em.'"

While Ez spoke Jim'd sat with such a fervent expression—with such a hectic flush on his cheeks, and such a wet sparkle to his eye—that I knew he was on the edge of tears; and Ben, between his moved interest in Ez's picture, and his fellow feeling for Jim, looked to be on the brink hisself. But the moment passed before Jim's constraint wavered; for what with Shad and Haggai making absurd banter, Ezra getting progressively drunker, and the macaw tossing in his two bits' worth, it was impossible to keep maudlin; and the talk soon turned to other channels. Before long Ben had brisked up again to his old blustery pace, and Jim had brightened up with that uncanny self-control of his; but for the better part of the night—and it was an uncommonly late one—I somehow stayed sobered up myself some, watching Ben's face and scanning Jim's. Maybe it was Ezra's story which'd cleared my head up, maybe just the damping effects of the food, sopping up some of the blur of the whiskey; but I seemed to see their faces with fresh eyes, as they eased back into the give and take round the table.

Now that I was paying close attention, I couldn't fail to see the new lines round Ben's mouth—lines which must of come since Jim's fall from the jib boom, and Matty's loss from the mainsail yardarm; and Jim, how much more mature he looked since Cape Horn! My blurring details of weeks of work was gone, the mellow haze of the whiskey also; and in a sudden odd orb of clarity, which circled just the two of them across the table, I seen the stern, chastened set to

Ben's mouth, the look of humility which must of sprung from Matty's death, or our clash of wills with the Horn; seen a new candor about Jim's eyes, a directness which did battle with his old reserve.

As if he sensed my gaze on his features, Jim suddenly cocked an eye in my direction, a half-smile playing whimsically on his lips; and in a rare lull—with Ezra and Shad caught up in a jest, and Haggai and Ben making a raid on the saloon cupboard—he held up something he'd been keeping at his side: a carefully-wrapped, cylindrical parcel, out of which poked the folds of a fine silk, the color of a salmon fillet. Nodding at Ben to show it was from him, he gave me a conspirator's wink; and the two of us shared a victorious smile. Then Ben set back down with a dusty bottle, which Ezra uncorked and handed to me; and that was the end of my clarity for the evening—and along with it, my train of reflection.

When at last old Ez had had enough, Ben trundled him swayingly off to bed—refusing to let him row back to his sloop, and bunking him down instead in the sickbay where Phillip and family had so recently languished; while the rest of us got to our feet with an effort, and steered an uneven course back to our cabins. More than glad to turn in myself—vaguely aware I'd be the first one up next morning, to commence port routine and broach the cargo—I was brung up short by the sight of a package, tidily set in the midst of my pillow, with a large, scrawling note readable in the moonlight: "For the Ship's Preacher—with love from Jim." Unwrapping it, I broke into laughter, a long, rolling chuckle stowed up with fondness, and with resolve never to underestimate his wit; for there in my hands, big as life, and twice as devilish, was a finely-made earthenware jug—and damned if it didn't have two handles.

Next day as I began discharging cargo—plagued by the world's most infernal headache, unseasonable heat and delays in the lighters—Ben and Jim lowered away and followed Ezra, back toward the wharves to check out his sloop: coming back around noon dinner to report it to be as neat and handy a little craft as ever sailed deepwater—all that Ezra'd cracked it up to be, and more. Plunging into his plate with the appetite of an oarsman, Ben gave me the details with an envious shimmer, full of admiration for its simplicity and compactness; while Robertson, equally delighted, said the cabin looked like the inside of a gypsy wagon: traverse berths, a small stove, cubby holes for storage, a cupboard or two for pots and dishes, even some sturdy bits of curtains.

Though Ben went back to work with a will after dinner—though he appeared to put the boat out of his mind, and along with it, Ezra's visit—I knew from the churning silence of him that he was full of schemes, doubts and dilemmas; and when, late that night, he hauled out his clay pipe, and proceeded to smoke like a house afire, I was sure that he was cogitating still. To me the whole thing was as plain as a whale spout, or a headland on a clear horizon; but I figured this was one of them times when I could be most useful by simply keeping my trap shut; so I kept him company on the quarterdeck with a cigar, whilst Robertson cut out a silk shirt with Shad's help, and the men skylarked and sang songs on the foc's'le.

The unexpected news of Jim's past—the tantalizing tale that he was a gypsy, spilled without delay by Haggai—gave plenty of fuel for fresh speculation about him; and aware of the competing views soon making the rounds, Jim retreated straightaway back into his shell, and rode out the scuttlebutt in silence. In my opinion he would of clammed up anyway, after owning to Ezra that he was a gypsy—it being his habit to withdraw after frankness, as if he was somehow scared by his daring. It just wasn't part of his way to disclose much —whether because it was his nature as a Rom to be secretive, or because he'd later been burned by the gadje world; but or my part I couldn't blame him for his closeness; for so much'd hurt and hunted him since his youth that I wouldn't of expected him to trust his own shadow.

But for Ben, who looked for him to be open, as a result of their close friendship—who was honest as the day is long hisself, and frank as the sun on a cleared field or hilltop—Jim's new bout of buttoning-up hit hard; and he had to make do with the ship's speculation— much of which was wide of the mark anyway, no one being within miles yet of Jim's true story.

Sometimes I thought, as I caught the gleam of Jim's eye while he sat, taking neat stitches in his silk shirt of an eve, that his whole rhythm of disclosure and quiet was a kind of conscious flirtation, the purposeful plan of a first rate lover; but intended or no, his secretive reserve had the effect of snagging—hook, line and sinker—Ben, along with every other mother's son on board: all hands again caught up in the charm of conjecture about his shifty background.

Indeed it was for his skill at courtship that I felt the greatest respect, and seen the greatest evidence of his maturing: Jim having the patience, wit and restraint of a man twice his age. Sometimes as I watched him maneuver—and I was getting better now at detecting the ploys that had a first seemed unconscious—I felt myself in the presence of a sort of genius; and I shook my head at his artful wiles. That there was a new maturity about him, apart from the ripening of his heart, everyone, even Haggai, had noticed—his ingenuity in such matters as fishing a sprung mainmast or renewing damage as apparent as his expanded frame, and the firmer, more decisive trim to his features.

"Jim's becomin' a fine man," Ben'd said to me once, a trifle wistfully, as we watched him direct loading on one of the lighters; but I doubted if even Ben could see the subtlety of the heart which lay back of Jim's seasoning; and I knew he knew nothing of the cost of Jim's restraint—of the patience that checked his instinct and feeling. Sometimes it showed up—at least to me, since I was looking—in the dreams that'd begun to distress him: dreams that'd started up after Matty's death, but which harkened back to his own fall off the jib boom, and to the shock of his separation—from the ship, from Ben, from all he'd come to value.

Then again his stress showed up in the headaches which'd first begun to appear last autumn, in the aftermath of his restraint camping, and which now laid him low once every week or so—usually just after some time spent with Ben, like them treks to town and Ezra's vessel. At sea he'd manage to more or less hide them, from Ben if not from me; but here, in port, he missed an afternoon or two of work, and Ben begun to cast an eye at him. Convinced that he was working too hard, he urged Jim to let up a little, and turn in earlier of an evening; but I knowed that the real cause of his ailment was the strain of withholding his feelings; and I felt for the burden he carried.

"Ye've got t' ease up a bit—time's on youhr side o' the fishnet—ye've just got t' learn trust it," I encouraged, one afternoon as he lay resting, recovering.

"You think that's why I'm gettin' these headaches?" he asked, appealing to me with them blue eyes of his.

"A' course I do; it's plain as high wateh."

"An' Ben—what does he think about it?"

"He thinks you'hre workin' too much," I said dryly.

Jim smiled.

"Y' do work damn hahrd; there's really no call for it; we'll still get home sometime afteh ice-out," I told him. "Seein' ye go at it surprises me eve'ry day."

"It does?"

"Aye… I thought gypsies was s'posed t' take things a little lighteh, go for singin' an' dancin' an' such like…in fact, till I met ye an' heard youhr story, I wasn't sure they worked at all."

Jim's smile broadened; then he lapsed into thoughtfulness. "I really don't know how such talk gets started," he looked up at me, pondering. "From what I remember, we worked all day—seasonal jobs like hayin' an' threshin', or makin' an' stockin' potato clamps—occasional deals like markets an' horse fairs—an' family trades we plied all year, smithying, carpentry, an' so on. The women an' children worked as much as the men—lots of times, they made more money. We had fun by the way; but everything was for a purpose—there wasn't a sense of aimless driftin'.…

"But then, I never knew the gadje to see us in any kind of truthful light…They emphasize all the oddest angles—like me, concentratin' on what I might've been doin' in Liverpool years ago, instead o' seein' what I'm up to today." He shook his head on the pillow; but his dark eyes smiled. "Gadje! No matter how much time I spend amongst 'em, their slant on things still amazes me."

"I don't s'pose the Rom eveh makes the same mistake in turnin' around an' judgin' the gadje," I proposed, looking at him slyly; and he at once laughed his frank, hearty laugh—a laugh full of good will and confession. "For one thing," I smiled, "I don't really see m'self as the ogre that comes round an' evicts Rom families from their campgrounds ... an' for anotheh, I ain't neveh thought of m'self as a stodgy house-dwelleh."

He laughed freely again; but he took my hand in a tight grip, and squeezed it a moment before letting it go. "You're my brother," he said thickly, with a catch in the quick words; and bending over the pillow, I touched a hand to his dark hair, and gentled its waves in quiet kinship. Then picking up my hat, I nodded him goodnight, murmuring a few words about getting rest; and seeing the lashes obediently come down on his cheeks, I silently backed out of his cabin, and took to the deck again for the evening.

Always when he spoke of his people, or referred to his earlier life in Wales, a great home-longing come over him—a yearning that softened and pained his features, as it had that night he'd listened to Ezra, and again just now as we'd chatted; and as I put in a quiet hour on deck, I pondered on his deep sense of attachment. The rugged mountains and moors of his homeland, his gifted father and dark-eyed cousins, and his sharp-tongued, shrewd, tale-telling grandmother —the simple rhythms of his early days, breakfasting out of doors, breaking camp, moving on and stooking wheat-sheaves— seemed to fill him with almost intolerable feeling, the same pain my own early memories brung me; and I wondered if even he knowed how deep his roots went.

When I seen him so moved I thought how out of his element he must sometimes feel, in the midst of a pack of gravel-tongued downeasters; and I felt for him in the ban against his return home. But then there was times it took a different direction, this craving of his for his native turf—times when he revealed he knew many kinds of home, everything from fleet-footed *Charis* to the spruce-woods of Maine and the space at Ben's elbow; and then I could only shake my head in amazement at how mobile was his concept of home— how undetermined by a single spot or a roof. Home almost seemed to be to him wherever he was most deeply in contact with some secret source of belonging—a kind of a moveable salmon's spawning grounds; and though it was nearly always out of doors, the times was becoming more frequent when it was at the side of certain people, wherever they happened to be—even where they happened to of been.

Yet even so—even recognizing all this, and appreciating his love for Ben's birth site—I hadn't really managed to see how keenly his definition of home had come to include Cape Damaris, till one night just before we cleared the harbor, when—tired out from the day's work, nearly the last mad scramble of loading—he'd leaned his head back against the saloon sofa, and heaved a sigh that seemed to come from his toes.

"S'matteh, matey?" asked Ben at once, looking up from his stowage plans—the merciless sheaf of diagrams he always inflicted on me in port; and opening his eyes with a smile Jim replied,

"Homesick."

Looking over at me Ben met my eyes—both of us wondering, *Homesick for where?*; then—thinking he meant Wales, but not exactly sure, and wanting like always to draw him out—Ben tactfully asked, "What're ye missin', hm?"

"Don't know exactly," Jim responded, as if trying to put a lot into a few words; "maybe the sound o' the bell buoy from my window...or the smell of the rockweed at low tide."

Understanding all at once he was homesick for *our* home, Ben looked to be on the brink of swift tears, his gratitude breaking out on his face like a sunrise; and patting Jim's knee with a paw wonderfully gentle, he returned to his papers with a wordless nod, and a quiet lampglow of gladness.

If our year's worth of expeditions'd bound us up in one another, our officering *Charis* clinched the matter; for nothing bespoke the whole we'd formed up better than our quarterdeck teamwork. At the close of the first week of April, we was back on our way round the Horn— having bid a fond farewell to Ezra, who'd got off a couple days before us, dipping his ensign as we give him three cheers—and having set aside such trinkets of handwork as lanyards and silk shirts for freshly-slushed boots, and long-handled suits of wool underwear.

With the wind this time around in our favor—blowing a

dependable gale out of the west, even if it was laced with snow, which quickly piled up knee-deep on the maindeck—Ben's general walking instructions to me was, "Hang out all the laundry she'll bear—an' hold on"; and grim at the thought of a thousand miles of running before a following sea, I laid out to do my best, not expecting anything less than a wild game of tag. But to my surprise we at once commenced a swift and easy—if hair-raising—passage, contriving to keep ahead of the seas, and carry sail rap full to the reef lines; and no small part of our success was the correspondence that'd ripened between Ben, Jim and me.

It was my first crack in upwards of fifteen years of seafaring at working harmoniously with both master and second mate—all three of us knowing and doing our jobs, playing up to each other's skills and covering for one another's faults; and I was fairly amazed at how smooth our routines went. Jim especially'd developed a knack at reading our minds from our eyes and expressions, and getting across his with a few scaled-down gestures, almost as if he was an extension of our thoughts, or an addition to our limbs and bodies. Full of admiration for him, Ben confessed to me one night how he'd had his doubts about Jim's temper, and his ability to mesh his will with the ship's needs, or our own peculiar division of duty; marveled out loud at Jim's sense of timing—at the trusty sureness that'd sprung up between us, as it had ashore when we'd tented upriver.

For his part Ben seemed to have not a glimmer of hs own role in the picture—of how changes in *him*'d helped bring about this climate; but Jim seen with his usual long-sighted shrewdness, remarking to me on Ben's willingness to divvy up his old prerogatives between us, navigation being but one case in point. Ben was less likely now to climb over the whole ship and minutely inspect it hisself, more liable to trust to my judgment on such matters as day's work and repairs; and as Jim pointed out one watch-change, he seemed full of a fresh flair as a result—an observation I had to agree with myself, for I'd never seen Ben in better form. He loved scudding, which we set up for around the fiftieth parallel—topsails close-reefed and drumming like thunder, foresails and foretopmast staysail straining; and though like other sharp ships *Charis* did better on the wind than before it, she behaved like a charm for him, keeping ahead of the seas like a blithe child, and booming along at a gallant twelve knots.

Watching them greyhounds come after us, looming like bad dreams thirty-five feet high over our taffrail, and often as not, breaking on our heels, I always held my breath lest one of them catch us; but Ben'd just look at me over his shoulder, easy as a man in on some secret, and laugh out "You apple tree-er!" or some likeminded brickbat; and somehow he seen her though all the tumult, doubling the Horn in about half the time as the trek out.

Hell-bent to fetch home more or less when he'd planned to, Ben crowded her all the ways up the Argentine coast, trying to make up for lost time on the run out; and every day I seen some improvement in our effort—some sign we was getting to know each other's ways and adopt them. Once, ducking below, whilst Ben looked out for my watch, I seen Jim at the chart table plotting our position, handling parallel rulers and glass course protractor above the maze of scrawls and notes on the chart, with such a practised, thoughtful calm that I stopped in my tracks to look at his face; and not long after I seen Ben curled up on the sofa, barefoot and a-snooze in the middle of a slow day, in so perfect an imitation of a sailor's siesta that I had to look twice to make sure it was him. So used to each other did we become—so familiar with each other's form, and so trusting of each other's performance—that we could work on deck in the dark, out of sight of each other and out of earshot in the roar, with every confidence as we wore ship or tacked, just as if we could see each other's acts.

Not that our joint effort was flawless, or that all trace of conflict'd disappeared between us. All this cream and pudding was still, you might say, pretty much in the business realm; when it come to the touchstone of personal matters, we hit the corduroy road with our teeth set. *I*, of course, caused little problem, being bent, as usual, on smoothing wrinkles; but Jim's chin could still come up if Ben was high-handed, sparking another of them spells of "not speaking"; and once when Jim contested an order, Ben hauled off and gave him what-for, which pleasured Howland and a few others immensely. There was plenty of times when I said to Jim, "Well, how many handles does the pot want t'day, h'm?"—receiving a scowl of black brows in answer; and ample more when I cautioned Ben, and got accused of sticking my oar in. But none of these could match the time when Jim was laid by the heels off Rio, and tried to keep Ben from stepping in to help; and even then their show of self-will or cussedness or pride or whatever, was underwrit by a note of promise.

Fetching the latitude of Cape Frio in mid-May, we one day encountered a heavy cross-sea; and still a dollop on the lubberly side at the helm, Roan wrestled with his trick at the wheel, struggling to keep the decks dry. Managing smartly at the start, he begun to wear out near the end, at last shipping a cargo of green water, which boarded the fo'c'sle just abaft the knighthead, and hurtled along the length of the main deck, before washing harmlessly out the scuppers. Passing the hen coop just as the sea swept, Jim went down head-first with the green surge—breaking his fall instinctively with both hands, then disappearing a brief spell in the welter, before turning up a few yards down the main deck, motionless beside the uprooted hen coop.

Frozen to the spot on the poop, Ben waited for him to get to his feet; and when he failed to rise or make a move, Ben was down off the break of the poop, and at his side before anyone else —the first time he'd ever just deserted his post. Staying behind to keep an eye on the helm, I could see him kneel down by Jim, swiftly joined by several others—seen him peel off his shirt and hastily apply it, as far as I could tell to Jim's head—seen him suddenly bring it away blood-red, and actually wring it out on the deck planks, whilst Howland and one or two others quickly offered theirs. Straining to get a sight of Jim's body, to see for myself where he was injured, and whether he was as bad off as Ben's shirt made it seem, I realized a-force how much Jim meant to me—how much a part of us he'd become; and hovering betwixt the helm and the deckhouse, I tried to follow Ben's moves as he worked, and read any news of progress from his posture.

At length I seen Jim hisself vaguely stir, and come to a sort of sitting position, braced up by Ben as if he was dazed; then everybody made shift to rise, Jim getting shakily to his feet in their midst, and Haggai and Ben steering him aft: Haggai having appeared on the scene almost as immediately as Ben had, at the first squawk of his discomfited hens. Passing near me—Jim frankly leaning on him—Ben nodded briefly, "Be right back"; and good as his word he reappeared in a few minutes, still decked out in his blood-smeared trousers, but having scrubbed his hands after settling Jim in.

Nodding me off, he meaningfully took the wheel, something he never did except in port; and hurriedly ducking below I found Jim, quiet in his berth but conscious, lying on an India-rubber bed sheet, and dressed in a suit of dry linen—his wet clothes neatly handed up to dry, and Haggai fussing about the cabin. Looking him over I found a long gash on his skull, abaft the temple and well back of the hairline, then discovered he'd split the heels of both palms to the bone; and fetching the brandy—locked in Ben's medicine chest, the only spirits we carried at sea —I propped him up for a few pulls at the jug, which he managed with my assistance, looking pretty much white to the gills.

"I s'pose I look a sight," he ventured, speaking with a shaky effort; and setting aside the jug, I smiled down.

"You know a head wound always bleeds some," I encouraged, giving him a pat on the shoulder. "I'm jest glad ye ain't broke youhr wrists, or busted that thick skull o' youhr's open."

The twitch of a smile played round his lips, but he was in no shape to muster a comeback. "I won't be able t' use my hands," he fretted, as I lined up scissors and twine and clean cloths, and Haggai sped off to see to hot water.

"Not for several days, no: I'd say they was pretty much out o' commission," I said dryly, speaking lightly as I could to cheer him; and his lips twitched again in answer. "I've got t' cut away youhr hair some, an' shave it close around the wound's edge; but if ye'll lie still, I'll try not t' hurt much."

Giving him a pull now and then on the jug, I stitched away with my cotton twine, timing my moves as best I could with the vessel— which, in Ben's hands, was on her best behavior; but even with care it was a painful job, Jim bearing my work with his usual restraint, only uttering a low cry now and again. Done with his scalp—which

I dressed with honey, according to his mule-headed instructions—I next tackled both of his hands, taking in all, dozens of stitches; then as with his head, I dressed and bandaged. A pull of brandy, a bit of lacework, a pause here and there to allow for the ship's moves, or to give Jim a rest from the needle, I somehow contrived to get the job done; and as I meshed he valiantly tried to make conversation, gritting his teeth and falling silent between efforts. Lightheaded to begin with from loss of blood, and progressively more balmy from the effects of the brandy, he wasn't always too coherent to follow; but once as we rested he looked up at me, and remarked on *Charis'* smooth going.

"That's b'cause thehre's a masteh touch at the helm," I informed him, glancing down at his face warmly; and alert to my meaning, he gazed up in wonder.

"You mean Ben—?" he asked, his features working; and giving his shoulder a pat, I nodded.

"A' course. He knew I had some knittin' t' do," I said gently; and so intense was the look of loving pain on his face that I had to turn away for the moment, and take up my work again in silence.

For the next several days his hands was so swathed in honey and bandages that he was helpless—Ben scarcely daring to even let him on deck, since he couldn't grab onto a thing, if need be. Furious at finding hisself on his beam-ends—about as useful as an upended turtle—he was in no angelic temper; and Ben's safeguards only served to make him more volcanic. "Whyn't you just bend a leash t' my middle, the way mothers do their children down't the town wharf?" he growled, once when Ben was especially cautious; and "Good idear! Why didn't I jest try that out a year ago—would've saved me a heap o' trouble!" Ben shot back, at least half in earnest.

As he couldn't do a thing for hisself, Jim was all the touchier in mood; and time at sea being tedious without work, his ill-humor was aggravated— for there was no outlet for his frustration, nothing to speed the long hours with, not even his drawings of Abigail, or the carvings he liked to shape in his spare time. Like me, he wasn't much of a reader—disposed of the Portland and Boston papers

Ben'd picked up in Valparaiso in a matter of a couple hours, by dint of Shad's folding the pages, and rejected the rest of Ben's library—which, being mostly technical in nature, made pretty dry doing, save some selections from Shakespeare that he wanted to hear read.

Over-anxious hisself to be useful, Ben made matters worse by trying to do things for him; and his dander up at Ben's insistence, Jim looked mostly to Shad for help. Being by office anyway a servant—being devilishly fond of Jim, not just as Paul's best chum, but as a kinsman, a bond no whit altered by the recently published news that Jim was no more Welsh than I was—Shad ably stepped in and met his needs, reading to him from Shakespeare's sonnets, and kindly feeding him his favorite tidbits. In such tasks he was assisted by Haggai, the two fussing over Jim to such an extent that they fell behind in their work, much to Ben's pretended ire. Me Jim would turn to because I was a doctor, or because I had his heart's confidence anyway; but Ben he bull-headedly kept at bay, suffering doing without rather than ask him.

Maybe it was Ben's high-handed manner, which grated on a nature so self-reliant as Jim's—maybe just the stubbornness of shunning the one whose assistance he most wanted; but all of Jim's pride come to the fore when Ben tried to step in, and made him cat-and-doggish about help. Understanding all this, I tried to mend nets; but Jim balked at me and Ben was impatient, all the more so because he was envious of Shad. Upset he was left out, Ben hovered about, or stood Jim's watch the first couple of times round; but still Jim persistently held him off—so obstinately that Ben at last threw up his hands, and huffed at him once as he refused help on the poop ladder: "Damned if I won't let the ants make a meal o' ye, soon's they get onto the scent o' that honey!"

Finally getting wise to my words—about three or four days into Jim's recovery—Ben backed off enough to let him go to work, directing his men from the deck when it was his watch; and mollified a dollop by this gesture, Jim allowed Ben to help him pass the time off-duty, mostly by way of telling tales, which I'd long known was one of his chief forms of amusement. It being fine weather, Ben'd set up a couple of deck chairs, usually in the shade of an awning; and there they'd sit under the sultry heavens, swapping yarns with a child-like fervor, whilst my macaw—christened Jasper in jest after Ezra's visit—swung to and fro near them in the rigging. It was the only time in the whole of my life I'd ever seen Ben just sit on deck; and as the entire ship was a-ring with activity—the boys in the tops slushing and painting, four or five hands over the side scraping, and the rest ranged from stem to stern housecleaning—in the big push to get ready for homecoming, Ben's idleness was all the more show-stopping.

It being my watch when Jim was off-duty, I'd pace nearby when not needed forward, eavesdropping on their eager jabber: no amateur stunt since, what with the banging, heave ho-ing and scraping of the clean-up, the slatting of the sails in the flat calm, and the squawking editorials from Jasper, I was hard put to make out their chatter, most of which was about Ben's grandmother. As he couldn't sketch—as he'd been doing since Portland, by way of preparing for Abigail's figurehead—Jim encouraged Ben to recount tales, from which he might make a mental picture; and obliging, Ben spilled out memory after memory of the old fire-eater, stories even I'd never heard before: yarns of her taking the wheel of the brig after she'd broached-to off the Guineas, ignoring Winslow and the helmsman, knocked unconscious by the debris, for the claim of the higher duty; tales of her taking to task the shore bastards—the infamous yard hands of Port Stanley—for trying to fleece Winslow for repairs; accounts of her hiding their six young children in apple hogsheads down in the hold, when the brig'd been boarded by Malay corsairs.

Answering in kind Jim responded with a flood of recollections about Taw—stories of her endurance in winter, her skill at poaching or pilfering gold pins, her arrogance in dressing down a British constable: him and Ben delighting in how much alike, at bottom, the two old grand-dames was. So thawed out did Jim become as this tale-swapping went on that he even broke down enough to allow Ben to feed him; for as I returned aft one day after overseeing the lines forward, there they was taking their noon dinner, on a tray Haggai'd set up betweenst them, Ben busy spooning up plum duff for Jim.

You had to see these two big, stubborn men, one gravely feeding the other, and both chattering like macaws between bites about the did-does of their grandmothers, to realize that they was worth my patience—that I wasn't a lunatic to keep supposing they'd one day manage to brush out their lot line, the way they'd contrived to clear the bounds on deck. As I looked them over Ben deftly reached up and wiped the corners of Jim's mouth with a napkin, with such an unthinking, caring gesture that the tears suddenly popped out into my hot eyes; and I had to dig down into my pocket for my outsized calico kerchief, and give a couple of good honks in its yardage, before I was fit to walk up to them sea dogs, and bum a bite of two of their dinner.

After a herculean effort—the men in the tops down the whole Gulf of Maine, making sail at a moment's notice—we hove into view of Monhegan, Metinic, the Mussel Ridges and finally the Point light, dropping our hook off the Ship Street pier head seventy-two days out—a smashing record; but it wasn't the crowd's congratulations, the pleased excitement of Melchett Bros., nor any of the commotion of dealers or kinsfolk suddenly pouring over the bulwarks that riveted Ben's attention; no, it was the hull taking shape on the Melchett yard north ways, so big it already dwarfed everything that end of town. Putting up with the amenities of homecoming as long as he could—about two minutes—he snatched up his young ones down on the wharfway, piled them into somebody's buggy, and made it double-dash out to the shipyard, where I suppose he inspected his newly-hatched darling to his critical heart's content, whilst Jim and me made *Charis* fast and shipshape.

Hurrying over ourselves as soon as we was able—not any too quick, since we was delayed by Damaris, and a bevy of other young comelies at Jim's elbow—we found the keel already laid, plus the square frames: the keel hook-scarfed like Ben'd wanted, and the body frames marching like ribs toward the bowpiece, three stories high in the bright, cool sunlight.

On the framing stage set up at the stern, futtocks was waiting to be assembled—the cant frames with their sharp curves for the bow and stern; whilst on either side of the ways in the dirt, assorted timbers was lying about, some of them already marked from the molds for the adz-stroke. Hammering away on the shores high above us, hauling fresh timbers behind teams of horses, turning out planks with the steam-powered sawmill, or stantions on water-powered lathes, every hand in the yard was a-buzz with the effort to supply the new ship with the parts she required; and in the midst of the deafening commotion, we could sometimes catch sight of Melchett, over-towered by the structure around him, dragging a child or two at his pockets— climbing here, touching there, measuring with his square hands, or now and again applying the battens, like a midwife assisting some imminent birth.

Lying there in the cool June wind, the hull did look like a sort of live lattice, taking shape on some vast, outstretched palm—her keel and square frames pretty much like the backbone and ribs of a giant beached fish in the making; and as I looked at the sawyers and teams of horses, the shipwrights and adzes and undead timbers, I thought that she needed but the breath of the Almighty in her yet-unrove rigging and canvas, to take her place amongst the hierarchy of his creatures.

Caught up at once in the demands of his yard work—not only the new ship but the brig and two schooners, with all the hullabalu of construction and launching, on his list for the summer and autumn— Ben was re-plunged into the hectic pace of his shore life, a pace not mellowed any by the pressures of family; and Jim, feeling a bit cut adrift after the close spell we'd shared on board, had his own troubles waiting in the person of Damaris, who if anything'd heated up in his absence. "Time t' face the music," I says to him, that night as we parted for our respective hearths—him to the Inn and me and Jasper to my cabin; but not liking to hurt her he kept putting it off, thinking the news of his being a gypsy might one way or another serve to cool her, once such scuttlebutt'd made the rounds of the town parlors.

It still being a fairly small hamlet—a thousand souls all related, and even more given than usual to minding each other's business— the news about Jim did get around fast, and made something of a local sensation: most everybody having supposed till now the he had come of "quality" stock, even if he did hail from foreign ports, and even if he didn't attend church, or carry around much in the way of specie. Gypsies was seen as something less than civilized, certainly as something less than decent and moral—calling to mind them ne'er-do-wells who showed up at farm fairs, or figured in them yellow-backed flash novels; and to suddenly know that Jim was one of them caused a bit of an about-face in the ranks of several families.

But if Damaris' parents was all at once a mite distant—reluctant to have Rom blood, whatever that was, in the parlor, to say nothing of running through their grandchildren—Damaris herself was apparently all the keener, to judge by her forward behavior, which as always took Jim aback; and confounded by her unexpected reaction—liking her all the more, because she accepted him as he was, and liking even less to hurt her—wanting nothing to do with a family squabble, especially not one with Cy and Amasa, his befrienders—Jim was pretty much over a barrel, and stayed over a barrel with all the grace of a decked codfish.

If Damaris' folks and a few others was distant—if some of Jim's acquaintances added themselves to the list of those who'd never wanted his hat on their hall trees to begin with—most of them who really counted was steadfast; and after the initial jolt of having his origin publicly broadcast, Jim found he was glad he could be hisself. For one thing he had a concrete excuse now for the eccentric shore togs he favored—high-colored weaves and earrings and such like; and it wasn't long before he'd sunk some of his wages into the get-ups he'd hankered after: bright figured waistcoats; pantaloons cut sailor-fashion, tight at the hips and full at the ankles; and as always, bold-colored neckerchiefs, worn Roman-style at his open collar. They wasn't the sort of garb he wore working, any more than he'd worn them to tote tar aboard *Charis*; but in the evenings now, or of a Sunday, you'd spy him at Eli's or on the street turned-out thusly; and nobody sported dry goods with greater finesse than he did.

In fact so well did he carry hisself, with such a fetching yet manly flair, that to my surprise, instead of being put off, or taken aback by such unorthodox costume, several folks started taking an interest, and affecting similar touches in their dress. Not that old sober-sides like selectmen and deacons commenced to discard starched collars and tailskirts; but all the young jacks who'b been round the Horn, and earned a gold earring for their trouble, suddenly up and started to wear them, instead of stashing them away in their sea chests up garret; and there was all at once quite a flurry of neckerchiefs, in place of cravats or neckcloths in the young set.

But to my eye not one of Jim's imitators carried themselves with half the graceful charm of him; for there was an unmatchable something in his bearing—an excitement that seemed to come from his body, and light up all his clothes and motions; and it was not the sort of flame you could copy. "He must be in love," folks started to say, coming out of church or meeting over counters—and a' course they all thought it was Damaris; but I, who knew better, looked on with a proud eye, and now and then had my quiet chuckle.

As if this new freedom to be hisself wasn't enough to make his eyes sparkle, there was his new apprenticeship with Bart, and the challenge of *Abigail*'s figurehead: Jim spending his days in the joiner shop, and most of his eves in his wood carver's shed. Paneling, billetheads, rail stantions, sternboards, all seemed to equally test and delight him; whilst the pattern he was now cutting out from his drawing, with which he would in turn rough out his carving, served to daily stretch and bewitch him. Because the ship's name was still a secret, and a glimpse of her figurehead would blow the whistle, he worked on the sly like he had when he'd carved Ben's, doing his best with old tools and the old shed; but with characteristic promptness Ben went to work on the latter, making it habitable as a Cunarder's cabin.

One late June night when Jim come to unlock, he found that the roof'd been re-shingled, a new window installed and a stove set up, along with several additional lanterns; and not long before his birthday he opened the door to discover a whole new set of tools neatly hung from the wall pegs, in place of the old ones he'd borrowed from Cy: carving gouges, chisels, parting tools, punches, awls and turning gouges of every size and description. When Jim balked at the gift and wrote a promissory note to Ben, bull-headedly signing his name to the debt, Ben sent it back with a bold, black "Cancelled," and a "Happy birthday, you liar: you're finally nineteen"; and dazed nearly to tears by the well-stocked walls and the offering of wood from Cy, Jim joyously began to tackle his carving, dowelling together his sections and roughing out Abigail's likeness.

Watching him work I thought I'd never seen him look finer, or felt him give out a more confident sureness; and I begun to see before me now, taking shape more clearly each eve, *two* figures—the one an iron-willed old lady, emerging from the rough bulk of apple wood; and the other her eager young carver, blossoming into a manly blend of cultures.

Independence Day fell on a weekend, celebrated by the usual midday procession—led this year by the relentless temperance societies, of which there was by now several—then followed by an elaborate dinner, 400 or more gathering on Worthing's front lawn: the day capped by fireworks off the town wharf, and a considerable flow of traffic in the streets. To escape the commotion of wagons, dogcarts and horses all clattering off in different directions, Jim and me sought refuge in Jimmy's tavern, downstairs at the Seven Seas; and there we was joined by Ben and others, all bent on the purpose of banishing the taste of temperance, toasting the States and ushering in Jim's birthday.

Around us the square tables was overflowing, not only with folks but with mugs and opinions, snatches of chanteys and political wrangling; whilst over in our corner, ranged along the long table and depot benches, Longworthy, Worthing, Ben, Tom, me and others was swapping the latest on *Abigail's* progress. Out in the middle of the pine floor—half-blanketed now with swirls of sand and nutshells—Jim in his silk shirt and dark trowsers, and my cousins Obed and Lem in their worn frocks, was tuning up a couple of fiddles; and in betweenst glances at them three, I tried to pry news from Ben across the table. I'd scarcely seen him at all since we'd made port, for he'd worked day and night on the new ship, and overseen the yard's other half-built vessels, hardly even showing up for a Saturday night at Eli's; and beyond the impression he was even more preoccupied than usual, I hadn't a glimmer of what he was up to.

That he'd got his name in the New York newsheets, and received a letter from Capt. Maury—asking him for particulars of the Valparaiso passage, as well as for details of the run to Rio, and for the use of both logs in his planned publication—I'd heard from the scuttlebutt at large in the village; but now that I got the word from him firsthand, I thought that he seemed far less impressed than the town by it. Other topics, too, which would of riveted his interest, any other Independence Day the past decade, seemed pretty low on his scale of attention; and I had a hard time getting more than a grunt or two from him. His obsession with *Abigail*, and the frustrations of home and shipyard, could maybe of explained his relative quiet; but I had my own view of what was eating at him, or shuffling up his deck of priorities; and I gave him a long look as I refilled his tumbler, a sympathetic gleam that was entirely lost on him.

At any rate neither Capt. Maury nor *Abigail* nor Melchett Bros. was what was preoccupying him at the moment; for in our talk his eyes continually strayed from me to the center of the barroom, wherest Jim was holding forth with my cousins. In his salmon shirt, black stovepipe trousers, gold neckerchief and embroidered waistcoat, with Lem's fiddle deftly tucked up on his shoulder—with his blue eyes dancing, his fingers flying, and his restless feet rhythmically tapping, he was easily the center of attention; and I noted how Ben's eyes followed his movements.

Looking myself—remembering the half-defiant, half-desperate young sailor who'd stood before us at our table at Toby's little more than a year ago, I marveled again at the changes in him; and sighing I shook my head and drank deep—only to look up and find Ben's eyes waiting, smiling as if they'd read my meaning. Seeing that the kinks was beginning to fall from him, I put another dent in the bottle of brandy that happened to set at our end of the table, thinning things off with just a splash of water; and our glasses replenished, we leaned back in our chairs, and watched whilst Jim traded bars with Obed, then wound up with a playful flourish.

Clapping with the others, Lem bustled forward, calling for a sailor's shuffle—and his face if possible springing even more to life, Jim kicked off his pumps and stockings, handed Lem his fiddle and joined several of the boys, now forming a line in the midst of the cleared floor. Jumping, clapping, slapping thighs and turning— keeping in lively step with the others, meantime casting laughing looks at their faces, and now and then throwing a roguish glance our way—Jim gave his body up to the fiddles, dancing like a man who's drawn a fine hand; and fascinated by his prowess Ben looked on from behind his half-screen, too balmy by now not to openly gander.

Coming round with a bottle, seldom the one we'd called for, or passing round mugfuls of hot, steaming flip, Jimmy tried to keep up with our needs, and get back to his counter more or less unmolested; but somewheres along the line Jim caught his elbow, and brung him playfully into the shuffle. Doffing his apron he fell in with Jim's rhythm, obediently matching his spins, claps and heel-kicks, whilst the whole of the room roared its approval, and beat on the tabletops for an encore. Chuckling half into his mug with us others, Ben gazed admiringly at the antics—his face taking on an even ruddier shimmer, which I kept encouraging with whatever jug was near us. By now we'd all stopped ordering drinks, and taken to lurching behind the counter to choose ourselves a likely bottle, leaving money for Jimmy somewheres on his desktop; and I couldn't of said myself what we was drinking. Whatever it was it went with the music, and satisfied Jim when he stopped by our table long enough to wet his whistle; and it seemed to cut through the smoke in the lamplight, and take the edge off the growing racket.

At midnight old Jimmy called for drinks on the house, and a general toast went round for Jim: most everybody there knew and liked him, and we all become an anniversary party. There must of been nigh sixty of us crammed into the barroom by then—a steady stream of faces making noise; and between the heat of our bodies, the warm July night, and the undeniable flush of the likker, the place was not unlike a furnace. Jim'd by now had a bit more than usual— Jimmy's round putting him pretty much over the bay; and something in his slackening restraint, the crowd's approval or the ruddy shine to Ben's face seemed to trip a sudden openness in him; for he took the floor as if he'd all at once made up his mind to up the ante.

Catching up the nearest fiddle, he commenced to teach Lem and

Obed some fanciful tune, airy, quick-fingered, vivid—sawing away awhiles by hisself, then encouraging them to follow after; and pretty soon they was all three going at it, playing what must of been gypsy rhythms, the most fetching music I'd ever heard. I could barely set still to listen, and I wasn't hardly the dancing type. Obed and Lem picked up the tempo, carrying on a spell by theirselves; and I thought Robertson would simply catch fire, encouraging them on, clapping his hands, nodding his head like an over-proud parent beckoning on his toddlers' efforts, and tapping his feet with restless excitement. In the midst of the singing I heard Obed yell "Dance, dance!", his voice almost drowned out by the pair of fiddles; and next thing I knew Jim'd jumped in and begun to move into the rhythm, a little uncertain in the beginning, as if trying to remember something he'd seen a long time ago.

There was some faltering on the fiddles, as Obed and Lem tried to oblige his motions; and he gestured them to start again. In another minute or two he had it; Obed and Lem sawed a bit faster, and Jim was dancing in a way I hadn't never seen before, and ain't very likely to see again. He didn't cover much ground on the floor, but he moved his body enough to make up for it: hips, shoulders and knees all seemed to come unglued, and he went spinning, snapping, stepping and twirling, like a creature who's newly received the breath of life, and rejoices to caress the space around him: all the time keeping the beat with his bare feet, and beaming out a roguish promise.

After a few minutes of this he stopped to catch his breath, motioning Obed and Lem as he took off his waistcoat, and wiped it across his sweat-dampened brow; then tossing the waistcoat to us he nodded again, with a gesture to slow things down a little. Putting their heads together Obed and Lem conferred, then picked up their bows with conspirator's grins; and signaling his approval Jim commenced to dance, clearly to the same catching rhythm, but with the tempo scaled down considerable. Following the beat he'd turn a little, ease his shoulders or hips into some guess of a movement, usually about as serpentine as moves get, then stop it short: he was teasing us, and a few laughs broke from the nearby tables.

Then as the cadence gradually brightened he completed all the motions; but they was small, like mere suggestions: by the lift of a shoulder or the sweep of his arm, he seemed to tell us there'd be more. By now he was fetching cries of appreciation, and a few frank snorts of recognition; and he met one and all with an impish grin, as if to see and up the score. His eyes and lips smiling—his brow flushed and shining—he'd shake the hair away from his face, put his hands to his hips and step out a rhythm with all the telling grace of a merman, taking the shore from the deep with a slither; and the cries burst out more appreciative and faster.

As Obed and Lem picked up the cadence, he moved back into the dance as he had before, clapping his hands, twirling about, swirling his hips till I thought they'd come apart; while the sheen of his shirt sparked and flamed in the lamplight, and even his fingers seemed to be dancing. Turning around, he'd show us his back, all sinuous with a flood of motions, and sinewy beneath the light and fabric, till you'd of thought he had the spine of a snake, or the fluid brawn of a seagoing creature. Oh, it was a right indecent dance—the kind of a dance you could only do dead drunk; and nobody there could utter a sound now. Even I, who thought I knew him well, found myself flushing from far more than drink; whilst Ben, he'd long since put down his tumbler, and fallen back into the depths of his bar chair.

Finishing up in style, Robertson followed the fiddles, right up to the summit and then some—deftly contriving to hold hisself steady whilst, his arms outstretched and only his feet working, he spun his hips till they whirled almost too fast to see; then he stopped, all at once, with an exhausted laugh, and quit the floor with a playful flourish. Breaking up into a roar of approval, the place was soon a-ring with lewd calls, and an insistent chorus of "more!" from one corner; but casting a shrug in the direction of the cries, as if to say "What more could there possibly be?", Jim walked up instead to my cousins, and gave them a deep bow of approval. After years of sawing for sailor's shuffles, or strumming for dainty country dances, Obed and Lem looked fairly stunned, as if they'd got a bit more than they'd bargained; but clapping Jim brightly on the shoulder, they assaulted him with their chatter, till at last he broke away, and headed determinedly for our table.

Then he was standing before us, with that dazzling wide grin; his shoulders was still heaving as he tried to catch his breath, and his face was shining with sweat. Getting up at once Ben made way for him to pass, steadying him as he climbed round the chairlegs to take his seat further down the table, then handing him his discarded waistcoat as he leaned exhausted against the wall. Accepting it, Jim wiped his face, then dropped the damp cloth down again on the table, looking a shade overwhelmed and bewildered by the flood of response around him, and gazing sidelong at Ben as if to gauge his.

His face still the ripe hue of a boiled lobster, Ben's expression was easy to cipher; and if that wasn't enough, there was the warm flush of his regard. "Damn!" he said then in admiration, trying to make hisself heard over the others. "I ain't never seen anything like it! Was it a gypsy dance?"

"Aye, one of the wedding dances: the bridegroom dances it," Jim answered, trying to smooth the wet curls back from his face, and dropping his eyes before Ben's bright candor. "There's one for the bride too, of course; she wears a long skirt, and you can't see her knees work. It looks so effortless that way, though it ain't." Raising his eyes, he met Ben's with a long grin, one of the most disarming smiles I'd ever known him to dispatch; and reaching for the bottle, Ben poured him a fresh drink, more for something to do than for manners. Noting the whole exchange with satisfaction, I traded off a wink with Jim; then I realized that all the excitement had unduly cleared my head, and there was our bottle, looking plumb empty: Robertson had got the last of it.

Threading my way behind Jimmy's counter, I gazed for a whiles at the selection: a hundred jugs or more, all inviting, some of them with figured labels, some of them with handsome shapes. Finally I chose one with a fancy glass stopper and brung it back like a prize to the table; Ben did the honors, and poured us each a share. Neither of us ever did determine what was in it; and I still can't recollect whether I remembered to leave a few coins for Jimmy on his desktop.

XIX

BENJAMIN MELCHETT
Cape Damaris, Maine July-Aug. 1843

Jim was out of commission the entire day after, as I found out myself when I stopped by to see him—not just early on but well into the evening, at which time I finally managed to interest him in eating. It was one of the few times I'd known him to overdo it; but—it being a small town—word quickly got round about his antics, an account of his dance all but appearing in the *Recorder*. Before the sun'd set even Anne knew about it, Sadie being as efficient at channeling gossip on dry land as Haggai was in his galley at sea; and no sooner had supper been cleared that evening than she cornered me on the way to the study, taking me to task for having been there, and castigating Jim for such public license. In a bit of a haze still myself from the night's bout, I failed to see where matters were heading; but it wasn't long before I got the picture, for by week's end all four temperance groups were inciting for the repeal of Jimmy's right to sell spirits, and campaigning to dry up every tavern in the county.

There being guests under our roof for the fortnight—Anne's sister June and her three daughters from Portland—I was prevented from venting my ire, as was Anne, only her tight lips showing her dudgeon; but one eve when they'd gone to town to pay visits, and she and I were actually alone in the kitchen, we confronted the issue in short order, both the doors closed to stifle our voices. Calling on every constitutional right I could think of, I condemned the entire temperance movement, and demanded she once and for all break from it; and she just as staunchly decried Jimmy's, insisting again that I give up spirits, and forswear the company I was keeping. The

249

upshot of it all was that, maligning him as lewd, she actually forbade Robertson the house, to bar him from further contact with the children; and stung, I glared as if I hadn't heard right.

Thinking of Jim's incomparable influence—of his liberating affection, and the warm, loving ways that'd drawn out our children—then contrasting his style with June's materialistic rigor, and its priggish effect on her spoilt daughters—I cried, "If Robertson ain't welcome here, damned if I won't make my home elsewhere!"; then trembling, I stopped short, breathless.

Standing still, we faced each other, both of us appalled at my words—me at least as aghast as Anne, as if the awful truth of my feelings, felt for years but never uttered, only came home to me as I spoke. Assaulted by sudden guilt and confusion, I turned away and left the room, Anne directly taking the far door; and thereafter an uneasy truce prevailed, neither of us referring again to the matter, yet neither of us trusting the other. Robertson came and went on occasion, and her kin lingered on through July; but it was an exceedingly disquieting time, even the children clearly feeling the strain. So oppressed was I by present arrangements that it was all I could do to keep up my new friendship with them; and only when I was working on *Abigail,* or spending a rare moment alone with Jim, did I feel free of the weight of home life.

As if to keep up an almost visible pressure, and give expression to my wordless infidelity, an old classmate of mine—Stephen Percival, one of the most highly respected citizens in town, and to all outward appearances, a model of domestic success—suddenly up and deserted his family, simply leaving a note and departing for Boston, where he undertook to begin a new life. Nothing like this having happened for decades, it created a veritable sensation, the whole port preoccupied from the resounding pulpits to the ringing cracker barrels and bar stools. Apart from a compassion for his wife and children, left in the lurch with an apothecary and no income, there was the expected indignation toward Stephen—for abandoning his young ones, for ducking out on his marriage, for shirking his business ties and obligations. Running for once parallel with the majority, my sentiments echoed the town's—obliging me to work with others on 'Change to help manage Stephen's business, establish a new proprietor, and keep his dependents out of the poorhouse; yet rolling beneath my initial reaction was a treacherous counter-opinion, a surge I tried but failed to suppress.

No matter how I battled against it, a pained comradery for Stephen flowed in me—a half-wrenched understanding of the shapeless pressures, the unvoiced denials and disappointments which must have precipitated his action; and no factor I weighed could annul it. In common with the town I was shocked and dismayed, even condescendingly disdainful toward him; but my heart was so wholly in sympathy with him—simply because he had done what I yearned to—that when I entered a shop and heard folks discuss him; when I heard someone declare, "A man like that ought t' be hanged!"—I started and blanched in guilty discovery, as if I'd stumbled on a condemnation of *me*.

For days I wrestled with my convictions, one minute damning, the next envying Stephen; but no amount of thought seemed to steer me through my dilemma, or bring me closer to a resolution. As often as I condemned him for breaking bonds I held to be inviolate, so as often did I feel for his flight; and so as often did I feel my own urge to break free. As I found myself more and more in sympathy with him, and with my own unspoken yearning, I felt myself increasingly outcast—from the town, from convention, from moral laws I myself regarded as sacred; and more and more I was at a loss for direction.

Nor was my feeling of ostracism lessened by the situation of others I respected: men who, far from breaking any moral law, had simply defied popular concept. Here were individuals who, like my uncle Ezra, had thrown over convention to plot their own bearing, or who, like Jackson DeMille, had turned against the tide of the day's religious beliefs, without violating the principles of ethics; yet they were almost as reviled as Stephen, and easily as isolated. Old Ezra, absent now from the town for ten years, and out of contact of all but the few of us who'd stumbled on him accidentally, was almost as scathing a subject as he had been when he'd sailed off a decade ago; while poor Jackson had been in hot water literally since he'd first ascended the pulpit. Only having been engaged in his office ten months, he'd already survived two votes of censure, the second just two weeks ago for avowing allegiance to the doctrine of universal salvation—as highly-contested a bit of preaching as he'd yet delivered.

How could such efforts to to steer by an inner, not an outer compass bring down such a barrage of resistance and hatred, while blindly and unquestioningly following the plotted course of convention yielded such a reaction of praise? And what about the path *I* contemplated—how much smaller still was its chance of acceptance than the ones wrenched out by Jackson and Ezra? Not that public acceptance mattered, so long as I was backed by my own conviction; but how to ascertain conviction in the midst of competing claims; and how to weather its isolation? Even now, though constantly surrounded, thronged day and night by associates and family, I was indescribably lonely.

In my tumult I turned instinctively to Jim; for though by dint of first rate seamanship, gentlemanly address and comradery—not to mention plain old good fortune—he'd won himself a degree of favor, I'd sensed from the beginning some great rupture in his past, some cataclysm or confrontation through which he'd somehow persevered. Though he'd never yet said a word about it—though he'd neither confirmed nor denied such an event—I knew of its existence from the guarded restraint which had marked him since the early days of our acquaintance, and from his obvious break in homeland and culture. Just what had occurred, he'd never confessed—most of the town still speculating on the Liverpool barmaid and such notions; but I felt more and more forcefully that the breach represented an utter parting of ways through Rom law; and it brought me a degree of peace and assurance to think that he'd charted the same seas I faced.

Yet the irony of my situation was that he himself, and what he stood for—his independence, his freedom from objects, his earthy, unfettered sensuality, and his wholly unchristian spirituality— was a part of my dilemma, indeed the very centerpiece of it; and I couldn't lean on him as I longed to. Each day that passed my loneliness increased; and the pressure between what I wanted to do, and what I felt I must continue to do—what principle and prior conviction compelled me to do—became more and more intolerable. Once or twice I almost went to see Eben, knowing that for years he'd anticipated this crisis—but every time I stopped short on the threshold; for I knew that once I put my thoughts into words, there could be no turning back; and I wasn't prepared to embark on that passage.

Without actually coming to the point, however, I began to venture some forays—tentative essays like those of the early explorers, who took care in the beginning not to lose sight of land; and one of my treks was to Jackson's office. Since I'd been commissioned to deliver some papers—a sheaf of documents from John's legal stockpile—I had a reasonable excuse to stop by; and once I was inside he was bound to have me for coffee. It was but a few days since his vote of censure, and there was still plenty of rankling, even though the decision'd come out in his favor; but he looked as calm as if he'd just been out sunning, or returned from a quiet weekend fishing. Looking at him as he handed me my coffee, and a plate of fritters he'd baked himself—scanning his polished patent leathers, his sober attire and tidy neckcloth—I saw that there was not an undone button, not an unpressed crease or a loose tendril to suggest a flurried frame of mind; and I looked at him with awe as he composed himself on the sofa.

Meeting his eyes as he leaned back with his cup, and sent me his usual half-cryptic regard, I couldn't help but suddenly blurt out, "How d'ye keep from bein' rattled?"; and he smiled as if he understood not only the question, but the personal dilemma behind it.

"I ought t' be getting used to it, don't you think?" he responded, taking an unhasty sip of coffee. "Even back in our days at Bowdoin, I was always on the hot side of an issue... Well, seems to me I recall hearing that when *Charis* hit that hurricane, you were steady as a rock yourself; why was that?"

"Why, I was sure as taxes of what I was doin'... I knew exactly what ropes t' haul," I told him.

"Exactly," he said, with a gentle smile at me. "There's a steadiness that comes with sureness of mind. If I seem calm now, it's because I'm convinced that my interpretation is sound; I'm as certain about it as you were of your ropes. These are *my* ropes, all these verses and chapters and parables and psalms; and if I'm ousted for the way I haul on them, why, I suppose there'll be anotheh deck for me to stand on."

That he could be so serene when he didn't know exactly where he was headed—when he knew there wasn't much of a chance he could hold out here much longer—when he must feel at least as lonely as I did, and had no one I knew of to turn to for solace—filled me with quiet admiration; and I looked down at my hands in silence, pierced by a sudden dart of envy.

"Of course," he went on, "I'm realistic about it—I know I'm one of those sent not to change, but to initiate the questioning which precedes change; and on the whole that's an unsatisfactory business. You seldom see your efforts come to fruition; for by the time the questioning you've instigated beahrs results, you yourself've been tarred and feathehed, and sent on to do your dirty work elsewhere.... But that's the nature of the structure of change. Naturally, it's the one who does the jolting that's despised; no one likes to be jarred into direction-finding; we'd most of us like to rot where we are. But jolting's my task, and I accept it; and as you see, I'm not rattled about it."

He'd never spoken to me so frankly about himself or his work before, not even in our days as students when we'd sometimes been drawn to each other as loners; and I felt a yearning to confide in return. In particular I was moved by what he'd said about change—about the discomfort of direction-finding; for I sensed that—despite his unruffled words on the subject—he was no stranger to that pain himself; and I guessed he somehow knew about the high wind that was buffeting the sails of my old life.

"About what you said last week," I began cautiously, starting at a point where I felt not too threatened, and groping ahead for words unfamiliar to me; "this whole business about salvation...about everybody's bein' saved. You don't think then...that folks who ain't Christian...are damned foreveh t' some hell or otheh?"

"I couldn't have preached what I did last Sunday if I hadn't come to that conclusion... Just tell me yourself, Ben—apart from doctrine, or whateveh we're to call what's been handed down to us since our days in Sabbath School—if you can conceive of a God who torments with hellfire those millions who die not claiming Christ, simply because they neveh came in contact with Scripture."

"Those that die in ignorance, no...but what about those who..."—here I had to struggle, to keep my voice from becoming thicker—"who *do* have contact...let's say b'cause they live in a Christian community...yet still don't claim t' know Christ as Lord?"

"How would you say a person claims to know Christ as Lord?"

"Well....by whateveh it is we do here, I s'pose...by bein' baptised, or attendin' meetin', or keepin' the commandments an' so forth."

"Is that how *you* claim to know Christ as Lord?"

I couldn't check a candid twinkle. "No," I said dryly, the corners of my mouth twitching.

"How *do* you know him?" Jackson persisted.

I relapsed at once into sober reflection, wishing that I was wearing a collar, so that I could tug at it to get air. Never once had I actually posed to myself that question, even after nearly three decades of church-going; and I felt myself floundering for an answer.

"I don't know," I got out at last, groping to put darting ideas together. "I couldn't tell you in words... but I could *show* you... in the actions of someone like my brotheh John, when he passes up lucrative government cases...an' puts his time instead int' sailohs' rights, or exposin' the schemes of crimps up to Portland... Or in the miracles I see, y' know, out on the wateh—the schools o' fish all teemin' in moonlight, or silvery in phosphorescence....Or in..."—here I struggled again, to master my throat's ache—"in the closeness I feel, b'tween me an' my loved ones..." Pausing to steady myself, I tried a final push: "All that comes t'getheh in a sort of...holiness... that I c'n feel an' live, an' be a part of...and I guess I'd have t' say...that's how I know him."

A wonderful light had been growing in his eyes, along with a quizzical curve to his lips, which registered his lack of surprise; but all he said was, keeping his voice quiet: "Just as I thought, you know

Christ through the world...just as his early followehs knew him. Now, how are we to tell whetheh an experience of God, which may take as many shapes as there are men and women, is at the core of a person's heart or not? Such subtlety of perception is beyond us—beyond all but the Mind of minds, which alone has the full ability to see."

"Then that's why you've neveh said anything about..." Here I floundered again, for try as I might, I couldn't bring myself to pronounce Stephen's name: the very thought of it so over-flooded me with pain, that I could only trail off lamely.

He looked out at me keenly from beneath his fine brows, with a gaze that was both curious and understanding; and I felt that he knew perfectly well not only the man of whom I was thinking, but the reason I was too moved to name him. "Exactly," he said, passing over my reaction. "The matteh comes not within my purview, but God's. And that brings me back to the question of salvation, which we've now placed where it belongs. When Christ died on the cross, Ben, he died for all; and I take that to mean literally all. Whateveh our sins, or our failure to claim or to know, we're one and all already forgiven. *We* haven't the vision or the right to judge others; and God, who does, has chosen to forgive us!"

"Then...thehre's no 'heathen,'" I said, a light dawning.

"No, none—unless you want to so name those who willfully reject an experience of knowing God; and frankly, I suspect there are more such in Christian circles than there are out in our fields of foreign missions."

I struggled again with the ache in my throat, and tugged at my invisible collar. "Then...what Jim believes, that whole gypsy kind of religion... that's an experience of knowin' God...we're not separate, afteh all."

Jackson looked at me with understanding. "What does Jim believe?" he smiled, putting his fingertips together.

I brushed my hair back and, feeling its damp strands, realized that I'd been sweating. "It's not very coherent, really, as far as I c'n tell....That is, it seems t' change shape accordin' t' his mood, or the requirements of the moment. He told me, once, that there's a kind of a supreme God, though he's not by any means the only benevolent poweh—there's dozens more, all the way down t' the fairies—an' he's not the one that created being. *That* was done by a sort of a goddess, who dreamed the world an' everything in it—though whetheh or not she dreamed God as well, I've neveh been able t' figure. Eitheh way, he's the God of life—not a figure that's separate from creation, like ours is, at least in the minds of most folks around here; but sort of the force that fills creation, all the way from the ants t' the trees in the forest."

Jackson nodded, his eyes bright with interest.

"As far as I c'n tell, he don't demand moral behavior, or have any kind of a relationship with people: he just *is,* that's all...The Rom *do* have strict morals, stricteh than owehs; but they seem t' demand that of themselves...Then there's the devil, too, the Beng, who appears in a lot of different shapes an' disguises—sometimes as a shadow, sometimes as a deformed person; an' a whole spirit world the Rom are afraid of... They're too proud t' submit t' any of it; so they use all kinds of magical arts t' control it, an' bend it more or less t' their purpose—mandrake roots an' charms an' so forth, not unlike some of the old folk practices here."

"Do they believe in some form of aftehlife?" Jackson queried.

"No—well, Jim says not; but I notice the dead seem t' have a lot of poweh oveh the living, which the living have t' more or less rendeh harmless; an' there's a whole code built up around the dead's possessions, which have t' be destroyed so the dead don't b'come restless. It's as if those who've died *do* have a spirit, which b'comes active undeh certain conditions—if someone living speaks their name, for example, or handles their possessions; but there' nothing like a heaven or hell....There's otheh states, though, in between life an' death—like the *mullo,* the living dead, what we'd call vampires; an' there's all sorts and shapes of ghosts...

"I don't know if Jim knows himself how much of it all he still believes," I went on; "he speaks of God, sometimes, as if he was beginning t' have a settled notion of him as Creator; but he doesn't know anything of Christ at all, except for the little I've tried to explain t' him; an' he seems t' still believe in spirits.... Once, at night in the woods, he heard a loon, an' I could see that he was scared—that he maybe thought it was some supernatural being; an' I know for a fact that death troubles him—that he was shook by Matty's loss off the Horn. But it's odd, you know..."—here my voice trembled a little, and I cleared my throat to keep it steady—"in spite of oweh differences, we seem t' have a lot in common...a sort of worship for creation... and....I don't know that I've eveh seen anything more... alive...than the way he lives, so keen t' each moment.....as if his whole body was fresh with God in it."

"Yes, that's it exactly," smiled Jackson, who'd been leaning forward, fascinated. "I don't know him as well as you do; I've only run into him now and again. But each time I've met up with him I've been struck by the thought that his body's the tool of a worshipping spirit; and from what I hear lately, he knows how to use it."

"You mean...that dance at Jimmy's?" I half-gaped.

"Of course," he smiled, his twinkling eyes on me.

I tried a word or two, but only came up with a stutter.

"Don't you suppose that God dances in us?.. That when we dance, we show we know him, as surely as we do in prayeh?"

"Well...but that wasn't just a dance...that was..."

"Sexual innuendo?" he grinned.

"T' say the very least...aye."

"Don't you suppose that the God who made sex, knows sex—recognizes its expression as a form of worship, and uses it himself to woo us?"

Too stunned to come up with a single answer—entertaining a passing thought of what Anne's ilk would say, if they happened upon this conversation—I tugged again at my collarless work shirt, and even undid a couple of buttons.

"What do you think it means, 'to know'—what we've been talking about all this hour?" he kept on.

"Why, t' come t' be familiar with someone...t' recognize," I managed.

"With our minds?"

"Well...aye, with oweh minds, and with oweh hearts or spirits, or whateveh."

"I think you know perfectly well, from the way *you've* experienced

God, that we know and worship God with our senses, the windows of our bodies; and it's but a step from there to our sexual beings."

So close had he come in the past few minutes to the shoals which threatened to shipwreck my future, that I averted my eyes as if to avoid a collision; but he didn't fail to catch my evasion.

"Why do you think the scriptural writehs use the word 'know' so much in a sexual sense—as in all those begats, 'He knew her, and she conceived so-and-so'?"

"Well, I'd always s'posed they was tryin' t' be p'lite," I said dryly, still not looking up from my shirt cuffs.

"To know in the deepest sense is to know sexually—to know with the totality of the body...and it's not limited to our relations with one another. We know God, and he knows us, as marriage partners... so Hosea long ago showed us."

By now I felt I was suffocating—that if I didn't step outside and get some air, I would simply perish for want of a breath; and to my unutterable relief, Jackson suddenly got to his feet, and so signaled the end to the conversation.

"How'd we get started on all this?" he grinned at me, relieving me of my cup and saucer. "Salvation?...Well, I told you there were many ways of knowing, didn't I? We shouldn't be in haste to exclude the Rom; sometimes I think such folk are closeh to God than we are."

"What *I* think," I said, trying to speak lightly, but quavering a bit as I thankfully got to my feet, "is that the day you say all this from the pulpit, is the day you'hre shown out o' town on a rail...an' I'll remind y' I said so, as I'm pickin' the feathehs off ye."

Putting our cups down he threw his head back, and burst into an explosion of laughter— the pure, ringing gaiety of a man untroubled by doubts, and undeterred by the course of the future; and picking up my cap, I listened with envy. When had I ever heard Jackson DeMille laugh like that —Jackson, the sober, the meditative, the quiet? But then again, when had I ever heard him refer to such personal matters as he had discussed in the last ten minutes—matters never broached in any parlor—matters certainly never broached by a bachelor, a preacher!

Getting to the door I bid him good day, energetically clapping on my cap; and giving me a salute as if he was on deck, he grinned at me brightly, "See you on Sunday." As I stepped out the door he looked at me in the confounded way McCabe always did—as if he knew far more about where I was, and where I was headed, than I did; but giving my visor a tug I turned my back, and issued out into the July sun.

Heading back to the yard I went to work, supervising construction on all four vessels; but as I measured and climbed and ran my fingers along faired wood, Jackson's words and Ezra's face and Stephen's departure, and above all the dissension which held sway at home, sped through my mind like a line without an end. Neither that day nor the days after could I see clear to a conclusion; and I took to sitting up late at night on the shore, searching my thoughts as I watched the tide ebb. Bad enough that this point I was carrying such a workload, that I was fatigued and my judgment muddied; but making it even more difficult for me to resolve things—distracting me time and again from the issues—was a matter of which I'd spoken to no one: the state of my private thoughts about Jim.

He'd always figured strongly in my private musings—right from the beginning, when I'd wondered about his mysterious background; but over the months my conceits had taken on more and more of a provocative content, until by now they bordered on the indecent. As long as I hadn't thought about them, they'd remained more or less buried, hidden in amongst alternative sail plans, or personal memorandums to the riggers; but now that Jackson had called attention to them, by putting into words Jim's earthy responses, they darted into visible patterns, like schools of fish in phosphorescent night waters when someone taps the wales of a dory.

From a commencement to wondering about his past, I'd moved to a curiosity about his relations with others—with women especially, such as that Liverpool barmaid; and from there I'd wandered into Welsh barrooms or Mersey dockside dives and apartments, trying to picture him with his sweetheart. I'd let my thoughts drift, imagining what she looked like—conceiving her as older, a sort of a temptress; but embarrassed by my own thoughts, I'd always broken off early in their assignation, feeling like someone who ought to be arrested.

But now—daring to venture further, or drawn to do so—I began to picture them actually engaged in lovemaking, as if I saw them through some convenient keyhole; began to entertain an intense curiosity about his preferences in passion. Anything that I saw in his day-to-day living which would provide a clue to his habits as lover—the uninhibited devotion he showed my children, the caresses and love-talk he lavished on Dee, the manly comraderie he shared with his shipmates: all these became part of and fed my fancy, along with his rare unguarded surrenders. The time that I'd lifted him—ill with fever—to the stretcher, and felt his trusting, confiding submission; the night that I'd held him weeping in my arms, and experienced the fierceness of his deep feeling; the time off the Horn when he'd crawled into my bunk, and abandoned himself to sleep at my side: these episodes, too, fed the demands of my imagination. If I'd needed anything more to convince me that he was as I had fancied—ardent, responsive, playful—I had his dance at Jimmy's to draw from; and Jackson's words, like a chisel, kept his image in focus.

As if these private conceits weren't enough to distract my mind from the dilemmas which pressed me, word all at once went around, on the fifteenth of July, that Damaris had suddenly asked Jim to marry her. Though I'd long anticipated that this was coming—though I'd long supposed that she had the gumption to take the matter into her hands, if he didn't muster the spunk to ask the question—the news nonetheless struck me like a pole-ax; and for the whole of the day I struggled through my work, not knowing what had been his answer. Unable to find out through the scuttlebutt—too gutless to ask him myself, though he worked near—I inwardly writhed as I dragged through my duties, dropping tools and mixing measures, and cursing my carpenters in the heat.

What had he answered when he'd faced the question I'd faced myself when I was his age?—that was the query which drummed through my mind as I labored. Had he been moved by some quiet passion—some deep-run feeling he couldn't reveal lightly, and so had concealed from all save her? Had he, perhaps, been tempted by convenience—by some not unworthy mixture of feeling and seasonable opportunity or timing, such as might draw a man with a youthful vision of marriage? Or had he—could he have succumbed to the safe ease, the stability of established and accepted patterns— the risk-free propositions which had seduced me?

Damaris was a good match for him—I couldn't but see the truth of that as I worked: a strong companion, level-headed, able to keep him on the ground—a good manager, one who could keep tabs on his money—a sincere thinker, free of the class-consciousness he despised—a bit conventional with regard to lifestyle, certainly not a traveler or seaman—but on the whole one of the best women he could marry; and, moreover, she plainly cared for him. As a friend I should have rejoiced for his fortune—for the honor done him within a year of settling in this, a town both staid and narrow; but instead I hated him for it, and detested her even more. That holy tie that Jackson had described— that intimacy of body and spirit—was all of this about to be hers? And was he to know her in return?—to give her children which would be theirs together?

So fiercely did I feel toward her—so forcefully did I resent even the possibility that her life could ever join his in this fashion—that when at last I got the word, through Sadie, at the end of this life-draining day, that he had reportedly refused her, I actually rejoiced in her pain.

But this was not the end of the chapter, as I discovered in the days coming; nor was it the close of my turmoil. I'd barely collected my wits together, and contrived to be civil—if not natural—with Jim, when the rest of the story buzzed past the town's ears, leaked out by one of Damaris' confidantes—maybe even by Keziah. According to the full tale, when Jim had refused her, he'd actually broken down into tears, pleading her parents' displeasure, his lack of background, his youth and want of preparation, and finally—when she remained unmoved by these answers—the fact that he'd already given his heart, and could never offer it to anyone again. "I'm not like other men; I've only got one heart t' give; and I could never live with myself if I tried t' pretend different," he'd supposedly said to her gently; and this response swept through the town's parlors on a veritable crest of gossip, throwing everyone—including me—into a fresh furor of speculation.

What, indeed, had these cryptic words meant? Was he referring to some love left behind in the vague years of Liverpool and Wales, before ever he'd set sail with Walker? Had everyone been right all along about that barmaid—had Jim actually married her, and later fled, like Stephen—was *that* the breach I felt in his past? Had there been a child, out of wedlock or no?—had she died in childbirth, been killed in some dispute? Or was the source of his affection to be found in New York or Boston—an affair brought to some abrupt conclusion—such as the fight that night he met us? Whatever the answer, far from removing him from romantic contention, these words made him even more the center of attention; and not one girl I knew accepted them as binding.

Some, like Damaris—packing her bags for Portland, where she intended to take refuge with her cousins—reportedly refused to wholly give up, moved, perhaps, out of sympathy for his old pain, each supposing she could be the one to ease it; while others, wondering if his words hadn't applied to the present—wondering, in short, if one of *them* wasn't the one he'd already given his heart to—could be seen jockeying into position around him, angling for invites to picnics and socials. Doggedly going about his business—carrying himself with his usual restraint and proud poise—Jim neither said more nor picked up the bait, refusing attentions with the excuse of his work; and no further news came from him of his story. Unwilling to leave matters dangling in mid-air—hanging out in the kitchen with Sadie, hoping to catch wind of some telltale postscript—I picked up all the scuttlebutt I could on the subject; but no bit of it held more promise of truth than any other bit; and every piece roused my fancies to a distracted pitch.

In the midst of all this the weather suddenly turned chill, with a predilection toward rain and fog that recalled spring; and an unseasonable attack of grippe swept in with it. Before long we were obliged to shut down the yard, so great was the number of workmen afflicted; and many of the shops and businesses followed suit.

Working on his figurehead, Jim still kept busy, managing to keep off the list of those stricken; but out at our house matters were not so lucky, Anne being one of the first to succumb. Having had no experience of her being ill—save when the young ones were born, which seemed to slow her down little—I was at a loss for a fortnight, trying to fill in round the edges with Sadie, and keep from clobbering June and her daughters; while the children wandered about half-aimless, moping or engaging their cousins in quarrels. Already on edge from the strife between me and Anne, which they somehow sensed despite our discretion, they seemed as crank as a shipload of muscovado; and the rudderless way they roamed made me restless— made me realize how much they depended on Anne for direction.

Climbing into my arms on the shore one evening, Jean gave the sigh of a weary creature, burying her head on my chest like a hare seeking its burrow; and thrilling to her soft, silky tresses on my cheek—to her slight, dainty form in the span of my big hands—I set aside my concerns to pet her. Thinking it was her mother she yearned over, I was brought by the lee when she murmured, from the depths of her warm perch on my shoulder: "Papa, you'hre not goin' away soon, are you?"; and guilty as if I'd just been caught packing, I tried to make answer brightly: "We ain't due t' sail till afteh Christmas ...thought you'd undehstood that."

Cuddling closer to me with her small hands, she murmured again, half-muffled in my shirt: "I neveh see you much, it seems like...you'hre eitheh to sea, or workin' in the yahrd."

Kissing her smooth hair—too moved to sound light—I answered her with a tremble in my voice: "Didn't know it matthed so much, mate...thought it was y'r Ma you children looked to."

Lifting one shoulder with a thoughtful, slow shrug, she muttered loyally, "I love Mama, but"—here her voice took on a droll tone— "she doesn't know a yahrdarm from a pawl bitt."

Bursting into a roar of laughter—the first unchecked hilarity I'd known in some weeks—I offered to her, rejoicing with heart's ease: "Well, in that case we'd best go have us a sail, eh?"; and instantly she was upright in my arms.

"D'ye mean it? Just you an' me? Right now, t'night?" she chattered;

and caught up in her elation I chuckled,

"Don't know why not, we c'n take Uncle Tom's sloop...Lord knows y'r Ma ain't fit t' stop us."

Taking the starboard tack in a fine breeze, wet with the day's rain and briny with sea tang, we swiftly filled away toward the east, and luffed out into the open bay: Jean for the most part by my side at the tiller, save when she now and again shifted a line. Watching her balanced, quick, nimble movements, I thought what a first-rate sailor she was, as good as her brother Tom, with an instinctive knack like Jim's; and I looked at her agile figure with pride. Though she was a fair swimmer, I'd put her in a cork vest as a precaution; and over its tan back her flaxen hair spilled, or lifted and rippled in the gusts of wind. Stroking it with my free hand, I drew her to me, and settled her against my shoulder; and thus the two of us sat for an hour, our eyes on the greys and greens of the mainland.

As she lifted her hand now and again and pointed, or looked up at me, her face alight with kinship, the faces of Stephen's children came back to me with a stabbing swiftness; and with them came my old doubts and dilemmas. But so sublime was the evening, so splendid the bountiful, tossing, brine-threaded sea, that I could forget the sting for a time, as if I found healing at work in the salt air; and I simply sat by Jean in acceptance, wordlessly rejoicing in our rest, and cherishing her in our common need.

Under the layered clouds the Camden Hills rose and fell like smoky carvings, a gleam of sun now and then on their profiles; while across our stern the blue-grey seas rolled away from our wake of silver. At this distance from land, the shore took on a sense of completion, an imaged fullness that'd been obscured by nearness, or by my own muddled self-involvement; and as I contemplated its unbroken visage, I bowed in homage to its panorama: what had been, and what was yet to be, insignificant in the vastness of its arena.

By the end of July—with Anne recovered, and her sisters Charlotte and Louisa in residence with their families, in a sort of colossal reunion—matters were back in high gear at our place; and my evening with Jean began to pale in me, like the outlines of an isle slowly falling astern. Driving home after a hectic day at the yard, I typically encountered the whole Howland clan, in addition to Anne and the children; and I scarcely felt at ease in my own house. The eerie feeling I'd had last November when Jim and I had returned from camping—the sensation that the rooms had all somehow shrunk—had never really dissipated; and now, with all my in-laws crammed in them, and portmanteaux, hat cases, and valises stacked head-high, they seemed as cramped and stifling as boxes. Though it was now mid-summer, the weather had still not improved, rendering it as oppressive outdoors as in; and I began to despair of sending *Abigail* down the ways by late autumn.

One chill, damp afternoon when the clouds seemed to lower, and the wind to blow the fog into my very bones, I suddenly felt I could endure things no longer; and I crept under a scaffold for shelter. As if I'd just ducked out on a fist-fight, I sat myself down on a bare plank, aching—reflecting that not even in the stiffest weather at sea, had I ever felt so weary. I wanted rest—but not only rest for my body; I wanted rest for the whole of me, for my fatigued mind as well as my limbs: repose of the quality I'd found sailing with Jean, but longer-lasting, the sweet rest of home. I longed for a haven, as an animal longs for its burrow; wanted the warmth of a fire, the seclusion of a nest.

Perhaps it was the dampness; perhaps I, too, was falling ill; but the thought of heat grew in my mind until was need was demanding as that of an addict. Blazing fires and cheerful hearths began to appear in my inward eye, while my body shivered in my damp work garb. But it was more than the radiance of a fire I longed for; I wanted warmth all around me. Something within me demanded a cover—craved the secluded withdrawal of sleep. Then suddenly I realized I needed to see Jim—that it had been days, too many days, since we'd sat down and shared a moment together. Somehow the mere thought of him brought a spark into my life; and getting to my feet, I ducked back out of the scaffold. Jackson, Damaris, unsettling fancies all forgotten, I left the yard without a word to anyone, and hurried directly to the Inn; it was late afternoon, and I thought I would find that he had returned to his room.

The Inn was as dark and cheerless as the day; not a soul roamed the halls, and the ladies' parlor was quiet. Hastening up the steep stairs to Jim's room, I knocked a couple of times on the door; when he didn't answer, I opened it with my key, and entered. He wasn't there—hadn't been there, I judged, since morning; and heaving a sigh, I dropped my keys on the table, and cast a weary glance at the hearth. The ashes in the grate were cold; I looked at them, and all at once felt too tired to set the nearby logs to burning. But Jim's presence was at work in the room; I sensed it, as I'd sensed it last fall, waiting day after day for *Amanda*; felt it as soon as I'd shut the door, and closed myself in the four walls which were his; and gradually it began to ease me.

As when one enters the bounds of a fir wood, and lets the boughs close behind like a gate, so now I felt the cushioned calm that somehow reigns in the sheltered heart of a pine grove; and I breathed the quiet breaths of homecoming. For a long time I stood looking fondly from one place in the room to another—stood contemplating the profound silence of half-animated waiting objects, the mute testimony they gave to his being. What a characteristic disarray!— the disarray of a man who has little concern for objects, beyond the passing pleasure they offer, and no thought whatever for their ultimate order. His clothes were strewn about on the floor in odd, crumpled heaps like jettisoned cargo; I saw his dungarees, his old red jersey, an assortment of cotton frocks and flannels—three or four days' worth of discarded outfits. There were more dumped across the back of the comfortable overstuffed chair: a couple of pairs of varnish-stained duck trowsers, a plaid workshirt that he'd worn to sea.

The sofa was wrinkled and looked much sat-upon, as if it had recently hosted a seal-pup; the pillows were lying as if abandoned, across the cushions or down on the floor. Over by the window, his desk was a hurrah's nest of books, half-open and propped up to show the sketches of ship's paneling, or the profiles of figureheads. Over the lot, like the calm eye of a windstorm, presided the placid shape of the window; through the half-opened curtains, I could see the fog moving on the face of the sea.

Looking across the room, I suddenly spied the wardrobe, a tall, strong pine cupboard whose doors now stood open; and curiously drawn, I went and paused before it. Inside I could see a regular cascade of clothing—jackets and sweaters hanging from hooks, neckerchiefs and scarves dangling down, duck trowsers, coveralls, stovepipes, and dungarees trailing from pegs to the cupboard floor. Quietly charmed, I bent to look at the colorful jumble—at the characteristic touches of red and blue—at the half-faded splashes of a checkered shirt, or the nautical stripes of a jersey—at the practical stretches of grey flannel. How diverse it was, this concourse of garments—how vividly it portrayed the complexities of the many-faceted man who wore them!

Soon I found myself considering the textures—the effusion of wools, with their rough weave and deep piles; the onrush of knits, with their broad, nubby webwork; the eddies of frayed cuffs and worn sleeves and shirt backs. Strange how I'd never noticed before the contrasts of the common needle—or the energies of garments lived and worked in! Almost I felt that the whole configuration might start moving, so great was the charge of his person in it—so intense the suspended motion in the draping of the clothing. The legs, the sleeves, the scarves might have been a waterfall, halted for a moment to permit me to see the individual droplets, and the foam of cloth at the bottom.

I suddenly thought of Jim's gypsy wagon, of his father and their belongings—imagined the chests overflowing with their garb, the tiered berths brimming with blankets and old quilts—and swiftly it seemed that in the wardrobe before me, I saw Jim himself, or part of him. Leaning forward, I touched some of his things—felt a variety of surfaces slip through my fingers: the scratch of wool, the coarse rub of twill, the softness of cotton and the filmy lightness of silk, all privy to his person and body. Like a man at a river, I scooped in my fill, burying my face in a handful of garments, as if they were some source of refreshment; then fabrics and forms began to blur before me—I realized there were tears in my eyes, and felt amazed. The thought that a tangled heap of clothes could make me cry! Reaching back in, I put his things down, with fingers that trembled as they grazed the cloth; then standing up, I turned away, and found myself looking at the bed.

Exactly as he must have left it that morning, tumbling out in a hurry to get ready for work, it was the very picture of comfort— the rumpled pillows supple and yielding; the jumbled blankets and sheet half-thrown back, revealing the expanse of the mattress, like an envelope opened to disclose its missive; and the mattress itself softly mounded and plumped up, the fattest and best in a feathered ticking. The bedclothes looked chaotic, but enticing and warm; and there were garments of his tangled in with the quilt—a nightshirt and night-socks, garb he only wore when—as he must have been lately—he was pressed to concede to the cold.

As I gazed an utter weariness swept over me, a yearning to capitulate to weakness and need; while the bed seemed to beckon like an invitation, a sumptuous promise of comfort and warmth. Somehow something whispered that to crawl inside it to rest would be to bring me closer to Jim; and before I knew what I was doing, I was taking off my cap. Jacket and boots quickly came next, tossed on the floor like their leather kindred, which were peeking out from beneath the bed skirts; and in due order followed twill trousers and waistcoat, too damp and work-soiled to sleep in. Then climbing in amongst the soft blankets, and pulling the whole nest of them close about me, I heaved the sigh of a hare in its burrow, and handed myself over to my slumber.

It was almost dark in the room when I wakened, with that vague uncertainty which lingers for awhile. Jim's key had turned and clicked in the lock; I heard him enter and shut the door, and stop for a moment—he must have seen me at once. Though my back was turned to him, I kept my eyes closed, feeling a bit foolish to have made myself so at home; but my senses on the alert, I listened, trying to make out his motions. I heard him sit down and take off his boots—heard the tug and pull of the buttons, and the clump of each heel as it hit the floor; heard him draw on a pair of slippers, then unbutton his coat and drop it on the sofa. Next I caught the soft pad of his feet as he went to the hearth to build up the fire; heard the scraping of logs and the rustle of tinder, the rubbing of bark and the dry snap of twigs, and the crumpling of newsprint or wastepaper; then finally I caught the strike of a match. At once the cheerful sound of crackling and burning filled the room—I heard the snap of pine needles and sparks, and smelled the pleasing odor of birch.

A few moments later, almost dozing again, I heard Jim's light tread softly approach me; felt him reach over me, and cup his hand to my face, very gently so as not to disturb me. His palm was warm; he'd held it before the fire first. Probably he thought I was ill, and looked for the obvious signs of a fever. I felt him brush me again, briefly, on the back of my neck with his deft hand; though his touch was light, his familiarity lingered. Then he straightened the bedclothes at my feet, and moved the blankets closer about me. A moment later his presence was no longer near, and I heard the sounds of him padding back and forth in the middle of the room, tidying the place up probably. I slept again.

When next I wakened more completely, it was wholly dark out the window. The fire and two lamps were burning; their reflections flickered on the wall near me. By now I felt I couldn't move to save my life; I felt as if I'd taken root, grown to the bed in a kind of luxurious restfulness. But something had to be said to Jim; I couldn't simply take over his room in this fashion. Summoning up what little energy I possessed, I managed to turn onto my back, and look across the way to the fire: he was sitting nearby it, sketching at his pad, with one of the lamps bright at his elbow. Something in his face put me in mind of other faces by other fires—put me in mind of my mother's expression, those nights she'd sat by me reading the Bible, while I'd lain battling scarlet fever as a lad—then harkened me back to what I'd felt on my own face, that first night in Boston when I'd watched *him* by the fire: not just a wakefulness but a caretaking, the vigilance of heedful devotion. In the warm quaver of the light his cast-down lashes, his sensitive lips and broad, gently-drawn brow gave out an attentive patience—a tender softness I'd never seen there before; and I drew myself up on one elbow, awe-hushed.

Hearing my movements, he put down his pen, then came and sat down beside me at once; and looking up into his warm, knowing gaze—seeing his understanding, and the sympathy which showed not in spoken expression, but in the tender incline of his head—I tried to beat down the hot pain which sprang in me. Having never seen him like this—having never marked before how soft, how almost maternal was his attention—I was thrown into confusion, a tumult which heightened the weaknesses of the day, and intensified my grateful feeling; and it was all I could do to fight down my response. Meeting his smile I tried to think of a place to begin, a starting point to explain my presence—but it was hopeless; and I merely met his eyes.

But it was enough; he smiled as if he'd read me—as if there was no need of words between us. "Like some supper?" he asked simply, as though coming home, and finding me in bed without an explanation, was pretty much the usual order; and grateful beyond words for his acceptance, I nodded. Giving another smile he got up at once, lighted the spirit-lamp, put on a teapot, set out a couple of cups and a small kettle, into which he cast some bark and herbs, probably preparatory to boiling one of his god-awful medicinal concoctions; then putting on his boots he slipped out the door, heading down to the kitchen to wrangle something solid from Jimmy.

He returned not long after, heralded by the clatter of dishes, and the occasional clinking of silver; and I watched his shadow as he entered the room, and carried a steaming tray to the table. Propping me up, he set the meal before me: hot soup, warm rolls and cheese, just the kind of supper I'd been vaguely dreaming of; but before he would let me touch a bite, he insisted "First this," fetching from the fire his villainous cauldron.

Pouring out a generous ladle—picking out the bark, and adding a bit of water to cool it—he handed me a simmering cup; and gazing doubtfully into its depths—not failing to take note of the herbs, flakes of which were a-swim on the surface—I saw that it had the consistency of brine, and resembled the color of a spring run-off. Finding some strength, I scowled my disapproval—but he scowled right back, his dark brows diving together; and I meekly drank the venomous stuff, Jim not letting me stop till I'd drained it all off.

Whatever it was, it didn't kill me; and grateful for that, I tackled the soup, and washed the works down with a cup of black tea: Jim's brew, always a fine one. Sitting beside me, he supped too in silence, occasionally passing me the salt or butter; and when I finished, he wordlessly took the tray, while I settled back into the pillows. Seeming to know I longed to stay, he took my presence in that casual way of his, acting as if I'd spent every night as his guest; and relaxed by his ease I again grew sleepy, nestling into the bed as if I lived there. Bringing me another pillow, he straightened up the wild tangle of bedclothes, then slipped into their midst two hot water bottles, which he'd just filled and wrapped in flannel; and soon the whole nest was a-glow with their warmth, as pleasing as the blazing hearth fire.

Feeling the occasional touch of his hands, the brush of his fingers as he helped me to settle, I reveled in being taken care of—something that hadn't happened to me since boyhood. How was it I'd never noticed before how gentle, how tender Jim's touch was? Had it always been so, and I hadn't seen it? Or had he just now slipped the veil from his fingers? Before I could ponder out any answer, I was drifting out into slumber, aided by all but one of the lamps being blown out—not even rousing into awareness by the thrum of a knock at the door, and the sound of someone asking for me. Vaguely I heard an exchange of murmurs, then caught Jim's half-hissed, stubborn rejoinder: "If you wake him up, I'll break your neck!"; and feeling all the more protected, I floated out on another slow thought, with the feeling that I wouldn't have to move now till sometime or other after dawn.

Perhaps it was Jim's villainous potion, perhaps the healing strength of his nearness; but whichever the case, when I wakened mid-morning, it was with some semblance of vigor. Looking around, I saw that he'd departed, but not without taking thought to my needs: a vivid fire was a-blaze on the hearth, and the makings of breakfast were laid out on the table. Hauling myself out of the bed, and finding he'd spent the night on the sofa, I wrapped myself in the spare comforter he'd left, set the coffee-pot on the spirit-lamp, and curled up in a chair by the fire.

It was here that I noticed another cupful of bark bilge, ready and waiting for me at my elbow, as if he had known exactly what I'd do on waking, and where I would light for a spell to come to; and exasperated, I muttered a Rom curse. Looking into the murky depths with distaste, I considered various options, such as pitching the whole thing into the fire, or summarily dumping it out the window; but at last, heaving a sigh, I drank it, following it up hastily with coffee. Even more unpalatable cold than hot, it was as bitter as wormwood, and oily; and it took three cups of coffee and the entire breakfast—brown bread and herring, a fisherman's mainstay, for which he'd probably gone to the market—to eradicate the persistent taste.

So relaxed from my long sleep, and still so bone-weary, that I needed a lengthy meal anyway to revive me, I took my time over my plate, scanning at whiles the patterns of fire, or the rows of bark-filled jars in the cupboard, wondering which was responsible for my brew. Then finally, feeling more human—feeling sated not just by breakfast, but by the whole substance of my visit—I heaved myself regretfully to my feet, and washed myself up in the basin; pulled on my work garb and worn-out brown boots, and searched beneath the bed for my cap. Looking around the room one last time—lingering again at the open wardrobe, and leaving the morning's clutter as I'd found it—I banked the fire and blew out the lamp; then picking up my keys from the table, I left this place that had been home for a night, and broke away from its warmth for the yard.

Here, too, in the chaotic noise on the ways, I found that Jim'd gone before me—that he'd sent ahead messages to Spooner and Matthew instructing them to expect my lateness, almost as if he'd known what time I'd arrive; and later on I discovered he'd spared me considerable hot water at my house, having sent Anne word the night before I was ill, and bedded down for the time being at his place. Since I was clearly still under the weather, and not just hung-over from the effects of Eli's, I found the opposition I'd expected withdrawn, and a caustic battle with Anne averted; and I retired that night so grateful to him I was heartsore.

Nor was that the end of his support; for over the next several days, as I dragged myself about the yard—as I camped by first one vessel, then by another, sitting down on the job for the first time in my life—he kept showing up at odd moments with his brew, never often enough to get my back up, and coaxing me into drinking the vile stuff, never obstinately enough to provoke my resistance. Like a bracing liquor or healing elixir, such visits as these sped the return of my full strength, and brought, with fair health, an easing of burden; and I found myself making progress on all fronts.

Yet underneath my returning vigor flowed a nagging counter-current—the persistent feeling that what I had called home, all these years with Anne and the children, and even before, with my own parents, had nothing to do with home as I now knew it— with home as I'd lived it that night at Jim's; and I yearned to live it again more fully—to wake up in the morning and fall asleep with its sureness, its certainty of place and belonging.

In particular I wanted to live it with Jim—to spend more time with him, to actually share space with him, to eat and drink three times a day with him, and partake of the ordinary events of life with him, as I had tenting on the river last autumn, or sharing the quarterdeck of *Charis* last voyage. As I went about my business—as August came in, and with it fine weather, hot and dry with southwest breezes—I tried to come up with a plan to free time; but so pressing was the yard, with the renewed pace of building, and so insistent were the demands of my home front, that I had scarcely an hour a week to myself; and even Jim seemed too busy to break away much. A night's talk with Eben—one of those maddening hearth-chats, in which I sat by silent, and he read my scowl-lines, might have produced the germ of an idea; but he was off on the Banks for a fortnight, setting trawl with some of his cousins, and there was no recourse to his place for the time.

So frustrated did I become, and so hell-bent for quiet, that I might have just taken off on horseback, leaving family and work to go to blazes, if matters at home hadn't suddenly taken a new turn; for Louisa and offspring were unexpectedly called back to Portland, prompting a general exodus of houseguests, and all at once it looked as if I might be able to hear myself think at our place. But that was not the only hopeful development; for as I packed trunks with Anne, sitting on lids as she locked them—as I was on the point of voicing good-riddance, with a fervent sigh of heart-felt deliverance—I happened to catch a glimpse of her face; and straightaway I was visited by an inspiration.

"Why don't you go along?" I asked her, giving the belts a pull as she latched them; and she looked at me as if she hadn't heard right.

"You mean...to Pohrtland?" she asked dryly, not supposing I'd meant it; but underneath her wry tone was a timbre of longing—an eager yen that must have been there for some time; I just hadn't before chanced to hear it.

"Why not?" I asked, as she started a band box. "They could cram you int' one o' them stages somehow...might even be room for y'r trunk on the stage top."

She cast me a wry look as she nested Charlotte's hats; but I could see she lingered on the idea.

"I suppose I could take the children...Nat's enough of a boy now to travel," she said doubtfully, knowing full well it was ridiculous to invite me, even if I could get way from the yard.

"Leave the children here; go youhrself and have fun—you haven't had a break in a spell," I told her. Actually it was over two years since she'd gone off, now that I stopped and thought about it; but in her astonishment she didn't even needle me for the remark.

"And who would mind the young ones?" she asked dryly. "You know Sadie's going home to the island this month, at least fohr a week, though I think likely longeh; and even when she's here, she'll need help with the housework."

"We could get some cousin of otheh of hers t' help out—an' the week she's gone, *I'll* look afteh things hehre," I put forth, as serious as I'd ever been on an offer.

For a moment she stood looking at me in amazement, having drawn herself up to her full height as I'd spoken; then she burst into a peal of laughter.

"What's so funny about that?" I blustered, deeply offended,

though I tried not to show it.

"You'd do the housework, cook the meals, dress and wash and mind the children?" she taunted, looking at me with derision on her face.

"Why the devil not?" I countered. "I could get Spooneh t' hold down the fort for one week, while I do whateveh needs t' be done hehre."

"Benjamin, do you have any idear of what it takes to run this house? The baking, the washing, the cleaning, the mending? Not to mention looking afteh the children, and teaching them their duties and lessons! I'lll wageh you couldn't keep things going a day."

"Hell, I run an entire ship, don't I? Look afteh 20 men in a gale o' wind, an' keep things from goin' t' pot in the meantime?" I cried, stung that she'd doubted my ability, and confident myself of what I could do. "*Charis* is two times as big as this house, an' I'll be damned if she ain't the cleanest ship in the merchant marine! Not a rope-end out o' place, an' the whole thing runs like clockwork."

"And I suppose you do the washing, know the difference between pinking and bluing, how much soap to whittle in each tub, when to scrub and how to sort, and how to heat and use the irons," she mocked, getting back with a shrug to her sandbox.

"I could get one o' the McCabe girls t' direct; Lord knows I've got enough elbow grease t' follow," I huffed, even more nettled at her aspersions.

"And the cooking?" she persisted.

"I c'n make the best johnnycake this side o' Boston...an' put t'getheh anything that swims or crawls in the sea...there ought t' be enough out thehre t' keep us."

"Benjamin, I'm almost willing to take you up on it all, so that you'll find out first-hand what I'm up against here, and how much I need a maid," she declared, filling a fresh trunk with her old hard expression, though I detected a twitch at the corners of her mouth.

"An' I'll be damned if I ain't willing t' seal the bargain, t' show you I c'n do it," I countered.

"You'd keep the children clean?" she pressed me.

"Within reason," I pledged dryly.

The corners of her mouth twitched higher, but she managed to keep her voice stern. "You'd look afteh their morals?"

"Damn right I would."

"No cursing?"

"Well....I'd restrict it."

"No drinking?"

"I don't drink at sea, do I?"

"No, I'll grant you that; I'd have heard about it if you did...You'd take them to church?"

"Every Sunday."

"Sabbath School aftehward?"

"Even if I boil in my collah."

She paused as if weighing invisible factors, my deficiencies on the one hand and my qualities on the other, to see if matters came out in my favor; and meantime she kept piling things into the trunk. "I *know* you'd make them mind," she muttered, folding in garb without much heed to order; but her eyes gradually brightened from cobalt to corn-flower. "I could stay in turns with June and Charlotte and Louisa," she went on, up to her elbows now in a cloth sea, "maybe a week or so at each place....a couple of days at Motheh's... a couple of days to travel... I'd be gone a month," she finished, smoothing out the folds of a dress.

"A month it is," I concluded, thinking we'd wrapped things up for the moment.

"I'd want to shop," she persisted, ignoring me as she started a fresh pile. "I'd want access to some of my money, Benjamin, to buy cloth... I could get some lengths of wool and some good broadcloth for the children for winteh...some nankeen and linen for undeh garments..."

"You don't need t' touch youhr money; I'll get you a letteh o' credit t' draw on in Pohrtland."

"I could check into some furniture," she went on, looking at me out of the corners of her eyes.

"Oh, no! Thehre I drawr the line. Not one more stick comes int' this place; ye couldn't cram it in if ye tried to," I retorted.

"I was thinking of re-doing the parloh...The style now is

different…and it's so much more ornamental; such pretty scrollwork and leg carvings—"

"What, you mean claws an' such, like that atrocious stuff in the dining room at John's place?" I bellowed.

"Yes, that's exactly what I mean! Depend on Cybil to be up-to-date and stylish."

"Anne, that god-awful stuff's a nightmare! It'd get up at night an' walk around while we were asleep; I know it would."

"Oh, get along with you," she huffed, slamming another lid shut and locking it; but I knew that we had struck a bargain.

It was the fastest packing job I'd ever seen her accomplish, twenty-one hours flat from laundry tub to locked trunk; but at the end of that time she was ready, and climbing onto the stage with Louisa and her daughters, the place so crammed full of dress skirts and hat brims, parasols, handbags, reticules and ribbons that I could barely get the door shut on them. Leaning back with her sisters she was giggling and chatting, her face bright and carefree as it had been in her teen years; and I thought as I looked at her how suited to this sort of life she was—to traveling and visiting, shopping and buying, eating out and socializing.

I knew what she'd do these next four weeks as plainly as if I was going with her: the trips to the import stores, the best in Portland, all up and down Exchange Street and Moulton; the stops at the dry goods shops, chock full of arrivals, light silks from Canton and cottons from Madras; the missions to the milliners, or the visits to dressmakers, where she'd choose hats and dressings, or be fitted and re-fitted, while Louise looked on from brocaded ante-parlors; the calling cards, invitations, sociables, visiting days, walking parties, croquet matches, lawn-parties, ship launchings, church services, recitals and concerts, non-stop from the break of day to midnight. It was far worse a pace than Cape Horn in winter; and for myself I infinitely preferred the latter. As they drove away, the glass down, gloved hands waving, I shook my head again at our difference; then I bent down to comfort the children, both Courtney and Seth having dissolved into wailing.

The first fortnight or so things went fairly smoothly, Sadie holding down the fort with one of her cousins while I worked overtime at the yard to get ahead; but on the morn in mid-August when I saw her off on the ferry and returned home alone with all five children, I got an idea of what I was in for. Having turned over the ship for a week to Spooner, and put Matthew in charge of supervising the schooners, I was free to devote my full time to the home front; but I swiftly found out how inadequate full time was.

Hauling in pails of water, heating them for dishes, scrubbing pots clean and straightening the kitchen, I, like any lubber, could manage; but coordinating such work with all five children, every one of whom seemed possessed with an unusually high degree of motion, proved to be a feat of epic proportions; and I battled to direct maneuvers. By the time Jean was pulling on my pant-leg, saying "Papa, I'm s'posed t' be doing my Scripture by now, an' Tom hasn't finished his Sabbath School lesson"; by the time I'd settled an upsurge of quarrels, mostly by standing distressed heads in corners; by the time I'd plucked the dog out of the parlor and Seth out of the flour barrel in the pantry, I still hadn't made much headway with dishes; and I called all hands aft to consider matters.

"Thomas," I said, tying an apron around him, "youhr job is washin', an' Jean's is dryin'; an' Seth, you ain't goin' nowhere till you've cleaned up the pantry. I don't care if it takes ye till suppeh t' figure out how t' go about it: here's the broom, the dustpan, a wet rag an' the scrap pail. Courtney, you'hre goin' t' help me put dishes away; an' for every one ye bust, you'hre goin' t' bed a half hour early. An' Nat, you'hre goin' t' bed right now, 'cause I'll be damned if I c'n figure what the hell else t' do with ye!"

From then on, with all hands working, there was no more fooling round—though every time I looked at the clock, it seemed to be unaccountably later than it should be, with fewer chores accomplished than called for. It was mid-afternoon time Seth cleaned up the pantry, with a final assist from me, and four time Tom and Jean sat down to lessons; and while I helped them with those Nat climbed out of his youth bed, and took a header down the front stairs. When I picked him up he appeared none the worse for wear, save a fair-sized goose-egg on his forehead; and I set Jean to watch him while Tom and I fetched kindling, and started up the stove for supper. The menu being exceedingly simple, about half the spread as usual, and all of us being too tired to care, the evening meal was soon over; and there was no fuss about division of labor for clean-up.

But all of this, I soon discovered, represented the easy part of the day; for next I had to make dinner for the morrow, baked beans and bread, which Sadie'd set, so that I wouldn't have to work on the Sabbath—something I'd sworn to Anne I wouldn't do; and then all five children had to be bathed, trimmed shipshape and Bristol fashion for church, dressed in their nightclothes and prayed over or whatever, all by a fairly reasonable hour. So great was the quantity of water which had to be drawn and brought in—Tom and Jean gladly taking it in turns with me; so large the amount that had to be heated, and poured with the cold into the brass tub; so demanding the actual bathing, both the girls first, and both of them with long hair, then Nat and Seth, then finally Tom, in water fast becoming dirty; and so exhausting the after-bath routine, nail-trimming, hair-brushing, night-dressing, fire-stoking, that by the time I got back down to the water, it was stone cold, and the beans were burnt to an unappetizing crust.

Sunday at dawn I woke feeling hung over, despite the fact I'd stayed on the wagon; and that was the best thing that happened all morning. Though I rose and dressed early, got the stove going, and even spearheaded a campaign for breakfast, things dissolved into chaos with the appearance of children; and three sheets in the wind things remained until church time.

As we ate I mulled over all our Sundays together, all our departures for church with Anne and Sadie; and I marveled that we'd got off on time, in our right minds. Just how did Anne coordinate the children? How was it they were always dressed for the table? Did she herself dress them, or did Jean help with the young ones, and how did they ever manage all the buttons? The dresses, the pinafores, the frocks, the round coats, the little kid boots and patent leathers—

all had hundreds and hundreds of buttons; and where there weren't buttons, there were ties and sashes.

And once dressed, how did Anne keep them clean till departure? Surely she didn't force them to sit still till called for—but what else *did* she do to keep them in order? How did she ever keep track of all the comings and goings: the trips to the outhouse, every one of the children save Tom and Jean needing help there—the tool shed, the henhouse—good Lord, I'd never collected the eggs!—the well, the springhouse, the stables? How was I going to get the horses harnessed and the carriage out, without one of the young ones setting the place on fire, or tumbling down the well? And where *were* those goddamned Sabbath School lessons, or quarterlies or whatever you called them?

"Papa, the clock's striking!" came Tom's voice into my thoughts; and dishes unwashed and plates strewn on the table, noon dinner still on ice in the springhouse, beds unmade and quarterlies still lost, and dog and cats still looking for breakfast, we piled ourselves into the carriage and got off—still brushing our hair—for church.

By the time I'd got through the opening exercises and sweated through the Sabbath School hour; by the time I'd heard from Tom's teacher about his unlearned lesson, and Jean's about hers, half-forgotten; by the time I'd herded all five heads back into our pew and suffered through an unmercifully long service; by the time I'd endured all the amused looks cast at us—at my unstarched collar, at Nat's mismatched stockings, at the dull, soapy film still somehow on the girls' hair—I'd made up my mind what to do; and I headed the horse not for home, but for Jim's place.

Pulling up with a jerk outside the Inn—hauling down all five from their seats, not daring to leave even Tom with the horse—marching them like a parade through the main hall, and up the two flights of stairs to Jim's door—I knocked for all I was worth on the panels; and when he—to my relief—cried "Come in!", the whole lot of us erupted into his room. Though he'd probably only been out of bed for an hour, and appeared to be drinking his breakfast coffee, he looked not at all surprised to see us—indeed looked vastly bemused beneath his welcoming smile; and he greeted us nonchalantly with

"Figured you'd be by here sometime t'day, Melchett."

"Cut the chat; pack youhr bag; an' be down't the carriage in ten minutes—you'hre goin' t' help me out," I told him; then hauling Seth away from his paints and plucking Nat out of the open wardrobe, I marched the whole crew back into the hallway, and slammed the door, followed by Jim's peal of laughter.

True to form, impulsive as always, and ready for a change at the drop of a hat, he was down in the specified few minutes, toting a seabag over his shoulder; and hopping up, he took Nat in his arms, while I whipped up the horse and headed for our house.

"I c'n handle it all if you'll mind the children," I told him while he mutely surveyed the kitchen, and took in the wreckage of the dining room; and he promptly threw his head back and laughed. "Hasn't taken you long t' sink the ship, has it?" he grinned, collecting the twins by their coattails and sashes; and "You'hre one t' talk, with that wallow you live in!" I shot back, stirring up the stove to heat water. Disappearing upstairs still laughing, he oversaw the changing of garments, sending down Tom and Jean to help me; then trooping downstairs he went out with the young three, probably down to the shore for a breather. Assisted by Tom and Jean, and for a mercy uninterrupted, I succeeded in re-claiming most of the household, and even in feeding the livestock, including poor Sam; then heaving a sigh, I turned my thoughts to dinner, though by now it was closer to supper than noontime.

Since it was so late, and we were so famished, I was about to venture another foray to the garden, despite the imminent risk of perdition, when Seth appeared on the scene and summoned me shoreward; and following him I beheld a campfire, and nearby it a pitched tent, a-wriggle with children. Nor was that all; for suspended over the blaze, from an iron Jim called a *kekaske-saster,* was the day's stew, which he'd fetched from the springhouse; and next to it, on a flat rock, was a bowl heaped with bounty, greens, carrots, tomatoes and what-not from the garden, arranged into a pleasing salad. With the cider he'd fetched while I was out choring, bread and butter and sweetmeats, it was a feast, better than Sunday dinner at Mother's; and we all immediately fell to it, sitting down in the sand and mumbling a quick grace.

"How will we eat?" asked Courtney blankly, surveying the primitive table-setting; and "Like this!" answered Jim, dipping a spoon in the kettle, and jabbing a fork into the greens. "Saves on dishes," he grinned at her when he'd swallowed, dispatching a devilish look at me; and soon the whole horde was following suit, slurping stew, spearing salad, and passing round cider, with a want of finesse which would've turned Anne's hair.

"This is fine!" cried Tom with satisfaction, as we tore off bits of bread, or sent around a wedge of cheese; "much betteh than all them dishes an' glasses, an' all them forks an' spoons t' remembeh! I'm neveh goin' t' eat indoors again!"

"Me neitheh!" loudly clamored the others, save Courtney, fussily brushing the sand off her cheese; while Nat, fully sated, climbed into Jim's lap, and fell asleep in the warmth of the sunshine.

Seeing no reason to return to the house—having everything we needed within reach on the shore—we whiled away the afternoon on the warm sand, alternately eating or swimming or dozing, or looking for hermit crabs in the tide pools; and when suppertime came, we gathered again round the fire. The menu being the same as dinner's, and still conveniently a-simmer, the evening meal was an easy effort; and so for that matter was clean-up, all seven of us simply sticking our heads in the sea, and leaving the few dishes to boil in the kettle, while we combed the shore for sea moss or goose greens.

Nor did bedtime present any difficulties; for Jim simply called the young ones round the fire, wrapped them in blankets to keep off the sea damp, and told them stories of his boyhood in Wales, tales of tending sheep in the uplands, or learning horseback tricks in the circus. Hearing them for the first time myself, I listened as raptly as the children, roaming in fancy steep hillside or bleak moors, or performing flips in bright costume to applause, while the shadows lengthened across the tide flats, and the beam leapt out to sea from the light house.

When the stars came out we all lay back, and tried to pick out the constellations; and I taught Tom and Jean how to spot the North

Star, and how to find direction from its faithful presence. That there were pictures in the heavens—that there were patterns of stars to steer by, patterns which revolved by season or hour, save for that constant center, Polaris—seemed to fill them with childish wonder; and I felt my old awe come alive with their low cries. Then having brought down armloads of blankets, worn-out comforters and old quilts, we made a bed for the seven of us in the tent; and one by one the children crept in, and nestled down in some pleasant burrow, till only Jim and I were left by the fire.

For a long time we sat, wholly in silence, tending the blaze and feeling the night deepen—watching the silhouettes of the isles shade to black, and the face of the sea take on the sheen of the moonrise; then stirring at last, we too retired, crawling into the blankets amongst the children. Covering myself, I yielded to the sensations around me; heard the wash of the waves, the lull of the wind, the rise and fall of low-hushed breathing; felt the incomparable gentle brush of Jim's nearness; then lost in the sheen of my own celestial center, I went out with the flow of the waves, and wandered far on unchartable seaways.

When I woke it was to a tangle of bodies, tumbled about in the postures of sleep, and I gazed in hushed delight at my young ones— at the flush of beauty on foreheads and cheeks; lingered on Jim's well-knit form in the blankets, and on the dark disarray of his hair. Climbing out into the dawn air, I built up a hearty fire, Jim soon joining me to brew up some tea; and not long after the children crawled out, dragging their blankets about their shoulders. Arranging themselves round the flat-rock table, they partook of their first gypsy breakfast, stick bread and cheese, tea and smoked herring—not even missing their usual fare; then donning the only reasonable garb for the setting, their short-legged, short-sleeved, big-collared swimwear, they immediately took to the tide pools, or dashed up and down the bracken-rich shore.

Changing into his work gear Jim left us for the time, saddling Dee and riding into town to the yard; but he was back by mid-afternoon, taking charge of the young ones while I went up to the house, and executed some of the chores on Anne's list. Feeling smug abut the state of things indoors—a conceit hardly warranted, since nobody'd lived there—I tripped back down to our tent on the shore; and there I found Jim making bread at the fire, while the children ran to and fro fetching driftwood, or green sticks to whittle for use at supper. Toasting bits of meat, digging potatoes out of the ashes, and helping ourselves to garden fare and goose greens, we sated ourselves on another feast, all the tastier for the tang of the seashore; then leaning back on our elbows, Jim and I digested, reviewing the news he'd brought from the yard, to the tune of shrieks and shouts from the children. "They look like a pack of coyotes," I said at one point, as a flurry of bare limbs and tangled hair flashed past me; and "They look pretty much like me and my cousins," corrected Jim with a grin, and a gaze of fond reminiscence.

Meeting his eyes, I saw dark-headed youngsters, darting about campsites long since abandoned, or up and down lanes long since departed; saw lurchers and spaniels, sheep, ponies and horses, answering Rom whistles and beckons; saw the banks of steep roadsides, the bends of side rivers, the melancholy slopes of broad moorlands, go flashing past manes and dark hair and bare feet. Then the scene changed, and it was the Maine coast I saw, but now the children were me and Charis, dodging about the net frames and fish flakes, or racing up the hard shore at low tide; and blurring by were the boughs of dark spruce or the hull of a schooner beached for repairs or the seaborne headlands of the Mussel Ridges.

Then this scene too lifted and Jim's eyes were before me, wide and wet with reminiscence, and beyond were the dashing forms of my children, ranging upshore now with the dog; and suddenly I saw in the depths of his blue gaze what he must have already read in my eyes—that his old life and mine had flowed together imperceptibly on this shore; that we had embarked again on the voyage we'd begun last fall tenting, and carried on this spring aboard *Charis*. Breaking away from his unwavering regard I realized that this was what I'd hoped would happen, when I'd first conceived of Anne's trip to Portland; that this was the shared life I'd secretly yearned for ever since that night in his room; and postponing all thoughts of the separation which loomed before us at the end of this week, I gave myself wholly up to the communion of the moment, to the knowing which takes place in simple doings.

What a succession of days we had—one summer morn after another rolling over us and drenching us, and leaving us waiting for the next. When the sun shone we dug for clams or swam, me teaching Courtney and Seth, Jim guiding Nat; and when it rained we all trooped up to the house together, and settled under a roof for a spell. Jim had the same impact here as he had on the shore; for wherever he went, rooms sprang to life; arrangements and utensils ceased to be still, and began taking on an animate force. There was a rhythm to living life this way, as there had been tenting on the river, or quarterdecking *Charis* at sea; and prepared to never again feel at home in my own house, I found that even here, in the place I'd so outgrown, I belonged as I never had before.

If he revitalized me and the house, he virtually breathed new life into the children, whether down on the shore or up within doors; for as the days passed they seemd to take root in his quick force, and blossom out like vivid flowers. Free from Anne's influence—from the strained relations between them, and the respectful distance he kept from the children in her presence—he behaved with them as he'd always longed to, in the Romany way which came naturally to him; and with me he tended them like a parent, as if they were the fruit of our past. In return they loved him—climbed into his embrace, heeded him with a will, gave him all their unstinting childish devotion; eagerly called him "Uncle Jim," and ran up in the midst of their play to kiss him; and sometimes it moved me to a wordless pain to see his glowing, happy face, or watch his open, impulsive responses. Under his influence even Jean by degrees lost her shyness—became more assertive, almost cocky, not unlike my sister Charis; while all the children seemed to grow closer—to play and tease and tangle more frankly, to the point of wanting to share the same blankets, or the same four-poster up at the house.

At the end of our week Sadie sent word that she would be delayed several days, due to an injury sustained by her sister; and overjoyed to postpone our separation, I simply arranged to swap roles with Jim, getting him leave from the yard for a short spell while I went back to supervise progress. Nor were we set back in the matter of church, or in Sabbath preparations, over which I'd last week come to grief; for that Saturday we all dutifully trooped up from the shore, attended to lessons and Sunday dinner, and scrubbed ourselves into shipshape order—Jim painstakingly helping with the bathing, even meticulously rinsing the girls' hair, though he himself went to Eben's empty cabin to perform his own ablutions: the idea of bathing in someone else's water as repugnant to him as sharing the same cup, or using the same chamber china or outhouse.

When he returned I saw he was carrying a bundle, some change of clothes he'd fetched from Eben's—where he maintained a spare bureau and cupboard—though he said nothing just then about it; but next morning as we dressed the children, buttoning up all those accursed buttons, and tying up bows and petticoat waistbands, Jim suddenly asked, "May I come with you?", holding up his best suit in his hand. Deeply pleased and moved, I simply said "A' course —ye c'n keep Nat from fallin' out o' the carriage, an' stuff peppermints in his mouth when he stahrts t' wriggle"; but though I'd spoken lightly, I watched him closely, wondering greatly what he'd think of his first visit.

Going into town—arrayed to the teeth, all the children except Tom in dresses, and Jim and me swathed in our best in the hot sun— was more or less like journeying to another planet, after our week of bohemian retreat; and mingling on the church steps, making all the proper responses, and submitting to the scrutiny of critical townsfolk, was not easy to bear up under either. Having never showed up in church before, Jim made an immediate sensation—heads turning as soon as he stepped through the entrance, and following him all the way to our pew; but he bore it all with his customary aplomb, composing himself with Nat on his knee, and looking about with familiar interest, as if he'd worn the seat smooth with past visits.

Throughout the long service, while others stared, I watched him out of the corner of my eye, trying to gauge his thoughts and reactions; but he gave me very little to go by, other than the direction of his gaze. Though he attended to the choir, appearing to enjoy the music, and sat politely through the Scripture, he never once registered an impression; while he appeared to glean nothing from the sermon, studying instead the pulpit and pews, or the bevy of faces and head-gear around him. Not that I blamed him; the sermon was indeed endless: another of Brewster's turn-of-the-century dissertations, dealing mostly with the nature of the sacred—though he had a tendency to wander off on tangents, dwelling now on the majesty of various mountains, the scenes of temptations and transfigurations, now on the mundaneness of the earth, or the transitory dust of our bodies.

What Jim must have thought of it all, I couldn't begin to fathom, neither from intuition nor from fleeting glances; nor could I soon after ask him, the post-church festivities and Sunday dinner all keeping us hopping right up until sundown. Not until nightfall, when the young ones had dropped off in slumber, and we were exchanging our customary murmurs, the moonlight streaming in through the tent flap, did I venture to inquire, "Well, what did je think of it all, hm?"; and a smile touched his lips as he regarded me from close by, his head resting on the crook of his elbow.

"You mean, your church?" he whispered, his lips still curved with gentle humor; and I nodded into my jacket, which, as usual, served me as pillow. Heaving a sigh, he turned onto his back, and studied the tent poles for a few moments, as if to get straight on the trend of his thoughts; then at last he turned back toward me, his eyes catching the glint of the moonlight.

"Well, if you mean about the inside, it was pretty much like I'd expected... not too different from the Welsh churches I've peeked into, though theirs 're built of stone and have painted windows, an' more furnishings inside t' look at... more music too, t' judge from what I've heard passing by. But it's very strange, you know, this whole gadje notion about the sacred; I can't seem t' get a handle on it at all."

Having though he'd got nary a jot from the preaching, including no concept of its main subject, I frankly stared at him from my jacket. "What d'ye mean?" I queried.

He ruminated again for a moment, brushing a strand of hair

from Nat's face. "All this business about particular buildings, or particular mountains an' other such places, even particular days like Sunday, bein' holy.... it's the oddest gadje idea I've heard yet."

"You don't think particulah places 're holy?"

"It's not that I don't think particular places are holy... it's more like I don't think there's any places that *aren't.*"

My lips parted with a swift understanding—with a sudden awareness of what I'd always myself believed, though knowing Jim, and hearing Jackson, had crystallized my instinctive thoughts; but for argument's sake, and to press him to say more, I tried to elucidate Brewster's position. "Y' see... the point Brewster was makin'...in his usual roundabout way, I'll admit... is that it's our encountehs with God that make particulah places holy...Them mountains he was referrin' to, like Horeb or Sinai... those're scenes in the history b'tween God an' us whehre there was revelations of ouhr bond, or manifestations of his presence... An' church t'day is the place where that kind of thing's s-posed t' happen again an' again... sort of like meetin' God in his house, y' might say."

Another smile flickered at the corners of his lips, as he bent to kiss the strands of Nat's sweet hair. "Is that what church is, the house of God?" he asked, drawing the blankets about Nat's shoulders.

"As much as *I've* been able t' figure, aye."

He smiled again, but said nothing.

"What is it?" I pressed, propping myself up on one elbow.

He grinned as he shifted onto his back, and looked up to study the tent poles again. "You see... the gadje have this idea of God breakin' in on things now and again... encountering us on mountain tops, or at the altars of churches or whatever.... though every time he really gets rolling, they bottle him back up again, with all sorts of buildings and dogmas and so forth... I've seen it so often, not just since I came here, but ever since I've been able t' read those Welsh tracts, or understand them wanderin' breast-beaters... It's just so completely different for us."

"How is it for you?" I asked him, eager, the hush of a breath held still at my lips.

"God for us...*O Devel Muro*....isn't anything apart—isn't anything like a separate power... it's in all of us, in everything around us... It hasn't got any dwelling place, so it never withdraws; it's just on the road with us all the time... Since it's in everything, everything's holy.... *develeskoe*, sacred or divine.... Life's sweet...day's sweet, night's sweet... It's only the *Beng* that c'n distort things."

Watching his face, I listened carefully, seeing again his form in the glimmering sunlight, walking the glades of Corcovado, or simply scrubbing the deck of a three-master on the glistening seas of the Western Ocean; saw all of this and the awe that attended the most ordinary of his motions—that transfigured the most ordinary moments for me. Turning away from his eyes, which'd come to rest on me, I struggled to find the words for my next thought—a question almost too close to my heart to utter; sought for a way to steady my voice as I spoke it, to conceal the extent to which it moved me. "If... everyting's holy... then for you... are thehre still some moments that seem...more intense than othehs...or is all experience just the same?"

He regarded me intently, as if waiting for me to explain.

"Y' see..." I attempted, trying not to sound hoarse, and clearing my throat as if that were the problem, "since I've known you...thehre's been times when... things b'come especially....bright.... as if.... as if there was a lamp turned on inside them, or as if they'd suddenly b'come alive."

"It's the same for me," he confided, husky-voiced, after a hesitation.

"You mean... things're bright like that for you all the time?"

"No.... things 're bright like that for me when you're near."

"You mean... *I* do that for *you*?" I asked, unbelieving.

"Aye. But you mustn't ever speak about it"—this as he saw I was about to break in. "Words rob power... Erode it, till finally it's dwindled an' weakened. That's the strangest thing of all about church.... the more you talk, the less there is." And with that he turned away toward Jean, and would say not another word to me, though I knew from the tenseness of his shoulders that he was still awake and thinking; and it was long into the night, well into the middle watch, before I finally caught sound of his quiet breathing.

Whether it was because of this conversation, of because of the drawing near of the end of our fortnight, he was unusually quiet in the coming days, helping me ready the house for Sadie's return—and Anne's arrival almost immediately after—with an air of preoccupation. Though the place was shipshape from stem to stern—though the pie safe was chock full of Jim's creations, and the lamps were trimmed down to every last wick— I'd decided to hire Anne help, one of McCabe's cousins, on Jim's recommendation; not because I considered my share of the experiment a failure, or was willing to signal to Anne the difficulty of her task, but because I knew what would be her reaction to Jim's living with us at the house, or to the children's bedding down on the shore, and all the other news that would be sure to get back to her; and I wanted to take the edge off her response.

Busy preparing for Anne's arrival, we had less time to ourselves than we'd had in the beginning; yet even our impending separation, and the preparations which kept us ever mindful of it, had no power to dim our last days together; for right down to the hour of Sadie's return we were celebrating the elements of our bond—the artistry of the everyday, and the rituals of our simple doings.

One day, just before Sadie and Anne were due, fell upon us like a vivid dream; for its clarity, its mood and color, recalled the vibrant glow of a vision. Already the breeze felt warm through the window; the curtains lifted and fell, then lifted and lingered, as if breathing in and out with the wind's flow; and I seemed to anticipate good happenings—seemed to know at the same time that these great events might be very humble, unpretentious, commonplace things.

We began the day together, Jim and I—drinking tea on the porch steps beneath the creepers, wordlessly taking in the sweet warmth of the new morn, then tackling a batch of chores before breakfast. Saturday had come round again, and we had no choice but to confront the laundry—two weeks' worth of play clothes and work garb, including some of Anne's and Sadie's things worn before they'd left, and mountains of bedroom and kitchen linen, all piled in odd heaps upon the porch floor. I hadn't the first idea how to proceed, but Jim evidently had some notion, pouring this and that into this kettle and that one—set over outdoor fires or hung from the hearth crane—as into a series of bubbling cauldrons, like one with past experience in such tasks, the knowledge which comes with lack of funds for labor.

Following the standard Romany pattern, he rigorously segregated the clothing—Anne's and Sadie's things going into one pot, and the children's and ours going into another, the girls apparently too young to matter; then fetching the washboards, he led the way scrubbing. Pinking, bluing, rinsing, wringing—none seemed to present any difficulties to him, nor any impenetrable mysteries, as to me; so leaving him to wrap things up in the yard—to dump the rinse water on the roses and put out the fires, and convey his finished product to the line—I commenced matters in the kitchen, firing up the stove and setting out dishes, and mixing a massive batch of blueberry pancakes. By then the young ones were trooping down from upstairs, in various stages of dress and undress; and Jim, coming in, took over on that front, while I flipped the cakes and hustled rounds to the table.

Seeing no reason to mar such a fine day with more chores, we washed up the kitchen mess in a hurry, like dancers whose feet itch to be off with the fiddles; and soon after we moved down to the shore in a herd, the lot of us decked out in bathing costumes, and Jim with an impressive armload of towels. The tide being low, we at once went for clams, digging mostly at our favored spots near the light; then spading a hole, we filled it with hot rocks, all manner of clams and potatoes and corn, a lobster or two from the shore right out front and a flounder we'd been keeping on ice—covering up the feast with a layer of rockweed, and a stretch of sailcloth to keep in the steam. The day's dinner on, and the essential shores done, we abandoned ourselves to the shore—to the warm of the sun and the sea damp of the breeze, and the sifting of sand grains across bits of stone.

At the urging of the children we took to the surf, keeping in close enough to watch over Nat, guarded as he napped by the faithful Sam, who'd bark if he started to stir or waken. Losing ourselves in the foam of the spilled crests, we went rolling in all directions. allowing our limbs to be tugged at the sea's whim, and washed up on the beach like bits of driftwood; then picking ourselves up, we plunged back into the surf, and offered ourselves up all over again. Teasing me and the children—disappearing into the wave crests, then coming up suddenly between our ankles, and toppling us into the breakers— Jim went darting and sporting about us, graceful and playful as a merman: the dark, dripping ringlets round his face and neck—the sea-wet lashes framing his eyes—and the brine-coursing collar and short sleeves of his suit, all bold against the blue sky and white foam, and stark as some figure fresh from the deep. How the children shrieked when at last I caught him, picked him right up into my arms, and tossed him full-length into a wave!

When at last we'd had an hour of this, our hunger was so sharpened by the sea air that we descended at once on our clambake—sitting together around the rock pit with our high-heaped plates and fresh-squeezed lemonade, helping one another crack lobster, or bone the fillets of steaming flounder. As we ate for the most part with our fingers, we dove now and then back into the rock pit, digging out deeper layers of bounty; then sated at last we sprawled onto the warm beach, even the young ones stuffed into stupor. \

Seeing my languor, Jim tackled the clean-up, waving my vague moves to help him quiet, and handing me instead my clap pipe, as if knowing what I wanted before I did; and obligingly laying back on my elbows, I puffed away in tranquil contentment, and watched him pile up plates on the jute trays. As he served me with these small gestures and glances a palpable glow sprang up between us—a luminescence which sharpened each sand grain, and warmed me as physically as a fire; and it lingered long after he'd lain down beside me, with Nat's drowsy head pillowed on his belly, and drifted off into a slumber.

That afternoon the weather changed. For some time the wind had come in warm gusts, starting low to stir the strands of my hair, then strengthening to bend the boughs of the firs; had risen and fallen as regularly as the surf, breaking and rushing in and then out, or as the breast-beat of some living bellows, breathing into me like the breath of a man. But shifting round to due south, the breeze dallied and died, then fell at last to a dubious calm; while the waves continued to roll in long swells, the surges that pulsate before a blow.

Over the sea a haze began to collect, then a smear of gold-grey off to the south; and an opalescence gleamed on the waters. Looking over at me Jim read my eyes, then propped himself up without waking Nat; and scanning the roads he spotted a sloop, one of the fishing fleet making for port. Reaching a lazy arm toward the umbrella—under which Courtney and Seth were dozing—I made a grab for my canvas seabag, out of which I fetched my glass; and focusing it on the near reaches of the bay, I struggled to make out the sloop's sternboard.

"Whose is it?" Jim murmured, lying back down on the sand, and pillowing his head on his hands.

"Kalkman's," I returned; "he always runs first—though I c'n see Shad's an' Pelham's out beyant, an' they appear t' be making for shore."

"Wish Eben was home," Jim muttered, eyes closed; and I brushed a hand across his bare elbow.

"He's got plenty o' sea room; he'll ride it out," I attempted to comfort flatly; but he cast a censorious eye at me.

"In that kindlin' chip?" he responded dryly; then falling silent he dozed again lightly, one brown hand across Nat's chest, while I kept an eye on the older children, and looked up from time to time at the sky. Though directly above the heavens were still blue, a brassy azure in the humid heat, the gold-grey smear to the south slowly deepened, casting a brazen hue on the billows; and the erratic toll of the buoy clanged more often.

When the gulls began to collect on the shore, in groups of two of three at first, and the wrens to dart under the eaves of the boathouse—when half a dozen more small craft within range of my glass began to show signs of wrapping up business, handlines coming in, lobster pots breaking water, sheets hauled taut for the run to the mainland—when, out of the south, came a hint, no more than a guess, of a distant droning or rumble—I sat up straight and brushed off my flannels, and stowed my eyepiece back in the seabag. Jim stirred at once and looked up at me, as if to judge our span of grace from my eyes; then sitting up slowly, he laid Nat aside.

"Want t' go into town?" he asked, knowing there'd be a commotion of work there, getting out extra lines and anchors, not to mention battening down *Abigail* on the ways; but I shook my head as I tied up my seabag. On any other day I'd've been there already, flying between the ways and the harbor; but now, come what might, I only wanted to be home; and the serenity that'd filled me since waking steered me.

"Nah, Spooneh 'n Matt're in charge at the yahrd, an' Tom an' Pa'll see t' the harboh; but I b'lieve I'll walk oveh t' Eben's, an' make sure about the windows an' stables... Be back in half an oweh."

At Eben's I found things strangely deserted, not just because he was on the Banks with his cousins, but because the whole place seemed to be mutely waiting, uninhabited and unprotected, for the advent of an uncertain evening; and the creak of the gate in the feeble air was unnerving. Entering the cabin I impulsively drew things back from the windows, tacked up an oilcloth over the south panes, closed and latched the indoor shutters, then bolted down the doors and outbuildings. Jasper being at sea with Eben, and his pair of bays temporarily housed in our stables, the place really was forlorn and abandoned in the creeping gray-gold of the storm gloom; and strangely restless, I walked on to the headland, from whence I could gain a fair view of the harbor.

There indeed I spotted a ferment—the bigger craft being taken out on scow-lines, and extra anchors got on their hawsers; the smaller craft being hauled up on shore, and housed in the lee of frames and boatsheds; and myriads of yawls, ketches, sloops and schooners coming in to moor and disburden. Turning on my heel I hurried back to my own shore, passing on the way the ledge below Eben's, a favorite roost of the gulls in all seasons, where dozens now waited heads down toward the south; and speeding my pace I climbed down onto the sand, while ahead at the Point the light flashed in the haze.

Though they were quite nearby on the shore, and not obscured by the thickening weather, the children sounded oddly distant and muffled, their shouts seeming to float in from behind a curtain; and coming up on them I found they were picking up their gear, while Jim was striking the tent and umbrella. Helping me haul the skiff up into the boathouse, Jim collected an armload and headed up the shore steps, muttering something about checking windows and laying out supper; and staying on the shore the children and I stowed gear and oars, and even rigged up some stout lines on the boathouse.

As I climbed up the shore steps and followed the wooden walk up to the front door, I took note of the dampness increasing in the air, a dampness which permeated even the sand hill. From the distance came again that half-guessed rumble, repeated once, for the uncertain of hearing; but this time I felt its vague echo in the earth, as if something stirred far beneath the dune. Pausing to listen, I tried to gauge the storm's distance; then recalled to my task by a breath of cool air, another brief but telling current, I went on up the walk to the porch, stepping into the house as one steps into a haven, a hollow protected from the elements without.

Here were no signs of the coming gale, save fore the damp and unaccustomed quiet; but rather the touches of Jim's presence at work—the traces I'd come to look for these past weeks. Pausing at the stove, I stirred the chowder, then stood before the dining room table and thought with hunger of supper; surveyed the setting of china and pewter with an odd, quick surge of warmth and delight.

The yard, construction, even the new ship herself, and what she might come to in the coming blow, after four months of backbreaking labor; even the sting of the future, with Anne expected back in a day, if heavy weather didn't delay her—none of this had the power to move me as I surveyed this setting for supper. Outside the sporadic rumble of thunder droned in now a little louder, rattling the china cups on the table; and looking out, I caught a glimpse of Jim through the windows: he was in the side yard, taking down the laundry, and Jean was stooping over the basket. Abandoning thoughts of the oilcloth and hammer I'd originally intended to fetch, I went directly to the back porch; and slamming the door, I scurried out to help.

How strange I'd forgotten, or never noticed, the pleasant ritual of taking down clean clothes from the line! Jim's face was smiling, and I could tell by the way his fingers lingered on the clothespins or caressed the cotton dungarees and shirts, that he found both joy and pleasure in this simple household task. Folding clean garments across his knee, he'd hand them gently on to Jean; and she'd look up eager, shining-faced at him, then find a place—with small busy fingers—for each fresh item in the deep basket. So Jean knew; she understood; I must have known myself once, and forgotten.

Now I inhaled deeply, and smelled the warm, clean cotton smell—the hint of dampness still in the cloth, and the faint suggestion of soap. Looking down the line, I saw the colorful garb remaining stir and rise in the gathering breeze—glanced at the worn sailor dress, and at once saw Seth—looked at the pantaloons and calico skirts, and straightaway saw Tom and Jean on the shore, lifting the rocks to uncover crabs. How they hurt all of a sudden, these simple garments—these bright forms which spoke of our fortnight together, or of my mother's long figured skirts, and me standing small and trustful beside her!

As if aware of my feeling, Jim turned and looked at me—I saw his fingers linger, almost lovingly, on some small blouse, and I took it to fold it carefully. In that brief instant his eyes had flashed, and met mine with that open, defenseless honesty of his—with that candor which sometimes flamed up unbidden; and before he could conceal it, his face tautened with pain. Looking away, he gave his head a toss, as if to shake the hair from his face—but I knew that this was a gesture he often made when he was deeply moved. Suddenly, with another quick motion, he handed Jean the last shirt and left us, half-running for the saplings at the edge of the sand-hill; and there he stood tensely with his hands in his pockets, studying the impending weather.

"Jean," I asked, looking down at her small hands, "c'n you take this big basket up to the house?"

"Aye!" came her ringing, spirited answer; and taking a handle in both of her hands, she began to half-tug, half-carry the laundry to the porch. I watched her for a moment—she looked both comical and determined—then I ran for Jim. Out of the corner of my eye I glimpsed Tom at the porch door; I heard the door slam, and saw him jump down to help his sister.

Jim was still standing with his hands in his pockets, scanning the signs of the seas and the heavens; the beech trees beside him shone starkly silver in the garish light of the looming storm. Coming up, I stood close by him, and laid one of my arms across his shoulders; but he made no move of recognition, refusing to speak or even look at me. For a long time we stood this way, neither of us speaking; but slowly he seemed to regain his composure, and I could feel him relax under my arm. Off to the south the gray-gold pall moved in closer, the sea below taking on a grotesque hue in contrast; a rumble of thunder boomed in the distance, and I felt the response in the ground beneath my feet.

When I could trust myself to speak, I said to him lightly, "We've maybe got an oweh... long enough t' eat an' wash up. Let's go tackle that chowdeh o' youhrs b'fore we batten down the hatches." He turned to me then with a shaky smile, a game look which showed in the lift of his chin—and a rush of tenderness swept through me; I took his elbow as he turned to the house, and clasped it tight as we walked back together.

While the thunder rumbled in gradually closer, changing from a distant boom to a nearer, more insistent growl, we ate a frugal supper together, clustered round the dining room table. Within the encircling house the faint clatter of china, the hollow drone of the sea and the fitful wind, were almost pleasant to hear when mingled in with our murmurs, the clinking of silverware and the scraping of bowls; yet growing on me was an air of disquiet, so much so that I'd said grace myself, praying spontaneously for those at sea. Ordinarily I was reluctant to pray before others; but now the words'd spilled out unself-consciously, as if such some other voice were using mine; and Jim'd bowed his head in his hand, as if such an attitude were his custom.

When at length there came a terrific clap, even the floorboards vibrating beneath our feet, we hastily cleared off the table; Tom and Jean gathered up lanterns, while Jim and I nailed up oilcloth over the south windows, and hauled back the furniture to the middle of the rooms. Bringing a hurricane lamp down to the cellar, Jim hastily laid out mats for the children, while I ran about closing shutters, then followed with the last pair of lamps. We completed our preparations none too soon; for as I shut the door behind me on the cellar, it grew all at once darker, the thunder-growls changing from a near-distant chorus to a sudden insistent roaring, and the fitful winds rising from a sullen calm to the onslaught of a gale.

The next moment like a cannonade came the hail, swooping down with a bombardment of white stones which battled the thunder and wind for supremacy; in a second every one of the south and west panes was broken, with a tinkling of glass not so much heard as guessed. Herding the children into their blankets, Jim settled them down with a kind word, then hastened upstairs to find me struggling in the parlor to hammer into place the blown-open shutters. Heedless of the woodwork and the lamps and bric-a-brac, which we knocked to smithereens in our hurry, we hammered boards in swift succession, the hail tearing at our hands and faces, and the wind literally whipping the curtains to pieces, as if the whole room were out of doors.

The hail spent, down swooped the rain, in a mass as dense and drenching as a Line squall; in a lightning flash, I saw a tree fall, and felt—rather than heard—its thud; saw its great roots project in another swift flash, and the cavern in the earth where they'd held. So unnerving was the incessant thunder and lightning, the latter diving down in spears from the heavens, that it was all we could do to batten the hatches; but at last it was done and we looked about us, mutely surveying the wreckage in the room. So this was the place we'd labored to keep clean, with a view to impressing Anne on her arrival! Looking over at Jim I found his gaze waiting, impish and mischievous as an urchin's; and I stared blankly at him for a wordless moment, with all that colossal upheaval around us. Then both of us simultaneously burst into laughter, sitting right down on the floor in the uproar—and there we would probably have remained till swept away, if the children's clamor hadn't recalled us to the cellar.

Down cellar the uproar was not quite so overpowering, the lightning bolts not quite so unnerving; and with mats spread on the floor, blankets laid ready, pillows at hand and hurricane lamps lighted, it was possible to collect one's wits, and give a thought to what should come next. Finding Jim'd brought down my pipe, I gratefully prepared a smoke, trying to suppress visions of *Abigail* on her beam ends, or the roof of the house turned turtle in McCabe's woods; while the children—bedding down with various dolls and ducks near us—began to view the whole thing as a lark. Striking up a song, the older ones caroled, in an effort to drown out the bedlam and clamor; and getting an idea Jim risked life and limb upstairs, fetching his guitar from the front room.

Soon bewitching rhythms, flamencos from far tents, flights of tones and chords and tempos were conjuring up our pliant fancies; and visions of bright skirts and flashing slippers, clapping hands and snapping fingers were weaving themselves in mid-air about us, or flickering upon the lamplit wall stones. Slowly the tunes waxed louder and stronger against the waning wind-roar and thunder, and the children one by one drew up the blankets, moving less and less beneath them, till finally their forms were still; then Jim at last set down his guitar, and sat by me in companionable silence.

The flickering walls—the smoky lamps—the rain trickling rhythmically down the windows, and the thunder and lightning rumbling from afar, diminishing as slowly as they'd come on: for a long time we sat and enjoyed their quiescence, an unearthly restfulness settling upon us. Then clearing a space for ourselves on the far mat—moving sleep-tumbled limbs one way or the other, and untangling a couple of blankets—we nested down amongst the young ones, and burrowed our heads gratefully in spare pillows. Jim was beside me: I felt his warmth, and the pleasant give of the mat as he settled himself; then I felt his arm briefly brush mine, before I drifted into sleep.

At once I fell into a vivid dream: I was wandering a rugged valley alone, a gully of land that wound by a stream, between the grass-clad slopes of low knolls, most of which were bare of trees. It was summer, early evening, and the air was warm and sweet with grass scents. Suddenly I came upon a tree, ancient and gnarled as an aged fig, yet hale with the carven beauty of wood: it stood alone near the banks of the river, bereft of its leaves, save near the ends of its twigs. One of its sections was about to fall—a broad lower limb, and its share of the trunk; an overpowering urge came over me to tug at it, to somehow break it down from the tree, and see what lay hid in the root-space beneath.

Clasping the limb, I tugged, wrenched and pulled, working away for all I was worth; but it soon became plain I couldn't succeed alone, and I backed away, pondering my dilemma. All at once I was aware of a child, who must have appeared while I was at work: oddly neither boy nor girl, it stood near the tree in the waning light, its long, loose garment free-falling like a nightdress, and its face strangely elfin and piquant and knowing . At once lending a hand, the child helped me to tug; our united efforts brought down the limb, and with it a portion of the trunk—a great cavern opening up in the ground where its share of the roots had been, a gaping hole like the one I'd glimpsed out the window upstairs in the storm.

Standing back, we looked on in awe, wondering what might issue from those ragged depths; but we were not kept long in suspense, for the next moment, up leapt a lynx—a fine, nimble creature who climbed to the tree's top, and took his place on an upper limb. In quick succession there followed after all of life's host of living creatures— tigers, weasels, rabbits, foxes—all leaping up and taking their places somewhere amongst the tree's gnarled limbs; till finally each branch held a figure, vivid and fur-rich in the early moonrise. Flowing silently by, the stream took on night-hues, dusk-greys and silver and moon-opalescence; the watercourse greens slowly faded to olives, then finally to deep-shadowed fir-tones; and still we looked on the storied limbs from our grass sward, while the creatures preened and groomed in the moonlight.

XX

EBEN MCCABE

Cape Damaris, Maine   September, 1843

Swearing off the sea'd been pretty high on my list as we made port that Monday after the storm—not too unreasonable a yen, since we'd just spent a fortnight longer than planned hand-lining in open dories, then half the weekend bucking the weather, hoping not be blasted to Kingdom Come by some storm bolt. Yesterday hadn't been any better, limping up coast with our dinged sails and rigging, fighting the after-storm rollers for headway; and talk of home sweet home, a warm fire to take out the damp, and something tasty off from the stove 'd been pretty constant in the mouths of all of us.

But we soon found out home's not always all it's cracked up to be; for there was Cape Damaris, looking like it'd been picked up and dropped: the shipping in disarray in the harbor, a schooner a-ground just below my cabin, and the fishing wharves stove in by the seas. Yesterday having been the Sabbath, nobody'd commenced on the clean-up, except to move life-threatening debris, or secure any imperiled shipping; so now, on Monday, folks was just getting down to business, and the place was as busy as Nahant in the summer. Hammering, hauling, shouting, swearing, they was crawling along ridgepoles, shinnying up masts, and cussing at buggies mired in the streets: the combined force of their racket almost as bad as the blow, and more than enough to trigger a headache.

In the midst of it all, plunked down in the middle of Water Street—my seabag thrown athwart my shoulders, and Jasper's cage slung from my elbow—I seen the Portland stage drive up, more or less in the path ground out by the traffic; and out, to my no small surprise, stepped Damaris, followed in royal array by Anne Melchett. With all the trunks that popped out with them, not to mention the bandboxes—fifty or more of every size, shape and color—it was impossible to get close enough to find out what they'd been up to, or how they'd fared on what must of been a wild ride down the Atlantic Highway from Portland; and they was off in hired rigs before I was any the wiser. But a timely stop at Eli's for a bowl and a quick one soon satisfied my yen for the latest; and it wasn't long before I found out that Anne'd been a month to Portland, and that Robertson'd been managing things with Ben up to the house.

Thinking that tale might prove highly interesting—well worth a trek out to the Point in the mire—I chucked the idea of stopping by the fishing wharves to check on the storm damage at my cousins', in favor of heading straight out to my place, and gamming with Melchett first chance he was free. When at length I hove into my drive—no small feat in the muck—I found that my cabin'd fared no better than the town; for even from a distance it looked pretty battered, whilst inside it was about as shipshape as a bait boat. Somebody—Melchett probably—'d been in and tried to brace things ready, to judge by the moved gear and tattered oilcloth; but in spite of his efforts the south and west windows was broke through, a snowdrift of hail was melting on the carpets, and slivers of glass was glistening on the cushions; whilst a tree'd toppled athwart the ell roof, threatening to bust down any minute into the kitchen.

Looking around, I scratched my head, trying to think where to begin; made an aimless move for the broom, then a couple false starts for the ax; and meanwhile got no help from Jasper, who'd screeched three times, "Sonofabitch!", then lapsed into moody silence. Whilst I was pacing about, trying to gather my wits, I thought all of a sudden of Melchett—thought of dropping by his place, cajoling him into helping with the tree, and posting me up on the news at the same time; and leaving Jasper in the lurch, I picked a path though the woods, less than a breeze what with debris and downed limbs. Coming up on Ben's house, I found the same mess—windows busted and shingles blown off, outbuildings listing and big boughs on the ground—though, a' course, as I'd expected, no tree'd happened to come down on *his* place.

Gratified to find he hadn't got off scot free, I drew up to where I could see the drive; and there I glimpsed Anne's rig still hitched up, luggage piled like hogsheads on the wharves, and a few yards beyond, running the length of the rose beds, a massive pine upended by the storm. Dancing along it, cavorting on branches, or exploring the uppermost boughs for nests, all five of the young ones was screeching and playing—except Seth, who was hung up by his dress, and cat-wailing; while Ben, with a set face, was carting in armloads, and Anne in the door was directing traffic. Robertson was nowheres to be seen; and concluding that Ben for the time had his hands full, I turned tail and went back to my place, where I stood bleakly surveying my ell roof.

I'd not long come back in and dropped on the sofa—had just reached the conclusion that broaching the keg was the only sensible solution—when the porch door banged open, and Jim busted in. "Aha, he'll help with the tree," I perked up; but before I could speak he ditched his bag at the threshold, hurled hisself full length on the sofa, buried his head in my lap with a low cry, and broke into a storm of sobbing. It wasn't his way no more to hold things back, at any rate, not around me; but even so I was took aback by his passion, and sat dumbly there with his head on my knees. Too struck of a heap to come up with a word, I simply patted his hair with my paw, noting with pity its torturous damp; while he sobbed on unabashed and unchecked, as if releasing weeks of restraint.

Though he said little in betweenst sobs, I gathered enough to know he'd just left Ben's, after the fortnight with him I'd heard about; and—barring some unguessed catastrophe at the house, such as words with Ben or a sword-crossing with Anne—I could piece together the rest. I knew by now that he wanted a good deal more than what he'd bargained for in the beginning; and it was pretty easy to see, from the force of his feeling, that the last fortnight had shown him what. But I said nothing just then about it, knowing he'd carve matters out without words, or any interference from me.

Quiet at last, he turned over in my lap, wiping his face with a clean kerchief; then regarding me with honest eyes—the eyes of a man who's spent and unguarded—he managed a characteristic wryness. "It was bad enough," he quavered, "in the beginning, when I would've been happy with a night now an' then... Now it's the days I want, an' everything in b'tween... I'm as bad as Anne in a shopful of china."

I threw my head back and guffawed frankly, a laugh as much of relief as wry truth, and patted his face as I would of my own kin. "Jest see to it ye keep that touch o' humor, matey....there's a lot o' laughin' needed in clay-pot makin.'"

He broke into a smile then, that radiant wide grin that always busted out so unexpected; and getting up for a minute, I fetched myself a stiff one, and him some powders out of the ship's chest, since he'd begun to see them flashes that was a sure forerunner to one of his headaches. Going upstairs, he laid down on the spare bed, pretty much the only dry spot in the house; and whilst he slept I poured myself another, and vaguely begun to sweep things up.

I'd about got the downstairs shipshape—except for the tree, a' course, which was still hanging fire, ready to bust down into the kitchen; had cooked up some early supper, fed Jim, and seen him off to town with a couple bucks, to buy hisself a good time at Eli's, when a heavy tread sounded on the porch, and I knowed at once it was Ben. "Good!" I brightened, "he'll help with the tree—there's still enough light t' get it down off the roof by"; but my thoughts quickly changed when I seen his face, which looked about like the onset of a Line squall. No passion of sobs or frank outbursts here; anything I wanted to know, I'd have to pry aboard with a gaff. Knowing right away he needed a drink—having got the news from Eli he'd been on the wagon, probably to pacify Anne whilst she was gone—I fetched him a glass with the merest afterthought of water, which he tossed off like a seal downs a haddock; and providing a re-fill, I left him the bottle.

Settling across from him, with my own glass to hand, I made a hasty survey of his face; took inventory, between discreet sips, of the various hints and signs of his mood. I had an idea myself of what was in his mind, if he didn't; but I was stumped for a way to get the ball rolling. Here we both sat, the roof about to come down on us, the state from Kittery to the Porcupines in tatters, and every ship in the harbor from *Abigail* on down needing repairs of an upper order; but he was as oblivious to it all, in his trouble, as if it was a cozy midsummer's evening; and I was as at a loss for an opener as if things'd been at a flatout standstill. As a rule I hesitated to flush him straight out, even when the silence'd become strained, like this one; but all at once the devil in me got the upper hand, and led me to dare things I wouldn't of if sane.

"I seen Anne t'day gettin' down off the stage, an' heard from Eli that whilst she was in Portland, you an' Jim was holdin' down the fort," I ventured; and he looked up from his glass startled, as if I'd busted into his inmost thoughts—which I had.

"Aye," he said briefly; but I knew I was warm, for his stony face'd taken on a tinge, the barest hint of a flush of fervor.

"Jim still oveh thehre?" I asked mildly, as if I hadn't just spent half the day with him, and sent him off to town to skylark.

"No," he answered, his voice gruffer; but them spots on his cheeks deepened a trifle.

"The place must seem right empty without him," I shot out; and for an answer he ran his hand through his hair, one of the few gestures he had which gave away his emotion or confusion.

"Aye," he said shortly, but he said no more because he couldn't, not because he didn't want to.

"I s'pose Anne makes it worse?" I asked him point-blank, trying not to let my words flinch. I knew this question would undo either him or me, and I half-shrank in my chair, waiting for him to give me the very Jesse for barging in on his private business; but alls he did was raise troubled eyes and look at me. The scowl I'd expected, with that lowering black brow, and that look in the eye of irate bluntness, never even begun to take shape on his face; only the look of a man fraught with his doubts, struggling at last to speak his thoughts out.

"She does...though I'll be damned if I c'n say why," he quavered, with a bit of a laugh at hisself in the wry words. "She...she does most of the same things....cooks, cleans just like anybody else, though more, a' course...even..."—he cleared his throat, as if it was too tight for him to go on—"even loves the children in her own way...but...nothing she cooks or does is the same." The unspoken words, *the same as Jim*, hung there in the air between us; but listening wordlessly, I kept my oar shipped.

"She's a fine woman," he grappled on, as if struggling to steer a straight course for what he'd spent years giving a wide berth to, "but we ain't really suited t' each otheh, I c'n see. I ought t' be grateful t' her... I *am* grateful t' her, for many things, especially the young 'uns. But suddenly I seem t' see the future stretching ahead of me—you'll laugh, but I neveh sawr it stretching ahead b'fore." He paused again, and looked at me as if he was about to ship the sum of his thoughts in a few words. "I can't see Anne in my future," he broke suddenly, in a rush. "I can't imagine growing old with her."

I understood he expected to be blown up on the spot, or struck down by a bolt from the heavens for voicing such infidelity; for he looked around him with a kind of dazed blinking, as if surprised to find hisself still in one piece—as if he'd been wondering, and 'd finally found out, what them words would sound like out loud. Seeing the fellow feeling in my eyes, he looked relieved, as though he'd expected me to condemn the unfaithfulness of his thought, or worse, remind him that I'd warned him of all this a long time ago.

"If I'd understood, eight yearhs ago," he hurried on, his voice hoarse and barren, "that marriage was...a kind of voyage...I'd never of married her...I'd of seen there wasn't a lifetime t' journey in her." He drew a breath, then spoke again, his voice trailing off with the bleakness of a wind soughing in the rock-walls of its prison. "Thehre's nothing' more t' journey in her even now. Maybe there is for othehs, but not for me."

"Have ye...have y' thought of leavin' her?" I asked, seeing no reason to pussyfoot around on this point.

"Y' mean...do what Stephen did?" He looked at me unbelieving, as if dazed that we was even saying such things—as if he hadn't expected such frankness even from me. Again he run his hand through his hair, and stared for a moment into the fire, a half-incredulous, half-wistful look on his face. "A' course I've thought about it... the way a man thinks about doin' things he knows he'll neveh really do." He gave a kind of hollow chuckle, the sort of sound the wind makes in the cliffs in winter, when the sun comes out pale and thin for a moment; then he growed practical and earnest.

"Y' know damned well I could neveh rate m'self so high as t' satisfy my needs at the expense of othehs," he went on, gazing again into the fire. "Even if it was just Anne an' me alone, I'd...I'd hesitate t' bring scandal on her. I wouldn't care for m'self, if I b'lieved I was doin' right, but...I respect her enough t' want t' protect her from othehs... from the damnation I know she'd b'lieve we'd face in the hereafteh... All that'd be hardeh for her than livin' with me would. An' it's not just her an' me alone... It's five young 'uns that need me as much as her... that'll neveh have what I want for them with just her...that have the right t' a life that's whole, unbroken by scandal or division."

"Don't ye s'pose they feel the division betweenst you an' Anne, even now as a family, careful as y' are?" I asked gently, remembering glimpses of Jean sniffling in her swing, or Tom kicking stones down the road.

He looked at me as if he'd like to dodge the question; but he was too honest a man not to face it, now that I'd come out and asked it. "I know they do," he admitted, his voice falling a degree lower with each word. He hesitated, as if he recalled some recent moment; then he went on, "But I think they fear my leavin' even more. At least, Jean does. Not long ago, she...she asked me, scared-like, if I was plannin' on goin' away soon... From any of the othehs, I know that would of meant shippin' out, but I know she..."—his great barrel of a chest heaved, as if from some labor—"she meant somethin' different, even if she didn't know it. I took her out in Tom's sloop, that same night, an' she...laid her head on my shouldeh a long time...."

His voice by now'd fallen so low, it'd begun to tremble and break; he hid his forehead in his hand, his big fingers all tense and knotted, while I simply looked on in pain. I'd barely survived Jim's earlier outburst; if Ben broke down now, I'd be a goner. But he steadied hisself as if years of training stood him now in ample stead; even managed the ghost of a chuckle, as he shrugged his shoulders and raised his eyes. "What's more important, her needs or mine? How's a man s'posed t' decide that?"

He shook his head as though the immensity of the question was too much for him to take on. "Anyway," he suddenly shifted, downing the rest of his drink with a quick move, and telling me—by the break in his gaze, and the abrupt change in his tone—that his brief exposure was over, "it's not me I came t' talk t' ye about...it's... it's Jim." He drew a deep breath, and heaved a sigh. "I'm...I'm worried about him. When he left the house, he—I sawr him, he stuffed all his things quickly into his bag, and left—he neveh said goodbye, not even t' the children."

"You know it was b'cause he couldn't say nothin', not b'cause he didn't want to," I soothed, wrenching inside all over again for Jim.

"I know it... It's not that that I'm worried about... I know he'll come around in time. It's..." He struggled with the uncharacteristic effort of launching his inmost feelings in words. "He's...he's lonely... he's not meant or made t' be alone."

"He's got good friends here—you an' me, 'long with half the town, though he don't know it; has more of a place t' call home than he's eveh had b'fore; I wouldn't worry too much about him."

"I know all that—an' I know at bottom, with his gypsy feet, he don't really want t' settle down in one place, or—tie himself down t' any one person," he said carefully, choosing his words. "Yet at the same time... I *know* he needs to...I... I c'n sense it as plain as if he'd said it. He don't say so, but...he wants a family, a place t' belong to... You should see him now with my young 'uns."

His eyes was wide, wide and grey as the bay when the dawn breaks, before the early mist 's scaled off; and he didn't look down or away from me either, as he foundered around with his worries for Jim. Trying to read betweenst his words, I guessed by now he must know Damaris was in town—guessed he feared that Jim, in his yearning, might make a hasty marriage like his; and leaving aside more hidden pieces, I decided to pick up these. "It's *youhr* children he loves, Ben," I said, just as carefully, "not necessarily his own he has a yen for."

"I just...I just don't want t' see him make the same mistake I did," he got out, his voice hardly more than a husky whisper.

"Y' mean, marry somebody like Damaris, b'cause he's startin' t' hankeh afteh a family, an' thinks makin' one's the propeh thing t' do?" I asked frankly.

This time he looked down, too moved to answer—tried once or twice to utter a word, but couldn't come up with anything more than a shrug.

"I don't think y' need t' worry about Jamie," I said kindly; "I'd say he's able t' look afteh his heart."

"You don't...think he'll break down an' marry her?"

"I think he's made it pretty clear that he won't—t' everybody except maybe Damaris; an' she'll get the picture sooneh or lateh," I said, puffing away at a fresh fill in my clay pipe. "Tennyrate, youh're right about one thing...he does seem more ready t' begin settlin' down some—even t' the point of talkin' t' me, b'fore I shipped last month, about filin' his intention t' become a citizen."

Ben set upright there in his armchair, completely surprised out of his troubles. "He said that? Y' mean it?" he scrambled the words out; then his eyes narrowed, and he looked at me, suspicious. "Why ain't he talked t' me about it?" he grumbled, as if suddenly wary of all the news I was privy to that he wasn't.

"I imagine he'll get around t' it," I mollified him. "For one thing, he's goin' t' need John's advice... It's been two years since he touched here in Boston, an' if I remembeh, he's got t' file now if he wants citizenship in three more."

He looked at me hard, as if trying to judge whether or not I was in on the Boston news, too. I met his gaze blandly and puffed away, as unperturbed as though I had no secrets; and he said nothing, though one of his brows twitched. "I'll speak t' John sometime t'morrow, an' try t' find out more about the procedure," he muttered, the gears clearly starting to grind on this one. "Lord, he'll have t' submit t' that test, an' he still don't know George Washington from Adam....It'll take the next three years t' teach him. What d'ye s'pose put it int' his head t' file?"

"Don't know f'r certain—but I 'magine it's b'cause he likes it here," I said dryly. "He's made it plain Wales is more or less b'hind him, even if it does still seem like home t' him...an' like y' said, he seems t' need t' settle in, or at least have some kind of place o' belongin'."

"I wish thehre was a way t' get him out o' that Inn... t' get him out here with us more often. Ain't there a way t' get him t' move into youhr place, without imposin' on his pride? We could fix up the upstairs room for him, an' he could pay rent, if it made him feel betteh."

"I've asked him b'fore, several times since you did, but he always gives me the same answer... He's scared of livin' in one place, that's what it boils down to—'s scared of givin' up the independence of his people, even if in his heart he wants to; an' I think we're just goin' t' have t' give him enough time t' work that through. It's enough he's come around t' settlin' down in one country, without expectin' him t' move into one house."

Ben sunk back down into the cushions of his chair, his glum look telling me he knew I was right.

"I'll tell ye what, though," I said lightly—understanding from his face that the solution now was Jim's nearness, even if it wasn't nearness of dwelling, and getting ready to play a card I'd long been holding—"seems t' me a betteh bet 'd be some new direction... someplace where we could get away t'getheh, without really callin' it anyone's home."

He perked up a degree, and set up straighter. "Y' mean, like the huntin' cabin?" he asked me.

"Aye, but it takes time t' get out there, it's hard t' keep it stocked an' so forth; an' when all's said an' done, we've got t' share it with Tom an' the othehs."

"What is it ye've got on the ways, then?"

"Well, how about the island? St. James, I mean—it's only eight miles out, an' we c'n sail it in a couple o' owehs. We've been promisin' t' ferry Jim out there f'r a year now, but we still ain't got around t' it."

He was back to being bolt upright in the armchair, and a light was playing acrosst his features, the sort of glimmer you see when the sun breaks along the billows on the horizon; but he said nothing, just looked at me, brows twitching.

"There's good fishin' there, good company too, what with most o' the McCabes in Spooneh Bay," I went on, trying to keep the grin of triumph off my face; "there's plenty o' supplies in the harboh, an' some kind o' place t' rent, I would wager. I could do me some trawlin' in autumn—ye could get some distance on things here, get away from the yard when ye felt like, even run the young 'uns out for a gander—an' Jim, he could have us around if he wanted, or just let them gypsy feet o' his wander, without havin' t' feel like he'd settled down some."

Ben was up on his feet by this time, pacing to and fro by the fire, his face looking like a rocket in mid-flight. "The island, a' course!" he was muttering to hisself, his features working with his excitement. "What a jackass I've been not to' think of it! We could rent that old place on the edge o' town—your uncle's cottage on the south shore o' the harboh—he don't use it f'r anything, does he?"

"Charlie's old place?" I asked, all innocent. "I b'lieve it's up for sale."

"F'r sale!" he roared, opening up like a Gulf blow. "Christ, we could buy it! If the three of us went in t'getheh, Jim wouldn't have t' think of it as his house much—not any more than he wanted to at first—Anne'd neveh want t' go out there, the children could pretty much run like they wanted—Good Lord! We've got t' get stahrted! What is the house like, c'n ye remembeh? It's big enough f'r the three of us, ain't it—room t' spare f'r the children if we brought them for a visit?"

"Bound t' be, Charlie was raised there, 'long with my Pa an' eight or nine others… It would be damned nice t' b'long t' the old place," I mused, perking away at my pipe to keep my grin hid. "I ain't been inside it since Pa showed me around it, ten years ago or more it'd be, now."

"What else d'ye remembeh? Ain't it right on the harboh? Ain't there a bit of a dock there below it?"

"Aye, it's set close t' the shore on a rise o' grass," I recalled, watching with pleasure the wheels go round in his head, and feeling their mates go round in mine. "Y' know," I went on, seeing sights in my pipe smoke, visions of me hauling nets off the ledges, glimpses of Melchett guiding the tiller, "if we're really goin' t' do this right, maybe what we needs is a boat, so's not t' have t' d'pend on the ferry."

His face—which was already about as ruddy as it ever got in a gale wind—all but turned geranium in his excitement. "Ye're right!" he gusted, coming down on me like a nor'easter, and giving my shoulders a shake with his great paws; "We've got t' have us a boat on the double. I've always wanted t' build a flash beauty, somethin' like the one Joseph's makin'—but no time now, we'll have t' buy one."

"My cousin Obed's sellin' his sloop," I offered, looking down to hide the glint of satisfaction in my eyes.

"What! That little gem he stahrted out with? Why ain't I heard till now about it?"

"He didn't d'cide till we was headin' home from the Banks," I answered, puffing hard to obscure my twinkle. "He wants t' take it out o' the fleet an' replace it with somethin' biggeh—some ketch or otheh he's seen f'r sale up the George's River."

Melchett didn't say a word, just reached dumbly for his jacket.

"Where the devil are ye goin'?"

"T' get Jim."

"What in blazes are ye up to?"

"Christ, I've got t' see y'r cousin, an' buy that boat b'fore somebody else does! Jim'll like t' help me bargain—them Romany *chals* c'n outdeal a Scotsman."

"You'hre goin' *now*? Melchett, it's ten o'clock!"

He was already out the door and halfway down the walk to the shore. Leaning out the porch I yelled, in one last vain but valiant attempt, "Melchett, b'fore ye go, there's this tree that's... Hell, he can't hear a word," I trailed off, watching him disappear in the gloom, "why in Kingdom Come am I hangin' out the door?"

Knowing he'd go to the Inn for Jim first, and probably get him out of bed, I heaved a sigh and banked the fire, then grabbed my jacket and hauled it on me; and looking ahead to an inevitable late bedtime, I went to prepare my cousin Obed.

Only the kitchen lamp was shining as I approached Obed's place from the shore. The cottage itself was up on stilts, to let the high tides pass underneath; what with the storm we'd had, and the uncommonly high water, there was a tangle of flotsam under there, wadded up with all kinds of spare trawling gear. The stilts shone out like slender yearlings in the moonlight, and the yellow curtains glowed with a welcoming shine. As soon as I stepped into the porch I smelled fish: the gear and old nets beneath the house; Obed's windbreaker and sou'wester and oilslicks; the baskets and hampers; the hods, diggers and buckets, some of them still gurried up—all of these gave off a constant odor of ground fish. Again I smelled it, and again I liked it: it was a smell that meant home and sea to me.

I found Obed setting at the table with our cousin Lem, a jug of ale, and the dog, a wiry spaniel; Obed's son Bryce was stretched on the kitchen sofa, sleeping the sleep of a six-year-old oarsman. When he heard Ben was coming, and in high spirits, Obed moved Bryce to his sisters' room; then he set me down with a spare mug, and poured me out a generous swallow. Clinking rims, gulling down ale, gnawing away at a plate of hardtack, and exchanging news of hogged docks and blown sails, we passed a handsome half an hour; and whilst I indulged I looked around me, taking in all the plain room fondly. The rickety chairs, the threadbare sofa, the corner stove and dry sink and cupboards, all met my eye like a bevy of old friends, the comrades I'd grown up with a cottage or two downshore; while Obed's and Lem's ruddy, lean mugs spoke of dear kin, parents and shipmates long since shipped for last harbors.

We'd just settled back with our clay pipes, and poured our second round of ale, when we heard voices outside on the beach, and then the stomp of Melchett's boots on the porch. He come busting into the kitchen in his usual blustery way—his big body always broke in on a room like a windgust, picking up to full force of a sudden; Jim breezed in just in his wake, and I noted with satisfaction the freshened shine of his eyes and face.

Once or twice in the hubbub of back-slapping and rum-pouring, Jim looked my way with a covert expression of gratefulness, as if he'd pretty much read my aims; I nodded back over my rim, as though in a conspirator's toast; but in all the commotion there in the kitchen it wasn't easy to get a word to him. He looked extremely well tonight— as fiery as he'd earlier looked downhearted; and I took time off from the business at hand to appreciate his return of spirit. Red-cheeked from the early autumn cold, he seemed to spark with anticipation, especially in the depths of them blue eyes; and his hands in the pockets of Ben's old red plaid sporting jacket gave his whole body an expectant air. Leaning against the kitchen cupboard—now and then quaffing a bit from his hot mug—he watched Ben bluntly open the bargaining; watched him with such a look of friendly pride, and indulgent love, that I paid more attention to his face than to any of Melchett's fast talking.

Melchett's bargaining was indeed lively, and punctuated by many a sweep of his arm in that old patched, faded brown jacket; nothing less than the hail, the licensed tonnage—displacement, gross, net and deadweight, plus the whole history of the craft from the ways to her berth now was the subject of his discussion. Where she'd been built, by who and of what woods —how the mast'd been shipped, how the keel laid—whether the keel was hook-scarfed or not—how fast she was—who'd rigged her and suited her—how she behaved in calms and coarse weather: these was just some of the relentless questions he bellowed out upon poor Obed.

Putting down the salt cellar and tipping back in my chair, I turned to watch him indulgently myself, and found myself thinking that any stranger to the group would of picked him out as a fisherman, and the poorest man in the room. Them faded pants—that ridiculous jacket—them boots with the gashes here and there in the leather; that wind-tangled hair, bleached out by the weather, poking out here and there round that visor; that hauler's build; them big, work-hardened hands; and above all, that broad, ruddy face, full of squints and lines and creases —what other clues would a stranger need? He lacked only one, the smell of fish; but since the whole place reeked of cod, the want about Ben wasn't much to be noticed.

There was a lull in negotiations: Ben was trying to talk Obed into lighting some lanterns, and taking us out to the sloop on the spot; and Jim was laughing and hobnobbing with Lem, and pouring everyone another round of ale. Holding out my mug, I smiled on his bright face, and his sun-warm, lively manner: he was teasing Ben for his hastiness, twitting him with a proprietor's pride, and sympathizing with embattled Obed, as he moved from place to place with the jug.

Uncorking the rum, he stood there for a moment chuckling,

the picture of easy poise and belonging, before he tipped the bottle and poured a generous portion in each tumbler. Lem came behind with the toddy iron; and glasses was raised once again with a vigor. Then the shuffling of burly boots on the floor—the general round of laughing and slurping—and finally a confused exit, with lanterns and questions and jackets: Melchett had got his way, a' course, and we was all five of us off across the beach to view the sloop.

She was a trim, handy craft just above 35 feet, with a single mast rigged out with a mainsail, a spinnaker and a couple of jibs; her topsides was flush except for a low deckhouse, and down below she had a galley, and a bit of a sleeping quarters forward. But it was hard to see her fair points in the clobber: Obed's nets was still draped acrosst her taffrails, and she was gurried up from herring, whilst her holding tank was still full of sea brine. "Not exactly the flash beauty ye spoke of when y' mentioned Joseph's," I said dryly to Melchett in an aside; but he shrugged his shoulders in answer, unmoved.

"Betteh yet, she's a workhorse," he grunted fondly, in a tone that showed no higher praise could be bestowed; "b'sides, I've an idear she'll go like hell-bolts when she gets the right trim, an' the right hands on the tiller."

As if to confirm his high opinion—his suspicion that she was not just handy enough to ferry us, but versatile enough for either speed or fishing—his fingers was everywhere touching and feeling, with the tenderness of a lover's; and his eyes was a-glint with a steely glimmer. He'd at once, a' course, begun to climb here and there, viewing her outfit from maintruck to keelson, since she was temporarily set up in dry dock; while Robertson followed him up mast and down galley, speechlessly amused, with the lantern. I'd already whispered sympathetically to Obed, "He'll buy her, a' course; but be patient, an' humor him"; Obed'd chuckled and shaken his head, and waited things out as I'd bid him.

Now Melchett begun to work on the price some, throwing out a new figure over the taffrail, or calling down a fresh sum from the masthead; him and Obed'd just about have matters worked out, and I'd figure we'd soon be back to the ale jug, when Robertson would slip in innocently, "But what about—", and the whole round'd start all over again. But at last Melchett jumped down and announced he'd settle; him and Obed shook hands as though neither of them 'd known this conclusion might be reached; and we abandoned the shore for the kitchen, and the satisfaction of a fresh refill.

Melchett, a' course, not being one to let the grass grow under his feet, had us aboard of Tom's sloop in the pitch dark, and out to the island well before daybreak—luffing up to Charlie's dock in the grey murk, and nearly scaring him into the drink with our sudden appearance. Getting ready for the day's trawl with his two sons, the only ones of his tribe old enough to help crew, he was clambering about nets and lines and tackle, looking as he always did, hungover; and it was no easy job to get him to understand our mission.

That he even had a cottage somewheres out the south shore of the harbor, he'd pretty much forgotten—that he'd put it up for sale, ditto; whilst if he'd ever had a key, it was certainly nowheres to hand now. Finally—to save ourselves a heap of trouble—we more or less bought up the place sight unseen; and before I knew it we was shaking hands all around, promising to come back tonight with a bank draft—which it'd probably take the old man days to figure out how to cash—and trusting to Eliot and Orin to remember the terms.

The deal shook upon, we drank a toast in the grey dawn, passing one of the jugs Charlie always stashed aboard the ketch; then—already looking more chipper—Charlie bawled as we cast off, "Neveh mind about the key—just bust int' the place when ye wants ter!" Though that was exactly what we itched to do, there was no time now for a look-see; but as we filled away—Melchett dipping his ensign—we made a slow circuit of the harbor, showing Jim the little village of Spooner Bay; and when we reached nigh the Point of the south shore, and come abeam of the cottage pretty much off by itself, we backed water and took a good gander. It was a sweet little cape, grey-shingled and weathered, with a couple of dormers facing the harbor, an overgrown dooryard a-mass with sea roses, and a small carriage house with a graveled drive; and good as it looked to me with my home blood, it looked like paradise to Ben and Jim, who could barely tear theirselves away for the run back.

We was back in Cape Damaris in time for Melchett to go on 'Change—still in his seaboots and windbreaker, a' course—and for Jim to report for work in the shipyard; but we was off to Spooner Bay again after supper, me some wore out from tackling that blamed tree, but Jim and Ben still a-roar as a fresh breeze. Making fast to the dock—what there was of it—and hopping the missing planks to the landing, we made our way through the weeds to the back porch, where Ben did the honors of forcing the door jamb; then standing back, he gave Jim a smile, encouraging him to be the first to step in. Following in Jim's wake, Ben and me crowded behind, for all the world as excited as treasure seekers; and straightaway we found ourselves in a small porch, pretty much cluttered up with Charlie's gear, but paneled ship-style with yellow pine, and lighted by a couple of windows.

From there we stepped into the kitchen piled high with lobster pots, but still with a cook stove, and a wide hearth with a mantle broad as a deck bean; and looking around we discovered a small pantry, a stairwell leading down to a root cellar, and doors opening onto a bed chamber and big front room. In the bed chamber I paused beside the four-poster, its ropes gone but its frame and pegs still solid: this was probably the same room my grand-folks'd snored in, probably the very bed in which my Pa'd been born; strange how I hadn't till now come to see it. Wandering into the front room I come on Ben and Jim, gawking out the windows overlooking the harbor, and eyeballing another broad-beamed fireplace mantle, this one decorated with a small brass plate: "From the bark *Maris Pelham*, Augustus Spooner, captain; hard a-ground 25 July, 1741."

"Well, I'm damned," I muttered, coming up to join them, and reading the plate over their shoulders; "if that ain't the very ship that's wrecked off Signal Point, not very far from where they've built the light now: Aug Spooneh got off'n her with a couple o' deckhands, includin' my great-grandpa Mather; an' takin' a shine t' the place, they decided t' stay here. It bein' James' feast day on the church calendar, they so named the island, since nobody else had; an' Spooneh Bay— both the harboh and the village they founded—took on the handle o' the skipper."

Eager to hear more about the island's history, Jim at once launched a whole fleet of questions, some about the McCabes, Winslows, Coombs and Pelhams who'd originally cast their lot in with Aug Spooner, some about the particulars of my kin line, such as how the Inn's Jimmy was related to old Mather; and still answering him we climbed upstairs, feeling somehow a-tune with others who'd trod them. Off the hall we found a large front chamber, facing the harbor with a broad, deep dormer, and blessed with a hearth, a rare thing in a shore cottage; whilst across the way was two smaller bedrooms, overlooking the road and the fir grove. As we nosed about, tripping over crates, lengths of line and now and then chair legs, or outdated utensils whose uses we couldn't guess, we chattered away to ourselves and each other, like diggers at some unlooked-for rich lode.

Once I seen Ben set a hand to Jim's shoulder, in a kind of gesture of welcome—seen Jim cast a grin of belonging back at him; and several times Jim took my arm in excitement, and tugged me off to some find in a corner. Having reached the point where he was actually gut-hungry for some sort of a place with Ben, he was looking longingly about him, as if imagining hisself carving out a home-life; whilst Ben looked like he'd come back to the stock that'd always been at his roots, the fishermen's blood that was his through generations of Winslows and Tuppers. As for me, old ties to kin who'd trawled these shores since before the first war with England come back to me as I trod these floors, and fleshed out the lonely life I'd lived; made me see my old incompleteness, and the wholeness that'd come not just from old moorings, but from newer bonds to these two big, eccentric men, lumbering about this musty room at the moment.

Needing to get the draft from the bank over to Charley's yet this evening, we hiked the harbor road to his place, passing scrub pines and straggling shore grasses, a few lamplit cottages surrounded by net frames, and here and there, a derelict schooner; then our business wrapped up —no quick undertaking, what with eight or ten of Charlie's young ones a-swing in the small place, complete with pigs and goats in the dooryard—we hopped back onto the sloop, and made for the mainland in a light breeze.

Hard pressed to spare much time from the shipyard—working pretty much from dawn to dusk, especially now that not only *Abigail* but the other boats was behind schedule—Ben couldn't get away again till the weekend; but come Friday eve we was back at the cottage, sleeping on the floor of the front room in bedrolls, plotting out our needs for furniture and dock planks, and luxuriating in the thought we could stay through Sunday.

For Jim and me that was no particular feat, since it meant little more than packing a seabag; but for Ben it meant a thousand preparations, everything from arranging a Saturday stand-in to ironing out details of work with him; whilst getting away from his house was a capital matter. At any other time him and Anne would of scrapped some; but now—fresh as a daisy herself from a month's play, and smoothed down a bit from his efforts in her stead, which even she had to give him credit for—Anne gave in gracious not just to this weekend, but to all four of them in September: buttered up, probably, by the appearance of a maid, and a full-time stableman-gardener. Feeling like he could leave justifiably, Ben was as buoyed up as a bobber; whilst Jim was so jubilant it wrenched my heart to watch.

Feeling for the first time like he had his own place—not just a part-time roof or a shared deck, but a visible sign of his permanence with us—he was a regular volcano of ideas: chattering on about firewood, dishes and bedsteads to the ceiling, long after Ben and me was a-snore. And me, sliding off into sleep on the hard floor—I was just as exultant as them: filled up with the grateful feeling that I was to be a part of this crew—not just as a net-masher, one who by nature stitches things together, but as a partner, one with his share of the hand on the tiller. My last waking thought as I trailed off from Jim's talk, and drifted away from the moon's path on the floor, was that after years of living lonely, and doing my stubborn best to win one, I finally had me a family.

We put in the month of September clearing out Charlie's gear, getting in our essentials, and driving new pilings along the dockway: four weekend treks out to the island, the last of the lot with Tom and Jean, who blew in and took root like pioneers. By the young ones' visit we'd set up the kitchen, cleaned out the various hearths, stovepipe and chimney, and hired bunks built in the upstairs chambers—more wintry jobs, such as laying in cords of firewood, banking the foundations and sprucing up the boathouse having been set aside for October, whenever we could spare time from the sloop in dry dock. Anne notwithstanding we worked like hell on the Sabbath, mostly indoors wherest no one could see us: getting in the elements for food, sleep and fire, good hearty stocks of quilts and potatoes, kettles and kindling and preserves—nothing more than what we needed, but nothing less, our rule of thumb in tenting.

By now I'd chosen the downstairs bedroom, once my great-grandfolks', and settled some gear in, re-roping the bedstead and hanging a lantern; the large upstairs room fronting the harbor, once a kind of dormitory for my Pa and uncles, and the only other chamber with heat, become logically Ben's and Jim's, and without squabbling they took possession. With a broad skipper's bunk built in at each end, an over-stuffed sofa set in the dormer, and a handy pine bureau and woodbin by the hearth, it was big enough for their wants—an imaginary line dividing the neat half from the messy; the two smaller rooms acrosst the hall, once my aunts', and now fitted out with berths and curtains, being even without hearths more than adequate for the children.

Maintaining a trim ship, we kept things simple, little more than cooking, chopping and sweeping; and keeping things streamlined we had time for the big jobs, the work necessary to salvage the old place. As we worked we developed a joy in belonging, a pride like the one we felt for *Charis*, a kinship as if the rooms was alive; and we established too a kind of routine, as we had to sea—an unspoken way of dividing up jobs, so there was no falling over each other's feet as we did things. If I'd had any doubts about how we'd get along, once the honeymoon glow'd worked off, they was quickly laid to rest, as they had been by the river last autumn; for even though we was so different, we had a knack of harmonizing our odds.

That we was all three as happy as we'd ever been, you could feel in the very timbers of these old rooms—there was straightaway a sort of shine about them, a glow that was more than swept hearths and bright quilts, firelight and the snooze of the dog by the blaze: the spirit of warmth that only springs up when all the elements of a place is not just used, but loved; when all the creatures under the roof is tolerated, and equally contented and at home.

Not that all was peaceful between us, or our weekends unmarred by any misfortune; that would of been too much to hope for, especially in a crew as mixed as us. One night after a late expedition for blueberries, Jim was laid low by another one of his headaches, which usually come in the wake of time with Ben, as if their intensity triggered a malaise; and on the lookout for a reaction, I wasn't caught off-guard none. But Ben—who'd only seen him succumb once at sea, and even then only from a distance, since we'd always been able to doctor things on his off-watch—hadn't any idea of the severity of his attacks; and he was completely floored by this one. Seeing Jim struck of a heap on the sofa, unable to move because of the pain, he was so wrenched with distress he was speechless; and he kept to Jim's side like a she-bear, dumbly guarding him at his shoulder. It took morphine now to block the pain; and though I was able to keep the dose low, and only had to resort to such measures once in every third week or so, Ben was thunderstruck I had to use it at all, and terrified lest he develop some addiction.

When Jim was finally safely asleep, his limbs relaxed with the limpness of comfort, Ben cornered me by the hearth in the kitchen, roaring at me for the use of the drug, and for keeping him all these months in the dark; and it was no easier to settle him down than it'd been Jim. "Whyn't ye tell me how bad off Jim was? Why d' I always find out such news second-hand? What the hell else are ye keepin' from me?" he bawled, his brow creviced up and gloomed with suspicion; and I had to hunt and fish a bit to restore peace.

Seeing Jim at the table next morning, bright as ever over his cup of tea, did something to ease up his anxiety and concern; but it was plain he wasn't quite as convinced of Jim's uncomplicated show of spirits as he had been; and there was a new wariness between us that hadn't been there before.

If Jim's illness had struck a disquieting note there was other discords, few and far between, and often as not the source of wry laughs; and most of them sprang from such innocuous reasons as the eccentricities betweenst us—as, for example, the matter of Jim's cup, which Romany fashion was his alone, to keep him from gadje contamination, despite the fact he shared all other utensils with us. But nothing riled up our household waters more than teaching Jim the ropes of American history; and frequently when Ben and me was alone we cussed—between guffaws—as we compared notes. By now with John's help Jim'd filed his intention to become a citizen; and thinking he'd pick up the principles of government and the essentials of history better if he began at once, rather than wait until the last minute, when he'd be obliged to cram his head for the exam, we took it in turns to tutor him up some.

That this'd be no small undertaking, I already had a fair idea, from my hair-pulling experience of trying to teach him the higher mathematics needed for navigation; for bright as he obviously was— however first-rate his intelligence—it didn't lend itself to book-learning; and I gave Ben the word to go easy with him. Optimistically starting out, Ben tried to teach him a little about the founding of the colonies, thinking that, since after all, much of early America had to do with Britain, where Jim'd lived and absorbed principles hisself, some of it would surely make sense; but as the weeks went by he taught little that stuck, Jim confusing the first war with England with the second, snafuing the branches of government and their respective tasks, and tangling non-intercourse with taxation, embargoes and rebellions with impressments and stamp acts. By the end of the month Ben was ready to throttle him—Jim no doubt thinking of responding in kind; and we was about to give up for the time, when one day, laying planks, I had an idea.

Remembering how so often Jim told things in stories, revealing what he knowed about hisself best in memories, and considering how eager he was to hear tales of the island, I hit on the notion of giving him history lessons in long yarns, tying up the early days of the colonies, and the war, with accounts of Ben's forefathers and mine; and I was astonished at how quickly he learned then, easily sorting out five or six generations of our kin, and remembering which generations'd been caught up in which times. The rebellion and its fights, the embargo and privateering, the separation of Maine from Massachusetts, all made sense when he seen them as part of the story of Mather McCabe, Winslow Melchett and on down; and once learned he didn't forget the yarns, loving to hear them over again for new threads.

Hammering planks in the warm sun, laying shingles on the roof, cleaning out the small rooms and readying them for the children, or drinking a bit of sugared rum after sunset, Ben and me took turns like spinners on a rope walk, giving fresh twists to the rope yarns we'd had; and slowly our past become part of Jim's tale; slowly our strand become bound up with his.

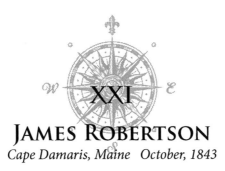

XXI

JAMES ROBERTSON

Cape Damaris, Maine   October, 1843

There was a fine sea on and the wind was making up; and too restless to hang about town—familiar enough with the weather now to know I'd be stormbound, if once I managed to make it out to the island—I jumped aboard the last boat heading out, Dory Pelham's, and made myself useful by tallying onto the mainsheet. Once in Spooner Bay I sped post haste for the cottage, shaking off anyone inclined to follow; and going straight up the stairs to my room and Ben's, I shut the door gleefully behind me. Out the window the trees, brilliant-hued, were tossing, the bay whipping up whiter and whiter; but on the hearth I soon had a fire blazing; and here I sat, knees drawn up, tea steeping at my elbow, in the hush of a calm surrounded by tumult, knowing I'd be wind-bound at least till tomorrow.

With the wind at the windows, or pulsing at the eaves, and the swash of the bay on the dock down below, I felt myself in a cabin at sea; and I wouldn't have known I was attached to the earth if I hadn't just clambered down cellar. All the details which now met my eye, as I gazed out from my chair, suggested the get-up-and-go of a vessel: the paneled walls, the built-in bunks, the practical readiness of pine trunks; Ben's eye-piece set at one of the dormers, the inevitable battery of barometers nearby it; and mounted over Ben's bunk the tell-tale, which shows direction first thing to one waking at sea. Though obviously rock-firm as any chamber, there was such an impression of movement about the room that I felt as at ease as if in a *vardo*, rolling down some lane behind a cob; and like the hermit crab which borrows its shell case, picks it up and carries it with him—only to shed it when he outgrows it, and commence a search for another—I felt ready to settle and grow here, and travel about within its shelter.

Nor was it only its appointments which gave the room a sense of movement; for there was something less tangible about it which suggested the tension between the two halves: not the strain of confrontation, but rather the force of give and take. Though the whole chamber mirrored the architecture of Ben's nature—solid, forthright, pragmatic—there was much that reflected my own as well, much that was airy, volatile, vivid; so that my love of color spilled over into his half, and manifested itself in his bright quilt; or my predisposition toward sentiment and memento showed up in the clutter of keepsakes on his bedstand. But in no way did I see the spark of my influence more clearly than in the impulse of the physical that erupted throughout his austere corner; for as I gazed about, thinking back to my first impression of his cabin aboard *Charis*—as I recalled its monkish order, yet its sense of hibernation—I realized I'd sprung him out; and I smiled into my tea as I sipped it.

His stacks of nautical periodicals and newspapers, dog-eared at every innovation—his flannel shirts, their sleeves still rolled up—his dressing gown, flung over the foot of his bed—the erratic jumble of puzzles to be worked out, everything from deckpins to be refitted to lengths of fishline to be unknotted: all these were visible where there had been scarcely so much as a hairbrush before; and to them clung hints of body and scent, the smells of machine oil, wood, hemp, canvas, and sand, so palpable that I could hardly bear to look at them.

Yet with all this evidence of our separate selves, spilling over and blending into one another, like the respective strands of a skillfully spliced rope, still there remained distinction enough to generate the action of commerce; and it was this ceaseless shoreline barter that I sensed in the room's intangible motion.

As if our room were a horse and carriage, I could ride it as well into Ben's inner spirit; for looking about me, I could see its pulse in the character of the chamber, in the incorporeal fabric of its assumptions; and I picked my way through this new terrain slowly. Now that I'd broken ground by attending church, not just at sea but on land, and conditioned folks to the freak of my presence—now that I'd commenced to try to read the signposts, or chart the patterns of his beliefs, I was determined to keep on till I'd grasped their essence; and I could see their invisible face in the air of this room, in the aura of hard work, honesty, moral straightness—of adherence to given word and duty, the very language of which seemed to speak through his work clothes.

Yet committed as he was to the pattern he'd been taught, I could see he was not without his doubts as to its shape; could see that he felt increasingly caught up in the clash between social commands, and imperatives of his own. I could detect it in the dogged strain on his face, or in his gradual increase in drinking; could discern it in the conflicts between his needs and convictions as he strove to interpret his place in his family. I could sense it here in his tidy corner, not so much in any lines of constraint, as in its atmosphere of escape; could sense that its peace had become his haven from those forces which did combat in him. Maybe it was the cottage silence, the snap of the sparks, the protective windows, and the tumult outside of trees and bay; but it was plain that amongst many purposes, this was the place of a man seeking refuge—of a man hiding out from a turmoil of spirit.

It would have pleased me to think that I was the sole cause of his upheaval—that I was that important to him; but I knew him too well now to suppose that it wasn't as well his contention with Anne, or his yearning to re-interpret his work in the light of Jackson's influence; and knowing only he could resolve his discord, and only with the tools of the beliefs he'd been born to, I looked on his half of the room with mute feeling—with the love of a ripening understanding, and the pain of a sympathetic waiting.

As I journeyed the furnishings to my side, riding the chamber into myself—as I looked out from the wings of my armchair, shifting a little in the cushions—I could see too the landscape of my own spirit; could perceive the maelstrom of unvoiced yearnings which pressed to rush past— unresolved—Ben's dilemmas, and confront him with their urges. Sometimes those yearnings were swallowed up—as just now—in my compassion for his pressures; but at others they asserted themselves above all else, till I felt I couldn't tolerate another day of the uncertainty of waiting. It showed in the impatient fling of the bedclothes; in the way I'd never fully unpacked, as if part of me were ready to throw in the towel at any moment, and hit the road for a fresh start elsewhere. Indeed it all showed, even my faith in the future, the hope which checked me from giving up the chase; showed in the whole structure of schemes in the room, the artifices I'd devised to bring him to the point.

Hadn't I just now hid under his pillow private hairs, the surefire Rom method of nabbing a wavering heart? Hadn't I tried every trick of body, every maneuver of spirit to net him in the bargain—every nuance from the tight breeches on the chair to the herb potions on the mantle? And wasn't this very room visible proof of my encyclopedia of wiles? Yet every time I sat back to await results, I despised myself for increasing the pressure on him; and so the whole cycle—yearning to stay, longing to quit—commenced itself all over again, usually with the onset of a headache.

So powerful was my physical yearning that it was an ache I could feel from my teeth to my feet; but even at my most optimistic, I'd almost given up on its venting; for it was so plain —even from my brief reading of his corner—that even if he were attracted, he would stop short of a confession, due as much to his steadfast religious convictions as to his respect for the commitments of his marriage. I wouldn't have come between him and those if I could; yet how ironic that what fettered him, bound me, though neither a Christian nor a spouse; and how ironic that adherence to the old prevented the emergence of the new—the final erasure of the bounds of this room.

To preserve my sanity I'd been forced to seek out that which most went against my grain, the make-do of a compromise; and so to that end I'd found an outlet in taking care of his things—in serving him as I'd certainly never before served, or expected to serve, another. This change in me too showed in the room—in the way I'd just now tenderly brushed his gloves, and set them neatly on the bureau; in the way I'd just picked up his work boots, and begun to scrape last week's sand on the hearth. Indeed now that I thought of it, I was acting like him, as if the two of us had somehow switched places; was acting in a way not inconsistent with the scripture I'd minutes ago thought so alien and removed. Pausing boot in hand, I took a look at me, then traversed the room again with a quick eye, seeing many signs not of my customary independence, but of service and interdependence. How many things there were that belonged to us both, things I'd helped pay for, or helped him discover! The sofa under the dormer, the hearth tools, the woodbox, the armchairs and braided rugs and ship's clock: how many attics had we raided for these goods, and what else besides them had we ever owned in common?

As if they, and my caretaking, had the power to transport, I suddenly saw my love of housekeeping; saw that I'd tried to find new ways to live out the conjugal roles I'd been pretending in our tent on the beach, here in this house, and here in this chamber; saw that I'd already looked ahead to our coming months at sea, and spotted a berth—not the second mate's—for me, a berth that would bring us more completely together, even if it did puzzle and perturb him. Then looking around with the eyes of my people, I saw with fear what I was becoming; and I felt an unsettled disquiet in me. As Ben clung to the old, I too clung to the Rom image of manhood, proud, self-sustaining, served rather than serving; and I feared to declare my need for another. Taking in the signs of tension in my share of the room, I saw not just the frustrations of one ready to quit, but the apprehensions of one longing to stay—the fear of surrender, of lack of control, of encountering one more potent and forceful; and asking myself what I would do if he ever took me up on my bid, I could see that I would decamp.

There was an atmosphere of poise in my corner, of hovering between open invitation and withdrawal, as if I were ready to flee if met; something which showed in the precarious balance between the personal allure of the bed, and the closed reserve of the locked trunk. Whether it was my fear of self-loss—or whether it was a lingering distrust for the new being I'd be if I yielded—whatever the cause, I vacillated; and I saw I was as much bound as Ben to the old husk —to the shellcase shaped by pride and convention.

Crawling into bed—not my own, but Ben's—I hid my face in an old shirt of his, one of his flannels, which I stretched over the pillow; but though I listened to the wind far into the middle watch, hearing its hollow rush at the eaves, I discovered no fresh wisdom from it; and I rose before dawn feeling drawn and ill sorted. Though the wind fell with day the bay remained wrought up, as feather white as the wings of a snow duck; and I couldn't set out for Cape Damaris till supper. When I finally arrived—on the deck of the mail boat—Eben and Ben were both combing the wharf front, convinced I'd gone to the bottom in the blow; and they nearly took me off my feet as I jumped down.

In no pleasant humor, Ben huffed and scowled at me, as if not altogether pleased to find his worries unfounded; and he marched off without so much as a handshake, snapping back something like "Ye might let folks know what you'hre up to, when you'hre jackass enough t' ship out in a windstorm!" But Eben remained behind to console me, with a comradely arm and a twinkle to his grin; and I soon found myself at a table at Eli's, cheering myself with a chowder and hot mug.

Abigail by now loomed over the town, dwarfing everything at the north end; and I gave my days —like everyone else—to her completion, working for a launch date at the end of October. Taking shape like a living being, which little by little attains its fullness, or realizes the potential with which it was first born, she daily fleshed out her frames and timbers, as if she, not we, had charge of her plan; while the days fled past in a restless peregrination, like the flocks of Canadian geese heading south, their distant, honking chorus cast at us. I could feel it in my heart like a call, this hoarsely-voiced summons to gather and migrate; could sense its effect in the way everything seemed to be coming together, woods, canvas, hemp, for the climax of debarkation; could discern it in the flurried congregating of workers, like so many trained hands convening to midwife, or in the plotting of potential sailors like me, hugging hopes for a particular berth.

As if racing to be off the yard dashed with workers: the mill and joiner shops a-scurry with carpenters, all rushing to fit out the decks and cabins; the oakum shop and pitch oven continuously raided by caulkers, pounding and pouring now in the last seams; the forges and bellows a-work by blacksmiths, turning out fittings from ring bolts to mast hoops; the rope-walk a-throng with combers and spinners laying up lengths of line and cable; and teams of horses generating power, the driving force for the saw and steambox. Joiners, coopers, sawyers, hoopers—all seemed to be turned loose in one last grand sprint; while Ben in their midst tromped from one project or another, decked out like a laborer in his high boots and pilot's cap, as at ease with the fine details of the cabins as with the stepping of the giant masts.

They'd shut the town down for a day, those masts, as they were moved from their water baths in the upper yard down along Ship Street to the Melchett ways—thirty-two oxen baulking sections of white pine varying in length from forty feet to a hundred; and now that the lower masts were in place, seated deep within the hull, and the riggers were on the scene, fitting tar-encased backstays and mainstays and laying out the network of halyards, the activity had reached its zenith. But Ben was as calm as if he was alone in his study; and whenever I felt unreasonably flurried—either by the pace of Bart's task-making, or by the general pitch of the yard—I'd simply seek out a glimpse of his face, capable and stoic beneath his visor, and imperturbably set as a seer's; and I always returned to my work steadied.

The figurehead completed, I was posted for the most part in the charthouse and after cabins, bodying out the hackmatack knees, live oak ribs and hard pine skin with unpretentious paneling, and supplementing the usual austere Melchett interiors with bits of fancywork I'd done on my own. At the door tops of Ben's cabin I set carved dolphins, the seagoing symbol of good fortune; while in the saloon I mounted a bracket—carved into the likeness of a sea serpent—from which to suspend Jasper's jute cage. As the days passed and my skills improved, I found more and more joy in shaping out visions; and I took satisfaction and pride in my craft, rigorous and fast-paced as it was.

But it was on Ben's work that I looked in awe, recalling my first feelings of admiration for *Charis* as she rose before me in her berth in Boston; and many a work break I sat on the scaffolds, watching him execute his business, or simply gazing on *Abigail's* unfolding. How this ship, with her frame now fused skeletal-tight with trunnels, and her rigging spun out from towering mastheads, had evolved from some yen of sight in his mind's eye—how it'd sprung to paper, to the layers of a lift model, revealing the lines of her hull from all sides—how it'd grown from a few points into curves drawn by battens, then into molds, full-sized pieces of pattern—how it'd burst into life here on the ways, joint into joint, hemp into hemp like sinews—was as mystifying to me as the compass rose with its network of rhumb lines had been, first navigating; and I watched each new stage evolve like a carver, conscious of a masterwork beyond him.

The mathematical vision, the geometrical concept, the meticulous measuring and piecing and planning, all left me in the dust as I looked on, and reminded me of the greater heights of Ben's mind; but I could grasp the outcome of his logic, the practical, eloquent symmetry of the ship; and as before I saw through it, as through a keyhole, the marrow of the hand that had laid it. A third again as big as *Charis*, the first ship ever built in Cape Damaris over a thousand tons register, it was the image somehow of him—big, clumsy woods somehow honed to reveal the delicacy of the spirit within. As if she were a vehicle not of the waters, but of knowing—of the commerce of the imagination—I would traverse her lines as I'd traversed our room, and see the oaken cast of his visage; and many a time my eyes blurred in the homage of one too moved to utter his heart's praise.

That she pleased him—that she was what he'd envisioned, and capable of the kind of sailing he demanded—I could tell not so much by words spoken, as by the unruffled poise of his weathered face as he proceeded from deck to deck, feeling, smoothing, measuring, conferring; but that he was troubled by her as well, I understood equally plainly, again not so much from remarks as from silence. Though the town was teeming with dignataries from other shipyards come to make out what they could of her secrets—though his name kept appearing in the Boston and New York papers, and it was obvious he'd begun to win recognition, not just as a master, but as a designer—he scarcely seemed to take any notice; and it wasn't modesty which closed his eyes to the furor. The upcoming passage—even though it looked to be to Whampoa, after a cargo of tea and fine porcelains, the *creme de la creme* of passages and cargoes, requiring crack ships and impeccable masters—seemed not to have impressed him either, despite the fact it was what he'd years worked for; and again it wasn't modesty which caused his obliviousness.

It was Jackson who lay behind his preoccupation; Jackson who'd led him to so re-interpret commerce that established routes and traditional patterns of traffic were no longer acceptable to him; Jackson who himself only hung onto his office by an eyelash. Though it was only a part of the great flux of confusion through which Ben was trying to find his way at the moment, shipbuilding was the cornerstone of his career; and he struggled to know how to apply his practice. With *Abigail* he'd found fame, admiration, the recognition justly due to one at the height of his profession; and he had as well his own sense of satisfaction. Yet with *Abigail* he was no longer on the right track, and he knew it; and as I sat beside him sometimes with coffee, looking on her unmistakable greatness, and watching the set corners of his mouth, I wondered how much longer he'd be able to bear the strain of his inner contradiction.

Nor was *Abigail* the only issue over which he floundered; for as I'd sensed in our cottage chamber, his conflict with Anne, and the precariousness of their marriage, had reached intolerable proportions; and they too could be read in the set corners of his mouth. About them, as about shipbuilding, he never said a word—though sometimes he seemed to be on the brink of a confession; but I knew of them from his silence at the end of a long day, from the reluctance with which he rose from Eben's hearth, and left me and Eben sitting by the fire; above all knew of them from his drinking.

He'd certainly never been a light tipper before, on shore when his duties were completed; but since his remarkable dry stint in

August—excepting only our times at the cottage—he drank after work without discretion. I'd seldom before seen him really well on, for he'd always seemed to have some innate restraint; but now several times we'd bedded him down at Eben's, with no small uproar of protest from Anne; and whenever he stopped by my room after hours, the first thing he did was reach for the decanter. Whether or not I played a part in his tumult—whether he struggled over what to do about me, as I certainly struggled over what to do about *him*—I had no sure way of knowing; and there was no way to get him to tip his hand either, for I'd tried every trick ever conceived for the purpose.

That he cared about me profoundly—so powerfully that his feelings flamed up, and took command of his brusque manner and voice, in those rapt moments between us, or on those occasions of fatigue or weakness, when neither of us was on guard; that my place in his heart was as deep as this, I knew without a doubt, and rejoiced; but beyond that I sailed without lead or compass. Even to get him to say out loud that he cared—words I'd longed for months to hear—had proved an impossibility; and I had to content myself with unconscious displays—with his warm, clumsy touch, which spoke for his mute lips—with the eloquent light which sprang to his face, whenever I came unexpectedly upon him.

That his hand sometimes trembled as it came down on my shoulder—that his silence perhaps betokened thoughts about me—filled me with a quick, poignant hope; yet though I couldn't but believe I was a part of his tumult, he so stubbornly held himself aloof, by means of his noncommittal quiet, that I never dared take his heart for granted; and in my frustrated efforts to bring things to a head, I more than once clashed wills with him, both of us on guard and touchy.

Once when he came alone to my room, after a particularly demanding day, and discovered that I still hadn't returned—for I was well into a secret project I'd commenced months ago for his birthday—he simply helped himself to the scotch, after building up a goodly fire; and I found him already half seas over by the time I returned sometime after twilight. Whether at last something in me snapped, out of my concern for him, or whether my disappointment that he looked to the bottle—rather than to me—for comfort, finally asserted itself, I couldn't have said; but next time he reached for the decanter I simply picked it out of his fingers, walked over to the nearest window, and poured it down onto the Ship Street boardwalk, narrowly missing two or three be-plumed bonnets which darted, startled, this way and that.

"What in blazes did'je do that for?" he bawled at me in his best quarterdeck pitch, his mouth still agape, and his brow scowling darkly; whereupon I picked up the rest of his stockpile, some fine West Indies rum, and some first class Madeira—worth a quarter of my month's wages —and dumped them out the window as well, while he glared from his chair, unbelieving.

"I figure you've had about enough," I told him, shutting the sash with a bit of a flourish, and setting three empty bottles back upon his shelf; and at that he got to his feet in a fury, with all the speed of a man scrambling to lash a split topsail.

"Well, I'm damned if I can't find a temperance advocate to home!" he roared, tossing his cigar into the fire; and snatching up his peacoat, he walked out.

For more than a week he kept up his dudgeon, the longest falling-out we'd ever had; and though I looked for him at the yard, at noon dinner or break time, and hung about patiently at Eben's, he never once showed up to make up, or act as if nothing had happened. On the new planks of *Abigail*, in the course of our duties, we frequently met one another in passing; but even then he refused to meet my eyes, or glance back over his shoulder to see if I looked at him; and when it was necessary for him to address me, he spoke gruffly.

Not since my month aboard *Amanda* last autumn had we been separated for more than a day; and stung by his distance I was forced to learn anew the fierceness with which I craved his presence— not just his touch, his offhand cuffs and punches, and occasional tender brushes, for which I literally lived as for food, but his simple blunt, earthy nearness, for want of which I now fairly languished. Never had I been so cross, so temperamental and out of sorts—as if the very mechanics of life had all at once been taken from me;

and so reduced was I by the end of a week that I actually considered humbling myself, and offering an apology to him: an unprecedented step I would probably have taken, if I hadn't had the wit instead to feign one of my unfailing headaches.

Hearing of my illness later the same day from Bart, or one of the ship's carpenters with whom I worked, he came marching up the inn steps—his familiar stomp immediately touching off my pulse—and bursting as quietly as he could into my room, his size and abruptness making any genuinely hushed entrance all but an impossibility. Finding me awake, and limply sitting up on the sofa, he at once crossed over to me, his face so full of unmasked concern that it was all I could do to keep from rushing to meet him; and as he sat down beside me I tentatively leaned a bit toward him, while he unhesitantly patted my knee.

"Somethin' t' eat?" he asked gently; and basking in his presence, the only nourishment I'd needed, I simply shook my head with a smile. Getting up for a moment he repaired the fire, and set a jorum of coffee to steep; then sitting down nearby—drawing a periodical from the heap, and hooking his spectacles round his ears—he settled himself to read for a while. Blissfully content, I burrowed in my quilt, healthily drowsy for the first time in a week; and knowing he was within reach, I drew a deep breath, then quickly consigned myself to slumber.

Our breach wasn't healed for long, however; for later that evening—after I'd wakened and found him gone, and eaten a bracing supper sent up by Jimmy—I heard his tread upon the stairs; and making haste to look ill I pulled the comforter around me, and meekly began to sip at my tea. Heaving himself into the chair and accepting a cup from the kettle—not without a telltale glance at his shelf, where the empty decanters still held forth—he began to look suspicious, like one about to try to maneuver; and on the alert I watched him closely as he poured himself a dash from the creamer. I could see that he was attempting to be tactful—could deduce it from his leisurely stirring, and the solicitousness with which he inquired about my progress, or added on the day's chitchat from the yard; but even at his best, he was about as tactful as a Line squall, and I waited half-braced in the quilt for his onslaught.

"My anniversary's comin' up," he began, with a giveaway clear or two of his throat; and at once—like one who sees a whole landscape in a storm flash—I knew exactly where he was headed.

"Oh, no, you don't, Melchett," I spoke up, before he could say another word; "you're not goin' t' get me like you did last year. No doctors, no needles, no gadje flimflam: save your breath for somethin' better."

Shooting me a sharp look over the top of his teacup, he took a few sips like a sparring partner who—finding the match more demanding than he'd expected—tries to buy time with intervening footwork; then apparently having decided on a fresh tactic, he made another bid to nail me, this time trying disarming frankness. "I seen McCabe t'night—had suppeh with him, in fact; an' him an' me got somethin' t' ask ye. We've...we've found a consultant up to Boston, a doctoh that specializes in conditions like youhr headaches... Let us sail ye up thehre once b'fore we ship out with *Abigail*, an' see if he can't do somethin' t' help ye."

It was rare for me to be able to find the will to resist that pleading honesty ploy of his; but the very thought of returning to Boston, coupled with the sense of betrayal I felt over the plotting Eben'd practised behind my back, made it easier tonight. "Not on your life," I told him flatly, forgetting that I was supposed to look ill, and sitting straight up in the nest of my blankets; "I'll jump off the meetin' house steeple first."

He looked down and hesitated, his face so frank an admission of the wheels spinning round in his head that I could feel my hackles rise up; then looking me in the eye he tried again. "Jamie, I... I can't stand t' sit by an' see y' suffeh. I'd... I'd ten times ratheh it was me that was laid up: honest t' God I would; y' know it."

Feeling guilty as sin—and not unlike one who's laid a trap, only to find he's fallen in it; feeling, moreover, contrite to the core, especially since he'd called me by that name, one of the few endearments he ever used in our talks, I interrupted as lightly as I could: "I ain't sick any more; I feel fine; look at me"—flapping my arms vigorously I spoke.

"It's bad enough I've got t' worry about ye ashore, whehre there's things we could do f'r ye if we had to," he pursued, ignoring me; "but what about when we're back at sea? What if them headaches just keep gettin' worse, an' there ain't nobody in a thousand miles t' turn to?"

It was true that, when they came, they were deteriorating, each more severe than the one before it; but so well did I feel now—so torn between wanting to confess I'd tricked him into burying the hatchet, and wanting to burst into a gale of suppressed laughter—that it was hard to focus my thoughts on the future; and I simply gazed down at my hands, without answer.

Looking at me as if trying to read my thoughts, he hesitated, then attempted—as delicately as he could with his brusque ways: "If...if ye'd ratheh not go t' Boston, we could maybe fetch him down here...y' wouldn't need t' have t' leave town t' see him."

On the point of forgiving the scheming that he'd done with Eben these past days behind my back, I became immediately defensive, the more so since I'd dreaded we might have to one day ship there, and even now felt ill at ease at the thought. "Why in hell shouldn't I want t' go t' Boston?" I barked, throwing off my covers and swinging my feet onto the floor. "Why, I could go there t'day if I wanted!"

Getting to *his* feet, Ben lost his temper, actually stomping his boot on the hearth rug. "Will y' quit bein' so gawddam stubborn an' jest let us do what we need to t' help ye? D'ye think I like sittin' by knowin' ye need t' resohrt t' morphine t' get through one o' them spells o' yours?"

"D'ye think *I* like sittin' by knowin y' need t' resohrt t' a bottle o' scotch t' get through one o' *youhrs*?" I countered, aping his accent right down to the dropped g's and the gravelly rasp of the consonants and the soft r's.

That line of his came down on his brow and just about divided it in half; but though he looked prepared to explode, he had no recourse to *my* accent, and he knew it; for he couldn't imitate so much as a trill. "You Romany weasel," he hurtled at me, about as benignly as a January bluster; "how much I drink's not the threat t' my health that morphine is t' youhrs, an' ye know it."

"Oh, ain't it?" I met him, on my feet too on the rug. "If spirits ain't just as certain a killer as morphine, I'd like t' know why we buried my uncle Arturos... An' it ain't just your health that's in danger; you're hidin' out in your drinkin', an' you know it."

For a moment I thought he'd actually hit me, and I braced myself to duck his assault—a gesture that'd once been as automatic to me as any other reflex of living; but suddenly his eyes took on a queer gleam, and I knew before he even spoke that he'd got me. "So you'hre interested in seein' me drink less, is that it?" he bartered, the thunderheads upon his brow lifting, and his whole being reeking of a bargain.

"Aye," I said limply, like one who sees a trap close.

"Interested enough t' sacrifice somethin' for it?" he kept on, his lips twitching in spite of the hard glint to his eyes.

"You Yankee bastard," I glowered at him.

He roared with delight and gave me a clap. "Damn, but it's a pleasure t' beat you at youhr own game! Well, there it is, mate: you see this here doctoh, an' let him advise McCabe how t' care for ye, an' I'll knock off drinkin': y' know my word's good."

I simply glared at the fire, speechless; but he took me by the chin and made me look at him.

"I know youhr word's good, too; so let me heahr it," he said, gently insistent. "Do us *chals* have a bargain, eh?"

I met his eyes and saw in their depths so much candor and honest feeling, so much undisguised love and worry, and—back of his concern, such mischievous pranking—that it was all I could do to check a succession of grateful sobs, not to mention, demonic laughter. "You...you won't let him do nothin' t' hurt me?" I asked dryly.

"I'll blow him down first," he pledged, determined.

It was such a Romany answer that straightaway the tears smarted in my eyes, even as the corners of my mouth twitched; and I had to bite my lip to respond. "Then it's a deal," I agreed, none too enthusiastic; and he gave my hair a rub with his warm hand before he drained off the rest of his tea, and bowed out with a smug light to his eye.

That he would stick to his side of the bargain I knew from ample past experience; and indeed he didn't let me down, wordlessly replacing the empty decanters on my shelf for full, and limiting himself to a drink or two from them those times he dropped by my room after work. At Eben's too he stopped with one glass, while he never even showed up at Eli's; so I had no choice but to carry through with my share of the deal. Determined not to let him believe that there was any reason why I should be fearful to make a return trip to Boston, I brushed aside repeated offers to fetch this sawbones down for a visit, and arranged to sail with him and Eben aboard Tom's sloop roundabout the third Sunday in October.

As we approached the environs of Boston, it all looked precisely as I'd remembered: Massachusetts Bay, Deer Island, Nahant, the narrow roads to the inner harbor; for though I'd arrived and left in a snowstorm, the setting was indelibly engraved in my mind. Hauling into the harbor with a host of vessels, of every sort from Dutch frigates to coastwise schooners, their red and green running lights plying the waters, we made fast to one of the vast wharves fronting Ann Street, the very same pier *Charis*'d been tied to; and jumping down we found ourselves in a bedlam of newsboys, tourists, stevedores, longshoremen, loafers, runners and seamen from every quarter of the globe. Conscious of the fact that any one of them might recognize me—feeling as conspicuous as if criers hawked my arrival—I felt my heart collide with my ribs; and it was all I could do to keep from ducking my head, or pulling my hat brim over my eyes.

It wasn't just that word might reach Lomond, from any number of runners still in his employ; not even that I might stumble upon him, in some freak chance of a meeting on Ann Street; what I feared most was the simple betrayal of recognition by one of a hundred crimps and sharpsters still holding forth in the neighborhood, or by one of the scores of seamen I'd known, unexpectedly in port, as had happened at Eli's. So powerful was my feeling for Ben, and the desire he should return it—so forcible my fear I'd now lose all I had gained, if he should discover prematurely what I had been—that it required my whole will to pace the wharf, and issue out into the crowd on the waterfront; but I kept my chin up somehow in a game bluff, and marched the busy wharf with my head high.

Buoyed up by Ben's nearness I made it to Hannah's, another landmark on last year's passage; looked, dazed, about me at the vivid details—at the chintz-covered sofas, the fireside bench, the kitchen table and fieldstone hearth, so emblazoned on my memory that I could scarcely bear to behold them. Upstairs in the same room I'd slept in before, and waited so tremulously for Lomond's knock at the door, or for my first chance to embark on knowing Ben, I managed to stave off the avalanche of feeling that had been building throughout the day; and Ben and Eben, stoic and calm, bid me goodnight and went to their rooms, each of them carrying a valise and candle.

So drained was I on setting out next day that I was scarcely aware of what was taking place—save that all was done with the utmost speed and convenience, Ben and Eben no doubt having plotted how to convey me with a minimum of effort and exposure. A covered carriage waiting at the door transported us—through brick-cobbled streets—to a handsome residence not far from Hannah's; and the ground floor containing the anteroom and surgery, we were directly seen into the former, where we scarcely had time to hang up our hats. I was still adjusting my neckerchief, standing before the hall-tree mirror, and Ben had just settled onto the sofa, when the doctor showed me into the next room; and there—with Eben standing by for moral support, as much as medical reference—I was cross-examined and studied, probed, scrutinized and tested, on a low-lying settee surrounded by cupboards containing a fearsome array of utensils.

Cutlery, forceps, pliers, lancets, tweezers, needles, bodkins, scissors—even a surgeon's saw or two: every one of them hung in plain view behind glass doors, with kindred of an even viler nature probably hidden behind the panels below. That he might fetch one of them out at any moment filled me with an unceasing concern; but he stuck for the most part to the settee beside me, examining my head and testing my eyes, and assaulting me with a relentless battery of questions, to which I replied with Rom imprecision. The blow I'd been struck a year and a half ago by Lomond was the principle factor

in question; and no evasive slip on my part fazed the doctor. "By
what were you struck?" he kept clipping at me, his hands busy at his
inkwell and notepad; and "By somethin' hard," I kept quipping right
back, in no mood to recall anything about that fight. "By precisely
what?" he badgered for more; and at last, fatigued, and too impatient
to keep up any further pretense for the sake of Ben's ears—separated
as he was from me only by a curtain—I simply snapped: "It's none o'
your bloody business!"

That pen of his was scratching again, dutifully recording my
answer; but other queries insistently followed—when the headaches
had commenced, how they compared in severity and duration, what
typical course of symptoms they ran; and I was hard put to read his
intent. I'd rather hoped they'd been caused by Lomond's blow, so long
as that didn't mean some unhealed injury necessitating surgery; for
that seemed simpler and more straightforward than Eben's notion
of emotional duress, and left Ben fewer questions to ponder. But as
I described the symptoms he seemed more and more to rule out the
blow as the culprit, and to incline his opinion to Eben's; and in the
end a new course of medication was prescribed, since the preferred
alternatives—the resolution of tensions, or an extended rest—were
manifestly out of the question. With the insistence I return in nine
months to a year, to re-submit to eye tests and such clap, the doctor
neatly put away his records; and making a mental note to be elsewhere
on the planet when the date of my return visit rolled around, I did up
my collar-ends, pulled on my coat, and high-tailed it out.

Meeting me in the ante-room with my hat, Ben wore an
inscrutable mixture of looks—amongst them satisfaction that he'd
won a round, at least as far as medication was concerned; but as our
glances met I saw in his eyes a contemplative curiosity or interest;
and he had the air of one who harbors deep thoughts, or who knows
a good deal more than he says.

Making our way into the hall we bowed out without incident—
save some lively discussion between Ben and me over the question of
settling the bill: Ben offending me by insisting on paying the doctor,
me pulling out my pocketbook like a saber, and the two us nearly
winding up fighting on the hall rug. Regarding me as one likely to

incur further head injuries with my temper, and, no doubt, further headaches with my moodiness, the doctor accepted my money—an atrocious sum by no means commensurate with my problem, or the consideration of our lengthy journey; and Ben glowered at me all the way to the wharf, declaring that—as the whole trip was his idea, and I'd lost three days' wages through it—he should be the one to foot the bill. Retorting that the headaches were mine and not his, I stood my ground—even when he snorted that *I* was his headache; and we were still wrangling as we set the jib.

By late afternoon we'd cleared the wharf, and threaded the inner harbor, tide-rode; but it wasn't till we'd left the city wholly behind without having been recognized or boarded, that I realized the strain of the visit, and the immensity of the relief of departure. So fatigued was I all at once by the long trip, and the constant uncertainties under which I'd labored, that by the time we'd negotiated the roads— in heavy workday afternoon traffic—I could scarcely haul the sheets; and as soon as we stood well out in Massachusetts Bay, and things were looking green to green, I curled up on a coil of rope on the bow, and slept away most of the rest of the journey.

If Ben had his doubts about *Abigail*, in spite of his confidence in her design, and his justifiable pride in her workmanship—if he unconsciously felt that he was on the wrong track, at least insofar as his place in commerce went—he had no misgivings about our little sloop *Idris*, on which he toiled with a clear brow and conscience; and I felt my own peculiar sense of delight in restoring her as I worked with him now and again of an evening. In dry dock between a bait shed and a net house, a stone's throw from the wharves and from Obed's, she was mine and Eben's and well as Ben's, for we'd all three pitched in to buy her; and I felt as loving as a parent as I caulked her hull and painted her. I liked to cast a glance down the scaffold and see Ben and Eben, decked in their oldest clothes, hard at work further down the hull—liked the feel of participation, the sense of rhythmic cooperation which marked our architectural effort; and as though rejoicing with me in my fortune, the weather conspired to lend its perfection, taking a turn to Indian summer.

At their peak of sassafras and russet, the rustling boughs nodded about us, swaying and bowing in the warm gusts; and as I labored beneath them with a high heart, crafting this vessel for her new course, I learned things about the art of shipbuilding I'd never known before as a seaman; learned things as well about the structure of Ben's nature I'd never have gleaned from sojourning on his decks. As if *Idris* and her harbor mouth environs were a lofting floor sketch done to scale, a chalk pattern of his contours and sheers, I rode their lines into his holds, those inner spaces of person and mind; saw the design of his oaken center in the configuration of our evening labors.

The wheeling, mewing, sea-searching gulls—the smokehouses with their raw hickory fires—the weathered sheds and derelict hulls—the great wooden frames with their meshwork of nets: these were Ben, were as recognizable a portrait as if they wore features, and configured a visage; compounded him out of their respective elements as surely as chemicals compose a mixture, in some apothecary's vessel; and more and more in their peculiar fusion I found my own particular alloy, as if my components had been stirred in the same flask—as if I, too, had been compounded of the same alchemy of spirit.

Frequently Tom and Jean—and less often the younger children—would come by to watch as we worked; and then I would see him as an instructor, his broad, outsized hands guiding their small ones. How they ever wrangled permission to put in even a brief appearance, with Anne so opposed to their associating with fishermen's children, I was never entirely clear; but probably Ben had laid down the law, either pure and simple, in the vein of a command, or as the byproduct of some obscure domestic compromise; for he generally seemed to expect them, cocking a brow —unsurprised—as they dashed by with a wave, or climbed up beside him on the scaffold.

As much like a deepwater master as a father, he grunted out instructions and answers, demonstrating the use of tools, and barking out orders as he handed them over; but there was a tolerance now in his dictates, and a glimpse of covert humor, that hadn't been present a year ago; and rather than criticize their fledgling efforts, he gently patched up their work behind them. Clambering up with questions and quick hands, Jean was as anxious to learn as Tom; and he did not discriminate between them, handing out the tasks they seemed able to master. I could see that they already had a feel for the tools, an understanding of the work their father did—slight Jean no less than sturdy Tom; for though she hadn't her brother's strength, she had her father's agile mind; and she almost immediately mastered his teachings—amusing him greatly, and affording him vast fatherly pride, by aping appropriate shipwright lingo, or by instinctively pointing out errors.

The twins, when they came, he set in the cabin, giving them wood scraps to build with or hammer; while Nat he allowed to climb at large, within sight of us near the tiller. Of them all young Nat looked most like his father, big-boned, broad-faced, sandy-haired, grey-eyed—even as a toddler, already brass-voiced and stubborn; and whenever I could, I was keen to hold him—knocking off work, if he wandered by me, and nesting him in my arms for a moment. Of all Ben's offspring, he was the only one in whom we'd both invested since birth; and he was doubly dear on that account. Since I knew now there would be no son of my own, his shared unfolding held me in thrall; and I looked on him, as I looked on the others, with eyes that saw children never to be born.

At the end of the day, when the ketches and schooners and sloops made fast, we'd sometimes help Obed and Lem with their nets, while they unloaded and salted the catch, sorting it for market and size. There was nothing I liked better than to feel the scaly net in my hands, and to look up to find Ben nearby me, leaning against a worn, creaking piling in that characteristic way of his, his weight on one leg, and his free foot crossed over his ankle for balance, while he examined the seine for tears.

There'd be a ripeness—all the more enticing for his unconsciousness—about his stalwart, stumpy thighs, his broad, weathered wrists and burly workman's chest; a readiness which made him look seasoned. He'd glance up at me then with that gleam in his grey eyes, with that expression of regard and contentment which it always gave me such hope to see; with a spontaneous light, almost of recognition, which swiftly evoked a flash from me—as if two travelers, long separated, suddenly hailed one another on the same shore. If I passed nearby him he'd reach out with a great palm, honest with work and forthright feeling, and lay it for a moment on my shoulder; or maybe he'd rub it briefly in my hair, as if touch were the signal of greeting in this land—the legitimate sign and seal of knowing.

Besides the cottage on weekends, *Abigail* during the day, and the sloop a couple of evenings a week, there was another project on which I was working, another vehicle of conveyance: an undertaking I was keeping secret, since it was intended for Ben's birthday. Because it was large in scope and time-consuming, I spent all my other scant leisure on it, including most of my dinner hours; and I called on McCabe for help with the hard parts. Having begun it immediately after making port in June, I was now, near the end of October, almost finished; and I could afford to dally a little. It was essentially a labor of memory, of recalling the colors and forms of days long gone; of recollecting arts my father and uncles had lived by, but which I had never come to maturity to practice.

The wheels hand-shaped, their rims of cut ash, their spokes of larch—the tyres metal, fitted red-hot, then cooled down quickly and hammered in place—the boxes and stocks, forged from gun iron, wed to the shafts, the wheels braced to run true—the undercarriage, its turntable of ash—and at last the uprights with a window at each side, and a low-pitched roof set ark-like on the chassis: all evolved slowly as they once had on the road. Each detail suggesting another, they put me in mind of days now long past—the glimpse of a stile, of a lane walled with stone, of the glimmer of a campfire at dusk. With such glances as these came the burn of old heartache, the inevitable tugging and tearing of change, of irreversible alteration and growth— the finality of old forms now shed; yet there came as well the longing to share them with Ben, these glimpses of past shells outgrown—a yearning to present him with some kind of vehicle with which to step into their abandoned halls.

It was late now in the season of migrations; the geese, eider ducks, summer birds had all gone, wheeling away in flight patterns southward; around me the pristine Maine autumn glistened, crisp, clear and still as a morning new-broken; but on the roads of memory, preserved unfaded, a line of carts appeared in the dusk, passed with a burst of song and a rattle, then—poised for a moment on the horizon—stood out etched against the dim heavens, before rumbling over the hill's brow into twilight.

It turned out to be well that I'd finished work on this secret project early; for a week or so before Ben's birthday—as a result of one of those freak Melchett bouts of one-upmanship sparked by a comment at Eli's—we were engaged in a county-wide contest involving half of the small craft in the harbor. It'd all commenced earlier on in the month when, sitting over a brandy cider with his brother Tom and me and several others, Ben spoke a few boasting words about *Idris*—predicting her strength, her hardiness, her smartness of helm once we got her out of dry dock; and Tom, cocking an ear, good-naturedly averred that she'd nonetheless never equal his sloop. Standing nearby, their brother Joseph—on one of his rare visits to Eli's, most of his leisure being spent in grander places—directly uttered an ungentlemanly snort, declaring that neither boat could hold a candle to his; that Ben's was too old, Tom's too broad in the beam to match the speed of his sleek cutter.

Getting predictably black in the brow, Ben asserted that helmsmanship was half the race; contended that he could beat reckless Joseph—known about town for his rash judgment—with an old boat and a good crew: naming me and Eben in the next breath without so much as a by-your-leave. Equally lowering—snapping out observations on Ben's monotonously steady nature—Joseph at once took him up on it; and before I knew it all hands at Eli's were shouting wagers on one sloop or the other, or worse yet, yelling bets on their own. From Eli's word swiftly sped about town, catching up half the village in racing fervor; till finally not only the three Melchett brothers, but every other boat owner in port, from fisher folk like Shad Talbot and Jeb Coombs to lordly shipwrights like Hull and Lombard, had tumbled out to take the challenge. Stalwart and hard-working, the jacks-afloat of the town were only too eager to snatch a chance not just to skylark, but to even up old scores and blood spats; and even the ladies got into the act, Keziah crewing for Tom and others setting up the hall for post-race festivities and a feast.

Of them all Ben was the most zealous, rushing Eben and me to finish *Idris*, then hauling us out into the chop of the bay, and keeping us out there wallowing around till long after the fishing yawls had put in; and when it was too coarse to sail he had us going over every tye and cleat, making infinitesimal adjustments in the halyards, downhaul and sheets till I thought I would go mad from precision. Scrutinizing his competitors every spare moment, running the course in all kinds of weather, rigging out wind pennants from the shrouds and masthead, bolting on straps for us to hang onto to shift weight, he was every inch the old Melchett; and watching him and his preparations from my station at the jib—riding the race like a craft into his thoughts—I marveled, bemused, at what he had been, and still was.

Overriding our protests—appealing to our loyalties, or whatever regard we felt for him as friends —he installed Eben, lean and quick, as mainsail trimmer; put me on the jib sheet because, though I wasn't light, I was smooth, the importance of which he drummed constantly into me; and small Orin McCabe he set in the stern near him, his sole duty to help him run down the starting signals, look out for shifts of wind in the pennants, and watch the other helmsmen for clues as to their next maneuvers and feints. As for his own role at the tiller, he had every confidence in his smoothness, efficiency and concentration; and he was banking on a hunch that none of the others could outmatch his peculiar mixture of instinct and scientific grasp of mechanics.

On the Friday night before the race he had us bunkered down at Eben's, going over the list of our twenty-odd competitors, detailing the various strengths and failings of each, and developing contingency plans to cover them all. That he was secretly gunning for Joseph—that this was somehow the final contest between them, one which decided old scores once for all—I knew from the almost offhand approach he took toward him; indeed guessed it from the very nonchalance of his brow, and the unconcern of his pen as he sketched moves to eclipse him. Yet he said nothing which might lead us to suppose that he wasn't simply out to beat the whole field; and what he expected of us—and himself—in the effort, he made plain as an opening volley, there being no guise of dispassion on this point.

"Some," he wrapped up, considering the ranks on his charts, and jabbing blunt fingers at our position, "like Talbot an' Coombs for instance, know how t' sail well, but not how t' sail fast; some, like Hull an' Joseph, have fast boats, but don't know how t' utilize 'em; that is, they think they know how t' fly, just b'cause they've got speed that's built-in. Only *we've* got the know-how t' sail both well an' fast; an' I'm tellin' ye boys, I aim t' show it, an' won't stop for nothin' short o' the Second Comin'... I warn ye right now if y' fall out o' the boat, hangin' out on the straps as we take off on a plane, some lubbeh or otheh'll have t' pick ye up, an' it won't be Joseph or anybody right on our tail; so ye'd betteh dress light an' get plenty o' rest, an' show up tomorrer sportin' some muscle."

So saying he picked up his cigar, charts and rule, folded his spectacles back into his pocket, and marched out the door like a grenadier armed for battle; and I watched him disappear with a bleak eye, and a remorseful shake of my head. "Do you have any idea at all why we're doin' this?" I asked, looking over at Eben with appeal; and he met my woeful glance with a wry grin.

"Can't think of a one, an' I been tryin' for ten yeahrs," he confessed, giving his pipe a tap on the hearth screen, then reaching into his pouch for a fresh fill. "Must have somethin' t' do with the fact that we love him...though just at the moment, I can't recollect why."

We woke up to the very weather he'd wanted, a fine northeast blow, with a brisk chop to the water; though it was a considerable mitigating factor that the breeze was not steady, canting to the north or even northwest, with unexpected puffs and gusts; while the short, steep waves, and the broken cloud patterns, which affected the sea's color in patches, were an additional test of mettle. Since few rules had been established save those regarding right-of-way—leeward boats over windward, starboard tacking over larboard—almost anything was permissible short of sinking one's opponents; and now in all the confusion of the pre-start, with a crowd of boats strung out on the long line, and the seconds slipping away with the signals, everyone around us was barging for room, or hailing to unnerve his neighbors.

In the bitter cold, with an eighteen-knot wind, and a chop to the sea liable to take one's teeth out—in the chaos of boats, all bent now for the line, all shoving for room and hurling insults—I only wished myself on dry land by a hearth; but Ben at the helm was imperturbable as a clam, computing Orin's count and deductions in one ear, shutting out the commotion of calls with the other, and bawling abuse at whoever was nearest, including two of his own brothers—trying to trick them into looking away from their tillers, or catch them up in a preoccupying argument, till I couldn't believe this was the man I knew.

This wily, conniving, treacherous schemer, ready to sell his own brothers for a race, capable of every trick and lie to advance, shouting at the top of his lungs vulgarities I'd never heard him use even at sea: this was the deliberate, honest, forthright seadog who'd skippered me aboard *Charis*? Nor was he the only one transformed; for as Joseph came barging over the line to buttonhook, carving out a hold for himself near Tom, Keziah—at Tom's jib—hollered out "You pimp!", in stentorian tones that must have carried to the shore; and so astounded was Joseph by her display that he actually lost a couple of seconds berating her, whilst Tom, on his toes, plunged ahead with a roar.

Over the line just at the gun and at good speed, *Idris* quickly jumped a length on Joseph, thanks to Keziah's inspired send-off; but as the field began to beat to windward, spreading out a little due to miscalculations, Joseph recovered, veering out of our backwind, and—counting on his speed—trying to overtake us to windward. In the position he'd worked for, to leeward and on course, with both favorable wind angles and unfettered air, Ben luffed hard and fast to cut off his attempt, tucking him back behind a good length; and from there he kept up a persistent cover, staying near to, and on the same tack as Joseph, dishing out dirty air from the angles of our sails, and at the same time trying to manipulate things to use him to cause our several nearest opponents—Longworthy, Lombard, Tom, Hull, and Sage Haskett—to stick together in a bunch, so he could cover them all at once.

For a spell we had a merry troop on a string, close enough to trade constant obscenities and jeers, Sage in particular jibing at me, and Ben threatening to drown me if I broke focus to answer; but giving up trying to pass close aboard to windward, for fear of being luffed out of the race—giving up as well trying pass to leeward, where we cast an effective wind blanket—Joseph split tacks, forcing Ben to match him; and we found ourselves caught up in a tacking duel, the very situation we'd hoped to be fast enough to avoid. With Ben obliged to cover, Joseph took the offensive, free to tack and try to make ground when he wished; and we had to respond to his every shift if we wanted to keep up our all-too-slim advantage, and prevent ourselves from being caught on the wrong tack.

A couple of times—to break the monotony—Joseph made a fake to windward, then moved on us to leeward, as if again trying to break away and pass; but at last, unable to get out from our cover, he split tacks and steered for the other side of the course, no doubt counting on his speed to get him first to the buoy. Having calculated his shortest distance to the mark that morning—one end of the line being slightly closer, due to its not being quite at right angles to the wind—Ben held onto his course with a grin, blithely covering Sage and Longworthy, a couple of lengths behind us, and scanning the waters for bunches of whitecaps, indicators of stronger wind currents; while Joseph, down on his lee rail as predicted, failed to make any significant gain on us; and most of the field fell further back, plagued by an occasional split sail or goosewing.

What it all meant to Eben and I—leaving the strategy up to Ben, and simply blindly following orders—was unrelenting work in the raw wind: Eben hauling in on the mainsheet, to keep it driving till the last instant, then easing it out as we settled onto the new tack, and setting it close again—for a second; me trimming the jibsheet more or less all the time, testing and re-testing to be sure it was just inside the point of luffing, then adjusting it for changes in our speed.

His eyes narrowed to slits in the spray and the glare, Ben sat on the windward rail with a tiller extension, himself as far over the gunwales as he could go, appraising me not so much as a seaman as dead weight—wishing it sometimes over the rail, sometimes amidships, and sometimes, quite obviously, no place at all.

Yet even this was not the most fatiguing part of my work; for me, keeping my mind for so long on one aim was quite the most exhausting stunt I'd ever tried. If this was the gadje method of getting places—taking the direct route, on land or in thought, without looking away to the right or the left—it certainly wasn't for me; and I marveled at Ben's ruthless pursuit of purpose. For him the work of concentration was endless—computing our opponents' moves, *Idris'* seat in the water, the performance of her sails, their effect on those behind us; calibrating the wind, not just by watching the pennants, but by reading the sea's surface, the language of spray, color, white caps; remembering water depths from soundings taken himself, and routing us over deeper channels to maximize currents—all this he managed without a break in focus; and I felt stricken dumb by his humbling display.

Rounding the first mark we found several boats in company with us, Joseph on the outside owing to his fruitless chase further afield, Tom over-standing the buoy due to a long final starboard tack, and Hull, Sage and Lombard all working for an inside berth, the latter two fairly close astern. Swinging wide a little to save speed with a smooth turn, Ben allowed Sage the coveted inside spot—till on rounding the marker, Sage was to windward, when Ben, to leeward, suddenly luffed to kill, knocking him entirely out of the race: Sage's torrent of language out-roaring Ben's laughter several boat lengths down the next leg. In the confusion of sails now trying to tag us—in the struggle to escape the peril of their wind blankets, the four of us now running before the blow—Ben immediately made ready to plane: setting *Idris'* course several degrees further downwind, getting her keel as even as he possibly could, then bawling at us to shift our weight aft a little and trim the sails in, to get her nose up out of the water, and give us a bit of a shove forward for take-off.

With the winds plaguing us by falling or canting—with Ben

hollering at me to now wing the jib, now bring it closer to luffing, now trim it—with him barking at us to hang over the rail, now ease our weight, now hike it, now shift it, till I was ready to brain him with the oar—we at last managed to time our sail-trimming, steering and wave-shooting with the wind; and *Idris* at once went surging ahead, leaving Tom open-mouthed several lengths behind us, and Joseph, Hull and Lombard laboring in our wake. From there it was simply a matter of keeping the sails trimmed fairly close in, watching out for an accidental jibe, and looking back at Joseph heeling, knowing he would never catch up to us now.

Too far down wind from any of our closest competitors to need to worry about their wind blankets—up on a good sustained ride for the most part, and able to take to the air on a fresh slant when forced—all we had to do now was round the leeward mark, which we had all to ourselves, close and smooth on the inside, then keep up our pace in the fickle gusts on the third leg, a broad reach; and Joseph was never again closer than two lengths astern. Guarding against broaching as we hurried along with the waves—picking up the deeper currents and wind gusts—Ben relaxed sufficiently to stop glowering at me; but he never for a moment allowed us to ease up our vigilance of weight, position and trim till we'd crossed the finish line, and all hands on the committee boat'd hailed us.

Even considering the handicap points allowed some of the boats for differences in hull length, sail area and rig, we'd won flat-out and square; and in all the celebrating that followed—Ben now being dumped in the harbor, now thumped on the shoulder or showered with champagne—we had the satisfaction of knowing our lead hadn't been eroded by mitigating considerations. Jubilantly riding the wave of acclaim, Ben breezed through the festivities unfatigued, drinking far beyond the limits of his pledge: colliding rims with a beaming-faced Galen, who'd wisely kept aloof from his sons' competition, and a still spray-drenched Keziah, who tossed off a glass at Ben's side like a deckhand, claiming she'd given him the winning edge with her starting-line send-off.

Though the attitude of his family was still the mixture of

condescending indulgence which for years had irked him, others were analyzing his moves like colleagues, and looking at *Abigail* with fresh eyes, thinking that if he could get such a performance out of an old workhorse like *Idris*, what might he not be able to achieve with the new ship; and he was plainly gratified by their response. So spent was I, on the other hand, by my exertions—so plagued by complaining muscles, and so chilled by my dank woolen waistcoat and pea jacket, which I hadn't the strength to walk home to change— that I crawled into a corner of the hall, mug in tow, and thankfully sat down near the stove, from which I refused to budge the whole evening: for once having no taste for the square and round dances and fisherman's jigs going on around me.

Sitting down beside me at one point—soddenly aware, perhaps, that I'd been avoiding his eyes, or that the stove hadn't yet thawed my feelings, Ben looked apologetically at me—or at any rate, as close as he ever came to it; and glass in hand, he said to me kindly: "Sorry t' have handed ye such a job, mate."

"Melchett," I said, taking a long swallow from my own mug, which'd made some inroads on my numb innards, "if it's made you feel any less overshadowed by your brothers...or any less in doubt of your capabilities...or"—here I hesitated, then hurried on—"any less likely t' be enslaved in the future to the idea that manhood's a matter of power...then it was worth it."

Giving me a long look over his rim, he regarded me speculatively, so intently that I had to break my gaze; but as Tom came up then, jovial and loud-voiced, decanter in one hand, steaming tray in the other, he said nothing in reply; and not till we parted company for the evening, on our way to Ship Street from the hall, did he speak to me again.

"Well, what didje think of it all?" he asked, comparatively sober from the masses of food consumed, and the lateness of the hour.

"Y' mean, the race?" I returned, listening to our footfalls in the quiet of the night, and the voices of home-goers dwindling in the crisp distance.

"Aye."

"I think that if it's the gadje way of gettin' places, it's not for me."

"What's the Rom way?" he asked dryly, trying to stifle the twitch at the corners of his mouth.

"Goin' in circles," I informed him.

"It's a lot sloweh," he was quick to point out.

"It has more charm," I countered dryly.

Next day I woke up so late in the morning, and it was so brilliantly, serenely autumn— yesterday's blow having shifted southwest, and fallen off to a few puffs and breezes—that I took to the hills with my tarp and bedroll, and pitched my tent by the banks of the river, where I tickled fish and cleaned and fried them, and cleared my head of gadje nonsense. For awhile, as I ate, I thought about the race, as a kind of monument to Ben's past; thought of it as I thought of the gypsy wagon I'd just finished making from the patterns of memory. In its way it too was a relic of my own days gone by, a marker to some stage of life shed on the road: a hall long abandoned yet still cherished, like the remnant of some antique civilization, such as those pillars called Karnak sketched on John Melchett's office wall.

I considered how we were still tied, Ben and I, to the series of husks which defined our beginnings; how we had only half-emerged from the latest, in spite of our months of contact and conflict; how we, like the shedders below in the harbor, were doubly vulnerable thus exposed, and would be till, freed, we carpentered new shells. Then at last, forgetful of past and future, I let my mind roll out across the hillsides, along passageways of burnt orange and scarlet, till it came to hover by miniature altars, the intricate artistries of seed by the river; and not until early Tuesday morning did I finally quit my boundless temple, and come down out of the hills for work.

It came as a complete surprise then to find that, in my unexplained two days' absence, the town—far from worrying about where I'd been—had instead gone up in a commotion over Jackson DeMille's latest preaching, heatedly convening in the meeting hall Monday night, and at last polling a vote of dismissal—in spite of Ben's staunch, if clumsy defense, and John Melchett's impassioned pleading. By the time I arrived on the scene at the yard, everybody was kicking up dust on one side of the issue or the other; and despite such hot topics as *Abigail's* launching, slated—with a Melchett ball—this coming Saturday, Jackson's dismissal was the one subject of talk.

What it was all about I couldn't grasp, knowing too little of Holy Writ to begin to gauge the importance of words said, even if I understood their meaning. But I understood the net result; for not only was Jackson stripped of his office, but directly after, expelled from his family—read out of his inheritance, and struck from the family Bible by Andrew DeMille, an old, lion-faced, iron-willed deacon whose narrow views seemed to speak through his bearing.

If I comprehended nothing of doctrine, I nonetheless understood better than anyone else how Jackson must now silently feel; and in the next couple of days, catching glimpses of him in the street as he calmly wrapped up his business—meeting his eyes once in the general store, both of us buying a cone of sugar—I felt an irresistible urge to speak to him before he left. What on earth I would say to him I didn't know, since I'd only once actually formally met him, and that just briefly, coming out of church; but I wanted to let him know I'd shared his sting; simply had to convey that I knew how he felt.

At last, unable to stave off the urge any longer, I walked over to his cottage one evening before supper, approaching the unpretentious clapboard frame with slow feet; and there, through the open doorway which entered directly on his sitting room, I found him quietly packing up his few things, sorting them into a variety of handbags, crates and valises.

Looking up—an unmistakably glad light in the surprise of his eyes—he gallantly did me the honors of a bow and a welcome, as if I were one of the most important visitors he'd ever received; and I felt more tongue-tied than ever by his kindness. "Won't you sit down to tea?" he asked, climbing over a few crates as gracefully as if they weren't reminders of the circumstances of his departure, and giving a nod at a well-filled tray, in the midst of which a clay-pot was steeping. "I made the rolls and scones myself."

"Well—you see—I didn't intend t' stay," I said, miserably turning my hat in my hands—uncertain whether to relinquish it and sit down, or have my say and make a run for it. "That is, I don't want t' trouble you with your packing… I just wanted t' stop by t' say—" I paused again for breath to consider, still turning my hatbrim around in my hands, and desperately gazing here and there for inspiration. Just what *was* it I wanted to say, anyway; what was it that'd led me to presume on his kindness—to suppose that, at the back of his assured calmness, there was the need to hear a word from me?

Seeing him close to, I saw again what I'd forgotten, the utter gentlemanliness of his person; and I felt the more abashed by his address—by the sober distinction of garments, even now when, in his shirt-sleeves, he was caught up in packing. With Eben and Ben, I could forget the leagues between us, the gaps in background I might have felt keenly, had it not been for their rough garb and plain language, and the leveling factor of the work we shared; but here, in the presence of such unmistakable fineness, I recalled sharply my rude beginnings. Yet as he looked at me kindly, waiting for me to go on—as he regarded me with neither hurry nor pressure, simply with an encouraging expectation—there was something in the curiousness of his gaze, the defenseless honesty of his eyes, which spoke of receptiveness, even need; and in that invitation to speak I took heart, and found the nerve to stumblingly say:

"I—for some reason I didn't want you t' leave town without my telling you… I don't know what on earth good it will do, but… I wanted you t' know that… in a way… I understand how you feel. You see, in Wales years ago…certain things I'd done were brought b'fore the Kris…a sort of tribunal of my people….and I… I too was cast out by them, and my family."

So swift was the rush of feeling on his face—not of pity or commiseration, but simply of understanding and oneness—that it all but brought me to instant tears; and I tugged again at the tarpaulin of my hat brim, wishing that I could made a dash from the planet. But he plainly labored under no such restraints; for he at once came warmly up to me, and gently took my hat from me, saying, "Sit down, son…take some of this tea, it'll do you good"; and even in my confusion of feeling I couldn't fail to note that, far from my consoling him, he was suddenly consoling *me*.

"So that's why you left Britain, and came here," he was saying, unhurriedly hanging my hat on a peg, and pouring me a cup on the tray. "How old were you?"

"Thirteen," I said, still fighting my tight throat, and trying to hold the cup steady in my hands.

"They...the Rom...and your family too...they ostracize their own at that age?"

"Aye," I answered, taking a swallow, and gratefully feeling the warmth spread through me. "You see, by the time we're ten or so, we're expected, anyway, t' be independent."

"Your motheh... no one took your part?" he asked, considerately leaving untouched what I'd done.

"My mother died when I was a child."

"Your fatheh, then?"

"No....he couldn't have, even if he'd wanted to—which he didn't." I hesitated, struggling for words to convey the principles of Rom convention. "You see, when one of us is judged *mukado*—unclean because of what he's done—then he's a threat to everyone around him... he contaminates them not just by his presence, but by his belongings. For my father to have so much as touched me—to have stayed at my side, and gone on living with me, which he might have wanted t' do, if he'd condoned what I'd done—he too would have been *mukado*, and everyone else would have shunned him as they shunned me. It would have meant the end of his life in the clan. It was best that I was sent out alone."

"You've neveh seen him since?"

"No." I cleared my throat. "Afterward....when I'd joined up with a traveling circus, and won some notice riding horseback...I used to wonder, sometimes, if he'd ever see my name on one of the posters... put up along the road to advertise...and maybe show up in the audience...but after awhile, I stopped looking for him."

"What if you should...want to return?"

"Oh, I... couldn't, you know. My sentence was made for life. Even if I wanted to...brave their scorn... I couldn't touch...or deal with any of them, you see—I'd bring ruin on them even now. In their eyes, I'm dead—no longer Rom, which is the same thing; and I guess in mine I'm no longer Rom either... I don't know what I am anymore, frankly."

His lips twitched at the dry note in my voice, as if I had sounded some like chord in him. "Do you miss it?" he asked, with his steady regard.

"Sometimes," I confessed, as my vardo sprang to my mind, and with it, unbidden, memories of dusk on the road. "But then I know that if I hadn't been sent out, I'd never 've started the journey that led here...and without what I've found here, I couldn't have lived." My voice was so thick now that I had to pause, and finish off what was left in my cup; but he continued to wait without hurry, his chin in his hand as it'd been since I started, and his eyes on my face with an encouraging shimmer.

"Have you neveh spoken of this to anyone else?" he asked, as he poured a fresh fill for us both from the clay pot.

"I couldn't," I answered, taking refuge again in the hot tea. "I... we were never raised, you see, t' confide in others...or t' trust anyone else, even other Rom, with our stories. I'd never taken that risk till I came here...and even here... Eben's the only one who really knows much about me. I don't know why I suddenly had t' speak to you...it was just...I couldn't see you leave town till I'd stopped by, and let you know part of my story's like yours."

"It was kind of you to tell me," he said, regarding me with a gentle smile.

"What will you do?" I asked him frankly, glad to change the subject from me.

"Oh, I'm not so unprepared as you might think...I've known this was coming for some time," he smiled, buttering a scone, and munching it with simple appreciation.

"What...what was it all about, that they should vote to dismiss you?"

"An immanent or a transcendent God: that's pretty much what it comes down to," he mused, still munching away as he pondered. "I've declared myself in the one camp, and most of the rest of the parish is in the other—that's what most of the past yeahr's disputes have been about."

"And what do those words mean?"

"Immanent and transcendant? Well, to oversimplify, the first describes a God who's within us, present so to speak in creation; the other a God who's out and above it all....the advantage of the latteh being there's no need to explain how the perfect Divine could be mucking about in imperfect conditions." He looked at my blank expression and grinned. "Is that clear?"

"I...simply never met anyone before who worried about such things," I said, struggling, as always, with concepts.

He broke into a forthright chuckle, frank with delight and appreciation, setting down his cup to keep from spilling. "How I wish I'd had you more often in church," he said, still chuckling and regarding me kindly.

"Is...is this the end now for you of your work?" I asked, waiting for my cheeks to cool.

"Of preaching and ministry? No, that'll neveh be done; but it's about to take a new direction."

"Where will you go?"

"Oh, when I was in Boston this summeh with John Melchett... seeing the homeless state of old seamen...it was fairly plain to me then that the next stage of my work is there. I have some money laid by from my salary...these things I've sold...and I'd like to put it toward buying up one of those old buildings on the waterfront... then get some local parish to renovate it, or betteh yet, some of those seamen themselves... There must be more to life for them than t' end their days in debt and care. Anyone who could rig up a jury mast could certainly prop up a wall; and as for those old stewards and cooks, why, I could put them to work in the kitchen... B'tween what I've got and what othehs have given, I b'lieve I can make a go of it... Why, just this morning I opened the door t' put out the cat and fill her dish, and found undeh the sauceh this envelope. Jim, thehre's five hundred an' sixty dollahs in it...practically enough to buy up a building."

I laughed with him at the thought of finding a year's wages in so incongruous a place as a cat's dish—then stopped, mid-chuckle, moved; for suddenly I knew where it had come from. Five hundred and sixty dollars was the precise amount that Ben'd been owed in wagers made on the outcome of the race, bets that he'd been collecting all week; and if the sum weren't enough to declare him, surely the act of putting it under the cat's dish—at some unearthly hour when no one was up—was. As if he'd somehow read my mind, Jackson all at once hushed too, on his face a look both wistful and touched; but neither of us said a word, and the moment passed in respectful quiet.

"What about you, now that I'm leaving—will you still come to meetin', listen to Brewster, an' try to find youhr way through it all?" he asked, leaning back in his chair with his cup propped in his hand.

I hesitated, looking down at his carpet, the only rug on any of the floors in his house. "I don't know," I said, picking out the colors, the cheerful reds and blues of the rag weave. "I can't make heads nor tails of what he says; he talks all the time like you did just now, about immanence and transcendence....He thinks so completely with his head; and I'm not sure I'll ever be able t' think that way."

"How *do* you think?" he queried, interested with a warmth which encouraged.

Still following the pattern of hues in his carpet, I foundered around in my mind for an answer. "Damned if I know...excuse me... Not in concepts...not in a straight line like almost all the gadje I've met do... I guess I think in...images....inner pictures that sum up somehow what I've understood...the way a figurehead sums up a ship. I don't know why, but...the world's more alive...more personally attached t' me that way." I raised my eyes and looked into his gaze, which regarded me still with warm interest and patience, and the sudden alertness of understanding. "Does that make any sense?" I asked, trailing off lamely, and seeking safety again in the carpet.

"Ample," he said vigorously, propping his chin in his hand as he looked at me. "Tell me, Jim, if you don't mind my asking, do the Rom believe in God?"

I hesitated, wondering how to answer, and anxious about the direction of our talk. "Not...not exactly like you do. O muro Del is... I s'pose you'd say a Supreme Being, but...Being's the wrong word...that makes it sound separate from everything else, like gadje talk about God as a person. O Muro Del isn't a...he, it's a force that...animates everything in creation, not just the living creatures, but the rocks an' the brooks an' the streams an' the moors. It's...it's not separate, but within, and...I can't talk about it like I'd talk about Ben, or the general store down at the corner."

He smiled with delight, almost as if he clapped his hands secretly inside. "Then you do know what immanent means, even if you don't understand the bald idear."

A feeling almost like comradeship, the closeness I felt with Ben in our silences, began to warm me somewhere in my middle; and I made answer with less reluctance. "I guess I do...but I know it without...words."

"Tell me, do you yourself believe in this God?"

This was a live one, and I looked around me like I expected a spook at my shoulder, a materialization of the sudden uneasiness in me. "I guess... I must," I said at length, wishing he hadn't spoken so plainly. "I'm not sure....I ever thought about it; but it fits with what I feel."

He waited, as if understanding that there was more I could add if I wished; and I foundered about in an awkward silence, feeling the sweat collect at my temples. "I...I can't talk about it," I finally blundered, as desperate as if I'd suddenly been cornered, or asked to disrobe in so many words by his eyes. "Words...words take away from what you're saying," I managed, again unnerved by a feeling of presence, and half-looking over my shoulder. "I...all these thoughts are...precious to me...and I'm...afraid of losing their sweet power in me."

Jackson laughed a frank, honest laugh, breaking, to my relief, the tension; and I drew a breath as if I hadn't in some time. "You and I are so different," he said, smiling on me with musing hazel eyes. "I believe just the opposite—words bring power into being."

I looked at him like this was the most outlandish thing I'd ever heard.

"The Bible is full of such demonstrations... In the very first verses God said 'Let there be light'...and there was." He smiled at my attentive expression, diverted, for the time being, from the rug. "Out of the void, there sprang the world...the realization of the Word. And Christ is the Word of God made flesh, which pitched its tent and dwelt among us...another way God is immanent in our world. The Word is the Cause, the prime moveh and shapeh of not just that which is already, but will be; and if that isn't poweh, then I don't know what is... Jim, why do you keep looking oveh youhr shouldeh?"

The sudden change in his voice caught me completely off guard, and I looked at him, terrified.

"If you think our words diminish poweh, why do you keep looking oveh youhr shouldeh?" he pressed; and when I simply couldn't answer—a fear like no fear I'd ever known gripping my throat—he said gently, "'Wheneveh two or three gatheh t'getheh in my name, there I am amongst them.' Don't be afraid, Jim, of the Guest in our room...Now what was it that I was saying?"

I knew, but couldn't begin to tell him, so choked off was my voice by the fear in my breast; and I looked at him like he was mad to be at ease—almost as afraid of him, in his weird calm, as I was of the Awareness in the room. There he sat, with one foot over his knee, and his cup of tea on the arm of his chair—with his chin in his hand, and his face full of mild ease, as if he was at home in this place, in this plane of experience where the Unseen broke in, and threatened to unseat the minds of those seen. Could it be that night after night he sat here, turning his pages or buttering his bread, with this Guest, as he called it, in the chair by his hearth, all but materializing before his eyes? I knew that I would have run a mile before I ever spent a minute alone here; and I regarded him with disbelief and awe.

"You only feel a threat to yourself, Jim, if you have a self to preserve...if you want to hang onto that which is still you, and fence out that which is another," he said, as if he'd plainly read all my thoughts. "When you break down the bounds—in effect, surrender—that which was a foe becomes a friend... As I was saying, words bring about poweh...and I think, in a way, you've always known it. What else could be at the heart of the incantations and the magical rites of your people?"

My eyes silently pleaded with him to stop, and with a compassionate gaze, he smiled. "There's a wonderful passage in one of the Psalms I think you'd undehstand—you in particulah, from all I've heard... Do you have a Bible of youhr own?"

"No," I answered, embarrassed to confess I'd barely got past the point where I'd grasped that it was in two halves, one before Christ, one after.

"Here, then, take mine...not with the insistence, mind you, that you forget youhr Rom teachings...but that you mingle them with these...and see what the final union looks like."

He made a mark beside a passage which he found with ease in all those passages, then handed me a leather-bound volume, worn and scuffed in many places; and I accepted it gingerly in my hands, thumbing briefly through its chapters.

"I...I never saw so many words in my life," I said dryly, moved completely out of my fear by the task. "It'll take years t' read all of this."

"It'll take you the rest of youhr days, b'lieve me...knowing is a life-long job, and it takes however much time you've got." So saying he got up and took my empty cup, then cleared away the empty plate between us; then fetching my hat he met me at the door, where I looked out across the tranquil harbor. "Thanks for coming," he said, with a hand on my arm, and a kindly look on his honest features; and understanding all at once I wouldn't see him again, I felt the wrench of a pang inside me. Stumbling over my farewell, I tucked his book under my arm, and tugged my tarpaulin hat in place; then without a final backward look, I ducked out of his simple cottage, and strode along Water Street in the twilight.

That night I set the book on my desk, but didn't so much as open its cover, as if it were hot, and needed to cool; nor did I stay alone in my room, but hightailed it instead all the way out to Eben's, where I slept on the bear rug next to his bed. The next night I managed to pick the book up, and thumb through it in a preparatory way, noting not its words but its dog-eared appearance, its stained, fragile pages and underlined verses; and I tried to read something of it from its worn look.

That it was a book known, used, loved and lived with—as vigorously perused as Ben's North Atlantic charts, some of which were almost soft from his touch—I could understand from the outset;

and I turned it around in my hands with veneration. Looking at the inscription, I saw that it'd been presented to Jackson by his father, on the occasion of his twelfth birthday; and I was touched all the more by the sentiment of its beginning. Afraid to read, but moved by last evening's talk, and by a longing to know what Ben knew, I opened to the passage Jackson had marked, and read to myself from Psalm 19:

> "The heavens are telling the glory of God;
> and the firmament proclaims his handiwork.
> Day to pay pours forth speech,
> and night to night declares knowledge.
> There is no speech, nor are there words;
> their voice is not heard;
> Yet their voice goes out through all the earth,
> and their words to the end of the world."

Never had I heard or read such music, or found in any book such grandness of vision; and for a long time I read on in other passages marked, picking them out the way one picks out an island, and hops from it to other isles in an archipelago, following a map some mariner has charted. Then at last I got up and sat by the window, and wandered for a while in my memories, or stared out over the mastheads to the harbor where the dock lights were quivering on the waters.

That Friday night, as I later heard, Jackson conveyed his few things to the wharf, helped by John Melchett and his brother Lafe, who edited the local *Recorder*; and while the town prepared for a gala weekend, *Abigail*'s launching and a ball, he quietly slipped away for Boston, aboard the ferry which'd stopped from Bangor. No one else had seen him off, indeed no one else had even known he'd left till he was gone; and passing the little vacant cottage, unsentimental and plain by the harbor, I felt his sudden absence keenly. Glancing through the darkened windows, I wondered if they lingered there still, the voices of our spirits in converse; wondered if some unseen Guest, terrible in its holy presence, wandered there looking for its host, the kindly, hazel-eyed gentleman in shirt sleeves.

But there was no time for me to ponder; for Ben had me up most of that Friday night, secretly mounting *Abigail*'s figurehead with Cy Spooner, while he went over last-minute preparations; and Saturday, dawning bright and fair, and promising as ever an Indian summer morning, saw me setting up tables on the Melchett family house lawn, in company with most of Ben's brothers, while the butler and footmen readied the ballroom, and the kitchen staff cooked up two massive dinners. Expecting a crowd of five hundred on the lawn, Sarah had commandeered every chair and table, ottoman, footstool, tray and tea wagon, linen cloth and napkin in the district; and my job was to help set them in some kind of order, under Keziah's inspired direction, while Sarah oversaw the kitchen, and Galen the supper room and ballroom.

Between the coming and going of servants, rushing off to the harbor mouth for clams and oysters, or into the village for ice, cutlets and staples; between the dashing up and departing of carriages, broughams and delivery wagons, as early guests arrived to lend a hand, or tradesmen breezed up to unload their barrels; between the cavalcading of kitchen garden vegetables, going up the side door steps in baskets, and the promenading of potted plants from local patrons, marching up to the third floor to the ballroom, I was a dazed and dizzy man; and it was no quieter over at the Melchett yard north ways, where a crowd of thousands from the surrounding region was massing on either side of *Abigail*'s stages, or pressing for views from the planks of the town wharf, and from dories and skiffs out in the harbor.

Arriving barely on time at the wharf myself, I found Ben in his work clothes—in laughable contrast with the fine garb around him, frock coats and beaver hats and gaitors—hanging around the ways with the tallow; and there he remained even after the rest of his family, including all the seniors of Melchett Bros., had come up to take places of honor on the stage. Despite the flocks of news agents asking questions, and the press of local shipping magnates, such as Cabot or Hull and Lombard, politely requesting details, Ben was off on another planet, his anxious eye on his wooden darling; and it was impossible to get more than a word or two out of him, or to elicit more comment than an uncivilized grunt. Too intoxicated already—from sampling the afternoon's punch, and the evening's array of port, gin and Madeira—for anything like a coherent answer, Galen was not very helpful either; and it was Amasa Spooner, master shipwright under Ben, or Seth Melchett who hosted the press, while Ben superintended the moves of the launch crew.

Till now he'd kept the figurehead shrouded, and had draped a linen over the sternboard, so as not to give away the ship's name, held secret all these months by a few; but as Abigail came suddenly up with Sarah, pecking away vigorously with her cane, and looking hawk-eyed at this, the umpteenth Melchett vessel she'd seen poised on the ways, he gave a signal to remove the coverings, and she saw for the first time that the ship was hers. Her face a study in noncommittal, neither a drop of sentiment nor a dash of censure on it, she scanned the hull with the sharpest appraisal, as if to make sure this one was good enough to measure up to her—the crowd meantime falling quiet; then piping out loud enough for all surrounding to hear, she simply cackled, "Well, it's about time, boys."

Marching over to the steps of the scaffold—undeterred by either their steepness or height —she came climbing up with her cane in one hand, Sarah's arm in the other and Ben just behind; then tramping over to the figurehead, she took my elbow, and scrutinized her likeness in wood, while I stood by trying to keep the grin from my mouth. Now that the moment had finally come, I was none too sure of her response; for I had blended her features with the gist of my grandmother's, the qualities of the two being so much the same; and though I'd carved her at her present age, I'd dressed her as Galen and Seth remembered, in the garb of the early days of the century. Bird-like, she looked her carving over, tapping away judgmentally with her cane, and rustling her dark taffeta skirts as she swayed; then pointing at the gown she said,

"I neveh wore a dress like that hussy in m' life."

"Oh, Ma, ye did so," countered Seth, "ye wore dresses like that all the time, in the old days—hahrdly so much as a yard o' cloth to 'em."

"I neveh showed my neck and my..." she insisted, rapping with her cane at the bosom.

"Oh-ho, if ye didn't!" wheezed old Jorab, standing by leaning on *his* cane, next to Galen. "*I c'n remembeh what they looked like.*"

"Why, you libertine...you common masheh, you!" she cried, turning on him and rapping him on the noggin, while everybody around her guffawed; then returning her attention to the figurehead, she jabbed with her cane at the heavy gold necklace.

"The jewelry," she crisped, eying the chain at her neck, and the broad gold band which circled her wrist.

"What's wrong with it?" blustered Galen, elbowing in for a closer look.

"I neveh owned a necklace like that... Winslow an' I could neveh afford it."

"Well, ye can now!" Galen bellowed in her ear, with a guffaw which sprang partly from good spirits, partly from drink; and his laughter was echoed in the ranks about him.

Shaking her head as if he doubted she'd really given birth to him, she returned her gaze to the carving. "I ain't that dahrk," she said next, giving my ribs a jab with her elbow.

"The weather, Ma'am," I defended my work, conscious of Ben nearby trying to keep a straight face.

"I neveh had that...come-hitheh look in my eye."

"Are you sure, Ma'am?" I asked her, droll.

"Why, you—you ring-tailed roareh, you—you're as bad as he is!" she barked, giving a jerk of the thumb at Jorab, while everyone broke into another round of laughter; then cocking a final glance at her likeness, and another at me as if to say it'd do, she turned to us all and said abruptly, "Now, the name, boys; what about the name?"

"Why, she's the *Abigail Melchett,* a' course; didje want us t' name her *Diana,* or some otheh goddess name like that?" grinned Ben, leaning against the rail in his work clothes.

"*Hera?*" suggested Jorab, still bold; and "*Aphrodite? Proserpina?*" ribbed Seth.

"Hmpf, might be more fittin' for that siren," she sniffed, with another side glance at the carving; "No, boys, what I mean is m' name, the first letteh of m' Christian name! Are ye going t' christen anotheh ship with a name that stahrts with the letteh A—and that just a yeahr afteh we've lost *Amanda*?"

"Oh, Grandma, you know there's nothin' in that old supehstition," roared Ben, sharing a belly laugh with the others. "If there was, then why're ships goin' down that stahrt with the letteh B, an' C, an'—"

"Oh, get along with ye," she cackled, as he headed down to commence the launch; but there was a pleased look in her eye as she followed his descent.

"We could call her *Gail*...just plain old *Gail*," he called up, wicked; and she gave her cane a fiery shake at him.

"Just get on with it down thehre!" she called at him over the rail. "Kick off the 'shores an' bust the bottle, an' let's see if this chunk o' wood knows how t' float!"

A laboring man to the last minute, Ben himself helped kick off the dogshores, after the tallow'd been poured down the ways; and as the final blocks were removed from her path, *Abigail* began to shiver, like some primal creature almost freed from the earth—from the clay that'd contained her visage for so long. With the last 'shore gone she quivered, still half-poised, as if uncertain she could move; then after an endless shuddering moment, she began to make her descent.

Three stories high, 173 feet long, 37 feet wide, a thousand tons in weight, $80,000 worth of oak, pine and labor, she picked up speed as she went along; and as she hurtled, groaning, past Amasa, he broke Keziah's champagne at her cutwater, shouting out to the crowd as he did so: "*Abigail!* You're the *Abigail Melchett!*" With a creaking roar down the smoking ways, she thundered headlong toward the harbor, past cheering throngs that yet waited, anxious; then silently, gracefully she took to the waters, her quiet wake rippling behind her.

In the midst of all the hurrahing on shore there was a sudden commotion and flurry, as all hands who could commandeered boats to row to her; and climbing her Jacob's ladder, tramping over her new decks, swarming up her lower masts and rigging, then admiring her windlass, binnacle and helm, they flowed below into the after cabins, carrying me like a stick in the tide along with them. There at last in the saloon—the only really decorative place in the ship—I came upon Ben clinking glasses with his well-wishers, answering questions freely, his tongue finally loosed: the gentlemen shaking his hand coming away greased, and the ladies nearby him pressing their skirts to their sides.

At length, quite tipsy, and done with our tour, we all descended again to our dories, like so many seas pouring back out of the scuppers; and making it miraculously back to the wharves, we headed ravenously for Sarah's. Having headed straight home herself from the launching, she'd had time to assemble on the serving tables the most marvelous menu I'd ever seen, steamed clams, heaped oysters, fried potato chips, roast turkey, herb stuffing; salad greens, baked apples, marinades and melted butter, kept liquid and warm on miniature spirit lamps—not to mention poached pears in mint sauce, pumpkin pie and dumplings and pound cake.

By the time I'd sampled it all, and washed the works down with the punch, which was well-spiked; by the time I'd taken a couple of promenades round the lawn, to generally promote digestion, or had a dash or two with the children—young girls like Jean in shaded silk dresses, young boys like Tom in dark velvet round jackets; by the time I'd admired it all in the sweet wind, I wondered how I'd ever have either the wits or appetite for the evening's ball and supper; and I made it back to my room at the Inn in a daze, crashing into an immediate slumber, from which I never wakened till Eben came to dress me.

I'd been sent an invitation two weeks ago, along with about a hundred others—friends of the family and associates who'd helped build the ship; and though I knew it wasn't really expected I'd come, since I was hardly of the town's upper crust—though I knew I couldn't afford the clothes, the height of formal wear, of which I owned none—though I knew too keenly the difficulties bound to arise from my presence at a social event with Damaris and her crowd—I knew as well that Ben would have to be there; and I longed to be with him at a ball, longed to see what a cotillion would be like. The very word filled me with excitement, a mysterious eagerness half of hope, half of memory, as if I'd once long ago danced its steps, or wooed a love in its strains, some past life; and I looked over my invitation with awe, tracing the graceful gold of the script, and reading and re-reading incredulously its message:

Mrs. Galen Melchett
Requests the pleasure of your company
on Saturday Evening, October Twenty-ninth,
at Ten O'clock.
21 East Water Street
Dancing.

Debating the matter for days with Eben, who pointed out mildly all the drawbacks I knew well, including the fact that I couldn't dance the german; arguing that I could wear my father's cutaway coat, which in style and darkness was formal enough to qualify for a ball, and put together, at some expense, the rest of the costume, a sort of half-Rom, half-gadje get-up; insisting that I could mind my manners, and avoid potential problems by taking no escort, thus freeing me from having to attend anyone closely, I finally made up my mind to go; and he shook his homely mug fondly at me.

"I think this'll be a lot hardeh on ye than y' realize; but if you're determined t' make a go of it, why, damned if I won't see ye do it in style," he said, giving my hair a rub with his lean hand; and he dropped all further argument on the subject.

That night after he'd left I counted my dollars, all too slim in denomination and number; but next day I found on my bed, after work, a length of fine white Holland for a new shirt, and another of lavender watered-silk for a cravat; and soon after his cousin, who could sew a fair hand, stopped by my room to commence the fitting, since no tailor took on inner garments of that sort. Feeling more hopeful, I laid out the expense of a new pair of plum-colored knee-breeches, buying up a nice broadcloth I could cut and sew myself; then I bought up as well a pair of silk hose, lavender kid gloves, and a new shirt collar and cuffs—doing without visits to Eli's in the meantime, and cutting back on candles and whale oil to get me through to the next payday.

Cleaning up my father's embroidered silk waistcoat, brushing up my beaver hat, blacking and polishing my Wellington boots, and fetching out my gold-headed walking stick, I managed to complete the outfit; and dancing attendance in my room at the Inn, Eben helped me to put it together, for I was too nervous to accomplish things alone. Shaving, brushing, polishing, buttoning—the kid gloves alone a job for the evening; washing, combing, tying, anointing, with the usual ministrations of SenSen and tooth powder, scented soap and cologne and hair jelly, we worked until I was finally ready; then pulling on my coat, I stood by the fire.

"Well?" I asked, smiling into his gaze; and he looked me over with a judicious eye.

"Ye'll be the only man thehre in such colors...the only one in knee-breeches...an' ye look like a head-on crash b'tween cultures...a cross b'tween George Washington in evenin' dress, an' them ne'er-do-wells at fairs with fiddles," he intoned, his voice as dry as the leaves out the window. "But somehow or otheh you...y' seem t' carry it off...I don't know how ye do it, but y' look like some fancy foreign prince, if I do say so as shouldn't."

Giving in to the excitement I clapped on my hat, and picked up my walking stick on the hearth; then at last, button-hook and keys in one pocket, invitation and silk handkerchief in the other—a bookful of reminders about etiquette in my head, and a flurry of nervous anticipation in my heart—I hugged him and set off alone down Water Street, already alive with closed carriages and broughams, all heading for the Melchett family house drive.

It was the sweetest of nights, the autumn leaf fires of the afternoon having sent up a smoke which hung in the still air, or stole out across the harbor in white wisps; and in the unusual, tangy warmth of the evening, the houses and trees took on a soft look, the nebulous, indistinct mist of an old dream—an aspect heightened by the muted orbs of the street lamps, and the feeble flicker of candlelight in the windows. Down the wooden walks by the shops, then along the cobbled lanes of the street, gentlemen escorted ladies through the haze; or now and again a pair or a team caught the indistinct beam of the moon on their flanks, as they clattered along before buggies or broughams.

Looking ahead I saw the clutter of carriages which announced the head of the Melchett house drive, then, through the mist, the brilliant-lighted house—whale-oil yard lamps, larboard and starboard ship's lights at the entry, and chandeliers with their banks of spermacetti candles, all illuminating the housefront and main hall. Coming up on the confusion—a score of carriages all trying to park, some being numbered and driven ahead, others discharging passengers at the blocks—I found myself in a festive crowd, a commotion of ladies in evening dress stepping down from the blocks with their escorts' aid, or with the help of serving-men in the blue and tan livery which declared their employ at the Melchetts'. Joining with their ranks, tipping my hat to those I knew, I walked up to the house in a sea of mantillas, knee-length palatines of black satin, and shoulder capes of embroidered muslin—our way leading us along the bordered brick walk, and under the canvas vestibule specially erected for the occasion.

A part now of the scene I'd yearningly watched from the street, that faraway night across from the Melchett house in Portland, I removed my hat as I entered the front door, held open to all by the welcoming butler; then following the crowd up the elliptical staircase, I detoured into one of the second floor chambers, which had been designated as a dressing room for the men. Here in the cranberry glow of the lampshades, I set aside my hat and walking-stick—not without glances at the tall highboys in the shadows, and the warm patterns of the paper in the lamplight; then pausing before the ornate mirror at the dresser, I smoothed my hair and tried to look calm, tugging at the wrists of my gloves. Across the hall in Sarah's bedroom, the ladies were doing much the same; and mingling with them as they came back into the hall—passing decorative touches and family heirlooms on the walls, hair wreaths of infinitely fine detail, shadow boxes of magnificent old ships—we swept together up to the third floor, where the strains of music and shuffling of feet announced the opening quadrille was underway.

Waiting in line at the entry to the ballroom, which covered one half of the third floor, I made my manners to diminutive Sarah, indefatigably receiving guests with Abigail—herself still going strong after a dayful of events: the two of them resplendent in family jewels, and brocaded gowns of sober hues. Next remembering to seek out my host, I threaded past ladies in gossamer dresses, with low-cut necks and frilly berthas, and wide, full skirts with lace-trimmed flounces; dodged gentlemen in full evening dress—black cutaways tailored with tight waists, black cravats above white satin waistcoats, and dark, slim trousers strapped off with gaiters; skirted the orchestra of eight pieces, playing away behind a partition of spreading ferns and potted plants, then the refreshment tables, laden with platters of crystal and silver, till I came up to where Galen held forth in a knot of cohorts.

Intimidated by now by the assault on my senses, by the perfumed bare arms and scented hair dressings, and the complexities of the code of manners; almost wishing I hadn't braved the event, and anxiously wondering where in the crowd Ben was—I bowed to Galen and presented myself; and he at once burst into a guffaw of comradely, hail-fellow delight.

"So y' showed up t' feed an' dance with some pretty afore ye ships aboard that monsteh we launched, an' spends six months dinin' on hahrd tack!" he bawled, no more sober than the last time I'd seen him; and taking heart from his forthright bluster—from the evidence that he, at least, was no different here than he was on deck—I grinned with unrestrained delight.

"I wouldn't miss the chance, sir," I said, feeling my spirits buoy again in my breast.

"Now what's that rig you'hre wearin'?" he pressed, forgetting his manners to the gentlemen around him, Amasa and Seth, who looked on grinning; "is that how them gypsy lads dress up ashore?"

"Aye, sir."

"Ye looks fit t' make a killin'. Y' ain't by any chance afteh my daughteh?"

"I'm not afteh anyone, Cap'n," all but dropping my own r's, so thick was his accent.

"Smahrt man! Smahrt man! Though as I remember, ain't ye the one that's a bit of a liah?"

"D'pends on what you call a lie, sir."

"I call a lie anything that's not true," he snorted dryly.

"The truth t' you might not be the truth t' me, sir."

He looked at me with a perplexed pucker—with the sodden confoundment of liquor. "Somebody'd betteh give this man a drink! Just one little drink hehre, heh-heh. This hehre's the claret-punch, son; the best I could convince m' wife t' do till suppeh. It'll give ye a bit of a kick, at least, an' straighten out youhr muddled thinkin'. Don't monkey with that otheh malarky—that's lemonade an' such crap for the teetolahs. We got plenty o' them here t'night. They ain't really human, but we got t' treat 'em right, wouldn't ye say?"

"I'd say so, sir," I said, trying to keep a straight face, and longing to laugh out loud with relief—with release from the pretense, the artificial mantle of manners which this man's flesh and feeling so forcibly stripped off.

"That's what the Good Book says....treat 'em right. But it ain't easy....It's a conspiracy, y' know...this livin' life thing. Everything you'hre s'posed t' want ye can't hardly fetch nohow, an' everything you'hre not s'posed t' want, hell, ye can pick it off a bush! So watch out for that as ye gets oldeh."

"I'll keep my eyes open, sir."

"B'cause I like ye, y'know...yayuh, I do, even if y' does have a funny cut t' youhr jib. I like that bit of a chip on youhr shouldeh...an' that look in youhr eye that says ye got feelin's."

Suddenly I wanted to cry—wanted to hug this man who, with his drunken perception, had made me feel I belonged and made sense here, even though I hailed from a different world. "I like you, too, Cap'n," I managed thickly, my voice so hoarse I could scarcely speak; and he at once lapsed into humor.

"Heh! Ye'd betteh!" he laughed, straightaway bright as a dollar, and convivial as ever. "I'm the one that's feedin' ye dinneh!" And with that he picked up the tray he had just filled, hoisting it aloft with a spill or two, and bowing off into the midst of the crowd; and there I could see him beaming and handing out drinks, or jovially picking up empties, for all the world as if he was the waiter.

Buoyed up by his example I took on the rest of the crowd, feeling there was nothing I couldn't accomplish; and as the figures of the quadrille ended and a round dance got underway, I mingled with those not on the floor, greeting the young ladies to whom I'd been introduced, asking them for the favor of a dance later on, and signing their cards before their chaperones or mothers—meantime eagerly searching the festive room for Ben. Most of the throng I knew from the yard, or from occasional parlor invitations; but amongst them were a few out of towners who were strangers, connections of Melchett Bros. in Portland or New York who'd journeyed all the way down for the launching; and to these I was introduced by John Melchett, who kindly took me under his wing for the ordeal.

In his fashionable, almost foppish attire, with his quiet, understated dry wit, he was as different as could be conceived from his father; but he shared old Galen's familiar ease, imbuing me with calm afresh as he marched me up to dowagers and shippers. Jacob Melchett, Galen's older brother, liason man for Melchett Bros. in New York, his sophisticated wife and handsome daughter Claire; Elkanah Melchett, who ruled the roost in Portland, two of his daughters and three of his sons, including Reuben, whom I knew only too well; John and Courtney Howland, Anne's father and mother—these made up the majority of the new faces; and I managed to keep them sorted out in my head, despite the Madeira Galen'd set in my hand.

But of Ben in this flurry I caught not a glance, until at last I stumbled on him in a secluded corner, sitting with old Jorab and a couple of cousins; and as apprehensive as if this was our first meeting, I walked up to him with John still at my side, trying to conceal my nervous fluster.

Getting to his feet—helping Jorab rise too—he stood waiting for me as formally as a stranger, an impression heightened by his attire; for coming up close I saw that his dress clothes—a dark cutaway with a pinstripe of pearl, and pearl-colored trowsers above white gaiters— were new, transforming him into a Ben I'd never seen; while his manner was stilted and awkward with unease. With his hair neatly parted and combed to one side, his beard freshly trimmed and his big hands gloved, he looked manly in a way he never had before, almost frighteningly genteel; yet despite his perfection of dress and bearing, he appeared manifestly uncomfortable—almost laughable, had it not been for his massive dignity of person. The only sober-faced man in all the gaiety about him, he looked definitely "walled," as the saying went: on the outskirts of the festivities, with nothing whatever to contribute to the light talk which passed for conversation at such an event.

Nor did my appearance on the scene help any; for he had not a word for me, as close a person to him as there was in the room—shaking hands with me as stiffly as if we'd never met, and falling mute after his greeting; and to my dismay I found I had nothing to say to him either, my tongue cleaving to the roof of my mouth as I stood, waiting for some thought—any thought—to inspire me.

Here was a man with whom I'd just launched a ship, with whom I'd just spent half a night mounting a figurehead; and I could not come up with a word to address to him! Formerly our silences had been full of meaning, the intimate thoughts of men close in heart; now our quiet was agonizing, full of side glances at one another. It was with a relief of immeasurable proportions that I suddenly realized I was being hailed by a voice, and had an excuse to cross the room; and as I walked away I found that beads of sweat had actually collected at my temples, and were now drying in the cool breeze from the window.

If Ben was indisputably one of the most miserable guests present, Anne, on the other hand, was one of the most vivacious; and as I caught sight of her—opposite Joseph in the round dance—I came to an amazed halt, my mouth open. This young woman with the flushed cheeks and bright smile, with the sparkling eyes and light feet as she danced—this young woman in the dust-blue flowered brocade gown, and the dainty white gloves trimmed with swan's down—this was the sober, almost severe matron I'd met time and again at Ben's house? Before tonight I'd wondered what Ben had ever seen in her cool beauty to make him desire her in marriage, and I'd felt almost sorry for her children, wondering if they ever missed her warmth;

but now I could see how sunnily pretty she was, how vibrantly alive and gracious.

As I danced the minuet with Sabrina, the waltz with Keziah and the quadrille with Kate, avoiding Damaris for all I was worth—as I led each of them in turn out onto the floor on my arm, remembering to let go till the sets were lined up, and the strains of the music had started—as I worked my way through the figures and steps, remembering how to hold their hands in a clasp, never with intertwining fingers, as Claire and Jonas were so obviously doing—I turned again and again to eye her; but never so frankly as the few times she danced with Ben, always the waltz, the only step he'd attempt.

At first I was simply struck by the contrast between them, by her easy style, and his formal, stiff effort; and I felt again the contentions of their marriage. But as the initial surprise of her warm beauty wore off—as the nervous delight of watching him dance for the first time began to fade—as I continued to feel like a stranger toward him, and he toward me, neither of us meeting eyes—a searing pang announced itself in my middle; and the buoyant lift Galen'd given me departed.

How it stung, all at once, to see them as partners—how it stung to see the right she had to him, the awkwardness with which he tried to match her steps; how it ached to dance with someone else besides him—to feel the separation between us, as we danced with separate partners! How I envied her the brace of his big arm, the attentive incline of his head—all that propriety allowed; how I envied her the clasp, however awkward, of his cumbersome gloved hand. Oh, there were leagues, miles to go yet between us; walls of convention we could never scale in public, even if we ever surmounted them in private! So great was my pain that, directly after seeing Kate back to her mother, I went out into the stairway hall, and stood before the great arched window in the bit of an autumn breeze from the sea—so full of unanticipated yearning that I simply wanted to flee to Eben, to confess I knew now what he had foreseen.

On the winding stairway Sabrina was flirting—in a daring moment when no one was looking—with Sage Haskett, who'd met her coming up from the dressing room; down below, in the smoky gleams of the moonlight, ripples of laughter were dreamily wafting, as couples, with chaperones, took the sweet air on the lawn; but here in my heart I knew I was debarred from such public knowing with Ben for all time; and no ostracism I'd ever felt so denied me.

Till now my whole will had been so directed toward winning his heart that it'd never once occurred to me what it would mean if I succeeded; and in my double burden I only wanted to hasten away from this place and hide my despair. So compelling was my need that I would have left straightaway if I hadn't caught a glimpse, on turning to go, of someone in the corner of the semi-darkened supper hall—someone who, by lowered head and bowed shoulders, told me that she too was in pain; and hesitating, I paused in my flight, long enough to see that it was Keziah. Till now I'd never had more than a light word with her, certainly never a serious moment; and I vacillated, wondering if I should make an effort to cheer her, to maybe find surcease from my pain in hers.

If she had been any of the others—sophisticated Claire or worldly Sabrina or even good-natured, straightforward Kate—I would have been abashed to try; but I knew that, underneath that white organdy vision, with its flounces and frilly bertha and ribbons, and its delicate embroidery of pink roses—underneath that coronet of braids, with its intertwining of gold cord, and those disconcerting mathematical brains—was the same woman who'd worn Abby's breeches reefed in with a length of sinnet, all the way back from the loss of *Amanda*, and who'd cussed like a foremasthand at her brother Joseph; and I wasn't anymore intimidated by her.

Coming up beside her, I touched her arm, in a quiet, sympathetic gesture; and she looked up quickly with neither distress nor censure, simply a mute expression of hurt. As I realized that she, even she, with her bright ways, had a secret need which she carried within, I felt a sudden closeness to her, an inexplicable bond of kinship; and in that closeness I found comfort.

"Things not going so well for you?" I asked, offering her my handkerchief; and as she took it she squared her shoulders and gave me a little, shaky laugh.

"It's...just Claire," she said, dabbing at her eyes, and giving me a game look as she spoke. "She doesn't know how I feel about Jonas, so it's not her fault...but oh, how I wish she'd stayed in New York!"

"So it's Jonas, is it?" I asked with a smile, finding a degree of lightness to cheer her.

"Yes...it has been for some time. Nobody else knows...certainly *he* doesn't."

"Moves a bit fast t' deserve someone like you, don't he?.... Not t' mention the fact, he hasn't got any money."

She laughed Ben's frank, appreciative laugh, and blew her nose without embarrassment or pretense. "It's...Claire's influence, I guess; he never behaved like that around us, any of the otheh parties we've thrown here....and as for money, I've neveh noticed that anybody's heart really took such factohs into consideration...You're not from one of the 'first families' round here youhrself, and everybody's simply mashed on you."

"Oh, they are, are they," I murmured, wary.

"Of course; did you think that Damaris was the only one?"

"What I think is that I should never have attempted t' come here; and since I have, I'd best bow out early, b'fore I get into any more trouble."

"You'hre lucky you can... If it was anybody else's house, I could just up and leave and go home myself, and have myself a luxurious cry...but this *is* home, so I guess I'm stuck." Looking up at me she gave a wry smile, and a searching gaze as she smoothed her hair; and she seemed to read my quiet face. "Things not going so well for you eitheh?" she asked, assuming an expression she could present to others.

"No," I confessed, keeping my voice light.

"With you, I neveh can tell; you always manage t' keep youhr chin up."

"I've had plenty o' practice," I said dryly.

"Anything I can do about it?"

"No; I'm afraid my problem's even more hopeless than youhrs... so we might as well go have an ice."

Throwing her head back, she frankly laughed—a little thickly, but nonetheless fully; and giving me a curtsey, she gathered up her skirts, and preceded me to the refreshment table. There we found Galen still holding forth—if possible, even more congenial than the last time I'd seen him; but apparently there was yet plenty of perception in those blurred eyes, for as he peered at Keziah, leaning forward, he gave her chin a fatherly pinch; and the glass he handed her was not without a kick.

Though I hadn't intended to take her in to supper—not wanting the rest of the crowd to think, along with its other misconceptions, that I was secretly fortune-hunting—I found that I now wanted her company in misery, while she seemed willing to tolerate mine; so when the meal was announced, promptly at midnight, we crossed into the supper room together, Galen escorting Abigail first, and the remainder of us following, wives before husbands, ladies before escorts. Because we were now all sitting down at the five long tables, each seating twenty, and obviously only needed to attend to those immediately around us—because Ben and Anne were mercifully on the other side of the room, Claire and Jonas somewhere in the middle—supper was something of a relief; and I drowned my feelings in the menu—hot canvasback, cold partridge, breast of veal, oysters and mutton cutlets and sweetbreads, herb soup, lemon pudding, and wine—six or seven empty glasses before me, and a new kind poured with each course.

With the busy coming and going of servants, the brilliance of the three chandeliers, and the brightness of the cheerful converse around me—with the preoccupying complexity of the meal, of silverware and plates arriving and departing, and crystal glasses multiplying—I felt my spirits rise a little; and I found myself exchanging thoughts with Keziah in a way we never had before, as if our common distress had allied us. Refusing all the wines save the Madeira, she even so, after Galen's claret, spoke with an unwonted candor: talking about her longing to sail, at least as navigator, and do a man's work, in contempt of convention—yet at the same time, marry and rear a family; and I listened with a kind of revelation.

Never had I heard any woman speak like this—save Damaris,

who was preparing to take up teaching; but then, I had never heard any man speak like this either; and as it was nothing less than what I wanted to do—to blend the conventional roles of the sexes—I supported her with sympathetic words: finding, in her resentment of social form, a restless rebellion which matched my own.

As the final dessert plates were cleared away and the ladies departed, leaving the gentlemen to smoke—as Keziah rose with my aid and gave her thanks, I intimated my plans to leave; but she emphatically shook her head, insisting convincingly that I hang on. "Stay and dance the german," she begged, with an expression of earnest friendship; "you pick up new steps easily; and thehre's all kinds of favohs for those who join in. A ball's not a ball without the cotillion—and b'sides, I'd make it through myself so much easieh if you'hre there."

"Don't I have t' have a partner?" I asked, glancing round the emptying supper room doubtfully.

"Ask Kate—nobody's asked her yet, and she's a good egg who wouldn't make anything of it. Just don't try to take the lead—let Sage or Reuben and some of the othehs, and keep well back whehre you can copy."

Longing to find out what it would be like—led on by the same kind of enchantment one feels, at a fair or a carnival or on a bright city street—I sought out Kate and spoke to her, with apologies for my unfamiliarity; and staying well back of those who pressed to the fore—allowing Sage to take the lead with Keziah, who threw a look of mock distaste at us—we took our places somewhere in the middle, while those not dancing seated themselves round the room. Presented with bonbons and carnations, we found ourselves caught up in a festive aura; and pinning on my flower, I glanced round to see who else was participating—spotting Claire with Jonas, Sabrina with Reuben, and not very far away, Damaris with Reuben's brother.

Since we'd all be exchanging partners numerous times in the sets, it was understood we were all introduced, with the various rights and privileges pertaining; and as I looked at Damaris in her pale green watered silk, I realized I'd be dancing with her, trading off the familiarities I'd avoided all evening. Though she hadn't said so much as a word to me, or indicated by even the lift of a brow that anything had ever passed between us, there was a look on her face now which I understood; and I bit my lip as I glanced away. Nor was she my only concern; for where Ben was—somewhere on the perimeter watching, or still in the supper room smoking—I couldn't tell; and as the first figure opened and the walls blurred with motion, I felt the lurch of nervous fear in my middle.

Though the steps were complex, I discovered they were not hard to master with time, especially with Kate good-naturedly helping; and things would have passed off better than anything else all evening, had it not been for the pain, persistent from the beginning, that I couldn't share this sweet vehicle with Ben. This bewitchment of keeping time to the music, of surrendering oneself to its rhythms—this allure of glances and touches and murmurs, of damp brows and moist curls and breaths of air through the windows: if only it was Ben's body which knew these with me, Ben's feet which traveled with mine through these circuits! As I danced I wondered if he was even looking at me, for I still hadn't spotted him in the flurry of watchers; and even as we at last came to a halt, and Galen stepped out into our midst—even as we stood clapping and bowing, and endeavoring to catch our breaths—even as special favors were given, I was still trying to catch sight of him in the corners.

By three in the morning I was so fatigued—not just by the mysteries of the night, but by the ironies which rendered them tasteless—that I stumbled out into the stairway hall again, thinking to take the air at the window; and there I at last found Ben by himself at the casements, looking out at the moonlight on the sea. Backing hastily into the ballroom, I stood gazing at him from the safety of the doorway, lingering on him in the light of the candelabra—dallying on his fine, erect back, his broad shoulders beneath the well-cut cloth—thinking meantime how manly he looked, how noble, how out of place, how alone. The strain and fatigue of the night were plain on his face; and his hair—perhaps it was just the silver of the moonlight, or the reflections of the chandelier, a hundred candles a-gleam on its tiers—but weren't those glints of grey at the temples?

He was twenty-eight now, a couple of years shy of middle age;

time was passing, fleeting quickly; suddenly I felt its pressure as never before. Men lived to be sixty if they were lucky, forty or fifty if struck down by one of the host of infections prevalent throughout the country—typhoid, consumption, lung fever; and those that plied the seas had no guarantee of thirty. What had I had of his life so far, and what was I to have of his future—I who still stood bereft on the outside, trying to shape a way into this enigma?

From the ballroom floated the melody of a waltz, lilting and soaring in its sweetness; and as if to resolve the pain of the evening— as if to complete us, as one completes a shadow box, visioning a whole ship instead of a half with the aid of the mirror which forms its backing—I pictured us dancing alone together, our shadows moving on the stairway wall. A completed whole, Ben's arm circling my waist, my hand at his shoulder and our gloved fingers poised—rounded out by our contact, Ben's head inclined, his lips a few breaths from the waves of my hair—entire for the time, we glided and swirled, our shadows swaying and dipping and twirling; then as the notes of the music drifted away on the night, we paused in our course for an unending moment, our profiles young and tender on the wall.

With a hush and a whisper of fragrance and brocade, Anne came out of the ballroom to join him, brushing past me with a smile and a nod; and seeing her take her place there beside him, solid and real before the frame of the window, I fled down the stairs without their notice, taking refuge in the dressing room. For the moment I had the place to myself; and as I stood alone on the figured carpet, I absorbed the whole poignant pain of the chamber: the dresser skirts, the comb and brush pairs, the Sheraton chairs, the bedstead with its cloaks—all moving me with the incompleteness, the irresolution of the evening. Upstairs, the last couple of waltzes floated out on the autumn breezes; while here, at the windows, the curtains stirred a little at the open sashes. Sweeping down the stairs, Ben and Anne parted in the hall, Anne gliding into Sarah's chamber to don her mantilla and bonnet; and slipping at once into the alcove, I receded into the shadows as Ben came in to fetch his hat and cape, and pause for a moment before the mirror.

Watching him in its dim reflections, I smoothed his hair and cravat with my eyes, and fastened the clasp of his cape at his shoulders; then as soon as he left I hurried up to the window, brushing aside the film of the curtain; and from there I could see them emerge below and stand by the vestibule waiting for their carriage, two indistinct silhouettes on the lawn. For a while I watched them mount and clatter off, till their running lamps were obscured by the smoke; then picking up my own hat and stick, not saying goodbye to Galen and Sarah, or even to Keziah, who'd shown me such kindness, I simply walked out—not just of the house, but of the whole illuminated facade of Ben's past; and taking to the street, I headed not for the Inn, but for the consolation of Eben's.

Closing in on his cabin I saw it was lighted, as if he'd somehow known I was coming; and stepping into the sitting room I found him by the fire, reading a periodical, though it was nigh four in the morning. Going gratefully to him I knelt by his knee, and laid my head in his lap, with a hush too deep for tears; and as he stroked my hair, his hand blameless and kindly, I said to him thickly, "I'm goin' home t' pack my bags; it's crazy t' go on like this any longer."

"Ye've packed youhr bags for the last time, son," he told me, gently pushing my head from his knee; "might just as well go sensibly t' bed, an' see how things look t' ye in the mornin'." So saying he got up and banked the fire; and heaving a sigh I went upstairs, fetched my nightshirt out of the bureau, laid my dress clothes on the bed, and dragged the comforter back down to his room, where I settled myself again on the bear rug.

"How much longeh is this goin' t' go on?" he queried, peering at me over the bedside; and I gazed up at him from my makeshift bunk, blinking.

"What?" I asked, thinking he meant the state of my heart, and prepared to deliver a bleak answer.

"This sleepin' on m' bear rug business."

"From what I've been told, for quite some time," I returned, with as much cheer as I could muster; then diving back down again under the covers, I pulled the comforter over my head, and burrowed my face in the depths of the warm fur.

XXII
BENJAMIN MELCHETT
Cape Damaris, Maine   November, 1843

That he was ill all day Sunday—with one of the worst headaches
he'd ever had—I understood Monday morning from Eben, who
stopped by the counting house to help me begin laying out orders
for *Abigail's* spare parts and sea stores; so I was surprised when he
popped up at my desk bright as a sunrise, and invited me to step
outside. What he was up to I had no idea—one of his maddening
pranks, I supposed; and I glowered at him, exasperated, for I was
up to my elbows in work. With Pa, Joseph and six others just off
for Portland, to haul back a part of *Abigail's* cargo —with Tom,
skippering *Charis*, due back from Liverpool, and a hundred freight
lists, incoming and outgoing, consequently tacked up around me—I
was in no mood for jest; and besides, I hadn't had time to forget the
discomfitures of Saturday night.

That he was the same man who'd squired my sister and made
once again such a hit with her set, at the supper table as well as on
the dance floor; that he was the same stranger who—decked out in
dress clothes, the special garb of his people only I had seen—had
breezed through the festivities so difficult for me, I recalled only too
smartly; and I was not anxious to see him alone. None too graciously,
therefore, I hauled myself out of my chair, and followed him to one of
the boat sheds, where he steered me suddenly around a corner; and
there before me—looking as out of place amongst the derelict hulls,
and the plain, weathered spars of the stored sloops, as if it'd been
dropped from another planet—was a magnificent gypsy wagon.

"Happy birthday," he said cheerfully, as I simply stood and stared at this vision; and dazedly I shook my head at him.

"It's...you mean it's mine?" I managed at last, still having made no step toward it.

"Of course. I like it a lot better than what I gave you *last* year," he chirped, meaningfully rubbing his arm.

As if released by his bright, cheerful tone and the winsomeness of his cocky humor, I broke at last into reactions, and words came bubbling to my lips without order. "Jim, it's...it's even betteh than I imagined, all them times I tried t' picture what you described... it's... you didn't make all this youhrself, did'je?"

"Aye," he answered, "all but the wheels. I needed Longstreet's help with those; and Eben lent a hand with all the assembly."

"But...how on earth did'je eveh find time t' build it?"

"Oh, at dinner hours, sometimes in the evenin'. It's been all this time out in Eben's shed; I'm surprised you didn't stumble on it."

By now I was caught up in such a flood of reactions—joy that he'd remembered my anniversary, which even I had forgotten; relief that there were still secrets between us, personal exchanges of gift and memory to which no others were privy; awe at his skill and power of imagination—that I could no longer stand still beside him; and I walked up to the nearest window, opening and closing the shutters. Like a child who gains confidence from his first touch, and begins to explore a strange object without restraint, I hurried on to adventure the wheels, examining the boxes, rims and spokes—then traversed the walls to the driver's seat, where I knelt in the dust to peer under the shafts, and study the arts of the undercarriage.

Canary yellow in the body, handcart blue at the roof, emerald green in the shutters, barnside red at the wheels, with patterns and scrolls of every hue in between, it was like no other vehicle I'd ever seen; and I shook my head in silent amazement, standing back a moment to view the whole thing, with alternate rushes of humor and appreciation.

Then finally—afire to see the inside, not unlike a boy about to view his first treehouse—I gave a nod at the door opposite the shafts, where Dee stood patiently in harness, and eagerly asked him "May

I?"; and at once he opened its cunning latch, saying sunnily, "Of course: it's yours."

Inside I found everything laid out as compactly as the cabin of a sloop, and I took inventory as delightedly as one about to voyage: a small stove with two burners, a teakettle already clamped in place; a small brass fuel box full of logs; two or three built-in seats, each with a cushioned lid for storage; a table which folded up against the wall; three raiseable windows, handsomely curtained; a hanging cupboard for dishes, already stocked; and at the far end, in a curtained alcove, two big bunks, one atop the other, each wide enough to sleep at least two, and both clad in comforters, quilts and pillows.

"So this is what it looked like," I murmured, transported to another time and place, and imagining Jim growing up in these walls; and putting his hands in his pockets, he chuckled.

"Well...not quite," he told me, grinning; and scanning the place from ceiling to floor, I looked at him.

"What could possibly be missin'?" I asked, trying to imagine various Rom contraptions.

"If you'll meet me at Eben's b'fore supper, I'll show you."

"I've only got three ships t' load, an' a channel t' dig out in the harboh," I said dryly; and giving a carefree laugh, he shook his head.

"This is more important," he said, his chin coming up in that stubborn manner; and too curious to resist, I surrendered.

"It'd betteh be good," I postscripted, on my way out.

"Oh, it will be," he said serenely, latching the door again behind him, and jumping up on the box by Dee; "I don't expect you'll ever forget it."

Promptly at four I showed up at Eben's, having left my desk in a state of upheaval; and there in the drive I saw the cart, visible from half a mile with its bright hues; while poking out from all three windows, raised in the warm late autumn half-sun, were the heads of five children at once recognizable—despite disheveled hair and disreputable faces—as mine.

"What's up?" I called to Jim on the box, where he sat in the sun with Dee's reins in his hands; and "Hop up, we're goin' for a ride," he answered, grinning at me as I climbed up beside him and tried to take the reins, which he promptly refused to hand over.

Touching up Dee, he headed her nose out the drive, then turned toward the Point and the harbor road, where sparse leaves and red berries brightened the sere fields beneath the gathering smoky grey clouds. "I thought, since it's so pretty, we'd head this way," he added, while mopheads crowded at the window behind us, and a quick bark or two confirmed Sam too was aboard.

"And just where is it you figure on goin'?" I asked him, leaning back on the narrow seat, curious.

"In circles," he returned cheerfully, with a meaningful look out of the corner of his eye, and an almost undetectable curl of his lip.

"An' when are we gettin' back?"

"Whenever."

I knew perfectly well that he was referring to the conversation we'd had after the race a week ago; and I answered him with the twitch of a smile. "You'hre not goin' t' forgive me for that bit of a sprint, are ye?"

"Not any time soon, no."

I smothered a grin as I gazed ahead. "An' how did'je manage this?" I asked, cocking a brow at the children behind us.

"Oh, Anne's in town for the Ladies' Aid meetin'—a quiltin' at Melissa's which won't likely end soon; and it wasn't hard t' bribe Sadie."

"This is crazy, y' know," I dolefully informed him; "Anne's goin' t' get wind of it, even if we don't pass nobody; an' ten t' one it's goin' t' rain."

"The rain'll hold off, an' Anne'll get over it; you know damn well she always has."

"So far," I amended wryly; and he gave me a sidelong look full of humor as, slapping the reins, he bid Dee down the road.

At first we simply followed our noses, taking the harbor road for a spell, while the sea gleamed a gunmetal blue on our left, and the oak leaves provided warm splashes of color against the somber dark green of the spruce. It was so warm I took off my sack coat, folded it and leaned back against it; while Jim at the reins held forth in his shirt sleeves, the old red and white check he'd worn to sea, and a simple woolen waistcoat.

As we drove there poured forth from all three windows shrieks of mirth and argument and protest, accompanied by snatches of song, including Romany ditties Jim'd taught whenever he'd spent time with the young ones: most of the lyrics about poisoning pigs, or filching horses or soliciting flirtations, though in Romany they rang as sprightly as dance tunes. Despite the fact they had no idea what they were singing, the children rendered each air with relish, and as much conviction as their counterparts in Wales—the lanes echoing with such foot-fetching nonsense as:

"Here the gypsy gemmen see,
With his Roman jib and his rome and dree—
Rome and dree, rum and dry
Rally round the Romany Rye!"

Caught up in their infectious skylarking, I fell in with their jubilant spirit, applauding their various musical efforts, and letting them help Jim decide our route: mostly a matter of such offhand exchanges as "Have any of ye ever been down this road?" "No!" "Then let's go down it!" In this way even I soon lost all sense of direction, though I knew we were vaguely heading inland; and when we finally stopped for supper, it was in a place I'd never been—at the side of what looked to be a disused wagon trace, beneath a giant oak whose copper leaves still massed against the blue-grey sky.

Clearing a space for ourselves in the leaf drifts, and the piles of acorns scattered around—firing up the stove in the *vardo*, and warming up the supper Jim'd brought—we contrived to picnic outdoors, dipping our bowls into the kettle, and perching slices of bread on our knees: not even Courtney complaining about sharing napkins, or picking acorns out of her tea, so appetite-whetted were we by the fresh air.

It was while we were eating that the first problems arose on what till now had been a country lark: the sky, half-grey, suddenly closing over, and a few drops of rain beginning to fall. Looking over at Jim

I cocked a wry brow, which he studiously attempted to ignore; and gathering up our gear, we moved into the *vardo*, the seven of us finishing up around the small table. Finding room for our bodies on the three seats and lower bunk proved no easy undertaking; while— what with our bowls and teacups, not to mention our spilled stew and bread crusts, which the dog was busily lapping up off the floor— we'd soon made a hurrah's nest of the *vardo*.

It was at this point we discovered Jim'd brought neither dish cloth, nor any sort of a rag to clean up with; and dishes, kettles, silver and what not ended up on the stove, or stuffed into some seemingly unused corner, while faces were scrubbed with napkins fast becoming unappealing. By now the rain was coming down in hard streams, making a miry mess of the wagon trace; and abandoning for the time all thoughts of dessert—a magnificent gold and silver cake Eben had baked—Jim and I were obliged to go out in the wet, and get Dee and the wagon back onto the main road before we became hopelessly entrenched in the mud.

Though Jim erected a tarp and we both shrugged on coats—mine, of course, belonging to my best work suit—we were soon soaked through to our shirts: the rain slanting down under the tarp on Jim, and cascading on me whenever I jumped down to help guide Dee round the mucky morasses. Nor was that the extent of our problems; for less than happy now in the small van, the children could be heard squawking like hens in a hen house—from the sounds of things pulling each other's hair, disputing territorial bounds or arguing over who'd hold Sam; and their screeches of protest little encouraged us in our work.

Our task almost accomplished—the main road, with its better grading, actually hoving into view—there came a sudden crash and a shrill shriek from the *vardo*, followed by a chorus of cries and laughter; and rushing to door the we beheld a woeful sight: Courtney spread-eagled on top of the cake, which Tom had got out and set on the table, apparently for them to snitch from. Reportedly she'd fallen out of the upper bunk as the wagon'd lurched out of a pothole, though I strongly suspected a timely shove from Seth; and there being nothing left of the brave silver and gold, it had to be summarily pitched by the wayside, the boys grabbing handfuls of frosted ooze as it went.

Courtney meantime had to be doused with a bucket of water, which of course was our only spare; and dolefully hanging out the empty pail—examining the solid grey sky, from which the rain was now pouring in torrents—I said dryly to Jim, "Well, it'll soon be re-filled, at this rate."

Trying to hide his grin and miserably failing, Jim attended to the squalling Courtney, handing me her dress and stockings, and attempting to get the globs of cake from her curls; and I hung the clothes out the back with the pail, there being no place left indoors to stuff them. Of course he hadn't thought to bring spare clothes for the children, so Courtney, shivering, and none too clean to look at even in her drawers, had to be wrapped up in Tom's jacket and a quilt, which we hauled down from the upper bunk. Leaving her to huddle in a corner with her sister—promising to take a strap to the boys, if they perpetrated any more trouble—I went back out with Jim to work on the *vardo*, which had sunk in the mud with all our jumping around; and we soon found we had to put our shoulders to it, if we hoped to free ourselves anytime before winter.

Pushing together from the rear, Dee straining ahead in the traces, we'd just begun to make detectable progress, when another commotion erupted inside; and this time when we opened the door we found that Seth—who'd looked a bit peaked after supper—had suddenly and without preamble become miserably sick, all over the quilt and of course, the pillows. Coming into the mess, mud-splattered ourselves, and oozing muck from our boots and pantlegs, we did our best to effect a clean-up—suspending the quilt from the eaves out the back, hanging Seth's clothes and pillows out likewise, and dousing his face in rain collected from the bucket.

The rain by now coming down like thunder, and occasional lightning even flashing in the dark, Jim and I went back to our work—me with accusing scowls and sideglances, he with the squints and gleams of suppressed mirth; but we soon found that, between the heavy rain, and the jolting and jouncing of our weight on the floor, two of the wheels were even more deeply entrenched; while there was certainly no hope of any passing traffic from which to beg outside assistance. Trying one last idea, Jim hiked ahead, and wrested a rail from an old sagging fence; but getting it positioned in the right place in the mud, with the aid of one puny lamp in the pitch dark, proved to be a capital challenge; and I lent my help with a skeptical glower, while Jim, on his knees, gave in freely to laughter.

In the midst of all our grunting and tugging, burrowing and digging and scraping and wallowing—in the midst of all the racketing or rain, howling of wind and cracking of thunder—Tom could be heard, if not seen, at the nearest window, summoning me with a note of insistence; and trudging over to him I hollered "What is it?", in no mood to deal with another disaster.

"Papa, it stinks somethin' awful in here!" he cried, opening the window wider for air.

"Well, we did the best we could," I growled; "ye'll just have t' beahr it—or come out in the rain!"

"No, not that; I mean it's Nat—Nat's diapeh! Can't we please do somethin' about it?"

Looking over at Jim—who'd come up with the lamp, and who now was looking indescribably guilty in its faint light—I asked drolly, "I s'pose y didn't think t' bring extra diapehs?"; and he collapsed with fresh spasms against the van.

"Didn't think we'd be gone this late," he managed, while from within I could catch cries of "Ough, Nat, get away!" and "You stink too much t' be my brotheh!"

"So much for the 'charm of goin' in circles," I said dryly; but he was too convulsed to retort.

Carrying out a final attempt at the wheels, I held the rail while Jim—fairly useless, due to incapacitating spells of laughter—tugged at Dee; then both of us pushed from behind—but it was clear we'd come to a halt. Totally soaked and mud-splashed to the waist, surrounded by the din of thunder and downpour, we looked at each other in the lurid flashes, me fit to be tied and Jim vivid with mischief; then I shook my head with wry awe at his spirit. "It's no use; we're hehre for the night; might as well make the best of it," I hollered, giving the rail a last kick with my boot; and openly grinning, Jim unharnessed Dee, and led her into the shelter of a grove.

In the lee of the *vardo* we pulled off all our outer clothes, hanging them in a clutter from the shutters and eaves, then standing out in the rain for a makeshift wash; then taking one last look at the van in the flashes—the whole crazy rig looking like some crash between a vendor's cart, a laundry tub and a kitchen cupboard—we hauled ourselves in to take care of Nat, and break the news we were bedding down in the reek.

Firing up the stove, we attempted to get dry in our under-flannels, at least to a tolerable degree of dampness—meantime pulling off shoes and stockings, plumping up beds and scrubbing down Nat, and sacrificing Courtney's nappie for a diaper. In all the accumulated reek of cooking, stale vomit and wet dog and soiled diaper and dishes—in all the jungle of tramped on bedding, hanging laundry and muddy carpets—Nat was the only one completely happy; and Jim, holding him by the stove in his wet under-flannels, surveyed the mess with a half-fond grin. "*Avali,*" he said, falling into his old tongue, "yes; *this* is what it used t' look like."

Gazing around at the wild scape of what had been—only a few hours ago—my magnificent birthday present; settling down next to him and warming my numb hands at the stove, while Tom, Jean and the twins fought under the blankets of the upper berth, I asked, "Is this really how it used t' be? How on eahrth did'je keep from killin' each otheh?"

"We didn't," he said cheerfully, cuddling Nat.

"You mean—?"

"A' course. My uncle a few years ago dispatched my aunt. Though everybody gave out she was indigested, we knew the pig poison'd ended up in her stew."

My hands poised at the stove I simply gawked at him, dumbfounded at the ludicrous sight of him in his wet undergear, glibly relating the details of a murder—and a family murder at that— in this storm-lurid hodgepodge of dishes and laundry; then as if the crazy events of the night had suddenly been put in a different perspective—a preposterous perspective which gave a slant of humor and hilarity not just to the everyday and mundane, but even to the solemn and lofty—I frankly yelped with pent-up laughter. Somehow catching my spirit the children laughed too, each with his own particular note and fashion, some giggling and chortling, others whooping and crowing; and shaking my head I said, "We betteh turn in; we're gettin' punchy, even though you brought no cideh, nor anything else hahrd t' drink."

Still rumbling and chuckling we climbed into our berths, Tom, Jean and the twins —all coveting the upper—crammed into its various ends and corners, me and Jim with Nat between us, tucking our sodden selves into the lower; and for a while there was considerable pitching and rolling as fourteen arms and legs sought nooks and crannies, or various heads ducked under the covers, usually to muffle peals of thunder.

Slanting in through the window a bit of moon revealed Jim, curled up on his side close by; and forestalling sleep I looked on his still face, half-turned toward me in the muted shadow. Usually so neat—liable to shave twice a day, even aboard ship, in any seas less than twenty feet—he now sported the smudge of a beard, or mud, or both, while his wild wet hair spilled onto the pillow. Yet there was a peacefulness on his face in the dim moon, a serenity which matched the tranquility in my heart; and I gazed on him, moved, unable to withdraw my glance—seeing things that, even after all this time, I had never really noted before.

In the uncertain light, under his eyes, there were smudges which were not the shadows of his thick lashes; and suddenly touched with concern for him, I ventured to whisper "Jamie?", not loud enough to waken if he was asleep.

Lifting the long lashes which were one of his chief charms, he drowsily smiled, and turned a little more towards me; and still whispering I inquired, "You feelin' all right?"

"Neveh betteh," he responded, mimicking my r's with a sly grin; then closing his eyes he half-drowsed again.

"Eben said you was mighty sick yestehday," I murmuringly insisted; and his lashes lifted and fell as he smiled at me.

"I'm fine, really."

"That new medicine help?"

"Aye; don't worry about me. It was nothing, really—just too much of your Pa's claret-punch."

"You Romany liah," I said, turning over; but I caught the answering gleam of his wry smile, as he slid wordlessly into sleep.

If getting to bed had been difficult, getting off again next day was more so; for the reek, not improved by a night at close quarters, and the addition of a wet diaper, still lingered; while there was little dry to wear, and still less available to eat. Some stale bread and plain tea in the early morning half-fog was the best we could offer the children, while Sam looked on in mournful disgust; and it was damned ineffective in manning two men to the task which awaited in the mud.

Of us all Dee was the only one who had an adequate meal, Jim having brought a huge bucket of oats; and I looked at him wryly while she ate her fill. Nor were our future circumstances such as to inspire cheer; for Tom, late for school, faced a charge for tardiness, while the rest of the family, no less delinquent, anticipated a feather-white Anne, and I, overdue at the yard, confronted a loaded desk.

Yet in the light of day, reinforced by a night's sleep, the job of un-miring the cart went easier than expected; and once on the main road we found the going better, the main challenge being to detour potholes, and find our way back through the maze of Jim's routes. Pulling up at Eben's to avoid shocking Anne more than necessary, we helped ourselves to a scrub and a brush, Jim and I thankfully changing clothes, and all of us enjoying space; then—having put a clean diaper of sorts on Nat, and washed and combed the rest to a degree—we walked over en masse to Anne, and cast ourselves on her icy mercy.

Unmoved by our tale, she thawed only a trifle, obviously holding me personally responsible for the storm, and eyeing Jim like a creature from some other planet; but caught up in her hurry to purge clothes and wash hair, and fumigate Seth and Nat of their ordeal, she said considerably less than she might have, or would later on when she caught her breath.

Slipping a freshly-dressed Tom into the buggy and a still-grinning Jim beside him, I clattered off for the school and yard post haste, the three of us devouring johhnycake as we went; and when Jim and I parted company at my desk, he looked as bright as if he'd spent the night at the Inn, singing out "Hope you enjoyed your joy ride, Pal; beats sailin' three laps in the teeth of a gale, don't it?", and dropping me a merciless wink over his shoulder.

Re-immersed in the complications of dredging the harbor and posting up various cargoes, I didn't see him again for a couple of days; and when I did it was in circumstances considerably less comic, if those just passed could indeed be described as funny. Getting ready to sign up *Abigail's* crew—expecting to clear for China in early December—I easily roped Eben into being first mate; and naturally I looked for Jim to tally on as second. So sure was I that he'd choose the berth in which he'd already met such success, and proved such a valuable addition to our leadership, that I even dissuaded others from signing, turning away such able hands as Jack Tupper and Percy Winslow, and mentally calculating plans based on Jim's abilities. Thus it was to my amazement, looking over the freshly signed Articles later on in the week, that I found Tupper's name penned next to second mate, and Jim's, further down, beside steward; and for a moment I simply couldn't take in what I saw, too stunned to even feel betrayed.

Stomping straight over to Seth's desk, where the book had been stationed, I collared Seth summarily from his work, and demanded to know how the mistake had occurred; but he calmly assured me that no error existed—that Tupper and Robertson had even approached him together, and taken on these berths by agreement. Too dumbfounded to answer—torching the Articles, throttling Tupper, or transporting Robertson straight back to Wales, all courses of action which silently flashed through my mind—I grimly picked up the book and stalked out; and marching directly over to the joiner's shop where Jim worked, I unceremoniously hauled him away from his tools, and speechlessly shook the pages at him.

"Robertson, what the sam hell is the meaning of this?" I bawled, managing to find my tongue in my anger, and vaguely aware of the dozen or so carpenters looking up from their work to indulge themselves in our confrontation.

"Of what?" he asked, trying to look innocent, but coming nowhere near to succeeding.

"Of *this*," I bellowed, opening to the Articles, and jabbing my finger at the freshly signed lines.

"It's the berth I want," he said blandly, looking where I pointed, and refusing to be perturbed by my outburst.

"The berth ye *want*?" I erupted, never in my life more confounded. "What about second mate? All this time I been expectin' ye t' tote the load with me!"

"I know it," he said fairly, beginning to look stubborn; "but this is more important."

"More important, hell! What's more important than shippin' as second mate? It's the berth that makes or breaks the ship!"

"There's otheh important ways of servin'," he insisted, the sapphire in those dark eyes taking on a dry sparkle, and that obstinate chin of his coming forward a trifle.

"Not t' match the mates there ain't!....Jim, this is my first run t' China; I been lookin' forwahrd t' youhr help!"

"Just the same, I'm shippin' as steward," he maintained; and now his chin was definitely jutting, while the dry sparkle in his eye was glinting with heat.

"Shippin' as...you....Jim, I ain't sayin' it don't have a prestige of sorts, but it's...damn, it's such a dihrty job!" I floundered, casting desperately around for reasons compelling enough to make him change his mind. "Cleanin' the waduh closet, washin' m' laundry, swabbin' the bath tub—think of all that Rom *mukado*! Not t' mention, you won't neveh use youhr seamanship—haul on the mainsheet in all hands work, that's it! It's crazy, man—ye can't possibly have any idear what you'hre doin'!"

"Oh, I can't, 'ey?" he flashed, getting angry, and all our spectators edging in with interest.

"Of course not!—you—why, anotheh voyage, an' you could go

for youhr first mate's papehs!"

"I ain't interested in bein' first mate."

"What d'ye mean?" I gasped, never having heard such like. "It's youhr chance t' advance—t' improve youhr standin'!"

"I ain't interested in advancin'."

I looked at him like this was the maddest thing I'd ever heard, too dumbfounded for a moment to spit out a reply. "Well, advancin' is how ye make more money!" I sputtered, certain that this logic, at least, would convince him.

"I ain't interested in makin' money."

"Why, you've got t' be interested in it, man—you spend it like waduh!"

At once his hands went to his hips and his dark blue eyes flared up like tinder. "That's my business, ain't it?" he snapped like a whip; and at the crack of his voice all hands drew in closer.

"What's youhr business is mine, an' always has been!" I cried, losing the thread of my argument with the fear that I'd never now be able to sway him.

"Damned if that gives you the right t' tell me what t' do!" he fired; and now I could see the blaze of his will—the all-to-familiar signal that my case was hopeless.

"I c'n tell ye what t' do if it's for youhr own good!" I hurtled, impatient.

"You don't have the pimp-payingest notion of what's for my good!"

Stung to the quick I simply flung out whatever came first to my heart and tongue: "I know betteh than you do what ye need—have eveh since the night I met ye!"

"You wouldn't know what I need if you met it on the street!"

Beside myself at losing him for the role I knew too well was indispensable to me— panicked at the thought I'd bitten off more than I could chew, with a bigger ship and a longer trek than any I'd sailed before—furious I'd not been able to bend him to my will, I simply instantaneously hit him, landing him one square on the jaw; then as he took a step back, his hand at his face—as our audience zealously gathered around, like so many tourists craning to see an accident by the road —I caught my breath; for I couldn't believe I'd struck him—I, who'd never before hit a man in my life, much less this one I'd have shed my heart's blood for.

For an instant his eyes proclaimed his hurt, a pain like no other I'd seen written on a face; then swift as a bolt came the look Eben'd seen in Rio, that Reuben and Sal'd probably seen on the dock in Portland—the volcanic rage of an alien, a stranger; and even as he coiled I realized I still didn't know him. Anticipating his strike I half-flinched in preparation, wondering what on earth I'd do if he drew a knife; but he didn't assault me with fists or a weapon—no, not in any ordinary gadje way; he simply hurled himself at my body, a hundred and ninety pounds of fury, knocking me full length on the floor; and before I could move he was on top of me, biting, scratching, kicking like a hellcat, while our onlookers roared out encouragements and wagers.

Nobody I'd ever known had ever fought this way before, without any concept of square play or standards; nothing was off limits— everything below the belt as fair game as everything above it; and no trick was too infantile or dirty. Though I had a good forty pounds on him, it was all I could do to grab an arm or a leg, or now and again a hank of cloth; and then all I got for my effort was an empty shoe or sock or waistcoat, for he slithered and twisted out of my hold as if he was greased. To pin him down, hold him still, if only long enough to gain some advantage or figure out what next to make for became my only design in being; while his seemed to be to change shape or locale just when I came closest to triumph. In his shirt sleeves and bare feet he fought on without restraint, as uncontainable as quicksilver— now sinking his teeth into my shoulder, now pulling my beard and scratching my eyes, butting me with his head or pummeling me with his fists, till I was forced to respond in kind, or forfeit all chance of bringing him to heel; and damned if I wasn't biting him in return, and kicking and scratching as if I was nine!

Beating him and pounding, or being pounded, I soon lost all track of whose blows were which, or whose arms and legs were flailing on what path; and for all I knew he was me, and I him, so equalized were we by the impacts of body. By the time I got his neckerchief in a grip and he my throat, or at least, my collar, I found to my amazement he was laughing—laughing! with the blood running down from his nose and mouth; and then I found I was laughing too, actually rolling on the ground laughing, as though I'd just had the best time in my life.

As if that weren't enough there was a mob of spectators four or five deep from all over the yard; and all of them were laughing too, all roaring and whooping and slapping their knees, as if this was the most hilarious display they'd ever seen; and the whistles and hollers echoed from one end of the shop to the other, and probably spilled out into the yardway.

Getting to our feet, we mopped our faces with handkerchiefs volunteered by the dozen; then as onlookers reluctantly began to break up, amidst chuckles and rumbles of "Damned if that wahrn't the best I eveh seen!"—as I finished pulling on my shoes, and began to search about for my hat—my gaze fell on Jim, opposite me, trying to catch his breath; and meeting my gaze, he smiled, his eyes shining.

"I'll be the best damn steward you ever had, I promise," he said, holding out his hand; and I just surveyed his face, shaking my head.

"You'll have t' do somethin' about the cut of youhr jib; I don't hire nobody with a mug like that," I said dryly.

"You did once b'fore," he reminded serenely, still patiently holding out his hand; and my heart suddenly cramped with the force of my love I not only accepted his hand but hugged him, drawing him to me right in front of the whole place; then smoothing my hair I picked up the Articles, and marched them back to their place on Seth's desk. Ignoring his exclamations at the sight of my face, I calmly pursued the rest of my day's work, now and then icing my eyes and my teeth; and that night at supper I brushed aside Anne's remarks about Jim's being the Devil Incarnate, tranquilly sipping my soup with a slow spoon, and retiring to bed with a poultice and hot ale.

That I'd never know what to expect from him—that I'd never really get a handle on him, or know him the way I'd once imagined, when I'd traversed his memories seeking clues, or the images of his trunk, that first night, searching landmarks—I'd by now pretty much concluded; and events soon bore out my opinion, for far from hostile and unbending, he next reversed himself completely, yielding himself up in a way I hadn't seen since that indescribable night off the Horn.

For a couple of days we'd tread lightly round each other, meeting now and again at the yard, and once sharing a brandy cider at Eli's; but too swamped with jobs to indulge in much leisure, I seldom had time for more than a few words with him; while he, needing work, was helping crew the steam derrick out in the harbor, and busy dawn to dusk with dredging. Mounted on a barge, and primitive in design, one of the few in operation on the coast, the derrick could only be operated in fine weather, its use in rough seas out of the question; and as we were caught up in a reasonably mild spell, he and the others were working it full time, trying to beat my late November deadline.

From time to time when I saw him, warming his hands at the counting house stove, and tipping his hat to me before going off to a late supper, I though he looked uncommonly fatigued —those dark circles under his eyes failing to fade with the bruises, and the other scratches and marks of our fight; and a pang of disquiet stirred in my heart, as I contemplated what they might portend. But that his health was declining—that he, with his fine constitution, was imperiled by some ill that wouldn't mend—I never fully appreciated, till one night, coming off the barge, the crew dispersed, one of them telling me Jim'd just gone home, unwell; and hot on his trail I made for the Inn, fearful with all the fears of the season, yet trying to reason my way out of their grip.

It being a raw night, the wind fresh off the bay, and coarse and wet with the coming of winter, I tightened my collar myself as I went; and as I came up on the entryway of the Inn, the arc-lights of the lamps swung crazily on the steps, the green and red feeble and bleak in the sea-gusts. Thankful to step within, where some semblance of warmth and the quiet, sane exchange of converse did something to soothe my senses, I hastened up the broad, carpeted stairs, passing women heavily dressed in capes and beaver bonnets; then mounting the next flight, I came up at last on Jim's door, which I unlocked myself and opened without knocking, in case he was already asleep.

Curled up in the armchair, which he'd dragged before the fire, and wrapped in every quilt he possessed, he seemed indeed to be dozing; and I knew at once—from the tense stiffness of his posture and the wan hue of his face, usually so brown and robust—that he had a severe chill, probably grippe. Keeping at bay thoughts of the diphtheria and lung fever already making inroads again into households, I quietly touched him and spoke his name; and when he didn't rouse I turned to the fire, stirring it up for all I was worth. Exposed to the northeast, our worst winter quarter, the room was chill with the damp and cold, the eaves vibrating with the rising wind, and the window frames whistling with each gust; and balancing a fortnight in this room against the risk of a ride out to Eben's, where warmer conditions prevailed, I got up from the hearth to find he'd opened his eyes, and was looking at me with grateful recognition.

Seen closer to those dark smudges under his eyes seemed to proclaim a crumbling defense, a resistance weakened by long-concealed strains, and by more obvious trials, such as his headaches; and frightened for him—longing now for the spit of his obstinacy, and the exasperating mettle of his maddening will—I plucked anxiously at the quilts around him. Yet looking up at me he conveyed a simple gladness for my presence, and a trustfulness which at once hearkened me back to the look he'd given me, that night I'd carried him to the sickbay aboard *Charis*; and even in my fear I was moved by his candor—one of the few glimpses I'd ever had into his unguarded spirit.

Stripped of my own guards by my sympathy I simply stroked his tumbled hair, trying to measure courses of action, and saying querulously, "Why didn't you boys send up a flare; if ye had, I'd of come out t' the barge m'self t' bring ye off."

Shaking his head as if any answer he might make would be too long for either his voice or strength, he closed his eyes and fell silent a moment, the only sound in the room the sough of the wind, and the kindly crackling of the fire; then lifting his glance once more he asked "Is this grippe?", his gaze meeting mine again with appeal.

"Probably," I said calmly, making every effort to believe it; "an' if it is, you'hre in for a spell: game for it?"

"Aye," he nodded, with a semblance of his old mettle.

"Listen t' me," I said, still bending over him, and all at once making up my mind what to do; "I'm goin' to get ye out of hehre, all the way out t' Eben's, where it's warmeh an' we c'n look afteh you: d'ye think that ye c'n stand the trip?"

Squaring his chin with another vague show of mettle he nodded; and giving his blankets a tug I went on, "I'm goin' t' go down an' rig Jimmy's carriage, an' drive you out t' Eben's m'self; now hang on here; I'll be right back."

Clattering down the stairs—fetching Jimmy out of the pantry, and getting him to make up hot bricks and flannels—I saw to the rig, harnessing it to my horse; then hurrying back up I roused Jim out of his slumber, unwrapping him and helping him to his feet.

"The fire," he said, taking an unsteady step toward it, as if long habit moved him to bank it; and steering him away, I held out his peacoat.

"Neveh mind that, or anything else; Isabel'll see to it as soon as we're gone," I soothed, helping him into the sleeves and tugging at the collar; then seeing he couldn't manage the buttons, I sympathetically did them myself, propping him between me and the back of the sofa. Trying to keep to his feet he waited, making an effort now and again to be useful; then taking me completely by surprise—the more so since, even ill, he'd shown restraint—he suddenly and wholly without warning leaned against me, bracing himself on my shoulder in so sweet a submission that my heart gave a twisting wrench in my chest. "Oh, Gawd, Jamie," I quavered, treasuring him in my arms as I had off the Horn, those unparalleled moments before the oblivion of sleep; and for a wordless moment we stood together, an immeasurable sureness steeling me.

As if somehow rested, and replenished with strength himself, he raised his head and stood apart from me, looking uncertainly about him; and raising his collar, I said, my voice shaking, "Whehre's youhr cap, honey?" So naturally did the word issue from me that I scarcely even noticed, preoccupied with caring for him; but he heard it, even in illness, his face suddenly touched; and his voice too faltered as he answered, "On the table."

Fetching the cap, I gave it to him—his face as he drew it on strained, as if he fought against feeling; and struggling myself—needing to find his other gear, but unable to trust my voice to ask for it—I turned away and rummaged in the wardrobe, sifting his clothes for his muffler and mittens. Coming back with them, I handed them over, snatching up spare comforters while he dressed; then giving him my arm, I helped him down the two flights of stairs, bracing him while he clutched the rails. Finding Jimmy ready for us I bundled him straight into the carriage, where a battery of hot bricks and flannels awaited; and surrounding him with them, I closed him safely inside, then climbed up and took the reins.

Clattering down roads rutted and frozen, we rattled and swayed for a quarter hour, me trying to avoid the frozen ruts, and by the time we reached Eben's, pulling up close to the porch, and I reached within to help him to his feet, I found him nearly asleep in the blankets, only half-conscious between fatigue and fever. So far gone was he that it took Eben and I both to get him out of the carriage and into the house; but when we'd finally succeeded and were met by the warmth typical of the stout, log structure, I was thankful we'd made the trip.

Settling him in Eben's room, the most sheltered and easiest to heat in the house, I poured a drink and waited, anxious, while Eben fetched his kit and looked him over.

"Well?" I asked at last, unable to wait any longer, and crossing over to him as soon as he'd snapped his bag.

"He's in for a spell; but he'll weatheh it all right," assured Eben, calm and imperturbable as ever.

"What about his throat?" I pressed, anxious.

"Thehre's no sign of it," he answered, knowing what I feared.

"Thehre's two or three houses in quarantine hehre already; an' Asiatic cholera in Searspohrt—I just heard."

"I know it; but let's not borrow trouble. Thehre's plenty o' this hehre gripped goin' round; an' he shows every symptom of it."

I heaved myself into the armchair by the fire and downed the rest of my drink as I settled. "I'll set up with him first—I'm too nerved up t' sleep yet," I offered, searching my pockets for my pipe and pouch.

"All right, I'll send word oveh t' Anne; but call me t' take my turn around midnight, an' see to it y' get some rest youhrself."

I gave him a cursory nod, throwing another anxious look at the bed; and he hesitated at the door.

"Now don't fret none about him, Ben," he said mildly, looking me over with concern. "His health ain't what it was last year, but he's still got what it takes; an' I calculate he knows you'hre settin' up with him." Glancing swiftly over at him I searched his face, but he simply cast me his usual benign smile; then catching up a few spare blankets from the chest, he went to bed himself down on the sofa.

We took it in turns the next several days, Eben staying home from work to nurse Jim, and me taking over around suppertime for the evenings, and one or the other of us checking on him during the nights, at least early on, when his condition was worst. Due to leave for Portland to wrap up business, several of *Abigail*'s cargoes originating from there—expected already at Elkanah's, where Pa and Joseph were established loading freight, and getting impatient for my appearance—I kept postponing my departure, not wanting to leave till I saw Jim was recovering. So ill was he at first that he scarcely knew I was around, delirious in sleep and blurrily vague when awake; but there were times when he woke up half-there, his blue eyes above his dark beard searching for me, and a radiant smile spreading over his face, whenever his gaze fastened upon me; and I wouldn't have missed that light of recognition for all the tons of freight in Portland. There were times too when my touch seemed to serve him the same way—times when he knew me simply by the brush of my hand, as I helped him to drink or shifted the pillows; and no satisfaction in work could equal the pride I felt in knowing he depended on me. On other occasions, coming clumsily out of slumber, he would rouse to mumble requests in Romany, or ramble as he had when ill with fever after Havana; and there was no match for the leap which raced through my veins when I found that I could understand him, even answer him in his own tongue.

"Ben," he would quaver, rousing vaguely from sleep—from one of the unhappy dreams which plagued him, or from the pain which he bore with his habitual restraint—"Tu san akai?", "Are you here?"; and I would answer proudly, "Avali," protectively anchored there at his side. Sometimes it was only a word he spoke—sometimes just "pani," and I'd bring him water; sometimes it was "My sherro dukkers," and I would bring him powders for the pain. Now and again it was I who asked, "Si tut bokalo?", tempting him with a bowl of broth, and he who answered with a shake of the head; other times he'd be alert enough to ask, "So se tute's kairing?" as I knelt by the hearth or poured over a book, and I would reply with the half-Romany, half-English gibberish not uncommon even to the Rom: "I'm kairing the yag" or "Just reading a lil."

Once as I drew on my coat and he saw me, I told him gently, "I'm jawing keri now," going home—though more and more home meant where he was; and sometimes I simply sat and listened to the peregrinations of his murmurs, managing to understand memories of the heath and moor, of roads and seas and rivers traveled—or the ring of the river buoys through the banks of the sea mist, rising up from the drifting streams of the Mersey.

When he was well enough to correct my grammar, or smile at my pronunciation—when he was improved enough to sit up against the pillows, and order me to mix up putrid potions, elixirs of leaves and stems and what-not he had me fetch from his cupboard at the Inn, in lieu of Eben's medications—when he was recovered enough to actually drink the vile stuff, without relapsing into illness—I knew I could postpone Portland no longer; and I took leave of him one mid-November morning when he was unaware in slumber: looking down on his dark, thick lashes and the curve of his fine, wide brow, before consigning him to Eben's care, then catching a south-bound schooner in the bay.

I hadn't been gone twenty-four hours—hadn't been a day installed in Elkanah's madhouse, with its perpetual breakfasts and high teas and luncheons, and its rafts of visitors and relations—before I missed him acutely; and I pursued my work with irritated distraction. Never separated from him before, except during last year's run to

Havana—never further than a few minutes from him, and usually within sight or hail—I hardly knew how to get on without him; for even if I hadn't seen him every day, I'd always known that he was within reach, and liable to pop up any moment. Now I longed for his irrepressible spirit, which found humor in the most aggravating situations; longed for his exasperating mercuric changeableness, as one would long for a tonic in weakness, or the warmth of the sun after the bleak blows of winter.

Caring little for hogsheads and hatches—caring still less for the ceaseless receptions presided over by Agatha and my cousins—I plowed through the mails which came from New York and the north, hoping for news from Eben as to his health, or epistles from anyone retailing anecdotes of his doings; and hence it was with a bound in my chest that I found, not very long before Thanksgiving, a pale blue missive which proclaimed with its script that it was from none other than Jim himself. Having never had a written word from him—save his brief note about liberty day in Havana last year, and even briefer scrawls left on my desk, by which he returned his wages or otherwise thumbed his nose at me—I pounced upon his letter with delight, studying the envelop, running my eyes over its address, even scrutinizing the seal for some hint of its sender; but I forbore to open it for hours, carrying it instead in my waistcoat pocket, till I could find a place alone to read it.

As if it were fuel, it inspired me in my work all morning, causing me to accomplish more in the space of a few hours than I had in the whole week I'd been there, and filling my mind with so many alternate imaginings of what he had said and how he had said it, that I felt almost beside myself in my labors. When at last—late that afternoon—I borrowed a horse, and rode out of town to a quiet inlet, where I sat down alone with a belated sandwich, my fingers actually quaked as they fumbled in my waistcoat, and drew the envelope out of my pocket.

Propping it against my knees, I read again every word on the envelope—slowly scanned the strong, slanting script, even dallying before breaking the seal:

Capt. Benjamin G. Melchett
c/o Capt. Elkanah Melchett
124 Congress Street
Portland,
Maine

Satisfied at last I hadn't missed so much as a comma, I slit the wax and drew out a pair of neatly written blue pages, my heart picking up speed as I noted their length, and spread them carefully upon my knee; then holding them against the searching gusts of the wind, I read with a broadening smile the following message:

21 November 1843
Cape Damaris
Dear Ben:—
I'm up and about and (though this will make you hopping mad) back out on the barge, the weather holding off for the time being. Another two or three days and we'll be through to the buoy, at five fathoms deep the whole length of the channel. If it doesn't commence to storm we should be able to wrap things up not very long after Thanksgiving, as per orders. Hope *Abigail* appreciates all our labors.

Not much in the way of excitement has happened here since you left. The harbor's looking fairly empty; a lot of vessels cleared last week (21), and not many are posted due. Eben and the chandlers have been stocking *Abigail,* and they're about the only ones doing out there besides us on the barge, the *Bangor* now and then, and the fishing smacks.

This past weekend we had another freak thundershower, like the one that damped us down that night in the *vardo,* and there was no preaching Sunday. Took the roads two days to settle. At the height of things the general store was struck, the bolt coming right down the stairs and knocking over a counter, and busting open a cask of brandy, which caught fire. The temperance societies (all four) seized on this as an act of the Almighty, and word has it next Sunday Rev. Brewster'll capitalize on it. Eli immediately mixed up a new drink, the brandy sizzler, in honor of the occasion, and won't tell anybody what's in it. A few folks've informed him he's bound for some place hotter than the Equator, but he doesn't appear to be too worried about it. Haggai, though, has sworn off drink, and walks up and down in front of Eli's and the Seven Seas, scaring off business. Last I heard, Eli had plans to roast him for Thanksgiving.

I'm due for turkey dinner next Thursday with Eben at Obed's, about 30 McCabes expected in attendance, though where we'll all sit I haven't figured. According to rumor even Charlie and clan are expected over from the island, if he can navigate the channel. Eben's not sure he can find the harbor, even sober. With Effie cooking and the likes of Lem and Obed for entertainment—not to mention me on the fiddle—the affair ought to be a capital success, worthy of a column in the *Recorder*.

And now I suppose you're having a rich time at Elkanah's? Living in the lap of luxury, eating dinner with four forks, and all the other customs dear to your heart? Eben says not to worry, Elkanah's got the best wine cellar in Portland, but still I can't help but wonder if you've managed to keep from throttling Reuben, to say nothing of Sal and company. You're such a hot-headed bastard. If you scrap with Sal, take note: he's got an uncommonly quick left.

As for me, I think my right canine's less loose than it was, and all the other effects of your drubbing have faded. Eben says I eat enough for ten men, so apparently I've overcome grippe as well. It's payday Friday, I expect a few dollars for freezing out on the barge. What can a man want more?

Just the sight of you. Jean says to say you can't come home soon enough, and I can't add that I disagree. Tell Elkanah to finish his own damned loading, and catch the next boat back. Eben pledges to try his hand at another cake, and there'll be a glad welcome from

Your *prala*—Jim

So strong a gust of his vibrant person—warm with cocky, playful affection—blew over me with the words of this letter, that I read it not once but many times, testing each line for sentiment and feeling, and searching for indications that he missed me—that he was as lame without me as I was without him. Then leaning against a ledge of rock, I dreamed for a while on the island-packed bay, the letter actually warming my pocket. Next to me branched a low, stunted rosebush—not likely to grow any taller or fuller, but hardy from its hold in the granite, and leafy still, though its blossoms were done; and as if it sensed and shared my bright glow, it took on a kind of presence beside me, a sympathetic force which caused me to turn to it, and touch its leaves as if they were fingers. Marveling at the life coursing in it—sensing that it, too, throve and flourished in its way, even rejoiced like a sentient being—I stroked the fading leaves, noting their serrated edges, and feeling an uncanny communion of friendship; then breaking off at last from our wordless converse— giving a final reluctant pat to a branch, as if I would miss its kindly commerce—I got to my feet and remounted my horse, riding back into town at a slow, even pace.

Too moved within to attend to small talk at Elkanah's, or concentrate on the amenities of another high tea, I simply dashed through the door and up the staircase, not caring if my eruption was visible to all in the drawing room; and taking cover in my private guest chamber, I cast myself down in the chair at the desk, and helped myself to the supplies in the drawer.

Not since Bowdoin had I put pen to paper for any reason other than to add up a column of figures, fire off an invoice or draft a letter of credit; and words didn't come freely now from long disuse— nowhere near as easily as the thoughts came to my mind, or as the news had come to Jim's breezy letter. Nonetheless I managed, after an hour of effort, to marshal together a few adequate lines, and slip them into the mail in the hall basket; then wolfing down a plate of odds and ends in the pantry—avoiding, again, a formal supper with the family, about the seventh I'd managed to boycott—I crept back up the darkened stairs to my chamber, and slipped into bed with Jim's letter close at hand.

Whether it was due to the energy of Jim's words, or to the warmth which still lingered from the days I'd cared for him—whether it sprang from my need to see him, or from some inexplicable gift of vision—I fell into a vivid dream, so immediate that I felt I was waking. I was standing at the train depot, ready to take the cars home, though no line as yet ran to Cape Damaris; and Jim was there beside me—a novice, like me, at train travel. Why he was in Portland in the first place, and why we were now going home together, was unexplained; but we were both dressed in our best, taking leave of Elkanah with satchels in our hands, as if we'd been here for some time; and Eben too was traveling with us. I felt worn out, not just from work but from contact with people, as I always did after a stay at Elkanah's; while Jim too looked tired, not entirely well from his illness; and though he bore his fatigue with restraint, I knew he was eager to settle down in the cars, and begin the lengthy journey home.

Boarding from the rear, we followed the conductor to our seat, toward the front of one of the cars; another seat faced it, and on this Eben lighted, while Jim sat down next to the window, and I took the place beside him. Gathering speed our train left Portland, with the usual ungodly commotion and clanking; but so glad was I to be near Jim—to feel the press of his shoulder against mine, and the vivid potency of his person—that all the noise and smoke and soot, and even the chattering of the passengers, faded away into a vagueness.

As we went along I was more and more conscious of my immediate surroundings—of the worn horsehide which covered the seats, of the prick of its nap and its dusty smell, of the bit of embroidery on which my head rested; but above all I was aware of Jim's closeness. His crisp white collar and shirt-front, well-starched; his greyish-blue traveling suit, smartly tailored; his newly-trimmed hair, so precise round the ears; his freshly-shaved face, straight nose, sensitive brow; his strong, shapely hands, now at rest on his lap: each in its turn cut keenly upon me. Self-contained, he seemed almost asleep, his eyes now and then closing as he gazed out the window; but within him I sensed an alertness to match mine; for from his body emanated such an awareness—such a consciousness of *me*, that I could almost see the radiance between us.

With a wrench in my heart I wanted to touch him—wanted to search that crisp dark hair, those delicate creases at his eyelids; and I sensed that, though he sat with restraint, he was fighting the same yearning—felt that he longed to surrender to me, as he had that night when I'd buttoned his coat. For an unmeasured time we traveled thus, neither of us stirring or moving; then all at once, as had happened in his room, he simply, sweetly capitulated—laying his head upon my shoulder as if he could no longer help himself, and nestling there with his smooth hair near my face; and in the rush of his warm touch and confiding closeness—in the race of his confession made not just before me, but before a crowd of onlookers—suddenly, unarguably, I knew.

I knew we were lovers, that we always had been, though I hadn't as yet dared to lay a hand on him; knew that I loved him, knew—even more incredibly—that he loved me; knew it as simply, as sweetly, as plainly as I knew my name, or the shape of my hand. So overpowering was this onrush of knowledge and the blaze of joy that came with it that instantaneously I was awake, sitting up in bed and feeling the pillows in a confusion at my surroundings; then recalling every detail of the dream—re-living it so as not to forget it—I felt a wild flame of excitement sweep me; and at once I was up and pacing about, too exhilarated to sleep.

Though it still lacked a couple of hours to daybreak I hurriedly dressed in the dim light of my lamp, which cast a quivering dance on the wallboards; then, ravenous, I sneaked down to the pantry, where I filched some bread and cheese from the pie safe—the servants, just stirring, happening in on my stealth, and eyeing me as if I were a crazed man. Longing to get out into the open—feeling I would suffocate if I stayed indoors—I erupted onto Congress Street and half-raced down to the wharves, gnawing my chunk of bread as I went: the southwest gusts of the wind carrying me on, and tantalizing me with their unseasonal tang. Craving the sights and sounds of the harbor, I arrived, panting, on one of the piers, where I bought up smoked herring—all that I could afford, since I'd come away with only the change in my pockets—from one of the early morning vendors; then wrapping the fish in my remaining bread slice, I paced the wharf from one end to the other, without the slightest aim or direction: eating my fish, when I thought of it, from my hand, and watching the dawn slowly flurry the skies.

Whirling above in hungry curtains and clouds, the seabirds mewed and clamored and screeched—gulls, terns, cormorants variously hunting the tide-wrack, or diving amongst the schooner and yawls; while pedestrian crowds—pilots, fishermen, stevedores, seamen—irresistibly began to collect on the planks, as if drawn, like me, to the stir in the east. Slowly pinkening the hem of the sky, the light began to gleam on the horizon, glistening upon the backs of the windswells, and flushing with rose the wan sails of the fleet; then gradually irradiating the heavens, it imparted its luminescence to all—sparking in the deadest wood a shimmer, till pilings, buoys, masts and hogsheads, planks and casks alike began to throb, even beat with an inner incandescence.

Ignited myself, like the faces around me, I paced in and out of the oystermen and dockhands, whose seasoned, knotty features breathed the dawn air; and longing to escape from the throngs for a moment, and commune alone with the blaze in my breast—having already abandoned the thought of working today—I rushed back to Elkanah's with the wind at my heels, saddled a horse under the nose of the groom, and rode to the quiet inlet where I'd yesterday sat and read Jim's letter in the lee of the rocks.

Arriving at high tide, the swells fresh and strong, I threw myself bluntly down on the ledge, and rocked to and fro next to my kindly rosebush; and alone, yet befriended, I looked back on my dream, and hugged my new knowledge close to my chest. In those early hours of my understanding, I felt a simple exhilaration—uncomplicated by doubts and fears, and unclouded by considerations of past and future; and I let myself drift and flow with the eddies which swept and battered my limbs in their swift course. I was in love!—frankly, wholly in love—I, who'd never imagined that I'd ever know the sweet elation of such abandon—I, who'd never dared risk jettisoning myself for another, or made myself available to the chance in the first place. The practical fancy I'd felt for Anne, the youthful mystique I'd known with Susannah, the boyish attractions I'd entertained from the distance of a school desk or a sidewalk or a meetinghouse pew—all faded and paled before the power of this newly unfettered emotion; and I simply gave myself up to its potence as to the force of a sea at my head.

He was mine, he belonged to me; he'd never belonged, never could belong to any other; how could I have failed to realize the mating which had been working its way since I'd met him? What it all meant, or would come to mean—that I was married, not free to love another, much less another who was a man—none of it posed a threat at the moment; it only mattered that I loved him, and knew it; that I wanted him with a yearning and fire like no other I'd ever conceived. Awakened now to my fascination, I wanted to know him, know every inch of his body, know him as the imaginary lovers in my fantasies knew him; knew he wanted to know me, always had; and swept with reactions too many to sort I simply laughed, laughed wildly, swaying there restlessly on the rocks. Then getting to my feet I paced to and fro in the bubbling hiss of the backwash, heedless of shoes, stockings and pantlegs; talked to myself like a babbling brook, recalling past events in swift succession, and abusing myself for not understanding sooner.

The blaze of his eyes that first night at Toby's—the protectiveness I'd felt, guarding him by the fire at Hannah's—our communion atop Corcovado—his confiding clasp in illness aboard *Charis*—the intimacy of his nearness in the tent, on the beach or camping by the river—his homing in my arms off the Horn: all came back and suffused me with the wonder and certainty I knew in their wedlock.

Overcome with a fullness too great to bear I passed imperceptibly from laughter to tears, sitting back down next to my friendly rosebush, and brushing my hot face against its sharp leaves; wept with a wrenching that plucked and tore, bowing my head on the rock at its roots, and cooling my cheek on the rough slab of granite. I'd cried once before, a year ago now, with my arms about the young beech in Eben's woods, in the void of Jim's absence after the tent trip; so surely there was nothing shameful in crying into the wintry thorns of a rosebush; and I abandoned myself to its ragged branches, as if it could hear and understand me.

Coming half-dazedly out of my retreat—smarting with a hunger I'd seldom felt before—I climbed onto my horse and rode back to Elkanah's, bent on sneaking a bit of luncheon, as I hadn't cash enough in my pockets to buy one; and slipping into the back door I crept up the servants' stairs, thinking of hiding till the midday meal was done. Half-way up to my chamber I heard the bell, and the creak of the floor as booted feet sought the dining-room; while from the pantry came the strident notes of Pa's bark, interrogating one of the maids as to my moves. Realizing they must be wondering why I hadn't been to work—anticipating they'd soon by wondering again, as I felt suffocated by the very thought of cargo, and had no intentions of showing up to help load this afternoon—I peeked over the main rail as they glided into the table; then seeing they were all— servants included—occupied, I tiptoed on up the hall to my room.

Dressing myself in a few more layers—remembering a shirt this time, though distaining a collar—I struggled with fingers still clumsy and quaking, now exasperated by buttoning, now stuffing and tugging; then too restless to wait for luncheon to finish—thinking of snatching a bite to eat in a tavern—I scrambled in the desk drawer for a bit more money, not failing to pick out coins of substance.

Replenished, I began to sneak back toward the hall, passing my dresser mirror on the way; and pausing a moment to peer into its depths—recalling it was perhaps time to run a brush through my hair—I gaped, astonished at my reflection. The hair, of course, I'd seen wild before, since it almost always looked like a gale of wind had blown it, even when I'd spent the day indoors; and the suit of clothes appeared no worse than usual, that is, as if I'd just come in from the woods. But the gaze—good God! and the expression! these were certainly enough to catch notice. Were these riotous eyes, reflecting abrupt shifts of thought, and these hectic features, expressing blunt swings of mood, those of Ben Melchett, the stolid shipwright? No wonder passersby looked at me like one succumbed! Checking another headlong wave of hilarity, I clapped my pilot's cap onto my head, and gave a bow to the apparition in the mirror; then slithering along the creaking hallway, I surreptitiously navigated the back stairs.

On my way out the back door—within inches of freedom—I heard the maid call "Cap'n Melchett?", her voice alive with inquiring interest; but since there were five or six Captain Melchetts in the house, I found it convenient to presume she meant someone else; and making a dash for the stable lane, I followed it post haste into the street.

Consumed with hunger, but having no idea where to eat, or where to shop where I wouldn't be recognized—equally ravenous by now to see Jim, to look on him with the light of new knowledge—I ended up back on the wharves, buying up herring from a different vendor, and sampling steamed clams with gratified vigor. Peering through the vapor which rose from the vats, I spied, on the horizon, the curl of steam which heralded the approach of the *Bangor*; and realizing it would make its return trip in a couple of hours—recalling it would touch briefly at Cape Damaris, before steaming on its way to Bangor—I jumped up from the hogshead on which I was sitting, and began to pace again with excitement.

True, I had no baggage with me, not so much as a toothbrush to take home; true, I lacked collar and cuffs, and looked like an escapee from the nearest asylum; true too, I'd always sworn never to take a steamer, and would probably cause my home port to faint, if I stepped off onto the town wharf from one. But if I climbed aboard now—just spontaneously took off, and impulsively appeared in Cape Damaris—I could spend nearly the whole weekend at home; could visit with Jim by the hearth at Eben's, or at our favorite table at Eli's; could see with my own eyes the face I now only dreamed of, and touch with my hand the man I imagined. What in blazes I would do when I saw him, didn't matter in the least to me; that I'd left no word of my intention with Elkanah, and that by nightfall they'd probably be dragging the harbor, or running to the constable to get up a search, mattered nothing to me either; it only mattered—urgently, simply—that I see him; and before I knew it I'd marched up to the office, and bought myself a four dollar ticket.

Pacing to and fro I watched the *Bangor* approach, enlarging at first by miniscule notches, then at last looming broad by the wharfside; and sitting down on a bench for a rest I watched the gangway come down with a thump, and the crowd of passengers debark. Mostly ladies and gentlemen of means from Bangor, they came off in a swarm of great coats and top hats, beaver bonnets, wool capes and flounced skirts; and watching them disperse I waited, impatient, tapping my boot restlessly on the planks. Counting the hats, the valises, the canes, then reckoning how many hours till I was home, I tried to speed up time to a degree; but stopping short, I jumped to my feet, startled out of my calculations; for there coming towards me—checking his initial path towards the street, and angling off in my direction—was a tall, blue-coated, tarpaulin-hatted sailor, whose jaunty walk and joyous expression could only proclaim him as dapper Jim.

Blithely unconscious of the importance of his advent—wholly unaware of the upheaval in me, and of the astonishment he'd triggered by his arrival—he walked up to me with a breezy wave, looking very well pleased with himself; and trying to rally my scattered defenses I stood staring at him, speechless. Fresh-cheeked, neckerchiefed, pea-coated, with a canvas seabag slung over one shoulder, he looked like the seaman I'd always known—looked carefree and offhand despite his glad grin, and the eager light of recognition on his face; and taking heart from his jaunty ease I struggled to look merely like an old friend, speechlessly pleased with an unexpected meeting.

Taking a step toward him, I held out my hand, on the point of actually choking out a greeting; but as he swept off his hat and accepted my clasp, and I saw that he had just had his hair cut, precisely as I'd seen in my dream, my heart collided again with my ribs; and any words I'd come up with immediately fled.

"What's the matter with you? You look like you've just seen a haunt," he sported, glancing over his shoulder as if he expected to catch a glimpse of something filmy and white disappearing.

"It's just...I'm s'prised t' see you," I gasped, wondering if anything casual had come out with my croak, and if my heart was written as plainly on my face as it felt. "I....I neveh expected t' see you get off a steameh."

"I never expected t' see you get *on* one," he grinned, looking at the ticket in my hand. "Elkanah-sick, or homesick, or what?"

"A bit o' both," I hoarsely got out; and catching my gaze, he looked curiously at me. Bareheaded in the sun, windblown and fresh, he was handsomer than I'd ever seen him—handsomer, and more cheerfully self-confident; and I broke off my glance in consternation. That I loved him, and rejoiced in it, I was still entirely sure; but I was not at all certain now of his sentiments toward me. It was one thing to wake up sure from a dream, and another to behold him standing unconcerned here in the bright November sunlight; and I floundered lamely with my misgivings. His head thrown back in gamesome delight, this man looked to be anything but pining, for me or anybody else; and I felt idiotic that I'd ever thought so.

"What's youhr excuse for spendin' four dollahs, an' comin' all the way up hehre?" I plowed on, breaking the silence before it became painful; and he stood back on his heels, looking at me.

"Well, I came t' tell you some news in person; figured it'd go better that way than in a letter," he offered, sticking his hands a bit awkwardly in his pockets.

So uppermost in my mind was the state of our feelings that I wildly wondered if he'd come to confess that he loved me; but trying to preserve some shred of reason, I simply asked, "Everything all right to home?"

"Oh, at home, o' course—they're all fine. I've got a pocketful of drawings from Tom and Jean, an' a note from Anne," he soothed easily. "No, it's about the barge."

"The barge?" I gaped, trying to remember what on earth he was referring to, the dredger's every existence having slipped from me. "What's wrong?"

"Well," he said, his chin coming up a hair, and his eyes taking on a half-guilty, half-mirthful sparkle, "it seems there was a bit of an accident."

"What kind of an accident?" I yelped, my lameness for the time swallowed up in my concern.

"The kind where the derrick slips off int' the harbor."

I gawked at him with my jaw on my chest, too taken aback to make connections. "You mean—it's—"

"Sitting on the bottom, aye," he said flatly.

"All the way undeh—the whole thing?" I got out, wildly trying to calculate how much it was worth, and how much I was liable for in damages.

"Well, all but the top; that part sticks up kind of like a sea monster."

Immediately I received a mental image of ten feet or so of iron neck protruding above the grey swells of the harbor; and that, with my dream, and the astonishment of Jim's presence, was enough to trigger a tidal wave of laughter somewhere in the depths of my middle. "Twelve hundred dollah's worth of...an' all ye c'n see is the top?" I quavered, trying to preserve at least a semblance of sternness.

"Look at it this way, it'll make a great aid t' navigation," he offered.

On the point of erupting with helpless guffaws, I just stood looking at him, quaking. "An' I don't s'pose *you* had somethin' t' do with this?" I cracked.

"I'm sorry t' say I had quite a lot t' do with it, since I was at the gears at the time: aye," he confessed, his lips twitching beneath the serene glee of his eyes.

About to choke on my gusts of suppressed mirth, I was forced this time to remain speechless.

"You c'n take it out of my wages," he suggested, cheerful.

"I can if ye live t' be four hundred years old, yes!" I roared, a monumental laugh at last surfacing; and seeing me give way, he let go with his own, the two of us peeling like bells on the pier. If I had looked fairly beserk before, with my riotous eyes and rabid pacing, the two of us together must have appeared truly outlandish; and then, too, there was the preposterousness of how I must have looked to Jim—I, who in the fresh throes of knowledge only wanted to appear at my best. Unkempt, unshaven, slovenly dressed, and reeking of a day's worth of herring, I must have looked and smelled like a bait boat, rather than a prospective lover; but even that realization only made me succumb to additional gales of laughter.

Subsiding at last, I took him by the shoulders, and shook my head at the picture before me—the very image of irrepressible caprice; and looking back at me, he candidly grinned—no more governable now than he ever had been. For a moment we simply regarded each other, our chests still heaving from our mirth; then catching my breath,

I managed to gasp, "Have ye eaten anything lately?"—spasms of hunger once again assailing my middle.

"Not since four this mornin', though Eben packed me a bite for the steamer," he answered, still panting as he pulled on his hat; and spying a tavern across from the wharf head, I straightaway draped an arm about him, and tugged him summarily across the street.

Though it was a fairly unruly den, semi-dark with smoking lanterns, and boisterous with the rowdy hoots of seamen, it was filled with the tempting aromas of chowder, lobster and cod cooked every which way; and not about to be choosy we sat down in a corner, and ordered everything on the menu. Our plates overflowing, and our glasses ditto, we indulged ourselves for a couple of hours: Jim regaling me with the full tale of the barge, or breezy news from each of the children, and me—no longer intent on going home, since home had just come here to me—listening and laughing at his carefree stories.

Though my initial astonishment at his arrival had faded, my eagerness at seeing him had increased—my eyes calm enough now to take in details; and I sat looking at him above my fork, noting the curl of a tendril of hair, or the mercurial blue glints of his gaze, as if I had never seen them before. Through the haze of oil lamps and acrid tobacco, his words and features cut vividly at me; and I lingered on each of them hungrily—trying to cover my fervent glances by darting off to the fireplace or rafters, and refusing to meet his eyes for long, for fear he'd stumble onto my secret.

That I wasn't actually my old self, I could see he'd already perceived—not just because of my spasmodic manner, but because of my unaccustomed vagueness; and more than once I found him staring curiously at me. Having no news about work, since I'd done little, or about Elkanah's household, since I'd scarcely seen them, and never once taken a meal with them, I could barely answer his questions; and I didn't improve the picture any by abstaining from hard spirits. When I passed my quota for the first time since our bargain, he promptly covered my mug with his hand; but I brushed it aside, muttering "Should've set a time limit," and helped myself to more; and his lips twitching at the corners, he grudgingly gave in, with a darksome hint or two about the future.

Finding it helped me to feel less self-conscious, I kept right on to the bottom of the decanter—Jim making no effort to keep up with me, but looking indulgently on from his plate; till finally—my cheeks beginning to burn above my beard, and my talk tumbling out wholly unconnected—he quietly asked, "Ben, are you quite all right?"—his words falling clearly in on my ears' roar. Somehow I knew, even half seas over, that he meant something other than my drunken state; but mimicking his answer to me in the vardo, I simply bawled, "Shure, shure, neveh betteh"; and stifling his grin, he subsided into his glass.

Intent on seeing me home—no easy undertaking, since it was now late and snowing thickly, and neither one of us was clear on our direction—he managed to steer me onto the street, and get the tavern door closed behind us; then propelling me forward he asked "Now tell me, which way is Elkanah's"—his laughter unmistakably shaking his hands.

"He's up there somewhere," I gestured, including the whole of what I thought was the hill in my arm's sweep.

"Up there by the signal tower?"

"Sounds right," I traipsed, clutching him to keep my keel.

"Congress Street…that's the name of his street, ain't it?" he persevered, panting as he helped me stumble along.

"Sounds familiah…why don't we ask?"

"Benjamin, anybody we ask'll think that we're drunk!"

"Well, we are, ain't we?"

On we trudged, following a course more or less uphill, to judge from the way the streets rose up at me—the driving snow gusting about us in whirlwinds, and a feeble window looming up at whiles through the blur, or a horse clattering by on the icy cobbles. Sloshing and sliding myself, and more than once needing to be picked up, I all at once cried out "Why, that's his gate!", dropping anchor abruptly by a white post; and puffing up beside me Jim gasped, "It is? Are you sure? How could you possibly know?"—his voice rising skeptically over the wind's howl.

"I recognize them mermaids on the gateposts," I bellowed, patting one of them on the head.

"Melchett, this better be right, or we'll be arrested for bustin' in on somebody else's house!"

"It's right, I tell ye, it's right," I trumpeted, half-dragging, half-leaning on him up the walk; and stumbling like a battalion of men on the verandah, we arrived pell mell at the door, where I triumphantly sounded the knock. Admitted by the butler, we erupted clamoring into the hall, me stomping my boots and beating my hat, and Jim fervently gesturing me for silence; and following his gaze I clapped eyes on the drawing room, where a sea of silks and brocades suddenly hushed, and paused gaping at us, cups mid-air.

"Y'see, what'd I tell ye? They'hre havin' anotheh one o' them damn teas!" I bawled, half-stomping in toward the doorway to see better; and Jim's arm desperately headed me round for the stairs.

"Aye, Ben, I see—keep movin' now," came his voice, quavering with helpless laughter; but even as he dragged me I made everyone a sodden bow, nearly hauling him over with me in my effort.

"They have them damn teas everyday, that's why I ain't ate here," I bellowed, as the stair carpet began to rise up in my face; and I felt Jim's body shake with hilarity against mine. "Fine, hush now, up the stairs now, come on," recited his voice, while a swarm of faces collected below us.

"Y' have t' dress for 'em, an' I hate it," I bawled on, the faces getting smaller as I mounted, for the most part on my hands and knees.

"I'm sure they know it," gasped Jim's voice, desperate, while he struggled to haul me in one piece to the top; "now, which way is your room?"

"Down that way somewhere," I gestured, wondering if we were being followed by any of the swarm, and recollecting suddenly, "Say, I should've interduced you."

"They'll meet me soon enough… Is this place your room?"

"It is if it's got one o' them gawddam beds that looks like it could get up an' walk," I blared; and as he peeked in to check someone looked up the hall toward us—some tall, well-dressed spark steering a course for the party.

"So *that's* what ye've been up to all day!" scowled a voice which sounded even more displeased with me than usual, and which I gradually managed to recognize as Joseph's; "should've known that this limejuicer'd be behind it!"

"What d'ye mean?" I barked, feeling my wits swing into focus, and resisting Jim's insistent tug into my room.

"I mean he's always got ye sidetracked someplace ye shouldn't be," hurtled Joseph, coming to a belligerent halt beside us.

"Oh, he has, ey?" I glowered, feeling my hands cock at my hips; and again I resisted the tug at my arm.

"Ben, it's nothing; come on," soothed Jim, not relenting a whit at his pulling; but neither of us paid him any heed.

"Aye! He's up t' no good, an' he always has been; an' now he's got ye up t' no good with him," blurted Joseph, tugging at his gloves as he swayed on his heels.

"An' who're ye t' judge what I should be up to?" I challenged, determinedly freeing my arm from Jim's grasp.

"Ye should be loadin' the schoonehs instead o' letting' us do youhr dirty work!" he flung back, gaiters, gloves and cravat all quivering in the hall light.

"You do *my* dirty work! I like that!" I hollered, years of resentment suddenly rushing to the surface, and finding an easy exit from my mouth. "Who is it that's always runnin' the yahrd, or roundin' the Horn or building' us ships, while you get the best route, the transatlantic, the best cargoes, even the family house—even though I've cleahrly established I'm the betteh navigatoh an' shipwright, an' even the betteh skippeh! *I'll* give ye dirty work!" I bellowed; and before I knew it, I'd punched him in the mouth.

"Benjamin Galen!" came Jim's gasp, half-aghast, half-overcome with explosive laughter; then before Joseph could strike back he stepped between us, and kept us apart with a fist at each chest. "Now, Joe, don't mind him," he gentled, patting confidingly at his lapels; "he's just had a bit t' drink."

"I c'n see that," condescended Joseph, his voice coming cool as the north wind in autumn; then giving me a long measuring stare from his curt eyes, he turned with icy dignity on his heel, and marched away, head up, for the stairs, never once casting a look back at us.

"Fancy *you* in the role of peacemakeh," I muttered, as Jim— getting back to business—steered me into my room.

"Fancy *you* in the role of hothead," he came back, still quaking with pent-up laughter; and too grateful at the thought of sleep to answer, I stumbled in soddenly toward the bed. Letting go his arm, I fell into the bed clothes; felt the tug of Jim's hands at my boots, the soft settle of the covers on me; then felt at last the blissful abandon of sleep—the kind of sleep I slept when I knew he was near.

When I came to the next day, struggling feebly for recollections, I found him sitting beside me with a potful of coffee, and a half-buried smile of indulgence on his lips; and as I painfully sat up and downed a cup, he cheerfully described last night's entrance, witnessed apparently not just by Portland's upper crust—including half of my Howland in-laws—but by the governor of the state and his wife. The fight, too, they'd heard, and could hardly mistake, since Joseph'd danced through the night with a split lip; and though Pa'd attempted to smooth things over—with one of his typical "Boys will be boys, and likkeh will be likkeh" bromides—the temperance circles couldn't have been much impressed; while Reuben and Sal had enough ammunition stocked up from the spectacle to see them into the next century. "Wait till they hear about the barge," I intoned, trying to choke down a breakfast roll; and he playfully grinned as he poured another cup,

"Oh, they got other business first; they're expectin' you t' show up for work."

Sending him away with a groan I rang for water, the servants— no doubt startled at my signs of gentility—bringing me gallons; and from them I discovered that Agatha had stashed Jim somewhere up on the third floor, in reflection of his social standing—his presence in the house at all apparently the result of Pa's insistence, since he'd offered in the first place to board on the waterfront. Not much more welcome than I, then, he saw me through the weekend—through one or two of the less formal meals, through the confusion of loading and the sullenness of Joseph's humor; and though the cards were plainly stacked against us—though Agatha was cool and Elkanah was distant, and Reuben inclined to bait us at every corner—we nonetheless managed to carry off the game, due largely to Jim's winsome ways with the young set.

Having had time now to adjust to—or at any rate absorb—his advent, I privately struggled to sort out the meaning of my position; but so unnerving was his presence across from me at the table, or beside me on the loading dock, that every time I began to get a handle on things, I looked at him, and lost my grip. Convinced one moment that he loved me, the next that I was imbecilic to suppose it—convinced one hour that he'd showed up in Portland because he'd missed me, the next that that was too conceited for belief—I swung like a gyroscope on a wild sea; and my oscillations hardly made me a fit candidate for work, much less for a mannered dinner.

Not least unsettling was my manic conviction that my dream was about to come true; for here we both were—welcome or no—at Elkanah's, Jim with his hair cut, and both of us soon due home; and if we did confront our feelings more or less as I dreamed it, what in blazes was I going to do about it? Was I going to fling to the four winds my marriage, and carry on with him like the lovers in my dreams? Or was I simply going to burst with their containment?

Now for the first time I began to conceive what it all meant—all those considerations and consequences I'd postponed by my rosebush; and their uninvited assault further demoralized me. I'd never known anyone in a situation like this, never read of anyone either; it was virtually unspoken in Cape Damaris; and even at sea it was no matter for talk, save for a few snide remarks now and then in foreign ports. A couple of vague memories of old bards like Catullus—from my Latin coursework at Bowdoin—filtered back to companion me; but, of course, we'd never translated those poems, only knew they were there by innuendo; and bent anyway on making a name for myself in shipping, I'd never paid them any mind. Now I felt as turned upside down as one of those crystalline paperweights from Bavaria, the snow falling back into the sky from the housetops; and I longed for the comradeship of someone like me.

Against the ludicrous backdrop of mannered society my

daydreams of Jim blazed all the more bizarre, my isolation all the more urgent and painful; and I could hardly make coherent answer to the few who still sought to engage me in converse. Nor did I fare much better on the wharves, where we struggled to work in the last of the cargoes so as to be home, after all, for the holiday; and hence it came as an incomparable release when Pa called me to the desk in his room, that Monday night before Thanksgiving, and bade me and Jim ride his new saddle horses home, a day early in order to ready *Abigail* for loading, while he, Joseph and crew saw to sailing the schooners.

Though they weren't a train, and the Atlantic Highway was no track, the horses were a means home alone with Jim, an opportunity to break for a while from the others; and so overjoyed was I to get away from the family that even my trepidations about my dream, and my suspicions that Pa was doing me a favor, couldn't serve to quell my elation. Enamored of horseflesh, as Pa knew quite well—always more at home in a stable than in the parlor, and already a friend to the new beasts Pa'd bought—Jim himself was in seventh heaven; and though our trip was to be longer, and more tiring, than the sea journey planned by the others, we set forth gladly early Tuesday morning amid farewells tinged with mutual relief, and promises that the schooners would be off in a few hours.

Hoping to reach Cape Damaris that night, a journey barely within reach of the horses, we paced ourselves carefully from the beginning, making frequent stops for brief rests, and not hurrying along faster than necessary; and noontime found us on schedule in Brunswick, where we feasted at an inn and pampered our escorts, and rode at a leisurely speed past old Bowdoin. Showing Jim the three or four ivy-clad halls which comprised my alma mater, I recalled memories of professors and classes, and former classmates such as Jackson; pointed out the boarding house where I'd lived for three years, while he listened raptly as he always did, especially to tales of my past.

Then heading out of town, we cantered in silence, me reacquainting myself with the road I'd traveled by stage those school day vacations, Jim regarding alertly the new sights; but despite our quiet a warmth spoke between us, a wordless rapport that knit our reflections—his eyes seeming to look where mine looked, his heart to lift like mine at our nearness.. So reassuring was our accord that for a long time my uncertainties took flight, and I dwelt only on the present, content with matters as they stood—asking no more, no less, than to be his companion, to share the search of the wind at our collars, and the gloss of the sun on the necks of our horses.

Though we'd originally planned to ride all the way to Cape Damaris, I could perceive, as the afternoon waned, that he was beginning to fatigue; and my concern for his health—almost forgotten in Portland, and in the joyous affinity of our trip—recalled me suddenly to my senses. It was past suppertime and, as in my dream, neither of us had spoken for an hour or so, though we'd communed often in gestures and glances. Now, with the weather beginning to close in, and a cold drizzle commencing to fall, I felt a return of my old anxieties for him, especially as I could see his shoulders set, and his expression steel itself against a confession; while I, too, was tired, as all at once worn-out as if I'd just spent a day in intent correspondence.

With Waldoboro ahead—with Cape Damaris ten miles beyond, and no inn or tavern in between—I began to think of stopping for the night; but knowing Jim's stubbornness, especially in the matter of conceding weakness, I was wise enough to know that I should maneuver him through the horses, that being the stock Romany means of excuse. Stopping for calls of nature, giving up for the night, or even for the mid-day meal, were all managed on the pretext of seeing to the horses; so suddenly I simply reached over and took his reins, and brought us to a halt by the road. Dismounting with him, and stretching my legs, I appealingly asked, "What d'ye think, matey? Shall we knock off and call it a day? They've done a fair stretch since we left this mohrnin', an' the weatheh don't look too promisin.'"

Stroking the horses, and searching their faces, then looking up into the northeast, he asked in return, "How much farther?"; and I smiled over at him as he nuzzled Cherry.

"It's two miles t' Waldoboro," I answered, "an' ten more t' Cape Damaris; an' thehre ain't nothin' like an inn in b'tween—though we could lay up in a bahrn, if that appeals t' your Romany taste."

He threw me a grin, then asked, visiting Mistral, "Is there an inn in Waldoboro?"; and I looked away to hide my delight.

"Aye, the Bell an' Anchor, run by Johnny Talbot, anotheh cousin of Eli's; an' thehre's a first-rate ostleh, too," I tacked on for good measure.

"It'd be better for the horses," he nodded, as if he'd conversed in depth with them; and concealing my triumph I simply re-mounted, and led the way up the road to town.

Uphill and down, then uphill again, on some of the biggest slopes of the highway, we found ourselves in the crowded inn yard, on the Cape Damaris side of the village; and scraping our boots in the entry—a sudden wrench in my chest at the thought there might not be two rooms vacant, and the pair of us obliged to share one—I marched up to the desk by the stairs, and rang the bell for Johnny.

Breezing in from a bedlam of throaty cries in the public room, Johnny engulfed me in his grip, then regretfully informed me that, far from there being two rooms, or even one available for the night, there were none—not so much as a windowsill vacant. Overcome with disappointment —all at once realizing how I'd longed to stay here, to be thrown into close quarters with Jim—I tried to make an offhand reply; but sensing something from my voice, or maybe perceiving our fatigue, the old shellback gusted, "If ye'll bide a wee, Cap'n, an' if youhr not pahrticulah, thehre might be somethin' small at the back."

Suspecting he was about to evict some member of his family, I vigorously endeavored to stop him; but he flung me off and shaped a course for the second floor, waving his hand all the way to squelch me; and soon a commotion on the back stairs, characterized by flurrying feet running both ways, confirmed my suspicion that some son or daughter was scurrying off with armloads of belongings for a makeshift cot in the kitchen. Bursting back into our entryway alcove, and ignoring my eruption of protests, Johnny announced, "It's not much, Cap'n, jest a bit of a bed an' a hearth; but it's betteh than a bahrn on a night like this"; and not trusting myself to look at Jim— too overcome with gratitude toward Johnny, and with the sudden assault of apprehension in my middle, to stammer out more than a word of thanks—I clumsily accepted the offer.

Ordering a simple supper of bread and cheese, chowder and mulled wine, and asking that it be sent up on a tray to our chamber, as we were too tired to undertake the public room, we left our bags for the moment in the entry, and took our horses round to the stable, Jim insisting on seeing how they were to be housed and fed; then stomping back in and picking up our gear, we followed Johnny up the wooden stairs.

On entering our room—a quaint, low-ceilinged, spartan cubicle over the back porch, commanding a view of the Medomak from both of its dormers—we discovered that the fire had already been built up, and that two mugs of mulled wine had been set out on a low table drawn up between two comfortably worn armchairs; and dropping our bags, we looked gratefully around us. In the gable end, the counterpane of the four-poster—somewhat rickety, but commodious and inviting—had been drawn back, revealing clean bedclothes and an overstuffed ticking; while from the pitcher and bowl on the linen-decked washstand rose a cloud of steam, betokening freshly-poured hot water. Out the lace-curtained windows we could see the darkening sky, with its lowering cloud mass and portents of sleet; and in contrast the hearth-fire flamed all the more welcome, the blaze in my chest all the brighter and hotter.

Shrugging off our peacoats and pulling on our dressing gowns, we took turns at the basin, our breaths puffing in the chill air, then drew our chairs up to the grate, as close as we could without setting them a-spark; and settling ourselves into the cushions—Jim half-curling up thankfully into his, and spreading his pea-coat over his shoulders—we sipped our hot wine, and bathed in the hearth-warmth. Now and then adding a log to the fire, or arranging those in the grate to better advantage—breaking up bread and cheese on our tray when Sal brought it, and pouring a re-fill of wine from the warm jug—we took turns tending one another; and I basked in our protective caretaking as much as in the flames at the grate.

As soon as we finished, he rose to turn in, while I returned our tray to the kitchen; and coming back in a few minutes—finding him already in bed, curled up on the side nearest the wall —I made ready to retire myself, putting on a night log and banking the fire, which continued to glow even when I'd blown out the lamp, and thrown my outer garb over the armchair. As I climbed in beside him the wind began to rise, and the sleet to clamor on the rooftop above us; and feeling that fire, tavern and weather were cooperating in bringing us together, I gave myself up to the sensations of closeness, hot bricks at our feet and coverlets around us.

Except for the quiver of firelight on the walls, the room was dark— dark as only a chamber on a cloud-thick winter night can be; and the darkness enveloped us at once in a kind of cocoon of comfort. Rolled together in the center of the mattress—covered with a plentitude of blankets and quilts—we settled ourselves in comfortable positions, Jim unabashedly turning his head towards my shoulder, and nestling his limbs in the ticking near mine with a sigh of contentment. For an unmeasured time we lay together in this fashion, neither of us sleeping nor wanting to sleep—listening instead to the clatter of sleet on the roof, and abandoning ourselves to the luxuries of warmth. So elated was I that I was almost paralyzed: afraid to move a muscle lest he turn away —afraid to move any closer lest I offend him—longing to lift a hand to nudge his fingers—avid to know if he was filled with the same desire and joy—fearful he wasn't—fearful to ask.

In an agony of curiosity to know how he was feeling, the subdued hush of his breathing the only hint of his heart—yearning to know whether he was simply quietly contented as he seemed to be, as any gypsy in a wagonbed of relations might be, or whether he, too, was ache-filled with need—I lay in the warmth of our berth unmoving, conscious of his fingers tumbled near mine; remembered other times we'd slept nearby one another—recalled nights when fatigue or the presence of others had obscured me from knowing what I knew now. With nothing between us save the last shreds of defense, I hovered between that old life and our new, half-torn how to venture over; and it was far into the night before I fell at last into a half-slumber, and he too drifted off without having turned, or moved away from the warmth of my shoulder.

Quick raps or rat-tats which thumped the walls and punctuated the howls of the wind abruptly tore me out of my sleep, and startled, I rose up on one elbow, bewilderedly thinking a loose branch knocked the eaves; then blurrily realizing it was Johnny at our door, I dropped back down again under the covers. "Aye, Johnny; I'm awake," I managed, registering next the dim cold of the room, and the rattling din which must have been sleet; and through the darksome confusion came his muffled voice.

"Sorry t' wake ye at this howeh, Cap'n; but I thought ye should know the weateh's makin' up. Unless y' wants t' spend Thanksgivin' with us, ye should shake a leg; even if y' stahrt now, ye'll barely make port."

"Aye—thank ye—I c'n heahr it," I got out, with another bleary glance at the window; and entering briefly he set out hot water and lighted a couple of candles on the mantle. In their feeble gleam the frosted panes, glazed with a combination of sleet and salt, revealed nothing at all of what lay without; but the slant of the wind at our northeast eaves told me everything I needed to know; and as Johnny bowed out, I quelled a moan. Reluctant to rise in spite of the need— aware all at once of the whole of the night, the warmth of the bed and Jim's nestled limbs—I lingered on in the depths of our nest, conscious of all I must suddenly leave: the warm give of the ticking and comforters and quilts, the confiding closeness of shoulders and feet, the soft press of knees in the abandon of dawn, the sweet tumble of hair in the neglect of sleep.

Carefully shifting my limbs from his, I thought to let him rest a while longer; but alert at once to my gentle stirs, he roused enough to murmur "Ben...what is it?", in his half-sleep turning closer to me; and wrenched by his move I tenderly halted.

"Wind's makin' up; we've got t' be off, mate," I told him, my voice coming strangely natural in the dim light; and "Aye," came his answer, calm and accepting, not a flicker of remorse sounding in his tones—though he, too, dozed on as if unwilling to move, as if to savor one last long moment.

"You stay in bed till I build up the fireh; no use in both of us gettin' dressed cold," I offered, when I could bear our closeness no longer; and untangling myself from limbs and bedding I rose, feeling an actual pain of detachment. Assaulted at once by the bite of the cold I threw on my dressing gown and peacoat, and hurriedly fumbled at the hearth—wondering every moment what he was thinking; and when at length he rose to dress, his eyes were averted and he had little to say, as if he too was experiencing loss and regret.

Though he partook of the morsels Jimmy had brought, washed in the lamplight and packed up his gear with the simple utility of the moment, speaking unemphatically of this and that, there was a stern restraint on his face—accentuated by the dark of the room, and the stark, abrupt shadows thrown by the lamp. There was an unusual depth, too, in his husky voice—a fervor which caused me to look up and wonder; but in no other way did he betray emotion, leaving our room in the end without a backward look, while I gazed over my shoulder at the rumpled bed, the vacant hearth, with an almost palpable stab of regret.

Once out of doors and trudging along over roads ice-hard and crusted with sleet, I struggled to pin my mind on our business—tried not to look back on the night before or to give in to the haunting conviction, taking shape now with each hard-won furlong, that those unutterable moments would never revisit; that even if they came to me in another form, they themselves were gone forever, in all their perfect imperfection. With the dark still pressing in around us, the relentless cold stinging our faces, and the wind whistling over our larboard shoulders, I struggled not to look ahead either—tried to suppress the discord of misgivings, urgent if vague in the pre-dawn dimness, which had sounded a warning in my chest ever since I'd been awakened.

What Jim was thinking as he rode beside me, his features barely discernible over his checkered muffler—what he was feeling as he considerately helped Mistral pick her way, I couldn't tell in the resounding darkness; but for me, alternately staving off pain and disquiet, questions were irresistibly forming—queries I at first welcomed because they brought surcease to my raw preoccupation.

How soon it would snow, how fast the temperature was falling; where the barometer stood and how far we had to go, there being scarcely a house or barn after Thomaston to lay up in: these were the speculations which loomed up in my mind. But these in turn led me to others, far more disconcerting to weigh; and in the stinging dark I could no longer postpone considerations I'd wholly forgotten since last night—recollections of the schooners somewhere off the coast, and of *Abigail* out in the harbor, riding at anchor in a shallow mooring. How many miles Pa and Joseph had done before the blow'd commenced last evening—whether they'd made port, or sought premature harbor, or headed to sea to ride out the gale winds— whether *Abigail*'s holding ground was good—or whether she, too, had been taken out to sea, or driven out before that by the tempest:— such contemplations as these reared up in my mind like so many rocks along a lee shore; and the thicker they rose the more urgent my pace.

Torn between keeping up with me and showing heedfulness to the horses, Jim began to hang back a few rods, almost lost to view in the hail sheets; but when the snows swept in we closed in together, and picked out the last couple of miles at a snail's speed. When at last we drew rein in the lee of Job Taylor's, the house at the crest of the hill above town—when finally, by some freak shift or thinning of the clouds, it became a shade or two lighter, and we could make out Cape Damaris and the harbor—we beheld such a sight as I had never seen in all my years on the coast; and I simply sat atop my horse, gaping.

Between the low tides and the northeast gale, the harbor was drained, simply drained empty, as if a plug had been pulled or the water blown out; and the whole harbor floor from the wharves to Winslow's ledge stretched bare as a crab out of its shell. Along the exposed mudflats a litter of small craft, the bones of drowned ships and the flotsam of centuries loomed up like signposts on a desolate dreamscape; while between them lay bare beds not seen by man, certainly never imagined by me, mapping the soundings in my boyhood dinghy. Out beyond the natural shelf of the ledge rode

Abigail in waters scarcely deep enough to float her; but no sight of the schooners or any other large craft broke the eerie manifestation; and too stunned to take it in, I simply stared.

"Have you ever seen it like this b'fore?" came Jim's gasp, on the wind, at my ear; and having almost forgotten for a moment he was beside me, I cast a dazed look at him.

"Neveh," I shouted back, the words whipped away, as the driving snows commenced again.

"What d'ye want me t' do?" he offered, stoic and calm in the shriek of the wind; and shaken out of my stupor I struggled to think what.

"I don't know," I grappled, half-driven to act, half-fraught with a wild inclination to laugh; "I don't hahrdly know where t' begin—but we've got t' get *Abigail* out o' the harboh—Christ—I b'live I could all but *walk* out t' her from Eben's..." Fumbling to a halt, I paused to think, to marshal my wits into some kind of order; then hauling out my watch, I considered the time. "I'm goin' t' Tom's," I shouted on the wind; "he ain't likely been up more than an howeh; an' if anyone's organizin' a crew for *Abigail*, he is. Ride out t' Eben's, fetch him an' Obed an' anybody else on the neck on the way back—an' meet me at Tom's—we'll carry his dory, an' row ourselves the rest o' the way t' the ship."

"Aye," rang his voice, all comprehending, as if he'd followed my logic without words, and come up himself with the same conclusion; and with a slap of the reins he was ready to be off.

"Bring some oilskins an' a bite t' eat—no tellin' when we'll be back," I called out to him as he turned his horse; and with a jaunty wave he was off for the Point road, without so much as a look behind him.

Going straight out to Tom's on the harbor near the mouth I found everything in disarray— the whole household caught up in the early morning confusion which erupts with an unlooked-for dilemma: the children, not dressed, dashing to the windows, or clinging, confused and crying, to Rachel; Tom in his oilskins, hastily greasing his seaboots; six or seven men overhauling their gear; and all the paraphernalia of tomorrow's Thanksgiving dinner, scattered hither and yon on tables and sideboards.

When they caught sight of me they directly sent up a cheer, as if I'd been specifically dropped down to order; and while we waited for others Tom's stableman had sent for, we swiftly made plans, and swapped urgent news. That we'd all—schooners and horses—left Portland yesterday, they'd had no earthly idea, for there'd been no word or sight of the vessels, and no expectations of any of us till after Thanksgiving; and with the additional worry of the schooners before them, all hands did their best to put their minds on *Abigail*. While we chose duties and routes, Rachel brought us hot cakes, an impromptu breakfast far better than my first; and as I packed away a plate I kept an eye on my watch, on the lookout for Eben and Jim. Having collected ten or twelve men—enough to bring up the anchors, and hoist the necessary storm sail—Tom was all for an immediate departure, heading out with the men to ready the shore boat; but still I delayed, holding out for Jim, and considering what on earth could have delayed him.

When after an hour he still didn't appear—when both the thermometer and the barometer had fallen a notch, and the weather shown signs of further deteriorating—Tom at last prevailed upon me to leave a message with Rachel; and hastily scribbling out a note— disliking to leave without him, and filled with misgivings, all the forebodings of the early morning taking on a new shape—I stuffed the paper into her hands, lashed on my hat and went out in the wind. On the shore I found several already hoisting the boat, the rest shouldering sea bags and packs of gear; and so thick was the snow that I had to hasten up to within a yard just to keep them in my sight.

Reaching *Abigail* after a hard pull, pelted by sheets of sleet, snow and spray—climbing her Jacob's ladder in the murk, and hauling up the boat to the rail—we took to the decks and lighted the lamps, manned the helm, cast off gaskets and seizings, threw down running rigging and overhauled the ground tackle, struggling with the new and unfamiliar gear; then rallying round the windlass with the gale in our throats, we hoisted first one anchor, then the other. Setting only enough storm sail for headway and balance—hoisting the jib, two or three staysails, and the spanker, each roaring in turn and tearing at its ringbolts—we shaped a cautious course out of the harbor, aiming to swing fair of the Mussel Ridge islands, then simply run before it for the day; but we hadn't yet even cleared the Point—hadn't as much as coiled up a halyard, when our lookout hollered "Flare ho! Stahboard beam!", a shrill note of alarm hastening his voice; and word sped aft to me by relay in the roar.

Knowing at once with uncanny certainty what it was—desperate not to plow straight into the wreckage, equally desperate not to take every stitch out of *Abigail*, or broach her by an untimely move—I put the helm down and brought her into the wind, hailing Percy and Haggai to take the wheel; then racing to the flare site, now over the taffrail, I peered out into the driving dark. Neither flare nor vessel nor headland took shape, nothing save the wailing, wind-rushing snow, and the thrashing of breakers nearby on shore, reminding us of our own peril; yet though no one said so, we all knew what was aground, as plainly as if we could read the sternboard. Struggling to keep her hove back on the wind, we hovered on the brink of our own loss, drifting precariously toward where we knew the shore must be; hovered, half-expecting to feel her lurch hard aground, till—loath to surrender, yet fearful to stay—we were forced to conclude we must shift helm, and be off.

Leaving the rail I was about to signal Tom, when "Flare ho!" broke loose from one of the men, still peering out from the gangway bulwarks; and "Where away?" clamored half a dozen voices, as Jack Tupper gestured into the dim.

"Lahboard beam! must be directly off the light," he bellowed, all hands save the helm crowding round him at the rail; and indeed, though the flare faded, we were near enough now to the Point to catch the periodic beam of the lighthouse, eerily diffuse in the cutting snow. Hastily consulting with Tom I decided to anchor in what I hoped to God was the new channel—had just worked her upwind a bit, to make up for ground lost, and given the order to let go, when the neck of the derrick loomed up out of the murk like a sea monster; and giving a cheer—Haggai booming out "Thanks, Robertson!"—we dropped our hook in the newly-dredged trench, taking care not to let it down foul of the engine below.

For the first time having a clue as to our position, we mustered at the helm to parley, Tom and me looking to Seth Wingate—as the eldest—for advice; and so fierce was the blast we were obliged to turn our backs, and confer at the tops of our voices. Struggling to pinpoint the direction of the flares, and deliberating the techniques of a ship-to-ship rescue—balancing the threat of the breakers to leeward, the potential for failure of one or both anchors, and the risk of being driven aground at the Point, or even up onto the wreck itself, against the claim of the lives at stake somewhere in the snow—we blustered and hollered in each other's ears, our debate all the more urgent for the unspoken conviction that we knew sight unseen who'd sent up the flares.

"Who's got the turn t' patrol the shore?" shouted Percy Winslow at one point; and like a bolt came my understanding of what had happened to Eben and Jim.

"Good God, I'll bet it's McCabe—no wondeh him an'Robertson ain't showed up," I bawled back; and as they barked assent my mind raced ahead to trace the inevitable chain of events on shore. Knowing perfectly well the machinations of the entire volunteer lifesaving service, I saw directly what must have taken place: saw Eben out patrolling the beach, taking his usual turn in foul weather, in conjunction perhaps with Tom Longworthy on the east shore; saw one of them run for the boathouse, to fetch the gun cart, breeches buoy and faking boxes, while the other dashed for town to ring the alarm, which must have pealed just after we'd left; saw Jim gallop up in the midst of the action, and—being Jim—decide to ditch me, and commit himself to the more urgent need of the flare; saw him setting up the gun or pushing the boat cart or maybe even, madman that he was, casting in his lot with an attempt to launch a surfboat, if the wreck was too far offshore for the breeches buoy; saw him in the breakers, pulling for the vessel, in the ultimate moments of trying to bring off survivors.

Once I'd seen this no force on earth could have wrenched me away from the invisible drama before us; and when time had dragged on without further sign of either a flare or a vessel in distress—when we'd paid out as much chain as even the stoutest of us dared, and doubts had begun to creep into our talk—when Tom finally came aft and broached the subject of leaving, his hand a-grip on the sleeve of my coat—I raised all the resistance of ten men, convincing him in the end not only to wait, but to take command while I went to the rail.

Pinning my entire mind on the snow, and scrutinizing its streaming rush for a break—fighting a rising panic and dread, an anarchy of convictions and doubts, amongst them the conceit that events were out of control, their chaos spawned by the failed chances of last night—I peered for an age out into the void; struggled for some gift of clarity and form, till—after an endless span without flare or movement—Jack Tupper beside me yelled "Boat adrift! dead ahead!" Immediately I too saw it, a capsized surfboat just such as the shore patrol used in rescue, and four men clinging to it: a shadowy bulk and thin shapes in the blizzard.

Coming athwartships they were but a moment before us, for the combined gale and tide swiftly carried them downwind; and wildly hallooing we sent up a flare to signal our presence. No faces, no signs of individuality or clothing appeared to us through the dim and the snow; no voices called to publish their names; but instantaneously I knew who one of them was, just as I'd earlier known who'd sent up the flares—knew it as plain as if I could see his eyes, or make out his checkered muffler. Desperately throwing out anything that would float—heaving life-rings on lines, fenders from the bow, benches, even lengths of hatch tackle and blocks—we scrambled and darted pell mell on deck; flamed up with hope as one of them waved, a feeble sweep to acknowledge our throws; then helplessly watched as our equipment fell short, or drifted aft at a slower pace.

Leaning over the bulwarks we could just make them out as they slipped into the curtain of snow—were just in time to see, as they faded from view, one of them let go and sink; and a panic flailing me like no fear I'd ever known, I panted like a beast at the rail. Clutching and unclutching the sleet-crusted wood, I frenziedly cast about for a plan; caught sight of, then discarded, one by one all the deck boats, as too time-consuming and too risky to hoist out in the wind.

Then all at once my eyes fell on the little dory, forgotten ever since we'd climbed aboard and lashed it to the main hatch; and straightway—as though I'd been granted a deliverance of vision, a precise map or chart of the one route of escape—I was clear on what I should do. Flinging off my oilskins and heavy boots—dashing for the long boat and clapping on a cork vest, the newfangled preserver I'd just ordered and stowed—I began to unlash the dory; and instantly—as if liberated from their stunned witness—the entire crew descended on me.

"It can't be done, man—it's too small—it'll fill as soon as it's oveh," roared Seth, trying to rip me back by the shoulders; and finding the strength of a steamer, I shed him.

"I've got t' do it; let go of me!" I hollered, as others fought to unhand me from the ropes.

"Ye'll freeze t' death, Ben' ye'll never make it—ye've got t' let them go!" cried Tom, in possession of one of my hands; and desperate only at the thought of being detained, I flung free.

"Let them go!" I raged into the blast, tearing again at the stiff, frozen knots; "for Christ's sake, don't ye know who's out there? That's Jim in that boat, an' I'm goin' t' get him!"

Stepping back a little—as if I'd gone mad, and posed a threat to others more sober—Seth gaped at me, then managed to gasp out: "Melchett, ye've—you'hre crazy, ye've taken leave o' your senses! Even if that was God Amighty out there, ye'd neveh contrive t' reach in that boat; an' if ye did, ye'd neveh make it t' shore!"

"I'll do it all right; now let go o' the line! Seth, b'fore God, I neveh struck an oldeh man, but—"

"Ben, for the time bein' I'm standin' here in the boots o' youhr Pa; an' I'm bound t' tell ye, this is madness—this ain't a sound or rational decision!"

"It's the *only* d'cision!" I stamped fiercely at him, nearly losing my footing on the pitching deck. "I'm still masteh aboard this vessel, an' shipped or unshipped, you'hre still the crew; an' by God, if y d'tain me any longer, I'll charge ye all with mutiny in court!"

"Ye'll neveh live t' see the day," groaned Tom, as the dory went over and landed upright, immediately standing up and down on the seas; and climbing onto the rail, I touched his wrist.

"Tom, take command o' the ship," I told him, preparing to swing my legs over.

Gripping me by the shoulder, his fingers quaking in a way I could clearly feel through my pea coat, Tom grappled out in one last attempt: "For God's sake, man remembeh youhr children!"; but my heart and nerve steeled with an unshakeable calm, I soothed him as gently as I could in the gale wind.

"I'll be settin' down t' dinneh with 'em," I called as I went over the rail; and taking my seat and shipping the oars, then waiting for my chance, I rowed.

At once I was assaulted by a much fiercer wind, a far keener spray and sleet-driven snow, the foam flying in sheets round my open boat, and the seas running black in chaotic swells; but explicable or no I wasn't afraid, my eyes on the curtain where they'd disappeared, and an unearthly calm timing my strokes. Because they were drifting and I was rowing, the joint force of the gale and the tide at my back, I knew I could succeed in closing in on them; had only to keep before the elements and stay upright, and home in on the draw which exuded from Jim.

In another state now where logic was futile, and only trust in the unseen availed—clear-headed for the first time in months, as if I'd cut adrift all unnecessary baggage, and jettisoned all top-hamper clutter—I reveled in a confidence never before known; rowed pure, light, direct over the breakers, possessed of an uncanny judgment and skill. With the stinging cold and piercing ice all but blanked out— not forgotten, but neutralized by my calm, and the concentration which sprang from it—I heaved and pulled for an unknowable time, not forcing my chances but taking them as they came, almost as if allowing the tumult to row me; and at last with a lurch of the heart I raised a guess, little more than a glint in the white whirl of a boat.

Capsized as it was it showed up as a sliver, a murky slant in the turbid seas; but it rose and fell with a detectable rhythm, gradually enlarging as I closed; and finally I could make out its shape as a keel, and clinging to its handholds, one or two figures, frail pencil forms splayed over the hull. Where the third man was—whether riding low on the lee beam, or sunk beneath, spent, like his earlier companion—I couldn't make out in the tempestuous dim; but from the blaze in my chest I knew one was Jim, knew it as plain as if he shone with a light; and I struggled not to lose the grip of my pace. Whether they'd seen my dory lowered, and hence were aware of my pending rescue, I couldn't begin to guess in the din—for the driving snows had by then closed them to our view, and the seas pitched like heights now, periodically shutting us out. But as I hove into sight one of them made a sign, as if I wasn't entirely unexpected; and timing my moves—gauging the force of each swell, keeping the little dory stern on in its trough, then more abeam with the lurch of its crest—I finally pulled myself close alongside.

In the snow-riddled dark I could now discern that there were indeed only two still holding on; but both had the strength to clutch my gunnels, and hoist themselves while I steered and held firm; and first one, then the other pitched forward into the bottom of the boat, then lay motionless, completely done in. Even now it was too dim to make out who they were—to distinguish whether one of them wore a checkered muffler; but I called out "It's me, mate; hold on!" as surely and serenely as if it was daylight, bright day on a warm, benign summer's afternoon; and lifting the oars again, I rowed.

Though I had them in the boat, the most critical leg still remained: that of landing inside the Point, where the hurtling seas slammed into the rock-ridden shore; and easing the bow, I hesitated, undecided. If there'd been any sign of the beach I was nearing—any clang of the channel buoy, warning me away from the crags near the light—it would have helped; would not only have provided direction, but served to further strengthen my nerve; but instead I could catch only the diffuse beams of the lighthouse, disembodied and vague in the streaking snow. Since all the signposts of reason had failed, or were rendered unrecognizable by the tempest, I had no course but to again trust instinct; and choosing a route toward the turbulence of the shore—looking for a break, then steering more or less for a place which seemed right—I felt my way into the tumult.

Several times, shipping water, I kicked the man nearest my feet, who roused enough to bail for a spell; but even partially swamped, both by whitecaps and spray sheets, I didn't give up my self-possession; kept my countenance till—reaching the inshore surf, with its thunder growl of booming and pounding—I from nowhere remembered another perilous landing off this coast; and straightaway my calm was shattered. No longer rowing me, the black seas turned vicious, menacing me with their frigid deep; while the blast of the wind bit into my back and gnawed at my hands as they gripped the oars. Suddenly aware that my wool coat was stiff, stiff as a topsail with frozen brine, my beard crusted and hoary and my feet unfeeling, I stamped my heels and beat my hands on the oarlocks, automatically losing my timing; then as if to further demoralize me, there pierced the night a wild, pitching wail, seeming to urgently beckon or summon, though no words could be discerned on the wind's howl.

Rising and falling, pulsing and failing, it came from nowhere that I could detect— simply beat and throbbed from the very depths of the night, the very lungs and throat of the wind; and paralyzed altogether, I yielded my pace. A-race on the seas, abandoned to their course, I was about to commit us all to the breakers; but just at that moment, through the gale cloud of snow, there loomed up a shade— the dark bulk of the shore; and more glorious still, the blurred lights of a house, my house, every window blazing. Hurtling ahead I could make out the beach—could snatch the hurried forms of men running, the glare of flares and a jumble of apparatus, probably the forsaken breeches buoy; and directly knowing precisely where I was—every pebble beneath me as plain as if I had eyes on the keel—I courted my chance for our final dash; awaited the promising lift of a breaker, then feeling its power, drove in straight for the shore. At once we careened at great speed on the crest top, as if hurled along by an unseen hand, rooted deep in the maelstrom of water; then downward we plunged in a cascade of spindrift, our hearts flying into our mouths with the impact, and the seas drenching us in a torrential smother—a cataract of cold which burned us to the bones. Abandoning the oars I made a desperate grab for Jim, even as men streamed out into the breakers;

gripped him by the chest as we smashed into the wave trough, and landed dazed, but miraculously upright; then more than half-filled we lumbered on for the next roll, swept up and over before we capsized, and Jim and me straightaway went under. Floundering for my feet, for anything solid beneath me—flailing in the searing cold, and the rib-crushing pressure—I finally fought free, borne up by my cork vest; and gasping the air, I found myself still clutching Jim, though he tugged like a dead weight in the welter around us.

Struggling for the shore we went over twice more, wholly submerged each time by the surf; but staggering on we wrung a way through the surges, straining against the conflicting currents. Emerging into the wind—which instantly froze our clothes— we stumbled and fell at last in the backwash, then crawled like crustaceans up onto the beach—Jim at once sick with all the salt water he'd taken aboard. Pausing to help him—terrified by his long exposure, and by how listless he seemed as I strove to get him to his feet—I urgently propelled him towards my house, where I knew they must have set up a lifesaving station.

"Jamie, it's me," I tried to encourage, hoarsely battling to top the wind; "up, up higheh now, out o' the wateh!"; but sick again in the wallow he fell to his knees, me holding him and endeavoring to make him hear. "It's all right, matey—I've got ye—up higheh now," I kept on, trying to get him up out of the backflow; and succeeding once more I forced him slowly on through the snow crunch, stopping repeatedly for him to be sick: each time bellowing at him, "Up—up now, Jamie—ye've got t' walk—we've got t' keep movin'—no, ye can't lie down— we can't stop—keep movin'!"

Wholly alarmed about his condition, I finally maneuvered him up to the house front— floundered through snowdrifts and sand-blasted bare patches with the one thought of shutting out the wind's fury; but as soon as I'd wrestled him into the hallway I stopped, too stunned for the moment to go on; for the unreal bedlam of lights and confusion which met me was surely no place I'd ever lived in. From both the front rooms streamed a babble of voices—shouts, cries, moans—and flows of people, mostly women in stained gowns and aprons, hurrying basins and piles of linens; while the hall before me lay stripped of all save the stairway, through the rails of which peered the petrified faces of children.

So intense was the activity that Jim and I went unnoticed; and dazed, I wheeled him into an unrecognizable chamber, its carpets cast off, its fire black out, and its furnishings all swept back under the windows. From wall to wall sprawled the inert forms of men, wild, chaotic heaps of blankets, discarded boots, salt water oozing from them, and tangled upheavals of guernseys and jackets: Kirk and Eben, Anne and half a dozen others scurrying amongst them with pitchers of lukewarm water, which steamed nonetheless in the stark air.

Finding a place for Jim in the midst of the tumult—fumbling at his stiff boots, their buttons a torment, so frozen my numb, giant fingers couldn't work them—then flinging off his peacoat, soaked heavy with brine, I simply grabbed comforters, quilts, anything to hand, and bedded him down on the planks of the bare floor; pulled off my cork vest and crawled in beside him, and waited for him to commence shivering. Surrounded on all sides by the cries and moans of unknowns, coming to or regaining circulation, or grieving, perhaps, for those presumed lost—lying close by the sobs of a young man, dull, wrenching sobs I dazedly came to realize were those of my brother Matthew—I couldn't but take in the mournful commotion; but too exhausted to wonder I dumbly held Jim, with the one aim of simply keeping him conscious. Exhibiting at first the slow pulse and brief, shallow breaths of the long-exposed, he plainly knew neither me nor anyone else; but starting to shiver he gradually gained ground, me trying to warm him with my own wretched limbs, and babble encouragement to him in the clamor. Then finally with a shuddering sigh he spoke my name, even nestled closer to me for warmth; and his tongue loosed by the host of sensations which pressed him he began an incoherent mumble, a murmur of sounds full of distress and confusion which culminated in half-choked words I could detect: "Ben—he's gone—your Pa—I had him—but he—let go—" It was the first I knew for a certainty that our schooners lay out there—the first I realized that those around us weren't strangers, but kinsmen taken off, or townsmen or both—the first I understood

Matthew's sobbing; but still I held him, unabashed in the tumult, my whole mind pinned to comforting his distress.

When at last Eben came by—his face haggard above us, but measured and calm in the flickering hurricane lanterns—and asked "How far along is he?", I simply answered, "He's shiverin' now—look at his hands an' feet"; and checking his pulse—working him carefully over, then taking a hard look at me—he gave his head a noncommittal shake. "No tellin' what his body temperature is—but his pulse is still slow—an' his skin is white. He put out with the first boat, an's one o' the last I seen make shore. Keep him covehed, an' when Sadie comes by with the cloths, staht with the coolest an' work up t' the lukewarm. The pain should b'gin soon—I'll come by with laudanum if Kirk c'n spare any: he's got the worst cases across the hall."

Dismayed, I knew what he meant by this last; and fearful lest Jim should lose one of his feet, or worse, his hands, I went straight to work—fetched and laid cool cloths on his arms while Sadie came to minister to his legs. Slow and gentle as we were, beginning with damp layers the temperature of the room, and increasing their warmth by only the smallest degrees, we nonetheless caused him insupportable pain; and it was all I could do to keep on with the task—to continue a therapy which coaxed him to feel.

Looking with anguish on his restraint I finally moaned "Oh, God, honey, yell—everyone else is"; and freed by the extremities of the night he at last succumbed to need, yielding up cries which tore at my heart. Solid as a plank, Sadie worked on, as she had on unnumbered other cases; and battling to pattern myself on her conduct, I laid on cloths and stoically removed them, my mind meantime a perfect churn of disorder.

My father's loss, and the potential loss of others—*Abigail's* danger, and the hazards Tom faced—the schooner's grounding, and the threat to her cargo—Jamie's pain, and his nearness last night— my Portland dream, and my failures to act: all dove and circled and pecked at my limbs, while I struggled to close a grip on any one of them. But all I could manage was the same desperate calm I'd felt from the moment I'd lowered the dory, and the dumb pity that filled me at the sight of Jim's sweat. When at last Eben came by with a scant teaspoon of laudanum, administered it to Jim and looked him over—when at length he pronounced him tentatively out of danger, and ordered me off to find dry gear for us both—I was so limp I was almost unfit to walk; and I made for the stairs with half-seeing eyes, and knees that seemed to want to come undone.

Upstairs it was dark, luridly dark as befitted this freakish combination of day-night; and the walls reverberated like the skins of a drum to the beating of the hail sheets and gale wind. Dazed by the gloom, I looked witlessly around—went round and round the perimeter of my room, trying to find my chest of drawers; but though I circled and circled—though I came back to the same walls, and saw time and again the same mirror with the carved eagle, the same fire screen with the parrot and bough—I couldn't find my own bureau. How long I might have hunted for it, anyone might hazard a guess; but by chance—on one of my frenzied circuits—my eyes fell on the immaculate washstand, and the embroider-rich linen Anne always set out for visitors; and taken aback, I realized I was in the guest room—that I had been lost in my own house.

Clear-headed for an instant, I found the door, exited and crossed the hall; paused for a moment on the threshold of the next chamber, and studied it before I entered. This, I could see at once, was indeed my room and Anne's; but nothing here looked familiar either, and I fought another flood-surge of panic. Clothes, I had come for dry clothes— something warm for Jim to be ill in, something for me to wear back outdoors, where I knew I was duty-bound to head next; but though I found chests with drawers a-plenty—though I pulled them out, and tore hurriedly at them, my fingers like squirrels' claws in the dry leaves—there seemed to be nothing in them I needed.

Nightshirts, nightcaps, woolen stockings, mittens and flannels and knitted guernseys—these were the garments I'd come to search for; but though I threw things down on the floor, and scrambled and scrabbled in wardrobe and closet, nothing came to hand that was useful. Collars, cuffs, buttonhooks, corsets, waistcoats, cravats, reticules, handbags: these I met in every corner; and maddeningly, I ditched them in heaps on the chairs.

If the drawers were eccentric, the rest of the room was more so—eccentric with the shapes of the bizarre; and pausing in my search, I glanced on the bedposts and bureaus around me. Abrupt and stark in the day-night, the settee loomed tall-backed, the highboy hump-backed and freakish with scrolls; whilst there was something indescribably menacing about the armchairs, whose claws appeared unaccountably poised for a move. As in a dream when the familiar turns alien, the mantle seemed about to spring at me, the chair legs to secret some sinister purpose; and I had to force myself to recall that this was the same house in which Jim rested—that this was the same day on which I'd wakened at the inn, with him tumbled close and warm beside me. Now last night seemed like centuries ago, an event in some other life, some other epoch; and this house a stranger's I was attempting to burgle.

When at last I stumbled on a drawer I needed—when I'd pulled out an old flannel nightshirt that would do for Jim, a thick guernsey and woolen trowsers for me—I couldn't wait to quit the place; and I threw off my wet gear and drew on the dry with fingers that fumbled and caught in their hurry. Meeting me downstairs, Eben helped me dress Jim, the two of us easing him gently into flannels; then knowing that he was not in pain anymore—taking a last look on his still face, dreaming on some mute, faraway vista—I got to my feet and lashed on my hat, said hoarsely to Eben, "Look afteh him for me," and went back out into the night.

XXIII

EBEN MCCABE
Cape Damaris, Maine November-December, 1843

It was dawn the next day before the storm blowed itself out; and we was at work all noon and night at its height, trying for a chance to bring more men off the schooners, and giving first aid constantly to the surfmen and sentries, some of them coming by as much as two or three times. Kirk and me being the only two medical men in a radius of ten miles—and Kirk by far the more experienced—that part of the show was up to us; and we was kept at it without halt the whole time, treating frostbite and hypothermia, setting busted bones and stove ribs, and helping the grieving lay out the dead.

By now half the town was on the scene—some right out in front of Ben's place manning signals and surfboats, others scouting up and down the shoreline in pairs, latecomers driving up with sleigh loads of supplies, and a contingent hurrying together soup and coffee in the kitchen, or keeping vigil by those at rest in the parlor. That any of them'd even made it out to Ben's in the first place was not much short of a miraculous event—the roads clogging impassible with drifts by mid-morning; and once they'd got here they had no choice but to stay on, the inland routes fast becoming as hazardous as the seaward. Somewheres along the line Rachel—Tom's wife—showed up, and considerably fetched Ben's children off to the stableman's room above the barn, it being no fit scene for young ones; but otherwise we was all forced to stay put, the living together with the dead.

That we wasn't organized to handle such an emergency we all quickly seen; but it was too late now to regret we had nothing more than a volunteer life-saving service, everyone just tallying on wherever there was a need. Of all the disorder that abounded around us, the worst of it was, nobody really knew what was happening—it being no easier to collect and pass on news in all the screaming howl of wind, than it was in a screecher off Cape Horn; and it was hours sometimes before we all knew what one did. Tom Longworthy and Amasa Spooner, John and Ben and their uncle Seth was more or less in charge of the beach, handling the flares, channeling word to and from the relays and the lighthouse, passing the latest to us or back down again, and trying to coordinate another rescue; but even so it was almost impossible to keep track of who was where in what condition, what had to be done next and how.

Who'd gone out in the surfboats, who'd come back or failed to— who was reckoned to be on the schooners—who was patrolling what stretch with who—it was all herculean to keep straight: the hubbub of shrieking wind and bleak snow, the hurry of working against a deadline, and not least, the exaggeration springing from a mounting hysteria, as more and more come to fear for their loved ones, all defeating our best efforts. That both Melchett schooners was out there, and just to windward of them *Abigail,* the mystery newcomer we'd been unable to make out, till Ben made land in his hair-raiser and explained—that was the sum total of what we knew for sure about the state of things offshore; whilst we was almost as much in the dark about our own rescues. Of the first boat that'd put out, we'd still learned nothing, since Robertson was the only surfman who'd come back, and not in the lifeboat, but in Ben's dory; while the man he'd rescued, Marshall Pelham, was, like him, still too bad off to let us know what'd become of any of the others.

We could only suppose that, since Pelham was known to of been aboard Galen's schooner, Jim's surfboat had made it to the scene, rescued some of the men and been swamped—Ben spotting Pelham and Jim from *Abigail*; but whether the rest was still clinging to the wreckage in the water, or had struggled back to their stranded mates on the schooner, none of us on land had a glimmer. The second boat that'd stood out in the direction of the other schooner—more distant by some rods, as near as we could make out from the flares—had almost won its way through the breakers, but been forced to turn back, even so losing two surfmen, one of them Jeb Kalkman, my cousin; and our third and last attempt hadn't even negotiated the first rollers before capsizing and spilling its men, all of them gaining shore in rough shape.

That Joseph's schooner was in fact the second vessel aground out there we'd only learned by finding Simon Coombs' body, washed ashore far below the lighthouse— Matthew Melchett bringing him in, and affirming he'd shipped with his brother; but why he'd been washed ashore in the first place—whether Joe's boat was breaking up, or whether they'd been swept by a wave, or whether it was simply a desperate attempt by one man to make land—there was no sure way to distinguish. From our ill-starred efforts we had nearly a score of men laid up; while it seemed more than likely that, with the addition of *Abigail*, there was as many men still out there, about whose fate we knew nothing; and since there was hardly a household in town that didn't have kith and kin involved some way, there was no sleep for anyone this night, all hands finding strength through the mask of a job.

It was around mid-afternoon—or so I guessed, it being nigh impossible to tell in the dark—when Amasa Spooner come up to me in the hallway, put his hand on my shoulder and asked to speak to me for a minute; and getting us into a huddle out of the way on the stairs, he told me he had Galen's body down by the lighthouse—that they'd found him on the rocks and carried him up to the light, trusting him to the keeping of his old cronies, my great-uncles. Though he'd spoke to Seth and John, he couldn't bring hisself to tell Ben, who wasn't down on the shore at the moment; and would I somehow break the news for him.

My heart went like lead, but I promised I would; and when Ben come into the hall not long after—on his way to change his boots, and check Jim—I took him aside for a word in the dining room, that being the only place out of the line of traffic. Trying to shut out the turmoil of the kitchen—trying equally hard not to see the silent candles, and the still forms beyond the glass doors of the parlor—I stood by the cold hearth and looked him in the eye; and I seen him brace hisself for what I had to say. He looked grey in the lamplight, just about beat out, his boots oozing salt water and his oilskins soaked through, and his beard and brows under his hatbrim a-drip; but there was a strength for all that in the lines of his face, and the set of his shoulders as he met my gaze.

"Ben," I says as gently as I could in the uproar, "I just had it from Amasa, who stopped by for a minute...they've just found youhr Pa, down by the lighthouse...Ben, he's gone."

"I know it," he said simply; "Jim told me."

"He...had him in the surfboat, then?"

"Or on it...Pa let go. I didn't want t' say anything till...till we knew for sure," he stumbled.

I touched his arm.

"Any otheh word from Jim who was in that boat?" I asked when I could.

"No. It was almost impossible t' undehstand him, he was pretty much off his head, an' in all the noise an' confusion... But when I was still aboard *Abigail*, we seen him with three othehs, clingin' to a capsized boat... I think it was the surfboat, but I can't say for sure. We saw one man sink"—his voice caught, but he went on—"an' when I showed up by them in the dory, a second one was gone too. Thehre was only two when we finally made shore, Jim an' anotheh."

"Marshall Pelham; aye."

"He all right?"

"Smashed a shouldeh, probably in the surf; othehwise, about the same as Jim."

"An' Jim?"

"He'll rally; just give him time." I tried to speak lightly, but in truth I'd been keeping from him, ever since he'd first brung Jim in, a stubborn undercurrent of worry; yet though I'd fought not to show it, he immediately sensed it, even in his own whirl of concerns.

"What is it?" he snapped, his whole expression changing; and I struggled to manufacture a mild look.

"It may be nothin', Ben; it's too soon t' say."

"What is it?" he snapped again, not any gentler.

"His feet," I admitted, "pahtic'ly his left."

Another shadow crossed his face, but he said simply, "You'hre watchin' him?"

"Me an' Sadie're takin' it in turns."

"Gawddam ye for eveh lettin' him in that boat."

"There was no holdin' him back, Ben, he was hotteh t' go than any o' the othehs... I think he knew, somehow, it was youhr...it was the Melchett schoonehs out thehre...he told us they was ovehdue, the first we'd heard of it... an' y' know, from day one, he was awful fond o' youhr Pa."

He was quiet for a long minute; but though he didn't speak, I heard every word in his head as plain as if I was privy to it; and I followed along as if he was talking out loud. His old man's last thoughts, Jim's shaky condition, the rescue still needed and the impossibility of it— Jim's state and Pelham's enough to show that, even without the twin biers in the parlor: them was the lines that preoccupied him; but alls he said was, hauling off his sou'wester, "Who else went out with Jim in that boat?"

"Gideon Coombs—he guessed Simon was out thehre...Jonas Winslow, Saul Tuppeh, Hal Talbot, an' in the stern sheets, Sage Haskett."

"Sage, too... my Gawd."

"Aye... Ben, I don't think any of 'em made it."

As if hearing their names had made him realize the enormity of the night's losses—as if my bit of a roll call had brung home to him the sheer insanity of another rescue—he leaned against the mantle, dazed. "I don't see how we c'n put anotheh boat out," he said hollowly, his voice all but lost; "an' damn it all, I don't see how we can't... If them seas don't let up soon, we'll neveh get out b'fore night, an' they'll neveh last out thehre until dawn... they'lll...they'll freeze even if they don't break up."

"Ben," I spoke up, trying as gently as I could to help him—to ease him into taking a decision back down to the shore, "be realistic... d'y think thehre's anybody left on youhr Pa's schooneh t' bring off? Y' know he would of been the last one oveh the rail; an' if Jim had him in the surfboat, why, the decks're empty."

There was a twitch in the muscle along his jaw, but beginning doggedly to work on his boots, he only said calmly, "Unless they was swamped nearby, an' some o' the men made it back."

"That's the only chance I c'n see, an' it's a slim one... Them seas're man-killin' out thehre, ye know it... I'd give 'em twenty minutes in the wateh, not more."

"Twenty minutes...why, Jim was... I was...we was out thehre for howehs."

"It was minutes, Ben...it had to of been."

He looked more floored than he had by anything I'd said yet, his face a blank as if he just couldn't take the words in, and his fingers halted in their fumble at his boots. "Why, I could of sworn...it took me so long to...are y' sure?"

"They ain't above a hundred yahds out thehre, Ben."

His fingers went through his hair again in that half-shaken way he had, and I thought, in the lamp, how lost his face looked—how altogether uncertain and swamped. "I must be gettin' turned around, or tired out or...what time is it now?"

"Around mid-aftehnoon, though I ain't looked at the clock."

"Mid-aftehnoon...that gives us two howehs t' dark..." His fingers was back at work at his boots, hauling off the wet and pulling on the dry that Rachel'd brung along earlier in the cutter; and I could see by his look he was pushing hisself towards a choice—that lost, swamped or no, he wasn't ready yet to quit. "If we do tackle a rescue, it ought t' be Joseph," he finally murmured, as he finished a boot; "can y' remembeh...was it you who first seen his flare?"

"Aye, me an' Longworthy, when we'd met at the lighthouse, not long afteh I'd caught sight o' youhr Pa's...He's furtheh t' leeward than youhr Pa's boat, almost off'n the light... Tom c'n show ye." I hesitated, then carefully ventured, "I... I got t' caution ye, Ben, if y' try this... I know it's youhr brotheh out thehre in that boat, an' othehs too got close kin on board...but I... I seen enough hypothermia an' smashed bones for one night...Darcy Winslow's got one o' his lungs stove, an' I ain't lookin' forward, when Jim wakes up, or Marshall, t' havin' t' tell 'em about their feet."

"I'll remembeh," he promised, his face grim.

"Do ye...d'y have any notion at all what Joseph's doin'?" I asked, still trying to help him get all the factors in focus.

He shoulders hunched and he shook his head, too honest a man not to say what he thought. "I think Joe knows we'll neveh get a boat through....that we'll try, but that the odds just ain't in oweh favoh. He'll reckon the only way is t' launch his own lifeboat, an' hope for the best—it bein' easieh t' ride a rolleh in than it is t' fight t' beat past it. He's crazy enough t' do it, too. In fact, I think he's already done it—that he gambled on some o' the men that was ready, split the crew in half, an' sent two or three out... Simon Coombs bein' one ' that numbeh."

"In that case, his position is bad—he's breakin' up, or can't brave the cold—othehwise, he'd try t' wait out the storm."

His shoulders sagged as he tied up his other boot. "I... I'm stahtin' t' worry about Tom as well...he's got more protection, an' c'n take the surf betteh...but if this wind keeps up...Damn, but I should neveh of moved *Abigail.*"

"If ye hadn't, we'd of lost Jim," I reminded him kindly.

His face gentled to a wonderful softness, there in the haggard light of the lantern— relented the same way as a storm relaxes when at last it's of a mind to moderate a little; and in the letting go his voice slackened too, coming out hoarse as he lashed up his pantlegs. "Watch him for me, Eben...Gawd, I c'n only stand all o' this if I know that he's safe."

"He'll be safe," I pledged, because I had to—because I would of pledged anything to that face; and nodding, he held out his sleeves to be lashed up, then headed back down the hall for the shore.

In the end it was just one man that put out in the surfboat, not Ben as I'd feared, but Amasa—him claiming the job not just because he was stalwart, but because his children was all growed, and he'd no cause for emotion to impair his judgment, no close kin to him being on Joe's boat, the target. Instead of risking six lives to row out and back, the way we usually manned a surfboat, Amasa went alone with the aim of trying to set up a breeches buoy—the Lyle gun falling short in the wind, but the schooner close enough, by our best calculations, to mount some kind of a relay from the mast to the shore below the light, if once we could run the lines out. With the steering oar fixed as a rudder, a couple of oars shipped, and the breeches buoy and faking box lashed amidships—with the hawser end already fast to the beach, and Amasa strapped into Ben's cork vest, the utility of which we was just beginning to appreciate—the surfboat was launched, Ben and half a dozen others on lifelines guiding it out well past the first line of breakers; and after that, all hands took to waiting.

As the minutes dragged on, and Amasa didn't come back—as he slipped out of sight in the snow still upright, and no sign of him or his upended boat met us—we begun to entertain some hopes, John Melchett or Worthing running up to the house every so often and considerately letting us know things was still on; but all prospects was dashed when, an hour or so later, the surfboat was found below the lighthouse rocks, half-stove; and word reached us soon after that Amasa was at the light, alive but with his collarbone busted.

Going out to see him myself—making the half-mile trek in the dark, only able to navigate by following the shore—I set his shoulder and treated his frostbite, showing Solon and Darius how to care for him; and whilst we was gathered around him, he come to enough to tell us the seas was rising, and not to try again. So laced up with laudanum and fraught with pain and cold that he couldn't mutter much more than a few phrases, he just the same managed to pick me out with his eye, and murmur "Ye'll have t' tell Ben that... Joe's on his own"; and giving his grey hairs an encouraging pat, I soothed the best I could, "Hell, old man, y' give it a good try."

All further thought of a rescue put to flight, there was nothing more to do now but patrol the shores and wait, the storm itself the master of choices; and it was the worst stretch of all, the inaction, the waiting around and chafing till dawn. Aside from the patrols—arranged in pairs, with regular watches, each set relieved every hour at the light—all hands was simply removed into Ben's place; and the long night was broke only once, by Bill Worthing, who come in with the news that Saul Tupper'd been found, a few miles below Longworthy's, and laid to rest at his house. Surrounded by hurt men, Kirk and me was kept busy, mostly applying and re-applying dressings; but most of the others was at a loss what to do, dazed to no longer be on the shore, working. Going upstairs, some stretched out on the beds, or rolled up in blankets on the floor, thinking to build up their strength with a sleep, if they could; but finding it nigh impossible to drop off—what with their hauled taut nerves and the wind's howl, and the blaze of lanterns kept in every window, to aid any survivor in making a landfall—most tumbled back down again to concoct a meal in the kitchen, or help stoke the fires on half a dozen hearths, it being safe now for the recuperating to have heat.

Squatting down by Jim—who was still sleeping soundly, the insatiable sleep of the wholly exhausted—Ben set to tending his feet, the bandages having to be kept within a steady range, constantly dry, lukewarm and clean; and coming by him often I tried, without luck, to persuade him to curl up somewheres for a rest, knowing what waited for him in the morning. Of the others who was awake—folks who'd been on the job since daybreak, and who knew they had loved ones at stake—most went into the dining room to pray, some sitting alone in corners under lamps, others with joined hands at the table; and with them was most of the ladies who'd nursed, or held down the fort in the pantry and kitchen. Throughout the day they'd been unflagging—Sadie, Rose Talbot, Sabrina Winslow, Melissa Worthing, Keziah, Joe's wife Elizabeth, Sarah, and even old Abigail herself, her back unbent and her eyes clear and dry as she led in prayer; but nobody'd been more of a workhorse than Anne, who even now was helping me with the dressings.

All these years I'd thought of her as a compound of a nasty-neat housewife and a rabid shopkeeper—looked down on her because of the cross she was to Ben; but now I seen something of her mettle— seen she had something of the seaman's spit, after all. Ready to tear the whole place apart to clear a space or meet a need; sacrificing linens that'd been her grandmother's, and hauled over in some pokey bucket from England; instantly fetching what Kirk and me wanted, then unflinchingly holding limbs while we set them, or bandaging frostbitten flesh raw with blisters—she'd been everywhere to hand; and now here she was, her tidy lace house cap, embroidered cuffs and morocco slippers long ago ditched by the wayside.

Splashed and bare-armed, her sleeves actually rolled up, and her feet decked out in somebody else's wool socks, to protect them from the bite of the cold floors—stripped of jewelry and ribbons, her hands coarse and red, and her hair straggling out over her ears and forehead, she actually looked kin to Ben; and once when I seen them exchange a word in the hallway, him haggard and rough, her rumpled and drawn, it was possible to say they was yarns of the same rope.

By dawn Thanksgiving Day the winds had fallen, the snows half-lifted and the seas moderated; and at the first hint of light two surfboats was pushed off, Ben steering in one, old Seth in the other—each of them with four men at the oars. Heading out for the schooners— both showing up as a blur now, their mastheads canted at a rakish angle, and their jibbooms chunk in a line off the Point—the two crews met up with an expedition from *Abigail,* Ben's brother Tom and two or three others in the quarterboat; and together they boarded first Galen's, which was deserted, the canvas and tophamper in tatters, then Joseph's, from which they brung off the dead, all of them clinging to the rigging: Joe and three of his seven men. Reckoning all the rest must of been lost in Jim's rescue attempt, or in a bid to launch Joe's dinghy, which was in fact found to be missing, they wrapped up the dead in the battered sails, then stood out for the shore, where we was waiting in a throng; and though I'd been like steel to the last, I couldn't look now as Ben and Tom slowly beached, and gave Joe into the keeping of Elizabeth and Sarah.

His face set and steady, Ben went straight back to work, overseeing the scouting relays on the shore, whilst Tom, after hiking briefly out to the light, to pay his quiet respects to his Pa, rowed back out to *Abigail* to bring off her waiting hands; and as if taking our cues from them, the rest of us dumbly dispersed, some shouldering our tasks, others carrying the dead. In the faltering snow, and the still bitter gusts of cold, we shambled in procession up to Ben's door—a couple of rooms immediately given up for those lost, and for the dazed, restrained vigil of their kin, already on the scene or arriving now by way of the shore; and by contrast with yesterday's chaotic frenzy, the house reigned oddly still and finished.

In the silent grieving that held forth it was almost impossible to take in what'd happened, or to reckon up the toll of the dead; but in the end, with those discovered in daylight ashore, as far as five miles up the coast, it was found we'd lost fifteen men—four others, Sage Haskett amongst them, never recovered, though patrols was kept up throughout the day, and the signals was flying to alert the islands. With twelve of thirteen lost off the schooners, five of six off Jim's surfboat, and two others from Tom Longworthy's attempt—with most of them fathers of young ones, and all critical to some work going forth daily in the port—it was the worst nautical disaster to ever hit the town, and one of the worst recorded on the seaboard; and not least in all the anguish of the mourning ran talk of how it could of happened, right in our teeth on our own shore in our own boats, and how it could of been avoided.

In the midst of all the hushed activity at Ben's, folks was gradually piecing together the story, and fitting each other into the drama of its lines; while some was already beginning the job of combing the harbor for further evidence of loss. That the Melchett schooners was taken aback by the sudden onslaught of the northeast gale, as they rounded the Point early yesterday morning, and straightaway driven aground on the shelf that skirted most of the headland with shoals, was pretty much taken for granted; but it wasn't till hands from Melchett Bros. come aboard, later on in the broadening daylight, that they was able to assess the full extent of the damage.

Inspecting Galen's vessel, they found the tophamper useless, though the hull and cargo still looked to be sound; but Joseph's craft, piled up just off the light, 'd been pounded to pieces, a total loss. Hardly a hundred yards to windward, *Abigail* was safe, though she'd dragged both of her anchors, and lost every stitch of her new suit of canvas, whole acres having worked adrift in their bunts; but just the same, between the loss of Galen and Joseph, key figures in the outfit— Galen for decades ship's husband, and Joe a sterling shipmaster— and the lesser blows of the schooners and cargo, Melchett Bros. was in total disorder: the trek to China, posted to clear in ten days, postponed now till Christmas at the soonest.

Nor was they the only calamity in the harbor; for the rest of the
shipping, from Hull and Lombard on down to the ketches and yawls
in the fishing village, had come to grief as well—hardly a vessel whole
and unscathed. It being too much to take it all in—to begin to think
of getting on without kin, to renew all the damage or even to tackle
the logistics of setting up a more permanent lifesaving service, folks
took to concentrating instead on what'd been done right—looked to
the valor of them who'd given their lives, and the fortitude of them
who'd engineered a life-service.

Though he didn't yet know it, Jim was hailed as a hero, for his
daring recovery of Marshall Pelham; for in coming to, Marshall'd
begun telling stories of Jim's clear-headed leadership and courage—
not just in helping to mount the rescue, but in preserving it when
it went awry—in rallying the others to right the surfboat, which'd
twice overturned in the breakers, and in maintaining calm when
some of Galen's crew'd panicked, and tried to grab the oars from
the surfmen. Yarns like these was soon abounding; but it wasn't
till Tom's quarterboat put ashore again, and discharged the rest of
the crew from *Abigail,* that we had the full story of Ben's staggering
rescue—all hands describing his dumbfounding recognition of Jim,
his resolution and irrational calm, and his seer's words about setting
down to dinner with his children, the way they would the enterprise
of some mystic.

Jim I was able to set by at last early Thanksgiving afternoon, me and
Paul Talbot having brung him by stretcher to the sofa at my place,
and built up the fire; and—though I was glad to finally hear from
his lips a little of what'd happened since Portland—the griefs of the
morning, the concerns for his feet, and above all the pains he suffered
for Ben, all clouded this first chance of ours for a word. When he'd
first opened his eyes earlier on in the day, he'd hoarsely asked, "What
news?", and I'd had to tell him about Joe; and not long after that,
when he again come to, I'd had to explain about his feet, the most
hopeful word being he'd be laid up quite a spell. With Ben constantly
at work on the shore, he hadn't been able to see him so far; but he'd
continually asked about him—about what he was doing, and how he

was standing up to it; and I could see my vague reassurances hadn't fooled him.

Now, laying flat on his back on my sofa, his feet raised a little on a couple of cushions, and his legs swathed in bandages to his knees, he was brung even lower by the clang of the bells —the tolls having begun for our losses; for though we was too far out of town to usually hear them, the northeast wind was still gusting strong, and fetching their clamor clearly to us. Trying to shut out that wailful sound, he wasn't the clearest at telling a story; but he was able to recall how things'd gone at Elkanah's, and how him and Ben'd come home on horseback. Realizing along the way that Ben and Joe hadn't parted friends, I guessed the guilt Ben must feel for not having been aboard the schooners; and Jim wept when he told me about their night at the inn, too weak not to give in to his frustration.

Their separation in town, Ben for *Abigail*, him for my place, and his valiant surfboat battle out to Galen's, he was able to relate pretty plainly; but his final capsize and the loss of Galen, and the mounting anguish of fatigue and exposure, he was mercifully already forgetting; whilst of the wild ride to shore he remembered nothing—nothing till being ill on the beach, with Ben's great bulk and command beside him. Nor was he much better at absorbing what I told him in return—seeming scarcely able to comprehend that Joseph and his entire crew, with whom he'd been loading just this past Monday, was lost—that even his old adversary from the first trek aboard *Charis*, Sage Haskett, was gone.

The only thing that held his attention, and seemed to make a lasting impression, was the story I passed on of Ben's rescue of him: his unaccountable recognition of him in the blizzard, his irrational daring in putting over the dory, and his mind-stumping row through the breakers, a yarn he wanted to hear over and over. But each time the mournful clang of the bells, and his anxiety for Ben and his losses, so overtopped all other considerations, that at last I gave him a few more drops of laudanum, and he slept through the rest of Thanksgiving.

Ben meantime, like all the Melchetts, was simply doing what

he had to—carrying out the necessities of the day to the finish; and though every time I run into him I begged him to rest, there was no stopping him or any of the others till everyone missing was accounted for. It being Thanksgiving, and Sarah being Sarah, dinner was on time, at three—all the Melchetts who could be spared from the shore meeting at the family house; while those who couldn't put in an appearance showed up to take their turn in relays, sometime or other before nightfall. Though I wasn't there, I had the story from Sadie, whose sister was one of the serving girls at Sarah's, that grace before dinner was one of thanks for Galen's gifts to the shipyard and family, and for Joseph's legacy of children—every one of his young ones dressed up, and in his right mind, at the table; and with a heritage like that I wouldn't of looked for Ben to buckle under, any more than I would of any of the others.

It was in his blood to carry his burden; so it come as no surprise to me that he rounded up his family and took his own turn later on at the table—stopping by my place afterwards to see Jim, still decked out in his top hat and dress coat. Though dinner must of been, in its own way, one of the most harrowing parts of his day, he wasn't thinking of hisself as he bent over Jim, peacefully asleep on the sofa; was simply thinking of Jim and his hardships—looking down on him with a face so worn by gratitude and sorrow, that I had to turn away for a minute, and fumble at the kettle and teacups.

Asleep like he was, so plainly marked with fatigue—the shadows under his eyes emphasized by his day's beard, which he'd been too tired to let me shave—Jim looked vulnerable, so much more unguarded than he had two years ago, and so much more comely, in a hurt way; and Ben, stooped over him, almost looked old, aged with exposure and burden, the way branches of scrog look after years on some headland, laying open to the windblasts and brine. Like lobsters in the growing season, when they split their shells and hide for a time, susceptible to whatever comes along, they was both more or less defenseless—beatable except for their stubborn persistence; and every instinct in me wanted to shelter them somehow—to harbor them with some kind of temporary protection, same as a cowrie houses a hermit, one of them bare crabs without any shield.

His big hands plucking a little at the blankets, Ben tugged them up closer about Jim, as if he, too, sensed the need for cover; tugged and tucked the thick folds about him till alls I could see was the tumble of dark hair, the curve of one cheek and the sweep of thick lashes—Ben's knotty fingers quaking so much with the clumsy care of a lover that I finally give in, and hauled out my kerchief. As though freed by my feeling he looked up and smiled, even accepted the armchair and teacup I offered; and taking a few sips he talked a little, sensibly and calmly there by the fire—mostly about Jim and how he was coming along, and what needed to happen next on the shore. But I continually sensed there was something brittle about him, as if he'd used up all but a shred of his strength; and my impression wasn't contradicted any by his cough, and the look of pain on his face whenever he moved his arms.

"Ben," I braved, "ye ain't well—I c'n see it; it's time y' had a rest, an' ye know it."

"It's nothing," he answered, "just a bit of the ague—I felt it comin' on when we was still at Elkanah's, an' bein' out in the storm's just flared it up some."

"You'hre in pain," I kept at it; "what's wrong with youhr arms?"

"I don't know," he admitted, "some strain or otheh—must of happened in the wateh, maybe when I was tryin' t' hang onto Jim...I...y'know, I neveh even noticed it till t'night, when I was settin' down t' dinneh."

Though I urged him to lay low, or at least to knock off for a bit, he simply smiled and shook his head, reminding me what I already knew only too well—that first thing tomorrow they had to move *Abigail*, and float Galen's schooner before more bad weather set in; and then, a' course, if there was any more time before the funeral, called for mid-afternoon at the meeting house, they had to make a start on transferring the cargo, and renewing all the damage. Promising to lend a hand—thinking to go in Jim's place, and help lighten the load—I was on the Ship Street wharf at daybreak; and what a load it was, as matters turned out—about twenty of us employed till dinner shifting *Abigail*, no easy job with them anchors, not to mention, not a whole sail to steer with—and bringing off Galen's schooner with the tide. How Ben managed in all the blustery cold, what with his meager sleep the past three days, and his arms paining so he could scarcely take a bar at the captstan, or tally onto the falls and tow ropes, I couldn't have ventured; but it all took the last bit of wind out of my sails, and left me ready for a long spell in dry dock.

That afternoon the funeral was to be held, one mass service for all the men recovered—the whole town expected save those still laid up; and Jim, on his back with his feet bandaged and raised, fretted not to be there to help Ben, if only with the aid of his presence. Dressed in my best—in black, like everyone else, though mavericks like Sarah wasn't going to keep up mourning, insisting Galen'd never had any use for it—I listened for the harness ring of the Melchett sleigh, Ben having promised to bring me into town with his family; and hearing them drive up—seeing him step down from the reins, and make his way along the plowed piles of my walk—I stood in the entry and waited, knowing he was coming in to check Jim.

It was the first time he'd seen him awake since he'd helped him up from the turmoil on the shore, the nightmarish morning before last; and stepping in, in his sober grey greatcoat and beaver hat, his driving gloves still in his hand, and his cravat and collar neatly adjusted—catching sight of Jim, half-sitting against the cushions, bundled up in quilts and comforters and flannels—his eyes lighted up in the plain calm of his face, touching it with comely concern, and transforming the whole of his tired expression.

As soon as he seen him, Jim held out his arms, too full of compassion and understanding not to; and his face flaming up with all the pain between them, Ben simply swept off his hat and went to him; set down by his side and went into his arms, laying his head beside Jim's on the pillow. Neither of them moving or saying a word— so intertwined it was impossible to say who was comforting who— they simply held onto one another, as though to trade off, without talk or glances, all they'd shored up since the start of the storm; simply held one another in silence, while the clock ticked quietly on the mantle. So long did they surrender so, that I thought Ben'd swooned, or fallen asleep; but at last, hearing the impatient stomp of the horses—the crunch of the snow, and the jingle of harness— and recalling the wait of Ben's family in the sleigh, I unwillingly stepped in, and touched Ben on the shoulder. Sighing, he stirred, and took leave of Jim slowly, drawing his arms out from under him gently, while Jim's fingers fell reluctantly from his shoulders; then not looking at him, but picking up his gloves, Ben put on his hat and accepted my arm; and not looking back, we left together.

In the days to come after things was slow to progress, folks getting back into the saddle by inches—most of the town in black gowns and bonnets, armbands or hatbands or handkerchiefs at breast pockets, with mourning wreaths in place of greens on their front doors, and festoons of crepe at their windows. Aboard *Abigail*, repairs was coming along slowly, bad weather several times interfering; whilst Tom and the others was feeling the ropes at Melchett Bros., trying to figure out just where Galen'd left things, and how to replace the lost cargo by Christmas. At the town meeting the pews was crowded, everyone subscribing what they could to a life-saving station, with a full-time keeper in fall and winter; but other than that, there was no social to-dos, all the end of the year festivities called off, and hardly the plunk of a piano to be heard of a still night.

In the midst of it all Ben was floundering along, so plainly under the weather that his own kin asked him to knock off, and so busy he could only show up for brief spells, mostly long after Jim was asleep; whilst Jim hisself wasn't coming on much faster, his worries about Ben dragging out his recovery, and dark dreams about the storm cutting into his rest. Though no gangrene developed—the great threat he'd faced—the tissues was worrisomely slow to heal; and he knew, in spite of my best efforts to hide it, that Pelham, in similar circumstances, would lose at least part of one foot—that being the one thing on earth he really feared, though he didn't never say so to me. The way he had it worked out, what he most had going for him with Ben was his looks, especially now with things coming so close; and though I tried to persuade him different, he held onto the idea like a limpet onto a rock.

"Jim, you'hre goin' t' get oldeh, y' know; ye ain't always goin' t' look twenty," I told him, one night when he was feeling particularly low, after being alone all day while I'd been out helping with *Abigail*; "d'y think Ben's the kind to stop carin' with age, or with accidents that happen along the way?" But arguments of that sort was too abstract, or based too much on the future to weigh much with him—matters to come of no count at all, compared to the vital issues of the present; and I didn't gain no ground with him that way, even with my whole heart put in it.

Besides his fear of being disfigured—his instinctive dread of the marred or misshapen, the by-product, maybe, of Rom superstitions— was his anxiety about his career: him being almost as scared he'd be forever barred from active sailing, as he was he'd be permanently maimed. Though he tried not to show it, I could feel his private panic at the thought of not being able to share Ben's work with him, since that was the chief way they come together—the one place in the sun he didn't have to share with Anne. Even at best, as he knew now, he'd be boarding *Abigail* on a cane—and his fear was, he wouldn't be able to keep up with Ben; and I hadn't the heart to tell him the other matter I'd been hiding from him, that a toddler could keep up with Ben nowadays.

At first he'd managed to keep pace, Ben had, out in the cold from daybreak until dusk, except when on 'Change or at noon dinner; but gradually that stopped, his arms almost useless, and his physical strength failing, though he wouldn't admit it; and I run into him more and more at the counting house, overseeing *Abigail*'s progress from there. Ever since the storm he'd been coughing, a dry, wracking cough I didn't at all like the sound of; and I suspected at times, from the dry glitter of his eyes, that he was suffering on and off from fever. Once, coming up on him at his desk—which was littered with narratives from other captains on the China run, none of them in the order that was his habit—I surprised that brittle look on him again; seen how his hands, which was always work-rough, had took on an almost fragile appearance, as though they was somehow thinner or see-through; and my heart gave a thud, though I greeted him calmly.

As Jim finally begun to show signs of healing, his right foot more than his left, but both enough to ease my cares—as he finally begun to progress, to the point where I'd made him a pair of crutches, and set them by to encourage him through his days on the sofa—I shifted my worries more and more to Ben; and I campaigned through Tom to get him to rest, though that didn't pay off any more than my own words. If ever he'd been stubborn, he was stubborner now, mule headed with the need to shoulder his share, and get his family and the shipyard back on track by Christmas; but more than that he was bulldogged with the same anxieties as Jim, the same fears of submitting to infirmity and frailness.

To not have his hand on the helm of events, but to be steered and shaped by some other pilot—and that pilot, his own weakness—was more than he could bow to, with his will to govern; and the toll of his resistance, on top of his labors and the losses suffered in the blizzard, wrought an almost daily change on his face. When at last he come by my place one day after breakfast, around the end of the first week of December, and asked me to lend a hand with the shipment that'd arrived by sloop the night before at the wharf, he looked so eroded that I threw friendship to the wind—ordered him straight back to bed, to which he agreed; but I knew, even as I watched him climb back into his cutter, that since he'd given in, it was already too late.

It was early the next day that Anne sent over a note, asking me straight by to take a look at him; and even though I'd seen it coming, my pulse gave a jump as soon as I read it, for she hardly ever asked for my help or Kirk's. Thankful that Jim was busy with breakfast, and so had no clear idea who'd called, I simply hollered to him from the entry that I was wanted at the yard; and hauling on coat and boots, I was out the door. Going over by sleigh, I found Ben upstairs, established in the spare bed in the guest room; and meeting me on the threshold Anne ushered me in, looking as pallid as seasmoke, and sleepless—not only Ben, but Courtney and Nat under the weather, the little ones with croup, which'd kept her at it all night.

When I asked her about Ben she shook her head, as if to signal he'd already got past her; and as soon as I seen him I could tell why, for not even my worst fears'd prepared me for what I found: the big bulk of him lying there as if toppled—senseless and soundless save for the rasping of breath—and motionless in every timber. Like some burly king pine that's withstood the years, and borne on its bark, or in the twists of its boughs, every carve of the clime, yet pegged away to the last, only to finally inevitably crumble, he was at that utmost transition—at that point where the pulp almost visibly yields itself over; and struck amidships, I stopped in my tracks.

Standing there I realized I hadn't never seen him lying down—all them times at sea or out hunting, when I'd shaken him awake by the shoulder, hardly counting, since he put out nearly as much energy and determination at rest as he did at work; and for a spell I just couldn't take it in, as if it was my sticks and beams, not just his, that was failing. Simply drifting a bit there at first in the guest room, I rubbed my chin and tugged at my pockets and remembered—out of nowheres—a few years back, when he'd busted his ankle and sat up while I set it, smoking cigars and taking pulls at my brandy, and telling me exactly what to do. There was no such barrage of directions from him now; and I rued all them times I'd wanted to break his neck, all afloat as I was a few feet from his bedside, scarcely even knowing how to approach him.

Setting gingerly by him, I at last looked him over—listened to his lungs, tapped his chest, felt his fever, then considered the remedies Anne'd applied, feeling the whole time like an intruder—like I should at least be asking his permission, never having had him put so completely into my hands. But even in all my clutter of feeling, I could verify my guess it was lung fever, and lung fever of the swiftest kind. Against such a foe we had few weapons; and weakened by the trials of the past weeks, he lacked the critical one, the constitution he'd once had. Calling in Anne, I said, "This is goin' t' go fast; I want ye t' do just as I ask, the first thing bein', send for Kirk at once"; and giving a wordless nod, she was off to dispatch Sadie or Jake the stableman with a note to town.

With Kirk on the scene I felt less out in the cold, as if two rattled heads was somehow more reassuring than one; and together we was able to improve on what Anne'd done—the timeworn remedies of a marjoram vapor, and a poultice of cayenne and bran to the chest—

by adding quinine as a fever-breaker, and agreeing to watch him in shifts, on and off every six hours. That'd free Anne to tend the young ones, who had to be constantly coaxed along with ipecac, infusions of mullein or red clover or hyssup, and still give Kirk time to look after others—lung fever and diphtheria having showed up in several households, along with the seasonal grippe and ague. That it wouldn't be long before things with Ben reached a crisis was just as plain to Kirk as it'd been to me; and leaving him to take the first spell, since he'd had to come all the way out from town, I drove my cutter up and down the Point Road, trying to settle my commotion of fears.

Spooked as I was I couldn't straight off face Jim—had to calculate how long I could delay the news, how long it would be before Sarah and the rest got wind of it, and word worked its way from town back to him; had to conjure up a calm face, and excuses to come and go at odd hours. Gliding up to my cabin I found I was in luck for the present, for Paul Talbot was there, having almost daily stopped by to see Jim; and in all the to-do of refreshments and dinner, my looking green round the gills went unnoticed. Slipping out for the afternoon I could pretty artfully manage, and ditto for midnight, since I could sneak out and snowshoe, trudging the path between our two houses instead of rigging up the sleigh with a racket; but even so, with all my tiptoeing, I could see he was on to me by the next day—could tell it by the way he studied my face, and said nothing at all about Ben or his absence.

Dreading it'd set him back if he heard—knowing full well just what he'd do, if once he got onto the story—I kept it up for another whole day; set beside Ben them long hours and waited, searching his features for any signs of a change, then went home and put on a show for Jim, trying to keep my head and hands steady. Whether word finally reached him from town—news of the prayerful vigils at Sarah's, or tell of the further slowdown at the yard, all hands trying to fill in around Ben—I couldn't of said; but long about the third day of the ordeal, when I could see myself things couldn't go on much longer, and had made up my mind it was my duty to break the news, he seemed suddenly determined to have it out in the open, as I could tell when I come home from my shift. Before I even opened my mouth, he asked "How is he?"; and setting tiredly down in my armchair, then pouring out the tea he'd saved for me, I told him.

At once he throwed off his quilts and stood up, then reached for his crutches, hell-bent to go; and though I actually wrestled him full force—warned him he'd lost all he'd gained if he walked, and let him know there'd be no welcome from Anne, who already had more than her hands full—there was no getting him down again on that sofa, or convincing him to delay his visit. Whether it'd been built up by his rest, or sprung from some sudden final reserve, triggered by the fierceness of his love, his strength was much greater than I expected; and I seen he'd go to Ben's alone, undertake it at a creep if he had to, if I didn't agree myself to help him. Fetching his clothes—wrapping rags round his feet, since he couldn't bear shoes, and would be too exposed in slippers—I steadied him on his crutches to the cutter, which I'd brung to the very door to save steps; then sitting him down with his feet on a hot soapstone, and bundling him up in a heavy lap robe, I drove him to Ben's, stopping again close to the porch.

Hobbling painfully in—struggling with the crutches, but still looking dead-ahead and undaunted, his mind bolted to the one thing that mattered—he labored past tables laden with foodstuffs, everything from gifts of blancmange to whole meals, brung in by well-wishers who'd tactfully withdrawn; made it as far as the stairway in the front hall, which run up a steep flight of twenty or more steps; and here even he was brung to a halt, no clearer than me on how to get up them. If I'd of been Ben in the pink of his strength, I could of carried him up in my arms; but lighter built than Ben by far, I couldn't alone begin to attempt it; while with two bad feet Jim's crutches was useless, worse than a burden to him on the stairs. Seeing it all at a glance, he simply handed his props to me, and proceeded to climb up on his hands and knees; and watching him crawl—guarding him from behind, so that no untimely slip caused a fall—I had to bite my lip as I followed.

As soon as he'd hobbled into the guestroom he took things over from speechless Kirk, as if it was him who was the doctor; looked quickly at Ben, at his senseless face and frail hands, a-droop with the peculiar limpness of the failing, not once flinching in his swift survey. Then glancing at the cayenne poultice, herbal vapor and other feeble paraphernalia of our effort, he turned to Kirk and declared without preamble, "We've got t' get him straight out of here, into a tent; if you'll carry him, I'll tell you what t' do."

About blown over, Kirk looked out the window, at the flurries drifting down in the bleak wind, then back at Jim as if he'd taken leave of his senses; and understanding the look—at once impatient— Jim stamped his ragged foot and insisted, "It's the only way—it's the way we do it."

Sitting him down, anxious to get him off his feet—Anne meantime sweeping in looking ill-pleased, and Kirk still sitting buffaloed by the bed—I soothed, "Try an' explain; you mean the Rom—what do they do?"; and struggling to calm hisself, he answered.

"We've got t' get him into a tent, build campfires around it, get kettles going, and funnel the steam into the tent through hoses; I tell you, it works; we've got t' do it."

If Kirk was appalled Anne was more so, flatly refusing permission to move him; and Jim, in his desperation at being refused, turned on her. "We haven't got much time; we've got t' move fast," he flamed up, getting to his feet again as he faced her; and her hands went to her hips in that cold threat. They'd never been friends, but he'd respected her with the same untutored politeness he showed to all folks, while she'd been as courteous as any well-bred matron; but now they squared off, her chill as a floor in January to his fire.

"What time we've got, we'll spend indoors, and not in some foolish gypsy contraption," she frosted, her face strained and white above her black dress; and Jim's fiery eyes blazed up all the hotter.

"You'll be the death of him if you won't try it," he burst out, too stung by her words to think out his reply.

Overwrought from the past weeks, she met blade for blade. "Let me tell you this, James Robertson, you've—*you've* been the death of him already—why, it's because of you he's so ill—if he hadn't gone afteh you in that boat—"

"Anne!" Kirk and me both cried out, stunned into rebuke; but she stabbed on,

"Get out of here while he still has a chance!"

His face stricken white all the way to the lips, Jim just the same heroically blazened, "He's got no chance at all without me"; and in answer she rang out another defiance,

"Get out, or I'll send Jake for the constable t' carry you out!"

"For God's sake," he pleaded, "let me at least sit a while by him"— and I realized, even in the midst of my aghast dumbness, that I'd never before in these years heard him beg.

"No," she snapped, "you've no place at his side; you'hre not even kin; you'hre—you've no business here."

Finding my tongue, I tried to placate her, sticking my oar into this withering exchange; but overtaxed by the misfortunes of the past weeks, and now by the additional stresses of illness, she was immovable, as fast as a ship on a bar; and to make matters worse the children across the hall, waked up by the clamor and clang of our voices, began to whimper again and cough, the sharp, ringing barks of the croup. Having had it with us, Kirk ordered us all out, Anne to the young ones and me and Jim back downstairs, till peace was restored and reason established; and in no position to overrule him—thinking to buy time by obliging—I said gently, "Come, Jim," taking his arm, and trying not to look at his face.

Standing there undecided—as if, after all, he'd take his chances, and hold out for the arrival of the constable—he didn't budge an inch for a moment; then all at once a peculiar look crossed his face, a look I knew meant he hadn't had the last word, and 'd just come up with a way to get it; and shuffling out on his crutches without a glance at Ben, he got down on all fours and crawled down the stairs—Anne not there to see him, or even she might of had a change of heart.

Heading straight for the door he kept up a fair pace—hobbled directly along even when I plucked at his sleeve, and whispered we might not have to leave the house, if we set by a while quiet and played our cards right; and getting into the sleigh he was still mum as a post, looking off into space as though deep in his thoughts. Giving in to his mood, I picked up the reins, and drove the two of us back to my place; and a quieter run I couldn't of made if alone. Not till

I'd gotten him back onto my sofa, his feet up and warming on a hot brick, did he speak; and then it was to calmly order, as if he'd just walked into the chandler's:

"I'll need a couple yards of canvas, some middle-weight duck; three of four lengths of India rubber hoses; three kettles at least, and spirit-lamps to go with; a sheath knife, some sinnet, and five stout sticks for a frame"—looking at my dumbfounded face meantime with the quirk of a brow, as though to get me moving.

"Jim," I managed at the end of this manifest, "just what is it ye think ye're up to?"

"It's simple," he said; "if they won't move him out to a tent, we'll bring the tent into his room."

Bamboozled by the very logistics, not to mention the matter of Anne's reaction, I got out through stiff lips, "Good Lord, man, are ye crazy?"; and squalling up his brow, he huffed at me just like Ben would.

"We can do it, I tell you; we'll rig the tent up over his bed, set up the spirit-lamps in place of campfires, get kettles going and channel the steam in through hoses."

"Jim," I hesitated, "I've heard an' seen a lot...an' it's not that I doubt youhr word it's worked...but—"

"You've got vapor goin' in his room now; how is it that this is so different?"

"Well, marjoram or lavendeh oil, they dry up the mucus—steam's just—"

"Moist warmth; I tell you, it works; I've seen it myself a dozen of times."

"How're we goin' t' keep from burnin' his lungs?" I pressed him.

"The length of the hoses; we'll adjust 'em for heat."

"An' how're we goin' t' get all this set up there when Anne an' Kirk 're both dead set against it?"

That he'd figured it all out in the sleigh was apparent from the ease with which the plot spilled from his lips. "T'night," he laid out for me, "when your shift comes around, we'll drive over t'gether with everything packed in the cutter... You'll leave me by the springhouse so no one'll see me...stop the cutter close by the porch an' go in...an' when Kirk has left I'll slip in the back door, unload an' carry things into the pantry, where I'll wait till Anne has gone t' bed... she'll *have* t' sleep sooner or later.:"

"Son," I said gently, "you'll ruin youhr feet."

"For God's sake, Eben, this has got t' be done...you know it, you saw him, you..." So far he'd managed to keep up his spirit, standing up to trials that would of unknit me; but now his features begun to crumble, and his hand come up to shield his face; and going straight to him, I put my arms round him. "It's my fault," he kept on; "Anne's right...I've brought him to this...you see, I've *got* to come up with some way t' help."

"Oh, God, Jamie, you—ye can't possibly blame youhrself for this," I soothed him, feeling his shoulder a-quake in my hands; "Anne was off her head, she didn't mean it..." For a long time I simply sat and held him, waiting for the tremors to ease up in his body, and listening to the fire crackle on the hearth; then feeling him quieten a little, I looked for a word or two that would help him, yet caution or check his expectations.

"Jim," I said plainly, "I'll do this for ye, so there's neveh any doubt in your mind, aftehward, that ye did anything less than your best... that we neglected anything on the books, or off 'em, t' help give him the winnin' edge in this fight. I... I want ye t' undehstand, though, speakin' now as a doctoh... it's. ..things're about as bad as they could be, mate...lung feveh's one o' them things we got no more control oveh than a squall...it might be there's nothing, not this tent, not anything, that c'n bust it...ye've got t' begin t' try an' face it."

"I know what t' do," he wholly ignored me, lifting his face and gripping his knees with his hands in order to quell their insistent shaking; "just get me back over there with these things, an' leave the rest up t' me"; and giving in to the smile that fought its way to my lips, in spite of the currents of worry against it, I gave his shoulder one last encouraging pat, and begun to hunt for the gear on his list.

Following his directions I got the whole lot together, packed into a neat inconspicuous bundle in the sleigh; and when my turn to watch come around at eleven, I drove him as far as the springhouse near

Ben's drive, which was out of sight—thanks to some pines—of the main place. Shuffling off in the snow—his feet wrapped not just in rags, but in strips of oilcoth I'd cut up from an old coat—he slipped noiselessly into the shed door, not forgetting to bring his crutches in with him; and pulling ahead to the porch—looking instinctively up at the shutters, and thanking God they wasn't drawn, the sign I'd feared every time now for three days—I climbed down and hurried into the house, which was quiet and dark except for a few lanterns.

Meeting me at Ben's door, Kirk took me aside, his shoulders slumped in the rumpled folds of his frock coat, and whispered he expected the crisis tonight; added that I should call Anne when I thought it best—that he'd given her a calmative to help her rest, since Courtney and Nat both seemed easier, and was sleeping; and looking at Ben I seen he was right—the changes in him visible almost hourly now. Oxygen-starved, his face was bluish, the tint plain to behold in the room's feeble light; whilst a tap to the chest yielded almost no resonance at all, and his breath come even shorter than it had. Giving a nod, I set my bag down by the bed, whilst Kirk picked his up and stole softly downstairs; then glancing around, I took stock of the room, plotting our needs for the next six hours.

In bottles and cups, Ben's swarm of medications—the infusions of hysup, the syrups of horehound and elderberry, and the tonics and elixirs the apothecary had compounded—all stood forlorn and untouched on his nightstand, as if his requirements had long since outstripped them; and I seen we'd no reason to concoct fresh batches. In the porcelain pot the lavender oil still vapored, as it did in the children's dish across the hall, near which the young ones, and Anne, was sleeping; the fires still burned handsomely in both rooms, and a plentitude of water showed in the basins. Clearly there was nothing more to be done except rig the tent and wait for the crisis; and privately making up my mind not to call Anne—not just because of the deception we was about to practise on her, but because I'd decided, selfishly, that if we lost him, I didn't want her by him, nor anyone else, save me and Jim—I tiptoed to the children's library at the back of the house, and parted the curtains to look out the window.

Scraping off the frost, I was in time to see Jim as he hobbled up to the sleigh in the moonlight; and slipping quietly down the stairs—taking special care near the kitchen, off which Sadie slept in the old borning room—I met him at the porch door with our gear, which he'd somehow contrived to hoist without crutches. Taking the load from him, I stepped slow while he crawled, that being quieter than stumping along on his props; and by dint of good planning we managed the whole in one trip, with a minimum of fuss and commotion.

Together in Ben's room, we shut the door; then sitting down by the bed—his face a mix of pain and clashed feelings, relief that he'd actually arrived with the tent, and urgency now that he'd seen Ben's changes—Jim begun to whisper directions. Setting up the frame, then covering it with the canvas went relatively quick and easy; but finding suitable tables for the spirit lamps, getting their individual flames going, filling the kettles and hooking them up to the hoses— which Jim hisself cut into the walls of the tent—was more difficult and time-consuming; and conscious of the clock, we fumbled and hurried. Checking the steam as it come into the tent—considering its temperature and amount, and searching carefully for leaks—took more time; but satisfied at last, Jim set down once again, heaved a sigh and pronounced the job finished.

Covering Ben's face—taking one last look, and stroking his brow with my gnarly hand—I bent low and whispered, "Come on, old man...wind's up"; then enclosing him completely in his canvas shell—leaving only his hands outside, so that I could occasionally feel them, and know from their touch how he was faring—I stood up and turned my attention to Jim's feet, which was still encased in wet oilskins. Unwrapping them, I warmed them with my hands, and looked at them in the light of the small lamps; then finding strips of flannel—in the bag Anne used for making bandages, or the layers needed for poultices and plasters—I wrapped them again in a soft, dry thickness. Oblivious of me, Jim'd taken Ben's hand, and cupped it in both of his with a sigh; and as I cleared things away he thanked me with a smile, and begged me to leave them alone together. Knowing what he wanted to do, I picked up my coat, and bent down close to him for a moment; then shrugging into my sleeves, I crept up the hall, and settled myself in the children's library.

For an endless time I set there in my coat, shivering head to toe from the cold, the anxiousness of the wait or both; and though I strained my ears to the limit, not a sound met me save for my own breath, and the occasional spark of a log on the hearth. Out in the hall, at the head of the stairs, stood a magnificent old clock, a lofty pine timepiece that'd once been Ben's grandfather's; and with the library door open I could also hear that, not the ticking so much as the quarter hours, which rung out in a series of chimes. These I kept track of till I growed drowsy and confused, even mixed up as to the hours—one sounding like two and two, like four, since the old gem was a repeater; and finally I found, in spite of my worry, and the numbing cold which caused me to chatter, that I could only stay awake by moving about.

Getting up a ritual, I rose every quarter hour to scrape off a fresh layer of frost from the window, look out on the night and consider the moon's progress; then tiptoeing to the children's room I checked on things there, regularly putting another log on the fire, or adding hot water to the porcelain pot to keep the lavender oil well-steaming. Propped up on their pillows, the young ones seemed restful, whilst Anne—on a cot between them—looked shadowed and strained; but the longer they slept, the more hope for Jim's contraption, and, maybe, the more chance for Ben; so I took care on my walks to make no more than a hush.

The rest of every quarter hour I passed looking back on my years with Ben—recalling old memories I'd scarcely known I carried; recollected all the way back to our boyhood, to the big, tow-headed lad he'd been then, scaring up lobsters with me a few yards from the shore. The congregation of mussels we'd harbored in a sort of miniature tidescape— the jettisoned crab-backs and legs we'd collected—the additions we'd made to our assembly of shells, still on display downstairs in the front room: all of these I called up and fingered and handled, with the same boyish wonder I'd hosted then. Of what we would come to, Jim and me, if he left us—of how Jim'd bear it, or how I would help him, I thought nothing—in fact, kept the very ideas at bay; actually fought them off with old memories or my walks, like the Rom ward off evil factors with rites.

Half the time pacing around, half the time harking back, I must of passed a couple of hours, all the while in the dark as to what was transpiring; but at last, between the bone-chilling cold and the numbing wait, and the befogging fatigue that sprung partly from my fight, partly from the hypnotic sounds of the clock, I simply had to know how Ben was faring; and the next quarter hour that chimed I crept down the hall, and gently cracked open his door.

Looking in I seen that all was as before: the spirit lamps burning brightly, the teakettles steaming briskly, the hearth fire sparking occasionally, and the chill air condensing—little droplets of moisture from the kettles' heat settling out in a film on the fixtures and tables. Still in its place, the tent looked to be working, Ben's legs under the covers motionless at the far end; whilst the woodbox and basins showed supplies almost as ample as they had when I'd earlier left them. Atop the cluttered nightstand, or along the mantle, the cups and bottles of medication still huddled, flickering in and out of the flame-light; and the ragbag, my valise, Jim's crutches and trappings hunched likewise in the corners we'd set them. Even the fire screen with its bough-perched parrot that Ben'd repeatedly confused with Jasper, the first night when he'd been off his head and mumbling, still held forth undisturbed near the armchair; while the curtains and walls continued to harbor the uneasy quiet that'd clung there for three days.

The only difference that I could distinguish was a new air or crispness at large in the room—an alertness that met me at the door like a force, and seemed to heighten the colors and sounds, even to set up its own uncanny crackle; whilst Jim, who I'd left setting by Ben's side, bundled up in his peacoat and muffler, was now down on his knees by the bed, his head bowed over Ben's hand on the covers. As soon as I seen him I knew he was praying—knew it as sure as if he'd said so, or as if I'd spotted him at meeting, his shoulders stooped to some hush of a plea; and touched to the heart by the sight of this gypsy attempting his friend's ways to fight for his life—humbled that, while he'd been battling in spirit, I'd only been counting off quarter hours—I gently, silently clicked the door shut, and crept back down the hall to try it.

That it'd been years since I'd really prayed—if I ever had, since I'd mostly listened to others, or calculated the Lord could tap my head when he wanted; that I was accordingly rusty at it, and not very comfortable getting started, goes without saying; but I figured that if Jim could do it, and him not even brung up as a Christian, I could. At first I found myself feeling out of my depth, and coming up for air every so often, still counting the chimes or thinking of the fires; found myself at an initial loss for words, since I was afraid to directly name Ben, or confess my fear for his life—having staved death off so successfully the past three days, by keeping busy or thinking other thoughts, that to pronounce it now seemed like a surrender. Even to pray, "Lord, spare Ben for us" was to concede we stood to lose him; and I hadn't really said as much to myself yet, in spite of how I'd cautioned Jim.

But somewheres along the line—after my first ducking of fear that acknowledging death would somehow make it happen—I started to feel like I was underway; like I was being heard, or more like I was speaking for Ben, feeling for him, and so fending off his illness; and then something like a battle commenced, a battle I couldn't quit on once I started. It wasn't a contest between my will and God's, if it was indeed God's will he should die; wasn't a combat made up of words, at any rate, not once I got going; wasn't a war of memories or hopes for the future—in fact, had nothing at all to do with words or pictures, or anything else I usually thought with; it was simply a struggle and I was in it, and Ben was, and Jim was, and my body suffered. As if I was hauling a flailing yardarm brace against the bucking pound of a windblast—as if I was fisting a half-frozen main course in all the pitch and hail of a blizzard—I was wracked and wrung in every muscle; was so tugged and wrenched in every direction that at last my whole being ached, busted up by the effort. So obliterating was the pain, and so extinguishing my weakness, that at last I simply gave myself up to them; surrendered to the blankness of their surge as I would to any slumber; and putting my head down on the library table, then closing my eyes, I went out on their flow.

Coming to all at once—maybe with the chunk of a log, maybe with some instinctive awareness of the lengthy passage of time—I jerked my head up, realizing I'd been asleep, and fuzzy with the dark and exhaustion, I groped for something concrete to pin to. As I struggled for my wits the clock struck six times, and I recollected Kirk would be here in an hour; then a pang of dread swept me as I thought of the night passed, and what it must of meant to Ben. Getting to my feet—untangling myself from the quilt, and finding my limbs was almost numb—I tiptoed up the hall to his door; heard nothing within, no perk of the kettles, no sound of Jim; and not sure what I would of expected anyway—whether he would of been weeping if we'd lost Ben, or whether he would of been dumb in the first shock—I was terrified to enter the room. Nothing I'd ever done before took as much courage as simply turning the knob, and quietly cracking open the door; and it required what seemed like hours to do it.

At last, looking in—the caps actually jumping in my knees, and cold flurries assailing my midriff—I was still none the wiser, for everything was just the same as before: the fire still burning, though much lower now; the kettles still going, albeit slower, the whale oil in the spirit lamps just about spent; and Jim still on his knees by the bed, but fast asleep with his face cuddled against Ben's hand, so again I couldn't see it. Not wanting to wake him till I knew how Ben was—thinking I could even get him out of the room before he fully come to, to spare him the sight if the worst'd happened—I tiptoed to the far side of the bed, where I could look into the tent without disturbing him; stopped by the mantle and fetched down a lantern, which I lighted with one of the spillers; then approaching the tent, I lifted its flap.

Raising the lamp, I looked within, steeling myself as I peered into the mist; brushed aside the steam, my knees braced as I did— but it was life, not death, that my lantern beams fell on, the tranquil hush of a living face. In the light of the rays his forehead was moist, not tortured and bluish as it had been, but peacefully damp with the broken fever; and his chest rose and fell with easier breaths. In the puffs of the steam and the shadows about it, it was the finest face I ever seen—shaggy with its beard and unkempt hair, but broad and tender and steadfast; and I bent and kissed its noble brow. In the rush of my joy, I simply needed to cry—needed to sob as I'd never sobbed before; but fearful of waking someone wherever I went—mindful of everyone's health-giving sleep, and desperate, anyways, to be alone for a moment—I at last noiselessly crept down the stairs; and softly springing the latch on the front door, I slipped outside, and flung myself onto a snowbank.

His recovery was slow and dotted with pitfalls, for he was so weakened he was vulnerable to grippe, and any number of other ailments that could just as easily of carried him off; but as soon as he started taking food—which was almost at once, Sadie that same day sending up broth—his progress was steady and unbroken. About brung to his knees, Kirk at once copied Jim's tent, and tried it on old Abby Taylor, where it worked as well; and given to skepticism even at the last minute—more inclined to attribute Ben's recovery to prayer, than to such an outlandish contraption—I come around to the view that both'd played their part, and apologized to Jim for doubting. As for Anne—who'd stumbled into Ben's room that pre-dawn still blinking, probably startled out of her sleep by Jim, who'd broke down as soon as I'd touched him awake with "Jamie, he's safe"—she was so torn by relief at Ben's turn, and indignation at the sight of the rig she'd forbid, to say nothing of the man who'd brung it, down on his hams on that freezing floor with me—that for once she was flat out failed of words; and she set down in the armchair, speechless.

Hoping to minimize ill feelings, Jim soon after collected his gear and bowed out, leaving the tent for me and Kirk to maintain; and with Kirk behind me I was able to persuade her—low in her graces as I was myself—that the set-up was worth keeping, at least till Ben was out of the woods. Though she never come around to confessing its value, even after it saved Abby Taylor—her being one with Ben when it come to stubbornness—she put up with the mess of the kettles and whale oil, hoses and canvas and smoke stains on the ceiling, not to mention, frost an inch thick on the windows; and when at last the tent was took down, the second or third day after Ben'd gotten the turn, it was Kirk—advised by Jim—and not her, that was behind the final decision.

Done in hisself—not just by the vigil, but by his feet—Jim soon had to come to terms with the fact that his own health was the price he'd paid for Ben's; for the hours of premature walking and standing, hobbling in the snow and kneeling on the cold floor—all of which'd impaired his circulation, or bruised the new tissues we'd worked so to build—had set him back just as I'd cautioned; and Kirk, looking him over, decided we could delay no longer, and insisted we remove part of his left foot. It was the outside corner with the small toe, which'd never healed well in the first place; and Jim—with no sure idea what it'd all mean for his work, and the active life he expected to lead—bore the decision uncomplaining.

It was while he was in Kirk's surgery that Ben first asked for him, in a voice so weak I had to bend over to hear; and though I managed to put him off for the moment— reminding him that Jim needed sleep, after his long watch—I soon found myself running out of excuses, for he asked for him day and night after that. So feeble in the beginning he had to be tended like a babe, even propped up and fed with a spoon, he was just the same relentless about Jim—too needful, maybe, to check his want, or mask it with the silence of pride; and finally I told him about Jim's foot, encouraging him with hopes for his progress. Fretful nonetheless—struggling to get up on one elbow, as if he thought he could head straight for Jim's side—he inquired for news even more anxious than before, though he seemed to give him a space to recover; went two or three days without asking to see him, then at last, started in all over again.

By now it was obvious that something was up, for he was receiving all kinds of visitors for short spells: at first his children, long enough for a hug; then his mother, Keziah, and brothers, long enough for the gift of a newspaper, or a brief account of doings at the yard; then finally folks who mattered far less to him, and to who he mattered far less in return, than Jim. Looking me in the eye next time I stopped by—well enough now to smell a rat, and squinting up at me with all the spark of his old vim, even if he did still have to be sat up—he demanded hoarsely why he hadn't seen Jim; and this time I had nothing more to put him off with, for Jim was up and using a cane, and he knew it—having weaseled the news out of Kirk.

Looking him over in exchange—judging him well enough for the story, and ready to take the rap for telling tales out of school—I spun him the whole yarn of Jim and the tent, his run-in with Anne and her heaving him out—watering it down some and giving her the benefit of fatigue, but just the same, spelling out the facts.

That the tent'd been Jim's scheme and that it'd saved his life—that it'd been Jim beside him praying that long night, he'd already heard, since I'd took care to tell him, as soon as I'd figured he could bear his response; but that Anne'd refused Jim—that she'd ordered him out when he'd proposed his tent, and made it necessary for him to sneak back in like a thief, at the risk of his feet and the success of his scheme—was all news; and he had to see that that's how things stood now, with Anne still up in arms that she'd been over-rid, and Jim in effect cut off from the house.

At once it all seemed to give him a jolt, as if it'd made clear how far apart him and Jim still was, and how complete a hold Anne still had on his rights; and setting up a little against the pillows—his knotty hands a-quake with the effort, and the ire that was writ as well on his brow—he growled directly, though in a mere ghost of his old bawl: "Send her to me." Glad that I wasn't her—glad I was anybody else but her—I found her sewing in the sitting room, her fancy work in a heap on her knees, whilst Nat and Courtney, well enough now to be up, played nearby on the hearth; and telling her Ben needed to see her, I stayed down to mind them, partly so's I wouldn't be tempted to overhear. What he said to her—whether he simply asked her to reconsider, or flat out threatened to pack his bags when he was well, and leave the house if Jim wasn't welcome—I'd probably never know, though I figured the latter; but whatever it was she was back down in a minute, asking if I might run a note over.

A' course I would, and I did, trying not to look guilty—trying not to reckon up all the underhanded roles I'd played in the past weeks; and giving the message to Jim—who was still more or less living at my place, in order to be near Ben, if not by him—I set down while he read it, merriment tugging at his mouth. "Ben put her up to it?" he smiled, and I nodded; and later that day, when we knew Ben'd be taking his tea, we drove over to see him, the two of us, in the sleigh.

Meeting us at the door, Anne let us in, the picture of everything expected and proper—black afternoon dress, white lace shoulder cape, smooth manners—nothing showing she'd backed down, or had cause to; and acting hisself like he'd been by a hundred times this past week, Jim asked leave to take tea with Ben, if he was well enough to sit up. Bowing us in, she called the maid to see us up; and not meeting her eyes—not meeting mine either, for fear of shattering the charade—Jim limped along on his cane up the stairs.

Looking up when we walked in—a litter of papers spread on his bed, more for show than for work, since he'd made no progress on them I could detect; looking at Jim above the rims of his spectacles—taking in his mismatched feet, his good right in a slipper and worsted stocking, his left still in a swathing of linen—then noting his cane and worn expression, Ben simply said dryly, with a bit of a hoarse rasp, "We're a fine pair, you an' I"; and meeting his look with his chin gamely up, and no sign at all of what either of them'd been through, Jim answered simply, with a droll smile, "Always thought so."

That it'd all given him a hearty scare—not the lung fever so much, or the fact he'd always be vulnerable now to such ills, as Anne's control over the ultimate matters of his life and death—I could soon see for myself; for the first night he was able to step out for a spell, I found him falling quiet by my hearth, where we'd been going over his charts for our route. Jim by now was back at the Inn, preoccupied more with concern over his place in Ben's future—over what he would ever do again, if Ben's health failed when he was on land, and he was once more cut off from him—than with worry over the adjustments he had to make to his foot; and we was alone together, Ben and me, him as close to the fire as I dared set the chair, and wrapped in a comforter to boot.

Glancing up from his notes—setting aside his spectacles and rubbing the bridge of his nose, still looking a long ways from a man who could stand up on a quarterdeck, and bawl out the orders to shorten sail in a blizzard—he cleared his throat; and I could see he was about to get something off his chest. Maybe he'd been fetched up by all his recent near misses—by his lung fever and the disaster of the schooners, and the chest pains that'd troubled him earlier in the fall, when *Abigail* was still on the ways—one of the few secrets I'd promised to play close, and kept. Or maybe his will and other final arrangements was just not looking as airtight as he'd once thought, before his close shave and the losses of his kin. Joseph's affairs—in spite of the fact his brother was a lawyer, and he was a man of complicated interests, one of the few men worth six figures in the State of Maine—was found to be in an exasperating snarl, the disorder of one who obviously expected to live yet for decades; and that'd pretty much brung the Melchett clan by the lee, and resulted in a scramble to caulk up existing concerns.

But whatever it was that'd first got him going he suddenly begun, out of nowheres by my hearth, "If it's all right with you...if I'm eveh ill again, on land, I'd like t' weatheh it here at youhr place"; and struggling to conceal my delight—thinking what it'd mean to Jim, to have him on some neutral ground where he could nurse him, or help shape the course of his last hours, if we lost him—I tried to say lightly,

"A' course. Jim'll be relieved...he's been some distressed it might happen again, and him not able t' get near, b'cause he's not kin."

Looking calmly into the fire, Ben said "I'll take care o' *that*, too"—with finality; and correctly reading my inquiring look—catching my eye, then obstinately squaring his jaw—he simply announced, as if he was about to take a walk: "I'm goin' t' adopt him."

About as floored as if I'd been pole-axed, I managed to bust out blankly "Adopt him!"—barely able to get the words out; and he looked at me as if annoyed with my slow thought.

"Aye; why not? He's still a minohr. I thought it all out when I was sick, an' I've already been an' asked John about it."

"Have ye thought of consultin' Jim?" I asked dryly.

"Not yet; but he'll come around—he'll have to. With him as my adopted kin, no one'll have any legal right t' separate us; an' what's more, if I should peg out first, no one like Anne'll be able t' cheat him out of his inheritance, or contest his claim on any grounds whatsoveh. We'll be legally related with all the rights that entails; an' no process on earth'll eveh be able t' undo it."

"Old man," I cautioned—torn between my joy at the direction his thoughts was tending, and concern for how it'd all set with Jim—"it sounds good out loud; but I ain't so sure he'll come around so easy."

"Why in blazes not?" he scowled, almost as squally as when he was hale. "Ye just said yourself how it scared him, the way Anne was able t' cut him off when I was sick."

"He's touchy as t' how things set with youhr family," I reminded; "an' he'll know some'll think he's fortune-huntin.'"

""Well, he'll just have t' put that notion out o' his head," he huffed.

"I'd approach this slow with him, Ben, I really would. He's....he's a proud man, when all's said an' done; an' this'll mean a hot fight t' him b'tween his principles, an' what he wants in his heart."

"All right, all right—but I've already got the papers, an' damned if I ain't takin' 'em with us when we sail... Don't ye go an' tip him off, now."

"I wouldn't," I protested, indignant.

"The hell ye wouldn't!" he hooted, with a snort. "You'hre a regulah baskit, with as many leaks as them ladies at the sewin' circles." Turning over his charts in his lap, he set his spectacles back on his nose; and next thing I knew we was back to our routes, to the timing of tides and trades and monsoons.

It was the first of the year before we'd packed ourselves up and managed to totter aboard *Abigail*—me doing most of the final work of loading, trimming the cargo and ordering sea stores; and there we was in all the bleak cold of a coast January, surrounded by supplies of wood and water meant to last halfway round the world, and a floating barnyard ditto, the pigs about as dejected as we was. Not even to sea yet, the old girl'd already won the name of a bad luck ship —what with the losses of the schooners, Ben's illness and the difficulties of all connected with her; and most of the crew'd been busy trying to make up by buying their luck from Worthing's ancient Aunt Bess, or stowing coins to toss as soon as we broke out our anchors. Carefully calling her "Gail," some'd even been campagined to have her name changed on the sternboard, or at any rate, to have the "A" accidentally dropped; and nobody'd been rooting louder than Abigail herself, though Ben'd tried time and again to squelch her.

Not in much better shape than the ship, we all three took to our stations on weak pins—Ben with orders from Kirk to keep below most of the time, and with newspapers under his peacoat to stave off the cold; Jim on his cane, not able to rally for all hands work; and me so fatigued from Ben's unfinished jobs that all's I wanted to do was hole up for the winter. This being the first voyage of any of the lot of us to China—and there being almost no modern information on routes, passages and trade technicalities and customs—Ben was relying on letters from shipping acquaintances in New York, clippings from Topliff's agents in Boston, and newspaper accounts from 1837 on—a whole file of stuff he seemed hardly to know what to do with; and with no one more experienced than him to ship as supercargo, he was on his own with that chore too.

So feeble still that he could only keep to the deck long enough to see her to sea—so frail that he had to take to the chair that'd been bolted to the poop near the helm, and deliver his orders through his speaking trumpet—Ben was not much more fit than the cabin boy to command; whilst Jim wasn't serving in his full capacity, either, confined as he was to the deck until China; and it looked to me, mastheading our topsails that grey day, like the real burden of the voyage was on my shoulders.

XXIV

BENJAMIN MELCHETT
North Atlantic, Sandwich Islands Jan.-June, 1844

I knew that they were both filling in for me—that Jim was going out of his way, as steward, to keep matters below as shipshape as possible, and that Eben was running the show up on deck in a way that required little attention from me. On any other trek I would have hauled them up by the ears and insisted on having my hands on the helm; but now, too bone-weary to carry out a tithe of my duties— too played out by illness and loss and confusion to be ashamed of my poor show—I just more or less let them take up my slack, even allowed myself to be tended and pampered. Coming below that first day—after an hour and a half on the poop, breaking out anchors and cracking on sail, then squaring our yards before another raw nor'wester—I fell into my bunk exhausted, with orders to Eben to call me if needed; and settling thankfully in I found hot bricks at my feet, extra quilts on my coverlet and a pot of tea at the bulkhead.

Too grateful to Jim to trust to words, I drank a cup under his watchful eye, then quietly turned in for a time; but each day afterwards it was the same, those long three weeks across the Atlantic, running down our easting towards the equator: a brick-warmed bed, a super-abundance of comforters, dry, mended clothes and hot soup or tea, not to mention a host of delicacies no ship's master on any liner could have dreamed of.

With even more laying hens than on past runs, Haggai was coaxing production great guns; and as long as there were eggs there were concoctions to tempt a king. Where all the other supplies had come from—the pumpkins and apples, spices and raisins, jellies and sweetmeats and condiments and preserves, not on this or any other vessel's bill of fare—I feared to ask; but they were stashed somewhere in the pantry, and Jim knew how to put them together; and I found myself gaining ground and fresh strength in spite of all the cold and stress of our first weeks.

Nor were food and warmth the only things Jim provided; for my cabin, the saloon, the pantry and lockers all were maintained shipshape and Bristol fashion—the epitome of maritime order. Privately expecting him to run our domain aft much as he ran his room at the Inn, I'd been holding my breath all autumn, wondering what freak of upheaval I'd be living in; and I'd come aboard this spotless new vessel and unpacked my chest in my tidy cabin wondering how long it'd last, and what'd go first. Long before we'd sailed—earlier on in the fall, when I'd first learned he'd shipped as steward—I'd said to him, in an attempt to forestall disaster: "Jim, y' know I keep things in ordeh—not just my clothes, all the gear in m' chest layered for weatheh—but my desk, especially m' desk, all them dockets for invoices an' lettehs o' credit... I c'n stand the clothes, if they get mixed up or lost—but so help me, if you foul up my desk—"

Yet I soon found out that, by some mysterious process, he knew where I wanted everything, and what my system of order was; and he kept things up far better than I could have managed, given my present forgetful weakness. Surprised by how competently he fell in with my habits, I discovered he carried out all the other aspects of his duty equally well; and amazed and gratified, I watched him perform. The first of the "idlers" or all-nighters wakened—called by the watch at four in the morning—he had the pantry stove fueled and going, the officers' coffee and breakfast underway, and me tumbled up on deck at five; and I never could have made it through that long stretch until noon, when I took the sun, ate dinner, and at last napped, without his countless acts of assistance.

Cleaning, scrubbing, washing, mending—scouring pots and companionway ladders, concocting the saloon meals and maintaining the table, or doling out supplies to Haggai and Tupper—-these were no more than what was expected of him; but helping me keep straight my day's work—managing my sheaves of papers, everything from manifests to Lloyd's List, to the heaps of charts layered in their long box—even assisting me with my correspondence, or keeping my personal log when I was too tired—these were tasks not customarily his; and between the two, proper jobs and improper, he was constantly at work for me.

How he managed all his work on his cane—his foot now quite healed, but his balance affected, so that he had to acquaint himself with a new walk—I couldn't conceive; but grateful beyond measure he'd shipped as steward, for his sake as well as mine—thankful to have him below for the night, rather than slaving watch and watch—I rejoiced in the foresight of his choice, and blessed the timing of its arrival. Watching him through the last of his duties each night— seeing him put out all but one of the lamps in the saloon, then slip in to light the little globe of my compass, with that soft warmth to his smile that'd never really been absent since last summer, when he'd first taken care of me at the Inn—I always felt a profound sense of well-being; and I slept as I'd never before slept at sea, knowing he was safe and nearby.

If Jim was my mainstay below, Eben meantime was my stand-by on deck, carrying out jobs I'd always claimed as mine—shinneying over the whole ship before breakfast, laying out the day's repairs on his own, working out our position and keeping the official log, along with his usual diverse jobs as mate; so that all I had to do was take the sun, review our course and oversee all hands work, responsibilities which required me topsides seldom.

Though it wasn't the way I'd ever run things before—though I was fortunate our crew were all kinsmen or townsmen, who understood the change and knew its reasons—actually *Abigail* was run now more like a regular New England merchantman; was run more according to custom, with the captain the largely unseen command, and the chief mate the organ in charge. As I was learning to adjust myself to receiving from Jim—to depending on him to help me complete tasks, and create order out of the welter of each day—so too I was learning to share my command, to entrust Eben with forging direction; and little by little I gave up decisions that affected our course and the way we achieved it.

Sympathizing all, from the cabin boy on up, they thought it was my health that'd changed me—the double blow of loss of kin and lengthy illness; and indeed they were right, so far as they knew. But if I could have spoken I would have told them that above all it was Jim, and my feelings for him, that'd so altered my way of being, as it had been since that day I'd waked up from my dream in Portland; and on top of my battle to win back my physical strength, and adjust to the passing of Pa and Joe, I was struggling to sort out my heart, and hide it from Jim till I knew how to proceed. Near him all day—in effect, living with him; fresh from the extremities of loss and death, my head was in a whirl; and I sought out anything to steady me—to anchor me down in the plain and concrete.

Especially I longed for converse with anyone who could share with me anything at all about the romance I craved with Jim—yearned for descriptions, accounts as any voyager would, about to embark on new climes; and with that need in mind I'd sneaked aboard my old volume of Catullus, that being the one easily accessible source which sprang to mind. There were, I supposed, illicit materials on the same subject floating somewhere around the back streets of Portland, or more likely still, the waterfront in Boston, if I'd had the time and know-how to seek them out; but Catullus was compact and ready to hand, and sufficed, in lieu of an actual acquaintance, for news. Lying in my berth these wintry afternoons, my lamp swinging to and fro in its gimbal, and the telltale gyring likewise above me, I endeavored to work out translations—striving to look, whenever Jim or Eben stepped in, as though merely bored, and trying to pass time.

Never an outstanding Latin scholar—higher mathematics having been my strong point, the basis upon which I'd managed to make any kind of a show at all at Bowdoin—I nonetheless managed to plow my way through a fair number of passages that'd never been marked off for us to recite. They weren't much—certainly not so racy as they'd been rumored, nowhere near racy enough to satisfy my insatiable curiosity now—but they were enough to add fuel to my fancies, and to ease my sense of isolation; and I poured over the least nuance and fine print like a traveler hungering ahead for new towns. Reassuring me with their plain words that here was an eminent thinker who'd long ago experienced what I yearned for and thought of, the passages yet, in the long run, added to my upheaval; for looking up from their lines I would see Jim, passing by my door with fresh wicks for the lamps or a pot of coffee bound for Eben on deck; and straightaway I'd lose all sense of my work, what little of it I was still up to.

Frustrated by all that was unspoken between us, I still, even after the crises of last month, and the extremes which'd torn the shreds of time and reason from us, had no idea what he was really thinking; had no clue as to how he privately felt, beyond his obvious loving support—a fault I shared with him, for I revealed little myself; and between that uncertainty and the arousal of my reading, I was in a steady state of commotion, alternating betwixt excitement and doubt. Underscoring my agitation was my vague conviction that things were on the wrong course—that they had been ever since our night at the Inn, when I'd failed to act on the chance of our closeness; and now that we were at close quarters at sea, I tried clumsily to right things.

Once, waking up in the chill of the night and finding the cabin thermometer had fallen below thirty—discovering a film of ice on the water in my basin, and instinctively feeling his cold as he slept—I got up and carried a spare comforter to him, yearning to care for him as he had for me in my illness; approached the little compartment he shared with Haggai between decks, even caught sight of him in his upper berth; but I quit on the threshold, feeling idiotic. Maybe it was the unromantic snores of Haggai bringing a mundane humor to the situation; maybe simply the picture I suddenly had of me through Haggai's eyes, pampering Jim a bit there in his sleep; but no one at sea ever performed such acts for another—the necessity of appearing manly being greater here than anywhere else; and though we aboard *Abigail* had more latitude to display affection, still it was hard to overcome the force of custom, even with a heart as full as mine.

Another time I tried to approach Jim with my idea of adoption, but trailed off again, disconcerted; for what was there about this strapping young man, sitting at his ease in my desk chair, and regarding me with unwavering blue eyes, that had made me suppose he'd want to belong to another, much less to a blunderbuss like me? Visibly matured by the trials of the fall—always older than his years, anyhow, and seasoned now with subtle new strengths—he hardly looked like he needed adopting, by me or anybody else; and I ended up hiding away John's papers in the ship's banking chest, to which only I had a key.

Above all I endeavored to touch him familiarly as I always used to—to lay my hand on the back of his neck as I came up on him at the saloon table, or punch his arm or tousle his hair; but even these proved impossible now, time and again though I got up the nerve; for in spite of the longing which kept me awake nights, and gnawed like an actual hunger at my deep, I was wary now of his body. Partly it was my fear of giving myself away, partly awkwardness now that I knew what they meant, all those fondlings I'd traded so readily in the tent, or in the sickbay, tending him in fever; but I couldn't so much as brush his fingers now, if he handed me the salt cellar at the table, and he, for his part, seemed to be alert to my new unease, for he never touched me anymore either. Sustained by his touches for years, I couldn't live for a day now without them—craved contact with him more than food, more than sleep; and so great did my internal upheaval become, as day by day we sped toward the Line, that its tumult began to appear in my dreams.

At first they were dreams about the crises just past, about anxieties uppermost in my mind from the last weeks; and I would wake up drenched with sweat in the cold, those wintry nights still crossing the Atlantic. Sometimes it was Joseph's face, no longer that of a dandy, but chiseled and blackened with the death throes of ice, that rose up at me in the regions of sleep; sometimes it was Anne's face which hovered above me, cool and efficient as she tended me in illness, while my whole inner being cried out for Jim. But more and more often it was the sea, and not just the sea, but giant breakers, which loomed up at me out of the deep; and night after night now it was such titans that figured in and troubled my dreams.

If it wasn't enough that my nights were beginning to take on the character of my days' tumult, there was a further complication, wholly unlooked-for; and it came at the end of the second day out, when I'd turned in for the evening in my berth. Wtih Catullus to one side, a sheet of foolscap on my knees, and Jim's faithful pot of tea at my elbow, I'd just dipped my pen into the inkwell, and embarked on the passage beginning, "O Gellius, why art thy red lips like snow," when there came an apologetic knock at my door; and responding to my call Jim stepped in, with something obviously concealed behind him.

"Ben," he commenced, looking vaguely guilty, "b'fore I tell you what I've got here, promise me you'll keep your temper"; and I merely looked at him, nonplussed, and nodded, fumbling to cover up my translation. "When Jack an' me was b'low just now," he went on, with one hand still behind him, "t' broach a new cask of ship's bread for t'morrow, we heard a noise that sounded suspicious, an' got up a search with a couple of lanterns; an' at the end of it we found these two, hidin' out b'hind the barrels o' salt pork."

So saying he pulled out from behind him, to my no uncertain amazement, a pair of ragged, disreputable-looking children, cobwebbed and rumpled as it they'd slept days in their clothes, but recognizable nonetheless, beneath all those layers of ship's dust, as two of my own, Tom and Jean.

"Gawd Almighty," I intoned reverently, for once too dumbfounded to come up with an outburst.

"We wanted t' come with you, Papa," they both tumbled out at once, their eyes bright and huge beneath their wild mops; and I simply looked from them to Jim and back again, speechless.

"What kind o' time we been makin' since noon?" I asked Jim, finding my tongue at last in my dazed hush.

"From ten t' twelve knots," he supplied promptly.

"Well, that's…why, that's…seven an' a half hours since we did 220 miles… we're… we're 300 miles off the coast o' Maine, not less."

"Aye; not a doubt of it," he assented cheerfully.

"Too gawddam fahr t' turn an' beat against a headwind."

"Aye," he nodded again, while Tom and Jean took on the faintest countenance of hope.

"Any sail in sight?"

"Not since that outbound brig we passed this noon."

"Jesus Christ, even if there was somethin inbound, we couldn't hoist these two aboard some heathen vessel—Anne'd kill me," I muttered, knowing she'd so dub any ship not hailing from the state of Maine; and Tom and Jean looked more hopeful still. "It'd mean they'd have t' take anotheh vessel out o' Boston or New York, an' sail down the coast with anotheh set o' strangehs... Can't be done," I concluded, at a dead end on that route. "I'll have t' think this thing through with Eben...As for you two, you'hre turnin' in... What the devil did you bring with ye, an' did you leave youhr Ma any message?"

"We left a note, sir, but not whehre she'd find it right away, for fear she'd send somebody out t' chase us," spoke up Tom from his safe berth near Jim.

"Hmpf, as if anybody on the coast was fast enough t' overhaul us...D'ye understand she's probably gone grey from worry?"

"Aye, sir."

"I ought t' keep you two aboard an' work ye ragged t' make ye pay."

"So you ought, sir."

Tom met my eyes and we exchanged will for will.

"We've come prepared; we've brung our schoolbooks....I have my readeh, an' Tom has his arithmetic; and we've tooken some of our workclothes," volunteered Jean, producing a knapsack while Tom exhibited his; and I had to work to restrain a grin.

"Any food in thehre too, or have ye et nothin'?"

"We've et some apples an' a round o' bread, sir, an' a sweetmeat or two this mornin."

"A sweetmeat! D'ye recollect what it is the crew eats at sea?"

"Aye, salt pork an' hard tack...but Uncle Jim says he's just baked a pie."

"Oh, he said that, did he? Well, the good grub gets served to the first table, what's left goes t' Tupper at the second, an' I don't expect he'll leave much for you at the third... Now set youhrselves down an' eat what Jim puts before ye, then wash up an' turn yourhselves in for the night."

"Aye, sir; where'll we sleep?" Jean chirped.

"You'll sleep in the sick bay next t' my cabin at least for t'night, so's I c'n keep my eye on ye."

"Aye, aye!" they sang out lustily, and saluted; then doing an about-face they marched into the saloon, knapsacks wagging over their shoulders. Still leaning on his cane, Jim watched them fondly, their heads passing by him about the height of his midriff; and something in his eye suddenly fetched me up short.

"*You* didn't by any chance have anything t' do with this, did ye?" I blurted, as he was about to make off for the pantry; and he kept a straight face as he cast a glance back at me.

"Benjamin, what an idea!" he protested, managing to look as guileless as a newborn.

"Aye, what an idear, just like all youhr otheh idears, you Romany bastihd—pumpkins in the pantry an' peppermint in my tea, an' Lord know what all else you ain't confessed yet."

"It's about time you had a little spoilin," was all he said, as he limped out the door; and in the sweetness of his words I let slip my awareness that he hadn't come up with an actual denial.

Weighing all the options with Eben—not that there were very many—I at last concluded that, barring our speaking an inbound vessel which hailed from some port in Maine, we had no choice but to take them with us, at least as far as the crossroads at Java, where we'd planned to stock up on fresh provisions anyway, and where the odds were good we'd meet up with some ship out of Searsport or Portland which could be trusted to see them home. A journey so far—around two and a half months, if we played our cards right—shouldn't prove too arduous for them, barring unforeseen hazards; should even prove beneficial and instructive, in the long run; while the work should more than enough satiate their premature appetite for sea life.

Beyond Java, the uncertainties of the South China Sea made their continued presence ill-advised; and I fervently hoped we'd have safely dispatched them by then, though there was no guarantee at this point. Having made up my mind on this much, at least, I swiftly drew up a letter for Anne, reassuring her and outlining our plans;

then setting it ready to be tossed aboard the first westboard vessel we happened to raise, I shook my head, and put out my light.

First thing after breakfast I called them both to me, Eben having already left the table, though Jim was nearby, clearing and setting for Tupper; and before they'd so much as tasted a bite, I broke the news to them, waving aside their glad cries.

"Don't get too excited till ye've heard the terms," I damped them down over my coffee. "You'hre shipped as cabin hands, Jean included; nobody, man or woman, with the name of Melchett ships as passengeh while I've got breath."

"Aye, we know that, Pa; work's just what we want," they testified, all but lost in the broad chairs.

"Oh, it is, ey; well, there'll be enough for youhr taste. Ye'll work for Orin an' Jim, an' Haggai too, if he needs ye; an' you'hre directly answerable t' all three. When you'hre done here b'low, scrubbin' an' what-not, ye'll lay up on deck, where I'll b'gin t' teach ye the ropes; but no all-hands work, ye'll just get in the way; an' no climbin' the masts, or I'll break youhr necks."

"Aye, aye!"

"On the Sabbath, ye'll sit at meetin' with the rest; Spooneh's the one that leads in the worship. Ye'd betteh write down all the texts an' the hymns or youhr motheh won't eveh let yet back in the house... As for youhr lessons, ye'll do 'em in the dog watch, or on Sunday aftehnoons an' recite 'em t' Jim, since he's the one that winked at this in the first place," I wound up, loud enough for him to hear in the pantry.

"We didn't neveh say so, Pa."

"Ye didn't have to... Now, what kind o' gear is it ye've got? Not any o' them velveteen suits youhr Ma dresses ye in, I hope, Thomas!"

"No, sir. I've brung three paihrs o' my oldest breeches, worsted stockin's an' my coat an' muffler."

"An' Jean?"

"I've brung my oldest frock, it's a wool one, my calico dress for summeh, an' two aprons—" displaying the dress from the depths of her knapsack as she spoke.

"Good Lord, ye can't swab the decks in such tripe, ye'll break youhr neck or get tangled up in the riggin'.... Ye'll have t' wear trousehs; even youhr Aunt Keziah came down to it in the end. Jim, d'ye think ye can make her a pair patterned on Tom's?"

"A' course; there's plenty o' twill stashed in the slop chest," he smiled, just in from the pantry with a fresh tray load.

"An' I ain't got no sea-going hat, Pa, only my beaver bonnet," Jean spoke up.

"Jesus Christ, their grammah's goin' already.... All right, we'll see about a hat. Now, wash up for breakfast—in salt waduh, youh're on an allowance o' fresh; an' don't let me catch ye cussin' like the sailohrs!"

"Aye, aye!"

With them in the sickbay or at the captain's table, underfoot in the pantry or playing tag in the after passage—with one of them popping up every time I settled down with Catullus, or got up the nerve to join Jim on the sofa—there was even less of a chance for intimacy with him; even less of an opportunity to bring our feelings to a head, or to broach a private subject like adoption. Teasing Jasper, cleaning lanterns, sanding floors, scribbling lessons, they were everywhere, overhearing everything, and bringing ill-timed interruption or touches of absurdity—like Haggai's snores—to every potentially tender moment. Yet I was bound to admit they also brought a relaxation, especially as time wore on and I gave up trying to maintain a hierarchy at the table, or in our stations on the quarterdeck; brought a spontaneity that somehow diminished the threat of my being alone with Jim, and so made me a little less anxious around him, less wary of his physical presence.

With Tom's battalions of toy boats, whittled out of stove chips, scattered hither and yon on the saloon rug—with Jean's impressions of mermaids or whales or ghost ships littering the margins of the course slates, or with old Bo'sun the cat rigged up in some doll's dress careening along the break of the poop—it was impossible to be constantly on alert; impossible not to let down my guard a little in the midst of all that chitchat from Jasper, or that childish prattle at the dinner table. And the relaxation affected not just us aft—me and Eben, Orin, Haggai, Jim and the children all sitting down at the first table together, in defiance of every maritime custom—but the forecastle too, all hands seeming more vulnerable and human, more able to show feeling and pull together, and to put on their best face before others.

The livestock, too, were becoming part of our wholeness—suddenly all had names, from the bullocks in the long boat to the pigs in the sty and Haggai's hens between decks; suddenly all were as destined for the plates on the forecastle table as they were for their traditional final home aft; and they were as mourned over in their parting moments as any old shellback shipped for Davy Jones. It was as if all the beings aboard ship were subtly becoming a unit, a community of shared responsibility and spirit; while the four of us aft who spent the most time together, me and Jim and the two young ones, found ourselves merging into a family. Though this too eased me—though it took some of the edge off my daily tumult, and injected me with new heart and strength—it yet filled me with an inexpressible yearning, a longing to live for the rest of my time with Jim and the children as one body.

Industrious and eager, the young ones did their work well, not tiring of it as I'd expected —especially since I drew up regular accounts for them and recorded their pay each month along with the rest: at eight dollars a go, half the standard rate for an ordinary seaman's wages, the most money they'd ever seen at one time in their lives. Working with me, they learned the ropes, how to tell a main skysail halyard from a royal, and where all the lines were belayed on the fife rail; while frequently Eben would take time out to explain the principles of a maneuver. But it was Jim who was their primary influence; and I thought once again how fortuitous it was he'd shipped as steward, for a finer instructor they couldn't have had. Adept and practiced, he knew how to do everything, from bake up a pie to construct his own clothes, to lay out the position and course of the ship, or repair a sail a half-acre in size; and he demonstrated by his mere presence that no task was out of reach of, or beneath the dignity of man.

The relative benefits of the long or the short splice, they were soon debating at the dinner table; and they would unnerve crack hands like Tupper by asking why he favored one type of seizing over another. Nor were direction in the maritime arts, and the supervision of their cabin duties, the full extent of Jim's instruction; for he heard all of their lessons too, helping Jean with her reading and Tom with his ciphering, and teaching both of them how to write a clear hand; and in accordance with my wishes he'd added geography to their course, so that they'd have some proper image of where we were going. It was in the latter instruction that I found once again how unlike we still were—how his gypsy migrations had schooled him differently from mine, mostly maritime as they were; for when he proudly showed me maps they'd drawn of all the land masses we'd be passing—the West African coast, the Cape of Good Hope, the southern tip of India and Burma, and the shores of Sumatra, Java and China—I simply shook my head, bemused.

"No, no; I meant *geography*, not this," I chided, jabbing a finger at the continents and islands.

"What's this, then?" he protested, offended.

"Why, this is land, man," I asserted dryly.

"An' what the hell else d'ye think geography *is*?" he gaped.

"Why, it's... it's the Gulf Stream, an' the NE trades, an' the doldrums, an' then the SE...it's the Beneguela an' the Indian Ocean, the Sunda Strait an' the NE monsoon."

"Oh, you mean *currents*," he gasped, seeing the light.

"Aye, aye! A' course—sea lanes an' routes; that's what geography is—how ye get whehre ye're goin'."

"What about land?" he insistently kept at it.

"What about it?" I asked blankly.

"Well, roads, you jackass, roads on land; that's how most folks get where they're going; at any rate, that's how *I* do."

"Not with me ye don't; an' I'm not even sure ye do by youhrself, judgin' by the last time I let ye drive."

"That's b'cause you always have an end-point in mind."

"An' don't you?"

"No; unless my end-point's not to have one."

"Are we back t' the 'chahrm of goin' in circles'?"

"Aye; an' I figure that, sooner or later, I'll seduce you."

On edge as I was, constantly thinking of Catullus, and transposing what I read into fantasies of him, that word struck me like a cat-o-nine tails; and I quickly looked up to see if he knew what he was saying—but he merely gave me an airy wave with his free hand, and carried his maps back off to the children.

Coming up on the Line—26 days out, as good as the best I could have managed—it was his other qualities that shone out as well; not just his attributes as an instructor or parent, but the traits that distinguished his form of manhood, the tenderness that softened his self-restraint; and I basked in them along with the children even as we emerged from the cold, and all hands threw back the companion hatches. Sitting out on the quarterdeck in the kindly sun, with Tom and Jean whittling nearby me, or practicing knots in the lee of the skylight, I gazed covertly on him as he sat close by, repairing a studdingsail as a favor for Wingate; drifted over the seamarks of body and nature that yielded up clues to his perennial depths.

Back in the well-worn white duck trousers, red checked shirt and faded straw hat in which I'd first learned to love him, he was still as much an enigma as ever, as inscrutable and unfixed as the sundance on the waters, or the mercurial routes of the dolphins; but I knew him nonetheless by his manifestations, as one knows a harbor or sea; and I looked them over as one mulls the stages of a well-remembered journey. The sun on his throat as he looked up at the sails; the breeze in his hair when he took off his hat; the aptness of his hands as he plied his craft; the tenderness of his gaze as he watched my young—all revealed facets of his still unfathomable deep; and I sighed as I savored their familiar shapings.

Even as I watched I was re-living with them, new as they all three were to this passage, the discoveries of my first voyage as a boy—all the monuments and peoplings of the deep: the Cape Verde Islands, rugged and barren, their mountains erupting from the sea lanes to larboard; Gough's Island, with its abrupt rise and bold cliffs, and myriads of seabirds encircling its skies; St. Helena, in the great shipping thoroughfare to the Indian Ocean, emerald green and lofty-ridged; the grampuses, or the whales or black fish, unexpectedly surfacing and spouting. All these denizens and outcroppings marked the unseen banks of our route; and we looked on them with hush-stilled wonder.

Round the Cape of Good Hope, 43 days out, we met cooler weather—met albatrosses and Cape hens, the latter scrambling for Jean's crumbs, and raised a range of low hills, a-smoke with brush fires; then came the Indian Ocean, ceaseless palette of the sea, body of shifting wind flows and currents, and vermilion or peacock-hued clouds; came sunrises like a torrent of lava and moonrises like an upblaze of sparks, the horizon blood-red and pulsing with light. Here came nights of glimmering phosphorescence, the whole sea a-dance with bewildering sheens, great pools and sheets of incandescence, and the quivering wake of our ship, a lurid, flickering trail behind us, a map-trace of fireballs and bright streaks.

Here too came the afternoons of stillness, the perfect calms of wind and water, when the ship appeared line for line on the surface, and the clouds too puff for puff about it, as if in wordless evocation of what lay shrouded in the depths. And here came the breaths or airs of evening, the merest cat's-paws on the water, rippling the flat sheen in the distance, then wrinkling the frail reflection, till one by one all the spars, all the rigging wavered in an uncontainable shimmer.

By now my health had improved to the point where I'd taken back on some of my old duties; and I'd even started in on some of the repairs myself, helping tackle the upper maintopsail yard, which'd parted its tye in a colossal thundershower. Jim, too, done with his cane, was up at the same time in the rigging, helping Wingate overhaul the mainsail; and it seemed good to be working aloft with him, to have the wind in our hair and the slender deck far below us—to have the sails thrumming in a vast chorus around us, and *Abigail* rocking us like a giant cradle. With the return of my vigor, my passion for him had redoubled, making his hardy form as he laid out on the mainyard or labored in the top beside me more desirable and alluring than ever; and I searched as I worked for some way to engage him.

That he loved me I knew—felt unshakably sure of, as sure as

when I'd waked up from my dream in Portland, but it was one thing to know how deeply he cared, and quite another to suppose he'd want me for a lover; just as it was one thing to know I'd betrayed Anne in principle, and quite another to practice infidelity in deed. Sometimes, in the semi-seclusion of the cabin, I wondered what he'd do if I touched him, not in any way I ever used to; wondered what would happen if, one of these nights when he was putting out the last lanterns, I suddenly just threw all reason to hell, and drew him down beside me on the covers. The children's proximity, the absence of locks on the doors, the utter lack of privacy in our quarters aft, almost any sound made audible in the other cabins, I'd simply conveniently forget; just as I'd forget my personal convictions and prior commitments back home.

Would he be appalled and offended, kick and bite me with all that Rom impetuosity I knew only too well from past experience, when we'd tangled over a simple conflict of wills; or would he resist me at first, and then surrender; or would he surprise me by taking me on? I'd dreamed it all out in so many ways, and it was always so uppermost in my mind, that I began to find it hard to look him in the face, as if my bedrock of thought was transparent; and the end result was that, far from being able to engage him, I couldn't now even meet his eye; and the energy I missed from his touch was doubled by the loss of his brilliant blue gaze.

About 60 days out, long since out of fresh provisions, we began to see the effects on the children—on Jean especially, who ate sparingly anyway; so that when the chance came to speak an American ship, standing off to the westward and by its course from the Spice Islands, we backed the maintopsail and begged for produce; and receiving an invitation—learning the vessel was New York bound, and only 10 days out from Anjier—I lowered away the gig, and rowed over. Climbing aboard, I met the captain, starch-collared, tail-coated, quivering-fingered and red-cheeked, the latter undeniably the effects of liquor; but he was courteous enough when it came to meeting my needs, directing me to the steward, who filled several baskets of bananas, pineapples, cocoanuts and sweet yams, none of which had the children ever tasted.

While below I learned from the chief mate that one of the sailors was laid up with coast fever, or so they thought, there being no doctor aboard; and in return for their generosity I offered to take a look at him, and row over the proper medications if they had none. Looking a little dazedly at me, as if he thought such efforts wasted on a common seaman, the mate nonetheless saw me into the forecastle; and I found myself in a dismal, dark hole, equipped with neither adequate light nor ventilation, and minus both table and spitbox— the watch all sitting around on their chests, and darning stockings in the feeble lamplight. The stricken seaman lay in a leaky berth, forgotten, to all appearances, by his shipmates; and as I looked on him I couldn't but remember Jim, in the grip of fever off the coast of Cuba.

Stung with pity for him—not just for him, but for the wretched many of the merchant marine he represented—I marched back to the captain in his quarters aft, finding them not unexpectedly resplendent; and taking in the velvet hangings and sofa, not to mention the absurd Persian carpets, I knocked. Inviting me in, he looked up from his desk, where he was amusing himself by reading the mail; and jovially he offered me a drink.

Declining his offer—watching him toss off a glass—I instead began, "I wanted t' thank ye, sir, for the baskets of produce. My children are much obliged t' ye for it."

"Well, now, what else're us Yankees for, eh? Brothers we are, that's what, brothers at sea."

"In that spirit," I picked up, "I went forward with Mr. Hastings just now, t' take a look at the seaman who's down with coast feveh, since apparently you haven't a doctoh aboard."

"That's right," he rumbled, "extra wages, you know what they are... I take it you know how to treat him?"

"I know enough t' know he ought t' be removed at once from the fohecastle an' housed separately aft; othehwise youhr whole ship'll be swept, sir."

"What, house a common seaman aft?" he bellowed, looking me over as if he found me even more eccentric than first thought, when he'd clapped eyes on my twill trousers and worn shirt and straw hat.

"We have a sickbay built right off the saloon for the purpose...If ye haven't a place that'll answer, y' could contrive one b'tween decks, so long as there was adequate ventilation."

"Well, well, we'll see about that... D'ye have an idea what medicines 're needed?"

"Aye, two or three, if ye've got them in stock."

"Well, now," he grunted, fumbling with a key at his locker, and drawing out one of those standard chests with a false bottom, "here's the medicine box; pick out what you want."

Lifting the lid, I found the contents dismal, a few elixirs and purges, not one of them half full; while the really vital medications showed scanty or empty. "Cap'n Brown," I said sternly, "there's no calomel at all, an' little quinine—I'll need both; an' are ye aware there's not a drop o' laudanum here?"

"Well, well," he brushed aside, "it's the trek home, y' know.... an' not very likely t' be called for."

Catching sight of his pipe, I guessed why it was missing—guessed that the opium, customarily stocked in the false compartment, was gone also; and I thought of a few things John would say, if he were here. "It'll be called for if one o' youhr men suffehs an' injury, an' you'hre needed t' set or amputate a limb.... Could ye' do that?"

"Look here, Mr. Melchett," he started to rankle, his eyes focusing a degree or two sharper, and the red thatch of his side whiskers commencing to bristle, "you mind your ship, I'll mind mine."

"In return for the fresh provisions," I ignored him, "I'll row back with the calomel an' quinine."

"That won't be necessary," he huffed, trying to look dignified, and brushing off the velvet lapels of his coat.

"I think it will be," I returned, just as dignified, in spite of my rolled-up sleeves and bagged-out knees; "you see, amongst otheh things my brotheh practices maritime law—an' I happen t' know exactly how ye could be prosecuted; an' don't think that I wouldn't do it."

Over the bay as he was, he was fairly easily cowed—the more so since, in the variable light winds, he couldn't make a quick run for it; and putting on a mollified air, he saw me over the side with my baskets, waving as if he welcomed my return.

Appalled I'd been exposed to coast fever, Eben no more favored my return visit than Brown did, trying to talk me out of it the whole time I was fetching our chest, and filling up a couple of fresh vials. Assuring him that I'd quarantine myself—not that that in any way cheered him—I rowed quickly back and treated the seaman, leaving the surplus medications with one of the crew—an old Swede—I'd already picked out with my eye as a leader. Accepting them gratefully, he promised to administer them faithfully, especially when he understood his own skin might be next; and collecting my hat— stopping to take one last look at the sick seaman, a young Briton, and surreptitiously slipping my card with Jacob's New York counting house address in his pocket, on the chance that, if he recovered, he might seek for a better berth—I touched his damp brow and climbed back on deck, thankful for a breath of fresh air.

For two days I more or less hid out in my cabin, carefully keeping Jim and the children at bay, and letting Eben stand part of my duty, while I worked up our position and kept the logs; and by the second night I was congratulating myself, thinking I'd both done a good turn and escaped the fever. But in the middle watch, waking up in the pitch dark, and feeling the ship rock and lurch in the low swells, I unaccountably rolled and swayed with it; and my cabin seemed oppressively hot, hotter than it had, though by midnight things usually cooled down a little, and we could look for a comfortable sleep.

Lulling myself, I fell back into a drowse—into something like a half-dreaming slumber; and in it at first I was alone in a dory, handlining for cod off the banks in a long sea. Rising and falling, dipping and swaying, lifting again and rolling and drifting, I felt almost hypnotized by the broad swells; till subtly their green shine took on a verdure, the mossy wrinkles of pastures and hills.

Then as in an old dream, the earliest I could remember, I was hovering above a patchwork of meadows, a landscape of field slopes and stream beds and hedgerows; and following the contours of the earth I was flying, rising and dipping and rising on air flows. Paralleling the earth's shape, my flight patterned the ground's roll, pandering to gulches and ascents and shoulders—till suddenly the fields all at once stopped short, poised like a headland on the brink of space; and I was awake, sweating, dizzy, confused, trying to think where I was, and in whose berth.

Fumbling for my thoughts, I heard Jim's voice, calling out the time from afar; and dimly knowing that I must move, I struggled to heave myself out onto the floor. Concentrating my forces, I strove to brace up on one elbow; yet though I put forth the greatest effort, I only succeeded in moving my hand a little; and worn out by the effort, I dozed for a spell. The next thing I knew, Jim was sitting beside me, though I hadn't heard him enter; and with my last resources I managed hoarsely, "Keep the children away....move them int' the steerage."

"I've already exchanged cabins with them," came his voice from somewhere distant above me; and I marveled again with an odd detachment at the pure, well-pitched, foreign tones of his accent.

"An' you," I kept up, "don't ye dare come near me."

"I'd like t' see you try an' stop me," came his voice again, steady, tranquil, unswerving.

"You ain't obeyed one o' my ordehs yet," I graveled, as a glass of cool water came to my lips.

"I know it," he said, "an' I ain't plannin' on startin' now"; and with that, I slipped off again to the meadow.

How long I was gone, I had no idea—time a matter of heat and less heat, light and less light, noise and less noise; of hovering bodiless above green meadows, or of rocking back and forth in a dory. Sometimes it seemed I was floating in the cabin, and I could look down on myself in my berth; could see with a curious dispassion my tumbled limbs and lips, and ponder the passage of dreams on my face. Sometimes we'd come to both together, my body and I, and I would try to reckon up the day, or get out a call for water before we went our separate ways; but so swift went the clock, or so slow my thought, that I seldom finished either—thirst, time, heat, delay, all fading into the meadow. Yet always with even the slightest awareness came the thankful perception of Jim's nearness—of words meaningless, but calm, reassuring; of strong limbs and staunch, hard-muscled presence; and best of all, hands, hands brushing and soothing, laying cool cloths on my face or helping me drink.

In all the haze and heat my head fully cleared only once, and even that for a brief duration; but it was long enough for me to see his face—to attach brow and eyes to the tender ply of his hands; and eagerly I searched his expression for the same gentle calm I'd felt in my daze. Clear-cut and fine, his strong features took shape, resolving themselves into the familiar pattern of old friends; but belying his ease his visage looked strained, unaccustomedly tautened and white; and I understood all at once he was scared—as dumbly frightened as he was reassuring. As if inspired by his fear—as if visited by an uncanny knowing—I said quite clearly, "Jamie, don't be afraid... the feveh's goin' t' break in four or five howehs, an' then I'll be myself again"; and I saw his lips part in silent awe. How I knew was a mystery to us all, then and after; but in that space exactly the fever was broken, ebbing as dramatically as it had flowed; and once more I was convalescent.

Throughout my recovery—which lasted another week, and brought us almost up to the latitude of Java Head—he nursed me just as he had from the start, insisting that, since he'd had the fever, he wouldn't get it again no matter how long his exposure; and guessing that I wouldn't have contracted it myself if I hadn't been so pegged out from lung fever, I re-built my strength, content to let him care for me. All the tenderness he never demonstrated at any other time around me—either because it was inappropriate aboard ship, or because of his own innate restraint—he showed now, even though I was becoming aware; and I laid back against my pillows watching, drinking in a facet of him he'd only fully revealed in brief flashes, such as that day tending me in his room last summer.

As I regarded him I thought he seemed happy, happier than he ever had been, as if he welcomed my needful weakness—as if he'd found himself in serving me, and celebrated his transformation;

and I marveled myself at the attentive softness which heightened the appeal of his strength. Infusions made from our fresh produce, pineapple and citrus juices, melon slices and the sweet milk of the coconut: all these he brought me with the care of no other; while of an evening with the breeze through the hatchways, and the late afternoon sunny glow through the skylight, he gladdened me with yarns of the children, or posted me up on our progress with the slates, his fingers tracing the day's knots and courses.

But best of all he came in once with a basin, early on in my convalescence, and set it down on the stand next to my bunk; and taking first one hand, then in turn the other, he bathed them in the lukewarm water, unhurriedly stroking my palms and fingers. Too weak at the time to move or talk, I simply wondered at the pleasure of the liquid, its soothing wash and the ply of his smooth touch; attended as I never had before to the range of feeling of my hands. Twitching aside the bedclothes at the bottom of my berth, he next washed my feet, his hands firm and cool, gently sliding and flowing, almost indistinguishable from the water; and moved beyond words by the love of his act, I gave in to tears despite my resistance, my chest burning with an intolerable ache.

Turning my face, I hid it in the pillow, hoping that he wouldn't see me; but somehow he knew, for he hesitated, fumbling a bit awkwardly as he re-covered my feet; then as if making up his mind he swiftly came to me, and stooping, gathered me up in his arms. Encompassed by him—by the strong slopes of his arms, and the warm, salty-sweet, gentle give of his breast—I gave way, succumbing to all I'd held back since that night at the Inn; wept for its loss, for Pa's and Joseph's, as I'd never wept before in my time; but throughout he held me with unparalleled tact, his embrace warm but unstifling, loving but manly, full of wordless understanding. If he felt anything at all toward me as I did toward him, it must have wracked him to restrain his feeling; if he didn't, he gave no sign he was abashed, or embarrassed—merely sure and steady, compassionate and knowing, till at last, hushed and spent, I lay back on the pillows.

On our 74th day out I was sitting up for the first time—writing letters at my desk to the yard and our consignees, to be posted at Anjier village—when "La-and ho!" rang out from someone at the masthead; and moments later Jim appeared at my doorway, beckoning me up on deck for a sighting. Taking his arm—which he offered with a smile, and an intimacy that was never absent now between us, as if my tears had leveled our last walls—I accompanied him up the companionway ladder, and thence to the starboard rail, where Eben and the children were already gathered; and together we gazed on the high beauty of Java Head, rising up like a staircase from the heart of the blue depths, luxuriant with burnished verdure. Running in close to the land, we followed the shores in the morning wind, passing sumptuous tropical growth which clustered right to the water's edge, thick clumps of palm and brush which fanned out in broad fronds, and mangrove trees which throve far out in the water, spreading their boughs to shade prows and dories.

In the intense heat of midday—which rained down from the nearly vertical sun, and sent up a haze from the lush damp of the forest—I rested below, unable still to get through a day without sleep; but at nightfall I was back on the quarterdeck beside Jim, watching the darkness come down like black velvet, starred by the occasional swing of a lantern, or the fireflies whose flight skimmed the treetops, and interwove the branches of foliage. From the shores came the strange sounds of a far land, hums, calls, choruses of alluring music; while above and all around the soft light of the stars shimmered in unciphered patterns. So majestic was it that Jim woke the children and hustled them back up on deck to join us; and worshipful we stood at the taffrail, watching the flickering coast slip by us, or dreaming on the red and green glades of our ship's lights.

Arriving early in the morning watch, dawn came like an outburst, an eruption of sulphur and crimson and saffron, so poignant that Eben this time knocked on the skylight, and roused us up to admire the display; and tumbling up we stood on the charthouse, to find we were coasting along a palette, a mother-of-pearl of land mass and seaway. Trailing behind us, the occasional showers, irridescent in the early daylight, shimmered and shifted on the face of the sea, the waters now silver, now wine in the sun's touch; while far off to larboard, in the midst of Sunda Strait, halfway between Java and Sumatra, rose Krakatoa like a great cone from the seabed, its slopes abounding in an outrush of flora: a sporadic puff of smoke, or an ominous vapor, the only portent of its dormant power, unrevealed since 1800.

In about 24 hours since we'd first sighted Java Head, we raised Anjier Point, and saw the small village; heard the dip of oars, the swish of prows, and the half-mourning chants of the natives rowing—scantily-clad Malays come to barter their goods. In a matter of moments we were surrounded by boats, crafts loaded to the gunnels with baskets of fruit, crates of fowls and eggs and seashells; jute cages of doves, lorrikeets, and parrots, their feathered tufts like wisps of rainbow; and tethered to the oarslips, chattering monkeys, or miniature deer, which caused the children to shriek and dance. Before we could signal the decks were teeming with silks, crepe shawls and scarves and sandalwood boxes, ivory curios and tortoiseshell cases—one monkey escaping in the midst of it all, and immediately taking to the rigging; and it was all I could do to bring us to anchor, my first official act in my capacity as master in the two weeks since I'd come down with fever.

Seventy-five days out from the coast of Maine, a record—much to McCabe's surprise—against the NE monsoon, and a fine endeavor of almost 14,000 miles, we dropped hook in the holding ground a cable's length from the shore; and neighbored by brigs and ships we eagerly looked on Anjier village, an array of thatched huts and European dwellings, the latter including a hotel and post office. All hands aboard aching to set foot on shore, and our time here limited to 24 hours, we soon arranged for half-days for the watches—me meantime taking possession of the gig, and commandeering Jim and Haggai to row it; and having got out tackle on the yardarms and stays, we immediately lowered away, Jim and Haggai pulling at the oars, the children bouncing in the bow, and me laying back in the stern sheets with the mail, a passenger for the first time in my life.

Arriving on shore—beaching the boat on the hard sand, and taking leave of Haggai at the market, the good man already feeling the hens for the fattest—Jim and me each shouldered a share of the mail, and managed to rein in the dashing young ones. Taking it slow—the heat already intense, and my pins from long disuse not the strongest—I showed the way to the village post office, a long walk through dense groves of coconut palms, on which the children looked with wonder. Resting now and then—Jim helping me sit down by the road, his hand at my elbow insistent but gentle, and his glance when it met mine unreservedly happy—we came out at last on the small outbuilding; and leaving our letters we took a different route to the hotel, passing thatched bungalows and groups of shy, naked children who eyed Tom and Jean as they pranced in the road, or ventured to touch the lush fronds of the palms.

Ebullient with their zest, and Jim's, I felt such an intimacy with him that it was as if we were already lovers; as if we had reached an understanding which bypassed all that lay unresolved between us; and as I walked with him—the children now racing before us, now dashing back and forth behind us—I exulted in the certainty of his love, and the uncomplicated joy of his presence. In and out of the bright glades of the sun—now drenched in green shadow, now bathed in gold quivers—he looked more alluring than ever, there in his simple sailor's loose trousers, worn checkered shirt and straw hat, the corners of his neckerchief lifting in the light wind; while the looks he cast at me told me he, in return, found in my plain shape ample fairness.

At last reaching the hotel we ordered a fine dinner, delicacies of the sea simmered in fresh produce, then ladled upon a savory rice platter; and not even the commotion of captains and mates nearby, punctuating their meal with shouts of French, German and Spanish, nor even the antics of Tupper and the starboard watch, anchored stem to stern on the verandah, could diminish my sense of our private oneness. As if surrounded by an impregnable shield, an invisible scarf of tranquility and well-being, I peacefully ate and sipped my Madeira, noting the tang and taste of each morsel—now dwelling with fatherly pride on Tom and Jean, on their eagerness as they essayed dinner, their first hotel meal on this, their first foreign venture; now resting on Jim's dark blue gaze, openly attentive, and candid with his confiding closeness. Though one after another they all swept up to our table—every ship's master in the room, not only out of the simple courtesy which brings seamen together ashore, but out of the inevitable quest to compare times, runs and weather— even these interruptions failed to ripple our accord, or disturb the intimacy which intermarried us four. One of the captains indeed proved an old friend of John's, a brig's master out of Searsport, hearty, self-restrained, steady, the ideal candidate to sail home the children; but even this knowledge, that we were to place them on board first thing in the morning, and entrust them to him on the long voyage homeward, cast no shade on the glow of the present.

Taking leave of the company, we at length stepped outside, Jim rescuing me from further social obligations by the suggestion of a walk; and in the late afternoon sun we roamed the beaches, looking for shells or hop-scotching on the hard sand, then wandered into the market for treasures. Buying up a pair of lovebirds in a jute cage for Tom and Jean, we carried them to the hotel verandah—quieter now, with only a couple of women in European dress and stylish hair in residence; and scraping together four cane seats in the shade, we sipped at our tall glasses of lemonade, spinning out the incalculable minutes.

Drawing close to Jim, Jean leaned once on his shoulder, and he hugged her—on his face an indescribable sweet pain; but the moment passed, not to revisit till he slipped into my palm his find of the day, a venus-comb, its fragile spindles intact. Looking swiftly at him I tried to speak, but he smiled and turned away as the children beckoned; and carefully wrapping the fine shell in my kerchief—taking a long time about it, and quivering over its frail curves—I gently slipped it in my breast pocket, and followed the rest of them up the beach.

Dusk descending upon us, we rambled in the cool wind, the fireflies roaming like wandering lights through the palm fronds, and the soft gleam of the stars a-pulse in the heavens; then sitting on the shore we listened to the surf's wash, and took in the spices and scents of the rich earth. In the moonlight beside me Jim sifted the cool sand, as cool and smooth as silk on my bare arm; while the children waded and danced in the white crests, shrieking and dashing as they toppled ashore. So sweet was the night, so perfumed and soft, and so exquisite was Jim, a breath's brush away—so tender the clime, with its gentle wafts, and so unveiled his eyes, in the candor of dark—that by the time of our departure I was raw with their touch; and if it had not been for Haggai, sitting self-importantly on the quay, atop a heap of hen crates and produce no ten boats could convey, I would surely have broken under their gift—Jim and me instead wordlessly looking at each other, and giving way to the balm of laughter.

That night back aboard ship, I was troubled by another dream, a vision in which the crust of the earth trembled, and a giant wave loomed up in the offing; and I woke with a longing to look on Anjier, to spend my last hours here admiring its beauty. Why the need was so urgent I couldn't have said; perhaps it had something to do with the children's leaving, perhaps with Jim's eloquence, or our unfinished hours ashore; but it seemed wasteful to sleep when I could worship —when there was time now, unthreatened, and the most poignant of vistas lay unmarred and matchless, awaiting praise. Quietly rising and dressing, I climbed up on deck, which was deserted except for the look-out; and giving him a wave I turned to the skylight, on which I could sit and see the whole harbor.

To my surprise Jim was camped there before me, sitting with his chin in his palm, and his gaze resting on the peace of the village; and looking up at my footstep he smiled in the moonlight, as if he had been expecting my visit. Making room for me on the platform he leaned back on its casement, while I settled down close beside him; and together we sat in the homage of silence, waiting for dawn to stir the harbor. Pacing out his watch, Paul walked in the waist, back and forth from the main hatch to the fore, while the waves gently washed against the sternboard; but no other sound met our ears on the light wind save our ship's bell on the half hour, and the distant ring of the others', drifting from bark to brig over the water.

Rising once in the night cool, Jim disappeared, to return before long with our monkey jackets, and a pot of tea he'd brewed up in the pantry; and carrying a mugful forward to Paul, he settled back down on the skylight by me, shrugging into his jacket and accepting a pour. Sipping, we watched the dome of the sky lighten, Jim so close by his shoulder brushed mine, and his knuckles my knee as he raised his cup; and I could see the fine shadows of his lashes slowly fade as the day broadened out in the heavens, and a warbling note greeted it from the forest. Touching the hem of the sky first with pearl, then with silver, then with the vibrant gradations of rose, dawn overflowed in a gush of vermillion, green feathered palms and the throaty response of birds, trilling amongst the monkeys' chatter; and hushed, we looked on the timeless pageant that had always been, or that had been only now—that would always be long after these shores washed away, and all these frond-starred hills tumbled under.

Reaching dumbly out I touched Jim beside me—touched the man that'd sat by me on Corcovado, or worshipped with me at the rail in Havana; touched the man that'd wondered with me on the stark seas of Cape Horn, and the glimmering sheen of the Indian Ocean—the man that'd always been beside me, my heart's blood, my other. It wasn't much, just my hand on his wrist, but it was more than I'd ventured on the whole voyage; more than I'd ventured at any time before, except in the pressing need of misfortune; but it was enough to at once speak our closeness—to confess both my heart, and our oneness.

As soon as my fingers closed on his wrist, I felt the leap of him in my pulse—felt his vivid stir in the quick of my frame, as surely as if I held his breath in my lips; felt him tremble in turn, and swiftly looked at him; but he looked away and as he did, the bells rang, and Paul called all hands to start the sea day. In the minute before they took to the deck to rig the head pump and wash down the planks, I slipped my hand up to the back of his neck, and caressed him hard, stroking his long hair; then not glancing back I made for the companion, and missing half its steps, went to waken our young ones.

In the flurried press of the needs of the morning—both the children to see off, and our own leave to prepare for—there was no turning back to that hush on the skylight; and his eyes and mine when they met simply reflected a close calm—the accord of two men who know what to do to help one another. Packing valises, bundling up lovebirds, then partaking of our last breakfast together—through it all he was a stalwart aid and support; and by no waver or hoarseness did he betray his own heart, or any need he might have felt from the night.

To see Tom and Jean aboard the brig with a minimum of fuss— with a loving swiftness that would make parting easier for them, and for me—seemed to be the chief thing on his mind; and he took them forward and stood by them in their goodbyes—all hands having come to dote on them fondly—with a steadiness that heartened us all. Trying to brace up myself—assailed all at once by a hundred misgivings—I ordered the quarterboat lowered away, and called for a couple of men to row it; and tucking tidbits into their knapsacks and cooing farewells to the lovebirds, Haggai helped them over the rail—many long faces lining the bulwarks as we sculled the short distance to the *Mary Fales.*

Climbing aboard, Jim and I unloaded the boat, while Capt. Beale came forward to greet us; and standing uncertainly in the waist of the little brig, Tom and Jean looked up at the rigging, and eyed their new home with tentative awe and interest. Shaking hands with the mates—downeast men both, plain-spoken and hearty—and entrusting them with a long letter to Anne, I hugged the children, half-gruff with my pangs; but getting down on his knees Jim took them in his arms, his face so expressive that I turned away. Springing into the quarterboat I took one last look at them—and for a moment saw them through Anne's eyes, when they hauled into port three months hence; saw their wild hair, bleached tow, their bare feet and patched trousers, their sunburnt faces and wholly uncivilized look, through her aghast gaze on the wharf—and as with Haggai on that pile of hen crates, a sudden hilarity uplifted my spirits, and helped alleviate the sting of parting.

As if he'd had the same thought at the same moment, Jim turned and flashed me a grin, a buoyant grin full of delight and mischief, almost as though he'd caught the squawk of lovebirds during Anne's attempts to say grace; and feeling my heart rise, I ordered us off. As we pulled away their woeful faces were on us, watching us from over the taffrail; but now and then giving them a cheerful wave, we sculled along till me reached *Abigail,* where I immediately commenced operations to get underway.

Heaving short, loosing canvas, overhauling the rigging and running up the ensign, we fired our bow guns, which we'd run out in preparation for the South China Sea; and receiving a salute from the *Mary Fales,* we hoisted sail, and fished and catted the anchor. Skimming out with the slack tide and freshening breeze in our favor, we filled away for the Banka Straits, having taken aboard, after some debate, a pilot; and the morning sun at our bow and Krakatoa astern, sending forth is vaporous portents—a couple hundred bunches of green bananas swinging from our yardarms, a ludicrous note in the glories around us—we ran on: Jim standing and waving at the taffrail till the *Mary Fales* was but a speck, and Anjier village but a thimble nestled in the tropical hills.

On the third day from Anjier we made Banka Straits, after raising a succession of small islands which shot abruptly up from the sea; and expecting a long and difficult passage—the Straits rife with conflicting calms and light winds, and irregular tides from the monsoons—we prepared ourselves to lose time in the next weeks. Our pilot, whom we'd taken aboard to work his passage to Singapore, and whom we expected to drop off in the latitude of Lingga Island, warned us the trek could take a month; but it being late March, and the NE monsoon having abated, we made it through in just under five days.

Throughout the passage—from its commencement at the island of Banka, covered by an eruption of mountains, through the whole length of the Stanton Channel, one of two available for ordinary navigation—we skirted along incomparable beauties; and it was all we could do to keep up a lookout for the treacherous banks which littered the seabed, recognizable by their paler waters. In all the splendors of the passage—in all the garlands of lagoons and beaches, and tufted banks slipping by in the moonlight—I regretted that I'd sent home the children; and I missed their quick scamper and outbursts of wonder in each of my own awe-hushed trips to the rail. If it hadn't been for Jim, and the complexities of my situation with him, I might have missed them even more keenly; but so precarious were things now between us—after our day and night in Anjier—that the children's departure lost some of its sting; and it was mostly on him that my reflections lingered as the myriad shores slipped by us.

That it'd been what it seemed, that caress on the skylight, I knew that he knew even as the days passed; but in the constant shifting of sails and braces, and changing of courses and tacks in the light winds—at the quieter supper table below, partaking of curries and rice from Anjier—he was plainly waiting for me to make the next move; and what that might be, I had no idea. I might have ventured another touch—might have endeavored to invite a response, still ignoring my whole host of responsibilities at home—might even have tried to say something to him, if I hadn't one day, just as we entered the Channel, overheard Tupper and the pilot jesting with him at the second table. They'd just started in on one of Jim's pies, another of the benefits from Anjier, when Tupper, his mouth full, and his appreciation immediate, cried enthusiastically "Robehrtson—marry me!"; and in the raucous laughter which followed, Haggai and the pilot both bantering Jim, he shot back with his usual unflappable wit, "Not till you quit chewin' t'bacco, Tupper!"

Turning away from the saloon which I was about to enter, I slipped back up the companion to the deck, my thoughts in a turbulent reaction; for not only had their exchange burst in on my heart, invading my most intimate fancies, it also surprised from me two swift understandings, the one following quickly upon the other. That I wanted him as my mate, not merely my lover, I saw now with uncompromising clearness; saw that the alliance we'd celebrated in Anjier—the marriage that'd included my children—was the goal of my life, my courtship, my heart; and quick doubts as to the longevity of his response—even if he accepted my offer—crept into my heart when I considered his youth.

But more compelling still was the comprehension which broke over me not long after, when—watching him at the taffrail, leaning out in the soft wind—I saw once again the sensuality of his face; saw not just how comely, but how knowing he looked; then thinking back on all the scuttlebutt about his past romances—jarred to life by the offhand exchange prompted by Tupper —I felt a sudden question as to his partners, a sudden mistrust as to their gender. It was the first time I'd ever wondered if he'd ever been with other men; for since my discovery dream in Portland, my one thought had been that we were both new at this together. Now I wondered if this weren't the whole root of the mystery that'd enticed us from the start; from wondering went to certainty, with a jealousy that cut deep, and with even keener feelings of inexperience and ineptness; and so great was my confusion that I let slip my notice of March 31, the second anniversary of our meeting, which fell on the eve we left astern the Straits.

Nor were matters with Jim the full extent of my worries; for just as we dropped our pilot off Lingga Island—not an hour after he'd disappeared in a sampan—Tupper took a fall from the main shrouds, and broke the same leg he'd fractured on Tom's run to Havana; and we were without a second mate. Moving him into the sickbay—still echoing from the children—Eben and I gave him a brace to hang onto, an opiate for the pain and a bottle of scotch; and tugging and pulling, we set the bone. Preparing him for a long stay—eight weeks at the least—we transferred all his belongings from his cabin; then calling Jim into the saloon we held a short conference, the subject of which he knew even before he'd sat down.

As long ago as last fall, when he'd first signed as steward, I'd told him that if anything ever happened to Jack, I'd expect him to stand his watch, since nobody else aboard was as qualified for the berth; and he'd agreed and shaken on it. What he'd promised then hadn't seemed likely to materialize, or had maybe seemed easier to bear then than now; but despite how he felt when I called in the bargain, he lifted his chin and gave a nod, and promptly rising, moved his gear into Tupper's cabin.

Though he embarked on his new duties with his usual fervor, I knew he was hurt—that he deeply missed his old berth; and he wasn't the only one to suffer, for with Haggai filling in as cabin cook, and Orin taking up the slack as steward, I was a long way from the care he'd given these past weeks. From the moment of wake-up to the putting out of the lanterns, I missed him—missed his warmth, his voice, his humor; missed the companionship of having him on the same schedule as me; and I felt as though our domestic ties were broken. Nor was that the only rift between us; for I knew too that he'd sensed my fresh consternation—the confusion I'd felt ever since I'd guessed at his past loves; but having no way of knowing the source of my upheaval, he could only fall in with my mood—and the sure closeness we'd shared at Anjier began fading.

If all this weren't enough, we'd scarcely got used to our new duties, and embarked on the waters of the South China Sea, when we met with a species of tropical storm, the worst gale we'd encountered since the Atlantic; and somewhere in its midst we sprang the foremast, then shipped a sea that unmoored the long boat, and sent it hurtling into the galley. Rescuing the long boat we dusted off Haggai, whom we found on all fours inside the stove galley; but our hope that our spell of misfortune was ended proved unfounded within a day or two of fishing the foremast; and this time around, the victim was Jim.

Though the day'd begun fine, with no sign of a cloud in the offing, the wind'd commenced to make up by noon dinner, and a strong head sea to put in an appearance; and now, with the spray flying aft along the fore channels, it was plain we were in for some weather. Wrapping up business, Eben instructed all hands to get supper by the watch, and Haggai to ready the meal a bit early; and having ordered the studding-sails in, he sent the royal halyards over to windward, and got tackle upon the martingale backrope.

When the watches were again shifted, the helm relieved and the log hove, Jim should have immediately taken his post with his men, who were already finding their stations; and when he didn't appear I offered to stand duty for him, while Eben ducked below to see what was the matter. Waiting for him—watching the clouds make up in the northeast—I wondered what had happened to Jim; wondered if he'd been laid low by another of his sick headaches, not one of which had afflicted him since we'd put to sea; wondered more uneasily if he'd taken coast fever, the thing I'd most worried about in Anjier with the children. Beyond these speculations I had none whatsoever, so likely did one or the other seem; so I was ill-prepared when, after a long absence, Eben emerged from the aft companionway, and took me aside for a conference in its lee.

"What is it?" I asked, keeping my voice deliberately cheerful, as if that would guarantee nothing more serious than what I had guessed; but as soon as I saw his face I knew something critical was afoot, and a churning began somewhere in my midriff.

"Ben," he said simply, his words unemphatic in the wind's rise, "I've checked him out, and it ain't coast feveh, ain't anything like what I thought it might be at first...I'll stake my life on it, it's his appendix."

So taken aback that I nearly upended, I merely stood and stared dumbly at him, too staggered to get out a response.

"I was worried this mornin when he mentioned the pain, though he didn't want me t' say nothin' about it—an' then this aftehnoon, when his feveh stahted t' climb, I stahted puttin' two an' two togetheh... But now there ain't any doubt in my mind about it...an' we've got t' decide right now what t' do."

"What...what else c'n we do besides sit tight an' wait?" I stumbled, still struggling to take in what had come upon us.

"The longeh we wait, the greateh the chance for a rupture; an' you know youhrself we'd certainly lose him. There's only one other course an' I think we should take it.... Ben, it's got t' come out."

All the air went out of me and I found I was sitting down, not by the companionway but on the platform of the skylight, though just how I'd got there I had no idea.

"Does Jim know?" I at last asked hoarsely.

"Aye."

Again, in the face of his calm assertion, I felt my wits and resources scatter; and again I tried to focus their forces. "D'ye... d'ye have any idear what t' do?" I got out.

"I... I neveh tried it m'self, a' course, nor met anybody who has... But Kirk an' me once read the account of a doctoh who took out an appendix, a yeahr or so ago it was now; an' I pretty much fixed the procedure in my mind—havin' the feelin' at the time I'd some day need t' know... Anyhow, I b'lieve I could do it if I had the anesthetic right." He hesitated a minute with the wind in his rough hair, and the whirl of the gathering clouds above him; and when he spoke again, his shoulders were sagging. "I... I can't guarantee it'll work—that is, even if I do the job... there's so many things that could go wrong afteh... but it's a chance we c'n take an' t' me, it makes more sense than just doin' nothin' an' losin' him for sure... It's got t' be up t' you though, Ben."

"Oh, Christ, Eben, you... y' can't make me be the one t' decide this—"

"Youh're the skippeh, an' that's what it means t' be so."

For an intolerable minute the whole course of Jim's life was in the fragile span of my hands, as it had been that November day in the dory; and I balanced the certainty and pain of one route with the uncertainty and still greater pain of the other—all the while trying to waken and urge my dazed reason. In the end it was not reason, but instinct that decided—my paramount need to prolong his life, and so mine; for with him gone I was but a husk, a chambered shell without an inmate; and knowing that, I said gently, "All right... we'll do it."

"Thehre's just one otheh thing," he hesitated, bracing a hand on the casement as if it nerved him, "I... I don't know that I could attempt this without you, Ben... I'd tell ye what t' do, an' ye'd have t' do it; an' we'd have t' have somebody like Haggai fetch for us."

"Aye... of course," I said shakily, running a hand through my hair, and instinctively steeling myself for the ordeal. "I wouldn't have it any otheh way. I'll... I'll get Percy t' stand Jim's watch, Amasa youhrs; an' in the event of an emergency, they c'n send t' us for advice... unless y' think that'd be violatin' some law or otheh... I can't think of a single one of 'em now."

"Damned if I c'n eitheh," he smiled, with the gentle bleakness of a sun in December.

"All right, then... The first thing, I guess, is t' turn tail an' run b'fore it; she'll go a lot easieh an' make workin' smootheh. I'll call all hands an' give them the news, an' direct Amasa t' bring her about."

Calling all hands aft I dispatched orders, feeling every moment more like a cyclone; and it did nothing to calm me when the crew responded with an urgent, hectic hurry—Amasa dispersing men to the sheets and braces, Percy whipping them up at the bars of the windlass, and *Abigail* herself shivering and shuddering as she came up to, then fell off the wind, finally tearing before it with such a commotion that she seemed possessed with a feverish energy. Taking one last look at the skies in the northeast and the seas now crowding close behind us, I quit my post and ducked below, glad enough to leave the tumult on deck; but in our after quarters I found the same evidence of hurry, the utensils rattling with Eben's work in the pantry, the lanterns swinging to and fro in the saloon, the table stripped except for a rubber sheet, and in the midst of it all, scuttling to and fro like a rabbit, the unprepossessing figure of Haggai, setting out piles of towels and pitchers of water.

His arms loaded up to the chin with clean linen, he was white to the gills and nearly popeyed, his apron—a large coarse towel—still wrapped about his middle, while swathed about his forehead, the kerchief he always wore like a turban in the tropics, to keep the sweat from running into his eyes when he cooked. With his shirt sleeves rolled nearly up to his shoulders, and his broad arms bulging out with their India ink tattoos; with his stubble of a beard and his Cape Horn earring, and his cowhide boots, nearly out at the toes, he was about as unlikely an assistant to such an endeavor as could be pictured; but something about his nervous haste calmed me, and cleared the fog that'd descended ever since Eben'd first spoken.

Going straight to Jim's cabin I found him resting, tightly curled on one side with his back towards me; and if I'd had any doubts about Eben's verdict they were dispelled with my first glance at him—for he lay oddly crumpled there on his covers, as if he'd just been clipped by a wagon; and there was a yellowish hue to his still face which I'd never seen on anyone before, but which at once struck a chill in me. All the things I'd never said or done swirling and diving simultaneously at me, and threatening to disperse my newly gained calm, I hesitated a bewildered moment; but collecting my courage I simply bent over him, smoothed back his hair and said in a low voice, "Jamie, we'hre ready; I'm goin' t' cahrry ye t' the table; hold tight."

Though there was nothing he was more afraid of than gadje

medicine, he held up his arms to me with complete trust; and as I gathered him up my heart gave a wrench, and momentarily stopped in my chest. Here was this man, who could hardly withstand an inoculation, much less a trip to Boston to have his headaches looked into, consigning himself to me for an operation by two men who'd never performed such a deed before, all the while submitting to an anesthetic so untried its effects were still unpublished; and if his confidence weren't enough, he was calmer than I was—his expression, though strained, tranquil, almost serene.

As I lifted him from his berth he cried out; but once up in my arms he nestled his head on my shoulder, and curled his hand about my neck; and I wordlessly stood and cherished him to me, bracing myself against the frame of the berth, and burying my face in his hair. So good did he feel, there at last in my arms, that it took Eben's call to rouse me to haste; and painfully raising my face from his hot brow, then waiting for a smooth chance in the ship's way, I carefully carried him into the saloon, and laid him as gently as I could on the table.

Already on hand, Eben made him as comfortable as possible, bracing his head and chest up a little to keep his breath free; and he obediently listened while Eben explained the anesthetic, its properties and initial action, and how it might make him feel upon waking. When the mask came down over his face—a sort of pad in which Eben had inserted a tube to convey the vapor, a clumsy enough device, but answerable to our purpose—he accepted it without protest; and though he at first tried to turn away, because of its odor, he obeyed Eben's instructions to breathe regularly and slowly, and his hand in mine was relaxed. For a moment or two his eyes were open, and his gaze above the mask was on me, as if he were preparing his memory to take me on a far journey; but gradually his lids grew heavy, his glances more hazy and sporadic; and at last he appeared to be sleeping deeply, his lashes thick and dark on his cheeks.

Turning the responsibility of the vapor over to Haggai, we undertook the final stages of preparation, timing ourselves with *Abigail's* motions, then called up through the skylight that we were about to begin; and Paul, stationed there, commenced his watch on the seas. "Smooth chance afteh this lift-off...here's the rise...now," came Paul's shout, filtering down to us with the wind's rush; and feeling the corresponding surge and settle of the vessel, Eben picked up his surgeon's blade, a strong, thin knife presented to the ship by Kirk, and began his first incision.

Till this point there'd been time for neither doubt nor regrets—only time, in the little over half an hour since Eben'd told me the news, for a frenzy of preparation, and for a show of spirits to keep up Jim's courage; but now a vast wave of fear swept over my whole frame, and left in its wake a backsurge of panic. So overpowering was it that my fingers could scarcely hold the towel—that their quivering made Haggai's look calm by comparison; and my face felt as drained, as completely run out as if it was my blood, not Jim's streaming freely.

Petrified, I looked at his features, finding it inconceivable he couldn't feel the incision; but he seemed quiet and still, and Haggai's homely, thick voice, with its rasping strains and rugged accent, came comfortingly, "I'm watchin' him, Cap'n." At the same time soothed Eben's "Stiddy, Ben," while above sounded Paul's "No good now...two big seas... watch the roll... smooth chance comin'..."; and into their play came *Abigail's* motions, as if in answer to Paul's evocations, and the hush of Jim's soft-drawn, regular breathing, till it all became like a conversation, a commerce of sounds which helped steady me to our task.

"Try not t' think of this as Jim," came Eben's voice kindly into the exchange, as my fingers trembled around the edges of the long wound; and looking at his lean, brown hands—not an artisan's hands, but a netmaker's, a fisherman's, hardly a flicker to them in the patience of their work—I was awed into a kind of quiet. "Now when I point t' a vein, tie it off; the thread's right hehre, as clean as I could get it," he went on; and this command was added to the stream of converse that ebbed and flowed by turns around us: "He's sleepin' fine, Cap'n"...."Smooth chance"..."Tie hehre, Ben".... "Anotheh combeh"... As we slowly crept deeper into Jim's middle, I began to lose my fear; began to feel a knack almost akin to seamanship, in the delving and splicing of our repairs; and as my anxiety lessened my concentration sharpened, till Paul's voice seemed to sound from farther and farther away, the lamp's glow to broaden out undefined, and the whole universe to become my hands and Eben's, poised above the labor before us.

How long this stage went on there was no way of knowing; but it ended when Eben made the second incision, cutting deeper into the layers of muscle, which it was my job to help pin back. So fiercely was I concentrating that I hardly heard the cry of "Sail ho!" which came and went with the sound of Paul's voice, varying only with the shape of the seas: "Rough spell…wait a little…betteh now…" Sometime later I became conscious of an unusual commotion above, a louder thumping and thudding as if making and bracing sail, and the more distant creaking of the head pump, all of which struck me as being out of place now; but slamming ropes, drumming feet, anxious hails alike I managed to drown out for the time, till there came a resolute knock at the door, and I heard the sturdy voice of Amasa.

"We've got a sail on oweh weatheh beam that I don't a-tall like the looks of," he told us, standing stiffly nearby in his monkey jacket; and trying to pick up a pin my fingers fumbled, suddenly clumsy and big, though they quickly recovered.

"Any colohrs?" I asked, reaching for the next pin.

"No, an' no signal neither; she's just makin' for us, changin' course every time we do."

"Brig, bahrk or what?"

"A hermaphrodite brig."

"Any guns?"

"Not that I c'n see through the glass; but a crowd o' men—must be a hundred—an' enough boats t' get 'em all afloat."

"How fast is she gainin'?"

"Fast enough t' have caused me t' ordeh the men t' commence wettin' down sails."

With the wind shrieking at the portholes and skylight, and worrying at every chain, sheet and halyard, not to mention, hurrying this brig towards us, my one thought was, thank God I'd sent home the children; and swiftly meeting Eben's eyes, I reached a decision.

"All right, hehre's what we'll do," I said, my gaze already back on the next pin and tissue; "Bring her about an' up again t' her old course; we'll head back into the storm—*that'll* surprise 'em. If they c'n match us on the wind, I'll be damn well staggered; an' if they *do* catch us up, they'll have t' work for it... Got the guns run out an' ready?"

"Aye, an' the shot an' powdeh's ready t' hand."

"If it comes to it, fire a wahrnin' oveh the bow, but don't engage 'em if ye don't have to... Send someone at once t' break out the ahrms, a rifle t' every man—ye c'n set 'em by in the coach house; an' see to it Jack has a weapon in the sick bay. Set the pistols here for us with everything we'll need; an' have a man constantly at the glass, lookin' out for the minute they loweh away."

"Aye; it's as good as done," he responded, already on his way.

Timing his moves with the ship's Eben worked on, his fingers as firm as ever at their blade; but he quietly spoke in between Paul's shouts, and all the clatter and clamor on deck,

"I take it the specie's b'low us?"

"Practically undeh oweh feet; aye," I muttered, trying to help him by stemming the blood flow. "There's a hatch that lifts up t' a false hold undeh my cabin floohr; so b'tween that an' Jim, I ain't leavin' this table."

"How much?" he asked, pausing again at Paul's shout, and waiting for *Abigail's* shudders to settle.

"Specie? More'n ye want t' hear; that's why I ain't said nothin' about it."

"More'n we've carried b'fore?"

"About three times as much; aye."

"Jesus Christ," he quietly intoned, while Haggai sucked in his breath beside us; then meeting up with a smooth spell, we again commenced work.

As *Abigail* came about—with a tumult of cries, a pandemonium of thumping and creaking, not to mention, wrenching and pitching, which frequently obliged us to stop for whole minutes—Ephie came in for the key to the gun locker; and taking it from the ring at my belt, he calmly fetched my brace of pistols, which he set, together with ammunition and powder, on the sideboard. Then stopping by at the sickbay with another pair, he finally disappeared down the passage with as many rifles as he could carry, coming back twice more for additional armloads. Losing speed at first as her head came up to the wind, *Abigail* was at her most vulnerable instance; and there was no need for Paul, shouting down through the skylight—which he and another were hastening to board up—that the other sail was closing on us.

Struggling to keep our thoughts solely on Jim—striving to trust to the teamwork of the watches, and detach ourselves from the dilemmas on deck—we heard the sudden scamper of boots forward; felt the ship lurch twice with the discharge of the bow gun, which echoed below with a lingering shudder; but working on we shut out the commotion, even as a more distant discharge signified the other vessel was armed. In all the noise we could no longer hear Paul, who was straining to jury rig a speaking tube through the deck; could barely make any headway ourselves, the lantern above us erratically swinging, and everything loose fetching away with the ship's plunge; but bracing ourselves till even our toes ached, we crept by degrees deeper in Jim's side, painstakingly timing our advances. When Paul's voice at last garbled down through the new tube—when over the boom of the thirty-pounders we heard "'They're lowehring away,'" and—as if in confirmation—the crack of rifle fire, filtering down to us through the thick planks of the deck, Eben again lifted his eyes, and met mine.

"Shall we move him?" he asked, turning back to his work; but pausing to listen to *Abigail's* swing—knowing, from her angle and the sound of the wind, exactly where she was, as plainly as if I was standing on deck—I deliberately shook my head.

"No," I told him trying to make myself heard over the uproar, and struggling to command my hurtling thoughts; "once we're on the wind, there'll be no stoppin' us; an' it can't be more'n a couple more minutes. If Paul shouts down they're boardin', which I can't conceive they could do, b'tween oweh guns an' the seas, unless a lucky shot stops our way—I'll... I'll go with Haggai t' the companionway passage, an' leave you an' Jim right hehre... I... It'd be safeh for him in my cabin, but I just don't see how we could move him."

Giving a nod, he simply went on with his work, as tranquilly as if there weren't the pound of the deck guns, the blast of rifle fire and the tremendous throes of *Abigail*, as she painfully came up to her course; and following his lead we did our part, me trying to think over the drum in my ears, and Haggai unconsciously sucking his lips. When at last *Abigail* heeled over on the wind—when at last, by degrees, she began to pick up speed, and to announce her progress by an almost deafening strumming, as she worked her way back into the storm—we looked for the concussions of deck fire to diminish; but in all the intensifying tumult of the gale, it was impossible to distinguish their outburst from the tempest.

With the ship working even harder now on a taut bowline—with the gale increasing to a roar over our heads, so that we had to raise our voices at our work, and Paul to holler hoarsely down through the tube—we felt an odd shudder at the starboard bow, a shaking which rattled the lantern chimneys, and toppled all the books on the shelves; but assuming we'd been swept, we labored on over Jim, Eben closing in now on the final incision. When a moment later Paul shouted down, crying out we were hauling ahead, and the boats turning back to the sail, now astern, we halted long enough to rejoice; but our elation quickly paled before a new threat, broken to us by a different call through the tube.

"Ben?" it came with a garbled firmness, distorted by a sudden downfall of hail; and with difficulty I recognized Amasa.

"Aye," I called back, not looking up from Eben's hands, which were hovering undisturbed in their work.

"They're turnin' back for the time; but we've been hit."

"Aye; shhaboard bow?" I returned, too numb for surprise.

"B'tween the cathead an' the bitts, above the watehline; aye."

"B'tween the cathead an' the bitts; I hear ye; how bad?"

"Don't know till I get int' the forecastle; I've sent the lahboard watch on ahead; just need youhr permission t' quit the deck."

"Quit the deck, aye; leave Percy an' the otheh watch in chahge; an' have the man at the helm keep her off a little."

"Aye; keep her off a little," he confirmed, the hail pelting down even harder on the planks.

"Have Percy shorten sail all he can, till he gets word from you repairs've been made; an' have Ephie post up Paul on youhr progress meantime," I bawled up.

"Shorten sail all he can, an' have Ephie post up Paul; aye, aye; we won't make much time, but then, neitheh will they."

"Have they been hit?"

"Don't know; can't see; storm's closin' in... How goes it b'low with oweh boy?"

"All right; but not more'n half done."

"Not more'n half done, aye; I'm on my way; hehre's Paul."

A shipwright of the first order, he was more than equal to his task—so long as he had enough men, and could control the flooding from the head seas at the bow; and putting our trust wordlessly in his ability, we shut out once again every dilemma save the one before us, and persevered with the needs of our work. So rough was our way now that there were long pauses in which we did nothing but watch Jim's breath, check his pulse and vapor supply, and staunch the bleeding; and we fretted and chafed against the delays which every minute rendered him more fragile.

When at length—*Abigail* laboring on at a steep angle, and her hull resounding with mallets—Eben pulled back the last layer, and I carefully pinned it with the others, we finally could see the intestine, and part of the appendix, large, white, and swollen; and though there was no sign of a rupture, it was awkwardly placed, our incision having been high, causing Eben to have to struggle to cut it. Bracing myself all the sharper beside him—harboring fears we'd have to broaden the incision, or worse yet, commence with another—I stood by with one hand widening the wound, the other staunching the blood; while patiently, cautiously, Eben worked with a small probe, trying to maneuver the infected tissue.

Not till it was removed did I at last breathe a sigh—as though, with that stage, the operation was over, and his eventual recovery assured; but not pausing to exult, Eben hurried ahead, snatching up thread for his first set of stitches. Painstakingly sewing the stump—hardly more than a stitch a minute—he turned it; then still timing each step with Paul's voice and the seas, he closed the wound by delicate stages. When at last the edges of the incision were closed, neat with Eben's line of stitches, the bleeding stopped and a clean gauze in place, I felt a relief akin to an explosion; and my hands actually shaking like wands in the wind, I unstrapped him and eased him onto the stretcher. With all the pitching and lurching it took us all three to convey him into my cabin; but finally we got him safely to my berth, and slowly, gently we slipped him down on the mattress.

Altering our course to the NNW—partly to correct our running, partly to throw off the sail astern —and promising supper to Percy's men, who looked ragged and worn out, but who still showed considerable spirit, sending up a cheer at the news Jim's surgery was over—I hurried down into the forecastle; and here I found Amasa and the larboard watch gaining on repairs, fresh futtocks scarved under a jury-rigged shield, and a start made on the inner planking. Augers, mallets, adzes flying, they were hurrying against the head seas, which every minute threatened to undo their labors; but though the forecastle was in upheaval, there appeared to be no serious loss; and pausing to consult with Amasa about shifting the watches, to give Percy's a respite from the exposure of deck work, I hastened back to the poop to oversee matters there.

For endless hours that was my pattern, going from the quarterdeck, where I kept an eye on our headway, to the forecastle to aid Amasa, to the saloon to figure and re-figure our position, wrestling with our two about-faces—and finally, always, back to my cabin, where Jim was still sleeping deeply. Worn out from the double demands of the gale and the skirmish—oppressed by the uncertainty of Jim's condition, and asking me continually about him—the crew finally got supper at midnight, a fine batch of scouse, albeit cold, from the galley—all lights, even the binnacle, black out to discourage pursuit; but before I could begin on my own meal Eben called me, and my heart at my throat, I made for my cabin.

Partially awake now, Jim was drifting and moaning, so pale I all but fell to my knees when I saw him; and so ill was he, and in so much pain, that far from rejoicing at his regaining consciousness, I cursed myself as I helped Eben with him, wondering if I'd been right to go ahead with his surgery. When—after hours of miserable sickness, the ether wearing off with maddening slowness, and his half-conscious battle wrenching me like my own war—it was at last safe for more medication, Eben gave him laudanum for the pain, and he kept it down, going off in a drugged sleep; but by then it was dawn and I stood on the deck, watching the light on the hem of the horizon, the turbulent, sleek seas and *Abigail's* rent sails, with such a yearning for respite and rest, that it seemed a hundred years since I'd slept.

His recovery was slow, hampered all the more by fever, which began climbing the next day, rising till it was sky high; and packing him round with the little ice still left in the chest, Eben and I hung on and waited. For another two days of hellish sailing—gale-force winds and storm-damaged decks, the struggle of repairs and the arduousness of makeshift—things hung in the balance; and the best that could be said was, there was no reappearance of the brig, and a diminishing chance of its show as the time passed. Taking turns on deck and below, Eben and I traded off duties, barely snatching time for a quick meal; and while he slept I sat by Jim, aching over his wan face and thin hands. Casting about late the second night for a way to help, I searched my mind for something to do; but all I could think of was that I wanted to hold him, to cradle and comfort him like a newborn—to erase all his pain and unease with my touch, the leaven on which he'd always seemed to thrive.

Suddenly realizing that we were alone—that Tupper in the sickbay was asleep, the pantry shut up and the saloon vacant—I rose and closed my cabin door; and sitting down by him again, instead of speaking or entreating him to drink, I bent and kissed his quiet brow. Though he made no sign, his face eased a little, as though he'd understood my lips—as though, in some dumb region of fever and pain, touch spoke with the eloquence of words; and for the rest of the night, while Eben slept on, and the ship gradually worked her way out of the head winds, I simply did all I'd always wanted to do, but had been to constrained or abashed to try: stroked his face, brushed his lips, caressed the sweet hairs at his temples, or the thick, lowered crescents of his lashes—never taking advantage of his slumber, but never ceasing to touch, and never saying a word save "It's me, Ben," or now and then reassuring him, "Jamie."

All at once understanding all those wordless rhythms and gestures of generations of primitive healers—suddenly grasping the meaning of curing by touch, as Abigail had done with my grandfather Winslow—I gently kept my hands on him, moving; played over his arms and face and chest, as though my fingers could draw out his poisons, and replace them with the strength of my life flow. When at last dawn came and I saw by its thin light that he looked less pinched and haggard—when at last, too tired to keep on, I stilled my hands, and settled back to doze in the chair bolted by him—Eben rose and stirred in the saloon; gently opened my door and, pausing for a moment, looked first at Jim, then at me, all but asleep; then bending over Jim he drew a deep breath, an ease-filled hush that sighed out his dumb thanks..

While I rested that day, he fully woke for the first time, and took some nourishment from Eben's spoon; thought he was only just now waking from the operation, having no memory at all of the past three days, save for the vagueness of pain and illness; and he listened amazed while Eben told him of all that's transpired since he'd gone under with the ether. Sitting by him myself that night, writing out my log with a lift to my spirits that sped my thoughts and pen in the still room, I felt him briefly rouse again; and looking over at him I met his eyes, which smiled at me out of the half-drowse of sleep.

"Still there?" he asked, his voice the merest whisper, and his eyes closing down again with his slumber; and crossing over to him I reassured,

"Aye; an' I ain't goin' nowhere."

"Storm's done?" he murmured after another minute, as if he'd been trying to remember all that Eben had told him.

"Aye," I assured again, taking his hand as I sat down.

"Eben says there was a sail hot on our tail, the guns out an' shooting an' everything ...an' I missed it," he smiled, his expression half-dreaming.

"An' a damn good thing too," I said; "what with that hair-triggeh of yours...ye probably would've taken out our man at the helm."

After what'd happened to Jack and Jim—reinforcing the general notion that *Abigail* was a jinx ship—no one was terribly anxious to fill the second mate's berth; but I finally prevailed upon Percy to take it, and he settled into Jim's cabin, moving Jim's gear back to his old bunk; and I simply did without a steward. Displaced from my quarters for the duration of Jim's recovery, I slept on the sofa in the saloon; and not only did I do most of my own cleaning and serving, but I took on much of Jim's care as well, as if I'd been the one that'd shipped in his berth.

Nor did the ignominy of a master who waited on himself and others weigh very heavily on me; for at the first sign of Jim's appetite returning, I marched myself straight into the galley, and informed Haggai I was going to bake a chicken pie; and when he protested pies were his province, not mine, I told him to pick out the fattest, youngest hen in his coop, and have it ready for me in an hour. Sputtering and stuttering—partly over my presence in his galley, partly over my desecration of one of his chickens—he balked, "Well, I just ain't goin' t' do it"; and I glowered at him from his precious stove. "Ye've got t' do it; it's an ordeh," I stood fast, rummaging round the bins for a skillet; "I'm still the captain o' this vessel, even if every Tom, Dick and Harry *has* had a crack at runnin' her lately."

Going off in a huff, he made for his coop between decks, leaving me in possession of the galley; and having found my skillet and stoked up the oven, I pondered what on earth I should do next. Having cooked very little—aside from a pan of fish over a campfire, or an uncomplicated venture such as johnnycake at breakfast—something as abstruse as a pie was temporarily beyond me; but I calculated that if I could help Eben take Jim apart, rearrange his middle and stitch him back up, I could certainly put together a crust; and though I drove Haggai nearly over the brink when he came back, I finally succeeded in making up the dough. Potatoes and other stock we were now out of, but carrots and onions we still had in abundance, together with plenty of spices and flour, which cooked up nicely with the fresh chicken; and filling two or three shells with satisfaction, I set them on Haggai's clamped racks to bake.

When at length they came out, lightly browned and aromatic, I felt a pride akin to a shipbuilder's pleasure; and proudly carrying one in to Jim, I set it temptingly before him, and joyously watched as he polished it off. Feeling the strength returning to him with each bite, I fed him another pie at supper; and by the time the banks of the Pearl River were slipping by, and we were hauling into the wharves at Whampoa, he was sitting up in his berth a little, and politely asking me for my menu.

It'd been sixty years since the *Empress of China*—bearing a cargo of ginseng and otter skins, and braving 16,000 miles of unpredictable sailing—had hove into the same port below Canton; sixty years since trade had first opened between China and the American continent; but though there was now a throng of hongs, bedecked with the flags of a host of nations, lining the river up and down the wharves, all matters of commerce and exchange were still new, and girded about by many conditions. Closed to foreigners, Canton—where banana plantations and hilltop pagodas relieved the monotonous banks, and where British military and naval stations stood at the city's door— was out of reach; while the hongs were forbidden to women, and even the language was kept secret, so that business was conducted in a kind of pidgin tongue, a mixture of English, Chinese, Indian and Portuguese.

Added to these were the constraints of cargo—the Chinese interested in little westerners had to offer, and most transactions conducted in specie, rolled by the keg down European gangways; while unofficial cargoes such as opium abounded, and received unexpectedly easy entry. Simply tossing into the river bundles of hay and straw, in which were concealed packages of the drug, or bottles containing carefully sealed papers, in which were listed the prices current in London, traders quietly initiated business; and rowing in from the shore to pick up the refuse, natives quickly dispersed it amongst private networks.

If all these particulars weren't enough to bewilder, there was the commotion of a wholly foreign city, much of it thriving in plain view on the river—junk-board shops, prows of produce, teeming houseboats, even floating inns and taverns, gaily painted and decorated for the allurement of travelers—not to mention the chaos of the wharves, ringing with the tongues of twenty nations.

Getting ourselves acclimated, setting up business, breaking out what little of the cargo was negotiable—mostly ginseng and New England leather and yard goods—and rolling out, to my relief, every last keg of our specie, then making way for 1,500 tons of tea, a most delicate cargo, and other fragile ware such as silks and porcelain, took every bit of what strength I had left over from Jim; and if it had not been for Eben, steering me through all the harbor rules and regulations, I should not have been able to conduct business.

As it was we barely managed it together—missing, at every turn, Jim's capacity for language, and the sheer zest and enthusiasm he always brought to port work; and I found my chief joy in bringing news back to him, as he lay fretting at not seeing all these new customs and vistas. Passing up arrays of supposed delicacies—wryly informing him he had a choice between edible birds' nests and sea worms, and receiving, in answer, a Romany malediction—I brought back lengths of silk to delight him, and a dressing gown in the latest New York fashion, Cantonese attire being in vogue; and as soon as it was safe we carried him up on deck, and set him in a chair to watch the goings on around us.

Before long we were known up and down the Pearl not just for the design of the ship, which had created a stir as soon as we hove into port, but for all the broken limbs and recuperations going on board, and for the music of Jim's guitar and fiddle; and more and more frequently American captains, sometimes with their wives of first mates, came dropping by for coffee and concert, singing along with the sentimental airs they knew, or swapping the latest news from back home. Since there were nine ships in port from the state of Maine alone, not to mention a dozen more whose hail was New York or Boston, the traffic through our saloon was hectic—Jasper greeting all and sundry with a lecture about noise, and Jim obliging with music till all hours; while, with the addition of captains from Europe and the Near East, of whose tongues we knew little or nothing, there was a regular Babel of language, and a commerce of signs and signals and gestures.

Our last night in Whampoa there was one final high-go; and though by and large I loathed such gatherings, especially the night before a strenuous sail, I stuck it out to the last glass and cigar, in order to see Jim at the piano, a last-minute gift to the ship from Mother. Sitting up bright and well in his common sailor's red shirt, the sleeves rolled up above his elbows in the warm weather, he obliged by playing the pieces he'd learned, and by attempting requests with a good sense of sport; and I watched him covertly from behind a screen of faces, or the bank of McCabe's perpetual geraniums.

A month now since his surgery, he was not only past the initial dangers that'd threatened him, but the inevitable weakness and depression which followed; and his resurging vigor showed now in his bright gaze, and the returning fullness in his face and hands. Through with my port work, and the many hardships before it, I could well afford to sit back and admire; and admire I did, drinking him in without stint, and with few if any glances at those conversing around me. So busy had been the past days, and so public our life aft, that for weeks we'd had scarcely a private word together; but now there was something personal about the way he played, as if he could sense my glances on him; and all the guarded intercourse that had existed between us seemed gradually to be dispelled, as though his songs were intended for me. Now and again our glances met, as when he looked suddenly over his shoulder, and I roamed from the confines of some boring skipper, or worse yet, some well-meaning skipper's wife; and each time my cheeks grew a few degrees warmer, my confidence a few shreds thinner, as I took note of his returning sureness.

Accustomed to having the upper hand, especially the past month, when he'd been as meek as a lamb in his berth, I was suddenly unsettled to see his flourish—the self-assured zest of his performance; and once again I was uncertain how to proceed with him, as I always was when he rang out with a challenge. Adjourning to the quarterdeck for a spell in late evening—wandering around in his wake beneath the colored lanterns, suspended at intervals from the shrouds and stays—I admired the glints of light on his hair, always from a wary distance; while I backed away from any chance to actually speak with him, uncertain of what on earth I should say.

Once, when I summoned the nerve to bring him a drink—having broached a keg of brandy as soon as we hauled into port, Haggai's protests notwithstanding—and he accepted it with a smile, his fingers crept up to my wrist, and lingered there a knowing moment; and as taken aback as an unguarded vessel—as unable to mistake the gesture as he had been that dawn in Anjier—I nearly dropped the glass between us. It was the first such conscious move he'd ever made—certainly the first initiative since my Portland dream; the first signal he was ready to pick up from where we'd left off after Anjier, and my unspoken anxiety about his past affairs; and for the rest of the night I tossed in my berth, re-living the vibrant shock of his touch.

Perhaps it was his move which, once made, stood like an invitation between us; perhaps the agitation of departure, the excitement of being homeward bound; but as we hove in our anchor and threaded our way back down the Pearl—bound to Maine, not via the Indian Ocean, where we'd have to buck the SW monsoon, but across the Pacific to the Sandwich Islands, where we hoped to sell the rest of our cargo—another series of dreams burst upon me. Now alternating with tidal waves—which still swept my night visions in such regular procession that I bolted awake at the first hint of their rise—were strange Oriental dreams about gardens, mysterious gardens intense with pattern, perhaps inspired by vivid landscapes just left, but always associated in my mind with the sensuous power and precipitous surprise of Jim's touch.

In one I found myself near a fountain, admiring a nearby forest of pear trees, when a cascade of feathers came drifting down on me, a drenching of color and shape and design, of orchid and pink, dotted cinnabar and melon; then wandering on I came to a pool of fish, magnificently green and aqua and jonquil, their patterns flashing in the filtered light. Entering the forest, I looked with wonder on the pear trees, arrayed with precisely regular branches, stylized and graceful with ocher leaves; walked along, ever further into the woods' heart, as if drawn on by an irresistible summons, till I came to one perfect tree on a grass bank, the leaves of its five branches so arrayed that they lay along the boughs, not one of them overlapping another, but each individual fully visible, golden against the rich brown of the bark.

Somehow its aura of enigma and allure recalled Jim's, as I'd always known it; as did the air of the jeweled bird, which spoke to me in a later dream in words which fell away on my waking: a resplendent living bird the shape of a partridge, but bigger and feathered with a magnificent array of gems, of sapphires and rubies and topazes and emeralds, each one again individual and faultless.

Night after night as we embarked on the Pacific, in finer and finer vistas of weather, these dreams broke upon me while I tossed and turned, like images of the human past; and by day I sheltered them in my stronghold as if I bore an incalculable cargo.

If my dreams were in tumult so was the sea; for as we bowled along day after day with a fair wind on our quarter, hardly starting a brace of altering a sail, the swells rolled in a hurtling procession on by us, their peaks erratic and toppling with spray, and long trails of foam patterning their valleys and the indigo rises of their heights. Not a fish, not a ship, not an island broke their surges, just our cloud of sails heaped pyramid-like above us, from the base of the lower studding sails and giant courses, to the apex of the dainty skysails; and all alone on the heaving, up-rolling surface, *Abigail* bucked along at a headlong pace, despite an unusual array of repairs.

On the third day out, in the midst of a stiff blow, she parted her wheel rope—an event which might well have proved disastrous to us, had not Eben instantly sprung to the rescue; and though Amasa and I quickly rove a new rope, she was not answering her helm as she should, a frustration to all hands in the following seas.

Flying along with an uncertain helm, on the crests of dreams that roiled up from my deep, things for me were tumultuous enough; but added to their commotion was my upheaval about Jim—his signal in Whampoa, and his daily presence nearby me, filling me with an almost uncontrollable excitement, and nearly as much consternation as hope. He was back now in his old berth, which he shared with Haggai, taking on most of his duties as steward; but with Eben still refusing to allow him to climb, or to lift anything particularly taxing or heavy, he was barred yet from all hands duty on deck; and the better part of his days was given over to his old round of caring for me, the saloon and after cabins.

Since his face still went pale after any exertion, and he was always plainly fatigued by nightfall, I was glad to have him kept from the rough and tumble of deck work—glad to see him curl up of an afternoon on the sofa, and rest for a couple of hours at the day's peak; while having him back again at the pantry and table filled me with an unassailable contentment. With Percy up on deck in the dog watch, and the rest of us below wrapping up the day's work—with Jasper squawking nonsensically in his cage, Eben and me looking over the past twenty-four hours on the slates, and Jim nearby sewing under the skylight, I put in the pleasantest evenings I'd ever spent sailing; yet even in the midst of such seeming tranquility, my silent thoughts were surging with turmoil.

More and more as time passed on our voyage, and as unlooked-for events deepened our mute bond, any move I might make to unite us without the spoken commitment of marriage seemed unsatisfactory to me, and unfair to him; while all the while matters with Anne went unresolved. Looking over at me under lowered lashes, handing me slates with fingers that lingered, he seemed to know, understand and wait; yet even his holding back seemed poignant with promise; and this, above all, in the seeming serenity of our evenings, in the domestic peace of music, reading and sewing, agitated my inner waters.

Thus matters stood when, on the fifteenth day out—in the latitude of the Marianas, just a degree or two south of the Tropic of Cancer—

events took a swift and irreversible turn; and all our hopes that *Abigail's* fortunes were changed were within twenty-four hours wholly blasted. It was on the first of June, a fine, temperate night with a moderate head wind, and a rolling sea under the sheen of the moon, that the first in the series of events befell; and not uncommonly for me, they commenced with a dream.

I was walking at first, though I couldn't see myself; the grass was green and springing under my feet, and there were wildflowers clustered amongst the thick blades. Suddenly I rounded the top of a knoll, and looked down to see a fair hill-rimmed valley, with a gently curving stream wandering along its shallow floor. All the way to the stream the whole slope below me was speckled with a star field of flowers, blue and buttercup and white; while beyond on the opposite hillside I could pick out the panorama of their colored dots. I saw one place especially, not far from the stream, that looked like a living carpet of azures and golds, marked with white: something drew me down to that place, as if its fabric beckoned with light, and I walked slowly down to it.

As I drew closer the meadow grew ever more radiant; and lost in its display, I realized there were sheep grazing on it—dimly heard the occasional clank of their bells, and passed a gentle brown dog. As I neared the carpet of flowers I began to look down—ceased to see the dome of the sky, or the sweep of the hillside beyond; and I watched the blossoms go passing by my feet in streams of white and blue and yellow.

Suddenly I felt a strange presence before me, unnoticed till now in my downward musing; and slowly coming to a halt, I lifted my head. There, standing before me, was a boy of nine or ten: he was brown-skinned, strong and slender, and his blue eyes flashed at me as if in friendly recognition. As he stood looking at me he seemed wholly at ease; he was barefoot, with the bright flowers about his toes; while upon his person he wore old blue pantaloons, which tied at the hips with a woven cord, a worn beige shirt, and a broad-rimmed, frayed straw hat. In one of his hands he held a sturdy stick, and on this he leaned slightly.

I knew at once, evening my dream, that this was Jim—Jim as

he was a decade ago, tending sheep for the Welsh while his people wandered; and a flash of joy and recognition flowed through me—a joy so holy and powerful I felt like weeping. Ignorant of my tumult of feeling, the boy stirred, and called to the dog; then he turned, and went walking with a sure, even stride toward a little footbridge which spanned the stream. Not wanting him to go—longing to get to know him better, to drink in the details of a long-ago I was otherwise forever barred from—I found my voice; and urgently I called out "Jamie! Jamie!" When he didn't acknowledge my cry, unconcernedly collecting the sheep, I tried the Welsh name I knew he'd used, insistently shouting out to him, "*Gethin!*"; but though the dog turned, with an alert cock to his notched ears, still the boy kept on walking.

Desperate to make him see me, I at last resorted to his secret name; and "*Taliesin! Taliesin!*" I called to him, loud enough to waken the valley. Turning again, he looked at me, and gave me a jaunty wave of his hand; then he passed across the wooden bridge, the dog and all the sheep following in a line. I saw them pass up the hill together—saw the flash of the boy's bare feet in the grass; then I saw their forms, clear-cut against the sky, at the top of the knoll, before they passed over the crest and so from my view.

Suddenly I woke with the feeling that I could scarcely breathe; dazed, I found my face and pillow wet with tears, and understood only slowly that I'd been weeping. Dumbly reaching out I opened my porthole, and sat for a spell drinking in the night air; then quieted at last I lay back on my pillow, and gazed for an unknown time on the shadows.

Next morning Eben and I were eating breakfast in silence; the early sun streamed in around us through the skylight, and wavered with the ship's roll on the carpet. I hadn't seem Jim yet, for he'd served before I'd sat down, then departed to fetch something from the galley; and I waited his return with anticipation—with a mixture of joy and hushed expectation. At the sound of his step, I raised my eyes from my coffee, and saw at once how well he looked: he was bright-faced, and there was a spring to his walk; his dark hair shone washed and well-brushed in the sunlight; and his clean denim jean pants and jersey, though faded, brought fresh notes of color to his weathered skin. "Well, sit down!" Eben exclaimed when he saw him, shoving over a clean plate, and gesturing to a chair; and setting things out from his tray with a grin, he accepted a place at the table.

"Coffee, Jamie?" I asked him gently—so gently that he turned to look at me, with a quizzical crook to his brow; for my dream was still so heavy upon me that I felt uncharacteristically at peace and subdued.

"Aye; I'll pour; there's biscuits on the tray from Haggai," he smiled, uncovering the platter he'd set before us; and after a flurry of hands and silver, we munched companionably in silence, not even Jasper disturbing our repast. With scarcely another side glance at me, Jim fell quietly in with my mood, as he often did with his acute instinct; and not till Eben had scraped his plate clean, excused himself and headed up for the quarterdeck, did he refer to my preoccupation.

He turned to look at me oddly then; but though he wordlessly invited my confidence, I found I didn't know how to begin. For a while we spoke of this and that; of Percy's doings, and Eben's orders to stay the masts; but my mind plainly wasn't on what we were saying, and when again he paused to look at me, I decided to take the plunge.

"Jim, I've had a strange dream," I said to him, blurting out the words all at once; and in answer he leaned slightly forward, giving me his full attention as he always did. Hesitating now and then, I gave him every detail I recalled; and as I spoke an expression half like wonder, half like fear came over his features. He never said a word in response; but as he listened a look as of recognition—of recollection illumined his face, widening his eyes and parting his lips, as though he heard cries from afar, or the beck of familiar calls in the distance; and with a thrill of awe I knew he'd seen the same vistas—that he'd visited them too, as the boy in my dream—that I'd beheld not just him but some real place in Wales, some place he'd actually lived and worked in.

In some inconceivable way I'd crossed the border into his past, burst into the environs of his youth, and he knew it; and as the knowledge came home to him his look of fear heightened—an unreasoning fear, not like the apprehension he felt for gadje medicine, or for the order and direction of gadje thought, but like the terror he'd shown when he'd heard the loon, that first night tenting on the shores of the lake: a fear for the irrational guest on his threshold, the manifestation of his own spirit.

As if uncertain whether to welcome an outsider on his turf—an intruder into these, the private grounds of his people—he regarded me warily at first, almost as though we'd never met, much less shared the overtures of lovers; but as I described the whole scene—the winding river and footbridge, the grazing sheep, brown dog and flowers—as I dwelt upon the rolling hillsides, with almost as much longing as if I'd been born there—his unease seemed to gradually give way to yearning, the wistful reflection of my own feeling. And when I described his response to my calling him—his jaunty wave in response to his secret name, which I thought would terrify him most of all, and which I forbore to utter now—his wordless expression of wonder triumphed: the same awe I'd felt when I'd looked up and seen him, and realized the myriad channels of knowing.

To the end of my account he said virtually nothing; but as I finished revealing to him how he walked over the bridge, and on up the hill with the dog and sheep following behind, I could see he was struggling with some strong emotion; his hands trembled, and his eyes shone as if with tears. When at last I fell silent he sat still a moment, struggling yet, as if to find words; then suddenly he got up and left the saloon—I heard him dash down the passage toward the poop companionway, and didn't see him again for several hours.

When next I met him it was on deck: he was standing alone by the taffrail, looking out to the west where a bank of cloud had risen to blur the hard lines of the horizon. A couple of pails by his feet and the wooden hayrake told me he'd just been feeding the livestock with Orin; down by the longboat I could still see one or two hands dispersing hay for the bullocks. Having had an eye on that bank of cloud myself, I came up behind him to view it with him; but in the throb of the sails and the creak of the rigging, he apparently neither heard nor saw me.

As I drew close to him I suddenly halted a moment; he'd turned his face toward the bow a degree, and I could see every line of his features—every wave of his hair and curve of his shoulders framed against the hard blue of the sky, still crisp and bright immediately above us. Then suddenly he seemed to see me, and impulsively, he beckoned to me; and in a moment I was standing beside him.

We looked out together on the sea for awhile; then he turned to me and began to speak, without preface; and I knew it was in reference to my dream. "You know," he said calmly, with his resonant accent, "that used to be one of my favorite places. It looked just as you described it. We'd move our wagons there in the early spring—just the other side of the hill you saw me walk over with the sheep. There was a river there—the Dee, near Bala—the stream eventually joined up with it, in the next valley. Early every morning I used to lead the sheep over the hill, across the bridge, and let them wander—they'd graze, they'd stray, and later I'd eat the dinner I'd brought, and gather them back together. Sometimes I'd pass the time on the bridge—I'd pretend it was a ship, or a stage; sometimes I'd imagine it was a wagon. I'd paddle in the stream as well, or go running amongst those flowers."

It was a long speech for him, far more than he usually volunteered without questions; and as if aware of this and other considerations, he paused and gave a measured look at me. Wary again, as though about to test me, or the power of detail of my dream, he appeared to take stock a moment; and when at length he launched his inquest, it was at a place unexpected. "That...the cord you saw about my waist... Can you remember what it looked like?"

There was no need for me to look back, or strive to recollect; the entire scene was still at my fingertips, as vivid and immediate as if it were a recent memory of my own. "It was...why, it was blue, with a band or two of red running through it....and a sort of a fringe thehre at the ends."

His eyes grew a bit wider, but he made o comment, save "Yes, that was it... my grandmother made it for me. And the dog... what did he look like?"

I looked inward a moment, but again I saw swiftly. "He was

brown as I said, with a white bib and muzzle...and both eahrs were notched, as if he'd been in a few fights. He was long-haired like a collie, had the same shahrp nose; but—he was different, smalleh—like some kind o' lurcheh. He... why, he had on a collah like youhr belt, with a small brass bell attached."

"And the bridge?"

"It...it was just an ordinary footbridge, with wide brown planks rising a little from each bank, and meeting in a straight short span in the middle... But it had a rail on eitheh side; and it... thehre was a carving at the head of each rail... some kind of a bird... a goose or a swan, I think."

As if this were the clincher his fear returned, revealing itself in his darkening eyes before he swiftly looked down at the sea. "Yes... you know, I had forgotten that myself," he murmured, in words I could barely catch over the ship's thrash; but his look was unmistakable when he glanced again at me—was suspicious and wary as if I was a seer, a Rom *chauvihano* like his cousin Vanko. Not having the first idea how to take me, he flitted his glance from me to the sea several times; while both of us fell into an awkward silence, not knowing what to make of each other. Grappling about for something to say next, some wit to help relieve the tension, I all at once out of nowhere exclaimed, "Long tails!"—visited by another recollection from my dream; and mystified, he looked up at me.

"What's that?" he queried blankly.

"Youhr sheep are different from owehs," I marveled; "they've all got long tails."

For another moment he stared dumbly at me, as if conjuring up comparative images in space; then suddenly he laughed with me, admitting "You're right!" with his own admiration; and in our laughter he let me into his reserve—raised his remarkable eyes, and looked at me; looked at me as he never had before, wholly candid and unguarded. Peering into his gaze that vivid moment, I saw he was as confused as I was; saw his acute fear and consternation for the privileges our feeling gave us—privileges of sight that left no retreat, and no private borders; saw too, triumphing over fear and confusion, an undeniable offer of heart—an incontestable offer of tenderness and love.

A passion swept over me from stem to stern in response, and in its force I simply wanted to hold him—to kiss those frank blue eyes again, as I had when he lay heedless in China; simply wanted to embrace him, to wed him and myself to that dream—to marry us to the ecstasy of its vision. I felt myself clinging to the rail; vaguely it dawned on me that the entire crew, forgotten till now in the exchanges of my dream, were scattered about on deck in the dog watch—that we were in their ready view. Turning my back to them, I grabbed Jim's hand—saw he was looking at me in desperation, as though he'd understood without words; desperate myself, brought his fingers to my lips—brushed their work-hardened backs in a kiss; then too shaken to keep to the deck any longer, I made straight for the companion hatchway, my one thought being to get to my cabin.

I might have sheltered a bit behind closed doors—might even have waited for him to follow, to pick up below where we'd just left off; but now the events that'd commenced with my dream raced on to their swift and inexorable conclusion. I hadn't reached the companionway when a terrific blast—coming out far in advance of the cloud front, still distant—struck *Abigail* beam on without warning, nearly taking the masts out of her and shredding the sails; and in the chaos of rigging and canvas which followed, Jim tore off to rally with Percy's watch. Getting back onto my feet I gained the wheel, hoarsely hollering orders which came to me slow and hard; heard Eben far off bellowing commands on the forecastle, and Percy crying out in the waist.

Let go by the run the rigging ran free, whipping and flailing in total disorder, while the sails went slamming and slatting against the mastheads, nearly flinging the men each time from the yardarms; and in the flying welter and uproar of noise, I could scarcely think what to do next —old procedures and orders slipping out of my reach as fast as I could grapple for them. Though one by one sails came in, several split or in tatters— though agonizingly the topgallants were furled, topsails close-reefed and courses hauled up, the ship finally running fairly before it—I had far less than usual to do with it: Eben and Percy far outstripping me in speed and timing, and in managing procedures from their stations.

Matters at last about under control, I was just congratulating myself we'd got off no worse—little as I'd had to do with it—when out of the tail of my eye I caught sight of something, a shadow as it were dark and swiftly falling; while simultaneously "Man overboard!" rang out from half a dozen locales of the ship. Reeling as I still was from the line squall, and from my earlier encounter with Jim, I could scarcely bring my mind to focus; and it was Eben who stopped the ship's way, shouting out to the helm and bringing her up to the wind. For precious moments I floundered witlessly for my voice; then "Loweh away the quarteh boat! Three men aboard of her!" sprang from me, rising unbidden from years of seagoing; and at once every hand not bracing the head yards or backing the after jumped aft to clear the boat.

In all the confusion of men scampering and yards shaking, I understood it was Paul that we'd lost, with an unspeakable relief it wasn't Jim; but helping lower away I realized he was one of the ones heaving himself into the boat just as she cleared the rail; and a whirlwind of protests swept through my mind and attempted to battle its way to my lips. Frail as he still was from his surgery off China, he shouldn't have gone, and I knew it; knew I had the power to stop him; but suddenly I could command him neither to go nor to stay; understood that, next to Eben and me, Paul was his closest friend, and let him go—just as I let Ephie and Roan, the two of them scrambling aboard close on Jim's heels.

Never before in my life had I allowed two members of the same family to lower away in the same boat; but the same dumb respect that'd halted me with Jim, stayed my hand with them as well; and away they went over the rail. As Paul was a notably capable swimmer, and his fall by no means necessarily fatal, there was every chance he might survive to be picked up; every chance, as the seas were moderating and the cloud bank still distant, that further rugged weather would hold off; and throwing in the spare sextant as a mere matter of form, I knew no reason for any fear at all. Yet as they rowed away upwind and out of sight, disappearing soon in the troughs of the great swells, a dead weight settled upon my heart—an apprehensive dread of separation; and the minutes till their return ticked away like hours.

Abigail having turned nearly around in our maneuvers, she was in a position to more or less follow; and we set a course on the wind instead of lying to, in an endeavor to keep the gap between us at a minimum: me watching the boat out of sight through the glass, though Jim never once looked back over his shoulder. The final order that Eben had given was that they limit their period of searching until dusk, not more than an hour or two off now; and I at once commenced killing the time by filling all the lamps and making sure the foghorns were in order, in case we had to assist them back. Properly speaking these were Jim's tasks, or Orin's, certainly not mine; but I undertook them to keep my mind steady, and my eyes off the cloud bank creeping stubbornly nearer.

Getting more and more impatient as they failed to reappear, I periodically consulted with Eben, debating how much longer to keep on the wind—considering whether to keep closing in on their wake, or whether to lie-to, on the chance our tack would skew us off course: the little boat, with its greater mobility, probably zig-zagging by now, crossing and re-crossing the stretch near Paul's fall. Scanning the seas the look-outs could report nothing, neither quarterboat nor Paul nor the flotsam we'd thrown out; and they stood their posts at the mastheads silent, while the rest of the hands went about their business, methodically coiling up the rigging. Restlessly pacing I re-checked the lamps, the foghorns and binnacle clock and look-outs aloft, then the glass and thermometer in my cabin—the latter two slowly falling, as they had been all day; consulted and re-consulted with Eben, trying to restrain myself from swarming up the masts; then my round of imaginary chores complete, I started in on the lamps all over again.

Gotten by the watch supper came and went, though the officers' table went unattended, as there was no one to cook for it or set it, and no one with the appetite to eat if there had been. Slowly westering the sun went down, disappearing prematurely behind the cloud bank, and dimming all the seas ahead to a dead slate—to a dull murk that rendered scanning all the harder; while to make matters worse the cloud front now crawled near, faster than I would have predicted, though there was still no rise in the wind. Blurred and ill-defined, there was something uncanny about it, something that suggested neither a gale nor high seas; and elbow to elbow with Eben at the rail, I kept an apprehensive eye on it, with that old out of control unease that'd pursued me ever since the night before the blizzard. Watching it with me Eben all at once cried out "Why, it's mist!"—the same alarm ringing out at the same time from the mastheads; and peering ahead in disbelief, I saw he was right—saw it was neither rain nor wind approaching, but our worst enemy, fog, bearing down on us like a relentless curtain, and obscuring all things from sight.

In a panic lest we'd sail off in the wrong direction—or miss them even if we were almost within hail—we immediately hove the ship to, and lighted all the lamps that were to be found aboard, setting them like a constellation in the rigging; then manning the foghorns in the bow and the stern, we commenced calling them back. Knowing they'd light their lamp and send up their flares, we had a fresh hand at each masthead every half hour, peering out into the fog for some sign on the waves; but though we sounded and listened and watched—though even the seas fell to an unearthly calm—there was nothing in the void to behold, save for the indistinct glow of our lamps, and the plash of the wash at the bow. Groaning out at intervals our horns mourned on, their moans punctuated by an occasional voice, or the ring of the ship's bell every half hour; but even such nearby noises fell dead, muffled by the surrounding gauze.

Sleep out of the question I kept to the deck, pacing from foghorn to foghorn to listen, or pausing lengthy spells at the bulwarks to peer out, striving to will an answering flicker in the blank—to suppress my fears with my remnants of reason, which insisted that the boat, too, if out of sight and hearing, would lie to and wait for daylight. Anxious to keep records in spite of the blind night, I drew up two courses on the saloon chart, and calculated the likely position and driftage for each of us, based on our weights and the direction of current, and the occasional variable puffs of wind; checked and re-checked my results with the lead line, cast every hour and neatly re-coiled in its tub. Then my grip on data as firm as I could make it, I hurried back to the foghorns and lamps, seeing to it the former were alertly manned, the latter not running low on oil.

So passed the night with alternating watches as always, the men tumbling exhaustedly into sleep when the chance came, but Eben keeping dumbly beside me on the deck, as if to shore me up with his strength: hour after inconceivable hour slipping us by with never a glimmer of light in the dim hush, and not so much as a sigh on the waters.

At dawn the fog lifted on a sterling grey sea, rolling with swells long and regular from the west, but devoid of all signs of life save ourselves; and conferring grimly with Eben I ordered enough sail set to commence exploring the area myself, more or less in the pattern of an ever-widening circle. Too driven for panic—too determined to act to surrender to the stampede of anxiety which threatened to drum out my thoughts—I kept at it not only for the rest of the day, but for the ensuing evening as well, with a methodical, orderly sweeping that became gradually more futile, more hopeless as the daylight hours dwindled. Never before had the wide sea seemed so unmanageable, so inhospitable, so trackless; so hostile to my attempts to govern its elements, to bend its unwieldy mass to my will. Accustomed to regarding it as a thoroughfare of criss-crossing lanes, all on the way somewhere from some place else—long conditioned to thinking of it as a veritable network of trafficking currents and prevailing winds, graspable, chartable, and hence, in a sense, concrete—I shrank now before its vast, shapeless blankness; succumbed more and more to a helpless foiling, dwarfed by its sheer immensity and size.

From time to time like a squall terror broke upon me, tidal waves of unreason and doubt—inner upheavals which cleared away, leaving me confused and drained, but newly awake, convinced our loss had been but a dream; then some strained face or Eben's eyes would remind me the dream was real, and squalls of terror would seize me again. Determined to put down my fears with solid acts, I raced from the helm to the bow to the saloon charts, keeping tabs on the moves of all hands aboard; then back up on deck I commenced afresh at the helm, alternating between feverish despair and drive.

On one of my rounds Eben forced something at me, with the obdurate command "Eat"; and looking at it as if I had never beheld it before, I saw it was bread, a loaf of ship's biscuit—found it dry as dust, even with the coffee he shoved into my other hand; but I obediently ate it, and thought no more of it. Another time—passing the saloon mirror, and glancing into it to read the clock on the opposite bulkhead—I happened to catch sight of my face, unrecognizable with its great ringed eyes; but again it slipped from me like water from a sieve, and I never after thought of it.

Trying to second-guess their invisible moves—striving to imagine ourselves in their place, and base our response on our conjectures on their acts—we carried on into the night, continuing our regular sweeping with a battery of lamps, and the aid of our pair of foghorns, still manned; but though I at last took a turn lying down—though Eben and I perforce divided up, and the middle watch below fell to me—I lay tossing sleepless in my berth: the pangs of loss and separation assailing me in such powerful surges that I felt hurtled overboard myself. In the heat of the day's rounds, pacing and planning, I'd managed to ride them out; but now that I was still, I was easy prey; and I could no longer keep them at bay.

Most of my panic centered on Jim—on what was happening to him, what would become of him, and us; but I was not insensible to the potential loss of the others, Ephie and Roan being my cousins; and visions of my family's dismay—re-called so soon after the loss of Pa and Joe—added to the already intolerable weight on my shoulders. Whether I'd made the right choices, from the moment the boat cleared the rail—whether I should have commanded Jim to remain on board—whether, if so, he would have obeyed—whether I should have restrained at least Roan—whether I should have hove the ship to sooner, or anticipated the coming of fog, or the squall's blast— these uncertainties cascaded upon me, aggravating the oppression of worry; while all that I'd left unsaid with Jim rose up within and pained me.

Any moment I expected to hear Eben's hail signaling they'd

been spotted—heard, with my mind's ear, the glad hurrahs of the watch, the tumbling up of the men below, with the physical hunger of one long short on food; but as the hours passed and the chances of sighting them on the broad expanse of the sea grew more remote— as time went on and nothing but the mournful note of the foghorns met me—panicked surges redoubled upon me. All the tales of suffering in open boats that I'd ever heard came back to assault me now; and fresh from the anguish of separation from Jim, I suffered the additional pain of his physical and mental distress. Though the boat had been well-stocked, with even a sextant—though there was a marginal supply of food and water, no boat of mine ever lowering away without it—the chances were that, given their location, they would die before they were sighted, or perish in one of the squalls prevalent in the tropics. Tossing and turning, rolling with the ship's pitch, I was scared—blankly scared without him; terrified as a child lost in the dark, utterly torn from all it knows; was wholly bewildered that he was out of my life, as suddenly and inexplicably as he'd come in. Again and again I tried to adjust, like a man trying to take in the loss of a limb; but all I could feel was a vast hollowness in me, a vacancy as broad as the sea. When at last Eben came in and I saw by his face that another dawn had lifted to reveal nothing, I succumbed; fell ill with a violence of empty retching, seasick for the first time in my life; then with Eben's arms about me I wept, with a wrenching that twisted and tore at my throat.

After five days of searching Eben and I called a halt, and sat down at the saloon table to consider our options. We'd been 200 miles ENE of the Marianas when the squall struck, just before the disaster of Paul's loss; in our sweeping had swung back round 150 miles to the east now; and though the North Equatorial current flowed westerly— though the prevailing winds were westerly too, both factors rendering a course for the Marianas a challenge—nonetheless it was their best hope, far more attainable than the Marshall Islands, almost a thousand miles to the east. With the aid of a makeshift sail and fair weather, it wasn't inconceivable they might make the Marshalls; more impossible feats had been dared and won; but the daunting distance, the chain-like array of the islands, strewn for hundreds of miles into the Southern Pacific, most too tiny to attract significant shipping, all made them far less preferable a landfall than the nearby Marianas, where more notable ports studded even the small islands of the north.

In addition there was the consideration that shipping bound out from the Marianas—in particular for the Sandwich Islands—might even have spotted their small boat by now, and either returned them to Ascension or Pagan, or gone on with them to Honolulu, especially when they learned we ourselves were bound there, and could eventually pick them back up. Though the area was not a heavy shipping lane ever—certainly nothing like the Boston-Liverpool route—there were occasional tea clippers bound to and from China, or whalers charting their way north for the summer season, any of which would think of putting rescued men ashore at the Marianas if convenient; while those outward bound from Mariana ports could be alerted to look out for stranded sailors.

Consequently—after a hurried debate over my legal right to deviate from course, which we considered granted due to the extremity of the situation, and another dispute over the condition of the tea, a delicate cargo, whose potential loss was of no moment to me, but whose prospective blow to others Eben persistently argued—we decided to make for Pagan, and leave word and money while alerting the shipping, squaring away early light on June 8. My spirits lifted a little by the prospect of fresh action—by the sudden hope that they might even now be in port, picked up days ago while we still searched—I washed my face and combed my hair, and took to the deck with renewed determination; while Haggai, perceiving I might eat, brought me fried fish from the galley, and doled them out to me at odd hours.

We hadn't been underway half a day when out of the west hurled another gale, lasting twenty-four hours, and doing unknown damage to the little boat—making prospects for a row to the Marianas all the harsher, and tormenting me with a wild urge to turn back, and search anew; but we held our course for the northernmost islands, speaking one outward bound bark, which we alerted. When at last we raised the jagged peaks of Pagan, volcanic-black against the brilliant horizon, and sailed into the harbor, we found a small array of shipping; but though we visited every local official—though we scoured the several boarding cottages, struggling with our inept Spanish, and personally boarded every vessel in the harbor, we uncovered nothing, not a clue of their survival; and leaving letters of credit and messages in half a dozen places, we were forced to leave without news for the Sandwich Islands.

With the hope that we might yet come upon them ourselves—buoyed up by the thought of Jim's unfailing ability to surprise—we gave one last circling pass of the area of Paul's loss; but again we found nothing, no so much as a bird on the wave; and we stood off on a course for Honolulu. Our final chance was that they'd been picked up by some vessel bound east, or arriving after us at Pagan, shipped for the Islands themselves; and fueled by that glimmer we covered the Pacific like no one had ever covered it before, making 3,000 miles in just under fifteen days, our distress signal flying every yard of the way. In all that distance we alerted only two ships bound west, one a brig for the Marianas, the other a square-rigger for Hong Kong; though we overtook and spoke three or four bound east, none of which knew anything of the stranded men.

As the days wore on the hollowness within me burgeoned into an actual presence, a tangible scarecrow of Jim's absence—a manifestation as visible as the occasional glances I got of myself in the saloon mirror, a tall, gaunt figure whose garb hung upon him; and it required all my strength pinned on the hope of Honolulu to stave off the process of its consumption. His wit, his tenderness, his maddening obstinate will—these I missed like meat at every turn; but even worse than these losses were the poignant reminders of his life here, scattered about at every quarter. His cup, his brogans—these lay about like mute finds, the remnants of some long-vanished mission; and I guessed, though I never asked, that the belongings of the others wrenched the foremasthands with the same pain—the same poignant twists of the left-behind, the unused.

As if understanding their torture, Eben—on the third day out from Pagan, not long after we'd completed our farewell sweep—ordered the men's gear packed up in the forecastle, and sent aft to be stowed in one of the lockers—not a man aboard desiring the finality of an auction; and coming down from the quarterdeck I found him packing Jim's, his hands just folding away the striped shirt in Jim's mending basket. As though it were one of my offspring being snatched from me, I cried "Belay that!" and snapped it up, clutching it instinctively to my chest; and his eyes unoffended, he gazed upon me with a tenderness that burned its way through my panic.

"Ben, it's betteh so," he said simply, taking hold of the shirt with his lean, homely paw; and as I pulled away from him he bent his eyes on me, gazing now with an understanding that forced me to see him. Was it only my misery, my longing to sob out the whole account of my feelings for Jim that made him appear to look so at me; or was there a comprehension on his face that transcended the little I'd ever confided? Had it been there all along, that look of knowing, and I'd never seen it; had Jim ever, by any chance, said something to him—and if so, how could I have failed to note it, that unswerving acceptance at the back of his eyes? Bathed by that knowing, finding in it a balm, I relented my grip on Jim's shirt a little; and holding it before me, I folded it softly.

"Then I'll do it," I said gently, my gaze still bent on his eyes; "it's what he'd want—what I'd want, if oweh places was switched."

No man had ever looked at me with such unbounded respect as sprang into his eyes now, as I folded Jim's shirt; but he said nothing in response, only smiled at me wanly; and patting my arm, he left me alone to my task.

To this moment I'd thought that the hardest undertaking I'd ever faced was prying Joe's black, frozen hands from the shrouds of his schooner; but I saw now there was nothing more galling than the shutting away of these helpless objects. Folding them one by one in Jim's trunk, I saw that these same things which had once flowed in a cascade of animation and movement in the recesses of his tall wardrobe, were now passive, futile, disembodied—derelict as the cast off china legs of old dolls; and if they still had a force it was manifest in a voice that almost seemed to call out to him for his warmth, for the vibrancy for which they hungered.

His salmon-hued shirt from Valparaiso, which we'd bought at the market where we'd found Jasper; the jonquil yellow silk, so vivid against his dark hair; his Cantonese dressing gown, my get-well gift from Whampoa; his plain sailor's gear that I loved best, the duck trowsers and denims, the red checked shirt he'd worn at Anjier, his blue monkey jacket, his worn frocks and jerseys: all these seemed to cry out in failing voices for the form that had given them animation; and I buried my face understandingly in each, as if maybe my force could breathe new life in them.

Shamelessly I went through all their pockets and corners, recalling that first night when I'd been afraid to, looking at his clothes by the fire at Hannah's; found the box with the shell I'd given him at Havana, which I knew he always carried with him; numberless other small souvenirs and mementoes, which showed him to be the man of sentiment I loved; but the surprise came at the bottom of his trunk, where I found a leather packet which proved to be full of notes, and a couple of letters complete with their envelopes.

Touched, I found they were all from me—the most recent, the inane scrawl I'd written in Portland, in answer to his which had prompted my dream; the oldest, my invitation to supper on his arrival in Cape Damaris two years ago. In between was every scratch and scribble I'd ever penned, right down to an unsigned "God damn you!", probably written in one of our spats over money. Actually all in order, worn with touch, yellowed with time, they too spoke, too late, their testimony of his deep feeling for me; spoke, like some ancestor's papers from some other decade, their futile testament, long delayed; and holding them for a long time, I sat over them with bowed head, before locking them with their silent kin in his chest.

On June 26 we raised Oahu, and lay off Diamond Head for the night; and next morning, it being fair, and a pilot immediately answering our signal, we put into Honolulu Harbor, where we were straightaway besieged with commotion. Getting through with the custom house officer in record time, I left everything else to Eben, including finding a buyer for our still unsold cargo; and grabbing the mail I rowed directly ashore, where I procured a carriage and commenced my rounds. Honolulu being a sizeable town—with residences ranging from the handsome palace to a dozen or more boarding houses, mostly filled with the wives and children of American whaling captains gone north for the season—and the harbor being crowded likewise, I had a considerable job before me; but though I spent the entire day searching—though I scoured every deck and sitting room and wharf, from the Sailor's Home to the smallest schooner—I found not a sign or word of our stranded men; and I rowed back that night empty-handed.

Trying to stave off fresh waves of panic—reminding myself we'd arrived days ahead of slower craft, and that we had nearly a fortnight in which to explore, while Eben, who'd been fortunate to find a ready market for our mixed freight, discharged cargo, then took on additional ballast and produce—I made all the visits I'd put off the first day, sewing seeds of friendship that might be repaid later, should our men happen in port after our departure. Sitting on Chinese sofas and looking out on the mountains, forcing down pineapple and breadfruit and dried figs, I tried to keep my mind on polite chitchat; struggled to make coherent answers and betray a respectable degree of compassion for the circumstances and voyages and home news, when my heart was laboring and my ears roaring.

When at last, after a week, the mails were preparing to embark for Boston, and still no news had come in from the west, I knew I could postpone letters no longer; and sitting down at my desk, I personally wrote to the families of the missing men—declining Eben's offer to break the word for me, knowing it was my unmistakable duty. As I wrote I grew aware of the sound of guns in the harbor, of noise-making and celebrating aboard several vessels; and only slowly I realized it was the Fourth—the fact it was Independence Day having completely slipped my mind, there being no cause for jubilation aboard our ship.

Shutting out the celebration I went on with my work, thanking God I at least needn't write a letter for Jim; but I had to face up to the reality the next day, when—preparatory to our departure—I went ashore to the American consul, and reported the loss of our men. Watching them list them one by one in his ledger—Paul first, then Ephie and Roan, their names in incontrovertible black and white, their lives reduced to birthdates and nationalities, and the latitude and longitude of their loss—was enough of a horror; but I simply could not bring myself to name Jim, as though that would somehow finalize the event.

"The last man—his name?" the consul had to prompt me; and even then I could scarcely get out "Robertson, James; July 5, 1824; Welsh"—each bit of information wrenching out with such hoarseness that he was obliged to ask me to repeat. "Ah, another young man; his anniversary today, too; what a pity," he said kindly; and with a shock I realized that he was right —that as yesterday had been the Fourth, today was Jim's twentieth birthday. A year ago, he'd danced at Jimmy's, with an abandon that had opened my eyes; two years ago, had sat by me at dinner in Havana, and held out his hand to the small shell I'd found; but tonight I sat alone looking west, trying to feel with my eyes for his presence—to know with my sight where he might be. As if the same gift that had enabled me to see into his past, might admit me into his present, I scanned the horizon for hours, searching; but nothing came out of the west, no sign or portent of where he might be; and at last I stood up and shrugged into my jacket, and bowed him goodnight from my place at the taffrail.

"We'hre goin' to Hilo," I broke it to Eben, next morning when we catted the anchor, and stood off for the southeast on a fair breeze; and though I had a pull to convince him—though the consideration of the state of the cargo and his concern for the wear of our search on the crew caused him to put up a stubborn protest, the strongest he'd ever essayed against me—I at last won him over, and we made the short sail to the nearby isle of Hawaii. Thinking that vessels bound for the Islands might have stopped here as readily as at Oahu, I combed Hilo as I had Honolulu, rowing from bark to brig in the harbor, and knocking on every boarding house door; but though I spent two feverish days searching, I turned up nothing, not a sliver of news.

At last, just as we were preparing to get underway—on the very day I again left word with the consul, and sculled the dull distance back to the ship—I spotted a brig standing in for the harbor; and on the chance they might be able to tell something, I rowed the additional mile to her side, *Abigail* meantime running down to her too. To my joy they met my queries with the news that they'd spoken a bark just ten days ago, the *Lucinda Snowe* bound for San Francisco Bay, with three men picked up in an open boat; and so wild was my excitement that the discrepancy in the number, pointing to the painful loss of Paul, was as nothing compared to the possibility the rest still lived—that Jim even now was hauling in for California, hale and decently fed and cared for. Like a flame the tidings sped through our crew; and I had no difficulty at all setting a course for the Northwest Coast, save with Eben, who confronted me on the poop.

"Ben, this is madness; it's got t' stop," he crossed me, his grip on my arm noticeable even through my glad daze. "We can't just keep followin' clues from pohrt t' pohrt; we've got a cahrgo down in the hold—almost seventy thousand dollahs worth of risky tea, enough of a profit t' pay off half the ship. An' it ain't just youhr money we stand t' lose, if we don't make Maine before it gets stale; it's half the folks' in town; an' without it, some of 'em'll go undeh, an' you know it."

"Oh, God, Eben—the Northwest Coast—it's only a couple thousand miles out o' the way— I c'n make it in ten or twelve days, an' haul int' pohrt while the *Luncinda Snowe* is still loadin'," I pleaded, my mind already charting the prevailing winds and currents.

"That's ten or twelve days out an' as many back down the coast, Ben, even if the wind's always fair, which it won't be. An' that brings me round t' the other serious point at hand, which is youhr legal standin' for all this deviatin' from course. The Marianas your consignees'll overlook, an' the Sandwich Islands was on the charteh, though Hilo was an unnecessary stop; but San Francisco Bay—why, thehre's no legal way ye can justify it; ye'll be sued the minute ye drop anchor in Cape Damaris. An' any more litigation on top o' the mess of Joe's schooner, an' ye know damn well Mechett Bros.'ll floundeh."

"The yahd won't have t' back any lawsuits; I will… D'ye think I'd let them take responsibility for my acts? Let's just say I'm ready t' set my share o' the profit against any actions forthcoming against me; that's how confident I am we'll make time, an' get the tea back in condition for sale."

His lips parted at the audacity of the gamble; but all he said was, with a dumbfounded look at me: "Good Gawd, Ben—that's youhr whole savings tied up—you're goin' t' stake all that on the wind, an' the chance we c'n still make a passage worth beans?"

"Ain't that just what I been doin', this ten yeahrs an' more?…The wind'll hold, an' we won't be long in the Bay—ye'll see; I'll just look up the *Lucinda Snowe*, I sweah it… Think what it'll mean, Eben, if we c'n bring oweh men home, especially afteh them lettehs I just wrote—think what it'll mean for them t' sail home with us, an' not have t' double the Horn with strangehs."

"Think what it'll mean," he pronounced harshly, "if they're not oweh men that's been picked up at all, but some whaleh's rescued around New Zealand, or—"

"For God's sake," I stopped him with a clutch at his arm; and he gave another hard and long look at me.

"There's no certainty about it, Ben—just one ship's vague report of anotheh's rescue somewheres b'tween the Marshalls and Asiar."

"Oh, God, Eben, don't you… don't ye miss him… don't you feel like youhr life's less every day we'hre without him?" I whispered, too wrung to go on with anything less than my true plea.

His face softened in a wonderful way then, and he actually brushed back the hair at my brow like a father would, or like an old shipmate at the pillow of another too feeble to tend any more for himself. "Just tryin' t' think of all the things you'hre not," he said gently, his voice low; and suddenly I saw him for the first time since I'd packed Jim's things away, more than a month ago now; saw how tired he was, how drawn and worn his expression, how deep the lines about the corners of his mouth.

"I'll hurry," I promised him; "trust me."

"All right," he smiled with the smile of old memories; "but this is the last time we c'n delay, Ben. If they're not in Californiar they're out of oweh hands; and we've just got t' find a way t' beahr it."

Scarcely hearing his last words I nodded, already on my way to the helm; and again we commenced to burn up the Pacific, rigging out studdingsails in places they'd never before flown, holding onto whole topsails when they should have been reefed, and hauling into San Francisco Bay in 11 days, averaging 200 miles per day port to port. I was sure in my mind no ship had ever made it faster; but too excited to bother about lodging news of the record, my whole thought pinned on sweeping the anchoring grounds just ahead, I searched the waters for the *Lucinda Snowe* as we rounded the presidio and slipped into the harbor, and dropped hook a cable's length from the shore. Only two other vessels of any size met my gaze, one a Russian trader, our near neighbor, the other—more distant—an American bark, by her colors; and immediately lowering away my small gig—rowing under the bow of the former, with a hasty salute to those of her crew at the rail, heavily coated and capped despite the warm sun—I laid on my oars with dispatch for the latter.

Blind to all the natural beauties of the bay—only dimly perceiving the sparkling waters, the forest-clad hills and myriad harbors opening out further on down the way—hardly seeing as well the Indian-manned small craft, coming and going with loads of tallow and hides—I slowly closed in on the sternboard of the bark, rejoicing to find she was in fact *Lucinda*; and my heart laboring so in my ears I felt faint, I pulled alongside and clambered up the gangway ladder.

Met at the rail by a kindly captain, clad in a rust-colored checked suit and beaver hat, and bewhiskered with sideburns all the way down to the jawline, I climbed aboard; and looking round eagerly fore and aft as we shook hands—searching the commotion at the cargo hatches, thinking any moment I might catch sight of Jim, then scanning the standing and running rigging, expecting any second he might slide down a stay—I swiftly went through the amenities of introducing myself, then plunged into the reason for my visit. Asked about the report of his rescue of three men in an open boat some weeks ago now, his face immediately brightened with pride; and my heart pumping so fast the ship gave a whirl, I steadied myself against the rail, anticipating his coming words.

"Three men in a boat, aye," he beamed; "they was whalemen, marooned as it were when their ship took fire, somewheres just south o' the Gilbert Islands. We come upon 'em on our course from Sydney, an' brung 'em here—but they're gone already; shipped with a whaler that put into the bay for supplies, three or four days ago it was now."

My heart cold in my chest with a swiftness that stunned—my midriff struck with the force of an actual physical kick—I slumped down against the bulwarks, dumb; and he quickly called for the steward to fetch coffee, then offered his cabin until I felt better. Drinking the hot brew through stubbornly stiff lips—answering his many questions with brief replies—I begged off, in spite of my silent longing to accept, to lay my head down in a place where I knew no one, and could anonymously be tended; explained all hands aboard *Abigail* were anxious for news, and bound away south for Cape Horn this same day; then thanking him for his kindness and accepting his mail, I handed my empty cup to the steward, and climbed the ladder back down to my boat.

Rowing back to the ship in a daze, with numb arms, I silently looked up at the rail at Eben, whose anxious face filled nearly the whole sky above me; and there was no need for me to speak, or for him to read my vacant expression, for my empty boat recounted the story. "I'll have the men overhaul the ground tackle," he said simply, "whilst you have a bit of a rest b'low"; but I shook my head, forcing out a reply. "I'm goin' ashore for an houhr, maybe; just need t' think; I'll be back by an' by," I said slowly; and like a father he gentled, "Don't be gone long," then turned back to rally the waiting crew.

Till now I'd been kept alive by feverish action—by the determination to take the course of events in my hands, to master it as I would captain a ship; but now I was forced to recognize that I'd done all that I could do—that Jim's life was literally at some other helm; and the grim obstinacy which had characterized me in past weeks suddenly departed, leaving me all at once drifting and aimless. Having no place to go, I made for the shore, and hauled up the gig on the embankment; and there I stood looking dumbly about me, taking in the dwellings and shops of the small town, a relatively new settlement called Yerba Buena, whose few hundred inhabitants— mostly Americans and British—appeared to be primarily trappers and traders, and merchantmen dealing in grains, beans and hides. Having never been here before, indeed having never set foot on the Northwest Coast, and possessing but a few words of miserable Spanish, I hadn't the first idea where to go; but my gaze fell upon a nearby hilltop, where sat a white-walled, red-tiled mission, which seemed to promise peace and detachment; and impulsively renting a horse for the rest of the morning, I started out for its quiet doors.

As if in a cloud I tied up my beast at a hitching post next to a couple of others; and climbing the steps and passing between the pillars, I found myself in a long, narrow church, silent and thoughtful with its half-century of witness. Around me marched pedestals with hand carved statues and rows of quiescent, wooden pews; above arched the lofty redwood timbers of the ceiling, betwixt paintings of Indian vegetable dye; while before me rose the tall, intricate altar from Mexico, richly worked with airy designs. Placing a few coins in the almsbox by the side door, I exited into the adjacent burying ground, surrounded on three sides by high, vine-clad walls, on the fourth by the thick adobe of the church building; and here I sat down on a stone seat facing west, toward the hidden expanse of the open sea.

To this moment I'd been torn by wild waves of resistance, alternating with periods of lucidity and action. Now, as if all my life forces had gathered together, I had one last turn of clarity, as I sat amongst the cloister walls that looked out yonder over the distant sea. Above me, there was a deep, brilliant blue sky; around me, a tantalizing sea breeze, not unlike the one that had awakened Jim and stirred him to action that morning in Boston over two years ago now: a fresh, clean air with tangs of moistness, the scents of early summer mornings, vivid and cool and sweetly refreshing, stirring memories of other such breezes in ports of call long ago.

Solidly present amongst the cloister walls, I felt, too, transported to other moments, other pasts—some of them not necessarily even my own. About me, there was an abundance of blossoming bushes and vines, clustering the walls and paths of the mission burying ground: a small place, small enough to make me feel enclosed and protected, yet large enough to give my soul rest and space. The cypresses and lilacs, morning glories and ivies, brought a measure of balm to my spirit; and the bright sunlight on the fading walls, on the stucco and marble, on the narrow stone pathways, brought serenity and calm of a sort. There was an atmosphere of age and naturalness about the place which comforted me: the vines rambling along the adobe walls, the bushes growing randomly amongst the monuments, the grass borders ranging unclipped along the paths, the gravestones themselves—worn with passing time—cracked and eroded and overgrown with lichens and moss.

Everywhere there were bright colors—the radiance of the broad blue sky, the violet of the morning glories, the dark green of the spiky cypress, the lavender and white of the lilacs, the gold and melon of nasturtiums and roses. But overall there was a feeling of the spirit that consecrated this patch of land to God, to the early dead of the church. The sheltered atmosphere, the serene sunlight, the quiet repose of monuments and stone seats and walls, the harmony of grasses and trees drawing nourishment from sunlight and coarse red soil, the casual intertwining of stone and leaf, light and space— all these made me feel that I was within a soul. Spirit was around me; the world, and my grief, were without; I was at the center of something still and quiet, whilst around me shadows trembled in the gentle, vibrant wind.

Standing at last, I looked out to the west in farewell, in a pain too deep-felt for either tears or words: the gentle sun, the waving shadows, the encompassing spirit dwarfing my fleeting visit with their eternal witness. Then turning away, I left the mission; and as if all the forces of my being had convened to yield the lucidity which had characterized my perception that morning, then all at once withdrawn or departed, I was left bereft and stumbling, numbed and visionless and deadened. Fumbling with my horse's harness, struggling to get up into the saddle, I made my way back down to the landing, never once looking back at the stucco walls on the hill; then rowing out to the ship, I climbed aboard, and embarked upon our voyage of darkness.

ABOUT THE AUTHOR

KIM RIDENOUR RAIKES is a member of the faculty of Maine Maritime Academy in Castine, where she teaches writing and humanities. An important aspect of her teaching career, which began 37 years ago in Marjoyoun, Lebanon, is global education, and she has led numerous study abroad programs for American students in Ireland, Great Britain, and India. As an ordained minister and student of world religious traditions, she has long incorporated spiritual themes in her writing and academic researches.

Beginning in Beirut in 1978 and continuing over the course of the next 30 years, Raikes worked on this novel daily, drawing not only from primary researches into historical records and sailing ship logs, but also from her personal experience of the working waterfront. Though these outer resources were important shaping influences, the key inspiration for this story came in the form of the three narrative voices which emerged from within, and the historical places which took shape though unseen.